"THE FACES OF THE DEAD ARE LIT

red

pur

fac

are

dea

sif

to

po

ve my

re are
there
ecome
don't

m out
n sup-
all—"

The Finest in Fantasy by
Michelle West

THE
SHINING
COURT

The Sun Sword: Book Three

Michelle West

DAW BOOKS, INC.

DONALD A. WOLLHEIM, FOUNDER

375 Hudson Street, New York, NY 10014

ELIZABETH R. WOLLHEIM
SHEILA E. GILBERT
PUBLISHERS

First Printing, August, 1999
5 6 7 8 9

This is for
Daniel and Ross and their father,
the three men I'm looking forward to sharing
the rest of my life with.

ACKNOWLEDGMENTS

Almost too many to go into, and the karmic burden will haunt me for lifetimes, I'm certain.

My mother and my father, my husband and my oldest son, were all particularly forgiving in the last eight weeks of the book's harried life when I didn't join them for lunch or dinner and turned the entire household schedule upside down.

My son's godfather, John Chew—also one of my closest friends—who picked my son up every day after school while I worked on this book, thereby earning me the envy of almost every mother in the neighborhood, and with just cause. He also ran interference by telling the *rest* of our friends that, in fact, I was completely psychotic with stress and should not be disturbed if one valued life, which I suppose was one way of putting it . . . but I hope not an entirely accurate one. . . .

And last, thanks to the usual suspects at DAW: Sheila Gilbert and Debra Euler who are busy trying to keep a business based on art and artistic temperament running smoothly, with the usual frenetic results one would expect.

I have no idea who the guys in the production department are, but if I ever see them, I imagine I owe them a whole lot more than just a round of drinks.

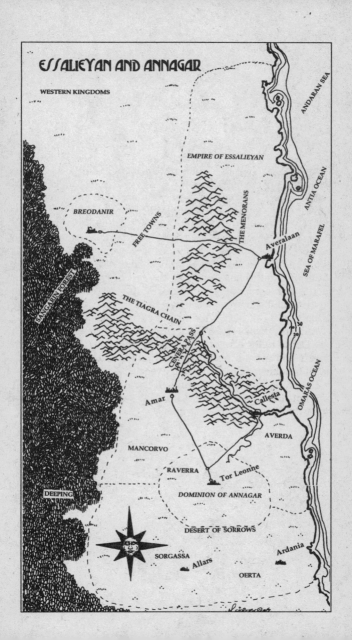

Annagarian Ranks

Tyr'agar	Ruler of the Dominion
Tyr'agnate	Ruler of one of the five Terreans of the Dominion
Tyr	The *Tyr'agar* or one of the four *Tyr'agnate*
Tyran	Personal bodyguard (oathguard) of a *Tyr*
Tor'agar	A noble in service to a *Tyr*
Tor'agnate	A noble in service to a *Tor'agar;* least of noble ranks
Tor	A *Tor'agar* or *Tor'agnate*
Toran	Personal bodyguard (oathguard) of a *Tor*
Ser	A clansman
Serra	The primary wife and legitimate daughters of a clansman
kai	The holder or first in line to the clan title
par	The brother of the first in line; the direct son of the title holder

The Voyani

In the Voyani clans, the men will often use their name and their clan's name as identifiers (i.e. Nicu would be Nicu of the Arkosan Voyani or Nicu Arkosa.)

ARKOSA

Evallen of the Arkosa Voyani—the woman who ruled the Voyani clan. She is/was seerborn. Dark-haired, dark-eyed; dies at Diora's hand, a mercy killing.

Margret of the Arkosa Voyani—The new, untested Matriarch of the Arkosan Voyani. Dark haired and dark eyed like her mother; she is not seerborn.

Adam—Evallen's boy, the light of her life, and much indulged. Charming, easily charmed, he is *also* very perceptive, very sharp of wit; he keeps it to himself, for the most part.

Nicu—Bearded, broad-shouldered; cousin in his early twenties. Son of Evallen's cousin. Looks older.

Carmello—darker in coloring than Nicu, dark-haired, dark-eyed, one year his senior. They're friends, sword-mates.

Andreas—Shorter than either Nicu or Carmello, but dark as the Voyani are dark; stocky and barrel-chested; one of Carmello's and Nicu's supporters.

Donatella—Nicu's mother. Evallen's cousin once removed; Margret (and Elena's) second cousin.

Stavos—Margret's uncle, much loved and crusty; gray beard, broad belly, laughs like a bear.

Caitla—Stavos' wife. Wide as well, but hardened by the sun and wind. Hair gray and long, eyes cutting and dark.

Elena—Margret's cousin; the heir to the Matriarchy should Margret perish without a daughter. They are both close and rivals, Margret and Elena, and it is Elena that Nicu loves. Elena is a firebrand in most senses of the word; her hair is auburn-red, her skin sun-bronzed, her eyes brown with green highlights.

Tamara—Margret's aunt. Bent at the back, older in appearance than her older (and now dead) sister, she is

Margret's support and strength, although she nags rather a lot. Closer than kin. She is Elena's mother.

HAVALLA

Yollana of the Havalla Voyani—peppered, dark curls, almost black eyes. She is in her forties, healthy, wiry.

CORRONA

Elsarre of the Corrona Voyani—long, straight hair, dark with streaks of white. She was, until the death of Evallen, the youngest of the matriarchs at the age of 36.

Dani—Slender, of medium height. His hair is long, thick and is always pulled back in a single braid. His beard is small, his face long, his eyes (as most Voyani eyes) are dark. He is Elsarre's Shadow; Elsarre has no brothers, and no cousins she chooses to trust with her life.

LYSERRA

Maria of the Lyserra Voyani—hair white as northern snow, eyes blue as Lord's sky, she is slender and silent much of the time. She has the grace of gesture Serra Teresa possesses, and for this reason is less trusted than the other Matriarchs. Her husband is the kai of the clan Jedera; *Ser Tallos kai di'Jedera*. They have four children:

Mika—Mika is broad-shouldered, dark-haired, dark-eyed as all clansmen; clean-shaven, as the Voyani are not.

Jonni—Jonni is quiet; large-eyed, clear-skinned; he wears a beard.

Aviana—The Matriarch's heir; she shelters with, and lives with, her mother's kin in preparation for her eventual role. She loves her brothers fiercely, even if they are of the clans.

Lorra—The family baby. Beautiful, but fair-skinned, she lives with her sister, and her mother's people.

PROLOGUE

The Serra Teresa di'Marano did not travel quickly. No Serra did, whose husband, or if unmarried, kai could afford to grant her the dignity of his rank—and his wealth. She had been ordered to the Terrean of Mancorvo, there to seek her kai, Adano kai di'Marano; the Widan Sendari par di'Marano had delivered into her keeping a message of urgency.

She was also, if she was permitted, to seek audience with the wife of the Tyr'agnate himself, the demure and silent Serra Donna en'Lamberto. Between women, or so it was thought by foolish men, there was ease, and much information might be exchanged. Thus did her brother, Sendari, hope to gain knowledge about the Serra Donna's husband. Tyr'agnate Mareo kai di'Lamberto. The man whose brother had, in the single space of less than an hour, so damaged the hopes and the plans laid out by Sendari, Cortano, and the General—no, the *Tyr'agar*—Alesso kai di'*Alesso.*

Serra Teresa herself was not married, had never been married, and would never be married; the dreams of that union, and what it might bring her, lay buried, seeking life when the skies were at their brightest, and the hand of the Lord at its height.

In the North, the darkest of dreams were night dreams, and in the South, it is said that men were also weakened by the Lady's thoughts—but the Serra Teresa di'Marano knew the touch of the sun to be the precursor to madness, ruin, loss; she did not meet the Lord's face.

There were no desert sands on the road she took, but the heat this summer had been scorching, and the grasses and wildness that often encumbered the road with their wealth of scents and hidden insects were a pale gold, dry and almost dusty. The Lady's rains had not been permitted to fall.

Upon the road there was talk, of course; in all things, speech. The Serra was a Serra, but she was only a woman, and the cerdan— free men all and of the clan's distant branches—made freer with their words when their superiors were not present. Her own cerdan knew better, of course; they were of a better breed. She had chosen them herself, although Adano's approval—a formality which no clanswoman had any choice but to seek—was necessary.

As much as she could trust any man whose sword served the Lord, she trusted them. As much as.

The tents had been erected, and the palanquin laid aside. It was hot for travel, and the midday rest had been decreed by the master of the caravan—not, of course, by its mistress. Sweet water was offered, and such food as might survive the heat of such a journey unruined; she partook of the first, and gave her gracious blessing to the men, who were given the rest.

Two days, and she would cross the Mancorvan border.

Three days more, with some speed, and she might see home—if such a mythical place existed, ever, in the heart of a woman who was sent from brother to brother and place to place at the whim of others.

And today?

She did not touch the samisen case, but instead reached for the lute, with its rounded curves, its musical tradition a thing not created by, or for, the Lord of the Sun. In the heat, she began to play.

When swords left their sheaths, she was not surprised at the sound, although it seemed sudden. Music often carried her to a place that could not be attacked because it could not be felt by any who did not possess her gift. Her gift, yes, and her curse, both.

But swords being drawn brought her back, as most sounds of war did. She carefully placed the lute in its case as Ramdan lifted the flap of her tent, offering his obeisance in such a way that it made the dirt and the dryness seem a gift as it clung to his knees, the palms of his hands.

"Serra," he said.

"Are we under attack?"

"No, Serra."

She closed the case with care, and rose with as much grace as Ramdan had bowed. "There is another traveler, then."

"Yes."

He did not offer what she did not ask for; there was that stillness, that perfect composure, about him. In all things, he took her lead; he was, of the serafs she owned, the finest.

Treat them well, she heard her mother say, at the remove of years, *and they'll be more trustworthy than blood kin.* It would have been a scandalous thing to say where other ears could hear it; it was said at the harem's heart, where only these two women dwelled: Serra Teresa and her mother.

They will certainly, her mother had added, *bring you more solace if you train and choose them well.*

Truer thing had possibly been said in time, but not by her mother. She waited for Ramdan to lift the tent's flaps, and she noticed, as she always did, how ageless he seemed, how perfectly unbowed by the labor of years.

For the first time, before she left the safety of shadow, the Serra Teresa di'Marano wondered if he was truly ageless, or if her eyes were deceived by some strange desire of the heart; Ramdan had been with her for all of her adult life, and she did not wish age or its foibles to force her to part from him, to force her to elevate any other to the position that he now held.

As she entered the domain of the Lord of the Sun, she raised her fan and opened it, shielding her eyes from the glint of new metal. Swords, helms. A Serra, after all, did not squint publicly.

Karras di'Marano bowed, and she returned this respect with respect of her own. He was older than she, and not so fast with a sword as he had once been, but wisdom and experience gave him an edge that no grindstone could. "Serra Teresa," he said.

"Is there a disturbance, Ser Karras?"

"A minor one, Serra, and if you wish not to be disturbed, you might choose to continue your vigil."

"Swords ofttimes disturb me."

He had known that would be her answer, of course; they were old friends, old almost-allies. "Very well. It appears, from what we can see down the rise of the hillock, that there are wagons encamped."

"Wagons?"

"We believe that they belong to the Voyani." He paused. "The Arkosa Voyani, if their flags are not false."

"Surely we are in no danger, Ser Karras."

"They travel in greater number than I have seen," he said. She waited for him to qualify the statement, to finish it, but it hung between them stubbornly.

At last she nodded. "It is the Matriarch, then."

"I believe so." His gaze was given to the ground. "But I have seen the Matriarch's van, Serra; there is something about this gathering that feels wrong." His shrug was eloquent; a way of saying that he could not say more than that, but that he would not be judged ignorant for instinct's sake.

They both knew, because it was a truth as old as the Voyani's homeless wandering, that the Voyani preyed upon lesser clansmen, and smaller caravans.

"If I may be bold, Ser Karras," she replied, "I would tell your young cerdan that this is not the place to earn—or to attempt to earn—the Lord's respect."

His smile was a thin-edged flash of teeth, gone at once; she felt the respect offered in the salute that he almost, but did not quite, give.

She liked Karras, and hoped that he followed her advice, for no cerdan would be likely to escape the wrath of the Arkosa Voyani who traveled in such great numbers should they attempt to exert their authority.

Margret, she thought, staring into the open sky.

Knowing that she had news to offer that would cause a far greater wound to the young Voyani woman than any cerdan's sword. And knowing, after that wound, she must then ask a favor that she could not afford to have refused.

Margret of the Arkosa Voyani was not a woman like her mother. She was a little too young, and the edges about her were sharper, harsher; it was just such a woman who made the greatest—or the worst—of rulers. To come to the clan as Matriarch, unblemished by the winds, unblunted and unscarred, physically, by the test of the sands, was an omen, and it was considered as such by both the Serra Teresa and the Arkosa Voyani.

Or it would be. It would be soon.

She did not wait upon the appointed hour; she did not need to. There was too much steel gathered here, beneath the Lord's sight, for the van to ignore. The Voyani did not often use horses as beasts for single riders; it was an expensive proposition, and one much resented by those who could not afford the luxury. They had, these wanderers, their pride, and much of their pride was a ferocity of fellow feeling with those they claimed as kin. In this case, the Arkosa Voyani. But a rider came out, on horse. The horse was Lambertan-bred; she wondered how dearly they had paid.

She thought the beast fine, and was certain that it would be kept only until a likely buyer was found for it.

Her cerdan stepped forward at the command of Karras di'Marano, barring the rider's way. He stopped short of them—just—and in a way that showed that he ill-loved riding as a form of approaching an uncertain situation. The horse, of course, could sense this, and she could tell by the tensing line of the shoulders of her guards that they could sense it as well. Young horse, and too newly broken to take kindly to the scent of any rider's fear.

Or too poorly broken, which was perhaps the reason he was let go at all. The Voyani rider stopped the horse, but at a lesser distance than any of them, save perhaps the horse, would have liked. A poor start.

Poorer still, he did not dismount, although privately the Serra thought it wise.

"Ho, travelers!" he said, lifting his voice. A normal greeting would have involved the lifting of an arm, a hand, some gesture that touched the open sky. A toss of the head was offered in its place; both hands gripped and held the reins a little too tightly. She wondered if the horse would throw the boy.

For she could tell, from the timbre of his voice, if not his build, that he was a boy. On the edge of manhood, to be sure, and with only a little time needed to push him over, but nonetheless, a boy.

It explained much.

Serra Teresa and Ser Karras exchanged a brief glance.

Karras stepped forward. "We are passing through Raverra to Mancorvo."

"You fly the colors of the clan Marano."

The cerdan nodded, neither well-pleased nor ill, although the Voyani did not always attend to the colors of the clans well enough to know them. Certainly not the Arkosans. The Havallans, perhaps.

"My sister sent me to offer you the hospitality of our wagons and our family," the boy continued.

Serra Teresa froze a moment as she studied the lines of the boy's face, seeing them as if for the first time, although she missed little.

"Your sister is?"

"Margret," the boy replied, with just a touch of pride. "Margret, daughter of Evallen, Matriarch of Arkosa."

Teresa closed her eyes then; it was a momentary reflex, and

the pain passed quickly beneath the heat of the Lord's regard.
Ser Karras, however, had turned to seek her permission, whether
desirous of acceptance or flat refusal, she could not—quite—
tell; she met his eyes as hers blinked open.

"Tell your sister Margret that the Serra Teresa di'Marano would
indeed be honored to accept the offered hospitality. Tell her—tell
her that the Serra is well aware of the honor offered."

He brightened, this boy, and she added—because she could
not help but add it, "And who is her brother?"

His cheeks shifted slightly in color, although with the Voyani's
sun-harsh skin it was often hard to tell, and he smiled; his face lit,
side to side, with the undamaged and unfettered charm of a child
who has not yet been broken or yoked. "I'm Adam," he said.
"Adam, Evallen's son."

She bowed—it was acceptable etiquette when the only mats
beneath her were formed of earth and dust—and then nodded to
the captain.

It was clear that he did not trust the Voyani; he was not paid,
after all, to trust. He chose three men—more than that, and the
lack of trust would be an open insult—and accompanied them
himself.

Serra Teresa began the descent from the roadside to the small
curve of grass that a desert dweller would call a valley and an
Averdan would hardly deign to notice. Where the land lay lowest,
there was some hesitant greenery; if the rains came, she thought
the golden dryness of the sun's reign would be cast off by under-
growth like so much ceremonial clothing.

She admired the Voyani their ability to maneuver, and keep,
their wagons, and as she approached the wagon ring, she saw,
standing above them as if it were a palace at the heart of a wheeled
city, a wagon that she knew, if not well, then well enough to never
mistake.

This was no merchant wagon, no van meant to carry creature
comforts from one end of the Dominion to the other; it was a
home, or as much of a home as the Voyani were allowed to
make. Canvas was supported in two places by carved lintels that
were oiled and tended; the canvas itself was not the only protection the wagon dweller was offered, for the sides of the wagon
were built up with a fine wood, and broken on either side by
panes of clear, thick glass, and bars of lead. Cloth twined and fell

to either side, ribbons of decorative color, and the wheels themselves were jointed in such a way that they absorbed some of the
rigors of wagon travel well.

Many a merchant would have paid the Voyani for the secret of
this construction, but the Voyani and the merchants were not
often friendly; death and time had given suspicion a hold that
goodwill did not dissolve. And that, she thought grimly, was for
the best, for goodwill rarely stood the test of the wind.

The Voyani had no manners, or so it was said, and for the
most part, it was true. They were a lazy people with regard to the
niceties of formal interaction. As if to prove her thoughts true,
several of the older men who attended the Matriarch appeared to
either side of the Matriarch's large wagon; they took up their
places by crossing their arms in front of their chests and lounging
against the wagon's side, staring at the cerdan who accompanied
the Serra, measuring them.

Sunlight aged them, as did the wind. They wore no armor, or
little of it, and three of the eight carried swords; they all carried
daggers, and Serra Teresa was certain that half of them were of
the throwing variety; the Voyani did not often like to close in a
fight with strangers, although amongst themselves the thrown
dagger was considered an act of cowardice that stained the honor
of the family.

Such as it was.

Some of the men shaved, although they retained either beard or
mustache; a smooth face was considered a boy's face by Voyani
men. Serra Teresa did not understand the rank that Voyani men
actually held, and wasn't certain if she wanted to dignify Voyani
pecking order with the word. It was the women she came to, after
all, and the women who entertained outsiders such as she stood
apart from their kin, if not above.

Margret of the Arkosa Voyani had not yet reached the age
where she knew how to maintain that distance. She did not understand the use of mystery, the use of silence, the use of sparing
truths. But she understood death; they all did, clansmen and Wanderers alike. These were the Lord's lands, and the Lady's, and
perhaps life was not such a mercy that it should be mandated, and
guaranteed.

Serra Teresa waited outside the large wagon for a full five
minutes before she realized that Evallen would not emerge to
greet her. Oh, she'd known it, of course; it was partly to convey

word of that woman's death that she had come into this dell. But knowledge of death and acceptance of it are often separated by time and experience, and she had had little time since the death itself had become known to her.

She lifted her head slightly.

"The Matriarch?"

"Is not with the caravan, as you should well know," a clear, strong voice said.

The Serra Teresa froze. And then, without another word, she turned. "Captain," she said quietly.

"No."

"Ser Karras—"

"I will not leave you with these," he replied, his tone low, his meaning unmistakable.

She hesitated a moment, afraid for him and now, because of this single sentence spoken by a woman who was always a little bit too obviously angry, afraid *of* him. But she did not choose to use the voice upon him, to force him away.

"Margret," she said softly, and she bowed her head.

The young, dark-haired woman paused, her mouth already half open as if to speak. It was grudging, this pause, a thing that the Serra Teresa was certain she had struggled for. "Come with me."

Karras was not pleased by the tone Margret took; he bristled, but not obviously—he was too well-trained to embarrass or endanger her that way. Although they were better armed than the Voyani, they were also outnumbered, and there was no question of surviving a fight started here, among these people.

He escorted Serra Teresa to the wagon in which Margret and her brother lived. Margret mounted steps whose upper hinge creaked with either age or want of oil, or perhaps both, and then flung open the small, perfect door. Inside, it was both shadowed and empty; the windows that graced the mother's wagon graced the child's as well, but they were smaller and allowed for less light.

"In here," Margret said curtly, "we can speak."

Such rudeness as this, Serra Teresa had witnessed once before in her life, from the mother. For a moment daughter and mother looked so alike that she felt, that she could feel, young again herself, on the brink of a mystery that she didn't—quite—believe in, and a mystery, herself, that Evallen couldn't quite believe in.

Perhaps, she thought, as she saw Ser Karras' small frown, *you will do well enough.*

* * *

Shadows provided mercy, of a type. Light was often harsh when sorrow intruded; it allowed for no privacy, no illusion of the strength of expression that dignifies either a man or a woman who understands that life ends, that death is inevitable.

"Where is my mother?" Margret said, as she found a seat in the high wagon, and offered the Serra her choice of worn but sturdy pillows.

The Serra was silent.

"She was to leave before the Festival's end, Serra. She was to meet us in Mancorvo."

"She—she told you this?"

It was the Voyani's turn to fall silent. When she spoke, her voice was flat, as inflectionless as the Serra might have preferred. "She told you different."

"Margret, your mother and I knew each other—"

"For longer than I've existed, yes, I've heard it before. But I'm her *kin*." She stood, and the flatness left her voice and her expression.

Evallen, Teresa thought, *I warned you against this: you have raised a wildness in your family.*

"What, exactly, did she tell you?"

"None of your secrets," Teresa said softly, folding her hands in her lap, taking up a posture that she was certain would both impress and offend the younger woman. "She told me nothing, Margret, that did not pertain to what little privacy a Matriarch is granted."

"What did she tell you?"

Serra Teresa turned her face to the window, lifted the fan that was wrapped, by a golden chain, around her wrist, protection against loss on the road. "She told me," the Serra said, pitching her voice as carefully as she could, "that she had come to the Tor Leonne to die."

The silence, as always, was terrible.

"She—she—" The attempt to speak was worse.

For Serra Teresa di'Marano was gifted and cursed, and where she could lend dignity to another by somehow refusing to see the weakness they could not help but show, she could not refuse to hear it. The voice conveyed a complexity of emotion that a word did not, no matter how good the speaker was at dissembling, at hiding emotion. Margret was not such a one, and oddly enough, that made it easier; she was not the eavesdropper, or worse, the soul's voyeur, she was the bearer of bad tidings to a woman barely more than girl and not schooled enough to hide what she felt.

"I wish you were someone else," Margret said, and it surprised the Serra.

"Why?"

"Because if you were, I'd accuse you of lying." The voice broke three times, as if the words were rocks it could not pass over, but must flow round. Bitterness, there. And beneath it, certainty.

"You suspected."

"Yes." She was tired, was Margret, and angry. "But I didn't have—what my mother did. I couldn't be certain." She began to pace the confines of the wagon, her long stride making it seem small indeed to the woman who was trapped there with her.

At last, she stopped. "How?"

This was harder. "I was not there, Margret."

"Was anyone?"

"Yes."

She fell silent again. "Who—who found the body?"

Teresa closed her eyes. "You are asking me if someone removed something from your mother's corpse. I can answer that question: If they did, it was not a thing of value. She *knew*, Margret; she knew what she must do."

"Then you have brought her home," Margret said formally, the words strange to the Serra's ears.

Teresa looked away again, wondering when the woman's voice had drawn her eyes from the Lord's light. "No," she said at last, knowing from the tone of the words, rather than from their content, that the younger woman spoke not of a corpse. "I have not."

"But—" For the first time, there was a fear about her voice, a loss of certainty. "You *must* have—have done what she asked."

"She did not ask it of me," Serra Teresa replied, coming at last to the second part of her duty. "She asked it of a young woman whom she met in the Tor Leonne. The young woman who—who witnessed her death, who was the only witness."

"You're lying."

She did not smile when she said, "You accuse me of something that you have just said—"

"This is your way, isn't it? This is your way of drawing us into your intrigues and your stupid battles. I *told* her—I told her not to listen to you—"

I know, Teresa thought. *You are much like your mother at this age; any plagues or curses we must suffer are our own, and we are welcome—at your pleasure—to suffer them with neither cease nor your aid.* But she did not say it.

"What is it, Teresa? What do you want from us? You've taken Evallen—and I have no way of knowing whether or not anything you've told me is true."

"You have the same method your mother had," was Serra Teresa's reply. She was curious, and she was not, for although she had always suspected that the pendant that Diora now held in her possession was a thing of more than just monetary value to the Arkosa Voyani, she also knew the price of sharing their secrets. There were places one did not, one could not, pry.

"Where is this—this other woman?"

"In the Tor Leonne. She cannot travel; even the freedom of daylight is almost prohibited her."

"But you travel. You could have—"

"I could not ask her to break her oath to Evallen of the Arkosa Voyani."

Truth, in that. Margret's sullen silence was acknowledgment enough. "What do you want of us, Teresa?"

"The young woman that she gave this great task to was the Consort of the Lord of the Sun."

"So?"

"Perhaps I betray myself; the court is my home, and has always been. You knew her, I think even you must have known her, by the name she once held: Serra Diora Maria en'Leonne."

Margret sat down, hard.

Into the silence, the sun fell, its shadows lengthening as its rays were broken by objects; tin cups, candle holders, lamps redbrown with rust around handle and base. Margret was white with the things she must leave unsaid; they were many.

Teresa made to rise, and the young woman stirred, restless as a caged beast—and as dangerous, Teresa thought, to a woman who had made the choice to enter its cage. She sat again, unmindful—if a Serra of her stature could be—of the darkness, the meagerness—of her surroundings. She felt oddly hollow as she watched this child pace; Margret was older than Diora in all things but experience, and loss.

Even this loss.

She had not thought to feel it, because she had felt it so little in the confines of the Tor Leonne, during the heat and the danger of the Festival Sun. She had seen the body; they all had; it was displayed prominently, and over the course of two days, it caught the wind unkindly, gave it the scent of early decay, of blood. They had taken it down as an offense to the grandeur of the grounds on the third day, but she did not know where it was buried; she was certain that no ceremony had attended the corpse.

She knew, as well, that the Voyani did not put much stock in the proper burial rites; bury the dead, by all means, but don't worship the corpse; the spirit, after all, had been freed from the burden of constant wandering, a homelessness decreed by fate, upheld by even the laws of nature.

Evallen.

But she had not thought, after seeing that body, to sit in this wagon, of all wagons. The grand wagon, that she could have brushed aside as easily, as nonchalantly, as serafs did the summer flies. But not here; it was in this wagon that she and Evallen had first met, when Evallen's mother, Violla, had been the Matriarch.

The circle closes. Yes. Around them all, an ambush.

"Teresa?"

She was embarrassed to be caught out, to be caught with no control, momentarily, of her expression. She knew the lines of her face were neutral because no loss could destroy that mask; it was part of everything she had been raised to be. But she also knew that it was vacant, that expression; she had gone, for a moment, into a past that contained Evallen and Teresa, a young woman who would rule the Arkosa Voyani as mother of them all, and a young woman who would never be a mother, no matter that either woman desired a different destiny.

She had seen the end of so many lives, but she felt, suddenly, the Lady's Night was falling, finally; that there would come a night so black that the inevitability of dawn could be struck forever from human memory.

And then she knew why, for she was not a woman given to the darker fancy of the Night's thoughts, especially not during the Lord's tenure. She heard it in a voice.

"I believe," she said, her own voice smooth as the silk that she wore, "you have a visitor, Margret. Or rather, your van does."

Margret turned at once, as if glad of the opportunity for action, or reaction.

Pitching her voice in the manner that she had been taught so long ago by a bard-born man, she said, "Margret—please."

The younger woman turned.

"Caution. Make no promises to him, give him no hint of your intent or your secrets."

"As if," Margret said, with a faint bitterness and angry but muted contempt, "we *ever* give outsiders anything of ourselves."

It was meant as a blow, and because it was meant that way, the Serra found it difficult to be offended. A difference, she mused, between the ghost of her younger self and the woman that she was now. So many differences—surely not all the product of age—but she knew how to do one thing well, at that age, at this one.

She knew how to listen.

In the artificial darkness of the wagon's confines, alone for the first time since the Festival of the Sun itself—for Ramdan's invisible presence *was* a presence, a comfort and a responsibility both—she closed her eyes and let the line of her shoulders dip, ever so slightly, groundward.

She shut out color and shadow and edges of light; shut out, as she could, the scents confined within the still cabin, and listened.

"I have come," this stranger's voice said, "to speak with Evallen, who protects the Arkosa Voyani on their voyage." Inflected slightly, the address was archaic and stilted—but there was, in the words, a respect that was truer than they were.

"She's not here." Margret's voice was thin and reedy when compared with the richness and the depths of this stranger's. Teresa could not help but compare the voices; indeed, the differences seemed to demand no less.

Grandeur, there. Power. Not Margret's.

If, Serra Teresa thought, folding her fan in the stillness by playing with its familiar edges, *you were a woman, you might even present a small threat. But the Voyani men don't follow men.*

"I . . . see. I am, perhaps, mistaken about the color of the flag that you fly. I was given to understand that such a flag was flown only in the camp of the Matriarch."

She heard the play of unruly hair against cloth that was the Voyani shrug.

"I assure you that Evallen would find it most—advantageous to speak with me; I do not seek to sell her anything—as you can see, I come with little. But I have word for her, of something she values, perhaps above all else."

"And if she were here, I'm sure she'd be happy," the Voyani daughter replied, in a tone of aggravated boredom; whatever this stranger looked like, it was clear that he had done two things by that appearance: He had impressed Margret with his bearing and confidence, and he radiated a certain authority.

Better to come as a man of earth instead, sweat-stained by labor, but built by it as well. Better to come as a sick man, or a father in fear of the loss of children, better to come as one fleeing from the unjust claims of the Dominion—for it was rumored, and the Serra was only barely able to remain uncertain about the truth of those rumors, that the serafs who fled sometimes found the Voyani before they found death—better, in fact, to come as anything other than a man of power.

For a man of authority and power could only be one thing: of the clans, and important to them. As if to prove the point she had not made, he was silent a long time. But to the surprise of the Serra, his tone, when he spoke, held none of the anger that she felt certain she would hear there. It held, oddly, a dark amusement, a certainty that this was both inevitable and unimportant.

"Tell her only this, then. We have the keys to Arkosa, and we are willing to grant them to its rightful owners."

She rose then, swiftly, urgently—rose with the grace of a lifetime of graceful movement, but without care for it, thought for it—and reached the window in time to see the cloaked hue of a stranger's back.

"Hey, Margret," one of the young men said, "should we stop him?"

She saw the young woman shake her head.

"But what's he mean? Is he threatening Evallen?"

She shook her head again; her hair was a cascade of darkness that still caught and reflected light.

"Why did he say—"

"I *don't know,* Nicu, but if you don't shut up, the answer won't matter to you." To punctuate the sentence, Margret drew a dagger that was slender enough to disappear as she turned it on its edge.

He shrugged, shoved his hands in the sash across his midriff, leaned back against the wagon. The Serra Teresa would never become accustomed to this; the man honestly did not take offense at the threat. None of the men would, with the exception of her brother, and indeed, had this Nicu—a fine young man with broad shoulders and sun-browned skin—drawn knife in return, the others would have made him regret it. Whether or not he survived that regret was entirely a matter of their affections—or hers—although in truth it was rare that the Voyani killed each other.

Usually, when they did, it was in a fine and black temper, and the memory of it lingered. There was, however, no love lost whatever between the clans; of the four, two were currently involved in almost open warfare. As long as that war did not spread into the villages owned by the Tyrs and the Tors, it was overlooked with some malice.

The young woman came back to her wagon, and as she turned, she shoved the dagger, with more force than such an obviously well-crafted weapon deserved, into its sheath.

But it was her face that told much; the expression on it heightened by a lack of color, a forced neutrality that must be hard indeed for a woman of her temperament to achieve.

The Serra was standing. "I will leave you, Margret. I am sorry to deliver so little news, and all of it bad."

The younger woman's anger was a guttered flame; gone. She looked across at Teresa as if desperate for guidance, even if it was not, and never to be again, her mother's. "Do you know what he said?"

"What who said?"

"That man—"

"Who was the man?"

"I—" She stopped. Flushed. "I didn't ask."

"Was he a clansman?"

"I'm certain of it." Then she stopped again. "I *was* certain of it. Teresa—you—"

"She cannot help you, Margret. But will you speak to an outsider of affairs of the Arkosa? If you will, speak to me, and only to me."

They turned at once at an unfamiliar, a new, voice. The wagon's flap lay almost shut and no one—save Adam, whose home it also was, or Evallen herself—disturbed Margret when those flaps were shut. Not if they didn't want a sound beating.

But Margret of the Arkosa Voyani—Margret, now protector of, and mother to, her clan—drew back as if she saw an apparition. "You," she said softly.

"You remember me."

Margret's face had lost the last of the color that was not granted her by the grace of the sun's harsh touch. "It was *you*," she whispered, the three words raw. "You. My mother—"

"I am not responsible for Evallen's choice," the woman in midnight blue replied. And Serra Teresa di'Marano heard the alloyed uneasiness in her voice that spoke of both truth and lie. "Nor am

I responsible for her death. She accepted the responsibility of
Arkosa."

"You took her away."

"She asked it, Margret. She asked me for vision."

"It's not your right—it wasn't your right—"

"She had the Sight, but not the clear ability to See."

"And you showed her her death, didn't you?"

"I? No. But I will not lie to you because we will speak again,
often, you and I: she saw it."

The Serra wished to leave, because she had never heard a
person speak who so clearly spoke with the wind's voice as this
stranger did. This woman, this intruder—her voice was the voice
of one who has seen enough horror to go completely mad—but
who, somehow, barely has the strength to remain true in the face
of the incomprehensible.

But the woman who wore a length of midnight blue that went
from head to toe, turned at that moment and bowed to her in the
Northern fashion. "Serra Teresa," she said.

"You speak," Teresa replied, "with the voice of the winds."

"Yes." Ferocity, in that single word; bitterness. Triumph perhaps, but one so tired there was no joy in it. She returned her attention to the younger woman. "You know what that . . . man meant
to offer."

Margret said, "You will not speak of this in front of the Serra,
or I will be forced to kill her."

"Kill her, and your mother will never return to you. Accept it,
Margret. You are not a fool. Your mother knew what she was
doing, and knows it still. She has given you the guiding hand."

"I never took her charity." Margret dragged the back of her
hand across her eyes. "I never asked to be guided."

"No. Perhaps not. But this is not a matter of charity. This is a
matter of the Arkosans, of *Arkosa,* and if your own jealousy prevents you from seeing it, if your own pride prevents you from
acting, you will have doomed your mother to a pointless death.
It is, of course, your choice; only the living can give a death
purpose."

It was a Voyani saying.

Margret was sullen, and she was fearful, and she was hesitant,
and all of these things were in her voice when she turned stiffly
and spoke—to Teresa. "What must I do to bring my mother
home?"

"I do not know."

"You know where this—this Serra is."

"I do know where she is kept, yes. Under guard, by the Tyran of the newly anointed Tyr'agar, in the Tor Leonne."

"And how are we to send word to her?"

"I will carry word, if I am able."

"You could have carried the—" She stopped; brought hand to eyes again, rubbing hard against the skin there.

"I am not granted free passage; I am only a Serra." She was silent, carefully weighing the words that she meant to speak. "I am certain," she said at last, "that your mother's death was indirectly ordered by the Tyr'agar, in ignorance of her identity. I am watched, Margret, but I am—barely—trusted. She is not. If I were to take anything from her, especially now, it might doom us all. It would certainly draw attention to—to things that are best left in the harem of an unmarried girl's father."

"Teresa—"

"I believe that war is coming. It was not announced after the Lord's Festival; it is likely, therefore, that it will be announced after the Lady's." She knelt into the faded cushions at her feet. "That will be our last night, I think, of freedom."

"We're not waiting until the Festival of the Moon!"

"I would prefer that you did not," Teresa replied. "For that is nearly six months away, and the armies that will gather in that time should never have been called to gather."

"What do you mean?"

"Night is falling, Margret, protector of Arkosa. I do not pretend to understand what links you to your mother, and Evallen to her mother before her. But Evallen came because she understood this, and this alone: That the Lord of Night has been awakened."

Margret was as silent as stone, and of the same shade, although her hair was still dark, and her eyes even darker. The eyes she closed; she drew breath as if breathing caused her pain, and then spit, once, to the side. When she opened her eyes, Teresa thought she had aged years; whether or not they were enough, the Serra could not be certain; only action would decide that, and action lay in the future.

"You are . . . brave, Serra," the stranger said.

"It is one of the many things one might forge out of desperation and fear," the Serra replied gravely, in the face of this stranger's boldness.

"We will meet again, I think." The stranger bowed. "I am Evayne a'Nolan, and in this, I serve the Lady's cause." Again, there was a strong thread of truth, of lie, woven into a single fabric: her voice.

"If you serve the Lady's cause," the Serra replied, "I have no doubt of that at all."

"Margret," Evayne a'Nolan said. "I will return as I am able."

"Don't bother," Margret replied tonelessly. Forcelessly. She didn't look as Evayne walked out of the wagon, to disappear before the window framed her back in open sunlight.

They were silent, Teresa and Margret. Silent, bereft a moment of the buffer the stranger had provided. It was, of course, the Serra Teresa who spoke first; she was trained to be, in all things, graceful.

"Margret, I do not know for certain if I will be able to return to you, or if you will be able to return to me; I am sent on the road as messenger for my brothers. Therefore, I bid you accept this, and accept it as a token."

"Of what?"

The Serra's smile was thin. "Of your will, and the truth of the offer you make, if you choose to make it at all." Her right hand covered her left for a moment, and when it withdrew, it held a single ring. Gold encircled emerald, and the emerald was a very fine one. Of such things had oaths been made.

She held it out to the young Voyani woman. "Have this delivered to my niece, and she will know that your summons is genuine."

"And if I sell it?"

"Then she will not know, and will make her decision based upon her need and her instinct."

"Just like that, eh? Are you made of stone, Teresa? Have you a heart of steel and harsh light, like all of your men do? Do you love nothing living that doesn't tread on four legs?"

"Would it matter to you," the Serra asked softly, her voice as calm and placid as it usually was, "if I had a heart as true as your own, but better hidden? Would anything suffice to prove its existence to you but gaudy display?"

"Maybe," Margret said grudgingly. "Maybe not. Did you plan it? Did you know I'd say yes?"

"Yes," Teresa replied. "When you knew who your enemy was—who *our* enemy was—I knew it. What other answer could you offer?"

Margret held out an open palm, and Teresa laid in it the only object that she valued, the only tie that bound her, personally, to the past, and to past deaths. Oh, there was the daughter, her niece—but she had not been a gift of oath and binding, not a gift to Teresa of love, although she had grown to love her.

Alora. She bowed, both as a gesture of respect and a way of hiding her face for a moment. The oath ring was gone. It was done.

Margret held herself in until the flaps swung open; until they swung shut; until they ceased to swing at all at the passing of perhaps the finest Serra in all the Dominion of Annagar. And then she turned in a rage to the low, flat table.

It had been her way, since the days of her childhood, to vent her anger on things that did not vent back—and it had been beaten into her early that those things best served her that also could not fight back. Because other children could hit and bite and scratch as they liked—*they* would not be the protector of the Voyani. Only she, *if* she was responsible enough to survive it.

Evallen had never been particularly kind to her daughter. Her son, Adam, she adored, and openly. Margret had thought to hate him forever when he first came into her life. She succeeded in hating him until he was two, and at two the fact that he adored her had thawed the ice of her anger in a way that her mother's remonstrations had—and would always—fail to do.

Still, if he came upon her now, she'd probably slap him, and he hated it when she was angry; he was always so proud of her. Aie, but his pride was already a heavy chain around her neck; it prickled her. She hated the responsibility of living up to it, but she loved the glow of it. Brothers. Kin.

In her hand, the ring was warm. She started to slide it on to her finger, and then noted ruefully that it would at best slide over the knuckle of her extra fingers—the small ones on the end. If that. She was tempted not to try because Teresa already made her feel old and ugly, and she was half the Serra's age or less. Spitting, she pulled out one of the several strands of gold that hung round her neck. She unclasped it and added the ring to its weight before letting it fall beneath the folds of her shirt.

This was her personal treasure; if the wagons met flood or fire or worse, she could flee and still be certain of survival in the Dominion. She knew its byways well enough. They all knew how to survive on nothing.

Nothing, they had a lot of.

More of, now that her mother was gone.

She sank to the floor, her hands in curled fists upon the scored

flat of the table. She couldn't cry; not yet. She couldn't link the
death to the Serra, the Serra to the death. Oh, Adam might suspect—he was so sweet, it was easy to think him stupid as well, and
he wasn't—but no one else should; she'd have trouble enough
when the word got out.

But she'd also have people to mourn with, to grieve with.

The clans—they were cold and hard and alone. They paid fealty
to blood ties without understanding the strength of them, the fire
that forged. She wondered—for the first time, for the only time—
if this was how Teresa felt, for this was the first time that she had
had to hide word so large from her kin. She wanted to speak it
now; she wanted to dissolve the lump of it from her throat with
word and song and the comfort of the arms of her kin; her uncle,
her aunt, her cousins. She wanted her mother to be respected, to
be mourned, to be *avenged.* And more. Much more.

The Lord of Night.

Ah, Lady, Lady—not now. Not on her head. Not on hers. What
did she know? She was not Evallen; she did not have the pendant,
and until she did, she was not *truly* Matriarch.

But to get that pendant, she must risk more than her mother
risked: the Arkosa Voyani in the Tor Leonne itself. She must make
the decisions that a Matriarch would make without the power that
had sustained the Matriarchs before her: the legacy of the line that
went, unbroken, from mother to daughter, mother to daughter.

Oh, she'd have to marry, too. Marry one or another of her
cousins or second cousins; she needed daughters now; at least
one, although most Voyani women had at least two for security's
sake. The thought made her grind her teeth, but it was easier than
thinking of death, of her mother's death, of the terrible need to
hide it versus the terrible need to speak it and have done.

They must move; they must plan. A month, she thought, and
her mother's death could be somehow discovered. No, two, to be
certain that the Serra passed above it.

Because Margret was not the only one to hate the clansmen,
and she could not add her mother's death to their list of crimes;
not now, not when they were necessary.

She wept, and she found that lonely tears satisfied none of
the ache.

Do you cry? she wondered, as she rose heavily. *Do you cry,
Serra? Do you only cry alone?*

Yes. Yet it had been to the Serra that her mother had spoken the truth. And it was the daughter who needed it who would have to do without. Anger was an important weapon in Margret's life; she used it now.

Wished she could use it against someone beside herself.

CHAPTER ONE

14th of Maran, 427 AA
Terafin Manse, Averalaan

She woke screaming.

It was nothing new. They'd been half expecting it, her bleary-eyed compatriots; she'd woken them, screaming, every night for the past eight days, and she'd remembered so little of the dreams that had sent her back to the waking world in such terror that she'd probably had no choice but to do it all over again.

Teller, Finch, Carver, and Angel—they were used to this. They'd lived with it for many years, first in the twenty-fifth holding and then as part of House Terafin, although it had seldom been this bad as she'd grown into her talent. Daine—given leave by a testy Alowan to sleep outside of the healerie—found it more trying.

"It's not the screaming," he said, as he joined the weary procession in the hall that led to Jewel's room. "It's the frenzy. It sounds as if she's going mad with helplessness."

"Unlike the rest of us, who are just going mad with lack of sleep." Light glinted off the surface of an expensive dagger. Shadows hugged the undersides of Carver's eyes.

"Hey, you know what they say," Finch told him, shoving a very stubborn swathe of hair out of her eyes for the fifth time.

"No. At this hour of night I barely know what *I* say, never mind anyone else. What do they say?"

"No one has a right to sleep. It's a privilege."

Daine snorted. "Sounds like you've been talking to midwives."

"Yeah, well. The cook's wife just gave birth to her first child, and the midwife gave a long lecture the entire time she was birthing." Finch snorted. Angel stepped around her with practiced ease, and pushed the door to Jewel's room open. "I'd've decked her, myself. Hold that thing steady. She'll want the light."

"She already has light," Jewel said, interrupting their conversation.

Of course. Avandar stood in her room, unwavering shadow that he was. His fist was glowing, or rather, the rock that sat cradled in the curve of his palm was. The shadows beneath his eyes made Carver's look handsome.

"You look like crap," Finch said sweetly.

He gave her the frown she more or less expected.

They'd grown around him, the way vines do around rocks, but they'd never managed to make him one of their own. Daine had already been swallowed whole. Of course, that might have more to do with the fact that he'd had to call Jay back from the brink of death, holding her soul inside his as he walked her back into the land of the living.

Which, she thought, only barely described the den this particular evening.

"Get anything this time?" Teller asked hopefully. What he meant, what he wouldn't expose her by saying, was, *Are you willing to talk about it yet?*

She shook her head. Stopped. Nodded.

The door to her room was open; she could see them so clearly in the lamp-dimmed dark, she wondered if her vision weren't augmented somehow. If it was her gift, it was a bad sign.

But the clearest face, pressed as it was between the shoulders of Angel and Carver—who would never lose the habit of drawing their weapons, even if the weapons drawn had changed, when they heard that cry—was Teller's.

"Jay," he said. Quietly.

Teller, to whom she could never lie. At least not successfully.

Avandar was in the habit of correcting her den when they questioned her too commonly; he was not in the habit of interrupting them when their questions—or accusations, in this case—were contained beneath the surface of a single inquisitive word.

Her shoulders slumped; she slouched into her height.

"Jay?"

"Kitchen," she whispered.

She dropped into her chair, sliding it against the rugless kitchen floor with a satisfying squeak. Her feet were bare. Everyone got to see them; she propped them up on the table's edge and leaned back on two of the chair's four legs. It was warm enough that slippers made her feet sweat, and she hated sweating

Angel dropped the lamp at its place by her side, or in this case, by her feet. Teller took a seat, quill in hand, inkstand long and shadowed by the flickering of burning oil. His hands were steady. Hers, oddly enough, were not; she kept them in her lap. They all knew that as a bad sign.

"You should be practicing," Avandar said quietly. "Whatever it is you've seen, it should be coming to you in your waking hours, and at your command. *You* are the seer; your visions are subject to your will."

"Avandar—"

"Or they should be."

"We've had this argument before."

"It is not an argument, Jewel. I merely state fact."

"I like your jaw enough to ask you to stop stating fact, okay?"

It wasn't entirely impossible that she'd lose her temper and slug him, although she almost never did anymore. House training had taken her temper away from her in bits and pieces and forced her to hide it in the strangest places.

"Very well," Avandar said, not at all bothered by the threat. "Your dream."

"It involves you, so pay attention."

That got their attention. She didn't really want it. "I've been having the dreams again."

Carver snorted. "So tell us something we couldn't guess."

"You know the drill. Three dreams. Three nights."

"You've had 'em longer than three nights, Jay. It's been— what—at least a week. I think tonight's the *eighth* night. If it's the same dream, that's some wyrd, all right."

"It's the same dream."

"What is it?" from Teller.

"I'm alone. I'm traveling alone. I think I'm the scout at the head of an army, but whenever I turn around, there's only one man behind me."

"Who?"

She raised her head. "He's wearing armor. But it's so bloody it looks like red steel. He's carrying a sword that's jagged and curved, a great sword—but he holds it in one hand. I know that I wouldn't even be able to lift it. A great helm hides his face, but not his eyes—his eyes—"

She could hear the scritch of Teller's quill against paper as she paused to draw breath.

"In his wake, as if he's a tide, there are just *so many* dead. I can only see them truly in the shadow he casts, but everything is there. It's as if he's just walked through all of history leaving a corpse behind for every year that's passed. Children. Women. Men in the strangest armor I've ever seen.

"He—"

Silence. They were waiting. She hated that they were waiting, but she appreciated that they could. "I've never done anything really important without you," she said quietly. Her voice was the dream's voice, but her words were her own. She saw Carver and Angel glance side to side; saw Finch frown. Arann wasn't with them; Daine looked—because he was smart—to Teller.

Teller continued to write.

"I realize that he only walks when I walk. That if I stand in place, his shadow doesn't grow any longer. So I stop."

"Then," she said softly, "I hear horses. Or something that sounds like horses. They come from where I've been heading. I look up, and I see her."

Silence. Edged now, sharp with things unsaid.

They waited while the oil burned.

"She is the most beautiful woman I've ever seen in my life. Her skin is fair and unblemished, her hair is long and pale and fine."

Teller frowned. *"Long and pale and fine, like a blade's edge, she pierced their hearts and led them, led them all, the fine chase, the dark road."*

They all turned, even Jewel.

"It's the poem. Shurtlev's 'Winter Hunt.' You remember it."

"I . . . remember it." Jewel closed her eyes. "But this . . . woman . . . She is mounted on—on a creature that was once human. At least I assume it was; it has a human face." Her eyes almost snapped open; she was denying the clarity of vision; replacing it with the familiarity of friendship.

"I want to run. But she's already seen me. She knows who I am. She *knew* who I was, even though I've said nothing. She lifts a horn to her lips and blows it; they appear at her side."

"They?"

"Her host."

"Jewel."

She turned to look at Avandar, who had only barely learned not to interrupt her.

"When you say host, what do you mean? This . . . hunt . . . Teller is correct. It is described in Shurtlev's 'Winter Hunt,' and it may be—"

"Thousands."

"Pardon?"

"Thousands. She's emptied her court."

"How do you know this?"

"It's my damn dream," she snapped back irritably. "How the Hells do I know anything in a dream?" But she choked back the rest of what was only hysteria trying to find expression. "She—gods, she was so beautiful—she says, 'We've come for the Hunt; the hunting has never been so good.' And then she calls my name.

"I know I'm dead. She's just so compelling, I'm not sure I care. But then he speaks, I mean, the man who's been following me. He says, 'Only give me the word, and I will save you.'

"He steps forward. And as he does, the dead pile up at his back. Only this time, I can hear them screaming; I can see them falling; I can see the shadows swallowing them whole. It makes him stronger. It feeds him.

"I tell him to stop. I tell him to *stop*. And she—she rides in." The lamplight flickered. She stared at it, into its heart. "The bodies appear to either side of her, as if they're some sort of afterthought, as if they're just dust from the road.

"And then he says, 'Do not challenge me.'

"She says, 'I have her name.'

"He says, 'The name gives you the right to combat, but it is power that decides her fate.'

"And she waves her hand, her unmailed, pale hand, and the land to either side of the road we're standing on is suddenly turned to desert; it falls away. Behind her, behind the body of her host, is a lake that glitters like diamond; cold, beautiful. She says, 'These lands were my lands, and I mark them still. What was given was given, and thanks are offered and my ceremonies performed, however weak those have become.'

"And he says, 'I will pass through, and I will take what I have claimed.' "

"Jay?"

"He lifts his helm then."

She turned in her chair.

Her domicis stiffened in the silent kitchen.

"Avandar?"

"Yes."

"It was you."

He nodded. Stepped back.

It was Teller who said quietly, "It isn't finished yet."

The domicis lifted a dark brow.

"No," Jewel said softly. "It isn't. He takes two steps forward. More dead. I tell him to stop. She stops as well. There's movement from the North—and as they look North, their faces are lit with a sudden light; red light, bright light. It seems to go on forever.

"A voice speaks out of that light.

"It says, 'This world is mine, and all deaths serve my purpose.'

"And then," she said softly, no longer looking at domicis or lamplight—or anything at all—"the killing starts.

"I'm in the middle of it; it's suddenly real. There are faceless people running around screaming in terror; there are dying children, dying women, dying men. They become dead so quickly they slip through my fingers, but if I don't sift through the dying, I won't find them in time.

"And that's why I'm there. To find them."

"To find who?"

"I don't know. *I don't know.* I've ridden this dream out to its end eight times, and I don't know what it is I'm supposed to know. I only know that I can't fail, or we all—"

Teller put the quill down. Rose. "Jay?" he asked quietly.

She looked across the table at him. Reached out with a shaking hand. "No."

"But we—"

"No."

"What's going on?" Carver's voice. Strained.

"She's leaving," Teller said quietly. "And she doesn't intend on taking any of us with her when she goes."

Moonlight. Darklight, nadir at its strength.

Why was it that she always came to be here when the darkness was strongest? She knelt. She was too weak to stand. The truth. The dead weren't faceless.

Teller knew. She was certain that no one else did.

"I can't do this," she said into the night, into the clarity of emptiness. Avandar had not even contested her desire to visit the shrine without him; although he hovered in the distance, he had chosen to retreat into a privacy as solid as any she could impose upon herself.

But that was acceptable to her. She knew that he understood her dream far better than he wanted to. *Knew* it. Did not choose to question him. She had her own ghosts, her own demons, her own guilty secrets.

"I can't do this," she said again.

"Then why," he replied, answering at last, "does Teller know that you're leaving?"

She turned, putting the altar firmly behind her.

In the moonlight, pale and thin though it was, she recognized the face he had chosen to wear. Teller's.

"I wish you wouldn't do that."

His eyes were like moonlight. "Why have you come, ATerafin? This is the altar upon which service is pledged. To my House. To me."

"I can't do what you ask of me."

"You have already decided to go."

She looked away. Cursed, not bothering to restrain herself. The night heard the words, and the dead. Neither of them were moved. "Years of dealing with merchants," she told him softly, "and I still can't bluff my way through a negotiation."

A brow rose.

"Yes. This is a negotiation. It just doesn't sound much like one 'cause it's late, I've had no sleep for a week, and I'm always at a disadvantage when dealing with the dead."

"A negotiation occurs when there is something to be negotiated. I fail to see that here."

"Yeah, well. Being dead probably doesn't help much." She tried for flippant. Got most of the way there. But her heart wasn't in it.

There was only one thing her heart was in. "I want you to take care of them."

"Jewel."

"Not the Terafin. I know it doesn't work that way. But them. My den. I want you to protect Teller. And Finch. I need you to watch over them."

"If I could, Jewel Markess, I would watch over *all* members of my House."

"There must be something you can do. You speak to *me*."

"Yes, I do," he said softly. "Just as I speak to The Terafin. You understand this, Jewel." He paused. His mannerisms were nothing at all like those of the man whose face he wore, and she wondered why he'd chosen Teller. "Why don't you take them with you?"

"You know why."

"Do I?"

"I don't know if anything is going to survive where I'm going."

"But you know there's no safety here. The truth, Jewel."

She knew why he wore Teller's face, then. Teller was the only one of her den she couldn't lie to. Or rather, the only one who knew when she was lying, and who seemed—by the complicity of silence—to understand why.

"If they're not here, the House falls."

"Yes."

"And if I'm not there, the House falls."

"Yes."

"Gods, I *hate* this." She spun to the altar and back. Once. Twice. Three times.

"And I," he said softly. "But I will tell you this: they must stand in your stead. Trust them."

She was stony faced. She'd never understood that expression before.

"They offered me their service. I accepted it." The night began to dissolve him. "It may surprise you, but you are not the only ATerafin of import; not the only ATerafin whose service the House depends on. You have surrounded yourself with people you trust. This is not uncommon.

"What is uncommon is that they are—all of them—worthy of that trust. You see clearly. You chose well.

"If I had any choice, I would keep you here. But it comes. Remember this: I left my House to ride with the sons of Veralaan."

"What am I going to tell The Terafin?"

"The truth," he said softly, his voice now as thin as the façade he wore. "She will accept it."

The Terafin sat across the length of the familiar, spotless table. Nothing adorned it; no books, no paperwork, no inkstands or quill, no lamp. But the lights that ringed the edge of the open glasswork above it cast soft reflections. Hers. Jewel ATerafin's.

She had chosen to forgo the domicis; Morretz, seldom excluded, had made his feelings plain by a slight compression of

lips even as he bowed. Avandar, on the other hand, had darkened. Had, in fact, turned from The Terafin to Jewel, forcing
them both to acknowledge that Jewel was his chosen master, no
matter whose gold had paid for—and continued to pay for—the
contract.

Jewel, however, was more politic.

Or perhaps more stubborn.

The two women sat in the room, experience, as always, the
thing that separated them. But not, The Terafin reflected, as much
as it once had. They were older. Wiser, perhaps.

Alone.

She waited for the younger woman to speak first.

Jewel acknowledged the right rank gave her; she spoke. "I'm
going South ahead of the armies."

Amarais inclined her head. "I suspected you might. Commander Allen will not, I think, be pleased."

"He might be."

"Oh?"

"If I don't go South, he loses the war. If I go, he has a small
chance of winning it."

The Terafin smiled at that. Commander Allen was not an obviously proud man, and he had never been boastful; his way, rather,
was to let louder men underestimate him until they had no choice
but to acknowledge his superiority. He was not, however, a man
to accept that he had either a slender chance of winning or that his
chance amounted to a single woman with no knowledge whatever
of the strategies or tactics of war.

"And besides, it means I won't have to deal with the Hawk
and the Kestrel, and I can tell you, he wasn't looking forward to
that."

The Terafin's smile was the only natural thing about the moment, and it faded. They sat alone as if they had always been two
solitudes.

"Avandar, of course, will go with you."

"Of course."

Silence.

"Will you take care of my den?"

"Your den, Jewel, are as capable of taking care of themselves
as my Chosen."

Silence.

It was awkward. It could hardly be anything but awkward. There
was an unspoken assumption that neither woman wished to touch,

but that had to be touched upon. The Terafin bowed her head. Took a deep breath. Smiled, the smile itself more of a wince than an expression of happiness or mirth.

"I do not think that I will be here to greet you upon your return."

Jewel had been fidgeting, her eyes drawn from one side of the library's expanse to the other, flicking here and there off book and shelf and table surface. It hadn't been obvious to The Terafin until the moment her words were exposed to the silence—because at that moment, Jewel became part of the silence.

She broke the stillness by rising.

"Isn't that why you came?" The Terafin said, pressing her, rising in turn. "To say good-bye?"

The younger woman's face lost all color, all movement; became a mask, but at that a poor one—one that was translucent, transparent, one that could so easily be seen through. If it weren't for its stiffness, it might have been no mask at all. There were tears.

She did not shed them. At least she had that much control.

"Yes. Yes, Terafin, I came to say good-bye."

"Without actually saying those words?"

The younger ATerafin looked away. "Without actually saying those words."

"Ah."

"You know."

"We know, but Morretz has difficulty acknowledging the eventual end of his service. It is why neither he nor Avandar is present."

Jewel sat.

The Terafin did not; she did not need to. "Have you no comfort to offer me?"

"I'm not much for comfort. Ask Angel. Or Carver."

"Or Teller? Or Daine?"

Jewel flinched. "I'm not much for offering comfort when there's no comfort to be offered. You don't want it. You don't need it."

"Oh, Jewel," The Terafin said softly, "you see, and you do not see. You're wrong. Tonight, in this room, between the two of us, I need comfort.

"I have looked; I have looked as clearly, as harshly, as I dare. I know the end is coming. Your dreams. The House's. My death is not natural. It is not accidental. One of my own will betray me, and if I could see clearly which one, I wouldn't be facing certain death. I see a war beyond the stretch and reach of my life that would have required all of my cunning and all of my experience to survive.

"This House—it is not me. But while I live, it is mine. I have been told by others with the particular experience I lack that my feelings are not unlike a parent's ferocity of affection for her child." She looked up; the stained glass was dark in the quiet night. From this vantage, the heavens weren't unreachable; they simply ceased to exist.

And it was not from the gods that she would make the only demand that would ease her.

"I had hoped that you would come to me. And you have." She looked across the table at the stricken younger woman.

"Terafin—"

"You know what I ask of you."

Jewel's mouth opened. Closed. She nodded.

"Offer me farewells, if that will ease you. But offer me something that will ease *me*. I have never asked it, Jewel. But this is the point of no return. When you leave, when you walk through the gates with your domicis, the ties between us are sundered although no one else will know it. I have given you all that I can give, and I have been pleased, even proud of what you have achieved.

"But what you have achieved pales against what you *must* achieve.

"This House—"

Jewel backed away from the table.

The Terafin thought she would flee. Was surprised at how much it cut when she did, in fact, walk quickly and stiffly toward the doors.

Was surprised at how much it meant when she stopped there, her hands on either side of the crack between them, her forehead pressed against the heavy wood. She lifted her head. Turned.

Her cheeks were wet with tears.

This, *this,* was why she had demanded, and received, privacy. Because The Terafin could not be seen to be weak, no matter how unnatural such a facade was.

She said, "I don't want you to die."

The Terafin said nothing.

"I don't want to accept what you offer because accepting— accepting it means that I've accepted your death."

"It is not an offer, Jewel. Make no mistake. It is a plea. It is a command. It is a responsibility. But an offer? No. Nothing so simple."

"Terafin—"

"No."

"Amarais."

The Terafin bowed. "Yes. Here, in this room, between us, that is all I am. I have no idea how I will die; I accept that I will, in your absence. It pains me. I confess a certain fear, a morbid curiosity, an unsettling anger. I will, of course, fight it. That is my nature. But I will have your word, here, or I will have your name."

It took a moment for the threat to sink in. She was patient. Wished that she could be more patient—but the time for waiting had passed. *I had hoped,* she thought, staring at this woman who, born into power, might have been her younger self, *that you would come to me on your own.*

Ah, well.

"This House means many things to me. But it stands for something. The Sword is *Justice,* and it *is* the House Sword."

"What do you want from me?"

"Everything. Protect Alowan. Preserve my Chosen, if they will it. Preserve my House from the war that will divide it if they do not. Become Terafin, Jewel. Become *The* Terafin."

"You're The Terafin. I know no other."

It was spoken so quietly The Terafin could have chosen not to hear the tremor in the voice, the break, subtle and slight, between syllables.

"You will know no other while I live," she said quietly, stating the obvious because Jewel ATerafin needed to hear it. "Isn't that what this is about? In you, tonight, I see my death. I *hate* it." The vehemence of the word surprised her. She swallowed. Looked away. Looked back; she owed Jewel that much. "But I also see life, of a sort. The life of *my* House. You are not who I am. But we value the same things. You will never destroy what I have built."

The younger woman was weeping now, silent and open-eyed. It was painful to watch. She watched, however; those tears were both for her and cried in her stead.

"Jewel Markess ATerafin, I name you my heir. You will serve the House and you will serve the Sword, and if the gods will it, they will serve you."

The tears were slow to stop, but they stopped.

"I will make no announcement. The House is already divided; the war is already in motion. But my death will deliver the news to the four least likely to accept it."

"To the five," Jewel said faintly, attempting to smile. The humor did not fall flat; Amarais accepted it for what it was. "Avandar will be so pleased."

"Yes."

"Morretz?"

She looked away. "He is not what you require. He will not, I think, serve another. Not for years, if at all. The option is open to teach, and many men who choose a life of service, rather than the contracts that are more common, often retire to teach others when the life of their chosen master is abruptly ended.

"Jewel."

The moment stretched out until it was so thin something had to break.

Jewel ATerafin slid, by painful inches, to one knee. "I give you my word," she said softly. "The House will *be* Terafin, and I—" silence.

Amarais waited.

The tears stopped completely, although their tracks lit her face in wide lines.

"And I will rule it."

Avandar was waiting for Jewel. The doors to the hall outside of this library had never seemed so heavy, and flight from them so necessary, in all of her years of service. From the first day, struggling for the perfect control that would give her the key to the House if she impressed the cold, forbidding woman on the other side of the table, to the weekly meeting called among the quiet walls of books, this had been the private recess of The Terafin, the place of judgment, the citadel of strength.

Gone, of course.

She wished, desperately wished, that The Terafin had chosen any other room in which to give her orders. In which to make her pleas.

"Jewel."

She'd been avoiding his gaze.

His gaze, she could. He served her, after all. She shook her head, looking at the floor as it passed beneath her moving feet.

But dammit, she was angry, and there was no one else to take it out on. She wheeled on him, disappointed for once that he'd kept his distance. "You wanted to serve a person of power," she said, surprised she could force the words from between her teeth, "so you'd better bloody well be up to it."

His gaze was cool. Condescending, in fact.

Just in case she missed this—and to give him his due, she often did—he said, "Are you finished yet?"

She almost slapped him.

"If I am to serve a person of power, Jewel, you had better be prepared to become one. This . . . display . . . is unbecoming, even in a person of the rank you have now."

She was silent because he was right. She'd even forgive him for it someday, although the aggregate of his offenses had piled up enough over the years that it didn't have to be any time soon.

"Let's go," she snapped, turning on her heel. "If we're leaving tomorrow, we've got a lot to do before we go."

"We do." He was quiet a moment. "I must speak with Morretz before we leave."

"Morretz?"

"I believe that's what I said."

"Why?"

Avandar didn't answer. He wasn't going to. He never answered questions about his past. But the futility of asking seemed comfortably familiar. She asked.

His silence, stony and completely impenetrable, made his annoyance plain. She shrugged. "Fine. Go talk with Morretz. I'm going back to the den."

To tell them what?

She froze a moment, hovering between choices that all seemed bad.

And because she froze, she was close enough to hear him.

"Jewel," he said softly, "I am sorry."

Torvan ATerafin came to her.

She had requested his company because she hadn't the right to command. Not yet.

But he came as if the request was a command, damn him.

"Jewel?" he said, as he came to a stop in the narrow doorway of her kitchen. A lamp was burning, even though the day was bright through the windows.

"Don't tell me. I look awful."

"Awful wasn't the word I was going to use."

"Oh?"

"It's politer." He frowned. At the lamp. Gods, he didn't miss a damn thing.

"Yes," she said, because she knew he wouldn't ask. "It's magicked. Avandar's little gift. What I have to say to you I can't afford to have anyone else hear."

"Where is Avandar?"

She was silent.

He matched her silence with a frown. "I heard that you went to speak to The Terafin."

"I did."

"I heard that you'd argued."

"Good."

"She hasn't revoked your name."

"No."

"Or your crest."

"No."

"Jewel?"

"Yes?"

"You didn't argue."

"We did, but it wasn't much of one. She has all the cards. I don't even have enough left over to make a bet."

"Why did you want to speak with me?"

"Because," she said, rising, "I'm leaving. Tomorrow."

His brows furrowed in confusion; she might have been speaking Torra. She could.

"We'll save the fond farewells," she said, after five minutes had elapsed and the oil had noticeably diminished. "I was to go South with the armies."

"I'd heard that. I hadn't heard they were moving."

"Well, now I'm going as . . . advance scout."

"There's a reason most scouts are well-paid and highly pensioned."

She laughed bitterly. "I'll be highly paid, all right."

"Jewel—"

"You're captain."

"Pardon?"

"You're captain. You're *my* captain. When the Chosen lose their leader, make them follow *you*."

She saw his eyes narrow. Blade's edge now; all frivolity, all humor, gone. "You're speaking about the death of The Terafin."

Gods, the words were *cold*. She wanted to cry again, standing here, in front of the man who had opened the House to her. Instead, she drew her shoulders back, achieving her full height. That brought her up to his shoulder. Almost.

"What," she said softly, "do you think we were arguing about? You knew what she wanted from me." It was an accusation, and it was the truth. It was also a surprise; a touch of gift that she hadn't even been reaching for.

He was very, very stiff.

"I haven't slept for nine days. I am *so tired* of this. If I had known what I know now when I first came to your gates—"

"You would have let Arann die?"

She looked at him, hating him for just that moment. "Gods, are you all sons of bitches?"

He surprised her. "Yes." There was something in his expression that she couldn't quite define to her satisfaction, but it replaced the cold anger that had framed the words that included Terafin and death. That had to be an improvement. "Answer the question."

She started to answer, to say something flippant, but the words got mangled by the emotion she was so bad at suppressing.

"Isn't that what I'm risking anyway?"

"Is it?"

"I'm leaving them behind." She looked at light's unnecessary reflection against the surface of the table. Easier than meeting his eyes.

He wasn't one of hers; he didn't touch her. He waited more or less patiently until she looked up again. "I'm leaving you behind."

Waited. Grim now.

"I'm deserting *her*."

"She can take care of herself."

His turn to flinch. She shook her head. She said, "You're the captain." Past caring now. "You're the only one who'll have prior knowledge. Start preparing." Her hands were fists. She didn't notice until she lifted them and forced them to unfurl; her fingers were literally shaking.

"Torvan—"

"Yes?"

"Protect my den."

She stood, ending the interview.

He said formally, "ATerafin."

"What?"

"Who will she leave this information with?"

"Damned if I know. That's one of the few things that isn't my problem."

"You've never been involved in a House War," he replied softly. "If it's not secure information, it will be far more your problem than any other worry you have now."

"Me."

"As interested party, your word will count for less than nothing."

"Torvan," she said, her voice as quiet as it had been all morning, "don't take this personally, but *get out.*"

He shut up. He left.

And one of the few good things she was certain about as she watched his back disappear was that he wouldn't take it personally.

One more. Only one more to go.

16th of Maran, 427 AA
Avantari, Averalaan Aramarelas

"Wait outside."

Avandar frowned. "Jewel—"

"This won't take long. I won't be in danger. And as far as I can tell—for the usual reasons—the Astari hate you."

"The usual reasons being no reason at all, I assume."

"Right the first time." Although to be fair—which she wasn't going to be—they seemed to hate everyone who had displayed even a trace of magic, and Avandar had certainly done that.

"Jewel—"

"It's only Devon," she said, before she had to hear the rest of the lecture.

"You don't seem to understand, all protestations and anger aside, that he serves another master."

"Oh, I understand it, all right."

"Jewel—"

"But maybe he serves another master just as obediently as you serve me."

That shut him up for the ten seconds she needed. She slid past him and into the office of Patris Larkasir's adjutant.

He rose at once, his eyes widening ever so slightly. That was Devon's version of unguarded surprise.

"Jewel?"

"ATerafin," she replied, setting the tone of their meeting with the formality of his title. "I hope I'm not interrupting anything important."

"It depends on who you ask. Patris Larkasir would consider these important." His hand touched a large pile of officially sealed documents.

"I'd like to speak to you in private for a moment."

"George. Please leave us."

The young man who was Devon's only obvious assistant bowed at once. Jewel privately thought he was one of the Astari, but she'd never asked. It didn't really matter. He left them alone, and that was all she wanted from him at the moment.

He waited until the door had closed, although from the way his eyes flickered over the frame, Avandar was practically standing *in* it.

"Why have you come?"

"To deliver a message."

"From The Terafin?"

"Sort of."

He waited. She was silent.

"Jewel, it's not like you to play waiting games."

"It's not a game."

"What is it?"

"Loss of words. I don't know what to say. No, not true. I don't know how to say it."

He waited.

She said, "I'm leaving."

"Pardon?"

"I'm leaving to go South."

"I'm aware of that. Unless," he added quietly, "you don't mean with the army."

"No, I don't mean with the army."

"What's happened?"

"It's not what has happened, it's what will happen. It's always what *will* happen with me. Birth defect."

"What will happen?"

She laughed, looking away.

He didn't.

"Jewel."

"End of the world. That sort of thing."

"You'll pardon me if the humor falls a little flat."

"Probably."

"Jewel, why *did* you come here?"

"Gods alone know. I want you to do me a favor."

"Have we had this discussion before?"

"Not exactly the same one, no."

"But this is House business."

Damn him. "What else?"

He leaned casually against the edge of his desk. Any other man would have hit the pile of Larkasir's documentation—it was close enough to the edge—but Devon knew exactly where to sit. She longed, just once, to see him clumsy. Gods knew he'd seen her trip over nothing more than her own two feet on several occasions.

"I'm going South. I'll join the army later."

His smile was thin and dangerous. "You aren't going South with the permission of the Kings' armies."

Devon, you are such a bastard. She smiled. "It's confidential; I prefer not to discuss it."

"I'm sorry, ATerafin. That wasn't a question."

Of course not.

She trusted this man. She knew it not because of the safety she felt when she was with him—it had been years since he'd offered her shelter that she could accept—but because of the anger.

Her smile didn't happen. She got it halfway up her mouth and let it drop. "Don't play stupid games with me, Devon."

He said nothing.

"Does The Terafin know that you spy on the House? Does she know that you—"

"Of course she knows it," he said, the snap in his words as obvious a sign of either anger or weariness as he had ever shown. "She's not a child."

"And I am?"

Again, he retreated to the sting of silence.

When he took up his words again, they were measured. Careful. He was, of course, no less angry. "The Terafin knows I spy on the House. It's one of the ways in which she proves her loyalty to the Crowns. Make no mistake, ATerafin. This *is* my calling. I *am* Astari. She could have released me from her service and taken back my name; it would have damaged my ability to hold visible royal office, and it would have changed the role of my life outside of the Astari, but it would not have changed my decision."

She was shocked into silence of her own, which had happened just enough recently that she almost instantly resented it. She worked off the discomfort her anger produced by walking across the room and yanking the curtains shut. The light that filtered through them anyway was muted, reddened; the material in her hand was stubbled like raw silk. She pried her fingers loose.

"You've never said that to The Terafin." The words, like the light just beyond her hands, were muted.

"The Terafin," he replied coolly, "is far too politic to ask. What do you think I am, Jewel? I am her peace offering; I am her pledge of allegiance. I am her willingness—in tangible form—to cooperate with the man whose life is the protection of the Kings.

"And in return for this, she partakes of the information I receive as a member of the Astari."

"You tell her nothing."

"I *tell* her nothing, but she is not naïve enough to believe that the value of my service is dependent on open words. Can you separate your knowledge, your experience, from yourself in any meaningful way? Can you act upon things that you know as if you don't know them, and never have?"

The silence lasted a full thirty seconds before she realized it was a question he meant her to answer.

It lasted a little bit longer before he accepted the fact that she wouldn't.

"No," he replied. "You can't. No more can I. You can, if you desire, lie about your knowledge."

Her lips thinned.

"The Terafin was always wise enough not to put me in the position of having to lie; she understands the politics of what she does—and doesn't—choose to do." He turned. "And perhaps that's not true. She has forced the issue once or twice in my tenure as part of Terafin. And each time I've managed to balance. The House is of value to me. The Terafin is a woman I admire, and she acts, in as much as any ranking member of the patriciate can, with conscience. Perhaps more so than Duvari." He shrugged. "Is this what you came for?"

Silent, she shook her head.

"So. You will go South without the army. But you will not go without the permission of The Terafin."

"No."

"And you will not take your den."

"No."

"Jewel, I fail to see—"

"I came to tell you that what one woman accepts with ease, another might reject."

"Were we speaking of women?"

His smile slid off the mirthless ice of her expression. "Here's something you can give to that bastard."

He knew she meant Duvari.

"You don't have to thank me. I imagine you'd find out anyway, in time. Does he have members of other Houses doing the same dance?"

"Of course. I am the only open member; the only ranking member. And to be honest, he does not put much of his effort into the Houses. They war amongst each other, but they have never had any pretensions to either of the thrones."

"True enough."

"Your information?"

"I know who The Terafin will make her heir."

"I hope she doesn't intend to announce that information prematurely; it certainly didn't extend the life of the previous heir."

Her laugh was an angry laugh, ugly with harshness, something that shouldn't have been able to go on as long as it did, it sounded so forced. She shoved her hair out of her eyes, catching strands of it in her House ring. Hurt, as she pulled them out. "The life of the heir is almost never at risk. Not this heir."

He was absolutely silent then.

"That's right," she said softly. "It's just me, Jewel the power monger. I guess I've gotten what I wanted."

"Jewel—"

"And what I *want,* what I want from *you,* patris of the fence-sitters, is commitment."

"Then ask," he said, and she thought he was paler although it was hard to tell, "when you take the title."

She hadn't thought she'd continue. Would have been smartest not to. But her words were tumbling faster than she could catch 'em; she couldn't shut up.

"I won't *be* here to ask. I'll be in the South, searching among the slaughtered for gods only know what. And you know what? It'll make what we found in Cordufar look pretty. It'll be—"

He caught her. Shook her. She didn't fight.

But she didn't stop. Flow broken, the words took a moment to reassert themselves. "Gods, worse; I can hear it now, and I'm not even on the road. And while I'm not here—while I'm not here, everyone will come *this* close to death—but I can't see who will cross over. I can't see whose bodies are lying in the wake of the Terafin War. And I want—I don't want—I can't save—"

"Jewel."

"I'm sorry, Devon," she said, her voice breaking, growing quieter and smaller in the wake of the command he had made of her name. "But I don't want her to die. And I can't stop it."

He said, "She knows." It was a question; he so seldom asked them it took her a moment.

She nodded.

"She knows." He stood, his arms on her shoulders, his face perfectly still. And then he said, "I'll do what I can to protect them."

"And if it's not in the best interests of the Astari?"

"Let your den know. Tell them that when I send word—or bring it—they're to follow that word to the letter."

"Devon—"

"Don't say it. Don't ask it." He turned to look out the window she had covered with fabric. Stopped. "We had better win this war," he said softly at last, "and it had better be worth the cost."

CHAPTER TWO

The most beautiful woman in the Dominion of Annagar faced her interrogators in a silence that they would have thought defiant had she not been so exquisitely deferential, so perfect in manner and grace. Had they not seen her make a weapon of herself—and she, a mere woman, unmarried and inconsequential—at the Festival of the Sun.

Yet in this room of Southern finery, she, visitor, ostensible prisoner, a woman, was the centerpiece, the thing to which all eyes were drawn.

They would have said, the four men in the room, that they would never underestimate her again; that once cut by her concealed edge, they would scar, and that edge would be the only thing they would see. And for one man in the room, that was true.

Cortano di'Alexes simmered as the questions asked by the other three—Sendari par di'Marano, her father but also the canniest of the Widan save himself, Alesso par di'Marente, the newly proclaimed lord of the Dominion of Annagar, and the man who laid claim to the lake of the Tor Leonne, and the Radann Peder kai el'Sol—lost focus, lost sharpness, lost the edge that the Serra herself, Lord scorch her and winds destroy her, had not once lost in the months of her captivity.

She sat, her hands in her lap, her hair a straight cascade of perfect black across her back and shoulders. Those shoulders were straight, her head slightly bowed, her lips and skin uncolored by the vanities of harem women.

Which was as it should be; she was, after all, not wife but daughter, and at that, a daughter returned to the father's fold by the death of a husband whose end was known from one edge of the Dominion to the other.

She *should not* have been beautiful. She should not have had that power, or any other power. She was dressed like a seraf, allowed no jewelry, no combs, no fragrances. Her father had barely given her leave to speak, but her silence, her modest evasiveness, her momentary pauses—these were parries, weapons, affects. He knew it. Her father *must* know it; the man was no fool.

But in the end, having answered all their questions in her own deceptive fashion, she had been dismissed, and Cortano was almost certain that the expression that passed from father to daughter was one of regret. Had he been certain, he might have actually given vent to his growing anger; he was not. And this was not the time.

But, Lord of Night, his jaw locked when Alesso di'Marente bowed and stared at her retreating back until the screen doors, rolled open by no hand but hers, as if she were no better than humble seraf—and closed the same way—banished all vision of her. Men could be such *fools*. Fathers. Lovers. Warriors.

Idiots. They were almost always one and the same.

To complicate matters, the Tyr'agnate of Oerta, Eduardo di'Garrardi—the biggest fool of them all, and certainly the least cautious—was threatening the alliance they had built. Over *her*. He refused to understand—and at his level of power, his lack of comprehension could only be refusal, it could not be actual ignorance—that she had made herself a symbol of the Tyr'agar.

Alesso di'Marente—Alesso di'Alesso—had given Eduardo di'Garrardi his word that, upon taking the Sword and laying claim to Diora, he would grant her, as promised, to the Tyr'agnate. Had it not been for Cortano's presence, had it not been for the calming influence of Jarrani di'Lorenza, Tyr'agnate of Sorgassa, Eduardo would not have accepted Alesso's word; would not have allowed himself to be mollified. Another gift from the very fine Serra Diora di'Marano: their alliance had almost splintered.

Eduardo di'Garrardi did nothing with patience. Having declared himself, it was weakness to recant, weakness to behave in any way with dignity and self-denial. Over a horse, it had been almost contemptible. But over a *woman?*

No, Cortano di'Alexes was not pleased.

She was sent from the room, and they, four powerful men, gathered, waiting upon a fifth. Not one of them was accustomed to be kept waiting, and in this case it wore on them all, adding to their irritation, their private thoughts, their differences and not the commonality which brought them here, to a place where the

Sword of Knowledge could control all witnesses, could prevent all eavesdropping.

He had not told them.

He had almost done so; in the days after the Festival of the Sun, in the days after the word of her actions had swept across the dry nation like brushfire, his anger had been sharp enough, hot enough, a thing that consumed.

But there was so little *to* consume; it burned in a flash, and because the court of the Tor Leonne was what it was, it was gone by the time he could seek the counsel of the new Tyr'agar.

What might he have said?

My daughter was born with a curse. Or, better yet, *my daughter's voice can command a man against his will.* Her death, certainly. He had wanted it—just for that moment; death and peace. But it was more than her death; it was Teresa's death—and that, too, Lady knew he had desired from time to time—and it would mean questions about his own knowledge, his own use of such a gift in the service of Marano. In the service of Marente's finest son.

Sendari par di'Marano sat upon cushions that were finer than even the Tyr'agar boasted; he sat beside waters that could have only come from the lake itself—with the inevitable grant of permission levered from the ruling Tyr—and wine that was both sweet and light. That fragrance, for he did not choose to imbibe, twisted 'round the scent of jasmine and spice, the scent of fruits cut and displayed in the cool night air, in such perfect proportion it could only have been planned. Opulence here, for those who knew how to appreciate it.

He did, and could, but distantly. Everything was at a distance now because things that were not were . . . costly. Cortano watched like a starving carrion creature.

Yet if there were only Cortano to be wary of, he might be more at ease.

"Forgive me, gentlemen."

Sendari rose at once; they all did.

"Lord Isladar," the Sword's Edge said, his voice thin but otherwise perfect. He inclined his head as if dealing with an equal, and not a ruling servant of the Lord of Night. "I will not take the trouble of offering you water; you never drink it."

"As you wish, Cortano, although you must know that I find these customs vaguely enticing. They linger at the edge of my mind the way all ceremony does: As a thing I might once have witnessed, might once have been drawn into or made captive by."

Just as, the Widan thought sourly, *we are now, of course. Captives to flesh. Victims of mortality.*

Ser Cortano di'Alexes stiffened slightly, but Alesso and the Radann kai el'Sol seemed to take the comment in stride. They did not, not quite, see Lord Isladar as an equal; he was a *creature,* a thing of the night, a thing to be feared, certainly, in the right measure, but not to converse with, man to man. Not to take personally, although both men would have died before they trivialized either his danger or his importance.

Not to envy for his knowledge and his power and his eternity— merely a thing to be used, as any weapon can be that has sharp edges.

Much, Sendari thought again, like either he or Cortano. In the eyes of most there was no distinction between unknown and unknowable; it mattered that they could be pointed, that was all. Enough to make a Widan weep with frustration or sneer with disdain—and either, here, would be a costly mistake.

"There has been," Lord Isladar said quietly, "news from the North. And my Lord requests . . . a change in plan."

The festivities that heralded the Festival of the Moon had not yet begun, and the preparations for even their beginning were sadly lacking. It was said that in truth this was due to the lack of any wife, any harem, on Alesso di'Marente's—Alesso *di'Alesso*'s—part, for it was always the women who were responsible for the court finery; the women who felt it necessary to insure, by seraf death if need be, that the preparations for the Festival of the Moon met clan expectations of a husband's rank.

And what rank was superior to Tyr'agar, first among Tyrs?

She wondered, idly, who his wife would be. It surprised her; the question itself would have been distasteful in every conceivable way had she actually cared about the answer.

The door slid open at her back; she stiffened into perfection— always perfection here—and watchful grace. This was her lot; this had been her choice. She was Diora di'Marano, and if she had hoped, half a year away, that the quiet torture of waiting was beyond her, she was still capable of, still expert at, the art of biding time.

But very few people were granted access to her private rooms, and when she heard the first footfall cross the wooden beam into which the sliding screens were set, some of that tension ebbed.

"Na'dio," a familiar voice said. It was shaded with concern; she could hear it in the timbre of the single word. Question. Fear.

She turned to see the oldest of her father's wives: Alana en'Marano. At her back, a beautiful shadow, the youngest, Illana en'Marano. Illana gently nudged her elder into the room and then slid the door firmly, quietly, shut at their backs. As if she had spent a lifetime doing no less.

They were, of course, allowed the freedom of the harem, but they were cautious; they rarely chose to exercise the freedom granted. They understood, as well as she, that her privacy was an exile, and that that exile was precarious.

Not even a fool could miss the malice with which the Sword's Edge spoke of Serra Diora—and none of Sendari's wives, with perhaps the exception of the Serra Fiona herself, were fools. How could they be? They had been chosen by the Serra Teresa di'Marano. Still, they were here.

She rose. "Alana," she said softly. "Illana." She kissed the cheeks they offered, and held their hands a moment longer than necessity or manners dictated.

The two women exchanged a glance. It was the younger who said, "I brought you a gift."

"Illana—I am in no position to repay you in kind, and I desire no difficulty for you. The Serra Fiona watches us all."

"Yes," Alana said coolly, "she does. But less so now. Part of the responsibility for the Festival of the Moon has fallen upon her shoulders—just as the responsibility for the Festival of the Sun did. And she is—"

The pause told Diora much. That was her gift, and her curse: To hear what the voice contained, when the words themselves could not or did not. She had learned, over the years, to hide such knowledge. She waited.

"She is almost beside herself," Illana continued smoothly.

That *was* surprising. There was no love lost between Sendari's only daughter and the mother of his only son, but Diora knew Fiona well enough to know that no little nicety would escape her, no attention to proper detail. "What has happened?"

"She has become sufficiently distracted by events that she . . . has less interest in watching us."

"That will not greatly please the Widan Cortano."

"No."

Silence again. Then, "She is not a friend, Alana. We both know this."

"Yes."

The youngest member of Sendari's harem—Diora herself, now an unmarried daughter—reached out and gripped the shaking hands of the oldest. They stood a moment in silence. "Alana," Diora said at last. "Tell me."

"This year—this year," the old woman said, looking her age, "there will be change in the Festival of the Moon."

She did not stiffen. Did not frown or offer this almost mother any cause to think she was concerned. The hands that she held, she held gently and firmly, as if she were the one who were offering support, rather than receiving it. "Yes?"

"They—there—" She turned to Illana, seeking help. It was almost hard, to watch Alana at a loss for words.

"They have decided that this year, for the first year, there will be a . . . Consort to the Lady."

"A Consort?"

"Yes. An . . . equivalent to the Lord's Consort during the Festival of the Sun."

It was a position she had held herself. While she could stop herself from trembling or stiffening, Diora di'Marano was not—quite—well-versed enough to stop her color from vanishing completely. In a Serra of her station, there was little enough of the Lord's color to begin with; the highborn were guarded from the Lord's vision—for the Lord was a man.

"They will call the Consort . . ." and here, Illana's voice dipped and almost failed her, but she was not Alana, and after a moment, she continued, "the Lord of Night."

Diora's hands froze; they lost warmth; they lost the strength that had sustained her. Alana bowed her head. "You see," she said softly.

"Yes."

"Do you know if—"

"No. My father will not summon the Serra Teresa. They have not spoken pleasant words—any words at all that I am aware of—since the end of the Festival of the Sun; she is with Adano this Moon's turning, and I think she will remain there."

"Diora—"

"Illana, Alana, I thank you for the information that you've brought me. I must ask—I must ask you to leave me a moment.

It is warm, this day, and I have spent hours in the presence of the . . . Tyr'agar and his counselors. I am weary."

"Shall we send you water?"

"Sweet water," Diora replied absently. Automatically. "Yes, that would be very fine."

She waited until they had left before turning to face the wall. Before kneeling into the flat, sturdy mats upon which she had lived out most of the last half year. Had she expected more? Had she expected, for some reason, that the Festival of the Moon would be allowed her? The laws of the land had already changed the moment the Leonne clan was assassinated. What the Moon meant, what the Lady's wrath entailed, to the men who now made the Tor Leonne and its Lake their Dominion, was to be lost to her. To be lost entirely.

It had been a long time since she'd felt foolish. She felt it now, and it was surprisingly bitter.

This was her home. This place, these walls that opened into no courtyard, no sunlight, no glimpse of open air or night sky or star.

She would be lowered into the sheets and the pillows, and then raised like a crown for all to see, all to acknowledge. A plan that she had been the architect of, in the end. An end of her own making.

She could not keep the bitterness from her face; the mask slipped for a moment as she faced a wall whose every flaw she had become familiar with over time. There were few indeed.

Across the breadth of the lesser Tor, Margret of the Arkosa Voyani shared the same expression. Years divided their faces; the sun-lines and wind-lines that a life of travel under the open skies forced upon the Voyani, generation after generation, made a mark upon the older woman's face that the younger's had never felt.

"Margret?"

The bitterness fell into a familiar grimace, easing and changing the lines of her face. " 'Lena."

Her cousin slid into view—and *slid* was the right word. She moved, had always moved, like a particularly beautiful cat. Long and sleek in line, she picked her way through the Voyani as if they were mice, playing as she chose and quitting just as abruptly. In everything she did, there was such a lovely mix of danger and attraction that one couldn't help but love her—and feel stupid about it.

"Well?"

"Well what?"

"Aren't you going to ask me what I'm doing in your wagon?"

Margret rolled her eyes. "If you want to tell me, I'll find out."

Elena made a playful face and swatted her cousin just that little bit shy of too hard. "Nicu," she said dramatically. "I'm avoiding him."

"You're too hard on him, 'Lena."

"Don't get motherly; it doesn't suit you. Besides, he's hardly a boy. He's past twenty this year."

"You were hard on him when he'd no underarm hair to speak of."

Elena shrugged. "Well," she said. As if that explained anything. Sauntering over to the window—for it was as fine a wagon as that—she pulled the drapes shut, plunging them into what passed for darkness here, at sun's height. When she turned, the playfulness had left her face entirely; she was all shadow, thin and straight as the blade Margret carried beneath her shirt.

"Tell me," Margret said, folding her legs as she unconsciously took shelter on the flat of the bench beneath which so many of her mother's heirlooms lay locked.

"You're not going to like it."

Elena never prefaced a report with those words unless they were an understatement.

" 'Lena."

"Festival of the Moon this year."

"That's what we're here for."

"There are changes."

"What changes?"

"First: All merchants must register with the correct official in the Tor Leonne proper."

Margret was quiet for a long moment. "Merchants?"

"*All* merchants."

"Unusual."

"Worse."

" 'Lena." Warning in those two syllables.

"Some of the merchants have been detained after making their reports. Their caravans have been either searched or seized—or both."

"Fair enough. We're carrying nothing contraband; we've picked

up no runaway serafs, and obviously we're not going to this
year." She shrugged; politics and expedience had always denied
safety to one or two of the merchant clansmen. Not often during
the Lady's Festival, though.

"You would think that would guarantee our safety, wouldn't
you?"

Elena Tamaraan was the cousin to whom Margret was closest,
but on days like this, the urge to throttle her was so strong it was
profound.

"Elena," she said, and her cousin smiled. Even in the darkest
of times, actually forcing Margret to acknowledge all three syllables of her name was considered a small triumph. It was a joke
they shared.

When Margret was predisposed to have a sense of humor.

"There have been three caravans taken so far."

"Three?"

"Yes. More significant: They are *all* Voyani."

"Any Arkosans?"

"No. Two Havallan caravans. One Lyserran."

"Matriarchs present?"

Elena was silent for a long, long time. At last she turned
to face the curtains that hid them from the light of day. Her
voice was so quiet, Margret could hardly hear it. But she already
knew the answer, even though the question itself had been
perfunctory.

"Yes."

"At the Festival of the *Moon?*" Margret drove herself up from
her seat with the force of her full weight against the ground; she
lunged around the darkened caravan like an injured beast. That
was her way; it had been her mother's way before her. "They
wouldn't dare!"

"Do you want the rest?"

"No, of course I don't want the rest!"

"It's Yollanna."

Silence. The beast was stilled. "Tell them," Margret said at last.
"Find Adam—he's at the Eastern Fount of Contemplation; tell
Nicu."

Elena frowned sourly. "I *was* trying to avoid him, Margret.
That part wasn't a lie."

"I don't give a damn, 'Lena. This isn't the time for it. Tell them."

"I'm not sure they'll let us pull the caravan back."

"We're going to try."

* * *

Although the Serra Diora was under the guard of walls and silence and near-isolation, she was still considered a part of the harem of a now-powerful man; she was no seraf, to be forced to tend to her own needs or the needs of others. Minutes might pass before she was allowed company; if her father's mood was darker, hours.

But serafs were never deemed company; they came and they went, delivering water, fans, food, changing pillows and sheets, sweeping floors that were already spotless lengths of wood grain, dark and light.

So it was that Alaya, the Serra Fiona's favorite seraf, came in through the one entrance to Diora's two rooms. She bowed before she crossed the line that the screens marked, kneeling until her forehead touched wood, and then, when Diora returned a silent nod for the gesture, rose, stepped over that line, and bowed again. Her hair was perfectly black, a sweep of knotted braids that were tied at the ends by flower and ribbon; the mark of a young girl. Fiona's work, Diora thought, with a mildly critical eye.

Just as her aunt would have done, had she seen Alaya. Alaya had been, indirectly, a gift from the Serra Teresa.

The girl rose, reached over the grooved lip which held the screens, and lifted a lacquered tray, bringing it very correctly into view for the first time. She placed this in the room, and then closed the door—silently, perfectly. She was so well-trained, Diora wondered that Fiona could not see the Serra Teresa's hand in her.

But Serra Fiona often saw only what she wished to see, and she wished to see her own power, her own ownership.

Alaya set out the water; it was soothing to watch her work. Soothing until Diora saw that her hands were trembling.

In a voice that only Alaya could hear—the voice that was Diora's birthright and birthcurse—she said, "Alaya, do you bring me news?"

And Alaya, born under no such shadow, and aware of the fact that the screens were thin and the walls had ears, nodded. She lifted a pale face, and Diora saw that its pleasing whiteness was underlined everywhere by gray.

"Did the Serra Teresa send you?"

She shook her head now in the opposite direction: No. Then

she spoke. "The Serra Fiona has sent you wine, Serra Diora; the day, she says, has been long, and if you would grace her with your acceptance, she would be pleased."

Fiona. Fiona had sent her?

"The Serra Fiona is gracious," Diora replied, letting the voice lapse a moment, so that others might hear. "Please. Tell her I am both . . . surprised and honored by her attention."

Alaya poured the wine. It had a pungent smell, at this distance. *I have not eaten,* Diora thought. Alaya passed her the goblet in a shaking hand, and where their hands overlapped, skin and paper mingled. Paper. Fiona had *written.*

It did not escape her notice: the goblets were Fiona's finest ware; the carafe in which the wine was contained, its deep, rich red glinting off silvered surface, one of the most expensive serving pieces her father's wife owned.

"If you desire it, she will send food as well; it has not escaped her notice that your interview deprived you of a meal."

"I—would be honored. I find I am hungrier than I thought I would be. Tell her—tell her that she has my gratitude."

Alaya bowed, ashen. But she bowed perfectly; the tremble, now that there was no weight against her arms or palms, had vanished.

Only when she was gone—had been gone for the space of at least five carefully counted minutes—did Diora look down at the paper in her hand. It was thin and fine, and traced with the delicate spiral of Fiona's unmistakable calligraphy.

The words, such as they were, made no sense at first; they were a fog of skillful, pretty lines. They reminded the younger Serra of her own days spent under the tutelage of Ona Teresa, learning the art of a pleasing hand, that she might one day return the letters of a suitable Tyr or Tor; that she might communicate perfectly with the wives of such powerful men; that she might impress, upon all, the gifts of the daughters of Marano.

But the daughters of Marano did not write letters in secrecy to disgraced members of the clan—disgraced and disliked rivals, if she were truthful.

Fiona now pitied her, where once she had resented, but pity alone was not enough to make Fiona risk not only the wrath of husband, but also of new Tyr, of the Sword's Edge.

The paper made a slight noise as she unfurled it further, willing the words to make sense. They did, but they were devoid of the prettiness that she had come to expect; they offered no

greeting, no apology for inadequacy, no news of the trivialities
of daily life; no joy, and no spite, no affection, and no rivalries.

*There is no time. If you have not heard, this Festival of the
Moon, there will be a Lord of Night to preside the Lady's
temples. There will be a change in celebration; the masks that
are worn at the Festival will be of a handful of prescribed
faces."*

More, there has been difficulty.

*The Tor Leonne proper is now the . . . guesthouse . . . of Yol-
lanna of the Havalla Voyani. She is alive, at the moment. She is
not unharmed.*

*I have sent word to the Serra Teresa di'Marano, but I fear it
will arrive late.*

That was all.

It was enough.

Serra Diora di'Marano sat in the empty room and very slowly
slid paper between skin and silk, so as not to make noise. Let it
absorb sweat and moisture; let it remain hidden, although in fact
the truth would be carried by wind and word across the breadth
of the Tor Leonne by morning.

She was silent for a time; the dead were with her, although the
sun was high.

So, she thought, the windowless world becoming both larger
and smaller around her, *it comes. The Lord of Night. General,
Sword's Edge, you have played this Festival poorly.*

And she smiled, although it was a smile edged with fear and
uncertainty.

Now Serra Teresa would come.

And before the Serra Teresa, her task was clear.

The Voyani were the sworn enemies of the Lord of Night and
Yollana of the Havalla Voyani the most famous of the four
Matriarchs. How to plan?

In silence. While waiting.

She bowed her head, and when she lifted it, the lines of her
face were unblemished by worry or fear.

This wagon had been in her family for four generations. The
wheels had been changed more times than she thought she could
count, and the walls had been replaced or repaired at least once
during living memory, but the glass in the windows had been
passed from one set of repairs to another—an heirloom and a
statement.

"Margret."

She turned at the sound of her aunt's voice. "Ona Tamara," she said quietly.

The older woman wrapped a protective arm around the younger woman's shoulder. "We've had . . . word."

"I know. I know it. Elena told me—"

"No. We've had word about Evallen."

Ah. Here, now, the truth could no longer be veiled. No longer *had* to be veiled. She was numb with it; had become numb with the hiding of it, the inability to seek solace or comfort. A new experience, for her. Probably one she should get used to.

Margret thought a moment, wondering what her mother would say or do now. Her mother was Evallen of the Arkosa Voyani, and needed *no one*. But she, she was only Margret. A Matriarch without the Matriarch's Heart: the stone. The line of blood.

"Tamara," she said at last, "come." She pulled away from her aunt and led her up the steps into the wagon, not certain how much longer she would be able to do even that. The wagon—it was the most distinctive of the Arkosan vehicles. It would half-kill her to leave it behind—and she wouldn't consider it at all if she wasn't certain that it *would* kill her to take it.

But Ona Tamara understood what it meant, this journey into darkness, and as Margret turned to face her in the covered room, the first thing she felt was the sting of open palm against exposed cheek: Her aunt's palm, her own cheek.

"You *knew*." Her aunt's accusation held a fury that a simple slap wouldn't dissipate. Margret took a step back, but made no move to defend herself. How could she? Had she been her aunt— her trusted, her valued aunt—she would have been *furious*. Might have pulled dagger where dagger would have helped nothing.

Ona Tamara was known throughout the caravan for her gentle temper. She left her weapons sheathed. "Margret. Look at *me*."

Margret looked. Looked at her aunt as she had never just looked at her mother, her bitter, her temperamental, her often angry mother. Their eyes, dark and dark, so similar in shape and size, met.

"How?" And then, after the silence had lengthened, Tamara said, "That clanswoman."

She wanted to let her aunt go on; her aunt, who had the freedom to express what she herself had struggled so hard to hide. But she heard herself, her voice dulled and weak even to her own ears, say, "No, Ona Tamara. No. It was—my mother."

"Tell me."

"I didn't understand it, not then—but she knew. My mother *knew* what she was doing. What she was going to."

"And she would leave you with the care of the clan—" Silence. Again silence. Tamara was known for her quiet temper, but she was also known for the sharp edge of her observation. She was no one's fool. Aye, the Lord had stained her, and the winds had made furrows in her flesh that grew deeper and more distinct with time—but nothing could reach the wit that lay hidden beneath simple flesh.

In the darkness, her aunt paled.

"The heart—"

"Yes," Margret said grimly. "You understand. You understand why I could not speak of it."

"Where is the heart?"

"It is—it is safe, I think." She paused. "That is what the clanswoman came to tell me. Where it is, and that it is safe. But I don't think even she knew what would happen this Moonlight."

She had turned from her aunt, in the darkness; turned to the wall and the window. The familiar arms of the older woman enfolded her shoulders again.

"Margret," she said quietly. "You are free now."

"Free?" Bitter word; it choked her, to say it. "Free in the Tor, when the clansmen have started to hunt us? Free in the Tor, when the Lord of Night has finally shown his hand again? I have no *heart,* Tamara."

"You have your own," her aunt said gently, "and it has borne the weight of grief far too long in silence. Grief drives a man mad," she added quietly, "when it is contained. It must be shared. It must be spread. It must be carried by the family. Grief is our measure, it is our strength, it is our community." She pulled her niece to her, and Margret resisted for a fraction of a second, no more.

"But she's dead. Grief won't change that. I have the responsibility—"

"Not even Evallen would have taken that responsibility. Come. She was your mother, but she was *our* Matriarch. We have the right, and you—"

Margret began to weep. She turned, blind, seeking comfort, and she found it. Only later would she remember that she had offered none in return to her mother's sister, her mother's much

loved, and much loving, younger sister. Tamara offered, and
Margret took what she could, although it wasn't quite all that she
needed.

"We will have our vengeance," Tamara said, over the storm.
"Remember, chia, remember what is said: *Only the living can
give meaning to a death.* We will give this death meaning, all
right. They will pay."

The Widan Sendari di'Marano felt the chill of wind in the stillness of a room that might have been at home in the iciest remove
of the Northern Wastes. Twice now he had gone to the wastes,
and he had discovered this about himself: that he would rather
face the heat and the parched, dry death of desert sand than the
ice and the wind of the North.

But these two men, his mentors in endeavors of power, felt
otherwise. He watched them uneasily; the man who now ruled the
Dominion and the man who ruled the much less wieldy Sword of
Knowledge. The sun had darkened Alesso's skin, but the wind
had not worn it much; he was unbowed in line by the burden he
had chosen to heft. Shoulders straight from right to left, he stood,
his hands behind his back—and as far away from the exposed
hilts of his swords as they could go. He was not given to finery
on occasions of war—and he wore *no* finery here; a statement.

A statement that was not lost upon the Sword's Edge. Cortano
di'Alexes wore robes that were deceptively simple; they were
expensive indeed if one knew how to look for the signs, but they
did not draw the eye to their wearer. Dark and gray, with hints of
gold that somehow never quite came to light, they draped from
shoulder to foot. Evening wear.

Not for the first time, Sendari found much about these two
men that was similar.

"I tell you now," Alesso was saying for the third time, "the kai
el'Sol will *not* cooperate. Whatever has led you to believe otherwise is illusory."

The words were not heated; they were cool. But they were
incautious enough to hint at the depths of Alesso's anger.

Unfortunately, they were spoken to the Sword's Edge, a man
known for the implacability of both his temper and his pride.
Cortano's pale hands stroked his beard rhythmically, as if it were
an instrument. There was a faint crackle of magic around the
edge of his fingertips; Sendari suspected that it was not entirely a

conscious use of the power that the Sword's Edge commanded. *That* would be a challenge too great for Alesso to ignore.

"He has cooperated with us in the past, Tyr'agar," the Widan replied mildly.

"Indeed. But we have never used the phrase 'Lord of Night' in our public dealings. I tell you, Cortano, it is *too soon*."

"And will you then return to Lord Isladar and Lord Ishavriel and tell them of our change in plan? Will you face the Shining Court? Will you face the Lord of Night?"

Alesso shrugged expansively. "If they wish to succeed, they will accede. If they wish to fail . . ." He shrugged. "Let them find another pawn."

"And the Voyani?"

"They have caused us trouble in their time," Alesso replied, speaking slowly. "But I foresee a greater difficulty. I had hoped to make use of them in the war against the Northerners; they bear them no great love."

"They bear us less."

Alesso shrugged again. "Yes. I will give the kin the Voyani if they so desire them. But the Consort *must* wait."

Evening.

Diora did not often pray; not to anyone. No sane woman prayed to the Lord, but even the Lady's face was often wreathed in darkness; no boon there, no comfort. When she had been younger, she wondered what it would be like to live in the North; to have the comfort of Northern gods; to be able to choose, among them all, a god to pray *to*.

Because she was only taken from her rooms twice a week, she seldom felt the wind; seldom saw the moon; seldom spent time beneath either the Lord or the Lady's face. Tonight would not be such a night; her father was absent.

Her father.

As a young woman in his harem, on a night such as this, she had often been seized by restlessness. It was the plague upon women; men were free—*if* they were freeborn—to excise it in a variety of ways, most of them energetic, none of them graceful or feminine.

Diora had been different: she had been gifted with a talent for music, and she would hold the wildness and the hunger—rare though either might be—in until her hands touched the strings, Northern or Southern, and her voice was given permission to accompany them. Then, oh, then, she might briefly experience freedom, under the watchful eyes of either Lord or Lady.

Her father had destroyed both the samisen that had been her mother's and the lute. He had forbidden her song, and she had acquiesced, thinking only that he was a fool for not forbidding her breath or life instead.

Thinking it, knowing it, knowing that had she, in fact, *been* the Serra Fiona, Diora di'Marano would be dead. She had wanted that death. It still lingered, like a vision of peace and a return to the warmth of the only home she had ever made for herself. But before that, the penance, the only act that might explain, might excuse, the fact that of all the women she had loved, she alone still lived.

Diora di'Marano did not pray because she did not know how. She did not play the instruments that she had been raised to because they had been taken from her. She did not speak in the darkness of a night that was supposed to—somehow—contain her sleep.

But she sang.

Softly, softly, her voice by some miracle not cracking as she forced it back into her throat so that it might be otherwise in-audible. Her father watched her closely, even when he was not present; he would know.

The silence her voice broke was broken.

"Diora," the voice said. **"Where are you?"**

She froze a moment, losing her voice as she recognized the distant tones that hinted at a power she had only once seen in full display: the voice of Kallandras of Senniel College.

The winds from the North had unexpectedly swept in beneath the night sky, blending with death and the threat of death and the Lady's neutrality.

She was speechless.

"I am in the Tor Leonne—the city, not the palace proper. If the Serra Teresa is here, she makes no reply. Things are more complicated than I had foreseen. Are you well?"

His Torra was perfect. She wondered what he would look like this time.

"I am well," she said, speaking as he had taught her to speak, unaccountably happy that walls and screens and distance aside, there was no way to separate her from his company, should he choose to offer it.

"There have been rumors that you are not free to travel."

"Rumors often have a grain of truth; this is rare. It *is* true."

She heard his laughter; her own lips turned up in something so foreign she realized it was a smile. How long had it been? Too long, and it would be longer still.

"Ona Teresa is not in the Tor. My father did not see fit to send for her. She attends the Serra Donna en'Lamberto for the Festival celebrations in Amar." She paused. "I believe that she has been summoned, but only recently. I do not know if she will arrive in time for the Festival of the Moon.

"But, Kallandras of Senniel, the situation here is not what it was—and I would advise you strongly against attempting to offer your services to the Tyr'agar."

"Understood," he replied, his voice shifting strangely. "I have come on the winds of war, Diora. I will be honest. You have made yourself so much a part of the war you must know that this is no social visit."

"I do know it," she replied, because she did, and because she did not wish to let either Kallandras or the use of the voice slide away from her. "But I do not much care. Listen. Let me be the wind's voice, if it is war you have come seeking.

"I do not know if rumor has yet reached the street. There has been a change in the celebration of the Festival—or rather, a change has been planned. The Lady's Festival does not have the significance of the Lord's, but it *is* Her Festival.

"First, the masks worn will be masks decreed by the new Tyr. Second, there will be a Consort to the Lady of the Moon. Third, and most important: Yollana of the Havalla Voyani has been taken captive in the Tor Leonne proper; where, I do not yet know."

"And is the third most important?" he asked softly.

"I—" she remembered the ruined, tortured face of Evallen of the Arkosa Voyani, and for a moment, a pendant invisible to the eye—to even the practiced Widan eyes of her father and the Sword's Edge—gained weight and warmth as it hung heavily round her neck. Remembered the servant of the Lord of Night who had looked, first through her, and then *at* her. He would never forget her; she was certain of it. Just as certain as she was that she would never forget him.

"Yes," she said, speaking as softly as he.

"Odd."

"Odd?"

"I would have said, of the three, that the most disturbing thing you have yet told me is the first: the masks. Diora, I am no mage. But I have had experience with the magi. My instincts bid me warn you: beware of the masks."

Silence.

She waited as her heart beat out three minutes.

"Kallandras?"

But if he could hear her at all, he did not answer.

CHAPTER THREE

The *Kialli* understood power, and they understood it well. When they had walked the face of this world last, they had served the Lord of Shadows in all his glory; he alone had had the strength to defy the greater gods combined. But they had been born, then; it was in rebirth, in the Hells of Allasakar, that they had been freed from all the folly that came with a life of earth and water and sky and flesh.

The fires burned it away, renewing them.

Garrak remembered the burning, and he shuddered, his body rippling beneath him as if it were an unknown and roughly made piece of clothing. He listened, waiting for the peace that often came with stillness; he stood, testing the charnel winds, trembling a moment with a desire that spoke of his long choice.

Emptiness.

He would not, he thought, become accustomed to the accursed *silence* of this place.

For in the Hells, it was not silence that reigned; the screams of Those Who Have Chosen were the winds' roar and whisper, the chill edge of morn and the arid heat of midday, the rush of the blood rivers and the ripple of the still ponds. When the Lord called forth more of his host, an echo of the damned touched the ears of all who listened—and Garrak had been one of the first summoned; he listened well indeed. It was his only thirst.

There were those among the *Kialli* who found their return to this place of blue sky and gray rock and white, snow-capped crest of mountain fascinating. He was willing to watch them in their folly; if it weakened them, they would be his, and he would rule.

That *was* the law of the Hells. That, and the guardianship of the souls of those who had fully, and finally, earned the judgment of Mandaros through their many, many lives.

When, the kin said, in sullen, muted whispers, *can we hunt?* And the Lord said, *Wait.*

He slid between the towering pillars that carried a great, curved ceiling the long-dead giants of the Northern realm—the Northern Wastes, in this diminished land—would have been dwarfed by. He paused a moment, but only a moment, before the guardians of the halls in which the human Lords lived. Their attention flickered off his ebon skin, measuring and dismissing the threat he might present.

Against these two, he would not test his power, not yet. But sooner or later, in the stretch of endless time, he would measure it against all of his brothers and sisters; measure and be victorious.

That, too, was the law of the Hells.

"Garrak ad'Ishavriel."

He paused and then nodded, bowing low enough to show his respect for a foreign Lord's power, but not so low that it embarrassed the Lord he served. The Lord he served, after all, was among the Five that the Lord of Night had chosen to serve Him personally upon the field of battle.

Of battle. "Lord Lissar."

"It amuses me to tell you that the young human woman, Anya a'Cooper, is alone in her room. The Lord Ishavriel has been summoned to a meeting of the Lord's Fist."

Garrak smiled, but the smile was a cool one. Anya a'Cooper was the lone human who did not choose to dwell in the human Court. "You know much of my Lord's activities."

"Indeed. But you will forgive us if we watch closely a Lord of the Hells who chooses to elevate a mere human over one of the kin."

It was meant as an insult; it was received as an insult. Thus did the strong treat the weaker.

It was the law.

And the weaker bided their time, waiting. Centuries could pass before the result of such an exchange might, at last, become final in one manner or another.

That, too, was the law.

Anya a'Cooper sat upon the throne she had carved out of the mountain's ancient rock. The act had shaken the Northern wall of the Shining Palace, which happened to *be* that rock; had, in fact, shaken the twin towers in which the Lord of the Shining Palace, and his daughter, singly dwelled. Here and there, in the surface of the stone beneath her feet, she could, should she so choose, see the welter of tiny fractures that spoke of the casting.

The Lord had been less than well-pleased.

She had thought the Lord might kill her then and undo all her plans, all those things that burned inside her, hot as molten rock, or hotter still, but hidden from sight. It had been interesting to see Him cloaked in all His power, the edges of his wrath shining like the deep shadow from which there was no return.

More interesting still was the effect he had upon the *Kialli;* they dropped to the ground like imps, cowering in absolute silence. Even Ishavriel. Even her master.

She was careful, now, not to speak His name, but his voice returned to her, carried in the shadows which pooled at her feet like a familiar—an overfamiliar—cat.

His voice, she thought, was deeper and more sudden than the voice of the thunder itself; certainly as beautiful, in its wild, un-conquered way. Even in anger, especially in anger. She loved the taste and she loved the sound of it, for it had depths of strength and power that the *Kialli*—that she herself—could only dream of, if her imagination was rich and dark and deep enough.

She thought it was. And besides, she wanted a big chair of her own.

She had carved here, taking care not to heat the interior of the rock so quickly that it shattered the whole. She wasn't certain why, but she knew that heat, applied too unevenly to rock—and marble, come to think of it—often had that effect.

And she had so wanted her *own* throne she chose to be careful. Her arms and her throat were scored with the shining white lines that spoke of her first attempt to melt rock. Lord Ishavriel had protected her from the worst of the scattering—but he was, and had been, slow to call his power. Slower than Anya, his pupil.

You know no fear, little Anya; you have no caution. Her par-ents had once said just that to her, but without her Lord's plea-sure and irritation.

Thinking of her parents always brought back the edges of wildness, of anger—because to think of them was to think of *him.* And to think of him was like fire itself.

No one had ever betrayed her as he had done, and he had promised everything.

You're known by your word, Anya a'Cooper, and when you give it, you make certain there's no call, ever, to break it. You break a part of yourself when you do, child. Mind me.

Her father's voice. Father's truth, in a world so different from this one, it might have been nightmare. She could smell his voice, now; see the color of it, the richness of brown and green.

But her father had been wrong. He was wrong about a lot of things.

After all, how had *he* been broken? He ran; *she* suffered. But he was alive; she was certain that he was alive, although he had never once attempted to come to her. He was burning the insides of her; his memory was blue and purple and red, red rage, and since she had given him her heart, since she had *told* him that he was the only reason it still beat, she was certain she would know if he died.

No one had learned to live without a heart yet, or so she'd been told. She'd experimented on the odd animal she could catch, but there were so very few in the Northern Wastes, she'd never managed to prove her master wrong.

The Lord Ishavriel disliked it when she thought of *him*. It angered and displeased the only friend that she had in this world, but even so, what of it? The throne had angered him, and she'd wanted it a hundred times more weakly than she wanted this: Justice.

Without a word, the heavily warded doors to her throne room flew open, winged by her power and her devouring, her just, anger. Anya a'Cooper was angry and bored.

She was tired of caution, and tired of remaining in the darkness, waiting on her master. If he was too busy in his councils, why should it be left to her to suffer? And what were his councils about, anyway?

A stupid boy, raised half-slave and freed only to be tossed away—or so Cortano said, and she probably ought not to believe him as he wasn't a very friendly man except for his beard, which spoke to her sometimes in a glint of color and light—a stupid boy, one that Etridian had tried, and failed, to kill.

Now she remembered what she'd been about: She wanted answers, and the Lords would give her none. None. As if their answers were too precious to part with. They were all powerful, and she understood that well enough; she didn't particularly want them to overpower and hurt her. That had happened before, just the once, but the scars there were deep enough that she could still close her eyes and feel the getting of them, over and over. She did not relinquish them, and would not until *he* was dead.

In anger, she blazed a little trail of fire into the floor, melting it. She thought of killing the imps, but they were suddenly gone, absorbed by the lightless shadows in all directions. Imps.

But the imps had never hurt her, had rarely even tried. No, no—it wouldn't do. She was *very* angry. It had to be something *bigger*.

And what else but the demons themselves? They thought they were so very powerful. They thought that, if she turned her back on them, they might catch her. And hurt her. She'd been hurt before.

This was why she didn't choose to live in the middle of the human Court. None of the demons dared to attack her *there*, and if they didn't attack her first, Lord Ishavriel was always angry when she destroyed them. He was one of her only friends, and she didn't *like* it when he was angry.

She frowned. He *had* told her not to kill any more of his followers—not that she could really tell the difference between the demons that followed one finger of the Lord's Fist and the demons that followed another—and that was a little more *tricky*.

But he always told her she could defend herself. Yes, of course. And he said it was good to learn things. So she would go and try to learn something new, and defend herself when the stupid demon didn't want to tell her what she wanted to know.

She laughed.

The colors of laughter, that day, were a brilliant blue, a brilliant orange, and a streak of rippling red.

The Widan Cortano di'Alexes was not amused. He had used his personal power to traverse the distance between the lands of desert sand and the lands of desert ice. It was a power he was not comfortable expending before he reached the Court, but he had little choice; he was not expected to entertain the council with his wisdom for at least another three days, and the summoning spell that would draw upon the Lord's power, and not his own, could therefore not be invoked.

The use of his power, however, did not bow him; he was not so foolish as that. Not here.

But he did not maintain personal quarters within the Palace. His early arrival meant that no rooms had been readied for his use. There was, therefore, no opportunity to recover. It irritated him, but much about the Court did; the Northerners were more firmly entrenched in the Lord's favor than the Southerners. That would change, with time, and with the coming war.

"Is that Cortano?" a familiar voice asked softly.

"It is indeed, Lady Sariyel," he said, bowing in the Northern style, his robes somewhat ungainly for such a maneuver. She offered him her hand, and he accepted it, bringing the pale line of her knuckles to his lips. It was not an art he was comfortable with, but she did him the courtesy of not turning her full attention upon him; if she had a natural prey among the human Court, it was Alesso di'Marente, a man who was both amused by and immune to her charms.

They were not inconsiderable; she was not old, but she had a power about her that would one day rival his own—if she survived that long. Her hair was still untarnished by time, her skin untouched by sun; her eyes were a blue that was pale enough to be as cold as Northern skies.

She had been brought to the Court as both apprentice and paramour, and her Lord had died early in her tenure; by attaching herself—momentarily and conveniently—to another, she had purchased her survival. Many of the lovers who had made their way—willing or no—to the Shining Palace found their way in the end to the sections of tower that only the demons called home. Not Lady Sariyel. Privately, Cortano wondered how she would have measured up against one of the Hells spawn—but very privately. Her temper was like the Northern wind.

She had been, and was, voracious; a student that he might have been proud of had he not found the prospect of teaching a young woman to behave like a man so disgusting.

And why, he mused, *do we waste power so conveniently? How many wars might we have won, how many lands might we have conquered, had we chosen to follow the Northern course?*

Then, because he was not Northern, he added, *And how many women might have brought down whole Tors in the wake of their duplicity and vengeance? Better as it is.*

"We were not informed that you would be summoned today."

"An oversight, Lady Sariyel; I am sure that you might confer with Lord Ishavriel if such an omission is of concern." Woman or no, Cortano did not play by the rules of the Hells; he hid his power, always, behind beard and mask, unveiling it to his advantage. Even here, certain that she was aware that the art of distance-traveling was his, he could not bring himself to share that knowledge. He bowed again.

"Enchanted as I am by your company, Lady, I fear that my summons here is of a nature that will not wait."

"No, indeed," she said, her dark, hard lips curving a moment in what might have been a smile had she been a cat, "one does not dare the wrath of the Fist of the Lord. But, Cortano," she added, as he turned, "you might give my regards to the General; he has been away from Court far too long."

"Indeed, as you say."

He left; he did not bother to cloak his exit in magics. She would trace them, and find him, with ease should she so desire.

Still, he hoped that she was bored enough that she did not desire to follow him, for he sought not Ishavriel, but Isladar; not the Lord's Fist, but the shadow beside His throne.

Finding him proved simpler than it often did: Isladar had taken up residence, temporary residence, within the human Court. It was not unheard of; as far as Cortano was capable of understanding, humanity was his study, his speciality. Had he been human, he would have been Widan—which would have made him more of a danger to Cortano than he was now.

"Widan," the *Kialli* said, voice deceptively soft.

The chambers were completely darkened; shadow lingered at the edge of Cortano's magical vision, pulling away from the touch of his fire. This shadow devoured light where it could, and all magic, as life, was light. Where it could not devour, it seemed to bide its time—and that, too, was very much like its summoner. Isladar.

"Lord Isladar."

"You were not summoned."

"No. May I enter?"

A dry chuckle. "Indeed. Enter. But leave the lights . . . dim."

Cortano returned a smile for the chuckle. He stepped into the room and closed the door firmly at his back, sealing it with a hand's gesture. He chose a simple spell for the sake of expedience; the travel here had been costly.

Of the *Kialli,* he was comfortable locking himself in a room with only one: this one. It made him more of a threat, and not less; comfort itself encouraged lack of caution. He was no fool; he had made a study of the lost arts, and he knew that there was not a *Kialli* in existence that deserved that level of trust.

"You look well," Isladar said, as the lights slowly rose in a beaded mist around the periphery of the room.

"And you."

The *Kialli* smiled. "You lie well, for a human. My residence here is . . . a matter of more than curiosity at the moment."

Cortano was absolutely silent. The shadows that he had long since learned were a signature of power in the Hells were tattered; cloth, and rent cloth, rather than the armor that so often obscured the Court's least obvious Lord. He thought he saw—although in the dim lights he could not be certain—actual wounds in the flesh that Lord Isladar wore.

"You are, of course, curious. It is your nature. I have miscalculated," Lord Isladar said. "At an unfortunate time. Lord Ishavriel will press his advantage."

"Has he that?"

"The advantage? At the moment, yes. I will seek to separate him from the source of his power—but I am not in . . . condition at the moment." Isladar did not rise; he rarely condescended to take a seat, and Cortano was certain that he would continue his quiet disdain were that seat the throne of the Hells.

Isladar was a curiosity, a thing beyond comprehension, but not beyond its edge. A puzzle.

"You did not come here to ask after my health." Not a question.

"No."

"Speak, then; speak quickly. There is to be a council meeting, of a sort, in a few hours."

"Very well. Alesso di'Marente—Alesso di'*Alesso*—has chosen, wisely in my opinion, to reverse the decision to name a Consort for the Lady at this particular Festival of the Moon.

"In all other ways, he is willing to consider favorably the suggestions the Shining Court has made to him."

"They were not," Lord Isladar said softly, "suggestions."

"They were orders?" The light in the room grew brighter; the shadows darker.

"They were . . . requests. Lord Ishavriel's."

"Has Lord Ishavriel not learned from Lord Assarak's presumption? The Tor Leonne *is* the General's. He will not be ruled in it, not by Northern hands."

"Or wise ones."

Cortano shrugged. "We have begun our inspection of the Voyani caravans, and believe that we will soon have in our possession one of the four Matriarchs." It was a lie; Cortano half-expected that Isladar knew that she was already their prisoner. "*If* we are able to detain her, she will be offered to the Court, as Lord Ishavriel requested.

"But we will make no such offer, and take no such politically difficult prisoner, if we are forced to accept a Consort at a time when it would be . . . unwise."

"I can guarantee nothing," Isladar said softly. "In this, I am a spokesperson for the Fist of the Lord, a lesser messenger. It appears," he added, with just a hint of dryness, something so mild it might have been imagination, "that many of the messengers the Lords send fall foul of the men to whom they deliver their messages, and they are loath to risk more of their lieutenants." He shrugged. "If you desire it, I will present your case."

"I will also attend."

"I will forward your . . . request."

Cortano stood in front of the door for a moment, his hand on its protected surface. Magic twisted beneath his palm, the feel of it frustrating—almost, but not quite, familiar. Old knowledge here, and none of it his.

He tried to remember how important that desire for old knowledge was; how important it had been when he had first been approached by Lord Isladar of the Shining Court. *Immortality,* he thought, as he stood in the shadows.

But not—*never*—an immortality lived upon his knees. He straightened his shoulders and looked back.

"It was not a request, Lord Isladar."

Across the length of demon shadows and human light, Lord Isladar gazed. And then he smiled faintly and bowed. Cortano thought there was an edge of fang, a glint of light off perfect, slender teeth; hard to see. "Very well, Widan Cortano di'Alexes. We meet in the Shattered Hall upon the morrow. I will have rooms prepared for your stay, and I will deliver your message."

The Shattered Hall was of a piece of great, carved stone; a single piece. Tables, chairs, floors; it was, as the Shining Palace

itself, the heart of a mountain exposed by the hand of a god. It
was meant to impress, and it did; from height to ground, it dwarfed
the occupants with its majesty. No gold here; no jewels—none
needed. They were, the room implied, the measure of man, and
the works of men were as nothing compared to this.

It was true; truth was something the Widan accepted.

But he wondered, idly, if it had always been true. The interest
that the Voyani provoked in the *Kialli* was of sufficient curiosity to Cortano that he had taken it upon himself to ask his own
questions. To date, the answers he had received were unsatis-
factory; the holding of the Voyani prisoners therefore served a
joint purpose.

And, he acknowledged, a singular risk.

Lord Ishavriel raised a brow as he entered the room; no more.
Etridian deigned to notice him; Assarak did not. Alcrax kept his
own counsel. Nugratz was actively irritated, which pleased Cortano; he was the least powerful of the *Kialli* who formed the
Lord's Fist. Lord Isladar offered a graceful—a human—shrug.

Shadows filled the hall; shadows blanketed the corners of the
room, rounding them and filling them until they lost all definition. He wondered if the Hells had rooms. If they had any solidity
at all. It was one of the few questions that he was not in a hurry
to have a definitive answer to.

"Generals," he said quietly. "I have been sent to convey a
message."

"Take a chair, then, if it pleases you. It is your custom."

"I see that this is not a session of the full Court."

"What we discuss today is not of interest to the mortals,"
Nugratz replied, his voice a high fluting sound that should have
been either irritating or comical, but which was, in fact, neither.
"Had it been, we would have presided over the meeting in the
Great Hall." He turned his head, narrow and birdlike, in Cor-
tano's direction.

"Come, Nugratz," Lord Ishavriel said softly. "It is of interest to
our allies, and the Widan is chief among them." He lifted a hand in
the room of shadows, and the shadows responded, carving themselves into a chair that was almost as grand as a throne beside the
wide stone table. "I will avail myself of a chair." He gestured
again; a second chair formed. "Sword's Edge?"

"Lord Ishavriel," Lord Isladar said, before Cortano could reply,
"How . . . courteous of you. A reminder, perhaps, of older times."

"Or," Assarak added, "a certain sign that the influence of your human pet is growing."

It was always cold in the Shattered Hall. The sunlight that entered the room—and there was sun, scant, cool light that came in through the pillars that rose from mountain's foot to the palace's lesser height—was never warm. The chill, however, had little to do with the weather; it settled about the Lord's Fist like a cloak of nettles.

Cortano broke it only slightly; he accepted the offered chair. "Gentlemen," he said softly, stroking his beard a moment as if in thought, although the words themselves were in no way spontaneous, "We have a minor problem."

He waited; Lord Ishavriel obliged. "What problem would that be?"

"After lengthy discussion with our allies in the Dominion, we feel it unwise to proceed with the crowning of a Consort to the Lady."

"Wise indeed," Assarak said. "I assume this means you intend to dispense with the pretense of the Lady altogether?"

This was expected; Cortano offered a brittle smile. "Assumptions, as often, play you false." The smile shattered; he thought he understood why the hall had been named as it had. "We agreed to your timetable under the assumption that the boy—the kai Leonne—would be dead at the end of the so-called Kings' Challenge. That did not come to pass."

"You do not seek to threaten us," Lord Assarak replied. He had taken no chair, and could not gain height by rising; it was the one advantage that a human chair sometimes offered. But his shadows deepened, darkening the cast of his complexion.

"No," Cortano replied mildly. He had discovered over time that a mild response—one verging on nonchalance—was an effective way of dealing with *Kialli* temper. It did not suit his temperament, but very little about dealing with the *Kialli* did; he was a man used to dispensing arrogance, not receiving it.

Lord Ishavriel did not rise, but it was close. "Widan," he said softly, "it was agreed upon after the Festival of the Sun."

The Widan shrugged. That was more of a risk. "It was agreed," he said softly, "but it was also agreed that the war would be called, and the *Kialli* joined—in subtlety—to the ranks of our armies. None of what we have agreed to, save aid in the assassination of the Leonne clan—an assassination that required no aid, in our opinion—has yet come to pass.

"There will be other festivals, Generals."

"It is after the Festival of the Moon that you will have your aid," Lord Assarak said, speaking before Ishavriel could.

"And it is after the Festival of the Moon that you will have your title," Cortano replied. "The Voyani, we are willing to cede you, provided they are not too costly."

"You are *willing?*" The great table bore the full weight of the furious *Kialli* claws; he could not be certain that the stone itself was not scored by the momentary rage.

"If we follow your course of action, we will lose the Radann," the Widan said softly, "before it is wise. We will lose some of the clans. We will lose the advantage of deploying the Voyani against the Voyani during the war with the Northern Terreans. Had we gained the death of the kai Leonne in the Empire, had we amassed our armies and taken the Terreans in question—*as we agreed upon*—we would not now face any danger by granting the title of Consort for the Lady's Festival. But now . . . what do you offer us in return?"

"Your *lives.*"

It came to this often with Lord Assarak and Lord Etridian. Embers glowed in the skein of magic that Cortano knew was visible to the *Kialli* Lords. His personal power was not negligible; not even here. To demand his death was easy; to cause it, costly.

He had no doubt whatever that they could, should they so choose, cause it—but the death that one Lord offered, the other opposed, seeking advantage. That he understood well, and not from observation of the *Kialli* and their lesser kin.

Lord Isladar rose. "Those lives," he said softly, bowing his head slightly to Lord Assarak, "are not yet yours to grant. The Lord will decide."

"Isladar—"

"And if I am not mistaken," he added, raising a brow and turning toward the doors that stretched from floor to ceiling in a long, flat sweep of something that might once have been wood before the hand of the Lord transformed it, "we are about to have a visitor."

The doors to the council chamber flew open, scattering the shadows of *Kialli* conceit in their wake. No simple doors, these; they were not of a piece with the Shattered Hall, but they were

formed by the same maker's hand. When closed by the will of
the Lord, they were impenetrable; when opened by His hand,
they were unstoppable.

The Lord's hand had not closed these doors; nor did he open
them now; Cortano would have felt his coming long before the
doors announced his presence. He had had reason to greet the
Lord of Shadows once, twice, and a third time; it chilled him to
the bone; made him long for the desert; made him desire to offer
nothing but obedience, and that, quickly.

But if the Lord was not present, the doors themselves contained
an echo of His grandeur; they were an announcement, both
closing and opening, that it was almost impossible to ignore.

He was grateful for the interruption. Even when the cause
became clear.

One of the kin fell at once groundward, cringing in a bow that
should have been impossible, as half his back had been seared
away by fire, and smoked still. "My Lord," he said.

Lord Ishavriel rose at once. "What is this, Garrak?"

"The mage," Garrak ad'Ishavriel replied, bleeding shadows
into stone formed by it. "She wants—information."

"And that?"

"To know what occurred when Lord Etridian failed his mark."

Lord Etridian rose as well, grim now, furious at the reminder
of his failure. He was probably, in Cortano's estimation, wondering if the interruption was Ishavriel's attempt to humiliate or
discredit him; Cortano thought otherwise, because he *knew* who
the mage was.

"Did she gain it?"

"No, my Lord. But she is—"

"I'm *here*," the voice of that mage now said, her words floating
above the noisy wheeze of the injured demon's voice.

"Go, Garrak," Ishavriel said. "I am pleased; if you survive,
you shall be noted." He gestured, and his servitor looked briefly
surprised before the Lord's magic carried him to sanctuary.

Such sanctuary as existed in the Shining City.

Cortano knew the spell; he had seen it cast several times during
the visits to the Court, and he envied the ease of its casting, the
lack of apparent cost. He was also keenly curious to know
whether or not it could be cast upon one merely mortal without
cost to the recipient; he was not, however, foolish enough to vol-
unteer merely to satisfy his own curiosity.

But if there was ever a time when he might relent to such folly, it was now, for Anya a'Cooper was, in his considered opinion, completely and utterly mad; there was no sense about her, nothing at all save a bitter rage and a child's destructive glee and acquisitiveness. She had twice killed human members of the Court, and for this crime there was no recompense, no recourse offered. The kin were destroyed should they breach the laws which allowed the humans and the *Kialli* to coexist in uneasy peace—but Anya a'Cooper was useful enough, and wild enough, that she could not be contained by those laws; she exposed their frailty.

She was also the only human he knew of to openly insult Nugratz, Alcrax, Etridian, *and* Assarak in the same breath and survive; the only one foolish enough to attack Lord Etridian without paying with her life. A close thing, and for what? She thought he had insulted the *color of her words.* She could not be controlled.

Only destroyed, and Lord Ishavriel—indeed, the Fist itself—was unwilling to see that happen. Cortano understood why, but he would not have exposed himself to the risk she represented; indeed, he wished to absent himself, but did not desire his movements to catch her attention.

The *Kialli* concerned themselves with power.

Anya a'Cooper was, in his opinion, the most powerful mage who had ever worn mortal guise beneath the Lord's gaze. Obscene, to waste so much in the form of a woman whose mind was—had been—fragility defined. But obscenity existed. And it had its uses. Her power was, he thought, in no small measure responsible for the speed with which the gate between this world and the Hells had been opened, and if the gate was small and unpredictable, it was growing daily through her efforts. Hers, and the Lord who commanded her.

If anyone did.

"Anya," Lord Ishavriel said.

She paused a moment, her expression openly shifting between glee and suspicion. At last, she said, "You can't hide him from me, Lord. I know where you sent him."

"Impossible," Assarak said flatly.

"That's what you always say, Assarak. That's what you said before I took the spell from your hands and sent—what was his name again?—something-or-other ad'Assarak into the cliff face to join with the rock." She laughed as she said it, and sauntered over to the table.

Lord Assarak stiffened.

Lord Isladar rose as well; Cortano did not. "Anya," Isladar said quietly, "if you wish information, you must join us at the table. It is," he added quietly, "quite black, but there are hints throughout of gold and blue. Come, you may have my seat, in return for which I ask only that you listen quietly."

She wavered a moment, half-suspicious. But there was about Isladar some quietness of manner that often lulled her tempers; he, of all the *Kialli,* had never fueled her sudden rage, piqued her angry curiosity. "I get your seat?"

"My seat," he said, nodding. "Come. I will remake it for you, if you so desire."

It was customary to add, *with your permission, Lord Ishavriel,* for Anya was clearly Lord Ishavriel's keep, but custom was often set aside when dealing with Anya. The great beasts that slumbered beneath the height of the Lord's spires were treated with less uncertainty than she.

"If you insist. You aren't talking about that boring boy again?"

"Which boy is that?" Isladar said, deftly and silently reforming the chair's back so that Anya might be seated in a throne of delicate beauty that better conformed to her diminutive size.

"You know the one—that half-slave that everyone goes on about."

"Ah. His name, Anya, is Valedan kai di'Leonne, and yes, I'm afraid we were speaking of him."

"But why?" She frowned. "I don't want to talk about a stupid boy. If he were here, I'd just kill him myself, and then there wouldn't be much reason to talk, would there?"

"He's not so easy to kill," Lord Assarak replied coldly.

"Oh, well, not for you. But I wouldn't have any problem I'm sure."

"But you might like him, Anya," Isladar said unexpectedly.

"I hardly think so. *I* am a mage, and *he* is a nothing."

"Ah. But he has declared himself a King."

"Well, maybe. But only of the Southern Barbarians, and they're all so stupid they don't even know about the real gods."

Cortano said nothing; she favored him with a side-glance that let him know how intentional the slight was. One day, Lord willing—which Lord, he didn't particularly care—he would see her dead.

"As you say. But he is . . . a danger to us."

"Etridian was supposed to kill him. I knew it! He failed again!"

One day, Lord willing, Cortano thought, they would *all* find the desire to cooperate for long enough to kill her.

"Yes," Isladar said, "and no."

"Which is it?"

"The boy lives."

"Then he failed."

"But apparently the boy has attracted the attention of a friend of yours."

"I don't have any—" Her eyes widened, and her lips lifted in what looked to be, inasmuch as she could have one, a genuine smile. Her face softened with a pleasure that had no malice and no triumph in it. She was lovely, in a vulnerable, happy way, for as long, Cortano thought bitterly, as it lasted. "Kiriel!"

"Indeed."

"But I haven't seen Kiriel for months!" Her eyes narrowed. "Lord Isladar, you aren't *lying* to me, are you?"

"No indeed, Anya. I see no need to lie. Kiriel di'Ashaf has found a home for herself in the heart of Averalaan." He paused, and looked out through the columns that defined the Shattered Hall's outer edge. "She will be traveling South," he said quietly. "To the Dominion. To serve the boy."

"But are you saying that she *likes* this boy?"

"I am saying only what we know, Anya. She either likes the boy, or she dislikes Etridian enough to interfere with his kill."

"She's done that before."

"I wouldn't know."

"You should. She *has*. I can't believe it! Kiriel! Isladar, this is the best news I've had since she left." A frown creased her loveliness, destroying it in an instant. "You don't think she likes this boy better than me, do you?"

"Anya, how could she?"

Again, her eyes narrowed, cat's eyes, crazed eyes. But Isladar's face was clear of malice, of amusement, of anything but truth. *Is this how you handle the darkness-born?* Cortano thought, not for the first time.

"When can we see her?"

"See her?"

"Of course. She's not as boring as the humans, and not as stupid as the demons. I miss her."

"Then we will make our plans, Anya, and perhaps we will indeed find her. I do not think it is time for her to return just yet."

"Why did she leave?"

"You will have to ask her, and I imagine that you will when we meet. Perhaps you should think about what you might want to do when you first see her."

She clapped, like a girl not yet burdened by age or responsibility, and bounced out of the chambers, wrath forgotten for a moment.

"Deftly done," Lord Ishavriel said, with a slight nod to Isladar. Allies a moment, Isladar nodded.

Then, as one, they turned to Cortano, the lone human in the cavernous, perfect hall. "You will tell your General," Lord Ishavriel said softly, "that his *Kialli* will begin to arrive during the Festival of the Moon; as he has requested, only those who bear human form will be sent.

"Tell him also that, should he choose to ignore our request, and our admittedly interrupted agreement, those *Kialli* will choose a different way of pleasing the demands of *our* Lord." He bowed.

When he rose, his face was a mask of slate and steel.

"I will tell him," Cortano said quietly. "And as you have not summoned the Lord and the Lord's wrath, *Lord* Ishavriel, understand that those *Kialli* will be destroyed if they attempt to hunt in the city in a way that does not please the ruler of the Dominion."

They did not choose to rise with him, and he stiffened. But only for a moment. Although he knew a dismissal when he heard one, wisdom argued against a confrontation with the Lord's Fist over something as simple as pride. He chose to ignore the slight. It was mild, a man other than he might have missed it entirely. A man like Sendari.

He left without looking back.

Lord Isladar chose to take the seat he had offered Anya. She had deserted it, but the lines, delicate and flowery to excess, remained, cast in stone. He was aware that the juxtaposition between his own power and hers was accentuated by his place upon the throne of madness. He did very little unawares.

Cortano's exit had left them with very few words.

Lord Ishavriel was first to rise; Lord Isladar second. Nugratz, third, was by far the most majestic; he took to the air, lending credence to the illusion of height in the arches above.

Lord Etridian, Lord Alcrax, and Lord Assarak rose slowly.

"The day will come," Assarak said at last, "when we are not required to bend to the whim of mortals."

"They serve their purpose," Lord Isladar said.

"Spoken by the *Kialli* who raises humans in his spare time."

It was, of course, an insult. Etridian's smile was sharply edged.

However, Isladar did not bridle; nor did any obvious sign of anger disturb the neutrality of his expression. He lifted a hand; the gesture, modified somewhat by a flash of blue light that hinted at a power he did not, immediately, possess, called all of their attention.

Which he held for another ten seconds at most.

One of the lesser kin appeared in a burst of gray-limned shadow, two feet above the table. He collapsed there, falling face first into stone with a force greater than gravity or weakness: fear.

His body was pointed in a straight line like a spear or an arrow; he abased himself in Etridian's shadow. That shadow moved, claiming him, name and all.

"Lord," the creature said.

"You interrupt me."

Self-evident; the lesser kin did not choose to speak.

"This is, of course, important."

Perhaps because he could not. Isladar wondered idly whose power had brought the creature here. Etridian's, in all probability. Or one of his lieutenants'. A moment passed. The shadow in Etridian's hands grew darker and more complex.

Sensing this, the kin struggled to raise its nameless face. "We've found him," he said.

Five Lords turned to face Etridian.

"Where?"

"In *Averalaan,* Lord."

"Impossible. I searched there myself after the death of Karathis. We all did."

"Accept my apologies for the intrusion," Isladar said softly, offering what only he could. "But *who* has been found?"

Grateful for the interruption, the creature nonetheless faced his master when he spoke, and he spoke only after Lord Etridian nodded.

"The Warlord," he said.

"And?"

"We . . . attempted to approach him. We are not certain what occurred during the watch of Lord Karathis."

"And?"

The sound of the creature convulsively swallowing was answer enough.

For everyone but his Lord.

"And?"

"He . . . was not interested in offering us his service."

"Difficult. But he has on occasion proved himself to be neutral."

"Lord." The creature hesitated.

Fire engulfed the flat surface of the wide stone table, surrounding him. Etridian had run out of patience.

"He was with a . . . human. A woman."

"And she?"

"She—wore a ring. They call it a House ring. It is . . . of import to the humans in the city."

Isladar rose, leaving Anya's throne to his shadows. "Which House?" he asked softly.

"Errador ad'Etridian said it was House Terafin."

"And it was gold? Platinum?"

"It was *human*," the creature snarled.

"We were once smiths," Lord Isladar said, "and of those things you deem *merely* human we created works of art and power that have not been rivaled since. And you cannot tell the *difference?*"

The creature's contempt was second only to its ignorance; they were interested now because Isladar rarely showed such a display of annoyance. It did not, however, last. He fell silent, and Etridian turned back to the creature who had shown himself to be of lesser value and power by his lack of memory.

"The woman. Was she tall? Short? Young? Did he *ever* speak her name?"

"Lord Isladar," Etridian said, "you question my servant too closely."

"My apologies, Lord Etridian. The Warlord, of course, was your watch. But the questions I ask are relevant to the responsibility our Lord gave to you."

"Very well. Answer him."

"Yes. Yes, he spoke her name—but we only recognized it as a name when she responded."

"That name?"

"Jewel," the creature said. "Shouted in warning."

"Then, kinlords," Lord Isladar said, "we have a problem."

"Speak, Isladar."

"The Warlord is not neutral in this battle. He will stand at the side of our enemies."

Silence.

Etridian and Assarak exchanged a glance.

"He will not stand for long," Etridian said at last.

CHAPTER FOUR

6th of Scaral, 427 AA
Averalaan

The dust was still in the air. It mingled with the stunned silence
of the crowded city street. Silence, that is, if you didn't count the
panicked nickering of horses and the screech of penned-up fowl
ten yards away. The people farthest from that swirl of dust had
already run as fast as their feet would take them, shouting and
cursing as they sought out the magisterial guards who were supposed to protect them from one of the least legal things in the
Empire: illegal public displays of magic.

Jewel had seen silences like this before; they would pass into
gossip and heresay as shock and fear gave way to the demands of
day-to-day life. Unfortunately, it would only pass that way once
she and Avandar disappeared.

Which they were doing by two expedient means, the first being
magic—his—and the second being a good, swift pair of legs.
Well, two. She hated running when she was, to the eyes of the
casual observer, invisible.

This was not an auspicious start to a journey.

Hells, it wasn't an auspicious start to just about anything. She
had never gotten the hang of disappearing in this fashion and
rammed into the elbows, backs, and legs of a dozen unsuspecting
pedestrians before she at last stopped dead and called a halt to
their flight.

Avandar's face was about as pleasant as the sky during a thunder-
storm when he turned; she had the certain knowledge that hers
was worse by his reaction. He opened his mouth to speak and
when no words came out, closed it with an almost audible snap,
as if he were biting silence.

Great.

They appeared more or less instantly, but no one seemed to really notice, and given that this had occurred in the streets of the Common, Jewel's frown was deep enough it threatened to become permanent. She had always known he was a mage, of course. But any display of his power annoyed her.

She was past annoyed now.

Avandar Gallais, her domicis, and a man hired for life by The Terafin herself, had killed a man in the streets of the city. Killed him pretty much instantly, and in front of more witnesses than she could count. She knew; she'd started.

"What *exactly* was that about?"

He was silent. But he offered her a shrug as he readjusted the heavy pack whose straps cut into his shoulders. "You will expect," he said, the words suspiciously like an order, "minor difficulties on the road we're traveling."

"Minor difficulties?" She turned in the direction they'd come from. People were now moving out of their way, which meant they could at least be seen; they were not, however listening, which meant they couldn't be heard. She could live with that. "I don't normally call a small speech in a completely foreign—and unpleasant, by the sound of it—tongue, followed by whatever-the-Hells you call that burst of fire, to be *minor*. I don't call loud, piercing screams, followed by complete and utter destruction, to be *minor*. Please correct the parts of these sentences you disagree with."

"You *are* aware that this is a war?"

"I'm aware that we're about to be involved on the periphery of one, yes."

"Well," he said, speaking slowly and carefully, "that was one of the *bad guys*."

Had he been one of her den, she'd have slapped him. It wasn't perfect behavior, but it was an old habit, and at times like this, old habits reasserted themselves the minute she forgot to pay attention.

"I haven't been a child for thirty years."

"No? Your pardon, ATerafin."

"What was that about?"

"Did you recognize him?"

"I don't know. There was something odd about him—and if I'd had more than a second before he turned into a human torch, I might have been able to place it."

He caught her hand, pulling her gently out of the way of a rolling wagon. No horses, not this far into the narrow paths of the Common, but wagons were still pulled by the next best thing: young boys and girls. From the looks of them, hungry as she'd once been. At least their labor was honest.

He pulled her into the stand of trees that was closest; she leaned against bark so broad it was easy to imagine the curve of the trunk went on forever. These were the Common's trees, and they were the one thing about the Common that still had the power to move her, no matter what her mood.

"He was a demon," Avandar said.

She knew, the moment the words left his lips, that he was right. Had known it on some level the minute he'd approached Avandar. He'd been perfectly attired for a patrician; his clothing fine, and enough in style that he was obviously a social creature; his eyes were dark, his hair darker still, and the line of his jaw was perfect and unbroken by years on the streets.

Just the type of man she couldn't stand, but he'd held her attention, made her uneasy. Hells, she was still uneasy.

"Jewel?"

"It wasn't him," she said at last.

"What wasn't?"

"It wasn't his death that bothers me. It wasn't the fact that you killed him without once referring to me that bothers me. I think— even if things did move damn quickly—that you saved my life back there. Thanks."

"But."

"But," she said, irritated to be so obvious, especially to a man like Avandar, "something does bother me."

"Or we'd be on our way to safety. Jewel, we must—"

Six inches from where her hand lay, palm against the rough grain of perfect tree bark, wood splintered as if struck by lighting.

Funny thing that. It was.

Avandar cursed; Jewel was already halfway into the head-and-shoulder roll that stopped the next bolt from demonstrating the effect of lightning a little more personally than she'd have liked.

She saw *fire*. She had only rarely seen fire quite so strong, and she had seen a lot of magic in her tenure at Terafin—a lot more than anyone should have, who still called themselves sane. She shouted his name; it was all of the warning she had time for. Steel bit her where lightning had missed, shearing cloth—and some skin—from her shoulder.

It shouldn't have hit her. She'd had enough warning. Bleeding, she drew a dagger of her own and turned to face her attacker.

It was sort of like having a sword while standing on the ridge facing the advancing army. Even if that army was an army of one.

Not only was he not human, but a chorus of screams at his back made it clear he wasn't her imagination either. She'd thought to face a creature that used a knife; instead, she faced one that wore them over every square inch of his body.

"Please," he said, in a voice that sounded like the clash and scrape of steel being sharpened, "don't take this personally." If she hadn't already pegged him as demon, she would've then: his voice was, clash and clatter or no, a thing of beauty, a thing sensuous and powerful. With anticipation. With pleasure. "You attend the Warlord. There is *always* a price to be paid for that service."

"Warlord?" She slipped out of the path of his arm; his blades gouged the side of the tree as he brushed past. Centuries-old wood gave before he did. Bad sign. Between lightning and blade, she thought, the tree that she had so admired was already dead. Couldn't be certain, but it angered her in the way that the helpless are often angered.

"The Warlord. The man to whom you were speaking before this . . . interruption."

Fire lit the demon's face in a glow that came from behind her. She didn't bother to look to find its source; she knew.

"You've got it wrong," she said, her legs tensing, her back bending slightly as the grip on her dagger shifted. "I don't serve him. He serves *me*."

The creature laughed. "Is that what he told you? He serves no one but himself, and he has a particular penchant for being the only man to leave the field of battle—any battle he joins—alive. Allow me to demonstrate."

"By dying?"

"You really are a clever creature; it must amuse him to have you."

She watched his face expand in a sudden stretch of thinning flesh across widening eyes, widening mouth, a visage of fear, of realization, of—surprise. Watched this expansion as if it were a natural growth, a natural outcome. It was. She knew the sight when it hit her, borrowing her eyes, subverting her vision from the here-and-now to the there-and-will-be. Unaware of this, his mouth kept moving, his arm swung back, his eyes narrowed in a way that only demon eyes *can* narrow.

She had time to return the cruelty of his smile with a demonic smile all her own. She didn't even bother to move out of his way. That caught him by surprise; he hesitated.

Even had he not, it wouldn't have saved him.

Fire ate him from the inside out.

His ashes hung a moment, bearing the form and shape he had occupied, before gravity and wind blew them away. The silence beyond the stand of trees was deafening. Satisfying, for just a moment.

The screams that followed it, breaking it, twisting it, were not.

She looked out; the city streets were, literally, broken; cracks had not only split the stones upon which much of the Common stood, but had uprooted them. And between these stones, above them, below them, trapped between living and dying, were the people who had been examining merchants' wares minutes ago.

She started forward.

A hand on her wrist stopped her. "I am sorry, Jewel."

"Sorry?" The word made no sense.

Avandar stood beside the scored trunk of one of the trees the Common was so famous for. A branch had snapped; hand-shaped, delicate leaves were caught in the lap of the fire he'd summoned.

But not, she noted, devoured by it. She wondered how he'd managed that. Wondered if it had to do with power. Wondered why she'd so carefully never asked him about his power before.

Framed, the flowers were lovely.

"These creatures are . . . past enemies. They occasionally appear to make life difficult. But," he said, turning to scan what was left of a crowd that was as broken as the ground beneath their feet, "I fear they wish more than mere difficulty."

"Then we'd better get the magi—"

The words left her as the shadows surrounded what was left of the crowd. *"Avandar!"*

He pulled her into the circle his robes made across the burning ground. "I'm sorry," he said again, bending his head, tucking hers under his chin.

The light shifted.

Jewel ATerafin *screamed*.

And then, there was nothing.

6th of Scaral, 427 AA
The Tor Leonne, Terrean of Raverra

You may have pride, or you may have brotherhood: decide.

In the streets of the Tor Leonne, old voices were far clearer than they had been for decades. Senniel College, the home of his adult, Northern life, was far away, by the shores of a sea that the Tor Leonne would never know. There, gulls and morning mist drew the mind and memory, made of dawn and dusk a song that had slowly—when?—taken root. He was not—had proved, although the voices of his brothers were still the strongest voices he heard, that even *he* was not—made of stone. Things grew within him, things changed.

He had taken great pains to straighten his hair; to alter its color and its length; to change the lines of his face. These were automatic precautions, and even the Astari would have thought of them. He had also changed his girth, added a few years to his age, pounds of appearance to his weight. Again, simple precautions; the cautions of a life that had almost—and had never—passed him by.

But Kallandras of Senniel had other gifts; the most striking change of pace was his movement. Catlike and graceful by turns, he had exchanged his gait for something slower and stodgier, something that weight or posture had broken.

You—you look like—

He had raised a brow at Solran Marten's total loss of words; it was rare indeed that a bard had nothing to say, and rarer still when that bard was the bardmaster herself. The expression brought her some comfort; it was his.

But if he could bring himself to change everything about his exterior life, he could not quite bring himself to leave behind the only possession he valued, and Salla, the lute that had been Sioban Glassen's gift, was tucked in the pack tossed over his shoulder. It was a risk; he acknowledged it. It was a foolish risk, a stupid one. It was, as his former masters might have said, prideful. Sentimental. Which of these was worse had yet to be determined. He had been both in life, and so far neither had killed him.

But death only happened once.

He thought, inexplicably, of Evayne a'Nolan. Of the young Evayne, striking in the narrow breadth of her white cheeks, her raven hair, her violet eyes. Those eyes, wide with horror or narrow with self-pity, would develop an underlying cast of steel as she aged, until the girl herself was buried beneath experience and expedience.

He had hated her when he was a young man. A boy. He had hated her more as an adult, first taking steps in the real world, and deprived of the only brothers to whom he wished to turn, to praise, to receive praise from. He was not that boy now, nor that man; and often, when she came to him as a young girl, he could not hate her. Could not clearly see the confusion that was now so obvious without feeling an almost protective twinge.

So much for vendetta.

She had come to him last night, her hands sticky with blood, her eyes wide and dark. The cloak that was her father's gift was already cleaning itself with an ease that profoundly disturbed her. It was not the first death she had seen, and it would certainly not be the last, but it was death, and she was tired of it.

Her hand clutched the lily that was her single adornment: a gift, a sixteenth birthday gift, from a friend in Callenton, the Freetown that had been her only home. He pried her fingers loose and found that she had cut them on petals and stem.

And she had watched him, as if he were a stranger that she hadn't the strength to stop. Looked at the blood pooling in her palms as if either all of it were her own, or none of it were. "Are you Kallandras?" she'd asked, and he realized that he was a merchant, with a merchant's clumsy gait and a merchant's Southern accent, heavy Torra.

"Yes," he told her quietly. **"I am. You are safe. You are safe here, Evayne."**

She did not pull her hand free, but she stared up into his face, hearing the truth he put into the bardic voice. Older and she could chastise him for its use on her. Much older, and she wouldn't even notice its effect. But last night, she hadn't chosen to speak at all about his gift or his talent. Instead, she'd said, "But you *hate* me."

And wept.

Funny, that the path would bring her to him here, now; strange that, as he got older, he saw more of her youth. *Have I gentled so much?*

Yes, perhaps. Truth. He accepted it as he had accepted all truths about his life save one: That, in the end, he had chosen to break his training and betray the Lady's command. It had taken him years to swallow the words, to practice them, to even think them clearly. Easier, much easier, to blame her.

She was so unlike Diora di'Marano; so unlike, and yet of an

age. In the one, Evayne, the trick was discovering the steel and honing it, bringing it to light. And in the other, in the other he thought, hearing her speak now, it would be a miracle to find anything *but* steel. He was bardic, and his hand had gone into fashioning her voice; she kept much hidden now. From a master.

"Hey, Matteo!"

"A man can't piss in peace," he replied loudly, turning in the direction of the voice.

It was Benito the merchant. "Up here, you fool, no one pisses at all. This is where the high clans live." He slapped Kallandras on the back with a broad, sun-wizened hand and mimed a man in obvious discomfort. "We're up, after Benazir's useless lot. I want you with me."

Kallandras shrugged. "It's bad this year."

"I guess the new Tyr isn't comfortable." But Benito shrugged, rolling his hand in a warding gesture that identified him as a follower—such as they were—of the Lady. "But as you say, bad. Bad. It's not the Lord's time; it's the Lady's—and this is the Festival of the Moon."

"We'll see."

"Matteo, you worry me."

They walked together back to the huddle of men whom Benito had brought for his own comfort; the wagons had been impounded. Kallandras had considered remaining with them, but he wished to see for himself the new lay of the Tor Leonne's famed lands. To see if there were compounds or outbuildings into which one might easily place a woman of Yollana's stature. To see, in a sweeping glance, how one might enter, unseen, and how one might leave.

Things changed, even here.

The Tor Leonne had been built in such a way that the parts were hidden from the view of the whole; that a man and his companions might walk into the forested, landscaped paradise and disappear, each into his own world.

But the pathways had been changed, the view widened, the leaves and their arbors making way for the sight of the Lord of the Sun, or the man who wished to take the mantle of his most powerful servant.

The mission's no different than Sioban would have given you, Solran said ominously. *You're not to interfere; you're to observe and report. We need the information.*

War was coming.

Breeze stirred in the cooling air; it would be evening soon, and if the Tor Leonne was no desert city, it was a city not far from the memory of sand and sun. No sea lessened its heat or its chill. He returned to the shelter of the awnings set up by the men with whom he'd traveled.

No Voyani caravan this; that choice, at least, had been a wise one. No, it was a merchant caravan from a minor Southern clan—a clan whose leadership was in dispute, and whose leader had come seeking redress. The man who ruled the caravan was Benito di'Covello, and his ire was so much drama and so much noise that he drew and held the attention. He invited mockery by such attention, but no matter; his existence served Kallandras' purpose.

Benito's wagons and been impounded and presumably thoroughly searched. Benito had been ordered to present himself to representatives of the Tyr'agar to explain his manifests—such as they were, as Southern merchants were less prone to keep records than their more bureaucracy mired Northern counterparts—to the Tyr's officials.

Kallandras watched, wondering. He listened.

The officials, as quickly bored by Benito's tale of outrage as any sane man would be, released the caravan with the usual warnings: Benito himself would be responsible for any murders committed by his men, or any damage done by them if they chose to partake of too much drink during the Lady's nights. Benito gave the usual replies: that his men were certainly well trained and better behaved than the cerdan of the high nobility themselves.

The low and high nobility here were a marked contrast in behavior. The comparison drew the expected, though silent, sneer.

"We will, of course, take your name, your clan's name, and your cut."

"My what?"

"You recognize this, yes?" The tall, well-uniformed man who had failed to offer the courtesy of a family name—or a personal name, for that matter—opened a large bag and set a wooden medallion upon the table that protected him from Benito's more forceful ranting.

Benito sputtered. "Of course I do! But I—"

"We require your oath of allegiance and your pledge to conform to the Festival rules. This," the man added slowly, as if speaking to an enfeebled man, "is the Tyr's mark. It is raised in the wood, but

room has been left for your clan's mark beside it. I have taken the
liberty, Ser Benito, of having a rudimentary representation of your
crest drawn up, and a suitable block will be here shortly. I require
your witnessed oath, and the proof of it, here.

"Masks, such as they are, will be provided you through the
generosity of the Tyr'agar. It is his gift to loyalty, and we *expect*
to see that gift appreciated. Do I make myself clear?"

"Eminently."

"Good. It has been a long day for both of us, but your day will
end with the crosscutting of the medallion; mine will continue
well into the night." He paused. "This is my way of saying," he
added, as Benito opened his mouth, "that I have no more time for
your explanations or indignation." He gestured, and a man came
from the tents at his back; three men in fact. "Your sword?"

Benito di'Covello unsheathed his sword less clumsily than he
did anything but ride. The official drew his a good deal more
gracefully, and cut first. The cuts formed a cross; a Southern bond.

"Your manifests—such as they are—have been approved; your
wagons are awaiting you, and you will find they have been both
undamaged and unplundered. I expect no difficulty, but if there
has been, you will report to the proper authorities in the city, not
upon the plateau. Is that understood?"

Before Benito could reply, the man turned and nodded; a name
was called out. Loudly. From behind the di'Covello caravan, an
equally surly group of merchants and their retainers pushed past
the heavily-robed Benito, seeking their audience and demanding
their due.

Benito blubbered silently like a water-hungry fish. Then he
snapped at his milling men and made his way down the single
road the merchants had been allowed to either see or use.

"We're to wear their masks? We're to swear their oaths? What
Festival do they think this is?"

Kallandras had turned a moment to the wind.

"Yollana," he said, **"It is Kallandras. Evayne a'Nolan bids
me tell you that she has sent me to your aid. I am coming."**

7th of Scaral, 427 AA.
Tor Leonne, Dominion of Annagar

The Widan Sendari di'Sendari—who, to his great and bitter
amusement, had to work hard to remember to use the name he
had struggled to achieve for himself—sat in an uncomfortable

silence; a silence made stony not by the disagreement between two powerful men, although Alesso di'Marente—he grimaced again, and corrected himself—Alesso *di'Alesso* and the Sword's Edge were often involved in such disagreements, but rather a silence made uncomfortable by a sense of helplessness. Two such men as these were not used to feeling the sting of another's will or power, especially not when it was used so gracelessly as the Shining Court chose to use it.

The sheathed sword was always better displayed than the unsheathed sword when dealing with men of pride—but the *Kialli* Lords seemed truly ignorant of even this most simple of graces. He wondered, idly, who would pay.

Sendari waited.

And waited.

And waited.

And then he realized that although the obvious was in the air like a sand-laden storm, it had yet to be spoken; had yet to be delivered into words that could be dealt with. Pride, here. Cortano's. Alesso's. His own—but his had been tempered by the loss of a foolishly loved wife, and the betrayal of an equally foolishly loved daughter. Tempered? He allowed himself a bitter smile.

And spoke. "It appears," he said, his voice as soft as Cortano's when the Sword's Edge was at his sharpest, "that we are at an impasse.

"We cannot allow the imposition of a Consort at this time; almost certainly our enemies will make much of the title Lord of Night, and it will hurt us.

"But we cannot allow the *Kialli* free reign in the city during the Festival of the Moon; their activities will announce the presence of the Consort we have refused them more forcefully than the ceremonial title would. It will be said that the fall of Leonne presages the return of the demons in force—and it will be remembered that there is a boy who acquitted himself with strength and honor, taking the service of Ser Anton di'Guivera under the bastard banner of Leonne.

"Clearly the Shining Court feels that they have the upper hand in this, and they mean to enforce their will in the Tor Leonne, having failed to do so during the Festival of the Sun."

Both men were silent; he expected no less. He rose from the hard mats; left behind the sweet water and the fruit that had been so artfully arranged by none other than his loving wife. His hands fell behind his back; he clasped them loosely and began to walk in a track that was decreed by thought alone.

"If the *Kialli* were unbeatable, they would have no use for us. They wouldn't tolerate the existence of the human portion of the Shining Court. Therefore they need us. But they now feel that they can dictate terms.

"We have offered them two things: the masks—which I will once again say I feel is unwise—and the Voyani. Of these two, I would say the Voyani have significance. Ah, forgive me for my sloppiness; we have offered them a third thing; in time: the Radann."

"And has your questioning," Alesso said abruptly, turning from Sendari to Cortano, "procured answers?"

"If you refer to my time with the Voyani woman, no. None. She is Voyani, and difficult."

"The *Kialli* come in forms that we cannot recognize easily— but there are ways. The Voyani have them, and carefully handled, we might have asked their aid. I believe we have lost some of that advantage," Sendari continued as if he had not been interrupted. "If not all.

"Certainly with the Havallans. There are rivalries within the Four Families which we may be able to exploit if we immediately cease impounding and imprisoning the remaining Voyani caravans. But we would have to go delicately, and I believe it would be in our best interests to . . . rid ourselves . . . of the liability of the Voyani woman we've already taken."

The Tyr'agar weighed the advice impersonally. His expression was completely impassive; Sendari guessed that he would discard it, but only because of the many, many years he had spent at Alesso di'Marente's side.

"And if not the Voyani?"

Sendari shrugged. "I do not know, Alesso, and I am sorry to have failed you. There are followers of the Lady who might be able to aid us—but which of the three of us, and which among our closest advisers or followers, would have the contacts necessary to bring those followers here? They will not trust us, and with reason; they are not the Lord's men."

Alesso rose. "They will not beard me in my own den. If they wish to take the Tor, they may take it in name or not at all."

"Alesso—"

The Tyr'agar raised a clenched fist and slowly relaxed it into an open palm; the gesture itself received the silence it had called for immediately. "Bring me my second sword," he said quietly.

Sendari nodded, although Sendari was a man of power and authority in his own right, and no seraf to be ordered to such menial tasks. Thus was their friendship observed.

"Tyr'agar," the Sword's Edge said, more formally.

"If it will not trouble you, Sword's Edge, I need more information."

"Information *is* our speciality. The *Kialli?*"

"I need to be able to detect them. They can take any form?"

"They can, I believe, take a human form. To take an existing form is far more difficult to achieve."

"But possible?"

"Possible, yes."

"Memories?"

"In theory. It is one of the magics that we hoped to make use of in the war against the North."

"One battle at a time, Widan. I need to be able to detect their interference. I don't care how it's done as long as it's swift and easily used."

Sendari and Cortano exchanged a momentary wry glance.

"Second: the masks."

Cortano nodded quietly.

"They are not ours; make them ours."

Another exchange of glances. Magic and miracles were never far apart in the minds of men—powerful or no—who had no practice in the former.

"And third: Summon the Radann Peder kai el'Sol." Alesso turned to look out toward the sunlight on the Lake. It was so bright it brought water to the eyes—and blindness. A sign, that. "He has been watched?"

"He has been watched. And aware of it at every moment."

"A pity. He is far more adroit than the previous kai el'Sol."

"And he has caused us far less damage. I will summon him, Alesso," Sendari said. "But I urge you to caution. The Radann—"

"*Are* the Lord's men," Alesso said, and he suddenly offered them the desert's smile: A glint of white, stark light in a harsh expression.

"Nicu, we are not having this discussion. Not now." Elena stopped short, pulled handfuls of thick, auburn hair out of her eyes, and rolled it all back into the kerchief that perched so precariously on her head. She rarely wore pins and nets—those were too severe for her, too restrictive—and suffered in the heat for the lack.

The heat today was combined with the job of carrying items of family value—and merchant curiosity—to safety. Their train had been noted; neither she nor Margret had any doubt of it. They had to move quickly.

And quickly didn't allow her the luxury of dealing well with anyone's ego. Not that it was one of her strong points to begin with.

"You had time to flirt with Peter and Adam—"

"Lady's blood, Nicu—Adam is a *boy!*" A wiser man than Nicu of the Arkosan Voyani would have seen the flush in Elena's cheeks for exactly what it was. She turned her glare a moment in his direction, and saw him: Handsome, in a pretty way, with wide, dark eyes, high cheekbones, a face neither too squat nor too thin. Unfortunately, handsome and petulant mixed poorly for a woman of Elena's temperament. She wanted to smack him.

Instead, gritting her teeth, she walked past him, her arms barely containing a bundle of silk cloth that was just that little bit too valuable to easily leave behind. White, with gold thread embroidery, and edged on either side by the deepest of blue.

Nicu grabbed her arm.

She gave him a face full of bolt for his trouble, and if the silk was soft, the weight of the whole was not.

He scrambled to his feet, his eyes wide. "Elena, I'm sorry—I just want you to listen to me for five minutes—I didn't mean—"

But the color had reached the height of her forehead. "How *dare* you?"

No rule stronger than this: You don't touch a Voyani woman without her leave. Not unless she's got no relatives, no temper, and no ability to defend herself if she's annoyed.

None of which applied to Elena.

"Elena, don't you understand? Can't you understand? I'm half-crazy about you, you know that. I only want to be able to tell you—"

"Nicu, *not now.*" Fortunately for Nicu, he *was* one of those relatives; a cousin. And Elena was fond enough of his mother—her mother's cousin—not to want to kill him or humiliate him publicly. She was certain, given the wide-eyed prurience of the Voyani, that this . . . altercation . . . would make its way back to Donatella, his mother, before he'd managed to finish rubbing his cheek.

And *then* he'd pay.

"Not now, not now, not now! It's always *not now!*"

"We're in the middle of moving what's left of the caravan, Nicu," Elena said, forcing a softness she didn't feel at all into her words, "And that takes precedence over everything else. It's easy enough to flirt with Peter. It takes two seconds, and there's nothing at all to it. But the discussion you want is bigger, longer, more serious. Let it go. We'll get there when we're safe. Yes?"

He was not mollified. But he was no longer mortified.

"Didn't Margret give you the task of guarding the periphery?"

"There are lots of guards."

She wanted to smack him again. But she was afraid she wouldn't stop. "And none of them are as closely related to Margret as you are. You're needed out there. I'm needed in here. Later, all right? Nicu, later?"

"Later, then." He stalked off, his face set in petulant agony.

She was going to have to talk with Margret about him. Either that or kill him and put them both out of his misery.

The worst part was this: In this mood, Nicu was a terrible guard; he took everything personally and was therefore likely to start a fight only his wounded ego could believe he'd win. They'd lost men before to just such a fight.

But Nicu was popular among the men; well-liked, well-supported. He had about him Margret's look, Margret's dark attractiveness—things, in fact, that Elena didn't like to think of at all. And, damn him, she was.

He watched. Unnamed, unnoticed, his arms folded casually across his chest in a mimicry of humanity that was completely unnecessary, he watched.

The Shining Palace was his home, but it was not the only home he craved; the world was larger than he remembered, but becoming smaller. Here, in this city that men deemed ancient, he might at last flex his muscles; here he might move small hills with the force of his Lord's gathering magic. Ah, the gathering was slow, but it was inevitable, and time had no meaning at all to the *Kialli*.

Power, as always, was the constant.

Lord Ishavriel watched quietly as the young man strode out of the busy encampment, seeking danger, nursing anger and pride. He was, as far as humans go, handsome in his fashion, burning with the pride and the folly, the light and the exuberance, of a youth he would never appreciate fully. Not as the *Kialli* might once have, in a different time.

That one, he thought, would do. They had waited upon Lord Isladar's efforts with the Voyani—and nothing at all had come to light. Not surprising; Isladar was a Lord even the cleverest among them did not quite understand. He exposed very little of his power, survived everything, and stood by his Lord's side almost as a monument, a thing that the *Kialli* drive for power and the wrath of God could not combine to destroy.

. But his influence had become weaker once the little half-god Kiriel had disappeared. It had become weaker still when she had arrived in force upon the side of their enemies, although in truth her attacks seemed aimed at Etridian, perhaps Isladar himself, and not the Lord of Night.

No matter. It was weakness.

Weakness was there for only one reason: Exploitation.

Ah, did they notice the sun, these little mortals? Did they feel its heat, and the luster it added to the beads of sweat on their aging, dying skin? Did they feel the dry, dry breeze? Did they understand how close to death they stood?

Not yet. Not yet. He lifted a hand—and the woman to whom his chosen vessel had spoken glanced up suddenly at the shadows that surrounded him. Her eyes narrowed into green-flecked brown, and the sun brought out fire in the brown of her hair. She stood straight as steel, strong as it, as unlike the man as day from night. How appropriate, here.

But her blood, he thought, was weak; all of their blood was weak. Only the so-called Matriarchs were a threat, and Lord Ishavriel knew well how to deal with them: Was this not, after all, the Dominion of Annagar? Was this not the land where women ruled nothing? Only the Voyani chose a different course.

Lord Ishavriel had once possessed the power to move rivers in their beds. His smile was a thing of perfect beauty and grace, where none at all might witness it.

The woman shivered, made a shaking sign with her hands, and moved away, shouldering her burden.

The Radann kai el'Sol had heard the news. It was clear from his expression—cautious, neutral, even friendly—that word had already traveled. Alesso di'Marente was beyond wondering how. The Voyani might have heard it, the serafs, the wives of Sendari— whom he could not quite bring himself to dispose of, for reasons of old friendship—and any of these would have carried word, eventually, to the Radann, or to those who served him.

No serafs among the Radann, of course. The Lord did not accept the service of men who lived on their knees. But the Lord also rewarded power, no matter what title it took.

Peder kai el'Sol had reached the pinnacle of his power; from here, it was only a matter of time until the next rival, the next ally, was cunning enough to take his place. But Alesso had been carefully observing the Hand of God, and it was clear that this particular formation was allied not against Peder, but against the coming night in the Tor Leonne.

He counted on it. It had been a dangerous play, all the way through, and the demons made it harder and harder to move. But he was—had been—the best of the Generals the Tor Leonne had produced in generations; he thought it without pride but with certain knowledge. He understood strategy, and he stared in the face of one of the most dangerous of his divisions.

Hard to utilize it now; he had hoped to hold it until the timing was more appropriate. But he now had the choice of putting it into play or losing it entirely. He was not a man to take a loss where the chance of a victory existed.

The serafs he dismissed the moment the kai el'Sol crossed the threshold. They were well-trained; well enough trained that he thought he detected the hand of Marano in their grace and movement. They had already brought the waters of the Tor Leonne itself, and had gracefully arranged those fruits which were in perfect season for the repose of their master and his guest. They left strategic fans, large and in keeping with the sparse decor of the General's preferred rooms, and they made certain the cushions against the hard mats were artfully arranged.

But they left when he ordered it, although the order was the merest gesture.

Which left the room to two powerful men, the two who best served the interests of the Lord, the two who were allowed the full sun in ascendance as personal crest.

"Tyr'agar," the kai el'Sol said, bowing.

"Kai el'Sol." He returned the bow, giving it the weight of his respect. "I have taken the precaution of insuring that these rooms will keep a conversation private. If you wish to have your own people inspect them, I will understand."

That caught the Radann kai el'Sol off guard; it was as open an admission of magic's use—and of the fact that the Tyr'agar also assumed the use of magic on the part of the Radann—as Alesso had ever made in his dealing with the former par el'Sol.

"I am confident," Peder kai el'Sol replied, "that what you say is true. You summoned me in haste, and I came in haste; I will not waste your time by returning for an aide."

"My time or your own?"

At that, the kai el'Sol did smile.

"Be seated; it is my belief that we will be here several hours. Take your ease, and if it pleases you, take the waters of the Tor Leonne and drink them. I find they ease me in times of darkness."

Peder frowned slightly, as if listening to the echo of the Tyr'agar's words. After a moment, he spoke. "We are being watched, but not listened to?"

"That is my suspicion, yes. I do not have time to have it confirmed."

The Radann bowed again; the bow was deep. When he rose, his face was a constructed mask of geniality and ease, even of self-indulgence. It was an unusual expression on the face of the Radann, although Alesso saw it often on the faces of lesser men.

He sat, taking characteristic care to arrange his swords. Alesso joined him.

"We have," he said softly, "been betrayed."

The Radann kai el'Sol did not waiver; he reached for the goblet that held the waters of the Tor Leonne. They were a miracle, one of the few that the Tor Leonne consistently boasted: they had healing properties, and they were always sparkling, even given the absence of direct sunlight, and always cool; they quenched a thirst no matter how fierce, and calmed hunger. Even madness was put at bay for hours at a time—or so it was said; the last had not been tested in years.

"Continue."

Alesso was struck by the composure of the man; struck and momentarily annoyed. But he had called for it. He accepted it with as much grace as he accepted anything that did not please him in time of war: as part of the terrain.

"Our allies have decided to impose on us a set of tasks and a set of creatures that we cannot accept."

Silence.

"We will not, of course, accede to the demands that they've made."

He watched; the lines of the kai el'Sol's face hardened slightly. Hardened and relaxed, as if at one and the same time the man were becoming the Sword of God and dispensing with pretense that would have irked the man who last held the title. "There were rumors," Peder kai el'Sol said neutrally.

"As many rumors, they bear some grain of truth, no more."

"Why have you summoned *me*, Tyr'agar? Why have you not summoned the Sword of Knowledge? They seem to hold more of your regard and your favor than the Radann."

"A good question," Alesso replied, taking up his own goblet having made his opening move. "The answer is simple: If we do not accede to the demand for a Consort to sit by the Lady's side—as if a Lord could sit by the Lady's side and not rule—they will send the Greater Servants of the Lord of Night into the streets of the Tor Leonne."

"I see." The Radann kai el'Sol was pale now, bleached of the sun's harsh touch. "It was to be expected."

"Perhaps. It is not the ideal situation, however; I thought to have more time in which to plan."

Silence. "You would have us deal with this threat?"

"Yes. I would have Radann deal with it—in a manner that befits both themselves and the Lord of the Sun."

"And the new Tyr'agar."

"Of course. I will be judged by the theater that unfolds in the city below. If the Lord of Night returns to the Festival of the Moon, if the worship of Lady is lost due to the fear of the death he brings, they will think, they will speak, only of Leonne."

"The Tyr Leonne could have no more handled such an invasion than you."

It was flattering, and Alesso di'Alesso had no time for flattery. "You do not say all that you think, and I choose not to hear what you are wise enough not to say." He rose, although it was unwise, and took the water with him. "But *I* will say it, kai el'Sol: that Markaso kai di'Leonne, weak and incapable though he was, had the single advantage in a night such as the coming night that I do not possess.

"The Sun Sword."

Peder kai el'Sol bowed his head.

"The Radann were chosen the Hand of God. I am no servitor—no servant of anyone but my own interests, as men of the Lord must be. But even I have heard that the Hand of God was granted, in lesser measure, some of the gift Leonne was granted in greater. You have the five swords," he said quietly. "And the vision with which to use them.

"We have not always seen with the same eyes, and we will not; that is the way of men with power. But in this, I believe our needs and our goals coincide, and to that end, I will direct all aid and obedience to you."

"I am to be given privacy."

"I am not in control of everything the Sword's Edge does, but I believe that privacy can be arranged."

"Then let us eat, Tyr'agar, let us drink. The night of the Festival Moon is not yet upon us."

In the pale light of moonless night, it glowed.

Set in its cradle, perched atop the steep stairs upon which incense braziers were set to burn in its honor, protected by the Swordhaven that was famed throughout the Dominion, the curved crescent of flawless steel spoke in a ringing voice that none could hear: *Demon. Kialli. Kin.*

7th of Scaral, 427 AA
Evereve

Nothing was an easy thing to be.

Nowhere, just as easy a place. Safe. Quiet. Devoid of the things that she'd last seen: the dead, the dying, the creatures that made them from the living like sculptors or mad artists, in their frenzied rush to stop Avandar from making his escape. From making *their* escape.

So she kept her eyes closed when she heard her name. This had the added advantage of keeping the world where it should be: at a distance, and stationary. Seen through the crack of a barely open eye, it spun in a disconcerting blur of light that immediately reached for the contents of her stomach.

Which she had no intention of letting go.

"Jewel."

The voice was louder.

But that wasn't what made her open her eyes. At a distance, at a remove, the voice itself had been what she expected: male. Worried. Quiet.

Now it was simply disturbing. She didn't recognize the speaker, but there was something distorted about her name as he spoke it, something cumbersome, uncomfortable. She forced herself to look. Saw ceiling, sort of. At least that's what she assumed it was, as she was pretty certain she was flat out on her back. *If I ever own this much gold,* she thought irritably, *I'm not going to waste it on interior decorating.* Or at least not on ugly interior decorating. Gold, in sculptured leaf, lay everywhere that wasn't surfaced by dark blue-green opal. The combination of colors was striking; unfortunately there was so much floral work in the patterns those colors were put to use creating, the effect was cloying. The possible exception to this gaudy rule was the central pattern in the ceiling's peak, of a distinct and powerful sun, which offered striking simplicity of line and theme when compared with the cacophony of the rest of the crammed images. All of which had nothing to do with the stranger's voice, but she found to her dismay that she almost couldn't turn her head.

"Jewel," the man said again.

She embarrassed herself by attempting to speak. Frogs sounded better.

"Avandar?"

"The master sleeps," the stranger replied. As if aware of her discomfort and her inability to easily turn her head a few inches to the right, he leaned over to offer her the comfort of vision.

She closed her eyes.

But not before she had clearly seen that the lines of his face were pale alabaster, shot through with smoky gray and blue; that his lips, full and soft in appearance were as perfect and uncreased as the stone they had been carved from.

"My apologies," he said quietly, and the stiffness of stone suddenly informed the tone of his words, "if I cause you discomfort. That was not my intent. I am here—at the master's orders—to serve any need you might have."

"I'm . . . fine," she managed to say.

He disappeared from her field of vision, which was so narrow it didn't take much work. She heard footsteps; expected them to be heavy. What else would stonefall sound like?

But they weren't, of course; they were light enough that she had to really listen to catch them. She closed her eyes, shutting out the gleam of gold in the curve of ceiling above. It was fairly easy; lids fell, gold, like magelight in a closing hand, turned off. But what she could not shut out—because it was already part of memory and her memory was such a badgering pest—was the expression on the face of the stone man.

He was upset; possibly angry, possibly hurt. Hard to tell; he was gone before she had the time to understand what the turn of lips and corners of eyes meant in this strange mimicry of a human face.

Briefly, she wondered if she'd managed to fall and *really* bang her head. And then she didn't wonder much anymore.

"Jewel."

That voice, she recognized. Out of habit, she scrunched her lids tightly shut and turned over, pulling the blankets up and around the swell of her shoulder. But the feel of the blankets in her hands stopped her in mid-motion. They were so soft that if it weren't for their weight she'd have wondered if they existed at all. She didn't deal in textiles—that was Ruby ATerafin, and both she and Ruby, for sad and obvious reasons, were often confused although they were different in every possible way if you didn't count the fact that they were both women—but she knew quality when she touched it. She opened her eyes. Stared at the light that lay against the surface of cloth as if it were trying to cling there.

"Jewel."

Warily, she turned.

Avandar stood an unusual distance from her bed. About thirty feet, in fact. It took her a moment to realize that he stood where he always stood—in relation to the wall. The wall that was only marginally more tasteful than the ceiling when it came to the use of gold. Someone had too much money and too little taste.

That wasn't the only problem.

Whoever had decorated this room had also apparently crept in and decorated her domicis. He was covered head to toe in some bright red robe that used gold the way fire uses orange light. His hair looked darker, his eyes brighter, his shoulders broader. He wore a crown, and beneath that jewel-encrusted circlet—which was, after all, no more tasteful than anything else she'd seen in the room so far—his expression was as grim and forbidding as any she'd ever seen grace his face.

"Great," she said, to no one in particular, "I've died and gone straight to the Hells."

His expression shifted like the light the silks threw off.

She had trouble standing, and realized that she, too, had been transformed into some nightmare of garish proportion: she wore blue silks, studded with uncomfortably bumpy little jewels which she tried to pretend weren't diamond or opal. It would have helped a lot if expensive frivolities like special rocks hadn't been part of her purview in The Terafin's merchant lines.

Standing wasn't really worth the trouble, but it reasserted old habits, and besides, she felt acutely uncomfortable enmeshed in silk. Her head *hurt*.

She reached up to rub her forehead, and her hand scraped something that was definitely not skin. "Let me guess," she said, looking across the room to a domicis who had not uttered a syllable that didn't contribute to her name. "This is a crown."

He said nothing.

She wondered if she was dreaming. This had that very strong blend of real and unreal which marked the dreams she had come to understand, in her youth, were prophetic. But, damn it, she *knew* she was awake.

"Avandar, what in the Hells is going on?"

There was something about his expression that she didn't like. All right, there was almost always something about his expression she didn't like—but this, this surfaced from an unseen place. She was not used to being surprised, not like this.

She'd known Avandar for half her life.

And wondered, as she took an involuntary—and creaky—step backward, what that meant. This man, this man was a stranger.

He stepped forward. She stepped back, into the bed.

He stopped. She reached for her dagger.

It was gone.

Think. Think, damn it. "Avandar." She kept her voice low. Formal. "You—you probably saved my life. Again. Where are we?"

She didn't feel threatened, not precisely, but the unease was so strong the only response she could give it was fear. She hated fear. Fought with it. This man was her *domicis*.

And what, exactly, does a domicis do with more gold than the merchants guild makes in a year plastered all over the walls and furniture of a single ugly room?

She really hated common sense at times like this.

Without speaking, she took the crown off and dropped it on the bed. It was very, very heavy. She'd've taken the dress off as well, but there was a lack of anything to replace it with—and although he'd seen her dress and undress more times than either of them could count, had, in fact, dressed her for every significant political occasion she'd been forced to attend, she suddenly didn't want to be naked while he was there.

"Where are we?" she asked again. The weight was off her forehead; she felt more like herself.

"We are," he replied, remote and cool, "in Evereve."

"Evereve?"

"My home."

She was absolutely silent.

"I apologize for your manner of dress. I hadn't realized how . . . ill it would suit you. I also apologize for your slow recovery. This . . . place . . . was meant to house only two living people. Myself and my—" He did not turn away; did not move. The words simply ceased.

That man had seen death, and he witnessed it again as he stood in front of her. She knew what memory looked like when it played across another's face.

She just didn't know what the memories were. Wasn't certain it mattered anymore. Pain was pain.

She waited.

"I—it took some work to stop Evereve from destroying you."

She sat.

"The compromise was your . . . current attire. I will have something more appropriate brought."

"Why exactly are we here?"

"Ah." His smile was his own, and familiar to her. Unfortunately it was also one of the expressions that she least liked. Not that she liked many of them.

"You are sensitive to the destruction done to your city and its people."

"Yes."

"To conclude our battle would have destroyed the Common— more of the Common," he added quickly, as her mouth opened and words almost spilled out. "I have no doubt you would have survived if it were, in fact, possible."

"And those demons?"

"Not friends."

She snorted. Shoved her hair out of her eyes.

"My clothing?"

"It—did not survive the transfer."

"And yours?"

He shrugged.

"Okay. One more question. The creature that looked like a walking blacksmith's reject. Why did he call you Warlord?"

"I was not aware that any of the demons did. Perhaps he mistook me for someone else."

CHAPTER FIVE

The masks had not been made by the servants of the Tyr'agar; they had been crafted—with care and attention to detail—by other hands, and delivered in a wagon, much like any merchant wagon, that had been detained for inspection, as agreed upon. What happened to the merchants who were responsible for their delivery, no one knew; they came to the Tor Leonne, and they vanished from it, melting into heat and sun and crowd, or perhaps into night's shadow: the nights were longest at this time of year. No matter; the masks arrived as planned.

Thus they came easily into the hands of the men meant to use them.

There were four faces.

The first was a study in elegant simplicity: A face, unremarkable in every way. Slightly narrowed circles for eyes, a nose that was neither too long nor too short, too wide nor too pointed, but that still somehow suggested imperfection. Cheekbones that were a little too high under the ridge of eyes, a width and a roundness that was perhaps a little too full for the whole, but that would guarantee accommodation of almost any real face beneath the facade. There was about the mask some of the softness that might be associated with a woman, and some of the edge that would definitely be associated with a man; it was a thing to hide behind. What made it interesting was that the mask itself was made partly of clay, smoothed into a fine, white layer and baked under a hot, hot sun.

The second face was smaller; the eye holes rounder, the features more delicate. It, too, seemed made of thin clay, and when placed against the brow and cheek was marvelously cool to the touch. Unlike the first mask, it covered the whole of the face,

Which was his way of saying he wasn't going to answer the question.

"There is food—or there will be—in the hall of welcome."

"You have a hall of welcome here."

"Yes."

"And this place, whatever it is, only lets two people enter it alive?"

"Yes."

"What if I told you I wasn't hungry?"

His frown was the most natural thing she had seen so far; although it wasn't at odds with the crown that split his brow. "I would hesitate a moment before I called you a liar, and I would have the food brought here."

"I'm not hungry."

He did, in fact, hesitate a minute. She counted. He turned and left.

Only then did she sink back into the comfort of a gaudy bed. Wondering who had last occupied it before her. Wondering—for there was no question whatever in her mind that it had happened—how that occupant had died.

leaving room for the mouth. The forehead was high, the cheek-bones less pronounced. Yet, Sendari thought, as he held the mask, feeling it almost as a lack of weight rather than as a substantial artifact, it suggested the delicate.

What it did not suggest, again, was the solely feminine. There was something about its line that hinted at steel, at something that women only possessed who—

No. He set the mask aside, but he had already seen, for a moment, the eyes of his most loved, and most hated, child staring back at him through holes that were meant for the moon in full-ness, and not the day's height. Ah, accusation. Anger. *Not now, Lady, not now; we two are doing your work; judge later, if at all.*

A prayer.

He set the mask aside.

Reached down to the low, flat table; spoke a word, and then another, the Widan's gestures of protection.

The third face was a broad face; exaggerated in detail. The forehead, in particular, was pronounced, and this mask—alone among the three—was adorned with a fringe of hair, or feathers, or silk, a flash and flare of color that made of each something unique, although it took little time to discern the sameness of face beneath the coloring. It was larger, wilder, a stronger mask. Not made of clay, but made of something more supple: leather, molded and hardened. The particular face that he now lifted had been painted with a thin sheen of bronze; it glittered in the daylight.

"Not," he heard Cortano say, "an inexpensive gift."

"No."

Sendari set it aside.

The fourth mask waited.

To call it fourth was not entirely accurate. The first three masks so exposed to scrutiny had been made from the same molds, and likely by the same set of craftsmen; they were finely done, not of the highest quality, but certainly better than the average Festival mask that one would see worn at the height of the Lady's Night. Poorer clansmen, offended by the edict and the gift, would nonetheless be drawn to the masks themselves for that very reason.

But the fourth face was not an identical face worked over with hair or feather, silk or lace. Each mask was subtly different; each face looked as if it had been made of clay in the same vein but set to dry in different conditions; humidity, little sun, light rain.

Storm. The face itself, Sendari thought, might have been a bird's face to start with; sharp and long-beaked, with a ruffled fringe carved or worked into the material that went into its making. He was partial to birds, for it was often birds that Na'dio had chosen to reveal herself in.

Yet there was about this bird a ferocity that he thought his daughter—his young daughter, of course—would have shied away from. He set it aside, and looked at what had rested on the table beneath it, something that in the North might be called dragon; the beak elongated, widened, the lower beak stretched thin and given not just tongue but sharpened teeth. Yet the size of the mask, and the general shape of it, was consistent.

In some, the beak was smaller; a nose, perhaps, or a ferret's jaw; in some, it was softer but still pronounced.

None of the faces were human, and in fact, he would have classified them as individual masks had it not been for the fact that they were made in similar style and of the same material.

They were also made of the most expensive external components: indeed the most gaudy boasted gems that to Sendari's admittedly less than well-trained eye were genuine. Paint had been used, sparingly and elegantly in some cases, wildly in others, and all to splendid effect: These were, of the four styles, the true Festival masks.

Yet they were in number evenly divided: One quarter for the blandest face, one quarter for the most delicate, one quarter for the smiling mask, and one quarter for the others.

He set the dragon's face aside almost with regret. "These last," he said softly, "are very fine."

"No doubt," Cortano said softly. "It is the last, of course, that most resemble the Festival masks of the Tyrs or the Tors." Sendari glanced back at the Sword's Edge; saw only the steel that spoke of the search for answers. He nodded and took to the edge himself. Of that, at least, he was capable; he was Widan, after all.

"Why four?" Sendari's question.

Cortano shrugged. "The elemental significance?" It was a desultory attempt at an answer; noise, meant to fill a silence of thought and deliberation. In and of themselves, nothing about the masks spoke of the elements—which were, in their way, Northern symbols of knowledge, not Southern ones.

So far, few spells had been cast, little magic spent in scrutiny; they examined by both jeweler's glass and naked eye the craftsmanship that had gone into the masks' construction. They had come with no instructions; women or men were allowed to choose the mask they wore, and no mask suggested simple masculinity or femininity to the two Widan who studied them.

But of the magic that *had* been cast, all spells were sophisticated and of a type that the Widan used automatically: a measure of protection or defense, of detection or information gathering on a minimal level. Greater magics than that, if these masks were indeed to be feared, would be too easily detected; Cortano was unwilling, without a clearer sense of the masks' purpose, to antagonize Lord Ishavriel further.

"This is your field of expertise," Sendari said at last, "but if you are willing, Sword's Edge—"

"Yes?"

Sendari fell silent at the edge in Cortano's voice. He flexed his hands, a reminder of old scars. Stood a moment in the scant light. "Mikalis," he said at last, deciding. "Mikalis di'Arretta would be of aid to us if any man could be."

"And the risk?"

Sendari shrugged. "Weigh the risk of failure against the risk of discovery. You are the Sword's Edge; the decision must be yours. I will, of course, abide by your decision."

Cortano's eyes narrowed beneath the frosted tuft of thick brow. But he was silent as he considered the matter of Mikalis di'Arretta. A Widan, a man as loyal as any seeker of power or knowledge could be; his was the study of antiquities. Sendari, too, had bent his considerable intellect to such studies—but Sendari was not a friendly man, and in the end, such studies required the ability to blend and mingle with the common man, the common seraf, or the common Voyani.

Cortano himself had studied objects, but never—not even in his questioning of the Voyani women—the Voyani at work. Only Mikalis had, and very, very rarely.

"You are certain that this is Voyani magic?"

Sendari shook his head. "No more certain than you. But we have detected no obvious magery, no understood art, within the confines of the crafting, and these *must* contain some elements of power, else why use them at all? It bears the hallmark of Voyani magic."

"But the *Kialli* are not Voyani."

"No, but the two things they fear are the Voyani and the Imperial half-gods."

Cortano's smile was small and chilly. "They are fools, then. And that is to our advantage." He turned toward the screens that, light and easily moved as they seemed, were still almost unbreachable when the proper words were spoken. "Very well. Mikalis."

She was fire and wind, sand and wind, sun and wind—but she was also the oasis and the coolness of dusk or dawn. Her hair was like sunset seen through a thin, brown silk, and her eyes, brown like most Voyani eyes, were flecked with green: life, there. Life, and he wanted so desperately to be a part of it he could almost taste it.

He had done everything he could to attract her attention; everything. It had been easy when they'd been children together. She, he, Margret—they were almost equals in the eyes of the clans. But Margret was Evallen's daughter, and destined to be the Matriarch of the clan. If death took her, than her aunt's daughter, Elena, would take the title and responsibility.

But he, Nicu, stronger and smarter and less quick to anger than either of the two women, would always be passed over. Because he was a man. Because he could not bear life. His mother, Donatella, much favored by Evallen and Tamara, would likewise be passed over.

He had never thought much about it as a child.

He thought about little else now that he had the full growth of his hair—although he kept the beard tightly cropped because Elena didn't care for length in a man's beard. Not, of course, that she noticed, that she ever noticed.

"Hey, Nicu!"

He looked up from the dirt in which he'd been absently cutting lines with the tip of his curved blade. Frowned at Carmello—his second cousin, father's side. Carmello was a year old than Nicu, and at one time—a long time ago—that had mattered. Not now; Carmello had stayed the same, and Nicu had grown up.

"What?"

"Heads up—to the East!"

Nicu swore. There were four men—clan crested, but not easy to tell which clan at this distance—approaching the loosely formed caravans. They walked with an easy gait, two abreast. Sheathed swords. He cursed himself, and Elena for good measure, and then took to the rim of the nearest wagon, using its frame to lend himself about four feet of immediate height.

He swore again.

Carmello's turn to frown and look up. "What's wrong?"

"West—farther down the road—and Southwest. Four men from each direction. I'd bet the Lord's balls we've got 'em coming in from the Southeast as well. Hey, Adam!"

Margret's younger brother suddenly appeared between the flaps of one of the exterior wagons; he was carrying two glass lamps on poles that were probably older than Carmello, Nicu, and Adam combined. "What?"

"Go tell Margret we've got trouble. Hey, Uncle Stavos!" Before Adam could ask a question—and Adam usually did, and usually from underfoot, Nicu was in action, swinging down from the wagon's height and into the thick of his men. If this wind didn't smell of fire and blood in less than an hour, the Lord was napping.

They had almost everything they needed. A wagon or two on the outskirts of the city—left there, for *just* such an emergency, because you could never trust the hospitality of the clans— would have to house the most precious of the caravan's possessions; the men and the women would walk, and could walk. Lady knew, they'd done it before.

She didn't speak of her mother; no one asked. The assumption that she was dead had spread through her people like wafting smoke in a strong breeze—but Margret had put them all into action immediately, and they knew they had no time. No time.

Questions later. She couldn't stop them from being asked.

This wagon was the hardest to leave: Her mother's wagon. Her family home. Everything she had ever loved that wasn't flesh and blood was here, and the shadows, mingling with sunlight, were an accusation of neglect and flight.

There, when her father had been alive before a Lyserran raid, she would sit in the older man's lap, her brother in hers, her mother on the bench beside them all, knitting or working thread. She couldn't sit still; not Evallen. But her children could, for him, for the father she remembered so clearly and Adam remembered so poorly.

He told them stories of the old days while her mother snorted. Told them about a time when the Voyani—when *all* of the people of the Dominion—had existed by the Lady's grace, not the whim of the jealous Lord. They had had a home, and hard work to be sure, but it was *theirs*.

"Alexi," her mother would say, mock-stern. "You fill up their heads with stupid stories."

"I," her father would reply, puffing his chest forward in mock willful pride, "fill their heads up with pride for their roots, and hope for their future, you foolish woman."

"Aye, well," Evallen of Arkosa would respond after a moment, "and maybe that's what men do. But I'll thank you not to spoil the daughter who has to carry all of Arkosa on her back—or her lap, some days—when she gets older. Let the little one dream."

He would whisper into her ear, "*You* dream, Margret. Without dreams, we're a small, bitter people who eat dust and get worn by the wind well before our time. Adam is a boy, with a boy's heart, but you're almost a woman, and women have always carried the Arkosans. They've carried the Voyani. Carry us somewhere grand."

He was gone now.

She hardly ever thought of him. Funny, that losing the wagon would bring back so much of his pipe-scented, wine-sweet breath, and so little of her mother.

"Margret?"

She half-turned, clutching the last small box that she would take from this wagon with her. Wanting that bench, where her father's ghost was still warm, wanting that flat, wide chest over which she'd slept for years, cushions, pillows, and Adam by her side. Wanting the world to go back to what it had been when the decisions were easy because they'd belonged to someone else.

Lady, she was spineless today.

"What is it, Tamara?"

"Adam came."

The box pressed into her arms as her grip tightened involuntarily. "Trouble?"

"Nicu sent him."

"What word?"

"Sixteen men, at least." Tamara drew breath. "But I think there's probably more."

"Armed?"

"Armed."

"Tyrian?"

Tamara did not answer. Answer enough, from her aunt.

"Shit. Get Elena. Tell them—tell them all not to stand against the clansmen for the sake of pride and a bunch of empty wagons.

"If we've got something to lose, we can fight for it. But we've got a fight already, and it's a big one. I'm going to need all the men I have here, and more, before it's over. You tell them. Make sure Elena tells them."

"Margret, I think *you* should tell them."

Margret cursed. Reached for her belt and grabbed the hilt of her mother's best sword. Tamara was right, of course. The box faltered in her arms. "I'll tell 'em. You take this, and you don't let it be seen."

"Margret—"

"I'll follow my own advice. I swear it by—" By what? By the heart of Arkosa? She didn't have it. Some clanswoman trapped on the plateau did, and for how long—for *how long*—Margret didn't know. Wasn't dark enough to pray; she didn't bother. The Voyani learned early that cursing was a lot more fun, and just as effective.

She was the Matriarch now, and no one really knew it. Worse, she had no way to prove it; no heart to unlock. The pendant was more than her history, it was her crown, her staff, her rod—it was the only symbol of office that counted. Because she could make it do things that no one else could make it do. Eldest daughter. Arkosa bloodline.

It gave her pause for a moment, because it made her nervous. Men with swords had always made her mother tense, and her mother didn't get tense without good reason. So much pride here, and most of it for good reason. She'd felt it herself, time and again: They were *better* than the clans. They were the true survivors.

But she didn't particularly feel the need to prove it by burying her short sword into the chest of one; she'd seen her share of fighting, and she knew that the only rules between the clansmen and the Voyani were ones that ended in death.

Couldn't afford that, not here, not now. She thought that maybe one or two of the men could be winnowed here—they were trouble, and looked likely to get worse before they got better. But they were distant kind and *that* kind of attitude, before the fact, was exactly the type of thing that the clansmen had. Better to wait. Better to let the crime be committed for all to see.

Her hands shook. She didn't have the Arkosan heart, she didn't have her mother, and there were probably thirty armed men preparing a descent on the caravan as she wasted time striding from the remains of her home to the edge of their circle.

She saw Adam first. His eyes were wide, his sword was out, he was glancing from side to side as if in search of a commander. Of all the men in the caravan, he was her favorite—but sitting in her lap from the time you *could* sit probably gave a boy an unfair advantage. Sweet-faced, round-eyed, he came flying into her shadow, a frightened man-boy. A proud one.

One day, he'd have to be more than that. Probably soon.

"What are we going to do?"

"What wax does, when we have it. Melt."

"But Nicu says—"

"I know, and this is his watch. But this is bigger than this fight, and bigger than this caravan. I *need* you all, and I need you to do what we're best at. Survive." Her voice rose on the last word, because she knew the minute she started to speak that an audience had gathered. Waiting on her.

Aye, now was the time, and it wasn't the time. This was her first big choice. She weighed it.

And as she did, Nicu stepped forward.

Nicu, the cousin she'd grown up closest to. "We can take them," he said, his knuckles white around the grip of his sword. "We've got the wagon advantage, height where they don't expect it, cross-bows—they're not carrying them—and the edge time buys us."

She nodded. "We can," she said. "We'd injure them. But we'd have to flee, and we'd lose men in the process."

"Margret—"

"I know it's your job, Nicu, and I know if anyone can pull it off, you can."

"Then let me pull it off. Let me prove it."

Behind him, her Uncle Stavos was standing, his expression almost completely neutral. But his arms were crossed over his chest; he looked bearlike, grizzled, his dark eyes giving no light. She hated that look. He was measuring her and her worth, and he was withholding his judgment—because this was a test, damn him, and the judgment might be some sort of clue.

Lady, they had no *time*. She rose as Carmello took his place beside—and slightly behind—Nicu, his face devoid of Stavos' neutrality. Another man, Andreas, joined Nicu, taking his left where Carmello took his right. Choosing, she thought. Choosing Nicu, making his stand. Andreas, short, stocky, dependable in a fight—but only just.

She put her hand on her hip—some unconscious mimicry of

older Voyani women through the four clans—and said, "So this is it? This is your choice?"

No preamble; she was angry.

"Margret—" Nicu began.

She cut him off with the chop of a hand. "You think *I* like to run from the clansmen? From *them?* Is that what you think? You think I don't think we can win a fight? Is that what you're saying? You think I give you orders and you have to pull off your privates and sling 'em into little bags so you can run, tail between your legs, like some beaten dog?

"Is that what you think I'm leading you to?"

Nicu took a step back; Carmello and Andreas had already taken two. Adam, wide-eyed and pretty-faced, stood at her back, unmoving. She'd remember that later. Was vaguely grateful for it now. Her sword hand came up; steel flashed as she jabbed it into the empty air two feet away from Nicu's chest.

"Does this mean we fight?" he questioned, defiant.

"No, it means we do what *I* say."

"You aren't the Matriarch, Margret, not yet. And Evallen's—"

"Evallen's *dead*." She spit the two words out as if they were burning the insides of her mouth. As if they were burning her. She was dry-eyed now. "And the clansmen—or whoever it is who wants us to celebrate the Lady's Festival by *their* rules— also have Yollana. Do you understand what this means?"

But her first two words were a slap in the face.

Evallen. Dead.

She hadn't meant to say it, and having said it, she could not withdraw it. The Arkosan heart would have to be recaptured, and soon, or she'd lose control. But the heart had a way of coming back to its keeper; it had been lost once or twice before. The Lady made a path for it.

That was the story. She willed herself to believe it. Needed to.

"They killed the Matriarch?" Uncle Stavos' voice.

She met his eyes, the paleness of his skin unmistakable. "Yes," she said softly. "And I want them to *pay*. But they won't pay if we don't survive.

"Survival is what we *do*. It's what we *are*. We've lived with the desert for all of existence because we know when to stand against it and when to let it roar. You think *I* don't want their blood? You think *my* blood is that thin?" The sword came up, cutting a swathe through empty air. She was angry. "You think that, Nicu?"

He had been her favorite male cousin when they were growing up and the responsibility of the clan had rested—forever—on her mother's unbreakable shoulders. She met his eyes then, her face falling into an expression that spoke of that kinship, that special relationship, that history.

"If you think it, say it. Say it, and we'll have it out here, where it will cost us the most."

"You want us to run."

"I want us to vanish like shadow under bright light. We're not the Lord's; never have been. We're the Lady's. But we can find what we need in the sunlight, if we have to. I *need* you all. You're the men of the Matriarch's caravan. We're going to have to be here, and there—" she pointed up, and up again, to the plateau where the Lake lay nestled, "before this is over. Don't make me do this without you. Don't throw away lives we can't afford to lose."

He was silent. Shocked by her announcement. They all were. "And if we can't afford to let them take what we're leaving with?"

Her smile was the Lady's darkest smile. "*Then* fight, and with my blessing. And remember, while you're doing it: They're no blood of ours."

He took a breath. Then he tucked his sword into his sash. Shook his head, as if to clear it. "Margret—"

"You're my closest cousin," she said, relenting. Taking the free hand off the hip, where it was bunched more as fist than anything, she slapped his shoulder soundly. "My closest kin next to Adam, or you wouldn't have the important job. I trust you. Do it."

Then she lifted her hand to her face.

"We'll mourn," she said softly. "We'll *all* get our chance to mourn."

And they looked at her; she felt their eyes on the momentary shield of her hand. She was the Matriarch, for just that moment; she was what Evallen had been.

But it didn't make her feel any stronger; if anything, she felt weaker for it. She had *used* her grief, or the excuse for grief, to manipulate them all to do what she wanted them to damn well do. What kind of a daughter did that with her own mother's death? It made her soul shrivel in the heat of the Lord's merciless light.

"Margret," Uncle Stavos said, coming out from Nicu's shadow, his sword over his shoulder, "They'll be here soon, and they're probably coming for you, Matriarch."

She looked up at his face, at his sun-worn, care-lined face, and she saw neither shock nor grief. It came to her that he was one of the ones who already knew about Evallen's death. That he knew, that he accepted it, that she had somehow passed whatever test it was he had set for her.

"Uncle," she said.

He put his hand on the ball of her shoulder. "Margret," he replied softly, giving her, in a quick squeeze, all of his strength. "Trust yourself. You are your mother's daughter—and we need you to be that. To be worse, to be more, than that." He looked over his shoulder. "They're young," he said quietly. "And I'm needed. Take your own advice, Matriarch. *You* are Arkosa, heart exposed or no."

Things would have been different if he hadn't seen Elena. Her sword was out and her hair, as usual, had escaped the binding knot it was so artlessly shoved into. Her cheeks were flushed, skin glowing faintly with sweat and heat. She was laughing. In all of this, laughing.

Oh, not at him; she would never laugh at him at a time like this. But she was the Matriarch's cousin, and until such time as someone was stupid enough to marry Margret—or until Margret found a husband she thought worthy of the clan, Elena was the heir.

They'd given her the children; Adam was by her side and she'd looped an arm over his still-slim shoulders. *He* was too stupid to know what she offered. Boy.

"Nicu," Stavos said. "Come. They'll be here in ten minutes; less if the crowd keeps thinning. The Matriarch—"

He pulled himself free. Stood there, his jaw clamped. "I'd give her anything she wanted," he said at last, the words rushing together. Uncle Stavos was no idiot; he looked past Nicu's shoulder to Elena of Arkosa.

"Aye," he said, "and if it weren't for your Aunt Ellia, *I'd* join you in mourning." He winced, that mocking half laugh of his finishing the words. "Nicu, come."

"What do I have to do?" Nicu continued, allowing himself to be led. "What do I have to do to even get her attention?"

"Nicu, women are strange creatures. We men, we know what's

best in men—but women, they know *nothing*. My Ellia," he said, "she spent two years mooning after Pieter of the Havallans."

That stopped Nicu short. *"Pieter?"*

"Exactly. Told me he had poetry in his heart. Didn't matter whether or not his feet were on the road; he knew how to make a home of the *Voyanne*." The Voyanne: the homeless road. "I tell you now, I was almost ready to carry her off myself—but I liked living. Those two years were the hardest two years of my life. And," the big man said, laughing from the center of his chest, "I got what I wanted." He mimed a smack across the side of the head. "You be careful of what you want."

"How did you get her in the end? Why did she come to you, if she wanted him?"

"Lady knows," Stavos said. "If I knew, I'd tell you. Come on, Nicu."

Nicu followed his uncle.

But Elena was there with the children. "We should—we should help her."

Stavos actually frowned. A frown across his usually friendly face was very, very rare. "You want her because she can't take care of herself or her duties?" he asked, his voice thick with sarcasm. *"Nicu*, you have your duties. You choose between duty and desire."

"I won't leave the women and children alone," Nicu replied stubbornly.

"You sound like a clansman," Stavos said. He lifted an arm. "Do what you have to, Nicu, Donatella-son."

Nicu stepped toward where Elena and the children had last been spotted. The conversation with Stavos, curse him, had done its work; they were nowhere to be found. He ground his teeth—something Elena disliked intensely, and turned to catch up with his uncle. *Maybe,* he thought, *this is the Lady's sign.* The twist of anger in the center of his chest began to unknot. Stavos was right; he was being foolish. Elena had been given children as last duty, and she would see them safely through the streets if anyone could. Lady knew, she was good at slipping between clenched fingers as if she didn't even notice the grip. He reached up, grabbed the outer hood of a wagon that he knew he wouldn't see again, and took a deep breath.

"Nicu, Donatella's son. I have been waiting to speak with you."

His sword was out at once, twisting in air so that its curved

edge was ready for a solid swing. Nicu was one of the best
Arkosan swordsmen; he was proud of the fact. It was one of
the few things he was certain of.

But the man who stood before him, in robes as rich as the
Matriarch's ceremonial dress, did not flinch or move. He bore no
clan markings, wore no armor, carried no sword. In the far, far
North, merchants did that: wore no armor, carried no sword. But
not here, not in the Tor.

Nicu could take a glance to the side without moving his head;
his eyes darted to the almost deserted compound grounds. He'd
be one of the last to leave. Last, if the stranger didn't leave.

"I apologize for my untimely intrusion," the man said, bowing
gracefully. "But I believe that you will find it of benefit, and the
result of our discussion here will be proved there." He lifted a
hand, waved it to the street through which the first of the Tyrian
cerdan were approaching.

"I don't have time—"

"You do. I shall speak quickly, and perhaps too freely. Some
months ago, an associate of mine came forward to speak with
your Matriarch." He shrugged, silk rippling in sunlight almost
sinfully smoothly. "He offered her something that the Voyani
have long sought: an end to the curse of the Voyanne."

Nicu's eyes narrowed. "And you could promise that?" He spit
to the side, tightening his grip on his sword and looking, nervous
now but battle-ready, for the sign of the Sword of Knowledge
across the overly-fine silk breast. Nothing.

"I can," he said. "But *I* know better than to approach the
Matriarch. Think: When the homeland was open, *who* ruled it?"

"If it weren't for the Matriarch," Nicu shot back, "there wouldn't
be Voyani clans. We would have perished with the cities."

"This is the Dominion, Nicu of Arkosa."

Hearing his name fall off this stranger's lips made him crackle
with a type of suspended energy. He wasn't certain why, but he
knew, right at that moment, that he shouldn't listen to the stranger.

Knew, as well, that he would.

"In the Dominion, where else do women rule? Do serafs rule
their lords? Do clansmen rule the Tors, the Tors the Tyrs?" The
stranger's smile was slight. "No. Only the Voyani are ruled by the
weaker sex. Do you think that the women want to go back to their
so-called home? Do you think that they want to give up power,
any more than the Tyrs do?

"Think: In the cities of Arkosa, of Havalla, of Lyserra and Corrona, did *women* rule? No. Men ruled. Women married, they were fierce in their marriages, and they were loyal."

"We don't like our women weak," Nicu said, thinking of Elena, his Elena.

"No," the stranger replied. "And in that, there is much to admire; a weak woman does not make a strong son. But leadership? Rulership in time of war? In a fight, you could best your cousin. I have seen that much, and I have been watching for some time, waiting for a worthy man to finally present himself from Arkosa.

"That man is you; you are now old enough, now skilled enough, now wise enough, to know what it is that you want. I cannot immediately prove to you the value of my claim, but think carefully, and while you think, I will gift you with some portion of my power if you will receive it."

Instant suspicion, there. Nicu's sword, which had been slowly falling groundward, came up at once. "What gift? I will not have you touch me."

"No, indeed. The gift I grant you is a sword, no more, no less. It is almost exactly like the one you wield; you need explain it, and its existence, to no one should you choose to carry it."

"And what will it do?" Nicu said, his eyes almost as narrow as the edge of his blade.

"It will aid you in a fight. You are faster than most of the men here, but not all; with this sword, you *will be* undisputed." He lifted the folds of his cloak. "I ask only that you consider what I have said, and what I have offered. I cannot give you the city itself, of course; the city is not here, and we are not before its hidden gates. I do not know where the city lies: only the Matriarch and her heir do.

"But if the sword is what I have promised, and if you are willing to serve your people as ruler and leader—as the man who will *bring them home,* we will speak again, you and I."

His robes billowed in a clean, fresh wind. Nicu, spellbound, waited a moment. The wind took the stranger, the man who bore no sign of the Sword of Knowledge, no sign of the arms and armor that mark a man in the Lord's eyes. But at his feet, where his robes had brushed the compacted dirt, was a scabbard.

In truth, it was not fine; it was as he had promised: much like the sword Nicu had owned for all of his adult life. As if that sword—the namesword, the sword by which he had taken his adult vows—now burned him, he removed it, touching it carefully, removing it from its easy and familiar place at his left hip.

It was something he did every night; no reason to feel so naked in the doing. But he felt it: naked. He hovered a moment, between desire and desire.

And then Nicu of the Arkosa Voyani straightened out his shoulders. He was a *man,* not a boy. He was not afraid of a sword. Bending at the knees, so as not to look subservient in the Lord's eyes, Nicu retrieved the sword the stranger had left, like a harbinger of either war or glory, where his feet had been.

He girded himself with it slowly, half-expected a trap of some sort: fire, wind, something that would burn or scour. Nothing happened. He gripped the hilt; felt the leather, cool and new, in the palm of his sweating hands. He murmured a prayer, indistinct and inaudible, for the Lady's Mercy.

Then, taking care to be as silent as possible—as if noise itself would draw attention he did not desire—Nicu of the Arkosa Voyani, Nicu, the Matriarch's cousin, drew the crescent sword.

It was . . . a sword.

Perhaps more, certainly not less. It gleamed in the sunlight, and its blade was a bit too pristine, untested, unnotched. His kinsmen would know, if they saw it. They would know it had been unblooded.

Nicu did not carry an unblooded blade.

He smiled for perhaps the first time that day. Opportunity was here, in plenty; if he carried the stigma of an unblooded blade, he would carry it in private, and he would not carry it long: there were enemies about, and none of them were his kin, however distant.

7th of Scaral, 427 AA
Evereve

She was reminded of old children's tales as she wandered the cavernous halls of the great, empty manse. But it wasn't the splendor of those halls that filled her with that unnamed childhood awe, although they were indeed splendid in their gaudy, gilded way. The heights the ceilings reached rivaled—or exceeded—those permitted the Mother, Cormaris, and Reymaris upon the Holy Isle, and contained by the larger surface of such walls, the gold that had seemed almost ugly and tawdry in the confines of an admittedly large bedchamber almost looked tasteful.

Well, perhaps tasteful was going too far. But the silvered glass
the hall boasted, end to end, was larger than any she had ever
seen and it distorted no part of her image; the crystals suspended
from the ceilings above on chains of gold or brass and silver
were of different colors that caught light and held it at their
hearts, transparent magelights. There were paintings, tucked into
frames of gold as if to give the wall continuity and color, that
were so perfect they caught her attention and held it for long
enough that she could forget where she was, what she was wearing,
who she was with. A sure sign of a maker's hand.

And there were the statues.

It was the statues that reminded her of the stories she had heard
while she sat in her grandmother's lap, probably from before the
time she could speak, the safety of the old woman's arms not yet
compromised in her young mind with the encroaching age that
would take her away so completely, so devastatingly.

They were here; men, a youth or two. They stood upon pedestals around which were carved runes she didn't recognize. Age,
august and profound, was implied everywhere and visible nowhere in the unblemished stone faces; the hand—or hands—that
had birthed them from their encasement in quarried blocks had
chosen to be both truthful and kind. She wondered, briefly, what
Meralonne could tell her of what was written beneath their feet.

Might have wondered longer, but she recognized one of those
statues, and she stopped in front of it.

Marbled alabaster, white eyes, full lips, clothed in smoothly
chiseled stone, he stood two feet above her looking not down but
up, as if he could see beyond the confines of the vaulted ceiling.
Or as if he hoped to one day be able to.

He looked no more lively than the rest of the procession he
stood in the middle of; no more lovely, in truth, but no less perfect. The expression that had accompanied his parting words was
nowhere to be seen. She reached out; her hand hovered above
his chest as she hesitated, searching still features for some sign
of life.

At last she touched him; the folds of his shirt—embroidered
by a thin set of grooves that made a pattern—were as hard as
Arann's armor.

But hard or no, they rippled beneath her fingers as his arms bent
at the elbow and his hand trapped hers. "You are not Elyssandra,"
he said, and she understood then why the statues felt old to her.

She had heard one speak, had found his voice strange, had not immediately understood why. She understood now, standing this close; they had the weight of earth in their voice; the weight of earth's bones.

She pulled her hand back; the surface of smooth rock abraded the skin, although he made no move to tighten his grip. "No. Not usually."

"I have slept long indeed," he replied, his eyes unblinking, his irises alabaster and disconcertingly large, "if there has been such a changing of the guard."

He fell silent; it became clear to her that he was waiting for her, either to speak or to leave. His expression was completely devoid of so animated a thing as emotion.

"Who are you?"

A brow went up, changing the lines of his face but leaving them, somehow, a statue's. "An odd question."

"I was going to tell you who I am," she replied, cocking her head to one side and then pushing the resultant locks of unruly hair out of her eyes, "but you're the host; you can go first."

"You were going to tell me who you are? Or simply what you are called?" But his lips curved oddly as he said it.

Great. A philosopher. "What I'm called. I'm not sure my version of who I am would mean anything to you, although come to think of it, the name pretty much says it all."

"Oh?"

"I'm Jewel ATerafin. And I'm stupid. I wanted your name first." Against her will, or rather, against her intent, she smiled. There was something about this statue that she liked.

"My name, I fear, will tell you less than your name tells me."

"Try me."

"I . . . am Aristos Concaella. I was . . . Regent in my time."

"Here?"

He laughed. It wasn't a pleasant sound; too much like the fall of one stone against another. "Not here. There are no Regents here. There is nothing to preside over in the absence of my master."

"Were you—were you ever—mortal?"

"Was I a man?" He laughed again, and this time she understood why the sound was unpleasant—a rock slide started that way before it buried whole caravans. "I was a fool. Does that count? It was many years ago."

She knew the answer to the question she asked next, but she

had to ask it; she had to hear the truth cast in words, because otherwise it would be too easy to slip out from under it. "How did you become a . . . statue?"

"The Warlord," he replied quietly.

"And the Warlord is Avandar?"

His frown was lovely. "I do not know the name; he had none by the time I was chosen to serve him."

"He was—he wears the crown here."

"Yes. The Warlord is your master."

She snorted. "*My* master?" As his expression shifted, the contours of his face gradually taking on a line that she couldn't quite name and didn't at all like, the laughter that almost escaped her subsided.

"I don't mean to offend," she said softly, "but I've known Avandar Gallais for half my life, and it is most decidedly not as *his* servant. He serves me."

"Oh?"

"Trust me. He may not serve me well; he may serve within the letter of the law and not at all within its spirit, but he does serve me."

He reached out for her hand.

She was not normally a person who liked to be touched—not by her own, and definitely not by strangers—but he moved so quickly, her right wrist was in his palm before she had even realized he intended to grab it.

He caught the edge of one of the fine, gaudy sleeves she wore between his forefinger and thumb and, scattering the edging of pearl and diamond to the floor below where they tinkled and rolled into silence, he yanked the sleeve up to her elbow.

There, two inches above her wrist on the inner part of her arm was a stylized backward S, bisected in two places with small v's. The S was red, the first v gold, the second silver. She ran her fingers over the mark as if expecting the paint to come off.

It didn't.

She rubbed harder.

The mark was as fresh and as unperturbed as the face of a great lady just after she leaves her morning rooms.

"What—what is this?"

The hall was quiet enough that the grinding of teeth could be heard.

"You do not recognize it?" He was silent a moment.

"If I recognized it, I wouldn't be asking."

"Can it be that you don't read?"

The accusation—of stupidity or the poverty that enforced it—had always riled, perhaps because it had come so close to being true.

"I. Read. Quite. Well."

"Ah. My apologies. My master . . . made me . . . to be the best of all possible servants. I hear all language as if it were my own. This," he said quietly, gesturing to the wrist she now cradled, "is the oldest word in our written vocabulary.

"It is the master's name," Aristos added softly.

"You—you have this?"

"I? No. Not that mark." He glanced down to the flow of stone over his forearms. "And the mark that I was given before I was given the responsibility of this domain is, I fear, long since made inaccessible."

"But you've seen this mark before."

"Oh, yes," he said, and there was suddenly something in his voice, like a second presence; something that struck her as lightning struck the storm-heavy sky: there, blinding, gone in an instant.

She didn't ask him. She reached up for the sleeve of her dress—her ridiculous, much despised dress—and yanked it firmly down over the offending arm, the offending sigil.

But perhaps the discussion had gone far enough.

Or perhaps it had not gone as far as he desired.

He said, "I have seen it once before, on the arm of the Warlord's wife."

CHAPTER SIX

It should have been easy to talk to him.

Or rather, it should have been easy to turn on her heel and walk down the great hall, each step alleviating some of her anger. She started, but the voice of a man trapped in stone—*of* it now, in this hidden place—stopped her.

As did the weight of his hand on her shoulder.

She wondered how little effort it would take for him to crush that shoulder—not a pleasant thought.

But he offered her words instead of violence. "Jewel ATerafin." The whole tone of his voice, the demeanor of his carriage, had changed subtly—if stone could be subtle.

She turned; he lifted his fingers, breaking all physical contact. "What?"

"I do not . . . understand . . . your reaction. It is clear you are angry."

"That would be an understatement, but, yes, I'm angry."

"Why?"

"He is *not* my master, for one. He has *no right* to turn you into stone and keep you locked up on a pedestal until he decides you should be serving someone, for two—I'll have him serve me *himself* first. And three? We've got a very important mission and stopping off in this . . . in this whatever it is . . ." She felt as if she had been absorbing the silence of the rest of the hall, as if she could no longer speak in the face of it.

"Do not," he said, "risk yourself for the sake of your pity. I am not worth it, and it is I who will suffer for it should you choose to speak."

Luckily, silence, no matter how heavy, never lasted in the face of her curiosity. She tried not to remember curiosity's natural reward in her grandmother's stories. "And he could do something worse than he's already done?"

"I have seen far, far worse," was his soft reply.

She didn't ask. *Change the subject, Jewel.* "Where *are* we?"

"You are in *Evereve,* his home."

"Yes, well. What I meant was where is *Evereve?*"

"None of us are completely certain."

"None of *us?*"

"Yes."

"Forgive me, Aristos, but I must leave. I'll return."

"Jewel," he said, his voice the low rumble of distant, moving stone, "if you are not careful, you will return in a fashion you will not like."

It took her a moment to realize what he was saying.

"I'll worry about me, all right? You take care of yourself."

She found Avandar almost as soon as the great hall released her. And it was a release; until the moment she stepped from beneath its vaulted ceilings, its magelights, its statues—which had started, in her mind, as an homage to life and had ended as worse than mockery—she had not realized how much like a prison it had felt.

She might have taken a moment to appreciate freedom; to be glad of the fact that her feet were not attached to a pedestal, her life not burdened by that involuntary service. But she saw him instead, and the sense of exultation vanished.

In its place something uncomplicated enough—but barely—to be called anger.

He stood, vivid in blue and gold, the crown a mark across his brow, one that caught light and returned it. At his back, the mercifully less golden, gently curving wall that marked the boundary of the room she had entered. To either side, doors that led into a distance that hinted at visual splendor by casting it into half shadow.

She raised her arm as if it were a weapon. The sleeve—jeweled edges torn now—fell to her elbow and rested there like a gaudy flag.

Between them, the mark in red and gold and silver.

"You'd better have an explanation for this," she said, her voice so quiet any of her den would have ducked for cover. "And you'd better get it *off.*"

He was not, had never been, part of her den; she now understood why in a way that she'd never put into words. He *wasn't* a servant. He didn't need her, not the way a servant needed a master. And more, buried beneath the half lifetime they'd spent

together, the most important of the little truths: She didn't
trust him.

She was certain, now, the mark twining like a serpent on the
pale inside of her arm, she never would.

The rest of her den weren't servants, not like the dozens of men
and women who swept and cleaned and stabled and cooked for
the great House Terafin. But they served her. The understanding
itself was as much a surprise as the mark.

It wasn't that they did what she said—they did, if you didn't
count Carver's incessant need to sleep with anything that moved
and spoke half-intelligibly—it was that they did so because they
understood what the stakes were, and why the choices were made.

They stood at her back or at her side, depending on what she
needed. They let her take care of the big things, and they filled in
the cracks between one crisis and the next, waiting with the
patience of—well, maybe that was stretching it. But they were
patient.

They were hers.

Teller. He'd known. What it would cost. What she was leaving
them to. He had never once questioned her. He had never once
confronted her about the choices she'd made. The accusation,
you're leaving us could sting and cut and bite because it was
true—but only Jewel herself had ever made it, and only at night
when sleep refused to alleviate her guilt and anxiety.

Ellerson had been like them. They'd all known it, pretty
much the minute he'd corrected their poor manners and forced
them to take a bath before they gathered round the dining table.
There was a safety about him that in simpler times meant he
was trustworthy.

In complex times? Trustworthy as well.

Morretz was.

Avandar was *not*.

As if he could hear her thoughts—and perhaps he could; it had
always been rumored that some mages had that capability, although the Magisterium itself had dryly and precisely denied the
accusation time and again—he spoke.

She didn't understand the language, and she recognized at
least five, spoke two fluently.

She waited.

He spoke again, and again the language made no sense; it was
an ugly complex of snarls and clicks. But she was certain it con-

tained meaning. He lifted a hand. Pointed; she saw a light take the outline of his finger as if he were oil and it, fire.

Unfortunately, he was pointing at her.

She *knew* he wouldn't harm her. If it weren't for that instinct, the one that overrode every lesson and every experience that together comprised the wisdom she'd managed to attain, she would have leaped to the side to escape what left his hand: fire. Light.

Instead, she waited as it touched her skin. Was surprised at how warm it was, how mild and pervasive its heat.

"Jewel," he said.

She wore no crown. If it hadn't meant parading around the halls almost entirely naked, she wouldn't have worn the dress either. But the halls were cool, and the shifts and undercoat meant to be hidden between skin and jewel-stubbled silk were not proof against the temperature. She almost always chose practicality over pride.

"You didn't have any problem saying that before."

"Before?"

"When I—when I woke up. In my—in your—in that room."

"Ah. No."

"Why?"

He shrugged. "Does it matter? I have no problem now."

"If that was a spell you just cast, and I was the recipient, then *yes,* it does matter."

He turned away from her by the simple expedient of shifting his gaze. "This is my home," he told her softly, his words strangely slow. "But it was built by many hands, and some of them belonged to very talented men whom I found intriguing, and whom you, I fear, would find mad. They created works I had barely dreamed of, and even the dreams were the type that linger in shadow at the first edge of morning." His gaze rose as he spoke, eyes tracking the vault of the ceiling. "I gave them freer rein than I had realized. I set few conditions on their work.

"But understand," he said softly, "that I desired privacy above all else; a place hidden from all of the visions that even the gods possessed. To enter is . . . never easy. I find these visits disorienting, but I generally recover."

"Oh, good. I suppose that's more than you could say about Aristos."

He hadn't been smiling, and given the sudden narrowing of his eyes, there wasn't a chance in the hells he'd start now. "Do not meddle in what does not concern you."

"You sent him to *me*."

"I? Alas, I—previous commandments ruled his presence in your chamber. My apologies for the discomfort he may have caused."

"Discomfort?"

"Jewel."

"No, don't take that tone with me—what do you mean *discomfort*? As far as I can tell, he's a *living man* and someone's done something—*you've* done something—to turn him into a convenient block of stone!"

He did smile then. It wasn't pretty.

What he spoke next was not Weston; was so far from being Weston she didn't recognize it immediately as the language he had first spoken when she slid out of the great hall and into his vision. "It was not for my convenience that I so chose," he said, and the language *hurt*. But she understood it.

She stepped back. She knew it was the wrong thing to do, but there was suddenly something about him that spoke of death. Hers. Everyone's. She stopped before she could take the next step, and took a deep breath instead.

"It was," he said softly, "for the convenience of my faithless, cunning wife. A reminder." He turned. Turned back. "If you follow the gold-encased lights, you will find dinner served."

"I won't—"

"I suggest you eat. You will find that you are much closer to starvation than your body thinks you are." He left her standing there, clenching her fists, surrounded by tapestries in an anteroom that obviously led to the lord of the manor.

Later she would look at them; she promised herself that. She would look at them, try to glean some hint of the future from the obvious past the tapestries were made to commemorate.

7th of Scaral, 427 AA
Tor Leonne, Annagar

"There's trouble," Benito said, nodding casually toward the gently sloping streets that led up to one of about six merchant compounds.

"What trouble?" Kallandras replied, moving heavily in the heat of the afternoon sun. Feeling the extra "weight" that he had adopted, like so much personality, as he made his way home at Benito's side. He waited; Benito, as usual, was expansive. The loud, half-friendly chatter of the merchant demanded no response. Better, it allowed for none.

"Those four men, you see 'em?"

He did, of course. "No. Wait—those ones?"

"No, *those* ones. Armored, with drawn swords. Over *there!*"

One of the four men looked up; Benito's words, spoken against the wind, were easily loud enough to carry. It was one of the traits that would have endeared him to many of the Northerners he knew—none of whom would be in attendance at the Tor Leonne during the Festival of the Moon.

Kallandras recognized both the man's interest—unfriendly— and the crest he wore: Tyrian cerdan. He spared him a glance, no more; spared his companions less. They were exactly what they appeared to be: Men sent, judging by their direction, to weed out the Voyani among the merchants and bring them up to the plateau for questioning.

"Benito," he said, huffing and puffing with the exertion of movement, his thoughts as far from his facade as they could be, "I think we want to be somewhere else."

"Where else, eh? You think there's so much room in the Tor Leonne at Festival time?" The merchant swatted him heavily across the arm. "Use your head!"

But he could see, beyond the obvious four, another four men, and he knew as he watched them that they were far too confident in their numbers to be just eight. The clansmen and the Voyani clashed frequently on both the edges of wilderness the Terreans boasted and in society itself, and they had only one rule when facing each other: No quarter. None given, none asked.

Among their own, the Voyani infighting was fierce, but unless an actual clan war had been declared—and it had happened twice in his lifetime—there were niceties and rules that were observed most of the time. Not here. Not among these.

He guessed that the Voyani had had word from the plateau. Guessed that they were scattering even as the merchant, Benito, continued to drone on and on to his left, a sort of toneless, heavy chatter that might have become musical if uttered by a different voice. Benito's daughter's, perhaps. Or his son, a lad as sharp as Imperial steel, but hotter in temperament.

"You, you two!" The Tyrian cerdan whose gaze had passed over them shouted.

Benito froze. "Us?"

"You! Come here!"

Kallandras shrugged; he waited for Benito to move, and then, when the merchant finally found his feet, followed to his right and behind.

"Who are you with?"

"With?"

"Whose caravan?"

Red rose in the merchant's cheek. "My *own*," he said, his chest inflating with a bit too much air. "I am Benito di'Covello, and I—"

"Have you been to the plateau?"

"Yes. We just—"

"Do you carry the medallion?"

"I beg your pardon?"

"I said, do you carry the medallion? You were required to make an oath," he added, speaking as if to a simpleton or a fool. "And that oath was made over a medallion of the Tyr'agar's manufacture."

"I *am not* used to discussing the oaths *I* make," the merchant replied, heat giving way to Northern ice. "Oaths are between *men*. You have an oath you wish to force on me, then try."

The cerdan stared at him for a long time. Kallandras was mildly surprised when the armed and armored man looked away. Nodded. "We've had complaints," he said, "about Voyani thievery. This Festival is important to our Tyr, and we're about to end the offending behavior. I suggest you mind your manners and remain close to your personal caravan for the next several hours."

Before Benito could reply, one of the cerdan lifted his voice. "Attelo!"

The man turned. "You see them?"

"Some. There!"

"Men?"

"No—it's the women."

The line of the cerdan's jaw compressed into square disgust. "My apologies," he said to Benito. It surprised Kallandras. "It's hard on a man, to be sent hunting *women*." He lifted his sword. "Don't stand there gaping, stop them!"

They were almost out. Elena had seven of the children under her wing—and her wing was expansive. They were young, these; not a one had seen more than five Festival Moons, and two at least had seen far less than that. She carried one bundled under her arm; her mother, Tamara, carried the other.

This was her most important duty, to get the children to safety— or as much safety as the streets allowed for. And she knew her ability to handle duty was about to be sorely tested.

Fail this, and every other success meant nothing; she knew, had known as a child, that the children were the only real future the Voyani had.

Donatella was with her. "Dona," she said, handing the wine-sleepy child to her aunt. "I've work here."

Donatella nodded grimly. She was older now, although no Voyani woman was so old that she couldn't fight. "The streets here twist; we'll find our way out."

"I'll join you. Mother—"

"I'm staying."

"You're going."

"Elena—"

"That's not a request." Her sword, shorter than Nicu's, but sharper and lighter, came out of the scabbard that rested easily across hip and thigh. "Illa!"

The other woman her own age nodded grimly. Drew sword as well. "Over there, Elena."

"Shit."

The children said nothing. But they knew how to count; they'd have to, if they were old enough to beg or steal, and most of them were.

Four men. Four armed men. Swords. "Mama, *now*."

Her mother took a breath. Elena wanted to smack her. *Not now,* she thought. *You hold the future, right behind your skirts. You protect it, damn you.* There were no wagons to hide behind; no stalls; they were exposed. "RUN!"

Tamara of the Arkosans hesitated. Past her prime, she had never been one to run from a fight, and she left behind her her child—adult or no, still her child—facing four armed cerdan. But she knew Elena was right. Knew what she herself would have said to her own mother, had her mother dawdled like a senti-mental idiot and somehow failed in the duty—the foremost duty, the important duty—of protecting the future of the family. The children.

She swallowed. Two to one.

No joy there.

"Mikala," she said, to the child who had almost crossed the

boundary of five, "I need all your help now, with the rest of the children."

"I'm not a children," Pollo said; it was the phrase he used most often this particular month. It was also said quietly and without vehemence. His mother was gone; gone with the men and the women whose duty it was to carry the few items they valued to safety. He was alone with Ona Tamara, and Ona Tamara was frightened.

Mikala, bless her, grabbed his hand. Tamara shifted an infant in her arm, picked up the second. Took two steps.

And a man she had never seen before in her life, a man who wore no armor, and whose hair was the color of Northern demons, stepped into the cobbled roadway. "There is . . . no one to bar your way, Tamara of the Arkosans. The road to the East is clear from here to the Easternmost Fount of Contemplation. It will be clear for perhaps half an hour.

"If you are concerned with the well-being of the children, I suggest you move quickly."

She was stunned a moment. "Who are you?" she asked, sharply and quickly.

"I? I serve the Lady," he replied, speaking in Torra as if Torra were something that, like the finest and softest of silks, could be donned. He turned to look down the street, to look beyond Tamara's bent back. Paused. Knelt. "You are Mikala?" he said, to the five-year-old Voyani girl.

She nodded, unafraid, the suspicion that was completely automatic for Tamara waived in the case of this stranger.

"You are a brave girl," he said. "You will grow up to be part of the Voyani pride." He smiled. Lifted his head, so that he could see all of the children. **"Listen well to Ona Tamara. Do as she tells you until she tells you you are safe."**

They nodded, all seriousness, the youngest child barely walking, the oldest nervously glancing at the men who were drawing closer, closer still. He rose then. "I regret," he told Tamara softly, "that I cannot accompany you. But my skill is better used."

"We'll be in your debt," the older woman said gruffly. Wondering, as words laden with personal meaning and fraught with difficulty escaped her lips, if she *was* the older of the two. "They don't—they don't usually hunt the children. If we'd known, we would never have sent the others away. The children—"

"They are not hunting children," he replied, turning toward

the causeway where her daughter and Illa now hid in what little cover there was, swords drawn. "But women."

Donatella, silent until that moment, reached down and picked up one of the children whose feet had given out on him. "Tamara," she said softly. "It is time."

"They don't usually hunt women; they aren't that smart."

"No." The stranger shrugged. "But the Voyani—especially the Arkosans and the Havallans in this generation—usually know better than to take the Tyrians on in a street fight. They melt into the shadows they can find—and they can almost always find the Lady's shadow, even in the brightest of the Lord's light.

"Today, a handful have sought the Lord's light, and there is blood in the streets; the cerdan have called for reinforcements, and the men are out in greater numbers."

"Who would be *such a fool*—"

The words froze in Tamara's throat.

Her best friend, her closest cousin, bent her head. "Dona—"

"Enough, Tamara. The children."

Tamara nodded. Who was she to criticize one of their own in the presence of a stranger? Especially when that one, as she suspected, was the son of her good friend?

But she whispered a benediction to the Lady as she began to lead the children down the gently sloped road.

Their advantage was a simple one, but it had two faces. The clansmen didn't like to fight women. The first type of clansmen would happily kill them in village slaughters, rape them, enslave them, sell them—but *fight* them, that was beneath their station as men of the Lord. The second type of clansmen looked at fighting women in the same way the Voyani women themselves looked at fighting their children in earnest: It was killing the weaker, the helpless, the people in life who must be protected.

She couldn't tell, looking down the road, which face the four men wore; most likely it was some sort of combination. But they didn't look gleeful, hunting the Voyani—and their *children*, Lady's blood—and that was something.

Illa cursed quietly. It was hot; the leather and cotton grips that kept a sword safely in hand weren't proof against a profusion of nervous sweat. Elena looked across the road, willing the men to stop where they were. A handful of minutes, and it wouldn't matter.

But when the men did stop, she cursed.

The foremost among them drew his sword. It was clear that he had been marching in armor; it was the first time that day that she'd wished it were summer's height and not the Lady's season.

"Surrender," he said, his voice a boom across streets that were emptying quickly at the sight of the unsheathed sword. "We have no wish to harm you; we only wish to enforce the Tyr'agar's lawful edict!"

Illa met her gaze; held it a moment. Shook her head.

"By what law," Elena said, "does the Tyr'agar hold the Voyani at the Lady's Festival?"

"The Lord's law!" A second man replied. She couldn't tell, although the distance was not a great one, whether or not the first man was irritated at the interruption. She would have been, but she wasn't cerdan.

"You waste our time," the first man said; the second was silent again. "And your lives. So be it." He nodded; the three men who obviously followed his orders came toward them bearing naked blades.

"This," Elena said, through gritted teeth, "is *not* going to be fun."

Illa laughed. Unfortunately, she laughed the way she always did when Elena stooped to understatement: nervously. It was only in the most dire of circumstances—sarcasm aside—that Elena ever bothered to understate anything.

She took a breath; held it. Expelled it. Took another breath, a deeper one. Brought her sword forward; grabbed it in both hands. She'd never learned the art of fighting sword and dagger, although she could fight with two daggers at close quarters better than anyone but Margret and Evallen.

Evallen, who was dead. Dead at the hands of men like these.

That gave her some fire; it burned briefly where she needed it to burn. Elena of the Arkosan Voyani said, loudly enough for Illa to hear it. "For Evallen."

And then, before she could move, the three men approaching her staggered like a row of tall grass being trampled, slowly, by a sauntering horse.

Kallandras came out of the shadows.

The men who fell were not, he thought, dead—although he was slower than he had been at the peak of his agility, and there was some possibility that he had mistimed his throws. He meant what he'd said: the Voyani did best when they sought the shadows and left the fighting to the clansmen. They were used to Voyani who ran in the face of greater numbers, and in the history of the Tor Leonne, there had been no open fighting between the Voyani and the ruling clansmen. The lay of the wild land was different; there, the Voyani ruled in their wheeled strongholds.

The man who had ordered the cerdan forward froze; he looked around from side to side, and then, in a moment of foolish bravery, dashed forward through the street. He had not seemed young to Kallandras until that moment. Watching from shadows that were better chosen by far than either of the two Voyani women's had been, he saw the man kneel into the cobbled stones. Touch the bodies of his fallen comrades, looking for some sign of weaponry: bolt, quarrel, arrow. Something.

He would find it eventually, but by that time they would be gone. Or so Kallandras had hoped.

But the woman with a blaze of fire in her otherwise dark hair chose that moment to step forward. Her face, sun-bitten and wind-carved, was both lovely and hard. These odds, he thought, these odds she favored, and she meant to take advantage of them.

The stories about Voyani savagery were based, as most stories were, in fact, and if the clansmen distorted that fact for their own purposes, that fact remained.

He almost stepped aside. Here, in the Tor Leonne, there was no crime in such a decision. In the lands to the far North, the laws of the Empire and his own position there—master bard, unofficial servant to the Kings and the Queens of the land—would have forced his hand. But here power ruled, and the women, these two Voyani women, now held its balance on the edge of their short, curved swords. It was not Kallandras' duty to intervene should he choose to turn a blind eye.

We are all changed by the facades we have chosen.

Hearing them, the lone Tyrian cerdan looked up. His eyes widened; his sword, slack by his side, came up at once. He found his feet, and he moved—but he did not move away from them; rather he moved to stand before the bodies of his fallen comrades. They were alive, then.

The red-haired woman reached him first; she swung easily, swung low, feinting. He was off-balance; a man who, in Kallandras' opinion, had never been properly trained to fight the fight he was handed; he was cerdan of the city, and the high clans, and the high clans did not fight women. Her second swing drove him back a step; her third swing did not. Behind him, unconscious, his men hovered, and if they were intemperate, if they interrupted him, if they did not—quite—follow the orders that he had set them, they were his men. That much was obvious from his actions alone.

Loyalty. Ah.

Over time, loyalty had become a trait that Kallandras could not quite ignore. This was not his fight, but he had already intervened, albeit for his own purposes.

He stepped into the roadway now, his hands empty.

"Elena," he said.

She heard him; she stepped back a moment, sword still at play. Her companion chose to join her, changing the odds. Two to one.

The man looked toward Kallandras as well, his sword, as theirs, unbloodied.

"Elena, this man, his life is not worth your anger. You have won the victory you desire. The children are safe; you will be expected to join them."

Her eyes were brown-green, flashing with sunlight, anger, the last vestiges of fear as she faced him, her gaze flickering between him and the cerdan who stood so close to death. The sun was high, harsh; it cast her shadow down in a squat mockery of natural grace.

"Who are you to tell me what to do?"

"I? I am a friend," Kallandras replied, "and I have walked the *Voyanne* in my own way these many years. Slaughter him, and what will you achieve? His concern was for his fallen—as yours would be. Look at him."

"And if I want his death?" she replied, her knuckles ivory beneath the sun's bronze, her cheeks flushed.

Beside her, the other Voyani woman waited.

"If you want it, Elena of Arkosa, you will have it. But in the end, if the Dominion is to stand against the Lord of Night, the Tyrians and the Voyani who are, at heart, loyal or honorable men will be needed." He shrugged. "The three who lie felled are not dead. There are other ways."

"And you, so-called friend of the Voyani, what will you do if I choose to take his life? We are owed a life, at least that!"

"Make your decision," he replied, folding his arms almost casually beneath the fullness of the sun. "And I, too, will make mine. We live by our judgments, Elena, and we live, at times, to regret them."

The sword shook. Oh, the sword shook.

Had this . . . man . . . been Annagarian, had he been clan, she would have ignored him; he carried no sword. But his hair was golden, and his eyes were pale, and his skin was like nothing she had seen in her life. Tall, too slender to be a warrior, he seemed a thing of night at the height of day. A whisper of conscience, a messenger of the Lady.

Night pooled in her heart.

She met the eyes of the cerdan. "You were hunting our children," she said softly, her voice as sharp as her sword.

"We were hunting only the women," he replied.

"You take our children as serafs where you can find them."

"You take *our* children as serafs where you can find them."

Stung, she started to reply; her sword shifted.

"Truth," the stranger said to them both. "But this battle is over. You have defended your children, and you," he said, turning slightly so that he might fully face the cerdan, "have defended your men. The Lord has judged you. It is not the province of a warrior to seek the helpless to prove his strength against."

He bridled like a high-spirited horse.

But his sword came down.

"Elena," the soft-spoken stranger said quietly.

She did not sheathe her sword. Did not take her eyes off the clansmen, and that was wise. The clans were steeped in treachery and deceit from birth.

"Elena?" Illa's voice.

She badly wanted Illa's advice; the women often turned to each other for consensus. But not here, not now; such indecision was just another weakness she couldn't afford. *Aiee, Margret—how have you lived like this for all of your life?* It was possibly the first time she hadn't envied her cousin her position as heir to the Matriarch.

"Leave him," she said curtly. Her face hardened. "And you?" she said to the stranger.

"I will follow, with your permission; without it, I will return to my work."

She snorted; tossed her hair back because she'd forgotten it was pulled so tightly off her face. "I'd give Voyani song to know just what that work is."

His smile was light, mysterious, dark. "I'd listen," he said softly.

She turned, and then she heard it: the shout.

"OVER THERE!"

The sun was so damned hot and bright she could hope, for just a minute, that she was befuddled enough to mistake the voice. Teeth that she thought couldn't be clamped any tighter almost drove themselves through the opposite jaw as she gripped her sword and turned.

Beyond her, beyond the sole standing cerdan and the three men over whom he kept watch, she saw something that made her jaw slacken.

A man red with blood, slick with it, face and hands and chest splattered with things that were far too solid. Behind him, behind him others, five, six, seven—all cut and bleeding in the same way. Her face paled.

And the stranger said quietly—so quietly that for the first time she wondered how it was his voice actually carried—"It is not his blood."

Nicu of the Arkosa Voyani came down the street at a wild run, bucking like a mad stallion, his sword the only thing about him more obviously bloody than he.

"We've come to rescue you, Elena!" he shouted. "Stand aside!" His sword came up in a terrible arc.

"Nicu, no!" she cried back, lifting both empty hand and sword hand in denial. For it seemed to her, suddenly, that a cloud had caught the sun, banishing its harsh glare; seemed to her that she could see—just for a second—clearly. And she knew, she knew that what he was about to do was not only wrong, but dangerous. To him. To them all.

"NICU, NO!"

CHAPTER SEVEN

He stopped in the street; the men at his heels ran into him. Were it not for the fact they were sticky with blood—and their blood at least had been shed in the shedding of their enemy's blood—it would have seemed a comic thing, an act to make small children laugh. They were gleeful in the manner that small children sometimes are, and such a glee, in such guise, was hideous and wrong.

But it was fact; the bard did not argue with fact.

Nor did he argue with what he heard at the heart of Elena of Arkosa's voice. He knew who she was, of course, although the knowledge was recent. He knew what her position in the line Arkosa must be. And he knew that the Arkosans, the Havallans, the Lyserrans, and the Corronans all boasted their share of the seer's taint.

He carried no sword; it was true.

But he carried his weapons.

Left hand, then right, he touched their hilts, waiting.

The man called Nicu frowned.

"By what right do you tell me to stop? These men are hunting my kin during the Lady's Festival. They hunt my women, my children."

"*Your* women? *Your* children?" Her sword was a flash, much like her eyes. She was beautiful, beautiful, beautiful.

And she was correcting him again, in front of the men he had led to *victory* through the streets of the Tor Leonne. The anger warred with desire, but it was not such an even battle as all that; with Elena, desire was a part of his growing anger.

"I am the leader of the protectors; I was appointed by the Matriarch. The decision is *mine*, Elena!"

He heard the decision in Nicu's raw voice. Heard more, besides. But he was not ready to be the Wind's Voice; not yet. He

made a noisy display of pulling his weapons out of their hidden
sheaths. There were two. Glinting in the sunlight, they caught all
eyes, even Nicu's. Even Elena's.

In the North, they were considered extremely unusual weapons.
Very, very few were trained in their use. They had, of course, short
blades, and the Northerners preferred the straight reach of the long
double edge. But it was not the blades that made them unique. It
was the guard; for each side of the guard came up almost two
thirds of the length of the blade itself, and each tip was pointed.
Honed.

In the North, brows would have been raised. And magisterial
guards called, in loud and echoing voices, as they were often
called when weapons were drawn.

In the South, brows were raised, but voices stilled.

These weapons were the Lady's weapons. The weapons of her
dark face.

If he could have ordered the cerdan to flee, he would have,
but he knew that the man would run no more than half the
length of road before the duty to his companions drew him,
shuddering, back.

"This fight," he said, his voice as reasonable, as soft as it had
been when it reached Elena through her anger, "is unnecessary.
It is not an act of the Lord—your numbers are too great to make
it anything but a slaughter—and it is not an act of the Lady's,
who seeks no open battle."

"These men," Nicu said, his voice shaking with anger and
righteousness, "will serve the Lord of *Night!* Who are you to tell
us how to—"

"Mete out death in the Lady's service?"

The silence was the silence of the sun's height. Kallandras
stepped forward, moving silently, slowly, a single man in the
sun. He was slender, not overly tall; were it not for the weapons
he carried, his demeanor would have robbed him of all threat.

But threat or no, his intent was fulfilled; he came to stand between Nicu of the Arkosans and the lone Tyrian cerdan. Thinking
it strange, after all these years, to interfere in such a basic way. To
save the children had been easy; to save the women, simple. But to
save the man was fraught with difficulty. Kallandras was of the
brotherhood of the Lady, and there were no shadows here.

"Nicu," Elena said, her voice softening. "Please. They will send
others—"

"Not a single one of *these*," Nicu said, pitching his words so they traveled beyond the stranger who stood in his way, "has been capable of stopping *us*. Not today!"

Elena's voice was not a voice which took to softness well. "And because of your slaughter, they've started to hunt *us* in earnest. Because you have tried to play Tyrian games, they enmesh us in Tyrian tactics!"

"Then let them! Are we to spend our lives running like beaten dogs? We are Voyani! We are Arkosans!"

The men behind him took up the last word like a cheer.

"You, stranger, get out of the way. This isn't your fight."

"Nicu, he *saved* the children while you were out killing!"

"Then I'll do my best not to kill him if he *gets out of the way*."

Kallandras heard the death in the words. Softly, much more gently than Elena was capable of speaking, he said, "This man will face you to protect his fallen. It is an act of honor. I ask you to treat it with honor; this is the Lady's Festival, and mercy is often granted when the Lady holds sway."

"We will treat him with as much mercy," Nicu replied, his voice as bright as his sword, "as they have ever shown us." He lifted his sword. "This is your last warning."

Kallandras shrugged.

The man named Nicu charged.

And behind him, slower to follow, came the rest of the Arkosans. It would be a difficult fight, if he did not wish to kill them—and he did not.

But he did not count on aid, and aid came; Elena of the Arkosans and Illa of the Arkosans came to stand, blades drawn, on either side of him.

The cerdan stood behind them all, almost forgotten, but he, too, wielded naked sword—and well enough, by the look of him.

Nicu stopped ten feet from Kallandras, his jaw unhinged in angry shock. "You cannot mean to do this, Elena!"

She said nothing, which in Kallandras' opinion was wise.

"Illa, you cannot mean to stand by the side of a known enemy!"

"I stand," Illa said, from between clenched teeth, "by the side of the Matriarch's *heir*. She has chosen, Nicu. She would have died saving our future; if she feels this fight is as important as that one, I'll fight it."

Nicu took a step forward. But his men—his men did not. They were suddenly completely ill at ease. He knew it. He started to bark an order; stopped. In this mood, Elena was not one to offer mercy—and there was no way to fight her without some quarter offered. She was deadly. They'd all seen her in action.

And she *was* as close to the Matriarch and the Matriarch's will as any of them got.

"Nicu," Elena said. "The children are safe. The Arkosans wait. Let us forget this and go back."

"So they can continue to hunt us?"

Illa spit. "They'll hunt us *now*," she said, her sharp gaze grazing their bloodied armor. "They'll hunt us all for sure."

"Andreas!" Elena said, her voice a heavy bark.

Almost shamefacedly, all battle lust misplaced, Andreas of the Arkosans stepped forward. "Elena," he said.

"Put up your sword. Come. We've yet to find our shadows and make our way back to our own. Carmello?"

"Nicu led us to victory," he said.

"And I will lead you only back to the *Voyanne*," Elena replied. "Are you coming?"

He glanced at Nicu's back. Nicu had not moved.

"Nicu?" Carmello stared at his leader's back, trying to get something like an answer from its rigid line.

She called them one by one. With the exception of Carmello, they put up their swords, or sheathed them, the exultancy of their mood broken by hers. In the bright, bright street, only Nicu and Carmello stood apart; the Arkosans came together behind Elena's back—and well away from the Tyrian cerdan. She'd seen to that without being too obvious about it; Kallandras was impressed. Women of her temperament were often devoid of subtlety.

That left only Nicu.

Nicu stepped forward.

For just a moment, Kallandras heard Elena's soft breath at his back; heard, in the voice that carried that sigh, relief.

But he saw nothing at all in the face of Nicu of the Arkosa that didn't speak of anger or death; when the Arkosan sword swung out in a sudden thrust to the side, Kallandras was prepared for the movement.

Prepared for everything but the strength of it.

He parried, dancing forward, his blade the shield behind which the surprised Tyrian cerdan might momentarily find shelter.

The blade *snapped*. The guard did not.

But he felt it, as their blades met: a ringing dissonance. He brought his second weapon up, and for the first time in the city streets, began to fight in earnest.

So, too, did Nicu.

There were cries; there was anger; there was fear; words rushed around them, an audience of a type familiar to Kallandras and ignored by Nicu. But the fight contained them; the imminence of death spurred them on.

Kallandras had been trained to the kill. Nicu of the Arkosans had not. But Nicu wanted it; even—and this was an obvious truth—enjoyed it; he derived strength from it, where Kallandras had been trained to derive purpose.

Steel clashed, rang, sang in the open streets while the Lord looked on. Two men, reach extended by steel, sought an opening, a weakness, an exposure. They used the ground they were given to advantage; they *moved*, feet as precise as blades, eyes almost unblinking, backs exposed to friend and foe, friend and foe, in a twist that was not unlike a dance.

The Lord watched.

These were men, these two; they fought for his benediction, because like it or not, all fights between men who would claim power in the Dominion of Annagar *were* fights offered to the Lord, if they were given like this: beneath the open sky, the unfettered sun.

The Arkosans were Voyani; they knew the dangers the sun presaged; they sought shadow. And the Brotherhood served the Lady; they understood the demands of the Lord, but they preferred the subtleties and the intricacies of the Lady's dance; they, too, sought shadow.

But it was the Lord who watched.

The Lord who judged.

Nicu fought with heat, with ire, with an anger whose growth should have hindered him. Kallandras fought coolly, precisely; his senses came into a sharp, sharp focus as he found the five points of his personal style, and leaped lightly from one to the other.

There was, in this fight, nothing that should have reminded him of his youth—but he had not been tested like this since the days of his training. Nicu was good. And Nicu was *not* of the brotherhood; he was like a boy half formed but skilled.

Or so it seemed to Kallandras.

But there was a rhythm to the fight itself that was akward, ungainly; it was almost as if Nicu's desire to place his feet in one position was overruled by the whim of the blade he carried; he would set a foot down, or almost, and then lurch to left or right, forward or back. Not capering, not quite; not visibly hesitating. Visibly overbalancing to Kallandras' sensitive eyes.

He did not know, could not be certain, that he was correct— but the *Kovaschaii* were trained to prize instinct.

Kallandras, born Kallatin, trained by the brotherhood and refined by Senniel College, changed his tactics. He moved in, moved quickly, and shifted the emphasis of his weapon hand randomly, seeking not his enemy but the weapon his enemy wielded.

A different fight. A fight that was taught to the older students, those skilled in seeking a death.

The Lord's gaze was hot; it did not waver.

Neither did Nicu's blade.

As if it were intelligent, as if it could somehow divine Kallandras' intent, it avoided a certain type of parry, a thrust that led too far.

Kallandras began to fight more conservatively; to draw the battle out; to force Nicu to dance, or perhaps to add steps to the dance that had already begun. Nicu was trained to the sun and the road—and the shadows. He had fought in the streets of the Tor Leonne's city, and he had run. To Kallandras' eye, he was tiring, and if the sword itself could aid him in a combat, there was a price to be paid for its weight, its heft, its frenzy.

A price that Kallandras of Senniel knew how to pay.

He heard Elena's voice. He heard Illa's. He heard the man Elena had called Carmello. Around their cacophony of words, he heard Nicu's breath lose its smoothness; take on the ragged edge of effort.

Soon. Soon. He danced.

Sweat graced them both; sweat, the Lady's blessing at the height of Lord's heat. Words fell away; silence reigned, broken by metal against metal, foot against ground, breath, heavy and light. Soon.

He watched the blade, not the man. The blade rose. The blade caught sunlight as if the light were a weapon it could use—and it was, but not against an assassin of Kallandras' calliber—and the blade fell, but it was met by either the resistance of weapon or the emptiness of air.

Now.

He moved, opening himself up to the weapon's thrust. It was a subtle motion, a misstep, a heartbeat's poor timing. A brother would not have been drawn in by the display of vulnerability, any more than he would willingly have been drawn by a weapon's feint.

But Nicu's blade was.

It extended itself for the same amount of time that Kallandras' chest was exposed; pulled itself slightly out of the sure grip of the man who wielded it.

The assassin did the rest, catching it, blade and guard, guard and guard, both pulling and throwing it free in a continuous arc of motion.

Nicu cried out in pain and surprise; Elena cried out in denial.

But Kallandras' weapons, so effortless in their motion, were also effortless in their lack; they stopped, blade casting a thin shadow against the bloodied, sweat-stained fabric of Nicu's shirt.

"Elena," Kallandras said quietly.

She walked, a bit too quickly, to stand at Nicu's side. "He's my kin." Her voice held multiple things: disgust, relief, anger, shame. Affection. Worry. Protectiveness. It was the last that was strongest.

"He is," Kallandras replied. "And I return him to you. But in return I must ask you two things."

"They are?"

"First: remove the sheath that your—cousin?—" when she nodded, he continued, "is wearing."

"Done." She bent a moment; Nicu slammed into her, knocking her off her feet.

When she rose, her face was red with something other than careless exposure to sun. Her knuckles were white, as white as Lord's light on water; they balled into fists and then into open, stiff palms. Without another word, she slapped Nicu. Hard.

The sound carried. Illa looked away; the men looked to Elena. When she bent to remove the girded, empty sheath, Nicu was still—but her anger had traveled the length and breadth of her palm to his face, and he seemed to have subsumed it; he was shaking.

She rose.

"Thank you. Now, retrieve the blade that Nicu used, but do not touch blade or guard. Use cloth, use silk."

"You want his weapon?"

"No, Elena of the Arkosa. It may well *be* his weapon. But this is the favor I ask of you: keep this weapon until the Matriarch returns. It is said that it is difficult to fool Voyani eyes."

"Yes." She paled. He knew, from her sudden sideways glance, that she knew the rest of the saying well. She lifted her hand, as if to ward off the words, but they had been heard.

Illa said clearly, "But the Voyani heart, *never*."

"Yes." The bard's voice was almost gentle. "I am a stranger," he said. "I am not kin. But if you would allow it, I would be honored to walk some part of the road in the company of those who know it best."

Elena nodded. Then, unwrapping silken kerchief—blazing red, a thing that was a poor match for her hair, and an even match for her temper—she walked to where the sword had fallen. Bent. Wrapped her hand in the softness of fabric, and still hesitated a moment.

"It is not . . . stained," she said quietly. Softly.

He did not answer.

She raised the blade, taking its weight as if it were twice what it had been in Nicu's hands. He heard her speak, softly, a benediction and a prayer. The blade made no reply, and as if that were enough, her shoulders took on a straight, even line. She sheathed the sword.

But he noticed that she did not, not even for the sake of convenience, choose to wear what she had recovered.

He turned, then, to the lone Tyrian cerdan who still stood in the city streets. "These men," he said, speaking in the most stilted, the most formal, of Torra's dialects, "will waken soon. They are the Lord's men."

The cerdan said nothing; his face had shuttered, just as a courtesan's does behind the perfection of smile and grace.

"Be aware," the bard continued quietly, "that to serve the Lord of Night—in any guise—is to forsake the Lord."

"You have never served the Lord," the man replied.

"No?" Kallandras looked up into the sun's height. "Perhaps not. But I serve Him now, in a fashion. Remember my words."

The night sky was just that: lit by star and a moon that was nearing its fullness. The Lady's time was coming, and with it the shadows, the length of her sojourn. Outside of the Tor Leonne, the Raverran night was cool, and the insects that occupied the fertile lands that conversely reminded Margret of the desert were louder than she thought she had ever heard them.

The children had come with Tamara and Donatella; they were safe, and for that, for that single thing, Margret was grateful. She said her prayers, and she said them politely; said them with heat and fire, with passion and belief. That much, *that* much, she owed the Lady.

But she said other things with *more* heat and *more* fire, for the children were not the only people to arrive. In ones and twos, in threes and fours, carrying sometimes a thing of value or history and sometimes less than a whole life, her people returned to the wagons that were always kept outside of a clansman's city in case of an emergency like this one.

And they carried word.

Cerdan had been engaged, and the clansmen had died. She'd somehow managed to avoid losing any of her own—how, she wasn't certain, but there was some old Voyani phrase about the Lady's partiality to fools that came fiercely to mind—but the toll taken by clansmen was *high*. Some of the men came back jubilant, and some of the women took up their high, high spirits.

But Margret knew, instantly *knew*, what it would mean to her: they would be hunted, now, and thoroughly—while the heart of the Arkosans lay hidden—at best—against the skin of a foreign clanswoman with no ties, no loyalty, and no damned *power* to protect it until it could find its way home.

Ah.

She said her prayers again, her thanks, her anger, mingling like fire and oil, fire and wood. She poured wine from the skin that she habitually wore at her waist, invoking the Maiden Moon, invoking the wise darkness, and invoking, steadily, the brightness, the Mother Moon, the Lady in Her Power.

Because she needed these things to calm her.

She was going to *kill* her cousin.

"Margret."

She knew her aunt's voice in any of its multiple guises; recognized this one immediately. It was soft, neutral in a way that Tamara only ever managed when there were strangers about.

She took a deep breath. Looked up at the veil that draped itself lazily across the clarity of the sky above. Lady's veil, lacy stars, open moon. She bowed stiffly; anger made her stiff and graceless, as it did so many of her women.

"Ona Tamara."

"Elena has returned."

She met her aunt's eyes; the tinge and cast of skin beneath precious oil lamp seemed pale. Hard to tell. "Not alone."

"No." Tamara drew a breath. "Nicu and his closest men are with her. Illa as well. And the stranger I told you about."

"The one who cleared the streets of the eight cerdan—without killing a single one of them?"

She nodded quietly.

"Who is he, Tamara?"

"I think—" she started to answer. Stopped. "I think you'd best talk with Elena."

"I will speak with Elena," Margret replied evenly. "But deal with the stranger until we're finished. He knows where we are," she added.

"He is not a threat to us, Margret."

"Anyone who isn't kin is a threat to us right now."

Tamara's lips compressed into a sharp, thin line. "He saved our future," she pointed out, the words as sharp as the line of her mouth. "We owe him."

Margret shrugged.

Elena stepped out of the shadows at the back of the wagon.

"Were you followed?"

"Hard to say." Elena shrugged. "But Kallandras said no, and I'd trust him to notice."

"Kallandras? He's the kinless one?"

Elena nodded.

"Would you trust him with anything else?"

"Like, say, our location?" Elena's smile was as sharp as her mother's frown had been, but infinitely more attractive. She shrugged. "Yes, but I'm biased."

Which meant at the very least the stranger was pretty. "What's that?"

Elena's face lost its attractive smile; lost, in fact, most of the play around its edges. She glanced up to the Lady's face, down to the grass the wheels had compressed. "It's a sword," she said at last.

Margret snorted. Waited. Waited another minute. "I can *see* it's a sword. Why are you bringing it to me?"

"It's the sword Nicu was wielding when he—when he was fighting the cerdan in the streets of the Tor Leonne." She paused. "When he was killing them. You have to see his clothing, Margret."

" 'Lena—"

"You didn't see his face. I did. I've seen men burn with the Lord's light, but I've never seen the light look so much like darkness."

"And you think it's this sword?"

"I don't know, I don't know," Elena replied. "But he—the stranger—he told me, he *asked* me, to bring it to the Matriarch. He said—he said 'it is said that it is difficult to fool Voyani eyes.' "

"But the Voyani heart, never." She was quiet a long, long time. "You haven't drawn the sword."

"No. Not after that."

"Nicu?"

"Angry, but—but he's grown more subdued. He—" She bit her lip. "He disobeyed my order; he tried to kill another clansman in the open street. The stranger stopped him." She took a deep breath.

"You might as well tell me the rest, Elena. How much worse could things be?"

"The stranger was fighting with the Lady's weapons." She paused. "And I think—although only the heart would expose him for certain—that he bears the Lady's marks. The night marks," she added, although it wasn't necessary. She walked over to Margret and placed the sword at her feet. "I'm sorry, Margret."

"You realize," Margret said softly, "what he's done?"

"Nicu? Yes," her cousin replied grimly. "If the heart is in the city, the chance that we will ever find it now has all but vanished.

"But think, Cousin, think: someone placed that weapon in Nicu's hands. Did they know? Did they know that the heart has no body?"

Margret looked up the gentle slopes of a city that led, on all sides, to the plateau and the Lake. "I don't know. I don't know that they care. They have Yollana," she added. "And although I would never have said this to my mother—to any of the Voyani Matriarchs—Yollana, of the four, was the most powerful, the most dangerous."

Elena came to stand beside her cousin; she looped an arm over her shoulder and drew her close. "That," she whispered for her cousin's ears alone, "is why you are Matriarch, Margret, and why I am 'Lena. Because when you say it, just so, I *know* it for truth, but I would never have placed her above any of *my* kin."

"Ai, well," her cousin replied, staring into the night sky above the cityscape, wondering if the smell of burning wood and incense, the hushed prayers, the mix of boiling potions and thick unguents that would be used, eventually, to treat the wounded, would be carried by wind to an unseen enemy. "Truth hurts, or it isn't truth."

7th of Scaral, 427 AA
Evereve

She came to the dining hall by following the trail of the lights
that were, as Avandar had said, encased in gold. Not encircled by
it, but truly encased; the light and the gold had somehow been
blended together, and each gave luster and luminosity to the
other. In shape, they were simple enough: quartered, flat circles.
Along the lines that quartered them, light welled alone.

As Jewel approached, the few nearest her would blaze like a
natural fire, passing on the intensity of their brilliance just ahead
of where she walked.

She tried, twice, to get lost; the effect was a gradual darkness. The lights simply faded the farther she walked from the
path that he had commanded her to take, until she was surrounded by something that felt like night. Like night in the gardens of Terafin.

She wondered how much darker it would get, and wondered,
too, if it would make much of a difference. Remembered the
talking, moving statues and the old stories her grandmother
had told her about wizards who lived in—well, wherever it
was this was—and their penchant for preying on the young and
the helpless.

Neither of which she was.

Gods, she *hated* this clothing.

She hated these halls. She hated these lights.

She hated the *lack* of light.

Following halls lit by light and gold, she realized that she
hadn't once seen a window, and she knew, then, exactly how
dark it could get. She'd been underground before when the lights
were nonexistent. The memory drove her to the light, and the
light drove her forward.

The food was not simple.

She was used to simplicity when she dined in her own wing;
fancy food, with its complicated courses and the etiquette that
governed which men and women of which rank ate which of the
dinners—early or late—and how, was a political statement. Eating
fancy food was therefore a political act.

Facing Avandar across the length of a table so fine she was
almost afraid to pick up the strange utensils that framed her plate

for fear of scratching its perfect surface, she didn't wish to descend to politics. Not yet.

She waited.

He waited.

After a moment she realized that this was the act of a *host;* he couldn't—if he had manners—begin to eat until she had. So much for the crown and the jewel-studded silks; so much for the gold leaf and the gold lights and the platinum inlay across doors so gaudy with artwork and filigree they seemed to be made of something other than wood. She sat back in her chair.

He looked across the table as if he could see through her, and his eyes, darkened by semicircles that spoke of sleep's lack, were a black that absorbed light, that denied it.

He spoke a single word in a language she didn't recognize. Spoke again. Again.

The fourth time, he shook himself. "Jewel," he said quietly.

She picked up the sticks by her plate; they were longer than the ones she had often used at her grandmother's home; they were finer, lacquered black and gold—it was a theme—with a very sharp end. There was no point in refusing the political when you were eating with a man who seemed on the edge of collapse.

Or madness, and she preferred collapse.

He watched her eat.

Minutes passed in a silence that teetered precariously, as if it were some precious object that was almost certain to break.

At last she saw something shift in the lines around his mouth; saw a few familiar lines suddenly wedge themselves into the space between eyebrows and hair.

"That," he said, in his most irritatingly superior domicis voice, "is a complete disgrace."

All hesitation, all foreign syllable, was washed away by his familiar disdain. "*What* are you talking about?"

He rose at once, walking with that stiff elegance that she so hated it usually made her grind her teeth. The crown was on his brow and the robes that looked so out of place—no, admit it, the problem was that they looked *perfect* for him, she was the one who was out of place—became, for a moment, simple accoutrement, a statement not of power but of fashion.

He rarely touched her. In fact, he had only really touched her for two reasons in their sixteen years together. First, for safety's sake: he never trusted her not to do something stupid—and when she was in danger, he somehow felt that his title and his position gave him the right, no worse, the *duty,* to interfere. And second, for etiquette's sake, when he was at the end of his tether and had neither the patience nor the time to explain in small words—and words got smaller and more cutting as he got more annoyed, a habit of speech she detested.

He caught her hands as she stared up at him in very real confusion, met her eyes and rolled his. "This is simple enough," he said, in the clenched jaw sort of way that always made the hairs on the back of her neck stand on end, "that most children past five of the Lady's Summers can manage with grace." And he grabbed the utensils from her hands and began to demonstrate their proper use.

"I've been using these since *I* was past those five summers, thank you very much."

"You've been using them barbarically. You'll be in the South and you can't afford to offend—" His voice trailed off. His brow furrowed. Almost as an afterthought, he set the slender sticks down beside her plate.

And he looked at her as if he was seeing her for the first time. "Avandar?"

Looked through her.

"Forgive me, Lady," he said quietly, and turned, and left the room.

The food was awfully cold by the time she got around to eating it.

CHAPTER EIGHT

Evening of the 7th of Scaral, 427 AA
Tor Leonne

Yollana of the Havalla Voyani sat in a darkness stripped of light, of the ability to bring light. She was not young, not by any stretch of the imagination, but until the moment she first met the Widan Cortano di'Alexes, she had not felt her age; it settled around her now, an ailment and an affliction that she feared—in *this* night, unblessed by the Lady's radiance—she would never be healed of.

Her daughters were far, far away. She was glad of it, although they had argued bitterly. Still, she had no intention of ending her days in the Lord's citadel, this clansmen's home of wood and rock and prettified dirt. The *Voyanne* awaited her even now; it called to her, with its treacherous runnels, its open stretch of exposed twists, its heat, its rain, its terrible, terrible wind.

That was her home. The only home she had ever known, and the home she desired fiercely. Because, of course, in the wilds there was freedom.

What price, Lady? she thought, staring at the ceiling in the darkness. *What price will you exact?*

For she had heard hope; it was carried by windless air, through closed screens and walls and doors, into what she suspected was a room dug out of the earth itself, it smelled so much like the grave. And that hope was a voice, the voice a man's. She recognized it; it was not a voice she might forget, having heard it once.

Evayne's servant.

Evayne, called a'Nolan, called a'Neamis; the Lady's enigmatic face.

In the darkness, the thought conjured light, but it was an odd light: a thing of fear and mystery. Evayne a'Nolan carried with her, for all to see who knew how to look, the heart exposed:

the crystal formed of soul and pain and a vision that cannot be denied.

There was only one way to expose a heart in such a fashion: only one road to walk. And none, not even Yollana herself who was counted wise by the ancient Voyani standards, had dared to look for more than the footpaths to that winding road.

Evayne, she thought, the word a prayer, *what have you sent me, and what price will I be forced to pay this time?*

The Lake at night was a thing of beauty, and there was so little beauty in his life that he forced himself to appreciate it.

Carefully crafted globes, things of glass settled into bronze and gold and silver, fanned all of the water's edges that were visible from the platform of the Lady's Moon. There were other platforms, of course; some grander, some wider, some more brilliantly lit; listen, and one could hear the mournful play of samisen across the silence of night sky: The Tyr'agar was in session beneath the Lady's open face.

But the Widan Sendari—born par di'Marano and elevated into the rootless, history-less *di'Sendari*—chose to take his ease, if such a pained and dark contemplation could be called ease, in isolation. And because he was the Tyr'agar's closest adviser, his request was granted quietly and without comment from any man save Cortano di'Alexes. The Sword's Edge drove them all, and the days had sharpened, not blunted, his tongue.

The masks of the Shining Court remained a mystery, impenetrable and foreign. Mikalis di'Arretta had been introduced to the masks, but he had been forbidden to ask questions of their origin. Cortano merely said, "We wish your studies to be uninfluenced by our own work to date." It was, as far as areas of magical study went, the most appropriate course of action, and Mikalis di'Arretta did not blink twice. He accepted Cortano's edict as both the compliment and the precaution they would have otherwise been.

But the man was no fool.

It was Cortano's weakness and his strength: he could not abide fools. Sendari himself was far, far more tolerant—but Sendari had no desire to be the Sword's Edge, no desire to wield it. He gathered those young men who sought knowledge and answers that were not in and of themselves a road to power, and he protected them as he could from the scouring of the desert winds Cortano used to temper them.

"Who made these masks, Sendari?"

The question hung in the air, above the cool lap of water against artful stone, as if they were a companion. He desired privacy.

"I do not know." It had the advantage of being the truth, this profession of ignorance.

Mikalis took his silence, wrapped himself in it, and stared at the masks that had been laid out in the most private of Cortano's work spaces. "Does the Sword's Edge?"

"No. Do you—do you know what they are meant to do?"

"I? No." Mikalis' answer was not devoid of frustrated pride. Sendari was almost unique in that. His desire to know, and his pride in knowledge, were separate strands of the whole cloth; one or the other could be picked up or set aside as occasion demanded. "But I fear that you—or the Sword's Edge—have information that, far from influencing results, will *give* them."

Silence, then.

"Cortano will tell me nothing."

"It is Cortano's . . . assignment. I am, in this task—"

"As in all tasks, Sendari?"

"In *this* task," Sendari had continued smoothly and without pause, "his Designate."

"Why did he choose me to second you?"

"He did not choose you to second *me*. He chose you—"

"It was your idea, wasn't it?"

Lord's sight, the man was no fool.

"These masks—are they Voyani?"

"I have said, and if you desire it, you may ascertain the truth of the words in an appropriate manner, that I *do not know* their manufacture. I am ill-used to being called a liar, no matter how delicate the accusation."

Mikalis was powerful, but his power *was* in his knowledge; he had mastered fire, and some movement of air, but his strength was the deep earth, and the earth calling was a slow, steady magic. He bowed. "I . . . apologize for my intemperate remark." It galled him to say it.

"No apology is necessary," Sendari had replied. "The remark itself was not intemperate. And my offer stands."

"It is thoughtful, but I believe you. *You* do not know." He lifted a mask. "Nor do I. But I will say this, and I will say it to you, because you are adept with words, Sendari, and I am not. Under no circumstance are these masks to be worn on the night of the Festival Moon."

Quickening, then, of heart, of breath. "You know their purpose."

"No. And," Mikalis added, offering a rare smile, "I grant you the same permission that you grant me: You may ascertain the truth of the words I speak in an appropriate fashion if you so desire.

"I do not know their purpose. But bound into it is something of a night that is not the Lady's. I fear it, and I fear very little that I do not understand."

He had stiffened; he stiffened now. The wind was brisk and chill, as cold as wind ever got when it touched these waters. "You sense night in them? I have sensed nothing, Mikalis; I have studied ancient arts, and I am as familiar as any of the Sword but yourself with the undertakings of the Voyani craft. If there is magic there, it does not, it cannot speak to me." His frustration showed; he could not contain it, and did not try. Mikalis would understand it.

Mikalis was quiet; Sendari knew him well enough to understand the expression. He was weighing words, weighting them, attempting to understand the role of the man who would hear whatever it was he chose to speak—and more, would hear what he did not.

"Sendari," he said at last, "I do not know what game is being played, and if I knew it—if I *knew* it—I might have a better answer to give you. But it is clear to me now that knowledge is not an advantage in this particular game. The Sword's Edge has been sharpened almost to killing these past days, and once or twice I have heard rumors of Widan who do not survive seconding his knowledge when the knowledge itself serves a . . . political purpose."

He had bowed then.

Sendari had returned the bow.

"I will continue my studies for at least three days," Mikalis continued, neutrality seeping into his voice. "Three days, and then I will tender my report to the Sword's Edge. I would appreciate it if—"

"Of course. This is a discussion between colleagues; it serves the purpose of honing and sharpening thought, no more. I look forward to your report, Mikalis."

That, of course, they both knew was a lie. They had bowed, parted as peers, and the day had dwindled into the unease of nightfall. In fifteen days, the Lady's Moon would shine upon them all. She was not as harsh a judge as the Lord, but She was subtle, and no man, not even those counted wise, could tell you what Her judgment might be.

Her judgment. The judgment of women.

He had not wanted to think of his conversation with Mikalis di'Arretta, but he desired such solace now, because those words held a certain safety compared to the others that came, on the lap of waves, in the dark of the Lady's hours. He attempted to hold onto the day's unease, the fear of the plans of the Shining Court— a Court that frightened him and angered him, that intrigued him and captivated him, by turns.

But the Court was so far away to the North it might have been a child's story, replete with demons and evil magi in a world of cold, cold white that simply had no purchase in the South, and Mikalis slipped from him, washed away in the scent of night water, night plants, night air. The Festival of the Moon supplanted them both.

Because Sendari di'Marano—ah, Lord scorch it, *di'Sendari*— knew what he wished to say on the night of the Festival Moon.

Knew whom he wished to say it to.

Diora.

What he did not know, what he could not know, was what he hoped to hear in return: He could think of nothing that would, in the end, dim the pain of her betrayal.

Across the lake, Alesso di'Alesso watched the same waters and heard the same music. He was almost moved to silence the players, but he had his guests and he did not wish to join them in the discourse that was almost certain to begin once the music's final notes had cleared the air.

He had had scant word from Cortano, which ill-pleased him. There was pressure upon him to choose at least two Generals, and that pressure was slowly building.

"You will declare war," the Tyr'agnate of Sorgassa had said, almost upon his arrival that morn. "Unless the circumstances have greatly changed. I have heard rumors that the Festival of the Moon itself is . . . to be different." A question, there.

He looked up, met the friendly, convivial mask that Ser Jarrani kai di'Lorenza never removed, and nodded. The Tyr'agnate returned his nod.

Alesso had been able to quietly put him off; the day's final ride had been a long one, and there had been some minor difficulty

with the caravan the Lorenzan Tyr had traveled with; a difficulty
that had resolved itself with the death of an overly zealous official
and three of Alesso's cerdan. The loss did not upset him. The necessity of the loss—the embarrassment and loss of face that accrued to
him personally—enraged him, but the point had been made.

He knew what Jarrani wanted: Alef, his par, as General. And
Alef was not a poor choice—but his loyalty was, and would always be, to his kai. Jarrani had seen to that.

He deflected the request, as he deflected much else, by speaking
with Ser Hectore's sharp-eyed, sharp-witted wife. Hectore was
Jarrani's kai, the heir to the lands of Sorgassa, a man Alesso's
junior, but not by much. He was as arrogant as the kin, dangerous;
a man who would be a worthy foe.

She, fan in hand, her posture perfect, had blushed and folded
slightly like the silk and wood she carried. Pleasing, that.

But not so pleasing as the posture, as the perfection, of the
single woman he desired: Serra Diora di'Marano. The woman who
had, by lilt of voice and perfect—yes, *perfect*—timing, caused him
so very much damage.

With such a wife, with a woman of that caliber by his side
what could he not do? He smiled as he thought of her. It would
take time to bring her to hand, and during that time he would
have to survive her.

The reverie itself was pleasant; the music and the Lake, the
silence of his guests, the sense of the power behind the crown
and the sword—these combined to give him a sense of peace.

But it was night peace, illusive, a thing that changed shape
and color in an attempt to evade the grasp. He looked up,
although he could not have said why, and he saw, silhouetted by
lamplight and the manifestations of the Sword of Knowledge, a
single man.

The kai el'Sol.

Such a sight would not have been remarkable, except for this:
he walked with a naked blade to the edge of the platform, and
then knelt there, waiting, his head bowed. He did not sheathe his
sword; it glistened, flat and new in seeming, in the moon's light.

And in the moon's light, Alesso could see the darkening
shadows of blood. He thought it new, but could not be certain.

The young women who played their skillful duet in samisen did
not pause, but by a gentle tilt of head, a movement of braided,
beaded hair, they asked him their question. He was pleased, indeed,

with the subtlety of it, and knew from this that they, too, must have been the choice of the Serra Teresa di'Marano, although they came from Sendari's harem. Her hand marked her brother's life.

Alesso nodded, and the older of the two began to sing. Her voice was delicate and lovely; it did not have the power of the Serra Diora's, and for that he was both grateful and regretful. He rose.

The kai el'Sol rose to greet him, holding his bow to offer respect and an unspoken apology for the naked blade. It was long enough. Alesso did not bid him rise; they were, Peder and Alesso, the only two men in the Dominion of Annagar who could, by Lord's law, bear the sun in full ascendance as their banner, and one did not cast aspersion on the insignia, no matter which head bore the crown.

"I would speak with you," the Radann kai el'Sol said, as Alesso approached.

Alesso nodded.

The kai el'Sol turned, and Alesso followed; the paths of the Tor Leonne, clipped and tended, unraveled before their feet, widening into something less private and less hidden than the previous Tyr'agar's home had been. Alesso wanted no hidden ways, no unseen avenues of attack. Not yet. Not now.

When the Tor Leonne was secure, and the Lake indisputably his, he would repent, and return the trees and flowers to the care of keepers who better understood their art. Here and now, he was General.

As General, he was surprised when the kai el'Sol led him directly to the Swordhaven. The Radann paused outside of the heavy doors that had been built into the stone monument; he bowed there, and then, with some effort, opened them. He did not speak; had not spoken a word since they had met at the Lake's edge.

Alesso was, on occasion, good at waiting, although it did not come naturally to him. He entered the haven just slightly ahead of the kai el'Sol, and stopped there, transfixed in the open frame, the wait rewarded, in a fashion. Peder kai el'Sol gave him a moment's grace, no more; he then stepped in and began to secure the doors at their back.

"You see," he said softly, softly, as Alesso di'Alesso stepped forward into the haven's heart.

"Yes."

The sword was glowing. It had taken, or so it seemed, the

raiment of moonlight and starlight; had given them the sun's edge, the sun's harsh strength.

"You have been searching." It was not a question.

"Yes."

"And?"

"Tyr'agar," the kai el'Sol said quietly, "when the Sun Sword speaks in so loud a voice, the Lord's enemies are close."

"How close, kai el'Sol?"

"Within the Tor Leonne."

"The city?"

"And the plateau."

He saw them enter the Swordhaven, of course. Half his time was spent here, in the Tor Leonne, by the twin discomforts of the Lake and the haven itself. But the open night sky held its almost hypnotic beauty, so dissimilar was it from the frozen wastes of the North.

Lord Ishavriel, born of an age that had been buried beneath all but the memories of the *Kialli* and the gods they had either fought or served, watched. Waited. It amused him, and he had not thought to be amused by the endeavors of humans. It almost—almost— gave him a glimmer of insight into Lord Isladar's odd fascination with, and about, humanity.

They *could* surprise one. They often did, in the brief span before their lives ended. But frequently that surprise was one of disappointment; they were frail and changeable, and they did not understand the consequence of their mortality well enough to serve as the imps did: with absolute obedience. Still, their defi- ance, sometimes subtle and sometimes overt, made them vastly more . . . entertaining.

Failure, however, would make them more entertaining still.

The wind changed slightly; he felt it brush against his skin, carrying the moisture of the Lake. It caused discomfort, and if he remained long in its path, would actually cause pain. Such an enemy as this he had no patience for, nor had he ever had patience for it; there was no battle, after all, no satisfying death to end the annoyance it caused.

There was only destruction.

He smiled in the darkness, and the smile was almost affectionate.

There would be destruction.

The man, the Radann, was clever. He did not understand the

roots of his power—no one in the Tor Leonne did—but he understood some of its effects. There was no place, unless it be within the waters of the Lake itself, that was proof against the magics of the *Kialli,* save the Swordhaven.

Let them speak.

They played at their games, and if they did not play carefully—and who did in the end when compared with the Lord Ishavriel?—they would fail. In one week's time, less perhaps, they would see the cost of their failure in the city streets below, an orchestration of violence and release that had been promised to kin grown half-mad at the absence of the abyss.

For just a moment, he wondered what the General would do: appease the *Kialli* or stand against them in the face of the slaughter. It seemed unthinkable that he would choose to appease them—which suited Ishavriel's purpose, although he had plans for every contingency—but the humans often chose to weaken their political stand for reasons that the *Kialli* found incomprehensible.

He watched, and watched, and watched; shifting so that the Lake might pass beyond him. But an hour passed, and the two men, protected—*for now*—by the Sun Sword's glow, did not emerge.

Kallandras did.

He moved in silence, certain of the shadows now that evening had fallen. Certain of the breeze, and the direction the breeze chose to take as he passed. It carried no noise to his enemies, unless his enemies were airborne. And if they were, and they revealed themselves, they would not remain enemies for long.

He paused a moment as he descended, sliding between the hedge of trees that surrounded the plateau to the North. Here, guards were sparse; the Lake was in the East, with the palace itself, the sun's rise and fall. But sparse and nonexistent were two different things, and Alesso di'Marente was a man newly come—and insecurely at that—to power.

There was no immediate sound of footsteps.

In the darkness, he lifted a hand, beckoning both breeze and the gift that he had been born to—as if the two had always been intertwined; as if they had become inseparable. They were not; he was not so dependent on the power of a ring given late in his youth. But he felt its edges, its demands, its voice, an echo of what the wind desired.

They argued a moment; it tired him. But it was a niggling thing, this exchange of wills, this little testing, and when it had passed, the breeze swept out in a natural series of circles that touched the whole of the plateau, carrying with it the sounds of movement, near and far, the sounds of voices raised or lowered, the sounds of armor, swords, the movement of the men he must avoid. His own skill took what the wind had given him, sifted it, categorized it, let it fall to a level of thought that was almost beneath thought, it had become so instinctive with the passage of time.

Thank you.

It had become his custom to offer that benediction; the wind was graceless, as always, in its reply.

"Yollana," he said quietly. The wind had not carried her voice; she raised no cry, offered no pain, no anger, indeed no comment at all. But he knew that she could hear his voice, where hers might not penetrate the prison they held her in.

"The moon's face is not yet full; the Havallans have withdrawn; they have need of your guidance, as do we. I am in the Tor proper; I am searching for you."

He moved like a shadow, *with* the shadows, grateful that he had not chosen to bring Margret. He would probably pay for that later.

He spoke again.

She had been waiting for his voice.

Until she heard it, however, until it woke her from the light and restless slumber that had been her only sleep since the death of the Radann kai el'Sol in the Lake of the Tor Leonne, she had not known it.

But before her eyes were fully open, before she sat up in the windowless room, she knew what had awakened her. Waited, breath held, until it came again.

"Diora."

"Kallandras." She wrapped herself tightly in nightclothes, although she heard no promise of freedom in his voice. **"Where are you?"**

"I am . . . in the Tor Leonne," he said, and the pause spoke; it spoke loudly. **"I have come seeking a woman who is held captive. But not, not at this point, the Flower of the Dominion. I am sorry."**

Is it so clear to you? Is it so clear in my voice? Do I give so much away? She drew breath; held it a moment. Gathered the daylight about her, although the moon was high, and its face bright and compelling. She was Serra Diora di'Marano, and she *did not* plead.

There was only one thing, one life, for which she might have broken that edict—and herself—but it was gone now; nothing remained but the purpose to which she had devoted what was left her: Justice. Vengeance.

"I need you," he continued, "in the Tor. You are safe, or as safe as you can be, while you reside within those walls—and if we take you now, there will be no safety in the Tor, or beyond it, for as far as these words will carry."

She did not desire his pity. "Why," she said, as coolly as she could, as neutrally, "have you come?"

"To find Yollana of the Havalla Voyani," he replied without hesitation. She felt the wind in the words, although there was no way for the wind to reach her. A hint of freedom; of night air, of the Lady's Mercy and the Lady's cruelty.

"She is here," Diora said at last, with misgivings. "But she is in the private quarters of the Sword's Edge. I would not dare them—"

"The Sword's Edge is occupied for the moment with the politics of the realm. Diora—watch. Listen for me."

She nodded, knowing that he could not see it, could not hear it. She wanted to speak; to speak to him because there were so few people she could speak to.

She had not thought captivity of this nature would be so very difficult. But she did not speak; her face shuttered; her expression became, even in darkness, even unseen, her own: steel and cool water and pale, pale moon's light.

There was a smell to magic, a taste, a sensation; something as strong as the little details that followed an act of intimacy. But it was subtle, caught only if one knew the act itself.

Yollana both did and did not. Magic had defined her existence. It had placed blocks in the road; pits, spikes; it had forced detours upon her trek down the *Voyanne* that she would never have willingly taken otherwise. So had she been taught: the magic of the clans is the thing we fight *against,* not the thing we fight for.

And how, she had said, to her own gray-haired, sharp-tongued mother—a mother she had promised herself she would never grow up to become, and of course, had followed in the footsteps of almost exactly—*are we to be judged if we choose to take up the power offered us?*

Her mother, grim-faced, thin-lipped, angry, had said, had always said, *The blood knows.* She had thought it foolish then. They exchanged words, heated with anger and impatience—the one for the conservatism of age, the other for the inexperience of youth—and, again as always, her mother had won the argument.

Her mother, after all, had been Matriarch. *The* Mother.

And what would you say to me now? she thought. But the earth divided them. The Lady had taken her mother years ago, far too many of them now for Yollana's liking. *Aie,* she shook herself. She knew the answer; there would be more anger, and probably—although she'd long passed the age for it—the five white marks of her mother's fingers stretched out around the imprint of her palm; her mother had not been above the openhanded slap for which the Voyani women were so often known.

You have risked our entire *clan—on the word of an outsider; what else did you expect? You've exposed us all!*

Truth, every word of it.

It had seemed a thing of choice, a lack of choice, at the time. The risk, the highest she had ever taken—that any Matriarch had ever taken—the possible reward, slim indeed.

But without the risk. . . .

The chains rattled against her wrists and ankles, a reminder that the cage was more than earthen, more than gravelike. Evening; she was sure of it. They would come soon. They would come again.

Her hands had been injured, and her feet, the flesh along her calves badly scored; if she was freed, she would lope like a cripple. But her eyes, at least, although they had stooped to threaten, they had not yet destroyed. Dark, here, the steel across her wrists far harder than the gold that they had stripped her of. She wondered, idly, if they kept it because they were rapacious, or if they kept it because they suspected it had magical properties.

It did, of course, but it was a magic that was blood-bound, and she would never release that into the hands of clansmen.

Aie, the steel weighed her down. The darkness. The earth-encrusted air. *Lady, Lady, this is as close to your time as we come. Help me. Help me.* Pleading did not demean her. It did not weaken her. Weakness was only weak when it was exposed for the inspection of others, and there were no others to hear what she did not put into words.

But the Lady heard her.

Magic had its own smell, its own taste, its own lingering malice. She felt it, sudden and startling, as the door slid open in a silence so complete she wondered if she had somehow been deafened.

He stood there, in the flat, rough entrance, like a shadow, the essence of shadow; no light cast him.

"Yollana." He was there in an instant; by her side, his slender fingers roughened in places by work, and in others by nothing. He reached for her feet, seeing in the darkness as if darkness were no impediment. Truly, she thought, the Lady's servant. The chains came up with her ankles, but fell without them: a blessing, a benediction.

And, as always, Yollana was gracious when gifted with such a thing.

"You'd best hurry," she said, lifting her hands, creating more noise than her words did as the chain links rattled against each other. "They know you're here now."

In the darkness, she thought she saw the faint edge of a smile.

Cortano stood at once, stiffening. Alesso had not returned from his discussion with the Radann kai el'Sol, and the Sword's Edge had been left, in some fashion, to hold his own in the presence of Tyr'agnate Jarrani kai di'Lorenza and his overly-sharp son, Hectore.

"I would, of course, support such a suggestion to the best of my ability," he said, bowing. "But you must forgive me. I am . . . called away." His gaze turned North and East a moment.

"Surely the two men who are responsible for—"

"There is only one man," the Sword's Edge replied coolly, for even in times of necessity, he was a political man, "who is responsible for the Crown and the Sword, and he is otherwise occupied with the Radann kai el'Sol." But he bowed again, acutely aware that a second such interruption in an evening was unlikely to endear either himself or Alesso to the Tyr'agnate, a man they could not afford to annoy.

He would deal with ruffled pride later; they all would. But now the magehaven called him, and he repaired to it in a haste that would—just barely—not call the attention of the entire assemblage toward his parting.

As he stepped away from the Lake, he let his power build, calling it quietly as if it were an intelligent servant and not merely the manifestation of his will. Very few were the men who had seen such a display who lived to tell of it; each member of the Sword of Knowledge chose his own way of calling—and arming—himself, of focusing, of channeling.

Eyes attuned to it could see the colors that edged his skin, the line of his body, the folds of a fabric that had been woven, thread for thread, under his supervision. Orange, of course, because no man approached a combat unarmored. But above that glimmer of pale fire, a redder light, a darker one: Fire.

He had protected the spaces that he had claimed from unwanted intrusion. But it was easiest, when protecting his space from the distance-walking that could bring a man from one edge of the continent to another—had he the power—to protect it entirely; to leave no door to enter by. That he had left a door to *leave* by had been costly enough.

He did not choose to breach the spell he had laid into place; too costly, especially given that he did not know the nature of his enemy. But he suspected, and he was displeased. He was not a young man, to run from the Lake's edge to his haven.

He ran.

She watched him kill.

Around her, against the background of the finery so coveted and despised by the Voyani, the men circled; their hands formed a pattern of light across the air, intertwined like a fine, fine net, crackling with Lord's light, blue fire. From such an attack, such a threat, she had no immediate safety; all that she had worn had been stripped or shorn from her. They had not left her her hair, and she accepted its loss with poor grace; the man, the Sword's Edge, had been thorough in his fear.

But no power that she had invested herself with would have let her walk unscathed through that complicated spell. None whatever would have let her walk, with perfect, catlike grace, *above* it. He walked in air as if the air itself were his platform and his home.

They were stunned by it; they froze for an eye blink.

She would have done the same.

Paid the same price for the minute hesitation.

She watched him, her body as still as the shadows that hid her,

her thoughts turned inward when she could tear her eyes away from the terrible flash of his blades in the poor light.

They screamed, one or two of them; cried out in a fear that was almost too slow in coming.

Almost, in light such as this, he seemed inhuman, a thing of night, of the Lady's. Or the Lord's. But she had heard the whisper of his distant voice; heard it still, requesting movement to the right or the left, words that seemed to come from a different chest, a different throat, interrupting nothing.

She had never seen him fight.

She had known that he could, of course; he was marked in a way that could only rarely be hidden from one who had the blood, however dilute that blood was. Could never be hidden from one who wore the heart of the Havallans. But knowing it and witnessing it were two different things, and the latter made her uneasy.

What price, Lady?

The Widan fought with spell, when they chose to fight at all; he walked above or beyond the reach of fire, the earth's grip, the water—and there were few indeed who could call water in the Dominion. Five men died in a handful of minutes, and they died quickly; so quickly that their blood, when it left them in a spray of red, almost seemed to be moving, to be alive.

"Yollana," he said, and she stiffened. **"This is the last. The worst will follow, and we must be done. Can you run?"**

She grimaced. Tested her feet against the hard ground. Shook her head: Yes. Knew that he would take her at her word; that her word, once given, would bind her. Knew that she would stumble; that her muscles—those muscles not sliced or cut, would somehow, *somehow* hold her weight.

She had the blood, and with the blood came vision. She *knew*. It should have offered her comfort.

He separated head from shoulders, but not cleanly. Then, while the bodies of the fallen were still twitching, he added to their wounds, tearing their flesh with the tips and the guards of his blade. It was quick work, but bloody, and the only thing that kept her eyes upon it—besides the sheer stubbornness that was her most famous quality—was the cool stillness of his face. He did not smile; did not blanch; did not otherwise seem to react to the work he had chosen.

"Now," he said, his back speaking. He turned, then; held out a hand.

Wincing, she took it. Her own hands, she feared, would never be what they had been without a healer's touch—and they had few enough of those in easy reach. Aye, she'd lost two fingers, and the ones she'd kept had been broken. As if broken fingers would give the servants of the Lord of Night the answers they sought.

As if anything would, from Yollana.

She had made her oath; the oath, she kept. Even with the heart exposed, and gone from her these many years. Gone. She was not a young woman, but she could not afford to make Evallen's mistake: She could not afford to die and leave behind daughters bereft of power and guidance at a time when power and guidance were the only crutches daughters could rely on to walk the distance the coming war demanded of them all.

All.

He took her hand; she tried to accept his offer of strength. And she did run, as she had seen, her gait uneven but unbroken in its awkward stride. He adjusted to it, moving to her rhythm, leading her into the shadows she knew best, the evening's strengths. She added to the shadows as she could, whispering her own benedictions—if they could be called that—and blending in with the trees, the grass, the living things that were part of the Voyani hidden ways.

But his hand was slick with blood, and although she had shed blood in her life, there was something about its warmth and his coolness that jarred her. Distracted her.

Yollana, who had not been led since before her mother had raised her up from the waters of the riverbeds and proclaimed her the Matriarch-in-waiting, the Lady's choice, was led now, and she followed a man whose hair was pale silver in the moonlight, whose body was shadow defined, whose death—whose death was the Lady's coldest death, her darkest offering.

The Widan Cortano di'Alexes did *not* rage. Rage, in its most primal colors, its loudest expression, was the signal gesture of weakness a man of power might otherwise show: not only was it a severe loss of control, but it also implied the end of a battle, and that battle's loss.

The Sword's Edge did not lose.

But here, the facts were incontrovertible.

The five men he had personally chosen were dead; there, a limb, beside it a severed head, the flesh on the youngest scored in multiple places as if—as if he had been picked up, like so much limp refuse, and mauled by large claws, by inhuman teeth.

The heads that had been detached were not cleanly removed, and at least one appeared—for the moment—to be missing. But the bodies themselves had not yet begun to stiffen; the deaths were new.

Hands shaking, lips so thinned they should have prevented any sound from escaping, the Widan Cortano di'Alexes made his way through the wide hall to the door that led into his personal chambers. Here, the effects were different; fire had scoured the room, scorching fans and low tables, cushions and mats, into a blackened curl. They had been finely made, chosen for the perfection of their matching colors, their contrasting textures.

He recognized the fires as his own; recognized little else as such. He cast; he cast quickly, the words a bark, the edge of an angered roar. No footsteps had crossed these floors. None; not even hers.

But the woman—and her things—were gone.

He spoke; spoke again; drew his sigils in the air.

What he found there brought silence. He stood, at the threshold of his quarters, casting a shadow in the dim light.

At last he moved forward, moved on, his gait stiff, the anger sublimated beneath an envy, a desire for knowledge, that had defined half his life.

It did not surprise him when, after he had completed his descent into earthen darkness, he found only empty chains; did not surprise him that there had been so little sign of struggle. He might have cast again, but his thoughts were now upon the first of the rooms, the deaths, the quickness of the theft.

In silence, he returned to the room that his own fires had blackened and scorched. He touched walls, his palms flat and wide, the bodies of the men who had served him stiffening into the rictus of death and neglect. Let them wait. He would attend to them later, when he attempted to discern what had killed them—and what had not.

Minutes passed. Possibly an hour; he was Widan for a moment; the Sword's Edge turned inward, rather than outward. He wondered, briefly, where Sendari was; considered calling for him. Decided against it; he did not wish to interrupt the reverie that had taken him.

It was thus that Alesso di'Alesso, the Tyr'agar himself, found the Sword's Edge: kneeling in ash, his hands black with it, the remnants of finery scattered and inconsequential.

Evening of the 7th of Scaral, 427 AA
Evereve

"This is the first time since the death of his wife that he has come to *Evereve* with a visitor."

She turned at the sound of the voice, wary now with isolation. Jewel valued privacy; she always had. But there was a difference between the privacy you took in the cracks between contact with your family and the privacy that an underground castle, in which you seemed to be the only living thing—Avandar not excepted because, although she'd been searching for the better part of an hour, she couldn't find him—afforded.

She had gone up the scale from anger to worry, and it was when she was worried that she tended to see most clearly. Had to. Avandar had *never* asked her pardon for anything in their life together, and he'd done a damn sight worse than forcefully correct her table manners. So something was wrong—and it wasn't the crown on his head or the stupid clothing that, much as she hated to admit it, suited him far better than anything he'd worn in her service.

"Aristos," she replied, using his name because names could be neutral.

She hadn't expected to see him, not here; although she knew it was cowardly, she'd avoided what she now thought of as the Hall of Statues That Were Probably Once People.

"Lady," he replied, bowing so smoothly it seemed impossible that he could be made of stone at all. Even his garments, gray and marbled in their oddly Southern folds, rippled with the movement he offered her. It was not an obeisance.

She was silent; awkwardly silent.

"Are you searching for something?"

"Not—not something in particular, no. I'm—I probably won't get to see something as big and strange as this again," *if I'm lucky,* "and I thought I'd—I'd just explore it."

"And would you mind company?"

It came to her then that she didn't want his company. Why? Because the fact that he existed at all said things about Avandar Gallais that she really didn't want to know? She examined that thought for five seconds—give or take a few—and tossed it aside. She didn't want his company because there was something about him, stone or no, that she didn't trust. A pity, because she liked him.

And she trusted Avandar?

If any of her den had been there, she'd have probably snapped at them in frustration. She was good at it; it came easily. Too damn easily.

"I think I need some time to adjust," she said, putting as much of a breathless and harmless cadence into the words as her voice allowed. Truth to tell, it wasn't much. Even at sixteen she'd've had trouble manufacturing it.

Aristos stiffened—he was stone, so it should have been hard to notice—and she felt that pang again. Guilt. "As you wish, Lady. I have, of course, been given no purpose other than to serve, and should you require me, you will find me in the Hall of Conjunction."

She should have shut up. That would have been the smart thing to do. But she *hated* to feel guilty for no good reason. "Aristos?" she said, as he turned away.

He turned back at once, pivoting as if stone had no weight. "Yes?"

"Is it true that you slept with his wife?"

A stone brow rose. Fell. "He told you that?"

"Someone did."

The smile on his face was as far from the expression of hurt that had stopped her dead as an expression can get. She didn't bother to take a step back, although when she was younger she would have. "Oh, my dear, you are so different from Elyssandra. I had hoped to make better use of you in time, but I see that you are . . ." his expression was almost a sneer, "rather common. Rather simple. Far, far too uncomplicated. I can see that the only weapon you will make is a blunt one. Very well.

"In a manner of speaking, yes. She was a very proud, very powerful woman in her own right; he has never been interested in anyone who isn't."

"A manner of speaking?"

"She did not see fit to explain the circumstances to him, which was indeed as I expected. The liaison was not to her liking, my dear; it was not, in fact, her choice." His smile was soft with memory. It was a memory that Jewel never wanted to be a part of. "I might never have been so . . . ensorcelled . . . had I not become careless. I never marked her; I never bruised her; I never destroyed an item of clothing, a strand of jewelery; I did not so much as remove—by hand—the clasp that held her hair."

"I'm not sure I want to hear much more of this," she said, lifting a hand. "No, strike that. I'm *certain* I don't want to hear any more of it. We can leave it as a conversation topic for another century. Or rather, you can. I don't plan on being around that long."

He stepped forward.

"I wouldn't, if I were you."

"You wouldn't what?"

"I wouldn't try anything stupid. Stupider."

"And what can be done that hasn't been done? I live encased in stone; I serve his whim. He offered me as a gift to her; he thought to wound her. She was grateful; spiteful, even. I do not think it impressed him overmuch, to know that she could so casually turn against a lover she had taken.

"But she was proud. She never chose to explain her humiliation. And it was, indeed, quite exquisite."

"Well, plan on not repeating it," Jewel replied. "For one, I think your build would make it generally uncomfortable, if it were possible at all."

"Ah. Well, if that were a fear, you need not fear it; as you suspect, it was not an ability that was left me." He stepped toward her. She stood her ground.

Or she would have, if instinct hadn't suddenly kicked the edge of her spine with a resounding thud that made her legs *move*.

"But he was no fool." Stone hands, shot through with lovely, smoky marble, were raised in the well-lit hall. Fingers curled into fists, and with a casual gesture, Aristos smashed the brightest of the magelights into fine, thin leaf over shards of crystal. The light went *out*. "He did not assume that my time in captivity would sit well with me." He took another step; she took another. His eyes did not leave her face as he extinguished another light, following the trail the lamps made as they followed her. "He therefore bound my behavior in regard to his wife quite, quite thoroughly. I might speak freely—speech, after all, was acceptable, and any accusation, any lover's quarrel, any *pleas,* were all to his amusement."

Crash.

"But I literally could not act against her, or any item of value that she owned. I could not crush the stem of a leaf; I could not bruise the petal of a flower. I could not drop a stray dish when I stood by her and she ate from it."

Crash.

"I have had a long time to become used to this form of captivity. She took great pleasure in it. He, on the other hand, the author of my misfortune, took none. At least that satisfaction was mine."

Crash.

She had a sudden, very bad feeling that she was running out of hall. It wasn't a guess. It was a certainty. Enough of one that she didn't waste much time looking over her shoulder.

"As far as breaking things go, you, ummm, don't seem to have that problem at the moment."

"No, oddly enough. I don't. It's been a long time since I've bothered to test it, my dear, because it's been a *very* long time since I've been awakened. That was his one act of kindness. Theophan has been aware for every year of his entrapment; he is quite, quite mad."

You aren't winning any sanity prizes, she thought, but she didn't bother to say it. Two stone fists beat zero weapons any time. She wondered how much being made of stone would slow him down if she broke into an out-and-out run.

"You are obviously part of the enchantment that allowed her to be sent here and live."

"She didn't always live here?"

Crash.

He smiled lazily, and she knew he knew she was buying time. But clearly the company—any company—was worth prolonging. Gods, if she got out of this in one uncrushed piece, she was going to *kill* Avandar.

"My dear, no one lived here. He built it as his personal citadel, a way of defending those he cared for. His own life has never been in danger—but the life of his wife, and his children, should there have been any—a different story entirely.

"Those born here might enter and leave freely. Those who bore the mark of his consort: the Serpent mark. His oldest name. You bear that mark, but it is clear you have neither his blood nor his blessing. I . . . was not a man of little power. I had more than a passing acquaintance with the magical arts, and I had his trust, for what it was worth, for some time. But had I not been entirely

enslaved as a magical construct, I would never have survived
transit to *Evereve*. No one would. That was the entire purpose."

Crash.

"But here you are. You are obviously not dead; I may be stone,
but I am still a purveyor of the flesh. And to accomplish *that* he
must have unraveled a great deal of what was wrought."

Crash. Crash. Two, for punctuation.

"And now, my dear, I am going to draw this little encounter to
an unfortunate close. I am going to defile you, eunuch fashion,
since the other is beyond me, and then am I going to kill you."

Theophan, whoever he was, wasn't the only one who was mad.
Stone or no, Aristos' face had taken on an ugly rictus that defied
any connection with sanity.

"You don't expect me to stand still for any of that, do you?"

"Not at all."

"Good."

The hall opened into a huge gallery of some sort; she *knew*
there was a round wall twenty feet from her back that it would be
very, very bad to get caught by. The dress was awkward—another
thing she'd kill Avandar for later—but she was familiar enough
with skirts that she managed to roll while Aristos' fist was flat-
tening thick gold into thin leaf. Very thin leaf.

She was worried.

Not terrified; not that. There was no one else in the hall but
her. No one to protect—and worse, much worse, no one to fail.
This was survival made as clean and as tidy as it could be. She
could *see,* on a level that the word "sight" was too simple to
encompass, where he would go, where he would strike, what he
would attempt, and she reacted fifteen seconds ahead of each
action.

Of course she did wonder about the structural integrity of the
hall itself when she saw the first fissure snake its way from mid-
wall to ceiling. She also wondered how well he could see; his
casual destruction of the lamps he could reach had plunged the
hall into twilight.

And what followed twilight?

He was *heavy.* She was light on her feet.

But he was not, as she had so dearly hoped, slow.

"I was made for many things," he said, no break for breath in
the smooth flow of the words, "among them defense. If I tire at
all, it is not in a way that will help you."

She saved her breath; cursing worked just as well when she didn't let it out.

It was when she took the right turn into the Hall of Statues that she said a single word. *Kalliaris*.

They were waiting for her.

CHAPTER NINE

They were waiting for her.

Those forms that had been carved into perfect stone, alabaster, marbled smoky quartz, something green and heavy and shot through with veins of gold, those statues that had their places on pedestals over inscriptions she had no hope of being able to read, now gathered 'round the doors in a half circle.

Unlike Aristos, they were silent; it was not a mercy. She had ten seconds of lead time, and the momentary pause to stare at the faces, mute but no longer expressionless, of the men and women that she imagined had somehow managed to piss Avandar off cost her.

She ran into their midst; stopped ten feet away from the one that stood farthest from the swinging door. Not a good idea to let him touch her, if she could avoid it. That was the problem with having an imagination; she could imagine just how well she'd fare beneath those fists, given what one blow had done to gold.

Cormaris, she thought, *don't let me snivel.* Not that she had much in the way of dignity, but what she did have was important.

"You must be the young lady that Aristos spoke of," the statue said. It had a voice like thunder's rumble: Heavy and unpleasantly grating. It—he—also looked nothing like Aristos; there was no refinement at all in his features. Heavy cheeks, heavy chin, beard that, even carved in stone, didn't look like it would pass Imperial muster. He was also about twice the width of the more pretty Aristos, and very little of that was fat.

Well, okay, none of it was fat. But in real life—wherever it had managed to run off to, very little of it would have been.

"Well," she said, looking over her shoulder, "I'm the only new person here that I know of, although 'young' or 'lady' is probably stretching it."

Aristos stepped into the room. The hairs on the back of her neck stood on end. They didn't come down when he smiled. She hated people who used smiles that particular way. Not that her hatred ever made much difference.

She turned back to Big and Burly.

The statue standing in front of her frowned slightly. "True," he said. "The dress doesn't suit you, either."

"Well, thanks. I suppose I won't return the favor and criticize what you're wearing, seeing as you don't have many alternatives."

He laughed, then, and Aristos slowed down. "Sanjos," he said softly. "You've found something of mine. I'm . . . surprised to see you awake."

"Oh? The way you've been babbling? You talk so much Aristos, if most of it weren't boring, you'd wake the dead."

"Do not interfere in what does not concern you."

"Or you'll turn me to stone?" The larger man's smile was very similar to Aristos' but it wasn't aimed at her.

"We have very little time. Let me finish what I started, and you may do as you please with what remains."

"Judging from your expression, that won't be much."

"Sanjos." His expression stilled, the lines of it smoothing out into something better expressed by stone. "I will already suffer for what has transpired. I have no wish to suffer without due cause."

The larger man shrugged. "Not my problem, really. Come here," he added to Jewel.

She started to obey, but her feet stopped in place. She was too tired to think, but not too tired to react; her feet understood what she knew before it reached the rest of her body. Like, for instance, her brain. Instinct. No safety there, then. No safety anywhere.

"Girl," the second statue said, some of the rumble in his voice turning to jagged edge, "I said, *come here.*"

"Funny thing about life," she replied, standing where she was as Aristos—and the line of statues to either side of the one called Sanjos—drew closer. "Even when there's only seconds left of it, no one rushes to throw it away."

Sanjos frowned and stepped forward just as quickly as Aristos had done.

" 'Funny thing,' " a familiar voice said, softly enough that she had to strain to catch it, "if I were to illustrate that truth by example, *you* would not be the person I would choose as its proof."

The light came down from the ceiling like rain and even the statues flinched at its coming.

In a brightness that the height of day couldn't match—except for those rare moments when the sea was still enough that it reflected sun in white, rhythmic stretches—stood Avandar Gallais, shorn of crown, shorn of jeweled silk. But it was his voice that was the greatest of comforts: because it *was* his voice. There was no struggle with dialect, no speaking in tongues—as it were—no dull confusion; for the first time, he was completely himself.

She had never thought to be so happy to see him.

Aristos howled in fury; it was all he could do. He lunged for her and his body froze that way, as if a sculptor had taken a fancy to a man in a frenzy, and chiseled him perfectly to reflect that moment of his life and no other. Sanjos did not make the attempt; indeed, the statues that surrounded her became just that: statues. Immobile stone.

"You are," he said softly, "such a foolish girl. What did you think you were doing?"

She stood in their center, almost unwilling to move; they had come close enough to her that she'd have to squeeze between the columns their bodies formed, and she didn't want to touch them, to gift them with the intimacy of either her escape or her relief.

"I was—exploring. This place—"

"It is my home."

"Well, that would explain a lot."

"Jewel—"

"Could you learn how to use gold in a less tasteful fashion? Could you learn how to cram so many paintings onto a wall they *all* look cheap and insignificant?"

"Jewel—"

"Could you choose a site farther underground? Could you live in a place that denies light more than this?"

"Jewel—"

"And *these?*" she added, waving her hand in a ragged circle, "could you keep anything less safe just wandering around like a rabid dog or ten?"

He reached the farthest of these human columns, the first statue, a woman. His hands were pale in the falling light as he lifted them, as he stroked the underside of her chin. Illusion or no, the face seemed to rise a finger's breadth, the stone shifting in acknowledgment. His lips moved. Gray light flared around the woman's perfect form as he spoke a single word in a language Jewel didn't understand. She thought it was a name. The statue that had been so touched vanished.

He made his way to her side by repeating that gesture and adding different syllables beside every statue he reached.

"Did your grandmother tell you nothing of the dangers of exploring a wizard's home?" he asked, his expression perfectly balanced between annoyance and amusement.

In reply, she slapped him.

Later, she would understand that he allowed this, because she'd tried it a dozen times—two—in the years that she'd been forced to suffer his company and she'd never once come close to succeeding.

But he only allowed it once; the second time she raised her hand, he caught her wrist. Fabric fell along the torn seam of sleeve; the backward S, the serpent mark, caught gold and silver light. His gaze glanced off it and rose to her face. "I will take the punishment I am due, but not more. Come. I have arranged for . . . suitable attire. The dress is worse than wasted on you; it is actually unattractive. As well as inappropriate."

He started to move; she didn't. She might have been one of the statues that cursed these halls.

"Jewel?"

"Let them go," she said softly.

"Pardon?"

"These. Let them go."

His brows, dark and perfect, did the scrunch and dip that spoke of annoyance. It looked mild, but any expression that actually reached his face wasn't. "Jewel, did you not hear a word Aristos actually said?"

"You mean you did?"

He nodded grimly.

She hit him. Not a slap, not exactly, and not with anything that could be considered warning. A test of reflexes that; he caught her hand with the flat of palm and actually took a step back.

"You *bastard*," she said.

"This may come as a surprise to you, but I arrived as quickly as I could once I understood where you were and what was actually occurring."

She struggled for control of her wrist, but this time he didn't choose to return it.

"You haven't answered my question," he said coolly.

"Yes."

"Yes?"

"I heard every word he said. I could probably repeat them, but they'd be so laced with *my* swearing, they'd lose some of their effect."

"And you want me to, as you say, let *him* go?"

She was silent for a long time. Surrounded by the statues that he hadn't sent wherever to get through to her, she looked up—she had to—and said, "Yes."

His expression was not so much one of disbelief—although that was definitely there—but exasperation. "I will never understand the North," he said at last. "I will never understand how so insipid and so *weak* a culture can produce such strength that the Empire has managed to stand against its enemies every single time it has been under siege save perhaps one." He caught her by the arms and lifted her so that her toes were the only thing that anchored her to ground. "These men and women wronged *me* or failed *me*. And perhaps," he added, "caused me to fail mine. It was an illuminating discussion, and I thank you for your part in it. We were never so close again, Elyssandra and I, and perhaps that was just. Perhaps she resented my inability to protect her from what I had brought into her home. You did not know her—she was not a weak woman. She would never willingly have asked for anyone's help; it would have demeaned her or broken her. She was . . . very unlike you." His glance, lost a moment to the statue, made Jewel flinch. "He would have killed you, brutally and inefficiently. Why do you desire his freedom?" With every word, he shook her slightly.

"It's not his freedom I desire," she said, speaking through clenched teeth to stop the words from wavering. "Just his death."

"Do not play games with me, Jewel ATerafin. I know you well. You know that for this statue—for all of them—there *is* only one freedom. You do know that, don't you?"

She started to lie, and gave up before the words reached her lips. "I suspected."

"Then why?"

She took a deep breath and exhaled it, letting go the last of her strength. Aware, as she did, that she was giving herself over to Avandar; aware, as she did, that in some ways she had done no less in the last decade. "I understand the desire to kill someone. I've done it, once or twice, a long time ago. I've done it for vengeance. I've done it for safety. I was younger. I didn't understand, then, that the deaths didn't just reflect the dead, they reflected *me*. Pretty harsh reflection, years later.

"The fact that they're still trapped here says nothing at all about them, to me; it says everything about you."

"And what does it say?" he asked her, in a tone of voice that was unusually distant, even for Avandar.

She looked past him. "I don't know," she said at last.

"Come, Jewel. You disappoint me. I hear the judgment in your voice; it is, as usual, quite distinct. I assure you my ego is not delicate. I have survived much worse than your poor opinion."

"Avandar," she said softly, "these people are dressed in a style I've never seen, and I'm willing to bet money that the language they're speaking and the words I'm hearing aren't connected by anything but magic. So I can't know who they are. I don't know what you think they did. But—"

"Yes?"

"But I think they've been here for long enough."

He surprised her. He laughed. "They have been here for a fraction of the time I have been here," he said.

"I know," she replied, turning away from him as much as she could considering the death grip on both of her arms.

"Jewel—"

"I don't want to know any more."

He stiffened. "That is . . . unlike you."

"Not really. I . . . don't particularly like you, Avandar. I never really have, you've always been such an arrogant bastard." As it was something she said once every two months, and usually with more vehemence, she didn't expect him to be terribly impressed. "But this—this is worse."

"How?" His voice was never this casual.

She hesitated because of it.

"Because I *hate* power," she said at last, "and I should have known, if I could actually dislike you for this long, that you've got way too much of it."

"What," he said softly, "is power?"

"I'm not up for philosophy right now. I'd like my old clothing, and I'd like my old life. I'll live with the lack of ignorance."

"And you won't demand further answers?"

Her face was shadowed a moment by his height. "No," she said at last, "not here. Because it would only be in jest, and I'm not—I can't—" she looked at the stone faces of the men and women who formed his bizarre and subservient court, and she shook her head; brown curls fell into her eyes as they always did, but this time—this time she couldn't easily push them away.

"They should have been dead. That would have been cleanest. They linger here like old wounds, and you let them, you keep them. You don't understand that if you don't let go of them, they don't let go of you." Her eyes were unfocused a moment. "I've heard a lot of people say that hate and love are flip sides of the same coin. I've never believed it. But then again, I've never called love that stupid fanciful obsession that eats away at your insides like Bleaker's worst ale. They wronged you. Maybe that gave you the right to kill them—I don't know. It wouldn't have, back home."

"No; back 'home,' as you call it, I would be the criminal by my just and justified actions here."

"You would *both* be criminals. That's the point. In order to punish them for their crimes against you, you have to be at least as bad as they are—maybe worse." There was a sudden stab of an ugly fear that choked her words.

"You were," she said, to her great surprise and to her regret. "You were worse then they were." She saw, reflected in the gold and diamonds that were scattered so deliberately—and so unaesthetically—across his chest, the face of a screaming woman, young, and in her features a hint of Aristos' features. A family resemblance. *Daughter.* She thought it. Knew it for truth.

"His daughter never did anything to harm you. If you had to rape anyone in revenge, why didn't you just rape *him?*"

He dropped her then, as if the words were so contemptible he could no longer bear to hold on to their speaker.

"There's no point, if it's just about power," she continued. "If all power is is something to be gathered, hoarded and abused, you could be just *anyone.* Just any mindless, petty—"

For the first time in all of their years together, Avandar Gallais, the domicis chosen by both The Terafin and Ellerson to serve and protect her, stopped the flow of her words by striking her.

Her lip split; the single blow was harsh and effective. Without another word he walked away, if anything that fast could be called a walk. By the tingling that crept from elbow to finger, she realized how tight his grip had been.

They watched her, made of stone and impervious to something as simple as movement. He had not released them; he would not. She knew it. He would not give them leave to speak or attempt to touch her again.

But she thought she saw, mirrored in the faces that had been turned toward her, the same contempt that Avandar had shown.

Evening of the 7th of Scaral, 427 AA
Outskirts of the Tor Leonne

Kallandras waited in silence.

Margret had vanished the moment he had crossed the periphery that marked her personal space in this emergency encampment. She returned scant minutes later, her gaze dark and unblinking. It never fell on him; not from the moment that he had laid his burden down upon the night-damp grass.

Yollana was not accustomed to being anyone's burden, and showed the poor grace that accompanied such a privilege; he had weathered worse in his time, and merely smiled while her complaints grew louder. And they did grow in volume with every mile that separated them from the plateau of the Tor Leonne.

The woman who came in Margret's wake was a woman Kallandras vaguely recognized; it took him a moment, no more, to place name to face. Donatella, one of the elders—and one of the women who had accompanied the children who had been his first concern. He had grown sentimental with age and time.

The smile that he cast in upon himself was bitter and merciless. He had grown no such thing, although the temptation to believe it *had* become more fierce with time. He had rescued the children because in rescuing Voyani *children,* one incurred the greatest debt, and he would have need of their indebtedness before his sojourn here was done.

No matter. Donatella brought cloth and water—or something that looked like water at a distance. Upon closer inspection it was slightly thicker, its clarity marred by some sort of leaves, some ground powders, which had sunk to the bottom of the stoppered bottle.

They were, theoretically, two outsiders, Yollana and he, but Kallandras left theory to the dominion of the magi; he knew there was only one outsider within the inner circle of this encampment, and he, Kallandras of Senniel College. Kallandras of the Lady's brotherhood. He glanced away from where Yollana sat huddled with the other women. Reached down, unsheathed his weapons. They were not the blades he had trained with; nor indeed the blades that he had broken in the streets of the city scant hours ago.

But they were the blades he had killed with upon the plateau.

These had been a gift, one of the few he had ever deigned to accept for his services, and they were special to him for a variety of reasons, not the least of which was the giver: Meralonne APhaniel, member of the Order of Knowledge, magi, one of the wise.

Where wise, of course, meant something more rarefied and distant than it did in most other venues.

"You mean to go South," the mage had said.

Kallandras had said very little in reply, but that was his way; words were his power, and he used that power sparingly when there was little point. He had no need to be politic in the company of Meralonne, no need to impress; he had no need to influence—and, more to the point, little ability; the member of the Order was strong-willed.

"Who sends you, Kallandras? Solran? Sioban?"

Sioban, as Meralonne well knew, was no longer the bardmaster of Senniel. But Kallandras' lips curved up in a smile, a slight one; the moonlight shadowed and illuminated the curves of his face. "Both," he said quitely. "Although it was, quite properly, Solran's dictate."

"The face of the South is not what it was."

"That is what I am being sent to determine."

Silence. Then, "Has . . . she . . . come to visit you?"

She. Evayne a'Nolan. Meralonne's former student, Kallandras' former master in a fashion. She was a wall between them, a mystery; they each guarded their knowledge of her, although neither man loved her well.

He weighed his words. Shrugged. "Yes."

"You will find the *Kialli* there." Not a question.

"Yes."

"And you will not take me."

At that, for the first time, the bard's voice broke in a small swell of laughter; it was light and quick, a thing to ease the ear and heart. "I would take you in an instant, and you know it. But will you leave? Will you leave a half-god on the verge of collapse, a seer with no knowledge of the South and no defense against the *Kialli* but the strength of her instinct and her inability to ignore it? Will you trust your enemies not to take advantage of the weaknesses that we both see, continually, when we look upon the massing armies?"

The mage's response was typical of him: He snorted and lit his pipe. Embers curled, orange warmth in the darkness that was already a bit too hot. Smoke wafted up in a breeze that neither man thought to control—but that both men could, should they so choose.

They had that in common.

"No," the mage said at last, ringing the air with smoke, with rings that hovered in the serenity of stillness. "You are too clever by half, Kallandras, that's your problem."

"I thought," the bard replied, with exaggerated politeness, "my problem was that I was far too talkative?"

"Well, that, too. In fact, at the wrong times you are far too quiet." The pipe's glow lit the underside of a perfectly smooth chin; Meralonne was one of the few male members of the magi who chose to go beardless, although his hair was long and fine, the envy of young women who rarely had a chance to meet the mage face-to-face, and probably with good reason.

"You did not call me here to tell me what was wrong with me? I assure you, Sioban would be somewhat annoyed to see you poaching in her preserve." Wry grin there.

"No," the mage said, his smile lost to the stem of pipe, and then to the night itself. "I did not call you for that."

There was something in his voice that caught Kallandras' attention. It was meant to; Meralonne was among the most careful of men, and he could hide behind the mask of words more easily than most could hide behind impenetrable fortress walls.

"You think you have something that presents a danger."

"Very good, bard. Master bard. Yes, I do."

"And you wish me to defuse it?"

"In a manner of speaking." He rose, cast a stray glance to the full moon, the high moon, and then said simply, "Follow."

It was a request, of sorts, but one did not lightly ignore the request of the magi, and besides, Kallandras was stirred with a rare curiosity.

Beneath skies so Southern even the breeze felt foreign, free a moment from the memory of the mage's familiar tower, he stared at the blades, wondering about them, about their use, about their manufacture. Wondering just how much Meralonne knew, and how much of that knowledge he had chosen to disclose.

"You will never be fool enough or young enough again to enter the Kings' Challenge," the mage said, "and I will not warn you not to carry these weapons there because I see no need to insult your intelligence."

"That," Kallandras had replied gravely, "has never stopped a member of the magi in the history of the Order that I'm aware of."

Meralonne lifted his lamp. It was odd; a man of his power could light a room without thinking and keep it lit without noticing the strain. But in this tower, in these rooms—or perhaps only for this particular visitor—Meralonne APhaniel chose older, quieter ways. The oil lamp, glassed in and darkened with use. The shadows it cast shifted slightly as the mage said, "Take the daggers."

They lay, simply made, simply sharpened, in a black box.

But the box, which he would have said was ebony at a distance, was something far harder than that; obsidian, cold and heavy as a rich child's casket. He approached the box, and stepped back, almost in a single motion.

"Interesting," the mage said.

"Meralonne, I am not your experiment."

"Not as such, no." The mage shrugged.

"What are these?"

"They are daggers. For the moment. They are weapons."

"And their manufacture?"

"Old," he replied. "The actual forging of the blades themselves is something that has not been attempted since the last of the mad Artisans passed—quite thankfully—from our world."

"*These* are Artisan's work?"

"They are," Meralonne replied, in a voice with the consistency of steel, "the work of the man who once called himself Magellus." He snorted. *"Magellus."*

"It is not so ridiculous a name as all that."

"Not if you're a small child, it's not." He lowered the lamp.

Kallandras shrugged. "He was an old Artisan."

They both knew the fate of the Artisans. "Yes. And I will warn you that he made these at the zenith, not the nadir, of his power."

"They look very . . . plain."

"They do."

"Have you handled them?"

"I? Yes. I have." He was quiet a moment, weighing the words that would follow. "I created the box that contains them now. But it is not a safe containment."

"And I am?"

"Strange though it seems, Kallandras, I would trust the blades in your sheaths far more than I would trust them in my tower—

and I have had in them in my tower since before I could legally claim it as my own."

"You've never thought to give them to me before."

"No. And I would not—but you go South, and I stay North, and I fear that we will not have this chance again."

"Her words?"

The pronoun, said with just the right emphasis, belonged to Evayne a'Nolan, even in this tower. Especially in this tower. There was a long pause, a thoughtful one.

"No; I rarely take advice from my students, regardless of how well they've learned." His gaze was curiously intent; his eyes, silver-gray, flickered with orange lamplight, much as the surface of the blades did. "I will not press them upon you if you've the wisdom to avoid them."

"You make me curious."

"I? No. That is a function of the weapons."

Kallandras reached out then.

Reached out. Touched them. They were cool, steel and leather. "Be ready," he said, although he couldn't have said why.

"I am," the mage replied softly.

He gripped the daggers, left- and right-handed, and pulled them from their resting place.

They *shifted,* writhing in his hands like solid snakes. His grip tightened, where another man might have let go in surprise or shock. There was a battle here, a fight, a contest.

Steel bent itself up in twin arcs, reaching for the backs of his hands. He could not contain them, but he did not cry out; he stared at their bending curves, seeing in them liquid, gold, an iridescence and a magic that were at once familiar and chill. Darkness here; darkness beneath the surface of reflected light.

But he had faced darkness before, and this darkness was contained, girdled somehow by form, by function. The blades edged up, and up again; the tips bent down.

He was surprised when they touched his skin; more surprised when they breached its surface. But he held, and he held calmly, waiting.

They went no farther.

"Meralonne," he said, "these are—"

"Not yet finished," the mage replied. "Watch."

As if he could choose to do anything else. The blades shifted again, undulating and twisting, *growing.* Fascinated by it, awed by it in some fashion, Kallandras watched the conception of a crazed maker as it began its first work in centuries: the fashioning of a weapon. Of two.

Steel melted, but without the heat that would scald or cripple a man fool enough to hold it; leather vanished, absorbed by form. The daggers did what they could not do: they grew in size, in weight, they changed in essential shape, blades lengthening, guards lengthening, handles growing.

He recognized the weapons.

How could he not? They were the brotherhood's weapons of choice when they faced each other, or when the weapons to be used were not prescribed by the men and women who offered the target.

Meralonne said nothing for a long moment. Kallandras stared at his gift. "I . . . see. Kallandras, these present a danger. The magi have not seen them and they will not, I think, approve. Sigurne knows."

"They are?"

"Magellus, as far as we are able to discern, thought he might make use of demons." He offered no more.

Kallandras said quietly, "and will these weapons fight *me* in a fight?"

"Magellus was an Artisan, not a mad mage. They will serve their function."

Kallandras bowed. "I will think long on accepting your gift, Meralonne."

"You will not think at all. You have already accepted the gift, or the weapons would not have changed." The magi bowed. The pipe's embers guttered in a wind that was felt, but never seen. "And now, I am tired, and I have work to do. Take them South with you; you're inventive. You'll know when to use them—and why."

Truth, there.

He *had* known when to use them. And why.

Yollana was injured. Margret saw it from a distance; the old witch would *have* to be injured to allow some man—some strange man, mind, not kin—to carry her into the encampment of a rival family. She was a Matriarch, after all, and she had her pride.

But she was also known for pragmatism, and if she had never been loved for it—what Matriarch was, after all?—she was admired for it, and followed.

Margret left, and returned with Donatella, and when Donatella had finished tending to Yollana's hands and legs—and her legs were a ruin that made the younger woman flinch, first with that momentary pang of recognized pain, and then with anger and a desire for vengeance—she sent Donatella away.

"Matriarch," Yollana said quietly.

"You've heard," was Margret's stark reply. Yollana *knew* that her mother was dead. It shouldn't have surprised her; it did. But worse, it shamed her. Yollana was Matriarch, yes, but she was *Havallan,* and she should not have known first what most of the Arkosans barely knew. Their Matriarch was dead.

She bowed, half to cover the shame that stung her cheeks, and half because this was Yollana of the Havallans.

Of the Voyani Matriarchs, Yollana was the oldest, and the one most feared. Margret was now the youngest; they were theoretically equals, but they did not meet as equals, not here. Although it was Margret's encampment, and although it was Margret's directive that had saved the Arkosans the fate of the Havallan Matriarch, Yollana was a breed apart, and she had come to Evallen on the morn of Margret's birth; had aided in it, as she had known she would have to.

Evallen had some part of the gift, but it was weak; Yollana's was strong enough to need no embellishment. But the two older women had forged a bond that Margret felt, meeting the dark, inscrutable eyes of her elder, she and Yollana never would.

Still, she nodded. "My wagon," she said quietly. "And my tent. Both are yours while you choose to stay with us."

"I want more than that, Matriarch."

"What did you have in mind?"

"Privacy; the Lady's privacy. You can grant it, if you choose—this is your ground, and yours alone."

"You want—"

"I want the heart's circle," Yollana said starkly.

Margret paled. "I—"

"You were trained by Evallen of the Arkosans." Yollana's tone was a slap, stinging and sharp. "You were raised to *be* Matriarch. You are the heart of your people. Falter, for whatever reason, and *they* will pay the price." She drew a deep breath. "I ask you again, Matriarch: draw the heart's circle. We have seen enough this night to know that it is necessary."

"You ask for this in front of a stranger?" Margret replied, changing tactics, attempting to buy herself time.

"This stranger has already seen it; he has already been part of it; I myself cut and carried the blessed wood and drew the sigils. Will you do less?"

"This is not Havalla."

"You're stalling."

Oh, the old woman could be a bitch. She wanted to tell her the truth, then: that she didn't *have* the heart of the Arkosans—that it was hidden in the keep of some highborn clanswoman, given to her by Evallen for reasons that Margret could not begin to understand. But she could not tell her that—not standing outside of the heart's circle. The words would carry on the night breeze, and they would reach every nook and cranny of every wagon before dawn's full light, weakening her.

Just as the angry admission would weaken her. The Matriarchs were responsible for their own, after all—and family wars were not uncommon.

After Nicu's poor display in the streets of the city, she knew that she could not afford to be seen as weak in any way. Ona Tamara knew the truth. Elena knew it as well.

"I'll burn the circle's periphery," she said, struggling to keep the bitterness out of her words, "with heart's fire."

"Good."

CHAPTER TEN

She found wood easily enough; trees lived and died without falling, and the sun turned them into dried husks of former life, meant for burning and not much else. She carried her ax into a night brightened by a nearly full moon; the cutting of wood, time-consuming and menial, was hers. Had to be hers, if the circle was to be hers.

Thus, her mother taught her, and she'd learned.

This is the simplest of our magics, but it's the most valuable one you'll have, day to day. It proves your power, without actually costing much. You'll need it, if I die young.

Only the good, she'd told her mother.

The ax shook in her hands.

She buried it in the fork of the fallen tree's branch. The wood was cut in fury because fury was the only comfort she would allow herself to take; she put her heart into the task, pausing only to set the lamp down on the ground so that her feet didn't become victims of her aim.

Wood splintered cleanly; the ax was sharp, her aim true. This close to the moon's height, the wood had its own power—or so her mother had said—but she knew that without the heart in her hands, wood's power was dim and almost impossible to reach. Wood cut during the phases of the Festival Moon always held the strongest essence, the easiest to touch and invoke; they were the longest nights of the year—for the Matriarch—with good reason. Voyani wisdom.

She gathered the fallen wood, dumped it in the cloth sack, bundled it tightly. The stars watched; she hoped no one else did. The cursing that accompanied the lifting robbed the moment of all dignity.

Made her feel a bit better, though.

In moonlight, she made the trek back from the forest, although forest was a poor choice of word for something so thin. The

Arkosans traveled the heartland's ring; their road crossed the verdant plains of Mancorvo, the dimpling valleys of Averda where forests were so deep and thick they bruised the leg and scratched the face of men made careless by an evening's drink. She missed those forests now; it was there that she had first cut the wood by her mother's side.

Her mother's side, while her mother's hands curled 'round the haft of an ax that had been passed, mother to daughter, since the beginning of time—or so Margret had believed then. The haft itself was plain, dark wood, and it had been replaced several times; it was the wedge of metal, something that never lost an edge and wouldn't condescend to bear a notch, no matter what wood it was set against, that was the heirloom.

That ax had seemed so very much a part of Evallen that night. Everything had: the starlight, the full moon, the night's landscape, the trees themselves. In the darkness you could best make out the living from the dead, the wet from the dry, by smell, by touch. True then, true now. She'd peeled away bark, under her mother's watchful shadow, listening to her mother's sharp criticism and, more rare, her bare, stark praise—the rhythms of a speech that Margret had never thought she'd miss.

She missed it now; missed the nervousness and the wonder of that first night. It had been important to please the Matriarch, more so for the girl who would become the clan's leader than for any other Arkosan, and she'd offered her hands to splinters and calluses, swallowing pain and failure in the search for success.

She swallowed now.

Because at the end of the first gathering, her mother had drawn the heart of the Arkosans out of the folds of her shirt. No one who did not bear Arkosan blood in their veins could see the heart if Evallen chose to conceal it, but even Arkosans could be shunted aside when the Matriarch chose to practice her power in privacy.

That night was one of the few nights that Margret had been granted more than a passing glimpse of the source of her mother's power. *People want other people's power if it's under their noses,* Evallen would tell her. *They can't think of a single good reason why you've got it and they don't. And frankly, most days neither can I. Don't lord it over your own with anything but force of personality unless you have no other choice.* She'd pause, then. *And any daughter of* mine *had better have enough force of personality that it isn't a problem.*

Wasn't a problem, now. She didn't have the heart to expose.

She took the wood to the edge of the small brook that had been the deciding factor in the location of their encampment. Here, she gathered water in a bowl that she had fashioned out of clay with her own hands, had decorated with gold leaf, had painted with dyes that had been one of her mother's more practical secrets. She took a second and a third such bowl out of the folds of her shirt, unwrapping each carefully and setting it down in the clearing, beneath the open face of the Lady's Moon, three points of a triangle, or perhaps three points along the edge of a circle. Into the second bowl, she poured wine, the harvest of vine; into the third, she poured rice wine, the harvest of grain. She dedicated these to the Lady whose Moon lit her way, speaking slowly, trying to put the same passionate plea into the words that her mother had always managed.

It wasn't there. She *knew* it; the heart that defined the Matriarch lay in the grasp of a clanswoman. How was she to continue without it?

Yollana was cruel—but that was part of her character that was known by and to all. It would not be beyond her to set Margret a task that would end in failure because she'd decided that dealing with failure was *also* a test that needed passing.

Was that what this was?

Maybe.

Margret's mother had laid the heart in the center of the three bowls, and it flashed a moment as it lay against earth, the Lady's element, drawing power and granting it. She spoke in a language that was Arkosan to the core—ancient and hidden and shadowed—before she touched forehead to earth. It was the first thing she'd done all evening that had shocked Margret because it looked so much like abasement, and the Matriarch was the source of all power.

Her mother ignored her stiff-jawed open mouth. Lifting the heart, Evallen of the Arkosa Voyani placed the wood where the heartlight still burned the vision. Her prayers lapsed into silence, then, but they continued.

Silence, Margret could manage—although it would have surprised most of the Arkosans who knew her.

I have no heart, she thought, and for just a moment it meant something other than the Matriarch's stone. She did not know as much of the old tongue as her mother had; her mother's learning had been courtesy of Yollana of the Havallans, and it had come in bits and pieces when the Matriarchs met at Moon's height in the Tor Leonne.

I have accepted all responsibility, and I have already begun to fail it. But I will not let that failure break me, Lady. We are not always lucky. The winds howl. The sun burns the shadows into last night's pleasant dream. The clans hunt us, the families war with us. We lost children to the harems and the houses of the powerful, and we endure. We lose our parents long before they've had the time to pass on the truth and experience of their lives, and we endure. We lose our loves, our lovers, our partners, and we endure.

But we die before we abandon the oaths we make with our blood.

I have no heart to bespeak you, Lady, no power to be certain I have your attention. But I have this: and it is of me, part of all that I am, and that my mother was, and that my daughter, when she is born, will be.

I vow, tonight, that we will *endure.*

Margret of the Arkosa Voyani reached a shaking hand to the side of her hip and unsheathed her dagger. She ran it along the fleshy part of her palm, biting carefully enough to draw blood that would run without injuring muscle or reaching bone.

The blood, she offered to earth, at the exact center of the triangle made by the spirits of the Lady's night.

She'd hoped for some flash of light, some recognition of her offer. There was nothing but night and shadow, starlight and moonlight.

Her hand stung as she lifted the wood, block by block, and placed it where her blood had been spilled.

Her head began the long descent to earth, and when it reached the cool, moist dirt of evening forest, she inhaled deeply. Abasement.

Yes, but more: Here, she could smell the dampness and the greenness of the forest floor, the sweet sharpness of wine, the fullness of cut wood, as if they were a part of her. Almost against her will, her back relaxed, and her arms; she fell into the posture of supplicant, completely devoid of the usual powerlessness it implied.

And then, when she had swallowed the whole scent of a forest's peace and the Lady's libations, she emptied the three bowls carefully, taking a sip of each for herself, and offering the rest to the wood.

"All right," she said. She was startled into silence at the sound of her own voice. She slung the wood over her shoulder; it settled there, a comfortable burden—for at least thirty yards. It was a lot longer than that to reach Yollana of the Havalla Voyani.

The peace of the forest hadn't quite left her by the time she reached the wagons and found Yollana and the stranger waiting for her. She nodded to the stranger, and forced herself to bow—wood still slung over her shoulder—to the woman who sat on the ground.

"The circle," Yollana said sharply.

Just as, Margret thought, her mother would have, had her mother been alive.

The last part of the heart's circle was the easiest. She built a fire of normal wood by her own hand; no one offered to help—and she would have been honor bound to refuse any such offer. The fire started quickly enough—a child could start a fire with relative ease, given the right wood—and once she'd built it, she turned to Yollana. "Matriarch," she said, "I offer you the safety and the protection of the Arkosans. Join me by the fire that I have built for your comfort and your safety."

"I accept," the older woman replied gravely, "what only you can offer, Margret of Arkosa." Yollana shifted her weight as if to rise; her face froze completely. That was the Havallan Matriarch through and through; she never shared her pain when it was something as trivial as broken limbs.

Kallandras was by her side in an instant, offering aid without ever giving her a chance to refuse—and she would have, as pride demanded. He carried her into the circle that Margret had offered.

The eyes of the Matriarchs met.

"You, stranger," Margret said, her throat tightening, her body tensing with the wrongness of the words to follow, "we owe the debt of future to. I offer you the safety and the protection of Arkosa. Join me by the fire that I have built for your comfort and your safety."

"I am honored by your offer," he replied gravely, speaking as if he truly understood the honor she conveyed. "And I accept it for the moment."

They took their places by the fire; Margret held back a moment longer, wondering if the circle she'd offered was as much a fraud as she felt herself to be.

*   *   *

"Your hospitality," Yollana said, "makes you one with the Havallans, Matriarch." She did not speak quietly; indeed, she spoke loudly enough that any casual eavesdropper might hear the words. And if they did, it proved that Margret could not even draw the Arkosan circle. Margret wanted to warn her, to caution her to silence, but she could not quite bring herself to expose her own weakness. "And I am in your debt." Ritual, ritual that. But it eased Margret to hear the formality of the tone. Made her feel less the impostor.

"The debt," Margret said, her voice lower, the word less prone to be carried by wind's caprice, "is not mine to accept." She turned, then, to where the stranger stood leaning against her wagon, his profile lit by the orange of a fire that was not quite bright enough to illuminate his expression. "Kallandras of Senniel College brought you to us. He intervened to send our children to safety, and he brought my heir home."

"That much help from strangers," Yollana said wryly, "is *too* much help. And it's costly. I would far rather *you* held the debt, my dear."

"The Arkosans are less of a threat than a stranger with a pretty face and hair a Serra would kill for?" There was a touch of levity in the words.

"The debt of the Arkosans is a debt I understand," Yollana replied gravely. "And that one—he serves the Lady, and he serves the blue witch who comes like a nightmare and a doom." All humor fled her voice; she stared at Margret intently, searching for the jump, the stiffening of features, that spoke of recognition.

Only when she saw them did she continue. "The time is coming," she said quietly, "when all debts are due. Your mother understood this, and she paid the price."

"My mother—" Margret let the silence fold in around her. "Yollana, what is happening on the plateau? What is happening in the city? Have the clansmen gone mad?"

"Worse," Yollana said softly, "and your mother knew the truth of that. They have fostered an alliance that should have become impossible with the birth of the clan Leonne."

"The clan Leonne is dead."

"It is not," Kallandras said, speaking for the first time, "dead. There is a single survivor."

"We've heard of him," Yollana replied, careful now, her voice as neutral as Margret had ever heard it. "And I will say to you that if the rumors that have carried this far to the South are true, he is more than we expected him to be."

"But not," Margret added, following Yollana's studied neutrality as closely as she could, "impressive enough, in the opinion of the Arkosans, to carry the war."

"He is served," Kallandras said softly, "by Ser Anton di'Guivera."

"So," Yollana replied—Margret having temporarily lost her voice—"that rumor *is* true. Is it true that he has fought the creatures of the Lord of Night?"

"You know the answer to that, Yollana, and I will not be trapped in your testing games for another moment."

She smiled. "So be it, then. Yes, I know it for truth. But the Voyani take no sides in the war of one clan against another."

"No," Kallandras said softly, "they don't. But you know, you *must* know, that this war is not that war. I will not lecture you, Yollana, but I have stood at the side of the blue-robed witch, as you call her, and I know as much of your ancient histories as it is safe for one who is not controlled by the *Voyanne* to know. Your captivity must tell you that you are already at war."

"It must, must it?" But she folded her arms across her chest. "Tell me, then, Northern bard. Tell me what is happening in the city."

"Margret, with your permission?"

She started like a wild creature, and then blushed; that made her angry. Shoving her hair out of her face, she almost said, "You need my permission to speak?" But she stopped herself, because it *was* her circle, and she *was* the Matriarch, and technically, as a man who had no blood ties to either of the women sitting in that circle's ring, he *was* required to ask her permission.

She nodded; it was graceless, but it was enough.

Kallandras began to speak, quickly, of the masks of the Festival of the Moon.

She was silent a long time; first, while she listened. Second, after she asked him for details. As if silence were contagious, he caught hers a moment, transforming it by expression and stillness. After he'd accomplished this, he turned to Margret and spoke a word or two. She raised a brow, and then nodded, and he vanished into the cover of starlit night.

"Who is he, Yollana?"

"He is as cursed as any of us. I was . . . intemperate. He serves

Evayne a'Neamis, but he serves her as any of us do: by seeing
the death that she stands in the gateway of, by helping her, in any
possible way, to be the mortar that seals that death out."

"Pretty words," Margret said.

"They are, aren't they? And they impress, where they must.
But they also have the benefit of being the truth. I am not sure
that I like him—"

"You do."

Yollana's smile was a rare, rare gleam of teeth. "Very well,
then, I am sure that I like him, but I am *also* certain it is not the
wise choice. I trust him in this battle, and this battle will devour
my life. It devoured your mother's, and it will work its way
through the older generation of the Voyani before it is at last laid
to rest. But your generation? Yours, I cannot see. He moves at
the bidding of the only woman I have ever met who has found her
way to the first road, and beyond it, to the first seer. Imagine,"
Yollana added softly, reflectively, "being asked to slowly cut off
your own hand, and then use it, always, as your most effective
weapon.

"She has been asked; she has accepted the price. But she is
less whole than I am, than Evallen was, than Kallandras is. I try
to remember that, when I think of what she has cost me. Sometimes it helps."

"It doesn't help me."

"No. I suspect it won't help my daughter either. But there are
choices we make that drive us because they are the *only* choice
we can make. We—ah, never mind. He returns."

He carried with him four masks. Four finished Festival masks.
Margret noted that his hands were gloved, and that he did not
choose to set those masks upon a single blade of grass; instead he
arranged them upon a silk that would separate their clay from the
earth beneath it.

Yollana's frosted brow went up in the darkness; her gaze leaped
from masks to mask—the former, the craft of an unknown worker,
the latter, the completely neutral expression the foreigner wore.
"You are versed," she said quietly.

"I have traveled with the Voyani before," he replied, and if his
face was neutral, it was nothing compared to his voice.

"We do not give our secrets away so lightly."

He shrugged. "Knowledge," he said, "is often a thing that slips
between closed fingers. It is more like water than gold; it cannot
be held."

Yollana laughed; Margret was shocked. It was a Voyani saying. "And will I say, in return, that only a fool displays his riches in two cupped palms?"

"Indeed." This unknown Kallandras relented, offering a smile to the oldest of the Voyani Matriarchs. "But will you pardon me if I do not then fall into a discourse about the nature—and the power—of the fool?"

"I will pardon you," Yollana replied, "and challenge you, Northern wise man. When the time comes, and we can sit in a circle wider and deeper than this, you will sing your discourse and I will speak mine, and we will have witnesses who will decide which of us—you or I—better evokes the Lady's truth."

"I will accept that offer, Yollana, if only because I know how stubborn you are: Once you've offered a challenge, nothing will stop you from taking it up—not even the threat of death."

Her smile was fond, a momentary self-indulgence as she met the smoother face, the prettier eyes. "You go straight to my head."

But they both saw the steel beneath her smile; they judged for themselves the truth of her words.

"The masks, Matriarch."

"Indeed."

She reached for the first of the masks that Kallandras had so carefully arranged. Her hands hovered above it, fingers delving into the eyeholes, the places where breath passed mouth and nose. Her palms passed above the swell of simple cheek, pausing a moment over the tip of chin, the anonymity of nondescript forehead, a nose that could have been anyone's nose, and yet had its own distinct shape. Delicate in seeming, it seemed to draw the hand.

She did not touch it.

The second mask was a half-mask, a thing that covered eyes and forehead and nose. Like the first, it suggested anonymity; it blended elements of the first mask, but made them somehow more workaday. She paused. "Are they evenly distributed?"

Margret frowned. "Pardon?"

The Matriarch's gaze slid past her to Kallandras.

"I do not know," was his quiet reply, but he drew breath, and he continued, "but I believe they are indeed evenly distributed."

She frowned.

"You would have guessed otherwise?"

But she had gone back to her work; the dance of hands in the air above the clay masks changed in tone and texture as she reached the gaudily colored leather hide. The movements became jerkier, lost all echo of caress, of fascination.

She worked in silence. She asked no questions. But her hands lingered longest over the third mask, and when they left, it seemed to Margret that she had to tear them away.

The fourth mask, then: the gaudiest, the richest, the most unusual. It was shaped of clay, as the first two had been, but it was not shaped with a human face as a model; it was almost birdlike in its extension—but its ferocity was its own. Clansmen wore masks such as these. Rich ones, or powerful ones.

Even at the height of the Lady's Moon, Margret could feel power.

"Yes," Yollana said faintly.

"Do you know what they are, Yollana?"

"Masks," she said at last.

Margret grimaced. "Thank you. I meant—"

"Will they be worn?"

"That is the edict and the intent," the Northern bard replied. His gaze was leveled at her as if it were a crossbow.

"No," she said softly. "It is not Voyani magic, if that's what you've been hoping to hear."

"I hope for very little, Yollana. Information, however, would be valuable."

"As in, whose magic?"

"As in," he nodded gravely.

Thought had taken her where healing could not; she started to stand, to pace the periphery of the fire's circle, to cast her shadows back. But her legs had been scored and injured, and were it not for the interference of the bard—again—she would have fallen.

She said, at last, "I don't know."

He heard it: In the voice, in the tremor beneath the surface of the words itself. He couldn't see beyond it; couldn't catch the current. Yollana was canny; she was as aware of his power as one not schooled in the North could be, and she could deflect it.

But twisted 'round the three words she had spoken were words that she could speak and preferred not to, and they held knowledge. Not certainty—that, he would have heard—but fear.

She was afraid that she knew the answer to his question.

Unblinking, her eyes met his in the darkness.

"You will take word," she said, "to my people. They are

camped—much as the Arkosans are camped—outside of the city. If they weren't fools." The momentary irritation promised dire consequences if they were, and given her shifting mood, he almost pitied them.

"I will carry word for you, if that is your desire." He paused delicately, considering his next words, his next offer. "I will carry *you,* if you will permit it."

"They'll be skittish enough, thank you. They won't want to see their Matriarch in the arms of a pretty foreigner." She laughed. "All except the young girls and boys; they'll think it's romantic. Even at my age."

Margret snorted. "You aren't old enough to play the age card, Yollana."

"Aye, maybe not. But I like to try it every once in a while. No, Kallandras of the North, I ask you to carry word—and I will give you the signs by which my word will be known—but with the permission of the Matriarch, I will stay with the Arkosans for a time." She paused. "I intend," she added softly, "to send the Havallans back to my daughters."

"But—" Margret bit back the words.

Kallandras was no fool; he saw the significance of the gaze that passed between them.

"I—we—would be honored."

He almost laughed then, but it was not his way; he *did* chuckle.

The two women turned to stare at him at the same moment, the gesture almost identical. "You must forgive me," he said quietly. "I have traveled, as I said, with the Voyani—and I cannot think of many who would willingly journey at the side of not one but *two* Matriarchs." He laughed. "There is a phrase about two Matriarchs and a war—"

"There is also," Yollana said, with a chill that only the far North could embody, "a phrase about the wisdom of offending *a* Matriarch."

"Ah." He bowed, the smile firmly attached to his face. "But there is also the truth of expedience, and I have not yet delivered your message."

Margret laughed. "But you deliver no message for *me.*"

"No, Matriarch," he said, and the smile did slip away from his face as he turned toward the plateau. "But I know where your heart lies."

Silence then. The crackle of fire and snapping log, the breeze of a cool, cool night.

Mikalis di'Arretta rose. The Widan Sendari di'Sendari and the Sword's Edge were waiting in the open courtyard before which lay the bodies of the fallen, and beside them, stiller than the corpses of the dead, the man who had taken the crown for himself, and now waited to lay claim to the Sun Sword: Alesso di'Alesso, the Tyr'agar.

But beyond them, beyond the confines of the building which housed the Sword's Edge and the studies of the Sword's Edge— the shadows were *strong*. He was frightened, and he had walked the long and the deadly road to become Widan so that he might *also* become a man of power and escape fear's grip. A fool's dream; he realized it the day he was elevated to Widan after years of struggle—and hours of it.

But he had not understood then that his struggles would bring him to the heart of his fears, and expose him in a way that not even the Lady's harshest nightmares could. He had thought to learn ancient ways, to walk ancient roads, to better understand the whole of the Dominion's ancient history. That had been his moonlight prayer from his earliest memory to his latest.

But this, this was too much knowledge.

"Mikalis?"

He bowed at once, gravely. "Sword's Edge." Bowed again, no less gravely. "Tyr'agar." By small gestures, he made it clear that he was not comfortable in the presence of such illustrious men, and by small gestures, they accepted that lack of comfort as their natural due.

Only Sendari watched with narrowed eyes.

"Tell us."

"I . . . am not certain. I cannot be certain, you understand this? The magic here is not my magic, it is not a thing of my making, a thing I could imitate." The frustration in his voice was genuine.

"I doubt," Cortano said quietly, "that it is a magic that any of us could imitate. I accept this; you are not being tested by the steel, Mikalis. You are here for your opinion and the intuition that you may have developed in your travels with the Wanderers."

Mikalis bowed again. When he straightened out, he left hesitancy behind. "The magic that destroyed the inner and outer room was—and of this I am certain—Widan's magic. I would say it bears your mark, Cortano."

"Oh?"

"It is too powerful and too sudden to be almost anyone else's, and it is of the fires. These are also known to be your personal chambers; I doubt the Sword of Knowledge combined could lay such a spell in your domain without your instant knowledge."

The Sword's Edge nodded. "Continue."

"These," he said quietly, turning to look at the fallen, "were not the work of your magic. And here," he continued, turning away from the corpses as if the sight of them burned—and it did—"in the outer chamber, there is a hint of a magic that almost feels like our magic but . . . isn't."

Two sets of eyes narrowed immediately. Sendari and Cortano exchanged a glance. The silk of Sendari's simple, fine robe rippled as his shoulder rose and fell in a shrug. "I told you," he said quietly, "I am not as sensitive. I know the Voyani artifacts—such as they are—and their uses, *if* I have seen them before. But this—this is not my dominion."

Cortano nodded; it was what he expected to hear. "What would you say it is, or was?"

"I would say," he said quietly, "that it was the element freed from the magic that binds it." His hands moved across the air in an elegant gesture that seemed to take in that air itself, to mold it, to call it. "Here," he said softly.

"Yes." Cortano's single word was succinct. "You've seen as I've seen; the air is . . . unsettled." His pause was loud because it was almost hesitant. Almost. "Can you tell me what the air did?"

"Not with certainty." The scored and scorched wood grain beneath his feet—wood that had once been perfectly chosen, perfectly stained, perfectly polished and tended—held more of his interest as he made his admission of ignorance than floors generally did for Widan. "But I would say it carried at least one, and possibly as many as four, through the fires of your own power."

"Unscathed."

"It would appear so." He knew what Cortano would ask for next, and he strongly desired to avoid it. So strongly that he turned without permission to see the open skies beyond the personal chambers of the Sword's Edge. To seek the Lady's Moon, her face still shadowed and veiled, her power coming into its zenith as she approached the Festival that, in the Dominion of Annagar, signaled the one night of true freedom any man knew.

But that was Festival Night; this was a night, like and unlike any other; power dictated, less power obeyed.

"The bodies, Mikalis?"

He could not avoid them, then.

No spell of preservation had been placed upon them; the Sword's Edge desired—rightly and intelligently—to contaminate them with no foreign magic. Not until they had been thoroughly studied, thoroughly examined. But although the Lady's Festival occurred at the coolest time of year, it was never that cool in the Tor Leonne; the bodies had stiffened and then relaxed, and those parts of them that had been laid open with such casual violence—for it seemed, to Mikalis, that they had had little time to prepare for defense, let alone defend themselves, against whatever force had chosen to attack them—had already begun to decline.

He recognized two of the men. No, he recognized all of them, but two he had considered—inasmuch as any Widan considers another Widan to be so—friends. Men whose search was similar enough to his own that he might be unguarded in his zeal and his enthusiasm from time to time. They were, neither of them, from the High Court; nor was he. The manners of the Court confounded them all, embarrassed them at times, made them aware of their deficiencies. Magic was easy; politics was death. How many times had they said that, and laughed or smiled bitterly?

He had not counted. It was over, that easy camaraderie. He was left with death, and the order of the Sword's Edge. It made him wish—Lady knew it, even if he would never utter the words where she might hear them—that he had never set foot upon the *Voyanne,* for the dust of that bloodstained road now carried the name Mikalis di'Arretta, and he *knew* what his duties were.

He knelt, not beside a friend, but beside a headless corpse. He had studied the dead many times, and as he stilled his breath, he found his center, found the distance that had always served him well in the past. He placed his hand on the ruined, clawed chest. Closed his eyes.

Lady, he thought. *Lady, guide me. Give me a sign. Grant me your wisdom.*

His hands burst into flame.

Had he been any other man, he would have cried out at the shock of it, but he had faced flame before and emerged—as they all must, who have been tested by the Wind and the Wind's guardian—*Widan.* He held his tongue, held his shock, let that shock turn into something else in the temper of the fire: determination. Knowledge.

The fires did not burn him; after the shock of first heat, he spoke the words of the triad and they melted to either side of his skin as if the skin of a man who could speak the three were anathema.

He rose. Cortano's eyes were as black as the night sky that knows no dawn. No one asked him what he had found; he circumnavigated their perfectly still forms as if they were statues, some perfectly chiseled, well-placed stones around which he *must* pass to find truth. To find their truth.

The next man, then.

The next.

The next.

All burned at the touch of his hands, the taint of his magic. For he, Mikalis di'Arretta, had indeed walked the *Voyanne,* and he had seen the shadows that waited by road's edge. They taught him of those, when they would teach him nothing else, because the shadows were the enemy of *all* men, and not merely the Voyani. No private quarrels existed when the Lord of Night rose.

Was it true?

In the eyes of the Lord, private quarrels *were* all that existed, and strength was the test of the Lord's favor. Lose or win; that was his judgment. Day, Night—did it make a difference? Men with power fueled men with less power; the weak died, in either case.

Ah. The last body. The last.

He hovered a moment above it, knowing that once he had finished here he would face the men who ruled the realm. He had no desire to do so; no way of avoiding the task. Power had been granted him in his life, but it was never *enough* power.

In the search for enough, a man might do many, many things. He bent; his robes brushed dried blood and rent skin; his hand hovered a moment above gaping throat, wide, sightless eyes. It was almost a matter of compulsion with him, to leave those eyes open. As if the dead could bear witness to the crimes of the living.

The fires came. He expected no less.

They came in a pillar, in a column that spoke of blistering heat and scorched earth, of death as the only rightful dominion of the element.

They had been taught thus: let the elements take control and death *is* their only dominion. Fire will scorch you and water will drown you; earth will suffocate you and air—ah, air was the wind itself, and no one who lived in the Dominion of Annagar could doubt the howling fury of the winds. Even when they were gentle—even then—a wise man questioned the seedlings that they brought as gifts for another season.

"Sword's Edge," he said, his living eyes trapped a moment in the thrall of dead ones.

"Widan."

"My examination is complete."

"Are you prepared to discuss your findings, or is there work to be done before the results are clear?" Ritual, that. Performance.

"I am prepared to discuss the preliminary magics I believe to be at work—pending, of course, the results of subsequent study and possible correction." He did not want to rise; he did not want to remove his hand from the skin of a dead man. The dead, for a moment, were an anchor, and once he left them behind, he would drift away. Into the shadows, where men waited.

But the shadows, men or no, also waited; the Lady watched. He had trained all his life to uncover the knowledge that granted him power, and with that power came, if not notoriety, than at least reputation; he could not step past the name he had with such cursed pride made for himself. He rose, lifting his hand. Letting the dead go.

Lord knew there would be more of them, and in far greater numbers; after all, rumor had it that the new Tyr'agar would *finally* declare his war against the North at the Festival's height. It was not that war which concerned him, although it intrigued him because it so obviously involved the Sword's Edge, a man seldom given to the intricacies of the realm political when magic itself was not involved.

It was *this* war. These dead. This Festival. Those masks.

He bowed to the Tyr'agar, and then, as deeply but not more so, to the Sword's Edge. "These men," he said softly to the man who ruled his Order, wielding it as if it were the weapon after which he was named, "were not killed by a magic that you or I are capable of wielding. Here, and here," he added, bending at the knee without actually kneeling, "are the killing blows, and the killing blows themselves bear the taint of—"

"Yes, Mikalis?"

"Of the creatures that we would best know as demons." He had been about to call them something else: *Leonne's Wyrd.* He hoped that his lapse had in no way been obvious; it was a mistake that a lesser man would pay for with his life. He did not dare a glance at the Tyr'agar.

"And you say this because?"

"You know well why I say it," he replied, his voice as sharp as the Sword's Edge. "You summoned me for the knowledge that I might have gleaned in my passage through the Dominion at the side of the Voyani. This—this rudimentary spell—is one of the few they would willingly teach me; it is a spell that they teach to anyone who has the capability of learning it. Simple detection."

"And you are certain that you are detecting what they've chosen to tell you you're detecting?"

Cortano was silent. Sendari, silent as well, had the grace to wince as the man he served, both as adviser and ally, waited for the answer to a question that no Widan would ever ask. Significant, to Mikalis, that neither man moved to enlighten the Tyr'agar; significant as well that the Tyr'agar did not know enough of magic's practice to render the question meaningless.

He blunted the edge in his voice. Bowed, letting his knee hit the ground as his chin clipped his chest. "Tyr'agar," he said, the title heavier for the respect with which he chose to burden those three syllables. "No Widan—not especially one who has studied under this particular Sword's Edge—is capable of casting a spell whose nature he does not clearly understand. Our magic is a magic of precision."

"Granted," the Tyr'agar replied, unfazed. "But the Voyani magic is said to be," and he paused to take in the breadth and the rich, quiet darkness of the clear night sky above them all, "a thing of night and shadow, a gift of the Lady's, a power of *intuition.*"

"The Voyani are also said to be able to see the future, and they fleece the young and the old alike on the strength of that belief when they travel through our cities." Thankfully, it was Sendari who replied. Sendari, whose voice was as dry as desert night, but less chill.

Of the three men gathered, he understood Sendari best and least. A ripple creased the former General's brow; it left the shadow of displeasure across the whole of his face, although Mikalis would have been hard pressed to say why; this Try'agar was a more cunning man than the last one had been; he gave *nothing* away.

"Very well. The Voyani magic, then, has much in common with the Sword's?"

"It has enough in common that we can learn much of what they teach, and they, much of what we do."

"And did you trade our knowledge for theirs, Widan?" Now he spoke with an edge in his voice to rival Cortano's. Mikalis stiffened, glad for a moment to be on his knees: it made taking a step back impossible, and the step back would have been the greater gaffe.

"I traded *my* knowledge, Tyr'agar, and at that, the knowledge was not magical in nature."

"Oh?"

"I aided them in a matter of folklore, an area of study which has often led me to discoveries more germane to the Sword of Knowledge, and the Sword's Edge, than a more direct approach would." He stood slowly, unbending at knee and neck. "And, in turn, they offered me two spells." His glance grazed Sendari's; their eyes met. Between Widan it was understood that no man of power *ever* exposed the full extent of his knowledge; secrecy preserved power. He wondered if the Tyr'agar would view the . . . omission . . . should it come to light, as a lie. Wondered what kind death he would be *granted*, if that were so. "Two. One, they said, was a minor protection against their ancient enemy, and the other, a detection of that enemy's residual magic. The latter spell can be used as I have used it, but I believe that it is more commonly used to cleanse the corpse of taint than it is to determine the nature of the creature that caused the death. In fact, I would hazard a guess that the Voyani would not think of using the spell as a confirmation of a suspicion, or as a tool of detection; they would feel no such need because—"

The Tyr'agar raised a hand. The gesture stemmed the flow of words that might otherwise have continued for at least the quarter hour, and it evoked the evening's first smile across the face of the Lord of the Dominion. "You are, indeed, one of the Widan," he said softly. "And I have never been a man with enough patience to listen to the minutiae that rules the Widan's life. This spell is a spell to cleanse a corpse."

"Or an object, yes—although that object must be an object that has been casually handled or affected by the creature in question; it cannot be one of the creature's manufacture—such a spell as I have worked tonight would not be up to the greater task."

"What, exactly, does it cleanse the . . . object . . . of?"

He froze a moment. Took a deep breath, tasted the night air as it passed his lips.

"The demon darkness," he said at last. "The shadows of the Lord of Night."

Mikalis was certain, as he watched a different darkness settle into the harsh contours of the Tyr'agar's face, that there were shadows just as unpleasant, and just as deadly, as the shadows that had killed the men whose bodies he studied.

CHAPTER ELEVEN

Alesso did not ask for confirmation of Mikalis' information. He did not, in fact, ask any further questions. Sendari counted to himself beneath the silence of a quiet sky. When he reached a full twenty, the Tyr'agar bowed to both the Sword's Edge and the Widan who had given them all information of value.

He nodded to Sendari.

A world separated the formal bow and the casual nod; Sendari had been, by that simple gesture, summoned; Cortano and Mikalis, by full bow, dismissed. The Sword's Edge did not appear to find the gesture offensive; he, too, had the look of barely hooded anger about the cast of his features.

They repaired to the Lake for which the Tor Leonne was so justly famous, standing not upon one of the many platforms that had been built for the pleasure and privilege of viewing the moon—or the waters—at night, but rather to the edge of the water itself, on the eastern side of the Lake, where rushes were allowed to grow so that they might catch lilies and make a statement about cultivated wilderness that Sendari and Alesso understood well.

Their lives were here. On a night like this one, they had crossed the boundaries that separated the clansmen from the rulers, and they had stood, two men without attendants, by waters that lapped reeds and shore, speaking of death, of the will to kill, of the desire for power that did not demand the clan-crime of murdering their respective kai.

They had come far, these two.

Sendari bowed to the face of the Festival Moon. He did so automatically, the bend of body in a gesture of respect as natural as breath. Alesso, as always, waited; he was not a man who had ever granted the Lady her due, and as such, his respect was not expected, its lack no slight to her.

After the silks had stopped swaying in an echo of his motion, the Widan cast, speaking to wind, to water, to earth, and to fires that burned upon a distant pavilion. He trapped his own words in an envelope of magic that separated his friend and himself from the rest of the Tor; tested the casement that held them. After a moment, poised just so, he nodded.

"Well?" Alesso said quietly, aware of what that barely conscious nod meant.

"I am not the politician," Sendari replied. "That has always been your role, and Cortano's."

Alesso laughed. "So you claim. So you consistently claim. But *you* are Sendari di'Sendari, and he is as he has always been. Come, Counselor. I am in need of your advice."

Sendari might have snorted, but the deaths of the Widan cast long, dark shadows, and he had no desire to dishonor their new memory when their spirits—or so it was commonly held—hovered in breeze and wind, seeking, seeing, listening to voices that distance and wall and earth kept from their living bodies. "Will you take any advice that you ask for?"

"I will, as always," his friend replied, in a tone heavy with irony, "consider and weigh each precious word carefully."

"And singly, thus depriving them of their aggregate meaning, no doubt."

He was rewarded by laughter, although it was brief. It made him wonder how often he had heard the laughter of the previous man who had worn both Crown and Sword by the edge of the Lady's Lake. The dead kai Leonne had been a cruel and dour man.

"As you say, old friend."

"It *is* a moon night."

"The Lord has ruled my life; it is not my way or my whim to beg for the favor of a woman who might just as easily smile as frown; might just as easily grant me my desire and drown me in the waters that bear Her name. The Lord, a man understands. But women?" He laughed; the laughter was as sharp as the edge of his blade. "I will not ask the Lady for Her intervention."

"You will pardon me if I am not so . . . proud."

"I will, indeed, pardon you for any perceived plea you might make. But you are who you are and I, I am Alesso." His smile stripped the years from his face, or rather, it made the years ineffectual; it was the same smile, the same expression, that had so often attracted men and women alike, from the day that Sendari— no Widan then, but merely a seeker of knowledge and truth—and

Alesso had first met. Sendari had not been proof against it; was not proof against it now; there was an easy power there, if one knew power on sight. An easy power, and more: loyalty. To invoke it, on the other hand, was as easy as gaining the ear of the Lady; Sendari had it, but could not clearly say why.

It was the gift of Alesso's presence that the Widan never questioned that loyalty, or the friendship that had been tested by winds and fire over the years. Never questioned, no—but he had tested it, and Alesso had replied in kind. What they had built endured.

"What advice would you have me give?"

"What game, Sendari? What game are they playing?"

The Widan shrugged. "It is to discover the answer to that question that we have been working these past weeks."

"No, you have been working to discover *how* they will play their hand, if they choose to play it. The masks are weapons, no more, no less. I want you to turn your mind to the game itself."

"They play at games of power, Alesso. You are the Lord's man. What power will they gain by turning against us? Perhaps they have managed to damage the Northern Imperials in such a way that they no longer need to wage a good war."

"And they turn to us?"

Sendari shrugged. "The Widan were killed protecting one of the Voyani. She is gone—and the spells Cortano used to track her presence have been shattered like Northern glass. They were costly spells," he added, almost as an afterthought.

"And the *Kialli* chose this night to take the Voyani out of the custody of the Sword's Edge?" His eyes *were* the sword's edge, narrowed to death's sharpness. "And they gain from this how?"

"I do not know. I confess I find the maneuver surprising." He shrugged. Fell into silence for a moment, as if silence were a lake, and Alesso's questions the sun's height. At last, he said, "Or perhaps they do not realize that we are able to ascertain the extent of their involvement."

Alesso froze. Sendari watched his face; saw the lines of it shift and alter. "If they gain power here," he said, "what will they do with it? Will they grant the Dominion to another man?"

Rhetorical question; he knew it by the tone and texture of the words conveyed. He did not reply.

"Cortano?"

"It was not Cortano's work; if I can be certain of anything, I am certain of that. The Sword's Edge is adept at both the Widan's art and political machination—but he does not easily cast aside his own. Had the dead men been of less value, and less proven loyalty, I would concede the possibility."

"Good."

Silence, broken rhythmically by the lapping of water against reed stalk and lily. At last, Sendari said a single word.

"Kinlord."

And Alesso nodded. "But which one? Which one? They can wear the Crown—but they cannot claim either Lake or Sword." He grimaced. "They are here, of course. We are probably observed."

"We are observed," Sendari agreed casually. "At a distance of perhaps fifty yards, perhaps a hundred; there is a magic at work that is at the edge of my ability to detect, but only barely. Whoever observes us is clever and well-trained."

"Cortano's?"

"I do not think so; there is a taint to the magic that I have seen only in the Shining Court."

"Only there?"

His brow creased, folding into the familiar lines that more than age and wind had worn there. "There and perhaps in one other place: The artifacts of the Voyani. The vest that was the gifting of Baredan di'Navarre."

"It comes back to the Voyani. Men and women who have barely been considered more valuable than bandits suddenly become the focal point of far too much interest."

"I want *answers*, Sendari."

The Widan raised a single, frosted brow.

It was when she saw the sword that her expression folded in on itself, swallowing darkness; becoming, for a moment, a mask that Margret herself stepped back from. Almost, but not quite, breaking the circle she'd called for. She was well enough taught to freeze in mid-stride, to plant her foot solidly back on safe ground, to draw sigil in air laden with the smoke of blessed wood. But that was all she offered, that and silence.

Kallandras the stranger—she would always think of him that way, and he would give, in the end, new meaning to the word stranger; she *knew* it, then, but did not know how—said nothing, returning silence for silence, and in the same measure. He waited; he was, she thought, good at waiting.

"Where," Yollana said at last, "did this sword come from?"

"It came," Kallandras replied, as her midnight eyes met his and granted him—indeed demanded—speech, "from the hands of one of the Arkosan Voyani."

"Not possible."

Margret flinched. "Matriarch—" she began, but Yollana lifted a hand, imperiously demanding silence.

"It is truth," Kallandras replied evenly. "And I would not so easily dismiss any claim to the contrary. The Matriarch's heir," and he placed a distinct emphasis—not a comforting one—on the word *Matriarch,* "was present; it was her hand that lifted the fallen blade and prevented its return to the man who wielded it. No," he added, as Yollana's expression shifted and fell, "she did not touch the blade or the hilt with exposed skin; she took care. She is no fool."

Yollana closed her eyes, cutting off all conversation. "We should have had this conversation under the open sky," she said, when her lids lifted again.

"Or not at all." He nodded quietly. "What will you do with it?"

"I? It is not in my keeping; it is not my responsibility."

He lifted a golden brow—although the shadows and the fires robbed it of color, or lent it a false one; hard to say which was truth. "No? And you have sent your people to your daughters for some other reason?"

"Clever man." Her smile was thin. "Very well; I do not know *what* you know, Kallandras of Senniel, but I know that you know too much. It is a dangerous combination; it makes me careless."

His smile was as brief and sharp as her own. "Yollana, you will forgive me if I doubt—and strongly—that you understand what the word careless means."

She shrugged. "*I* was the one in captivity, stranger."

"Granted." He bowed. "If the Matriarch consents, I will break her circle; I will leave you to your conversation and your privacy."

"And you won't listen in?"

He met her gaze full on, which said more about him than almost anything else Margret had yet seen; most of the Voyani would have shunted their gaze left or right after half a second. Yollana's eyes were sharp and harsh, something best not confronted. She saw far too deeply, far too quickly; she took, when she looked at you like that, and you gave—whether or not you wanted to.

But Yollana had called him Evayne's servant—or pawn—and a man who served *that* one had probably given more than any of the Voyani who fell under Yollana's sight and stayed pinned there. He didn't flinch.

"No, Yollana of the Havallan Voyani, I will not listen in. You have my word, but if my word is not enough—and it should not be, in these troubled times, let me offer you another truth: The circle itself has been drawn with real power this night." He bowed to Margret. "You have the heart of the Voyani, and if it is distant, it is still yours. Release me, and I will return to the night."

Margret heard his words. Between pleasure and sudden terror, her face remained as masklike as his own. She *had* performed the ritual that she'd learned at the side of the only woman—in her opinion—fit to rule Arkosans; she *was* Matriarch; the Lady had heard her pleas and filled the hollow gesture with the water of life: heart's blood.

But this stranger, this Kallandras, also spoke openly of the loss of the Arkosan heart, and if he spoke his words of muted praise to her, he spoke them in front of Yollana as well. Words seldom failed her; they failed her now. Her mother had always said that the texture of a silence was significant.

Still, she wasn't her mother; she'd turned to look at Yollana's face before she could stop herself. Some people's mouths ran away with them; with Margret it was always her actions.

Yollana met her gaze without flinching; without blinking. But she waited until Kallandras of the North had stepped carefully across the threshold of Margret's circle before speaking. Voyani moonlight in her eyes, and shadows cast by Margret's fire, made of her face a foreign landscape; she looked *old,* some edifice hollowed by wind and sand until it was thin and worn. Wisdom and experience had always been the cards granted for the youth taken away; the Matriarchs had been living proof of that for all of Margret's life.

All of her young life, and she recognized that truth for the first time, staring at Yollana's bleak face.

"Aye," the older woman said, "I know, Matriarch. That's why I'm staying. And *he* knows, or she'd never have sent him to you."

Margret returned silence. She turned away. "Did my mother tell you?" she asked, striving to keep the bitterness from her voice. Failing. "Did she tell everyone but me?"

"Does it matter?" Yollana's sharp voice. "She's dead. She paid the price. Or did you have another one in mind?"

That stung. "I'd forgotten you could be such a bitch."

"Your problem." Yollana's voice was mild; there was no anger or censure in it. "Think outside of yourself for a minute, Margret. I've faced what you've faced. We all have, sooner or later. We've just been lucky enough not to have to face it on the eve of—" The words stopped; the wall of Yollana's lips broke them. "You've proved yourself here, with the fire.

"Never think that the obvious power is the *only* power, Matriarch. You have your aunts and your heir; you have your uncles. You have your cousins, their children, their parents. They *are* Arkosa. Are you afraid you'll fail them? Good fear. Worthy fear.

"Learn to live with it.

"You'll defend your family with your life—with more than your life, with resources that you won't know you've got until they're standing with someone else's dagger at their throats. *That's* all that's asked of you, that and that you bear daughters that will take the name and the duty when you've passed on.

"She was proud of you. Proud enough, certain enough, that she took the risk of leaving you in shadow while she stepped into the Lord's light."

Margret turned slowly to face her, to face this woman who gave a grandmother's advice. "Matriarch," she said at last, her anger muted. "If she trusted me so well, why did she tell you? She must have hoped you would watch out for me, and step in when I faltered."

"Would you have me betray her confidence?"

"Yes."

Yollana chuckled. "Spoken," she said wryly, "like a daughter."

"You aren't going to tell me." It wasn't a question.

"No. Because while she would forgive me the betrayal, in the end, *I* would not. She is dead; respect is the only thing she has now." The smile was there in the lines that framed her eyes and lips, even when it left her face. "But we have things to discuss before the fires burn low enough that others might hear us.

"The sword, Margret."

"It is—"

"Yes."

Her power was so impressive. She had not pulled the pendant from the chain or otherwise called its power and knowledge, and she *knew* the sword. Margret herself felt uneasy when the weapon cast shadow over her hands, but Yollana's shadows were the darkness of knowledge.

"Yollana?"

"I have seen such a sword as this," Yollana said, bitterly. "I have touched it, with these hands. It burned, and I bear the scars." Her eyes were darker than the paling night sky. "You are Matriarch in title, and it is your blood-right and your responsibility, Margret. I diminish none of that when I say this: You are not Matriarch in fact until you have crossed the sands as the heart of Arkosa. There are things that I cannot speak of with you until you are tested."

"Tested?" She bridled. "By whom? You? The other Matriarchs?" Her voice rose; it grated as it climbed and she forced it down as if it were Ona Donatella's worst healing brew.

"By Arkosa," Yollana said softly. "But it is my personal experiences that I cannot yet speak of; I am old and I wander."

Margret snorted, but she could no longer deny Yollana her right to claim age as a refuge.

"The sword was not fashioned by smiths; it was fashioned by magic, in forges that were old when the cities were built, and older still when they fell. It is said that they grant the gift of ability to a warrior, but never without cost. They were a gift to such warriors in times past."

"They are . . . demonic?"

"No. They were meant to be wielded by men."

"Yollana—"

"You will know it all, Margret. All."

"But not now."

"Now," she said softly, "we have a larger problem. There is only one place that I have ever seen such a sword; only one place where *you* will, in your time. Not a single one of those swords have been taken from either Havalla or Arkosa—I would bet my family's life, and yours, on it.

"That leaves us with a problem. Either Corrona or Lyserra have weakened, which is problematic at best, or—" and she turned her eyes to the fire's heart as she spoke, "the time has come when the forges that first created the ancient weapons have been refired, and we will see war."

"I'm about ready to see war," Margret said grimly.

"That," Yollana replied, "is because you have never crossed

the desert as Matriarch." She lifted a hand to forestall Margret's reply. "Yes, you've crossed the desert, but you've crossed it as her daughter. The secrets that we *can* teach our own, we teach. This is not one of them.

"Keep the sword, Matriarch. Keep it in the hands of either yourself or your heir. And be aware that the hand that has held the blade and blooded it is a hand that will seek the weapon."

I gave him an order, Margret thought; she said nothing. Because she couldn't be certain that that order meant anything to the Arkosan cousin of whom she was so fond.

"What do you do," she asked quietly, "when your kin won't follow your orders?"

"When the orders are serious?"

Margret raised a brow. "All of my mother's orders were serious; she didn't waste breath otherwise."

"Fair enough; I natter when I'm thinking; I order them about. Soothes my nerves. Of course, some of them are stupid enough to listen to every word I say when I'm nattering. But that's their problem, and it's an easy question. The most important thing to the family *is* the family. The Matriarch embodies that."

"Yes, but I—"

"I kill them."

It would have helped Margret if she could have believed—for even a moment—that Yollana of the Havalla Voyani was lying.

As if she could hear that thought, the older woman said, bleakly, "It's a test we all face, daughter of a Matriarch. And we pass it, or our daughters or sisters rule in our stead. Do you understand?"

But she couldn't answer, not easily; she was caught on the edge of a childhood's slender memory, and it cut.

Yollana faded into a grim silence; their eyes met.

"Evallen trained you well, but you're still very young, Margret. And now, right now, youth will kill you. Do you understand that? It will kill you, and expose the heart of Arkosa to anyone who seeks to injure it."

She nodded.

"You're thinking of your first death."

"An uncle," she said quietly. "Just that. An uncle. I don't remember him well." A lie. She remembered three things clearly: first, that he had stolen fragments of the festive cake for her four-year-old mouth, although it had been strictly forbidden, and had perched her on his lap while she babbled with pleasure at the gift. Second, that he had struggled and screamed and pleaded six months later, two days after her fifth birthday, when the Matri-arch's men had come to take him away. He had run for her, his face wild and white and his eyes wider than any adult eyes she had ever seen that had still had lids.

Oh, that had angered Uncle Stavos. One of her mother's men. One of her most trusted cousins. Who had she been, at five? Someone who could believe that her Uncle Rogos, favored uncle with the handsome face, all his teeth, and the most generous satchel in the entire Arkosan caravan, could run for her, run *at* her, and mean her no harm, although the threat of death hung over him like a rare, heavy cloud.

Uncle Stavos tackled him; they fell together in a tangle of heavy arms and legs, three inches short of her feet. The shadows of the night were brighter somehow than the shadows Uncle Stavos cast over Uncle Rogos' heaving back.

"Don't let them do this, don't let them do this, child. Tell your mother—ask your mother—not to do this. Please. *Please.*" The last word, spoken in the valley his body made of wild grass and tall, flowering weed, still had the power to immobilize her. She stood, the heart's fire dying in front of her eyes, the third memo-ry at the edge of her vision.

"First death," she whispered.

They both meant more than just death, of course: Margret had seen many before she was five; too many to count. But the deaths that scarred were always the ones that happened between family. Arkosans killed other Voyani when the families went to war; they killed clansmen; rarely, although it had happened, they killed serafs. But each other? Almost never.

"How old were you?"

"Five," Margret said, although she seldom spoke of it. "Five years old and two days. It was the first time I realized that there were things I couldn't ask of my mother."

"She spoiled you, then." Not a question.

Margret remained unruffled. "Yes. In her fashion. I felt the back of her hand more often than most of the kids my age." She shrugged. "But she was smaller than most of their mothers."

Yollana grinned.

"No. That day was different. I think it was the first time I'd ever hurt her, and I didn't know it, then. I barely understand it now. She had cause to kill—to execute—one of my favorite uncles. Uncle Rogos. I thought if I asked her for his life, she'd change her mind. I thought if she *knew* what it would mean to me—"

"And you asked her this when?"

Margret laughed, but the laugh was just this side of a cry. "When the blade was in her hand, Matriarch. When it was in her perfectly steady hand."

"You were her only daughter, obviously."

The humor helped. "I want to kill them, sometimes. I want that. But to actually do it—"

"Breaks a family, or it can. That's why it's in the hands of the Matriarch. And those hands are always steady." Yollana looked down at her own, weathered and wrinkled by sun's poor grace. "I'm old, Margret. Old and feeble. I need my rest."

But they both looked, as one, to the Tor Leonne upon the high plateau, and Margret knew that neither of them would sleep much before the dawn.

He planned ahead.

The sun's heat could not be denied, but it could be lessened. A breeze could be called. Water brought. Fans hefted by serafs. Should one desire privacy, an awning might be constructed, poles wedged into dirt that was, at the height of the moon's season, soft enough to accept them. He made the latter choice, instructing the serafs to build and then *leave*.

The free seldom disobeyed his commands; the serafs, never. He contemplated their work and wondered why it was that they, with so little to lose, could work so quietly and so well; they were like shadows, cast but not noticed. Much like his own shadow would be in a scant few hours. The sun had not yet fully risen. If there was work to be done, it was best done now.

Even bereft as he was, he was not without wisdom.

Cortano di'Alexes was not a sentimental man. He was, however, a powerful man, and the combination of these two traits meant that he had few friends, and the trusted ones were always those whose associations he had made in his youth.

With a single exception, they lay dead, their bodies arranged in a semblance of peace. What could not be gathered easily—blood and blackened ash—now adorned the floor and beams of the room in which they had made their helpless final stand. Magic still lingered; he could sense it, and could name at least three of the casters. It was the last thing they would share: Power and the knowledge of it, ineffectual though it had been.

One of the Widan had been dispatched to carry word to the families.

The Sword's Edge himself saw to the bodies.

He accepted no Widan's aid; no seraf's presence. Here, stripped of the need to *be* the Sword's Edge for the benefit of spectators, he labored as a man labors who has lost something of value: in anger, in pain, in privacy.

No wine, here, not in the growing light. No tears offered to the Lady—or to the Lord. Behind the sliding screens, both Lady and Lord were divested like so much jewelery; there was, after all, so little proof of Their existence they were obviously the province of the sentimental.

Not so the Lord of Night.

In his darker moments, Cortano wondered if the Lord's worship was not descended from the Lord of Night's, for they had this in common: the powerful ruled the less powerful. But such a descent could not have occurred within Leonne's time. Men changed, and their worship altered; this much, study had shown. But they did not change so quickly and leave so little trace.

The history lay somewhere, its answers waiting to be found. By the Widan. By the seekers of knowledge.

By the man who lay dead beneath his hands, his face bisected, his arm missing. Habit kept the anger from his face; habit so strong he could surrender to it and trust his reputation should any fool dare to break his edict by interrupting his work upon the shaded ground.

"My apologies," such a fool said, and the Sword's Edge froze in mid-motion, dirt on his hands, "if I interrupt a ceremony of importance."

"Apologies? How unlike you, Lord Isladar." He rose at once. The dirt on his hands was moist and not easily removed, although that would change with the sun's passage across the open sky. His robes were not fine.

Nor were Isladar's.

All of the *Kialli* were threats, but of them, only Isladar was worthy of Cortano's curiosity. Curiosity was, in and of itself, such a dangerous trait.

"This is not the appointed hour. Am I summoned to the Shining Palace?"

"No." The kinlord looked down upon the shade-covered grass, the shallow rift in the ground, and the bodies that would help to heal it.

"You do not seem surprised."

"I am . . . not entirely surprised. Word of the evening's events have traveled. The Widan, of course, were not of concern. The loss of the Voyani woman was." His shrug was slight, but obvious. "Should an event of import occur in the Shining City, I assume word would travel just as quickly."

He assumed, Cortano was certain, no such thing; the advantage was all theirs in this particular case. For their part, the Southern Court's sole advantage seemed to come from the fact that the *Kialli* truly had no understanding of their enemies or their enemies' motivation.

Except, perhaps, for this one. Not for the first time, Cortano di'Alexes wondered if he possessed the power needed to destroy Isladar. He had never doubted that it would be necessary.

"The loss of the Voyani woman?" Cortano said bitterly, the anger near the surface of his words as it so seldom was. His was a cold anger, after all; a thing that bided its time. "You claim no responsibility for her?"

The kinlord did not answer; not directly. That was not his way.

"You are aware," Lord Isladar said softly, "that the Fist of Allasakar does not favor this alliance—or any alliance—with humans."

"Indeed."

"You are also aware, no doubt, that among them, one Lord has chosen to intervene, weaving our Lord's goal and his own so that they are inseparable in execution."

"No, of that we were not aware."

"Be aware, then. I bring you information and warning, although you need neither. Lord Ishavriel is the most subtle of the five, and it is his game you play. Come the night of the Festival Moon, the nature of the Tor Leonne will be unalterably changed. Be prepared."

He turned to leave.

Cortano lifted a hand, and fire enclosed him in a thin, but beautiful, circle. "Lord Isladar, a moment more of your time."

"You have it," the kinlord said, tolerating the fire whose sole purpose was to gain his attention.

"You are not at Court."

"No. I have been sent here for a different purpose."

"You will not divulge it."

"No. But I will say this, Widan Cortano di'Alexes: I am intrigued by mortality. The *Kialli* make no friends, and their allies and alliances are often short-lived, although perhaps not by mortal standards; I will therefore not insult your intelligence by offering friendship where none is possible.

"But if we cannot share friendship, we share enemies, another time-honored *Kialli* tradition. Where I can, I will aid you and give you information.

"I have watched; I am aware that the masks are a problem."

"Are you aware of their nature?"

"I am aware of the purpose to which they must be put—but were you to gain that information with no other obvious source, it would be my destruction. I have lived longer than any who has served the Lord so closely; I have learned what may, and what may not, be offered in the games between His lieges." He bowed, and then of all things, smiled. "There will be an interruption, I believe, in the Shining City; it will delay those who seek to control the events of the Tor more closely."

"And that interruption?"

"Rest assured, Widan. Your curiosity will be satisfied. Now I must go."

He vanished almost at once, with an ease that spoke of power. Power that Cortano himself barely possessed. *What is your game, Lord Isladar?* He wanted to ask the question, but knew it was pointless. A better question would be, *And will we survive playing it?*

Deprived of powders and oils, of creams and the heavy black kohl that was only slowly falling out of favor in the Imperial court, forbidden the adornment of Lake's jewels, the lilies that had been her preferred flower, the Serra Diora should have been just another woman, one of the countless number who came and went, in the moment of youth's zenith, through the gates of the Tor Leonne. But her skin was naturally pale, her hair thick and long, her eyes wide and round and dark in a way age would not diminish. And the grace that she exhibited in all things was a grace that only death or crippling would deprive her of.

Serra Fiona en'Marano acknowledged all this with private pain, for the Serra Diora had been—perhaps still was, it was so hard to tell—the chief rival for her husband's affection. His favored daughter. The only woman alive who, having publicly humiliated Sendari, could nonetheless be guaranteed survival.

She was clever.

Serra Fiona envied that, and feared it. But there were things she feared more, much more.

Sendari, she thought, as she offered his daughter the most graceful of all possible obeisances, *you have driven us to this.* The shade cast by a bower of almost unnatural leaves protected them both from the sun; nothing at all protected them from the prying ears of the Widan, and the Serra Fiona was certain that the Widan would listen: she spoke with the Serra Diora.

Diora, whom Alesso di'Marente now called the most dangerous woman in the Dominion. And still desired.

And would I? Would I desire you if I were a man? The wind brought the question, laughing as it left the words to abrade her peace. In an anger that she was not quite controlled enough to school, but intelligent enough to hide, she turned to the seraf she had chosen—in pettiness, she now acknowledged—to bring.

"Bring sweet water. And another fan."

He bowed effortlessly, his body bending at knee and waist as if his joints were liquid. She did not immediately recognize him, but his manner of movement, his perfect silence, his immediate attentiveness—these spoke of Teresa's hand. No seraf in the Dominion could measure up to the best of the Serra Teresa's, and more than once, Marano had made a gift of serafs to the harems and the high pavilions of the Tyr'agar, at the request of the Tyr's wife. Serafs—their purchase and their training—were far beneath the concerns of men. But the men knew value and quality when they saw it, and by look or gesture might indicate success or failure.

Diora, of course, had been granted no serafs in the harshness of her captivity; had indeed been forced to dress herself with her own hands, a reminder of how little power and how little dignity any woman truly had when she did not find favor—or worse, lost it—with the man who ruled her life. Fiona had promised herself she would never be so disgraced. It was a fear of hers, loss of the little power that she had managed, with beauty and cleverness, to find.

And yet she had arranged to speak with the Serra Diora. To risk her husband's wrath—her newly important husband, adviser and friend to the Tyr'agar—by pleading with him after an act of love rare enough these days that she wondered if she was too old, and too worn, to please—for Diora's company.

He was suspicious; she, even she, his not so clever Fiona, had foreseen this. She'd covered his lips with the palm of her hand, gently pressing her well-oiled, scented skin against a beard-framed mouth that was dry and worn in the corners by the wind's work.

"She has always been the Flower of the Dominion," Fiona told him, knowing that she stood upon the sword's edge: his temper. "I have always been the wife that she barely deigned to notice. Don't—Na'Sendar, it *is* true. She's always been what I'm not, she's always had what I've wanted."

His eyes were sharp as steel, bright and hard. "And what, little Fiona, do you desire?"

"The respect of your wives," she replied.

"You have that, surely."

"I have it in small measure; it has always been given first to the Serra Teresa and second to the Serra Diora. I have been given what dogs are given: scraps and leavings and the occasional kick when I come too close."

His brows, the peppered and familiar frame to eyes that she both loved and feared, rose. "You are . . . truthful, this day."

"I am the wife," she replied sweetly, "of the second most powerful man in the Dominion. I am Fiona en'Sendari."

And he, he was Widan, not husband. The indulgence had been burned out of him by the grace of the Lord and the command of the Tyr'agar. She had always admired Alesso di'Marente; she had cause to regret it now, and thought, feared, that her regrets in a future she could not see clearly for shifting sands would be harsher and far more enduring.

"Fiona en'Sendari, Serra Fiona, you presume. It is . . . unpleasant." He rose from the silks, tossing them aside. She arranged them artfully almost without thought before rising. Before approaching the back that he had turned to her; his attention was upon the screen doors that hid the view of the lake from their eyes.

"Forgive me," she whispered, as she approached his back without—quite—touching him. "I speak a truth that has hurt me to a husband that has more to do with his time than notice such a petty thing. I would not have spoken at all, but you asked, and I always do, in all things, as you ask."

"Yes," he said, his voice still distant, his back still turned. "You have always done so."

"I want—"

"To humiliate my daughter."

She was silent. He still did not turn; she weighed the risk she took by the stillness of his back and the neutrality of his voice. Neutrality was always the worst; it was the steel that was never far from Sendari's eyes—or orders.

And yet she continued to take the risk, rather than cringing from the sword's shadow or the fear of its fall as she had always done when she recognized what the bitter shadow meant. "To show her, rather, what a *dutiful* wife is due. To show her that love and loyalty are rewarded.

"I have been loyal. I have spent my life in your service. I have wanted only what you want, what is best for your clan. She is your *daughter,* Sendari. Of all women, she should—"

"Enough!" He turned, his hand raised.

She could not avoid it; she did not try. Instead, her face absorbed the blow; the slap, the resounding echo of it, was both order and reply. She wavered; the tears that came to her eyes were only partial pretense. But she had learned at her mother's side: be like the Lady's element. Water can be struck, but the hand passes through it, and when the two are parted—water and attacker—it is the latter that bears the mark.

But not, the Serra Fiona thought bitterly, the scar. She had been a foolish girl; she was, she acknowledged, an often foolish woman.

She waited until he had seen her face, and had seen the wide roundness of her eyes. Timing, now, was everything. A breath. Two breaths.

She fell to the ground before the third had left his lips, pressing knees and arms and face into the perfect mats at his feet, huddling there as if she were child, not wife.

Will this be the day? she thought; she had thought it before. Although it was rarely spoken of, even when the Lady was ascendant, every wife knew that death by a husband's hand was common. Sendari had not yet killed a wife. But never and not yet were separated only by the thin edge of a man's anger. She saw his feet more clearly than anything else, and watched them as he turned, almost on heel, away from her.

"Very well, Serra Fiona. You have . . . earned the right to your . . . request. See the daughter whose love for me should have been as unswerving as your own. Prove your point."

She was no fool, although of his wives, she was the least wise. She did not rise.

"But, Fiona," he continued, after a slight pause in which she might have reignited the Widan's flame—his anger, her injury, *"do not ask again."*

CHAPTER TWELVE

It was almost a pleasure to speak with the Serra Fiona. Diora acknowledged it as truth, and she was shamed by it, but both acknowledgment and shame were buried beneath the perfect facade of her unadorned face. The sun on her skin had been warm when she walked by the Serra Fiona's side, exposed to wind and sky for the first time since the end of the Festival of the Sun.

To talk about nothing, shaded from open sky and the harsh, harsh glare of the Lord, in the pleasant way that women have who must speak when the walls of the harem do not shelter or protect them, had never been a freedom before; it was a privilege now. A privilege although she had heard, in the Serra Fiona's voice, a fear so strong it was almost terror. When the seraf had departed, Diora gazed out at the surface of the Lake.

"Do you miss it?" Fiona asked softly.

It was an intimate question, a question that not even the wives of her mother would have asked. Diora turned away from the waters to the woman who had never been her friend. She knew they were being listened to. She wondered if Fiona understood this.

"I miss," she replied, "my husband. My wives." There. Truth in that, if one knew how to listen. Only one man did, and he would never expose her. A delicate hand rose from a perfectly folded lap, and fell again; she had forgotten. No fan here, not for Diora; no veil.

The Serra Fiona was silent.

"Your seraf is very fine."

"Thank you. I believe, however, that he must have been trained by the Serra Teresa. We will have to ask her, when she arrives."

Diora almost missed the information the second sentence contained. Almost. "Your pardon, Serra Fiona; the sun is so warm and so bright, I am unused to it. It is . . . a marvel, and I am distracted." She bowed her head briefly, gathering her thoughts, focusing them. "You spoke of the Serra Teresa?"

"Yes. She has been invited to the Tor Leonne for the Festival of the Moon."

"You must be mistaken."

The Serra flushed slightly, and Diora realized that those words, coolly inflected, were the very ones that she so often used within the confines of the harem when she had been her father's daughter, and Fiona merely his wife. She bowed her head at once, gently, easing the neutrality and passivity of her expression. Vulnerability was often confused with atonement.

Fiona's expression did not change.

"My apologies, Serra Fiona. I was told by my father that the Serra Teresa had been chosen as companion to Adano's Serra, and that she would not be traveling to the Tor Leonne for the foreseeable future." The smile she offered was soft, a thing that hinted at regret; her voice did the rest, tainted by the gift and the curse that she shared with her Ona Teresa. The bardic voice. "But my father owes me nothing; not information, and not truth. Indeed, if you have been told otherwise, I am grateful that you are patient enough to speak with me at all."

The Serra Diora had learned to lie in every conceivable way.

Fiona's eyes widened at the acknowledgment, accepting it at face value. Diora had often wondered at her father's choice; she wondered now, and was as shamed by it as she had been by the desire for company. More, perhaps. Fiona had always played her games, and had Diora been banished, humiliated, or married to an inappropriate man, her father's wife would have offered wine at the Lady's shrines for the rest of her life.

That was gone now; what remained was both a fear and a determination that Fiona had never shown for anything that did not concern her harem or her husband's rise to power—both matters of her own status.

What game? she thought, as the sun's heat lingered. Sweat trickled down the whiteness of her skin as if it were rain and she a statue. *Fire doesn't have to burn to kill.* Who had said that?

"She should arrive within seven days, well before the Festival of the Moon."

Diora bowed her head again. When she lifted it, her glance was caught and held by the seraf who approached them both, carrying a lacquered tray with two perfect, delicate cups. Water, as Fiona had requested.

Diora was no longer thirsty, not for the water he carried.

She knew every seraf that Teresa had ever trained, and this man was not among them. But something about his eyes—dark eyes in an almost perfect face—was familiar. She did not meet them; instinct spared her that. But she did notice, as he drew closer, that his hands were perfectly smooth, his arms and wrists unscarred.

Fiona, of course, noticed little; he was a seraf. Diora herself would have ignored his presence had she not been searching for eavesdroppers.

"Serra Fiona," she said softly, "might I speak to the seraf a moment?"

Fiona's confusion was genuine. The concern that followed it was genuine as well, although it was more quickly masked. "Of course."

"I think," she said to the man, as he set the tray on the low table between them, "I have seen you serving before, possibly in the house of my uncle. You seem familiar to me."

He did not answer, and that was wise; no seraf did, unless commanded otherwise. But there was about his height and his bearing something . . . unusual. Familiar, yes.

Of a sudden, she had to hear his voice. She had to *hear* it. "What is your name?" she asked, the four words falling in a rush of sound, as if forced, as if only speed would see them said at all.

He met her eyes then, full on, as unlike a proper seraf as a high clansmen.

"I am called," he replied quietly, "Isladar."

She didn't flee.

His words brought the night; for a moment all she could see was the darkness she heard in his voice, and it was so utter, she forgot about heat and the consequences of fire. Her own voice left her, just as the day did.

Had she ever wondered why demons were creatures of night, but were never connected with the Lady? She ceased at once: such a power could never be under the Lady's Dominion.

Or, she thought, the Lord's.

She didn't flee; she forced herself to sit in the shade cast by the height of the morning sun. She'd had practice, she thought, and the thought was bitter enough to break through the fear.

"Isladar. An . . . interesting name. Was it given to you by your master?" Hard to speak the words. But she had been trained by a

master; her voice was her sole power. She would not be deprived
of it.

"No," he replied, the veneer of his words soft and deferential.
He bowed to her; she caught the sweep of his shadow upon the
grass because she would not meet his eyes.

Would not?

And why? Her shoulders, never stooped, stiffened impercep-
tibly. "No?" He must play his game; he was trapped in a guise
that she would never have thought could suit him.

"No, Serra Diora. I was not born a slave."

He faltered, with a single word. Slave was a very Northern
term, and seldom used, if at all, in the South. She looked up, as if
this single weakness was enough to make him fallible. Mortal.

"No? But you bear no scars."

"A wise man knows when struggle is futile and preserves dignity in the stead of a freedom he cannot have."

And she looked up because, in truth, she desired to see his
face in the unforgiving harshness of the day's light; to deprive
it of essential mystery; to destroy her single memory of Lord
Isladar. At night, his visage just strange enough to be other than
human, he had been so very, very beautiful.

It had surprised her; it surprised her now, although it shouldn't.
What, after all, was more beautiful than power?

"And do you look forward," she said, "to some day when you
are not a slave?"

He smiled as she met his eyes, as she saw the whole of his face.
"Very clever." He turned then, as she did; they both glanced at the
Serra Fiona.

But Diora's glance faltered; Isladar's did not. She could almost
feel his eyes rest against the sudden rigidity of her own expression. Serra Fiona had not moved at all. Her eyes were wide and
round; they stared ahead at a spot just beyond the Serra Diora's
perfect, plainly clad shoulder.

Fear was not as distant as it should have been. But it was not
nearly as close as it would have been, had she been wiser. She
was cool; she did not choose to dissemble or to play at being
helpless.

"Well met, Serra Diora di'Marano." The seraf bowed. "You
cost me much when last we met, and if I had known then whose
flesh housed the spirit that slipped the Voyani woman past my
bindings, you would not have aggrieved your father or your Tyr
in the days to follow.

"You are called the Flower," he added. "And in *Kialli* eyes, you are aptly named: In your season, there is an astonishing beauty about your delicacy. It will fade. You will wither." The lack of malice in the words made them the more chilling; she saw the ages in his eyes, and understood then just how little mortals suffer age.

He *was* beautiful, although the night had left his features, but his beauty was the beauty of distance. The mountains in the North of Mancorvo, the ocean at the height of the rainy season, the desert after the storm—they were beautiful in just such a way.

But she was certain that they were less deadly, or rather, that the bodies that littered the passes in winter, the ocean floor after the height of a storm or the desert's hot, hot sands, proved only the indifference of nature and the foolishness of man.

"I am called the Flower of the Dominion," she said, as harshly as she ever said anything, "by the romantic, the ironic, or the foolish." The sun shifted across the sky, and as it did, light lit the folds of silk across her perfectly folded lap.

As if it were water.

"And of the three, I am which?"

Silence was her answer; her face was almost as still as Fiona's.

"She cannot hear us," was his reply.

"I . . . thought not. If you will continue to play at servitude, I must tell you that you are failing in your chosen role."

"Oh?"

"The sun is rising, and the shadows cast by the bowers above are becoming too short for the comfort of the wife and daughter of your Lord."

She was not certain why she'd said the words once they'd left her lips; was not certain why she had spoken in such a clear, unfettered tone. But she thought it was because he was beautiful and deadly and outside of the experience that had so harshly shaped the whole of her life.

Or perhaps it was because she feared no death. Everything her enemies might have used to threaten her with they had already destroyed.

To her surprise, the creature who had captured Evallen of the Arkosa Voyani, and who had so successfully seen to her torture, moved elegantly, gracefully, perfectly as he set about arranging the poles and pegs above which cloth would be draped. The cloth itself was a white silk, painted by the hands of Sendari's wives within the walls of their suddenly powerful harem. She saw Illia's work in the leaves of the lilies that were otherwise implied by the silk itself, rather than painted.

"You are clever," he said as he worked, his hands taking to labor as if they were made for it, and no more, "and I admire clever. To a point."

"And you are here because you admire clever? I had thought that you were the ears and the eyes of your Lord."

"I am," he replied mildly, "both of those. But not, perhaps, this day. I am curious. I have been experimenting in my own fashion with humanity. You have evoked the anger of the Sword's Edge; he is not a mortal who is easily angered. Nor easily frustrated in his ambition." He stepped back to assess the success of his work. Frowned, the expression a ripple of lip and eye that passed above his face and was gone. "I was given to understand that the women of the South were not powerful."

"We serve," she said quietly.

"As do we," he replied. He bowed. "We will meet again, if you survive."

"I half thought you were sent to kill me."

"They do not send me to kill. I am not reliable." He smiled, his eyes narrowed, and for an instant he *was* the demon she had seen at the Festival of the Sun. "And you, little one, believe you desire death. We do not grant the desired without reasons of our own, and your death would serve no purpose of mine at the moment.

"In time, perhaps, but I have learned, when dealing with mortals, that indulgence of that particular hunger is . . . costly."

Truth, in the words; truth and darkness. She wondered, as the Serra Fiona suddenly began to breathe again, her pink lips shifting subtly with the rise and fall of her delicate chest, whether her curse and gift was capable of discerning truth from the lips of a creature who had served the Lord of Night before Leonne the Founder had graced the Dominion with his sword and his death.

Night was the Lord's time; darkness the Lord's element. Or so humans believed. They took elements of reality and made myth of it. In turn, time eroded myth and left story behind, and story was good enough gruel only for the minds of the young.

But if the minds of the young outgrew those stories, the hearts did not, and in the corners of memories as old as life—if any mortal span could be considered "old"—stories and shadows became one. Demons were the darkness, the darkness the only domain they possessed.

But the truth—as all truths were—was less simple and vastly less romantic than that. The kin walked the earth. They had always walked it in one form or another, no matter how small their summoned number, although only the *Kialli* could remember a time when the earth itself was alive with wild magics, all long since tamed.

Lord Ishavriel walked the earth in the heat of the midday sun. He cast a shadow decreed by the height of his body, no more, no less; he dressed finely, in the manner of the humans of the High Court, but not so ostentatiously that he drew attention or suspicion, and he loitered near the water's edge, as most people did who were occasional visitors to the Tor Leonne proper.

Only the last was difficult. The Lake—as natural at its source as he—caused him pain when he chose to approach it. He had chosen once to consume the waters when they were offered; proof, in deed, that no curse and no magic were his match. But he had been wise enough to test his measure, and theirs, in the Shining Palace, where any revelation of what the mortals so quaintly called his true nature was hardly likely to harm his plans.

A costly display.

But he had proved his point. These waters were among the strongest of the magics remaining in the Southern lands, and he was their match. He would be more than their master.

Provided, of course, that his plans went smoothly.

It was not in the nature of plans to run smoothly. Not in the demesne that he had ruled by dint of strength and power, and not upon the earth that had changed so much in the millennia that his feet did not burn at the power beneath them.

And so he watched. Across the width of still water, two women sat in a silence of breeze and midday heat. They were, by the standard of the Court, quite lovely; they were also the wives or daughters of men of power, such as human power was. They were both young, both delicate in seeming, both dark-haired and pale as the Northern snows.

But one of them spoke, and the other did not actually listen; she was frozen in place, unmoved by what she saw or heard—if she saw or heard anything at all. The speaker, her back toward him, her face therefore unreadable, moved deliberately and gently; he could not tell by the delicacy of her movements whether or not she was afraid.

Or rather, he could not tell *what* she was afraid of. That she was afraid, he could see clearly. He could smell it, it was so strong.

But although he had cast the spells and expended the necessary power, he could not hear a single word she spoke. Syllables were so muted and hushed that one was indistinguishable from the next; all that was left to him was the cadence of her speech. Interference.

Isladar.

He waited. Waiting was simple, although to fill the time with the disguise of human motion was not. Mortals did not stand and wait; they did not observe for any length of time. They lived by the night and the day, in their short, short hours. It was almost a curiosity to mimic them, but curiosity in the end was Isladar's curse, not Ishavriel's.

Isladar, who had bred the half-human godling and lost her for reasons not a single one of the Generals understood. Only Ishavriel made the attempt, and only because of the five he was the most suspicious.

For millennia, Lord Isladar, truly *Kialli,* had graced the side of the Lord's throne like an ornament, like a human thing of precious metal and jewelery. He had no demesne, no lieutenants, none of the unnamed; he took part in none of the duels that had shaped, scarred and defined the changing face of Allasakar's domain since its beginning. Of all of the *Kialli* to serve the Lord so closely, only Isladar had survived. Only he.

Why?

To watch him as he was now made him a creature almost beneath contempt. He dressed as the least of the blood-bound kin did, and performed a service—or so it seemed—that the blood-bound might be too good for: spying on a captive girl.

Lord Ishavriel knew it for fact: He had ordered the girl watched. But not by a kinlord.

The girl stiffened a moment; Isladar bowed with a subservient human's perfect posture. Then the other woman, the enspelled human, came to life. When she did, he walked away, skirting the water's edge.

Across the water, the eyes of the *Kialli* met.

"I did not expect to see you here," Ishavriel said, twisting his words into the wind and forcing the element to carry them clearly.

"I came," he replied, "to deliver a message and to satisfy my curiosity."

"At my expense?"

"It costs nothing," he answered softly, "and may yet serve your purpose."

Ishavriel waited. The shadows lengthened. But waiting served them both ill within these lands, beside these waters; the sun was setting, and their stillness would be marked. It angered him, to speak first.

"What message do you choose to deliver?"

"Just this: Anya a'Cooper has moved her throne."

"Impossible."

"Indeed, that is what we would have said. She is exhausted, and only through my intervention did she survive the . . . re-arrangement. She is not popular among the *Kialli*."

"Your intervention? Then I am in your debt."

Isladar's smile was dark and sharp; they both knew the value of the words when no blood had been spilled to bind them. "She suffers the fevers."

"In the Shining Palace?"

"No. I did not think it wise to leave her there; I was not in a position to protect her."

"Because of your curiosity."

"Indeed."

Silence. Ishavriel mastered his fury with effort, none of it visible.

"There is more."

"More?"

"She moved her throne," he said, "because she was tired of standing."

He felt certain that he would not like what followed. He was absolutely certain that Isladar found it amusing, although he kept all trace of it from voice or face. Rare, that, in the face of a rival's discomfort. He expected to hear at least a cold chuckle, a quiet laugh; open scorn was more common but unlike Isladar.

"Where is the throne?"

"It is at the head of the pentagram."

"The—" the kinlords did not pale; that was a trait left to mortals, a trick of their blood and their weakness. No; the kinlords lost all movement; they became as still as the stone out of which the Lord had carved his Great Hall.

"The—not the ground upon which the mages channel their power at the Lord's behest?"

"Indeed," Isladar said, his voice a whisper, a sinuous motion of air within air. "She has broken the gate's containment. For the last mortal day, not a single one of the kin has been summoned from across the rift.

"He is not pleased."

Without another word, Ishavriel turned into the shadows the sun cast and vanished.

Only when his shadows were gone did Isladar offer what every other kinlord would have given openly: A smile.

Had he seen it, Ishavriel would have acknowledged that it was *perfect*.

9th of Scaral, 427 AA
Evereve

She did not leave her room.

Not because she was no longer curious; the curiosity was strong enough that it forced her to rise, time and again, and walk to the closed door that led to the rest of the dungeon of wonders. But each time, through dint of a will and patience that she would never have had as the young girl who had first come in through Terafin's front gates, she returned to the desk that she occupied.

Her lip was no longer swollen.

Her temper was no longer heated. Unfortunately, it hadn't cooled; it had chilled.

You seduce my wife—well, that's what he had thought—*and I rape your daughter. Gods, I hate men.* Be fair, she added silently—the whole conversation was silent, which was uncharacteristic—he *had* taken out what was left of his anger on Aristos himself.

She counted to ten.

Well, that was enough fairness.

Unfortunately, nothing happened to take her mind off her anger; she blunted it slightly by throwing a few very heavy things—what exactly they were supposed to be wasn't clear—at the door.

They were, surprise, surprise, gold. They didn't break. She had never detested gold so much in her life; had, in fact, never dreamed she could. Gold, after all, was an important source of power.

Well, so was liver if you listened to her grandmother. She was sharply aware that she probably hadn't. Not enough. But then again, she'd been a child when her grandmother had gone to Mandaros' Halls, and what child listens well? She'd heard mystery, and danger, and adventure, all in the safety and warmth of her grandmother's arms and lap.

The smell of cinnamon and sweat came back to her; she stood a moment, eyes closed, thinking about old stories. During the day, she'd play them out: She, the wily hero, the brave mage, the healer, the bardic wonder, and the shadows her enemies, her forest of wonders, her ancient, twisting passages at the heart of which her enemy waited for the final confrontation. But at night, at night, without the control of her grandmother's stories to bind them, those shadows had come to her, jumped between the thin barding of make believe, laughing at the ill-fitting guise of hero or healer as they pushed it aside.

Five years old, maybe four, she had huddled, trying to work her voice up to a scream so that someone would wake her. A smarter person would probably have taken the nightmares as a hint and stopped playing at the heroics night's terror so thoroughly disgraced. But the night couldn't rob the day of strength. She had still played at being the hero.

She wondered if it were night now; there was no window to oblige her by offering her a glimpse and an answer. Her stomach, however, ever helpful, growled.

And she'd be damned before she went down to the hall for dinner. The one thing about years on the street: Hunger was a known evil, and she knew how much of it her body could take before it was dangerous.

Perhaps the room knew. She had an uneasy sense that it was alive and watching her, preparing a report to take back to its master, Avandar. Or whatever it was he was called here.

Kalliaris, she thought, the word more of a mantra than a prayer. She turned away from the door and trudged back to the bed. Sat, letting the weight of her chin drag her head down. Down. Down. Her lids were kind of heavy, too. Lashes brushed cheeks before she forced them open.

Prayer stopped. Anger, for a moment, let go.

Across from the bed, a section of particularly garish wall had been usurped. By a door.

It was a very, very strange door, and she stared at it for fifteen minutes before she understood what was wrong with it: It was hers. One of hers. Her grandmother's voice hadn't been so strong since childhood, but it whispered in her ear now, repeating every

Voyani warning she had ever been offered, Torran words lighting the corners in which shadows, like fears, waited.

Oh, Oma, she thought. *I wish the Lady had never taken you.* What would you do now if you were me? To that, there was no answer. Jewel ATerafin walked to the door and opened it.

Beyond the door, her rooms shimmered beneath a gauzy veil of light. She wanted them so very badly she almost let herself believe they were real. "And what," she said aloud, "happens if I walk through those doors?"

The doors that were not her doors opened at her back; she heard their smooth glide across fine carpet and turned.

The man who stood between them flinched slightly as he met her eyes. That was to be his only acknowledgment of what he had done. Avandar said, not unkindly, "I do not know."

She had been so angry moments before she could not quite allow the anger to slip from her grasp. But it was harder to hold than she had thought it would be, with her lip still sore.

He didn't seem to realize she was angry. Or perhaps he didn't know how to acknowledge it; he had rarely chosen to acknowledge any temper that had no outward expression. Of course, if she were honest, those had been few. Usually he had done the dance with the rest of them as they made their way through—and out of—the kitchen doors, avoiding any loose pot lid, any pan that wasn't too heavy, any spare utensil. The clatter of metal against stone had a much more satisfying voice than the one she'd been born with.

There was no wind in the room; no sea breeze; no open windows through which air could pass unimpeded.

But she felt it anyway, the movement of air, the hint of water's expanse, the warmth of sun that had burned away all cloud. He came to stand by her side. By her side and a little bit back, as if this were a normal day, as if this present danger was the merely demonic, this mystery the merely magical.

She turned to look back through *her* door; her room was solidifying as she watched, the details becoming less hazy. She stopped a moment. Bunched her hands in open-and-closed fists that seemed timed with necessary things: heartbeat. Breath.

"Jewel," he said quietly.

"Did you let them go?"

"No."

"Why are you here?"

"I . . . don't know."

Turning, she hit him.

Not hard enough to hurt him, of course; without training, she probably couldn't. But hard enough to test. He did not lift a hand to stop her. "Don't ever," she said, as coldly as she could. "Don't ever ever ever do this again."

They both knew she wasn't talking about the lip.

She didn't look at him. She looked at her rooms.

There, the chair by her bed where she habitually threw her clothing. Beside it, the chest of drawers, and across the room, the desk that she never used. Her bed, unmade, the canopy so simple and tasteful compared to the bed she'd wakened in she promised never to make young-girl cracks about it again. Her closet.

"Can I go there?"

"It's not your room," he replied softly.

"It's my room."

"It's your memory of your room. Wait," he added. He touched her shoulder. Withdrew his hand immediately when she flinched. "When the light dims, it will be as real as it can be in this place."

Disappointment silenced her. But only for a moment; silence was not one of Jewel ATerafin's many gifts. "I thought it might be—I thought we could—"

"Go back?"

Something in his voice made her turn. She caught only his profile; his gaze was there, upon the room whose reality he dismissed.

"Yes," she said at last. "Go back. I've never been so far from home."

"You don't even know where we are."

"I know where we aren't. That's enough for me." She folded her arms across her chest; jewels caught and pulled against each other as they settled into this familiar position.

"No," he said quietly. "There is no way back from here."

"Avandar—"

"You may enter now."

"Is there any point?" But she left him standing outside the doors, the simple wooden doors, when she passed beneath their frame. She walked to her bed, paused a moment in front of her chest of drawers, and moved on to her closet. Her breath was a wild struggle; her chest felt constricted, as if something heavy had been placed against it and was growing in weight with each passing moment.

He had never been denied her rooms. He entered them quietly behind her, reasserting the order that she had come to view as natural. She wondered, briefly, if it would ever be natural again. She'd always known he had power, of course, but she never been forced to confront it. Funny how the little lies of omission were the things that held the safety of her life together.

Within the closet hung the dresses she wore to those meetings Avandar deemed politically important. And beyond them, hidden by this patina of decorum and rank, the clothing that she wore when she worked with her den in her kitchen. None of them fine silks—she found silk just a touch too delicate—but all of them sturdy enough. She'd had the elbows patched, and after Avandar had finished having his fits, had seen to it that the reinforcements were not immediately obvious, although it cost more.

Without thought, she turned her back to her domicis, inviting him by gesture alone to undo whatever it was that nubbled her spine so uncomfortably.

His fingers moved the length of her back as he undid the small catches that held the dress in place. Southern in look, it had none of the apparent simplicity of the saris she secretly loved; it took time.

"Jewel," he said.

"Don't."

"Don't?"

"Whatever you were about to say, don't bother. We—thanks." She slid out of the dress, keeping her back to him. Gods knew he'd seen her naked before—and not like he'd ever noticed—but she'd never really *felt* naked. Either that or it had been long enough that she'd forgotten the early awkwardness.

Either way, it was there now. She was aware of every particular flaw her body possessed, every out of place hair, every extra bit of weight.

She dressed for speed and not for elegance, which was a good thing; elegance was something that was really only within her grasp with Avandar's help, and someplace between Terafin and Evereve, she'd decided his help was too costly.

The shirt she grabbed was hunter green; gold circles had been embroidered into the sleeves and the collar, and they caught the unnatural light, reflecting it. She almost put it back. Didn't.

The mark, the S with the two little v's, was an angry red, decorated by silver and gold. Precious metals. "What does it mean?" She would never have thought her voice could be so quiet.

"It is . . . a claim. A . . . falsehood."

"I know you put them on your wife. But what does it mean?"

When the collar of her shirt had cleared her head, and before its sleeves had cleared her hands, he started to speak again.

"I . . . expended much of my power to bring you here," he said quietly.

"Why didn't you just use it to take us someplace safe?"

He laughed.

She turned, yanking her arms into clothing's confinement and comfort. "Just what is so funny?"

"This was safety," he said softly. "The only safety I, or mine, had."

"Well, I'm not you, and I'm not yours, and frankly I don't feel particularly safe here."

"You aren't. You are not of my blood and you are not . . . consigned to my service. The direction service takes in our relationship was . . . never conceived of in the time that this fortress was in use."

"Good. If you could just arrange for us to go home, I'd appreciate it."

"If I could just arrange for 'us,' as you so ignorantly put it, to go home, I would have done so before you woke." He walked to the door and closed it.

They stood together in her room. The curtains were closed; she wondered what she would see if she drew them. Started toward them to find out.

"Don't."

Stopped. "Won't it just be rock?"

"I . . . don't know."

"Oh." Silence, awkward and uncomfortable. "Why?"

"I never attempted to force windows upon this place. And my . . . wife . . . understood its nature well. You are, as always, surprising."

"How?"

"This. This room," he added, when it became clear that understanding was not going to miraculously occur. "It shouldn't exist. That it does speaks either to your power or to the dangers of tampering with a spell that was complicated enough to kill two of the mages required for its casting."

The tone of his voice made clear that it wasn't her power he was worried about.

She'd promised herself that she wasn't going to beg him for anything. She'd even promised that she wasn't going to ask, because on some level she was smart enough not to want to know. But smart wasn't enough.

"Who are you?"

"Avandar," he said smoothly. No cracks in that armor.

"All right. This?"

"This is . . . Evereve. Aristos told you its name, and he had no reason to lie. As you should well know, lies are best used sparingly."

"I don't lie."

"You've always been too lazy to learn the art."

"It's not laziness. My memory's lousy."

"As you will."

"And we were talking about you."

"In a manner of speaking," he replied. "I did not make this place, but I did discover it, in a fashion." His steps were flat and hollow in the still room; rugs absorbed their sound. "I . . . had already lost one wife. Two, although the first was killed when she tried to kill me." He lifted his head, folded his hands behind his back. She had seen him stand in exactly that position countless times.

"I lost all of my children."

She approached him slowly, as if approaching a wounded, wild creature—one that had claws, fangs, and weight behind it. His gaze was so far beyond her the walls couldn't contain it.

"I was . . . I am a very difficult man to kill. An acknowledged truth in my time. I was not . . . I *am not* a pleasant man. 'Pleasant' is a goal that those who have to live with fear struggle to attain.

"But my children were vulnerable. My wives. During a time in my life when I thought I could somehow attain happiness by protecting them, I found this place. I struggled with its essential nature. I made it my own. To do so was costly." His shrug told Jewel that the cost was measured in the lives of outsiders.

"I brought my wife here. She agreed to this; she was well acquainted with the death of her predecessor, and she was with child.

"She lost the child here. She did not conceive again until she left these walls, and she left them in haste."

"Avandar, please. We haven't much time."

"Yes and no," he said quietly, rising.

"Yes and no?"

"We discovered, in time, that time—within these walls—is not an issue. My wife did not age. Nor would she."

He was lying about something; she wasn't certain what. There was so much to lie *about*.

"But time is a jealous god."

"Time's a god?"

He raised a dark brow. "They teach you so very little these days."

"Thanks. I'll take that as a yes."

For a moment she thought she had his attention; that attention dissipated with the criticism. *It really is as natural as breathing,* she thought, stepping slightly back so she could see his face without being forced to tilt her chin up.

"You said she left."

"She left," he said softly, "because she desired a child."

Jewel shrugged. "Some women do."

And the edges around his dark eyes narrowed, changing their shape and his expression. "She was not a sentimental woman." His voice was cool. "She desired my legacy, or rather, a claim to it."

"And did she have her child?"

"Oh, yes."

"She survived?"

"She survived childbirth, yes. The child survived as well."

"There's something you aren't telling me."

"I am telling you so little it might as well be a lie," he replied. "You have no context in which to put the information."

She walked over to the closet again. Closed her eyes. Opened them, and opened the door. On the floor, tucked into the corner she reserved for long dresses and skirts she couldn't stand, was an old backpack; cracks split leather that was shiny with sweat where her hands habitually rested.

There were blankets in the dresser drawers, and clothing fine enough for the Tor Leonne—if she came as a Voyani. She grabbed the pack's shoulder straps in her right hand and slung it over her shoulder.

"Jewel," Avandar said.

"I'm not really listening."

"You're listening to every pause in my breathing."

Damn him anyway.

She began to roll the blanket into as small an object as she could. It had been years since she'd done this for herself; she was rusty. "What happened to her?"

"To who?"

"The wife you don't even grace with a name?"

"She tried to have me killed," he replied softly.

"Oh." The blanket stilled. Jewel looked up, but Avandar's face was like a wall whose only gap was arrow slits. "I'm sorry."

"And she died for her mistake."

"Did you kill her?"

"Does it matter?"

She took the shirts and the very Imperial pants out of the drawers and began to fold them up as well, taking less care than she had with the blanket. Years of training slid past her; she wasn't certain if the colors matched, or if the style, such as it was, was current. Didn't much care. "Yes."

He didn't answer. He wasn't going to. She knew him that well. "We don't have much time, Avandar. We've got to go."

"I know," he said quietly. "But to bring you here almost killed us both. To take you out in a similar fashion will."

"You're lying."

"Very well. It will kill *you*."

"Does it matter?"

His smile was grim, unfriendly. "Yes."

CHAPTER THIRTEEN

He held *Saval.*

Its hilt was fine, and its scabbard finer still, but the grip that made the sword practical was unadorned leather. In his tenure as par el'Sol he had patiently remade the grip; he trusted no one else with the sword that had become associated with his rank.

It should have passed on to the man who replaced him as par el'Sol; the kai el'Sol's weapon was *Balagar,* sometimes called *Balagar of the Long Night.* It was gone. Fredero kai el'Sol had taken it with him, somehow, and if Peder par el'Sol suspected the how, he was consumed with the need to protect the Radann from far worse, in the end, than the theft of the kai el'Sol's sword.

Or so he told the others, and if they chose to believe it—as he tried to do himself—so much the better. Whether or not there was belief, however, mattered little; they chose not to question him. The loss, theoretically, was his.

The streets of the Tor Leonne opened before him like merchant tents before the wealthy; he expected no less. He wore the full regalia of the warrior-priest; the armor in perfect condition, the surcoat a deep blue, signifying the depths of clear sky. In the clarity of cloudless day, the Lord's sight was keenest, his judgment most dangerous. Blue was bisected by the curve of a weapon's blade: *Balagar,* although very few would recognize the sword should they otherwise see it. From out of the valley its curve made the sun in gold rose, and it rose with ten rays, ten full rays.

They bowed to him, the people of this city, or they fled, depending on their rank. How often, after all, did the kai el'Sol venture among them? How often did he do so accompanied by the par el'Sol, each fully armored, each carrying a naked blade?

There should have been four: there were three, Samadar, Marakas, and Samiel. When he had allied himself with Alesso—Lord scorch him, winds scour—he had already decided upon the man who would replace him in the Hand of God. Significantly, he had not called upon that man to face the Lord's fire, the Lord's fight, and the Lord's test. Why?

The three men who stood at his back now were men he trusted.

Trust was a fool's game; it was also the game of desperate men. Desperation had forced him to trust.

For once in his life, he cursed ambition, because no man became par el'Sol—with the exception of Marakas, perhaps—without ambition. He had chosen his successor carefully. Grego di'Erreno was brilliant, cool, and politically wise; the perfect counterweight for Samadar, a man too much beholden to the Lambertan-bred kai el'Sol. He had intended to replace Samadar in time.

No matter; he could not afford it now. Too much was at stake. Gregor was ambitious, and Gregor had thrown his weight behind the General. The so-called Tyr'agar. No doubt—*no doubt*—the Erreno-born clansman, when confronted with the same truths that Peder had been confronted by, would make the same choices.

But by then it would be too late. Thus, Fredero kai el'Sol's revenge. What had he said?

I am the Lord's servant, but the game that is played here is a game for men who understand treachery better than I. Had he thought Fredero a fool for accepting—and forgiving—his treachery? He repented.

It did no good.

Sun glinted off metal; gold, he thought, although the momentary pain would have been the same if the light was reflected off something base.

The three men he led understood the risks that had already been taken; they understood, further, the risks they *would* take. How long had it been since he had stood beside men who would die to protect him? How long had it been since he had stood beside men he would give his life to protect? How long—and this question stung him, for it was foolish, and it was painful, and he could not quite say why—had it been since he had believed enough in anything to do either?

The Lord values power, and we are the Lord's servants. But Fredero kai el'Sol, the man everyone called the Lambertan kai even though the Radann forsook their blood families when they

took their oaths, had been both powerful and above the squabbles
of the powerful; he had made no excuses because he had never
had cause to need them.

The winds howled in the ears of Peder kai el'Sol, and they
howled with Fredero's voice.

At his back, he heard Samadar's reasonable tones and Samiel's
quick ones. They were as unlike as two men could be who fought
for the same goal. Fredero kai el'Sol had always held them in
check; they both respected him.

Peder felt the lack of that unique respect keenly. He had never
thought it would bother him, because until this moment, with so
much depending on him, it never had.

He had never particularly liked Fredero kai el'Sol. He had
planned, with clear conscience, the death that would remove the
sole obstacle between Peder and the only position he desired.
And he had discovered that, with the success of the scheme—and
it was a very empty success, a bitter loss—he had instead achieved
the responsibility of saving the Radann from the plans of the Lord
of Night. He had always wondered how the Radann could have
once been so foolish that they could worship and respect that
Lord, but he understood it well enough now: The Lord of Night's
face was dark, but it was kin to the Lord's. They were both creatures of power.

And power exerted its own influence, its own seduction. It
was his bitter truth, because he had lived it.

Luckily, judgment was not his vocation. Nor atonement. Fredero had given him the Radann, and had made himself legend, by
offering a death that no one who had seen it—or heard of it—
could ignore.

"Kai el'Sol."

He turned slightly; Marakas, always soft-spoken, had lost the
gift of speech after Fredero's death. When it returned, it returned
somewhat broken. His face would bear the shadow of the loss for
longer, Peder thought dispassionately, than most mothers remember the deaths of their infants. Had Marakas not been gifted
in his particular way, Peder would have had him disposed of.
The Radann could not afford to be weakened by someone whose
mourning was so open and so against the Lord's grain.

But the Radann could ill afford to lose a man whose hands
could hold off all but death with a single touch. He held his
temper, although his words were often curt.

"Marakas?"

Marakas par el'Sol held up *Verragar*. It was hard to see it—or perhaps hard only for Peder himself—but when it was pointed out, there was the faintest luminescence along the edge of the blade. The cutting edge.

"I cannot make it out," Samadar said quietly. "My eyes have seen sun for too long. Samiel?"

"It glows."

Their eyes met.

Marakas said, "The sword is alive."

Significant words from a healer.

"I did not realize it, until today. Whatever it is we seek, we've found. And finding it has woken the blade."

The words should have been a comfort. Peder glanced at the shortness of his shadow in the height of the day's light.

Samadar spoke the words that Peder would not. "And what will put it to sleep again?"

But Marakas the meek, Marakas the quiet, Marakas the last shed the words as if they were dirty clothing and he about to enter the baths for the first time in months.

In, Peder thought, six months.

"I am not certain, Brother," he said, although his eyes lingered upon the line of the blade, upon *Verragar,* "but I want to find out."

"Well?"

The shadows were longer and darker than any the sun could cast. A man stood in their center, dressed in the finest of human conceits: silks of a brilliant dye, gold chains around throat and wrist. At his feet, literally paralyzed by her own fear, was a woman who would perish when her heart stopped beating. She bore no marks, of course; Lord Ishavriel had forbidden them all but the most invisible of torments.

He had forbidden them *this,* but this they could, with speed and delicacy, take. In a city of souls—especially souls with this blend of light and dark, this shade of peculiar gray, this uncertainty—that was as much self-control as they could muster. The rules were clear: the powerful preyed. The powerless served, in one fashion or another.

"Telkar," the creature said.

Telkar ad'Ishavriel never acknowledged his Lord's name when his Lord was not present. He looked down upon the prone form of the fallen woman; her hands were trembling as he forced her to slowly unwind the silks that covered her body. The humiliation was delicate; for one newly come from the Hells it was almost beneath notice.

But Telkar had arrived early, at his Lord's behest, and he had been held in check a long time. This was as close to freedom as he had yet come in a world so full of textures, shades, colors, *light*. The hunger was more than visceral; it had become so strong there was almost nothing left.

"I am almost done."

"There is . . . trouble."

"Ishavriel-Malak," he replied, using the subservient form of the name, "you are beginning to annoy me."

"A pity," a voice said, in a language that was not, and had never been, of the *Kialli*. "As a servant, he is wiser than the master."

The woman at his feet was forgotten in that instant, as was his momentary irritation; all hungers were taken by the so-called Southern winds. The shadows were torn from the wall and ground, from the element of sky he had taken, and from his victim, before he could finish pivoting in the direction of this unforeseen enemy.

The sun rose in an instant over the poorest streets of the Tor Leonne, and the clansmen there—men who were often forced, in penury, to sell their children to the seraf houses—saw the light, and *knew* that god no longer dwelled in the heavens alone.

They had seen evil before, but they had never seen it stripped of familiar form, familiar word, familiar gesture. They had seen it before—and behind—swords; had seen it in the evidence of butchery along the roads during the hungry season, where quick death might have served the bandit's purpose just as well; had seen it in the death a man gives his wives for the purpose of his guest's pleasure; had seen it in a multitude of ways, each act a shard of a broken whole.

They had seen it in themselves, had never named it, had perhaps used and worked with it in their time. Shadows, secrets, lies—elements of the foundation upon which power was built.

But when *Verragar* called the sun's light, and the sun's light *came,* the shadows were burned away in its harshness. They saw themselves, for a moment, truly—but before they could be broken by that vision, they saw something more: what they could, what they *must* become.

The Radann held drawn swords.

Verragar sang first, and perhaps because of it, hers was the strongest voice, the brightest light. Radann Marakas par el'Sol fell silent as his flame washed over the creature the sword called *demon,* and when the flames parted, there was nothing human left.

Saval, Arral, and *Mordagar* joined in.

There were two demons in the streets of the Tor Leonne. And four angels.

Peder kai el'Sol heard the screaming as the flames stripped the disguise from the only enemies that he now had. Politics were forgotten. The streets of the city consumed them; there was the creature, with his great, furled wings, his elongated body, the fine, long arms that ended in a set of gleaming claws. His skin gleamed in the sunlight as if it were forged and polished.

Ebony was paler than the whole of his eyes.

"You do not know what you interfere with, mortal," the creature said, speaking in a language that resonated with depth and history—a language that Peder both heard as itself and as Torra. *Saval's* gift.

Had he desired *Balagar?* He would never feel that envy again. No man would take *Saval* from him while he lived, nor force his hand to another blade while he could wield one.

"This is impossible. Telkar—we were told—"

"That the mortals had forgotten our existence." The creature's smile was a predator's smile, a movement of long jaw and sharp teeth that looked nothing like a human expression of enjoyment or mirth, but nonetheless suggested it. He gestured.

To Peder's great surprise, a sword came to his clawed hand, emerging from air and darkness. "Did you expect Ishavriel to tell no lie? You are blood-bound for a reason."

"Telkar—"

"They are mortal. We are not. They recognize us because they have shiny toys. But they are not among the wise; they do not understand the nature of their weapons, and I see that they are only barely fit to wield them. One of them," he said, and his eyes cut the distance between Peder and the men who followed his orders, "will not be tolerated long."

The kai el'Sol understood exactly what was meant by the words. The sword he held had a song, but no voice; no method of telling him that he was, or was not, worthy as a bearer. And if he was not?

Fredero kai el'Sol had died for less.

Had died, in the end—Peder understood it now, completely, exactly—for *more*.

"If I am not worthy of the sword," Peder kai el'Sol said coolly, "the sword will judge." It almost cost him his life.

The beast descended, as if from a height, the red flame of his sword a living creature.

A creature answered by white flame, by light, by heat. *Saval* rose at once, a hair's breadth faster than Peder himself. They clashed, these swords.

The screams at his back grew louder and lesser; most, wise enough to understand how close they stood to death, had fled, but those that fear paralyzed remained as a chorus.

The second creature, the one that had seen them and offered a warning, was as meek as the merely mortal. One moment he was there, and the next, gone; the shadows swallowed him, but did not hide him. Nothing could hide one of the demon kind from the Light of the Lord.

To the music of fear, they fought, four men and one demon. Swords rose and swords fell. White light, white fire, white heat; red blood. They were silent, and when the creature laughed—and he laughed once, they allowed him that—the silence became heavy with anger, with determination. The Radann were not Northern priests; they were the *Lord*'s men. They had been trained not to dither and plead and stay for hours on bended knee, but to fight. To kill.

Marakas, healer-born, the weakest of the four, took the creature's arm, separating it at the shoulder with a clean stroke of blade, a savage movement. The creature grunted and replied; the great pinion of either wing snapped shut and flew wide in an eye blink. Marakas was thrown wide; *Verragar's* light was extinguished as the sword skittered against the dirt and stone over which they fought.

Peder heard what he thought was the sound of snapping bone; over the clatter of mail it was hard to tell what, if anything, had broken. There was no other acknowledgment of pain.

But *he* was the kai el'Sol, not Samiel, who was next to wound the creature, and not Samadar, the oldest of their number. They cut flesh and were cut in turn, their armor becoming his weapon and not their defense as it began to take heat and hold it.

One of you will not be tolerated long.

He saw the flame in the creature's eyes, the flame on the edge of *Saval*. Fire such as this he had seen at the end of the Festival of the Sun, when the kai el'Sol had bearded the newly crowned Tyr'agar while standing in the very symbol of the Tyr's power.

Fredero had defined the Radann, and *Balagar*—he saw this clearly now—would take no less a man.

But he had *Saval*. He would prove himself worthy of *Saval*.

With a cry that was half roar and half something he would not—could not, for he was the Lord's man—name, he called fire and light. They came in a winding twist of motion that reminded him of the wind and the wind's price.

The creature's roar was a marvel of contempt and amusement. He called *fire* and the light of it dwarfed the bonfires made of bodies at the end of great wars.

Kallandras looked up an instant before the sun's light changed. To either side, his uneasy allies did the same, stiffening and paling in the glow of red light. It was day's height.

"Is this how it starts?" Yollana asked him.

"I thank the Lady every day," he replied, his voice remote, his eyes upon the Tor Leonne's lower streets, "that I was not born a seer. I do not know where it starts or where it ends, Matriarch."

Margret said nothing; the light faded, the blue sky of sun's height returned. Watching her, Kallandras was reminded that the harshest of shadows cast across a person's face were never banished by light.

Against such a fire as the demon's were three swords and three men. But the three were the Lord's men, and they were his most powerful. They attacked in concert, their white light not extinguished by his red, even if it could not be seen across as great a distance.

Samadar was pierced by steel, his flesh puckered by fire. The pain forced a grunt from his lips, but the sword never faltered.

Samiel took the creature's left pinion.

Peder took his right.

They struck as one man, and when the creature reared up, his throat exposed in a roar that would have shamed the mythical dragons of the Northern wastelands, *Mordagar* pierced his chest.

And *Verragar,* once again in Marakas' grip, rose to sever his spine.

The roar became a scream. The creature's form dissolved in the red, red glow of the fire it had summoned, eaten from within by both blade and light. Its last act was to lose form entirely; fire spread in a sudden blaze of heat, red leaving black in its wake.

It was meant to be their deaths.

Baptized by flame and fire, blackened by the ash of their surcoats and the tendrils of hair and beard, four men were reborn in the poorest streets of the Tor Leonne. Three stood, one knelt; the body of their enemy dissolved and was taken, as all things were in the Dominion, by the wind.

The Tyr'agar was resplendent in ceremonial robes; white and gold lay beneath the face of the sun ascendant. The merciless blue of sky edged his robes, and the fall of two swords, one long and one short, had been perfectly arranged so that the casual observer might understand that *this* ruler was prepared for war. They caught the eye first, before sun, before robes, before finery.

He noted this dispassionately; the seraf who had been bold enough to aid him had been—of course—trained by the Serra Teresa di'Marano. Like a Northern miner, she could sift through the driest of dirt and find, cast aside by Lord and Lady alike, a perfect gem.

This seraf, a young man with broad shoulders and absolutely exquisite grace, was bred for personal service. He had been offered to the Tyr'agar by the kai Marano, Sendari's older brother. He had been accepted, his name—Aaran—unchanged.

The Serra herself seemed neither pleased nor displeased by the offering—which meant, if Alesso was any judge of the sternness of her mood, that she was in fact ill-pleased. The seraf that she traveled with was now an older man, and almost at the end of his useful service. He could be consigned, as the serafs were, to the Lady, having fulfilled the seraf's course and acquitted himself with visible honor. He was attractive in the way that older men are: he had about him that aura of wisdom so unsuitable, and therefore so beguiling, in a seraf.

He was not embarrassed to know the seraf's name, although he would never speak it aloud in the presence of others. Serafs' names were matters of practicality, but only those valued as wives were acknowledged to have them. And Alesso had taken no new wives.

Ramdan.

The youth had the same breadth of shoulders and the same height that the older seraf possessed; he had hints of the same wisdom. A fine gift. A fine gift, indeed, and one he was pleased to have accepted.

It was the only pleasant thought afforded him by the day's events.

"Tyr'agar."

He nodded, cool as the waters of the Lake, but infinitely less pleasant.

The Tyr'agnate of Oerta, Eduardo kai di'Garrardi, bowed, the gesture as pleasant and voluntary as the Tyr'agar's nod. Three serafs moved immediately to offer this most important of dignitaries the waters for which Alesso had risked so much.

He accepted the water—and then passed it, untasted, to one of the four Tyran he was, by custom, allowed in the presence of his Lord.

Silence fell like a sword, stilling the words of any who had seen the Tyr'agnate's action. Like contagion the silence spread to those less aware; the platform, with its cerdan, Tyran, and serafs, with its high clansmen, and Widan, became more silent than the Lake itself.

Even the winds deserted them.

The Tyran so honored—and so singled out—took a slow, loud sip of the water, lifting a hand to mouth and back as if the goblet offered him were a common tin cup and not the finest of Northern crystal. Had any cared to think the Tyr'agnate's action a gesture of boorish ignorance, the Tyran's action denied them the ability. He handed the cup back to the Tyr his life was sworn to.

Then, and only then, did Eduardo choose to drink.

I will kill him, Alesso thought; it was an effort to contain the words, to cage them. But not so great an effort as it was to keep his hand from the hilt of his sword; to deny Eduardo the satisfaction of his anger.

An angry Tyr was seen as weak if he did not act, and he could not afford to kill this man, not yet. Nor could Eduardo openly move against him. They were separated—as if they were errant young men—from the fight they both desired. But that would not always be the case.

He waited a moment; when words did not return to the platform of the Summer Sky, he turned to the Sword's Edge. He had

the privilege of seeing a very rare anger minutely change the lines
of the older man's face. Eduardo would miss that, of course. He
would also miss the fact that when motion began to return to the
serafs whom Alesso owned, and from them to the gathering at
large, that it did not return to the hand that had stopped in mid-
curl around strands of a beard.

Unfortunately for Alesso—and Eduardo, although he neither
knew nor cared—that anger, on a day like this, meant one thing:
Cortano was thinking of the Serra Diora. And he only thought of
her—or spoke of her—when he wished her dead. He was wise
enough, political enough, to understand the folly of his desire.
But to see the Tyr'agnate behave so disgracefully over a *girl,* and
to see the Tyr'agar he had personally chosen to support join Garrardi in this struggle, was enough to make him think the political
risk of her death worth taking.

Sendari was utterly mute.

They were saved from further awkwardness.

Red light blossomed in the sky to the South.

Into the stillness the wind returned bearing two things: heat, and
the sound of screaming. Fire. Sudden, intense, and compelling
in its beauty—a beauty that Widan fire and hearth fire had *never*
possessed.

Eduardo was forgotten in that instant. Alesso turned to Cortano; Cortano's eyes were wide. His hand had left his beard and
hovered midway between chest and face. He had cast something;
Alesso was certain of it.

"Sendari?" he said, his voice deceptively calm.

The Widan who was his closest friend was gray as new ash.
But he did not answer the question.

And that was answer enough.

The flames grew higher, brighter, wider; they seemed capable
of taking the sky from the Lord himself.

Alesso drew his sword. He shouted an order, and then another, bowing to his guests before he departed in the direction of
the fire.

Too late: the fire faltered. Noise returned, silence followed,
words broke it and then retreated; the conversation moved like
the Averdan ocean. He had seen that ocean so seldom it still contained mystery and wilderness.

Conversation, on the other hand, held only danger.

Eyes to the sky, he watched as the fires that had reached for the sun itself were banked. In the glimmering death of burned copper light, he thought he saw lightning, although the skies were as clear as the Lord could desire.

Alesso gathered his Tyran to him, and dismissed Eduardo almost summarily. The Sword's Edge was his shadow; Sendari his second. They began to walk down the road to the main gates, and stopped when they saw the four men.

They were almost bald—in fact, to Alesso's eye they *were* bald, but they were still some distance away—and they wore full armor, which was unusual in the Tor. They carried naked blades, which were forbidden almost all men who walked that road, but they had passed the Tyran and cerdan whose sole purpose was to weed out the acceptable from the unacceptable when granting passage.

Obviously, they were acceptable.

Although the cerdan paid with their lives, and the Tyran with their ranks, for any mistakes made, Alesso was not completely certain that he would trust them to stop these four regardless: they walked abreast, they strode with purpose, they carried blades that not only reflected the sun's light, but seemed to have swallowed it.

Lightning, he thought, and as the distance between the four men and the waiting Tyr dwindled, he recognized at least one of them by gait: Peder kai el'Sol.

Only the man's features were the same; his hair had been singed off, and the resulting ash had dusted his face into darkness. His eyes were narrow, his lips slightly thinned.

"It would not be wise," a voice to his left said quietly, "to greet them."

He turned, then, to see a face that he had never encountered before in broad daylight, exposed to the eyes of his enemies and his sometime ally. He was, quite literally, speechless.

"They have been tested," Lord Isladar of the Shining Court said, "and they have not yet been found wanting. They burn with the fire; they are the instruments of their weapons, not the masters." As he spoke the words, he fell to bended knee, and only then did Alesso—Alesso who took in all detail in a single glance—realize that he was dressed, and had been acting *all along,* as seraf.

The two, kinlord and seraf, were separated by such a distance that he could not easily combine them; in the attempt, he was silent.

"If Peder kai el'Sol served you before—and I will not question his service, as you accepted it and you are more conversant with mortal politics than I—he will serve you no longer, no matter what he chooses to say. And perhaps *that* will serve you against Ishavriel, perhaps not. I cannot stay, General; the events of this day have already begun to cast shadows in the Shining Court.

"But I advise you to clear the road, and to allow no obstruction to the Radann. They are . . . almost new. The swords they carry have been invoked for the first time in centuries; they have encountered the enemy they were forged to destroy, and they have emerged victorious.

"The Radann will return to their residence, unless they see you first. If they see you first, I believe they will behave in a fashion that is both imprudent and unlikely with the passage of but a single evening."

His bow held for a moment longer, and then he rose.

"Widan," he said quietly, to the silent Cortano. "The Shining Court has grown too large for subtlety; we have always warred among ourselves when our numbers are large, and they have grown. There may be culling. Be prepared."

He was gone.

Alesso turned to Cortano. "Sendari," he said. "Disperse these men in my name."

Sendari bowed at once.

The General was known for his instinct; he trusted it when he trusted little else. He chose. "Let them pass unhindered." He turned to the Sword's Edge. "Accompany me, please."

The word at the end of the curt, short sentence was only barely a request; had he been speaking to any other man, it wouldn't have been spoken at all. Cortano chose to ignore the slight.

Even before they had found shelter in the cultivated wilderness, the Widan had bent his will to silence, enveloping and protecting the words they would speak from eavesdroppers, no matter how powerful they might be.

"Ishavriel?" Alesso asked softly, in a tone of voice that he could not quite make free of threat.

"I do not know. No two members of the *Kialli* cooperate for long. Isladar plays his own game."

"Isladar," the General replied, "would not—if I read him correctly—allow demons to fight in the streets of *my* city before he owned it entirely."

"Am I to suddenly understand the minds of the *Kialli?*" Cortano frowned. "I am not Sendari, Tyr'agar."

"No." The silence was long. At last, Alesso said, "I ask your opinion only."

"Then in my opinion, no. Lord Isladar is cautious. He has rarely if ever offered advice. He has never shown interest in the domination—the obvious domination—of the merely human." There was irony in the words he spoke; irony in the words that followed. "Had he been human, I am certain he would have been Widan—one of mine, in fact."

He was willing to let go of his anger. It was wise, after all. Cortano di'Alexes had his pride, but he was no fool.

"Cortano, I have trusted your guidance, and I have even taken your orders on occasion. Forgive me mine, if you find fault with them, but find out what game is being played."

The Sword's Edge bowed.

9th of Scaral, 427 AA
Evereve

The nature of Jewel's rooms shifted during the first four hours she managed to sleep in something that did, after all, feel very much like her own bed. It was the first calming moment she'd had in this place.

She rose slowly because she didn't want to leave the familiarity of that bed; she dressed in clothing that would never again be so terribly, expensively gaudy, and she walked to the door. Took a breath. Opened it. Gold and gaudiness, high, domed ceilings, the quartered golden circle of bright magelights—all had vanished as if they were a waking dream. His halls were outside, but inside—she'd somehow made it hers.

Almost. The curtains remained closed, and she didn't have the courage to open them. She turned her head to the side and wondered, eyes tracing their straight, heavy fall, if she would any time soon.

The day had passed; although she was afraid her absence would let the rooms revert to their former state, she was also hungry, and she made the trek to the dining hall, following the lights as if they were servants; as if, in fact, they were somehow alive, and trapped and broken by their service just as the statues had been.

After dinner, however, she took advantage of Avandar's

awkward silence, broken only by sentences he fractured with a word or two from a different language, to come back to the room as quickly as possible.

She saw the doors as she drew near, and when she did see them she felt her shoulders drop two inches as she relaxed.

That night, she slept with the oldest and most worn of the blankets closest to her skin, drawing them up to her mouth and tucking them under her chin. She made certain that no stray limb, not even a toe, was exposed; there was comfort in that. Home.

What was missing were the sounds of the wing itself. As magelight, in the halls of Terafin, was not considered too great an expense, Teller and Finch often worked late into the night. Even when their voices couldn't be heard—and as they were the quiet ones, that was often—the comfort of their familiar footsteps could. Here, the silence was absolute. She filled it with her breathing.

The pack, cracked leather now fully round and almost ball shaped, was tucked into the corner nearest the doors. Avandar had told her just how useful he thought it would be—not at all— but she felt safer having it ready, and she wanted to leave it that way. Or so she'd told him. It was half true.

The other, more practical half, was that she'd managed to cram so much into the pack that every piece of clothing, every small pot, every piece of flint, was like the keystone in a large arch: if so much as one thing was pulled out, the whole would follow in a messy, inevitable spill.

She sat up in bed and pushed her hair out of her eyes. Reached for it, bound it back, and watched out of the corner of those eyes as the shorter strands popped free immediately. Shaking her head— which freed half the rest—she rose and dressed. The clothing was hers, or as much hers as anything in this place could be. She was happy to have it.

Avandar came in through the doors carrying a tray.

"You've missed breakfast," he said, obvious disapproval in the lines of his frown. Familiar, comfortable disapproval.

Jewel had discovered, over the days that had passed, that Avandar was most himself—or most the man she knew—when he was in these rooms with her. The farther away from them she got, the farther away from himself he got, as if all that bound him to the man she knew *was* what she knew of him, until—at the edge of the picture gallery that should have collapsed under the weight of its adornments—he lost Weston entirely and spoke in broken something-or-other, the language he never identified. His mother tongue, she was certain of it.

His whole demeanor changed. If she had ever needed proof that words had power—in and of themselves, and not wrapped in enchantment or bardic talent—it was there in the way his voice broke around syllables, like water around river rocks.

She thought about this now, her sleeves unrolled right to the wrists to cover the mark on her arm. She rarely wore her sleeves full-length; she liked to roll them up. Made her feel as if she was about to start working, even if the work she was doing didn't actually require it. But rolled up, she could see the stretch of red and gold and silver that disquieted her. The anger had passed. The explanation—that the mark was necessary to identify her in a way that would save her life—had been offered. She'd almost accepted it.

But it bothered her.

It was going to cause problems. She *knew* it, but didn't know how.

"Jewel?"

"Hmmm? Oh. Food. Sorry."

Asking him questions was tricky. Ask the wrong question, and he'd start to answer in the wrong language. Language was the first sign. It went downhill from there. But ask no questions, and she was certain they'd stay here forever, or for at least the next two weeks, after which it wouldn't matter much. In a bad way.

"Avandar?"

"Food first."

"I can talk and eat at the same time."

His raised brow was a clear indication of how poor a liar she was.

"I didn't say I could talk and eat *neatly*." He put the tray down on her desk. "Look, it's not like there's anyone to offend by my manners."

He raised a brow.

She ate first. Picked up the tray and started to walk to the kitchen before she remembered that there was no kitchen here— or at least not one she had access to. Wondered what the kitchen here was like—if there was one at all. It wouldn't have surprised her if food had magically appeared from the ether. In fact it would have surprised her if it hadn't. Not much place to grow things here.

"Avandar?"

"Yes?"

"You've eaten."

"Yes."

"You look—you look better."

His smile reminded her of the shadow candlelight cast. But the gaze that followed it reminded her of nothing in their long—well, friendship wasn't the right word for it. In fact there *was* no right word for the way they related to each other.

"Avandar," she said, knowing this was a bad question, but not knowing how to avoid it, "you've already said I can't leave the same way I came."

"Yes."

"Is there another way for me *to* leave?"

Silence.

"Can *you* leave at any time?"

"I would have said yes," was his quiet reply. He rose. Walked to her closet. Began to methodically straighten the dresses and coats that hung there, as if he, too, were aware that it was the familiarity of his routine in her life that made him a part of that life.

"And now?"

"This room, Jewel."

"Mine."

"Yes. But not even my—wife—was able to exact such changes in so short a time as you have made here."

"Maybe she wasn't as desperate."

"Perhaps. It is not a matter of will; she was not a weak woman in *any* way."

"Meaning that you think I am."

"Meaning," he said, lifting the shoulder of the dress she least liked and carefully realigning it on its hanger, "that I've seen every weakness you have, and I can guess at those you've never dreamed of."

Her hair stood on end.

"You would be," he continued, no words from Jewel said to break the stream of his, "so easy to break. The right threat, and you would crumple; there would be no need at all to carry it out, although I confess a certain bored amusement might cause your enemies to consider it. When her child was killed," he continued, and the way he said the word "her" made it clear he spoke of his dead wife, "she did not so much as blink an eye, and by that time, the only thing in the world that commanded any of her affection, any of her loyalty, was that child."

"You say that as if it were a good thing."

He turned, the dress gripped in one hand, the hanger in the other, as if they were weapon and shield.

"It was . . . an admirable thing. She had no defense against her enemies. They killed the child to cause her pain, and only to cause her pain. The only attack she could offer them was her absolute, her unwavering, distance. She gave them that. They took little pleasure out of what should have been a pleasure."

"And the child?"

He raised a brow.

"The child died knowing his mother didn't care at all."

"The child, as you say, was not so young as all that at the time of his death. He understood."

"And this is a good thing."

"Yes."

"Something you want from me?"

He turned his back to her. Placed the dress on the left rack. Turned back. Spoke to her in a language that made no sense. She privately thanked the gods for their momentary mercy.

"So you won't leave me here because this place has made a room for me and you're afraid it will turn the entire place into Terafin behind your back?"

"No." Language reasserted itself quickly; they were in her rooms. "If it turned the entire place 'into Terafin' as you so quaintly put it, I would have little concern."

"But?"

"You have not walked the breadth of my vision," he said quietly, "and I am not—have not always been—sane."

"But I—"

"You have seen the world that I am willing to share with at least one other living woman," he replied. "There are parts of this mountain's vastness that I share with no one. And not because I hoard. Are there not secrets, Jewel, that you would guard from even yourself if you had the ability?"

"The ability?"

"To lie," he answered softly. "To lie to yourself."

"Gods, I hate it when you talk."

Both brows rose slightly.

"You never talk this much," she explained, as she turned away.

"Except when you're telling me why whatever I'm doing is political suicide. I'm used to that. I never realized—I never did—how little I knew you."

"Does it matter? I serve you. I have always served you."

She turned to look at him. "Yeah," she said softly. "It matters. I don't know you. I know everyone else."

"Kiriel?"

"Even her, Avandar." She faced him now, drawing the hair out of her eyes, resting one hand loosely on her hip. "I know that she's half the dark god." The words that left her weren't the ones she meant to say; a sign of the gift and talent that she had always struggled to control. Good thing control wasn't everything. "But I know that there's more to her, that there could be *so much* more. That she's not the one to stand by while her child is killed and show nothing or do nothing; there's a rage in her that comes from a place that love hurt."

"Eloquently put. Half a dark god," he said to himself. "I sensed the darkness; I assumed she was half kin. More, perhaps."

"I know who she is. I don't always know what she'll be—and I'm afraid of it. I admit it." She laughed. "I know my den, Avandar. I know Arann. I know that he'd die for Terafin, and I know, I know that he'd take her orders over mine if it came to a choice."

Avandar raised a brow. "I would not be so certain."

"I am. I don't think he knows it. I'm selfish. I don't want him to know it. It would change what *we* have, because he'd feel different, not because I would. Angel would kill for me and die for me without thinking. Carver would do the same, but he'd complain a lot more. Finch and Teller and Jester? They'd have different, quiet lives."

His smile was thin, sharp. "You keep them to yourself."

"Yes. I do." She shrugged. "But you—you I don't know. And I thought I did because I could predict everything you'd do. I knew what you'd say when I wouldn't wear the council ring to Alea's funeral. I knew what you'd say when The Terafin—when she—before we left." She turned, the thickening in her throat unexpected and painful. "But knowing what you'll do isn't the same as knowing you.

"I don't."

"No."

"There's a way out that doesn't involve whatever it was you did to get me in."

"Yes."

She waited. "You think it's worse."

"I know it's worse," he said softly. "But I think we'll have little choice."

"What is it?"

"It's a very simple door." He rejoined dress to hanger, contouring its shoulders so that its fall was perfect. Showed her his back while he put it away. "Twice my height, ten times my width. It is covered, from height to depth, with runic symbols, each speaking of mystery, promise, wonder, and at the end of each, death. It was the door I discovered when I sought a place of safety; it was shown to me by . . . by a woman with vision much stronger than even yours." His expression froze a moment. "It was not an easy door to find. The path that led to it had been lost for . . . many years. Or almost so. I encountered . . . difficulty in making my way here, and when I chose to return to the world without, it was by alternate means."

"And the door?" she asked, because suddenly she *knew* what it looked like. The words, in runes she shouldn't have been able to read because they seemed the epitome of ancient and she hadn't mastered most of modern yet, were glowing with a light that seemed part sun and part the blood it went down on after battle's end, when corpses were strewn as carrion for the waiting and the watchful. But she could read them.

"Jewel?" His voice was sharp.

She was staring at the door that she could see in a vision that had nothing to do with reality; reading words that she knew would make no sense whatever were she to encounter them in the solidity of the here-and-now.

Two words stood out. Two words, warning, homage, mystery. Ownership. A cold, cold wind blew through the room; one that she alone felt. She shook herself, hard, and then turned to Avandar.

"Who was the Winter King?"

He closed his eyes.

CHAPTER FOURTEEN

10th of Scaral, 427 AA
The Northern Wastes

The Lord had not summoned them.

Had he, they would have met in the throne room, and spent the meeting on their knees before a throne that was impressive even to creatures who had no use for, and no patience with, such obvious trappings of mortal power.

Or who had not had patience before their return to the mortal plane. It changed them all, subtly, and in different ways, infecting them like a mortal disease, crippling them, fevering them. Power, upon the mortal plane, had always had a multitude of meanings, but they had been winnowed of those meanings in the Hells by the passage of millennia and the duties—the only true pleasure—of guardians.

High upon the peaks of the Northern mountains, surrounded by the sparse life, the endless cold, the clarity of nights so perfect the desire to spend a decade caught by starlight was at times as strong as the desire for the single pleasure they'd been granted when they had chosen to cleave to their Lord, the world returned to them. The kinlords were awakening.

Perhaps the awakening would have been faster had the world been more recognizably what it was at the time of Moorelas' final ride. It was not. Even the flowers had dwindled in the long absence of the *Kialli;* the trees—on the rare occasion they were allowed to travel far enough to see them—had lost all voice; the earth had been struck dumb enough that only the great among them could hope to hear the whisper that had once been greater than the roar of dragons. Of the Firstborn and their children, of the brethren, of their ancient enemies, their ancient brothers, only the mortals had flourished.

Surprising, that. They had been the weakest, and the shortest lived. In their youth they were glorious, but their youth was short; they grew into their bindings, bending and folding under the weight, finding new ways in which to deny themselves pleasure and power—and finding a perverse pride in that denial.

They called it dignity.

Lord Isladar had seen that perversity so often that he had grown, in his fashion, to admire it.

They are like the flowers, he would say, *and not the rock; they are so brief in their bloom one can pause to admire the blossom itself.*

And humanity has become your garden?

It has become, he had replied, to the ironic levity of the Widan Cortano di'Alexes, *my wilderness.*

Oddly enough, he found the company of the man who called himself the Sword's Edge almost pleasant. It, too, invoked memories of an earlier life, summoning them when least expected. Or desired. Among the *Kialli* there had been those like Cortano. Seekers of knowledge. He had not, oddly enough, chosen to be one of them, but he had admired the quality—for it was beautiful—of their odd obsession.

They were gone now. Their time in the Hells had driven them inexorably mad. They were the charnel wind, their voices raised in a howl of pain and fury and fear as the years became a significant weight, for the whole of their world was now knowable; that they understood everything; behind them, in a past they had forsaken for love and pride, were mysteries they were never to discover. They had slowly given up their memories; they had become lesser kin. Demons, yes, but their names were now merely tools for the most powerful to use.

He remembered it well. Remembered it now, when those mysteries, when that tangled past, could once again be offered to them as a gift.

Morellius, he thought. A name. The past. Morellius would have despised him; the *Kialli* rarely chose to honor friendship.

He bowed his head; the wind was cold, not hot, and it was almost silent. Almost. But he had invoked the element, and it was restless. "Not now," he told it. "But soon."

He looked out from the heights into the depths of the basin the Lord had carved in a single motion. It was there that he took what He denied the *Kialli:* human life, human pain, human fear. It was there that He sustained himself, feeding upon the souls of the living, regardless of whether or not they had made their final Choice. It was there that He forced them to bear witness to His actions, for in consuming the living, He kept their souls from the Hells for eternity. Kept their souls from the shepherds. The kinlords.

And it was there that the pentagram had been traced against ice-covered rock by blood and unguent; there that it had been burned, in a flash of elemental fire, into the rock itself, a seamless scar that no foolish lesser kin could cross and destroy in its clumsiness.

But its five points were now four, and a vast sheet of thin, standing stone, the center point of which was a chair not unlike the throne of the Lord, now occupied its peak. It was empty, and the kin worked the rock itself in an attempt to appease the fury of their Lord. Anya a'Cooper's work was, indeed, worthy of the lesser effort of a god.

He understood—they all did—why Ishavriel had chosen to keep her. But faced with evidence of her power—and this was undeniable—they were unsettled. Sor na Shannen, before her timely destruction and return, had assured them all that no mortals of true power remained. The Cities had not risen, and their descendants, scattered around the lands that ringed the burning sand, had fallen into the smallness that occupied most of humanity. Mortals.

Anya, he thought, and smiled.

The Lord would rise soon and see to the throne. Anya a'Cooper would rise at the same time and take her place as anchor of the vast magical array necessary to maintain the fabric of the doorway to the Hells. She was wild and unpredictable, and she had grown to like pain—other people's, of course—rather too well, but she was afraid of the Lord's anger, and had she clearly understood just how angry he would be, she might not have been so foolish.

But she understood so little.

She did not understand, for instance, that to rip the wall from the mountain, and then—as an afterthought, when the Shining Palace began to crack and shudder—replace it, keeping only that section that contained her chair, would be so costly. She *did* understand the effort it took to repair the damage done to the Lord's edifice, because she was not in any fashion stupid, but she clearly had so little sense that she did not then realize the little shudders forcing her to clumsiness were the penultimate warning.

She *moved* the chair.

And her own weight.

Not even Kiriel would have that power at her disposal when she finally came of age and took her rightful place at her father's side.

Kiriel.

The wind sensed his weakness and buffeted him, howling in petulant displeasure.

"Not now," he said again. "Not yet. But soon; I promise it. The Lord's Fist meets soon, and I with it."

Although he knew the answer, he had the pleasure of asking Lord Ishavriel how long it would take to repair the damage that Anya had done to the gate.

It would distract them from the question that had driven him to the mountain's peak; distract him from facing the fact, yet again, that something in his plan had gone awry, and that he had not yet managed to discover how, or why.

He could no longer see Kiriel.

Lord Isladar was *Kialli.* It was undisputed. What was often the source of argument was the extent to which he had retained his power after the passage. His memory, as far as the surviving *Kialli* could ascertain, was perfect.

And it was memory, it was *identity,* in the Hells that had defined power. Those who had been driven mad by the loss of contact with the world had found new ways to define themselves until all that remained of them was a name, and that name deep enough, old enough, terrible enough to be invoked.

Isladar, therefore, should have been a power.

Instead he owned nothing, ruled nothing, fought little; he was like a mortal dog, but canny. The games he played they could not fathom, and they had made their attempts. Assarak, Etridian, Alcrax, and Nugratz had long since given up. Ishavriel had not, not yet. Because he remembered Isladar of old, and he did not trust him, although perhaps that was not significant; he trusted no one. But the others had games and goals that were obvious; their deviousness was spent in attaining them.

What are your goals, Lord Isladar? What is your game?

He had asked the question privately for the last thousand years, never coming close to an answer, but today he would be given a glimpse of either the game or the Lord, a reminder that some questions were not meant to be answered before one knew the cost the answer demanded. The Oracle's dilemma, if the Oracle still lived.

Lord Isladar came late to the Shattered Hall.

He drew the eye; there was something about him, that day, that was changed. He acknowledged the Fist of the Lord with a passing nod and took a seat.

Etridian spoke; Alcrax answered. Ishavriel remembered the sound and timbre of their voices, but he could not look away from Isladar—and he felt that he should. Something had changed, or was changing, and change was a force that was seldom contained or controllable.

The wind's howl was unaccountably sharp this day and he thought he heard—he thought he heard the voice of elemental air.

"The Lord," Assarak said quietly, "is . . . not pleased."

Lord Ishavriel was silent, his focus peripherally on the Generals, his intent entirely upon Lord Isladar. The kinlord sat in his chosen chair, forming and reforming rock the way nervous humans curl and uncurl their fists. *What game?* he thought. The movements could not be ignored; they were almost mortal, and while Isladar could be accused of many things, mortality was not one of them.

Lord Ishavriel was not the only Lord to notice; he was merely the first. As the minutes passed, they divested themselves of words; they were caught by the spectacle. Fidget. That was the human word.

When he had their attention, or perhaps when he had endured as much of it as he desired, Lord Isladar rose and bowed. "Your pardon, Generals," he said softly, and this was another of his traps or his lies, for *no Kialli* showed deference or tendered apologies that were not forced. "But I find of late that the containment of the hells is . . . difficult."

"Difficult?" Etridian said sharply.

Isladar's reply was a long while in coming, and they did not have the time to wait. But they took it; it was almost as if, for an instant, the concept of theater gripped them as strongly as it gripped the mortals.

"Difficult." He repeated the word as if he had tried all others and found them equally inadequate. "The Hells and the mortal realm have become so different I almost doubt my memories of life before the Choosing."

The silence that descended upon them all was bitterly cold, a thing not of the Hells. They were immortal. Time passed beneath their notice as they absorbed what he had said.

"You are . . . bold," Lord Etridian said at last, shaking himself free of the fascination that had been caused, after all, by mere words.

"Am I?" Lord Isladar turned and walked toward the Western wall. Touched it. Murmured three distinct words: a plea for permission. There was only one being of whom the *Kialli* Lords begged for anything.

The walls resounded with their Lord's reply. Rock moved as if it were cloth being pulled to either side of a great, glassless window. The wind came whistling across its width, but did not enter, or if it did, it was too slight a sensation to be worthy of comment.

"These are not the lands we walked," he said softly, as they rose to bear witness. "Nor the lands we ruled. Look: beneath us lie the streets of the Shining City reborn. They are simple rock and soil too poor to be called anything but dirt. They are crowded with creatures too slight to understand that all identity is memory. Where are our natural enemies? Where is our former glory?

"The Hells have changed us much."

Silence, silence, silence, silence. Only Ishavriel chose to break it. He had to; although Isladar utilized no obvious magics, his words were slowly binding them all—and Ishavriel was not to be bound by Lord Isladar of the *Kialli*. "And what would you have of us?"

"Of you? Nothing." But they clashed, these two, in the silence that followed, their expressions hardening into complete neutrality. The four remaining Generals waited in silence, sensing battle. "But I would call a *Kialli* parliament in which to hold our discussion."

Memory.

What Lord Isladar invoked, he invoked, and once summoned to the plane—as any summoned creature would—those memories fought for freedom.

Not even Lord Ishavriel, who had the most to lose in this meeting, could shrug off what Isladar had cast upon them. "You . . . play a dangerous game."

"Do I?"

"Were the parliaments ever anything else?"

"They were a way of weeding out the weak," Lord Etridian said unexpectedly. "A way of insuring that only the capable ruled." He rose. He rose and went to the window that Isladar had made in the wall. "You take a risk, Isladar."

"I call parliament," the *Kialli* Lord repeated evenly. "As was our custom, you are free to refuse it."

Etridian smiled. "I will not refuse it. Alcrax?"

Alcrax's smile was slow to come; he did not choose to mar it with speech. He nodded lazily, eyes half-lidded.

"Assarak?"

"With pleasure. I remember the parliaments. I led a few."

"I led many," Etridian said. He had lost the demonic seeming that he habitually forced his body into, reverting to something older and wilder, taller and infinitely more beautiful. Instead of spikes or spines, instead of steel blades, he wore two arms, long and slender; his horns fell away into strands of hair, and those strands fell longer and longer until they touched his back, his spine. He spread his hands wide, and then brought them back in a circular arc whose midpoint was the searing light palm-to-palm contact birthed.

"Nugratz?" Soft, now. The name was a threat.

Nugratz, of the five the one who had never chosen to take a human form, rose. He stretched his wings like the duke of the Hells he had very recently been, and fire edged his shadows. A warning to Etridian.

A warning to them all.

But having given that warning, he merely said, "I will join the parliament when it is in session."

They all turned then. "Ishavriel?"

Ishavriel's smile was slowest to grow, wildest to finish. He stared past Etridian, whose demand for an answer would have been a call to combat in the planes of the Hells, and met Lord Isladar's eyes. "Have you forgotten, *Brother*," he said, lifting his arms in what was almost a mirror gesture of Etridian's motion, right to left, left to right, "that it was *I* who convened the greater parliaments at both Scarran and Lattan?"

"I remember it well." Isladar was still as the stone; perhaps more still; the North was warmer than the light in his eyes, although there was so little light to reflect. "And I remember the last of the parliaments. I remember the call that went out into the elements and the wilderness. I remember the question put to us. Oh, yes, Brother. I have forgotten nothing."

"Do you seek to test me *here?*"

"I seek," Isladar said, placing his hands upon the new-made stone, "a parliament, no more, no less."

"Then choose," Ishavriel said. "All of you. Choose the element. I will convene."

"I think," Etridian said, his smile chill as Ishavriel's, but more contained, "that Isladar should convene. He is not of the Fist, after all. He is no one's ally."

Isladar bowed.

"Etridian, be grateful our Lord has forbidden the Contest." Ishavriel's teeth grew sharper, longer—but the beauty of his expression was unaltered. He was—they all saw it—*Kialli* in a way that they had not been since—

Not since the end, and the beginning.

"I choose the element of air," Isladar said.

"Air? Air is hardly an element."

"Think, Etridian," Isladar's response was quick, quiet, wild in the way that Ishavriel's face and voice had been.

"*I* should think? You play games, Isladar. This was your request."

"We have not called parliament since Moorelas fell. Call parliament in fire, in water, and the Lord will know."

"He has not forbidden it."

"No. Will you take the risk that He might?"

Silence. Then, "We might convene in the earth itself."

"The earth here is not wild enough to hold us. Can you not sense it? The Shining Palace was made of rock and earth, but there was no struggle."

"Perhaps the old magics are finally dead."

"Perhaps. But I would counsel against the risk."

"As you have always counseled us, Isladar. I would expect no less—or rather, no more. Were you less cautious, you might have ruled—"

"Enough. We have had this discussion."

Etridian's smile was obsidian. "I will accede. Air."

"Air."

"Air."

"Air."

Ishavriel nodded.

Had they been trapped by the Shattered Hall in the same way they had been trapped by the Hells? They had never sought to question their use of that place. Of all the rooms the Shining

Palace contained, none matched the Shattered Hall for grandeur; none made so plain the power of the Lord over the earth itself. Had His journey from the Hells to the mortal world injured Him? Had it weakened His power, denying Him the full force of the strength He had once displayed when He ruled this vast plain? Perhaps. But the Shattered Hall had been a work of power, and for that reason, they had chosen to grace it.

They could not convene parliament within the halls themselves, although Etridian had suggested it. Such an act would do one of two things: destroy the hall, or force their Lord to expend His power to maintain it in the face of the wild element. Either outcome was not to anyone's advantage; implicit in their choice was the mountain's heights or the Broken Plains beyond the citadel.

And once they had chosen the heights, they felt it: freedom. Memory.

Lord Ishavriel wondered if they would ever enter the Shattered Hall again.

Isladar convened.

He called the wild air, and it came, fighting every inch of the journey. They watched; they watched in a silence made of memory, but sharpened by observation. Lord Isladar of the *Kialli* did not use the powers he now displayed in the Hells because the Hells were not elemental.

Was he a greater power here? A lesser one?

The millennia stretched out before them as it had behind, and they realized that the question was not, would no longer be, rhetorical. They were silent, measuring the power of an enemy. Understanding, truly, that if they made their demesnes in this new world, power would mean something different than it had in the Hells.

Hunger, there. Lord Ishavriel felt its sudden bite. As the wild air washed over them, stinging and biting in a momentary rage, he wanted more than the Hells. Had he come here at his Lord's command? Yes. He had obeyed without choice, and with a cunning and a thought bent to the Lord's will, the Lord's purpose. But now . . .

Hunger.

Perhaps it had always been there.

Perhaps they had missed it because they were no longer exposed to their only sustenance: the torment of the fallen; the justice of the damned.

It made no difference; Isladar had called their attention to it, turning them at last from the insular world of the Hells and returning to them two truths. The first, the simplest, elemental power. Not in the way that they had used it since they first set foot upon the broken ground of the Northern Wastes. No, that had been simple—a tossing of fire, a slight puckering of the earth, a whispering of wind. Water, they had only touched to ward the fall of snow when they found it unpleasant or inconvenient.

But they had wielded the elements as big clubs, clumsily and thoughtlessly. Here, now, they were asked to do something different: to find the heart of its wilderness, and to merge with it, succumbing to its voice while maintaining their own.

To speak, to think, to act in their best interests while the elements attempted to destroy them.

"Isladar!" Etridian cried, as the wind's voice threatened to destroy the fabric of simple words.

"Not yet!" he yelled back, swaying, his feet two inches above the ground, his body at the eye of the growing storm. "But soon. Prepare yourselves!"

The convener was not required to give warning. But this was so old, so distant, that it had become new; it was new to them all. They accepted what he offered without comment, and when the winds came, they forgot it. No warning could prepare them.

The air itself tried to destroy them.

The convener began to speak.

The ground receded from their feet in a rush of light and swirling snow.

Above the mountain's peak, above even the highest of the towers the Lord had built for his own amusement in the Shining Palace, the Fist of the Lord and the Lord's shadow stood. It would tire them to stand thus.

But no Lord of the Hells could admit to such a weakness.

Formality was lost to wilderness.

Ishavriel spoke with the air's voice as if reacquainting himself with the niceties of speech. But snow and rock and fine, fine ice crystals could not obscure sight of his expression as he faced Lord Isladar and spoke.

"I wonder, Lord Isladar, if you know where Kiriel is."

Lord Isladar merely smiled and shook his head. It was clear that his understanding of the heart of the element had not dimmed with time; he spoke with his voice, and without apparent effort.

"She is my charge," he replied evenly.

"And have you been so careful with her?"

"As careful, it appears, as you yourself have been with yours, Lord Ishavriel," he replied, showing a hint of a smile—a *Kialli* smile, "I have Anya. And perhaps it is best that things remain as they are."

"Yes, Ishavriel. You've dropped the leash of the mage, and she runs too wild for the Lord's liking." Etridian paused. "And too wild for ours. Isladar's keep destroyed a *Kialli* Lord or two who had grown careless." He shrugged. "Your charge destroyed the pentagram that anchored the gate. The Lord caught and held the spell, but it was a test of His power. I am surprised you did not feel His anger in the South."

"She has not been destroyed," Ishavriel replied, forced to defend the most cherished of his discoveries. Forced, in fact, to retreat from his attack on Isladar's.

Kiriel was almost the pastime of choice for Lord Ishavriel in the lull between the battles of the Hells and the war that was—finally—to start in earnest.

"No." Before Isladar could gain advantage from Etridian's words, Etridian added, "And perhaps we should not be surprised. There is some precedent. Isladar has shown a surprising inability to rein in his bastard, and she is still indulged."

Alcrax snarled. "She is worse than indulged. The Lord has broken His covenant. He has *handed* her power, where all others are forced to prove their worthiness by earning it."

"Which, in most cases means a simple baring of tooth and claw." Isladar's correction was cool. "If power is defined by the struggle, she will earn her place. And if it is defined merely by killing, she has *already* earned it."

"We will never find out, will we? He has given her power."

"He has done the unthinkable: He has weakened Himself. His power is not what it was, and hers is not what *His* was. The extent of her ability to control what she now wears has not been tested. We will," Isladar said softly, the sudden narrowing of his eyes a signal, "find out. If the Lord's work is ever completed. What, Lord Ishavriel, was the mage thinking?"

"How can anyone know, with Anya?" Before he could be attacked for such an admission, he lifted a hand; ice swirled around it, drawing blood to the surface of skin without breaking it. Thus, the discourse of kinlords. "You have her, Isladar, has she not spoken with you?"

"I have her in a protected place. As you are all well aware, I am capable of protecting sleeping mortals." He shrugged. "She has not finished with the human fevers; she will either perish or survive. The words she has spoken, as often happens at such times, make little sense. Can she truly see the color of words? Can she taste them?"

Unspoken, the words hovered. *Is this the creature upon whom the success of the Hells gate rests?* And more, *Is this creature truly the prize of your collection?*

Lord Ishavriel was furious. He forced the fury back, but the winds buffeted him a moment before he gained, and held, his footing. Hard to concentrate here.

Isladar's face betrayed nothing; no hint of satisfaction, no amusement, nothing.

Still, there was a contest here, as there had so often been contests in the parliaments, hidden but deadly. The perfect game for Ishavriel and Isladar to play so casually.

Nugratz, wings stretched from tip to tip, was nonetheless uncomfortable enough in the element that he did not attempt to speak. Flight was his strength, but the air in the Hells was not as wild—could *never* be as wild—as this.

"Ishavriel," Etridian said, his arms stiff as he, too, fought the battle of wild air. "The question. Why did the mage breach the pentagram?"

"She was tired. I was gone. She was, I believe, 'bored' with standing." He turned a moment to Isladar, and said coldly, "I *will* have her back."

"If I so choose."

"You go too far, Isladar."

Etridian shrugged. "The question, Ishavriel."

He had no desire to answer it. "I have not spoken with her, Etridian. I do not have an answer."

"And you understand her so little you cannot surmise?"

"I assume she wanted a chair. She was told—by Vantinir, the human Northerner—that a chair would disturb the gate; that she was not to bring anything but rock and herself to the pentagram.

"From the spells at my disposal in her quarters—and they are few, as she tolerates so little—I surmise that she took him at his word, returned to her rooms, and removed the stretch of the wall that contained the throne. I admit my surprise that the Shining Palace itself survived." He paused a moment, then added, "She was wise enough to ask permission to shape the rock; she received it."

"And how long will it take before the gate is fully restored?"

"How long will it take for Anya to either escape or succumb to the fevers? There *is* a reason that we have allowed her her existence here, Etridian. The gate cannot remain anchored—could not have been opened—without her."

"The Lord's power was not what it is now."

"Then ask our Lord," Ishavriel said softly. "But as I said, He has not yet destroyed her, and He has destroyed two for failing him at the gate. We require her presence."

"So you say."

"If you wish it, challenge her. Unlike Kiriel, Anya *has* earned her rank, such as it is. She has power, and she has learned to wield it."

"To move a chair, and collapse the gate. The armies will be delayed."

"Perhaps you forget, Etridian, that I am a part of the Lord's Fist. I understand well the cost to the armies."

Assarak finally spoke. "While I find this discourse amusing, it is pointless. We do not have the luxury of a full parliament; we are bound by mortal time. If Anya a'Cooper was not destroyed for her part in the gate's . . . interruption, she is obviously necessary.

"And if Kiriel has not yet been destroyed, so much the better; she offered me challenge, and I will accept it at my leisure. If she lives that long. Isladar, is the mortal taint so strong in her that she will live—and die—in a limited span of years?"

Isladar did not reply. They knew the answer to the question. She was mortal; the god-born were all mortal. And she would live a shorter span of years than one who had never been graced by the blood of the Lord of Night. It was for that reason, among many, that Isladar was so poorly understood by the Generals; Kiriel had commanded his time and attention from birth, and there was so little to be gained for it.

"If you wish to discuss Kiriel, I am willing," Lord Isladar replied. "But it will take time."

Time caught in the pull of the angry, exultant wind. Assarak shrugged broadly. "I care little enough for your pet. Ishavriel's at least serves a useful function." His expression shifted; he dropped ten feet and shored himself up by dint of will and expenditure of power. "The war will be fought, and it will end; we will rule here. The Covenant, and the mantle, were never meant for the planes of earth." He smiled, the muscles of his face giving the expression the nuance of menace.

"Perhaps." Isladar looked up, lifting his head until his eyes were level with Ishavriel's. "*Telkar* ad'Ishavriel was killed in the streets of the Tor Leonne."

Ishavriel cursed, but quietly. Word traveled *far* too conveniently. "I was aware of this."

"I was not," Assarak said, speaking sharply. "Who killed him?"

"Humans."

"Mages?"

"No."

"Impossible."

"It was seen."

"And what of it?" Etridian broke in. "We have *power* now—perhaps it is time that we stop skulking in the pathetic shadows humanity casts. We will rule, but not by hiding. Not by waiting."

Isladar let his words fill the silence that was left between the cracks of the wind's roar. Then he said, quietly, *"Mordagar. Arral. Saval. Verragar."*

"What of them?"

"They are awake, courtesy of Telkar's inability to, as you say, skulk in pathetic human shadows."

"I did not hear their voices," Assarak replied.

"And they, no doubt, cannot yet hear ours; the distance is too great. But I have seen their light, and I have heard their voices. The Radann do not—not yet—know how to use them."

"In a day, it has become . . . interesting to be in the Tor Leonne."

"And what of the fifth?"

"*Balagar* was nowhere to be seen." His smile was soft. "But the Sun Sword is keening now. Listen, if you have occasion to approach the city."

"We need to kill the boy," Assarak said coldly.

"And," Etridian added, diverting attention from his failure in that regard, "the Radann. Isladar, tell the Tyr that the Radann must be destroyed."

"He is aware of this, Etridian. Our plans in that regard have been—"

"Now."

Isladar bowed his head.

But he did not, in fact, agree. Minutes passed as they discussed elements of lesser importance. But hours would not be wasted here: the air was too strong, and their own skills too atrophied, to remain long.

The air left Isladar last, swirling at his feet in such a leisurely fashion the edge of his robe seemed liquid to the eye. He bowed to it, offering what the others had not: a benediction. A gratitude. The wind's voice, here as in the desert, was strong. Much stronger than the earth's voice, although the earth did have a voice. Had he called it too weak for a parliament? Yes. And it was; but too weak and voiceless were not the same. The earth, beneath the surface of water and the force of air, was alive.

He bespoke it as the winds reluctantly let him go and his feet grazed the ice-covered surface. The shock of foot against living ground had dimmed with the passage of years. But he was *Kialli,* not human, and the passage of years had been slight enough to make little dent in the visceral reality of millennia in the Hells.

Millenia in a place that defied things merely physical, in a universe where sight, where sound, where sensation itself, was filtered through two things: The Lord and the damned.

The world enveloped him; the elements, slow to wake to his presence, now called him, faintly, by a name he had not used since before the beginning. The Hells were gone.

In a moment—less—he could be sent flying back to them; in the next moment, he could be called forth again. As if he and the rest of the *Kialli* were fragments of memory, hidden parts of their Lord's unknowable past. It was truth; he acknowledged it. He had always been the pragmatic Lord, in either universe.

When the air no longer held him, he whispered to its keening presence; it roared back, ice crystals skittering along the surface of his skin in the wake of its voice. He spoke again; air rippled the length of his arms, pulling at the cloth that surrounded them, snapping at the tips of his fingers in petulant demand.

He had raised Kiriel from birth with the help of a Southern slave. He knew what no other *Kialli* Lord had ever truly learned: How to deal well with petulance.

I am called, he told the elemental wind, *on all sides. You have taken the measure of my enemies and my allies. They watch me; they are cunning. And they listen. What they see does not concern me. What they hear does.*

Carry the words away from them, if you can, and when the words are well away, we will destroy the mountain's peak.

He waited; the wind bit at his skin. On the odd occasion, it had drawn blood, but he had never angered the element enough to fight—to *truly* fight—for his life. Just as he had never angered his Lord.

Not enough.

The ground in the North was cold. The water above it, frozen and thick, had a more accessible voice. But water was not useful, not yet; earth was essential. He waited until the attention of air was elsewhere, and then channeled his power through ice and water and into the ground itself.

The ground answered, rumbling and slow. *Here,* there was anger and a desire for blood—or war, he could not be certain which. The voice of the earth was sluggish, slow, thick with the cold and the presence of water. He had wakened it over the past decade, calling softly, coming at regular intervals to stand in the same spot, by the mountain's foot, while he relived his first attempt to call the earth to heel.

He had been young then, but not so young that he thought power was a substitute for intelligence; he watched the success and the failure of others before he planned his own attack. Lord Isladar of the *Kialli* had always been capable of absorbing the lesson in another's failure. It was considered cowardice in the Hells; it had been considered prudence upon the plane.

He weathered both with the same ease.

You are known by what you choose to hate, and what you choose to love. If you wish to have no weaknesses, you will disdain either.

Truth, there. The fierce love that the *Kialli* had once been capable of had been winnowed by the Hells; their passion was in hatred, and it was considerable.

Ah. There. He lifted his head as the earth woke. Spoke to it, the syllables forming slowly, as if speech itself were fighting against his use.

The element spoke his name.

Isladar.

He replied. In that exchange of syllables, two hours passed. The rest came more easily.

The mortal.

He felt, rather than heard, the earth yield to his request. Ice cracked at his feet in a ring; it was pushed aside in shards so slowly one might have thought the earth had no power.

Until one saw the ground continue to rise beneath one's feet, the movement slow as glaciers, but as inexorable. He stirred a

moment, the thrum of the earth's voice almost a comfort. Earth
had been his first element because in all ways it was the hardest:
it required, among other things, the patience that the *Kialli*,
immortal each and every one, so often lacked.

Youth was here.

Memory.

And all identity was memory.

"Thank you," he said softly, in his own voice.

The earth replied; it split down the middle, falling in on itself
as it crumbled away from a shape at its center. Prone, dusted in
rock and rubble, it lay; he watched it only until he could discern
the rise and fall that spoke of breath.

Then he walked to where it lay, prone, a thing carved of flesh,
not earth, not air, not water. Lifting a gentle hard, he brushed the
rockdust and dirt away from her face. There was familiarity in
the gesture of comfort, and more; it surprised him. He had forced
himself to it with Kiriel, learning, over the course of a decade
and a half, to offer her the comfort she craved. It was a binding;
he had created a need, or perhaps exploited one that already
existed, as just another move in the long game. But as she had
grown—and she grew so quickly—she had hidden the need for
comfort from everyone but Ashaf. He should have been relieved.

Odd, that he was not. He did not lie to himself; he had never
lied to himself. It served no useful purpose. But there were some
truths that were slow to surface, slow to demand the attention. As
his hands brushed the last of the dirt away from Anya's face, he
acknowledged that, in his fashion, he missed the child Kiriel.

Anya a'Cooper was not that child, but there were similarities
and echoes. Kiriel was *not* mad; he had seen to that with care.
But she was vulnerable, powerful, and unpredictable. And she
was, of course, mortal.

He did not touch Anya when she was conscious. None of the
Kialli did, save Ishavriel; she had seen to that with an efficiency
he admired.

In fact, the only person, with one notable exception, whom
she had been physically affectionate toward had been Ashaf,
Kiriel's nursemaid. The old woman, sun worn and careworn, had
not returned that affection; she had managed, on a good day, to
look at Anya a'Cooper with a tremulous pity, but no more, and
that pity had only barely risen above her fear.

And what, in the end, was there not to fear? Anya a'Cooper

was a law unto herself. She had more power than any human had ever possessed, with the possible exception of the mages of the Cities of Men, long dead, long taken by desert sand and sun, but she had no understanding of power itself. She had not struggled to hone it for the sake of supremacy, but rather, at the request of Lord Ishavriel, and when she was bored, she would often destroy the room she was taught in in a sudden flash of rage. She hated to be laughed at—and no *Kialli* Lord could deny her that weakness, it was so much their own—but what constituted being "laughed at" was a mystery to the Lords, for it often involved no malice, or even awareness, on their part.

The Lord had forbidden her death.

Isladar was not so certain that, had he remained completely neutral, Anya a'Cooper would not have survived. She had an animal cunning, a child's cunning, a vulnerability that shifted and turned into a strength.

She had no sense, and no ability to plan, but she was driven by a pain that the damned know, and few others. They could sense it, all of the *Kialli* who had served in the Hells for so long; pain was their speciality, their drug—as Lady Sariyel cleverly called it—of choice. It was their compulsion; it was the silk that was twined round the chains to take the edge off their bite when one pulled against them.

They therefore flocked to Anya a'Cooper's pain like moths to flame, and like moths, they were often consumed. Because, of course, no one who had harvested the damned could easily resist the desire to take up the challenge and inflict other pain, stronger pain, a pain that bore signature and name.

She didn't approve.

Yet she lived with the *Kialli,* not the humans. And the one friend she had at Court was the only other misfit: Kiriel, the Lord's child, the half-human godling who had been Isladar's keep.

Kiriel was allowed to touch Anya; Kiriel was the only denizen of the Shining City who had bitten Anya—albeit when she was a young child—and survived the act. Anya, twice Kiriel's age, had a sentimental weakness for children—one that her madness and her instability had not damaged, or rather, had not damaged in a way that was easily comprehended by *Kialli.*

She was their monster, for although she was powerful she did not desire power—but she was willing to risk her life in the contest, again and again. And what did she gain? Nothing. Anya desired affection. Love that she could trust.

What was trust to the kinlords?

What, he thought, was trust to anything alive?

Anya a'Cooper was not, in any appreciable way, intelligent—but she had that low animal cunning that is far more important than things intellectual for survival. She had walked through the fires. Although she desired love and affection, she knew better than to believe in either.

That was the mortal trap. He admired it. As a way of inflicting pain, it was long and slow, and so very few of the kinlords understood its appeal for that reason.

The kinlord brushed her skin clear of the last of the dirt; he took one long look at her face, and then bowed.

"Anya," he said. When she did not stir, he infused her name with just a hint of power. **"Anya."**

It was a calculated risk. Anya a'Cooper could smell magic almost before it was summoned, and she considered all magic her province; she was willing to share with Lord Ishavriel, and she never went against a dictate of their Lord. When, that is, she understood them.

Her eyes snapped open, sleep shattering like dropped glass.

"Anya," he said, wiping his voice clear of even the echo of power. He bowed.

"Was I under the dirt?" she asked. "Did you think I was dead? Did you bury me?" She was on her feet before she'd finished the sentence. That, she'd learned in the Hells.

His bow deepened. Her voice had the high, sing-song lilt that spoke of, that meant, death. "You were indeed beneath the surface of the earth. You were not dead, no—but, Anya, Lord Ishavriel has taught you of the dangers of using too much power. You were nearly consumed by the fevers."

"Lord Ishavriel," she said smartly, "also says there's no such thing as too much power. And what does that have to do with being buried?"

"The fevers were strong enough to last two days. You are in the Shining Court. Lord Ishavriel was not here to protect you. I apologize if I've offended you, Anya, but I had to put you somewhere safe. The other kinlords would not see you beneath the surface of the earth."

Her eyes were narrow as a blade's edge. He met them, unblinking. It was important, with Anya, to meet her eyes when one offered her a truth that one hoped would prevent her from entering the black rages that meant death.

"Where," she asked softly, "was Lord Ishavriel?"

"Anya, you know this already. He did not run; he did not desert you. Did he not tell you that the Lord had sent him South?"

She was momentarily nonplussed; her forehead creased. "Oh," she said at last. "You're right. I forgot. South where?"

"In the Dominion," he replied. "The Dominion of Annagar."

"Did he tell me why he was going?"

"I'm sorry, Anya, but I do not know that. He is a kinlord, as am I; we seldom share each other's plans."

Her eyes narrowed again. "You don't like him, do you?"

"No," he replied. "Nor he, I. The kinlords do not like each other. It is not what we do." He had had this conversation with Anya before, but it was never wise to refuse to answer her questions.

"Where is Ishavriel now?"

"He has returned to the Shining City, but he cannot remain here long." He bowed again. "I told the earth that you no longer needed protection while your Lord was present." He paused. Turned from her. Spoke quietly. "Lord Ishavriel had no desire to leave you behind, Anya, but you are needed here, and he is needed in the South. He works a great magic there, and it is important that it succeed."

"When will he be finished?"

"He will finish his work after the Festival." He could almost *hear* the sudden shift in her expression.

"*What* Festival?"

"Ah, I forgot that you have not made a study of the Dominion." He turned to face her again. "In Annagar, there are two Festivals every year. One is called the Festival of the Sun, the other, the Festival of the Moon. It is the Festival of the Moon that is important to Lord Ishavriel.

"He is at the very heart of the Dominion, in the city called the Tor Leonne. On Festival Night, all of the people in Annagar are allowed freedom from their fears. They wear masks, they dance or sing—or sometimes fight—in the streets of their cities, they speak to each other freely, regardless of who is lord and who is slave; the masks prevent them from knowing. They drink wine, they eat all manner of food, they sing, or are sung to, and the mages create bright lights and beautiful displays in which to celebrate the rising of the Moon.

"In the South, they believe that the Moon is the face of the Lady, and they pray to the Lady."

"I went to Festival once," she said, her eyes wide, her expression soft and distant. "I went with my father to Averalaan. It was the Kings' Challenge. There were so many people I could hardly move or breathe. I didn't like that part." Her hands curled into fists; those fists began a dance and jab in the air. "But I liked the music—there were bards, *real* bards, from Senniel College. And I liked the food.

She cocked her head to one side. "Do you think if I ask him, he'll let me go?"

"I do not know Lord Ishavriel well enough to say that, Anya. You must ask him."

She smiled brightly. "I will." The smile fell. "Or I won't. If I ask him, and he says yes, then we'll have *fun*! But if I ask him, and he says no, then I'll be *sad*. I don't like to be sad, Isladar. It makes me angry.

"But I haven't been to a Festival for years and years and why won't he take *me*?"

"You are needed here, Anya. The gate is not—not yet—stable enough. Or large enough. No one else can do what you can do."

She was pleased by the words, but her pleasure was only a shade less dangerous than her anger. "Well, then, maybe I'll have to stay. Or maybe I'll go. Don't tell him that you told me."

No danger, of course, of that.

"I might go and surprise him. He'll be happy to see me! Or maybe he won't. Did you say that everyone wears a mask? I'll wear a mask. Then no one will recognize me. Tell me again, when is the night?"

"It is," he said softly, "thirteen days hence, on the twenty-second night of the month the Northerners call Scaral."

"That's *Scarran,* isn't it?"

"Yes, Anya."

"Don't you tell him," she said. "Don't you tell him that you told me. I don't want him to tell me I can't go. Don't tell the Lord, either, okay?" She clapped with glee, bouncing against the surface of exposed dirt. Then she grabbed the edges of her dress, pulled them to a comfortable height above the ice, and began to run toward the city.

He watched her go, wondering idly what would come to pass in the very near future. With Anya, as with Kiriel, it was often hard to tell—and as with Kiriel, so many of his plans depended on her actions.

10th of Scaral, 427 AA
Evereve

Long, narrow halls opened up before her, ceilings as high as any
five members of her den standing foot upon shoulder—although
it looked a good deal more stable. But where gold and crystal,
opal and diamond, splashes of gaudy colors that the Empire's
current crop of artists would have disdained to call paintings,
adorned and obscured the walls in the halls that Avandar had
marked, these were austere.

Rising from ground to roof, obscured in the wells of shadow
there, were long, slender columns, like perfect stone trees. She
wandered among them, thinking of the Common's trees, feeling—
in the vast expanse of empty, dusty space—the hint of movement,
of bustle, of conversation that once might have graced these halls
as they did the market grounds. Gargoyles crouched at the heights
of the columns, almost like pigeons nestled in branches.

Although she didn't spend as much time looking at it, the floor
was stone as well; old stone, not marble, not the flat wide planks
of polished wood she was used to.

There were no windows, of course. No room, no hall, no place
in this vast expanse of underground terrain, let in a light that was
not artifice, not pretense. She hated it. Although everything else
here spoke of wealth, windows and glass were the things that
she had most admired about the Terafin manse when compared
with her early life; the shadows, the darkness, the lack of those
things reminded her of her early poverty.

Different, to stand out in the street, hand out, begging for aid
against cold and rain and wind, against heat and sun. But to
stand, observing all those things and separated from them by a
thin sheet of glass, held in place by lead bars, cut by masters
who understood the nature of crystal: that was wealth. Power.
Freedom.

There was none of that here.

This hall, and the halls before it, defied the light, and the power
they spoke of was a power that had no voice to speak to her,
although she'd learned with time that that type of power could
still kill.

The Winter King.

The words meant nothing to Jewel.

They meant more than nothing to Avandar, and judging by the

minute changes in his studied neutrality, she guessed their
meaning was worse, and not better, than nothing.

"It does not concern you, Jewel," he'd said.

And she accepted that.

Which was why she knew she was dreaming.

It was almost worse to be here in her sleep than in some
physical reality; she could not be certain of anything she saw, but
she knew that something about this hall, these visions, these
thoughts must be significant. The problem with dreams, and the
quests one undertook in that state, was that after they were over
she had to take every little detail and thresh it, looking for the
one or two things that had meaning for *her*.

One of the gargoyles took wing.

She swore, pressing her lips into a thin line to keep the words
from escaping. She had no desire to be made a meal of; even
though it wasn't permanent, dream-pain had the ability to scar
in places only she could see.

Another took wing. Another. Up ahead, above the fine, hard
lines of vaulted arch, they were flying in lazy circles, like giant
cats with wings. And maybe fangs; hard to say at this distance,
and she didn't particularly want to be enlightened.

Dreaming visions were nothing like nightmare, but they had
one thing in common: they could turn, at the step of a foot, into
something far darker than they had been seconds earlier. She
wasn't particularly worried, though; not yet. Her nightmares were
always brutish and obvious; they involved death; she had never
dreamed of her own death yet, and she was alone.

Then the gargoyles landed.

The columns in the hall, she realized, must be much, much
taller than they looked—hard to imagine, given the way her neck
bent in half when she managed to get a decent view of what was
at their height. But the gargoyles were about as large as small
horses.

There were three. They sat on their haunches, like the afore-
mentioned cats with wings, taking turns licking their forepaws or
the tips of their pinions.

I hate my dreams, she thought, as she approached them. One
was white alabaster, one was black, like onyx without the shine,
and one was stone-gray. As one creature they spoke, their voices
a blend of tones, harsh and soft, that somehow managed to sound
as if they belonged together.

"We know where you're going," they said. Jewel had never liked cats all that much; Finch liked 'em and Teller—inexplicably—loved them and even owned two, but she had consistently failed to see the charm in a creature who didn't do what it was told, destroyed a day of good work by lifting its leg and pissing in the wrong place because you weren't paying it enough attention, and took small chunks out of your face in the morning if you happened—horrors—to forget to feed it "on time."

Some of that affection worked its way to the surface.

"What," the onyx creature said, "you'd rather own something *stupid* that drools like a madman and thinks like an imbecile?" It turned its head to its companion. "I don't think," it said coolly, "that she is *at all* suitable."

"Well," the white one said, "you know what his orders were."

"But what if she just *fell* off our backs? It wouldn't be *our* fault if she couldn't hold on."

I really hate my dreams. "Look, guys, I'd like to sit here and listen to you argue all day," *as much as I'd like to get my liver removed and boiled in oil,* "but I probably only have a few minutes of dreamtime left, and I get the impression that you don't want to waste it."

The black cat hissed. The white cat hissed as well, but the tonal difference between the two made it clear that one was chuckling and one was, well, complaining.

The gray cat spoke for the first time. "Have you met us before?"

She started to say no. Stopped. "I . . . I don't know," she offered at last.

"And you say *we're* wasting time," the black cat cut in. "Does it always take you this long to *think*?"

She was *not* going to spend time arguing with a cat. Not even if it spoke, had wings, and was part of a vision that was probably necessary, as she rarely had ones that weren't. "What do you guys want?"

"Well," the white cat said, folding its wings and preening, "you, lucky *mortal,* get to choose one of *us* to take you to the end of the hall."

"My feet will . . . oh, never mind." The hallway stretched on into a darkness that somehow suggested forever.

The white cat snickered, the sound like the scrape of rough rock against smooth. "You are lucky," he said softly, "that we made *him* angry and he turned us to stone. We used to get hungrier."

The black cat sniffed. "But we were never desperate enough to eat something as unappetizing as *you.*"

"True, true. But we did—"

"Look, can we get going?" She walked over to the gray stone cat that sat, catlike but blessedly silent, between the white and the black. "Ummm," she said after a minute of staring at the tines—for want of a better word—of his decidedly unairworthy wings, "how do I get up?"

The wings came out, folding neatly to avoid knocking her off her feet. They did not fold nearly as neatly or as gracefully when they approached the cats to either side; both snarled as they were swept back, knocked off haunches that probably weighed more than Arann did. "Well," it said, as their shoulders bunched rather dangerously, and in unison, "you shouldn't sit so *close* to me." She managed to jump up on the spot between its pinions, tucking her legs around its neck, before it lunged up into air, narrowly avoiding the two cats that were still earthbound.

She could feel it snickering.

Great, she thought. She felt the wind rush by her, throwing her hair back in great bunches that, in the waking world, would then be tangled for weeks. Shouting against the wind, she said, "Where are we going?"

The wind served the gargoyle. He said, catlike but suddenly profoundly serious, "To see the Winter King."

CHAPTER FIFTEEN

She wasn't certain what to expect.

Anyone, King, Queen, noble, *anyone* who owned three quarrelsome gargoyles like these and actually got useful work out of them had to be two things at once. The first, very powerful, the second, extraordinarily indulgent.

No wait, she thought, as she closed her knees around the girth of ungiving stone, *this is the dream. Lord knows what they represent, but it's probably something obvious.*

The cat hissed to itself; she was fairly certain the hissing was an amused one. The wind went rushing past her face, carrying flurries of leaves at such speeds she was left with the impression of their colors and their textures—dry and sharp—rather than any distinct image. Here, they were silver, shining as they caught a light that was neither sun nor moon, but present, for all that she couldn't pinpoint its source. As the creature flew on, the leaves changed, becoming sharper again, but brighter and warmer: gold, and in handfuls enough that she almost—almost—reached out to touch one.

But the winds that howled and carried them, as if they were angry words, also harried the cat; she held tight, the temptation never stronger than mild.

"It's never wise to fly above the forest," the cat said; wind carried his words in a tumble that fell into place only after the leaves had been blown from her hair.

"Is walking any better?"

"What?"

"Is walking any better?"

He laughed, a dry coughing that mingled with sibilance and the sound of grinding stone. "It depends on what you want. But it makes the forest less angry, and the wind less bitter."

"We could walk!"

"It would take far longer than you have, and longer than would please my master."

She would have let him know how much she cared about pleasing his master, but the leaves came again, thick as rain, and this time they stung and scratched, thin, curled slivers of ice.

"Not ice," the cat whispered, catlike in its astonishment at her stupidity. "Look at how they catch light."

She didn't. She'd covered her eyes by shoving her face as close to stone as it could go. But when the leaves had passed by, drawing blood on the surface of her hands, the sides of her cheeks, she looked over her shoulder and saw them glinting with color. Diamond.

I've read this story.

"Stories start somewhere, and they have power at their roots, even when their trunks are long gone."

The leaves came again, and again, but there was no third time; the winds broke as suddenly as if invisible doors and windows in the sky had been firmly and completely shut. The edge of the forest was beneath them; she saw the creature's shadow become a flat, perfect patch as it cleared the jagged tops of glittering trees and landed at last.

For the first time since the journey began, the wind didn't take her words and whip them away; the vision did. There was something that looked like a palace might look if an artist had chosen to take paint and palette and brush to it and give it an other-worldly, ethereal beauty. Spires rose, so slender and tall Jewel wondered if a single person could fit within the rounded curve of its wall. The bricks—it had to be brick, although she thought at this distance it looked translucent—were white and blue and pale, pale gray. A flag flew, but no birds; there was a silence to the whole that felt like sleep.

Or death.

"There is no way," Jewel said softly, "that you live there."

"Of *course* not," the creature replied. "Do I look like an *idiot?* That is a people place. A place for crippled creatures that have only *two* legs and *no* wings."

"Oh, right. Sorry."

He batted her almost playfully with a paw.

Unfortunately, his paw was made of solid stone. She went rolling along the ground, colliding with the slender stalks of grass and small-blossomed wildflowers that marked the edge of the forest. It was going to take her days to get the flotsam and jetsam out of her hair.

No, it wasn't. This was the dream and the vision.

But it was peculiar. As she progressed, it grew solid, more real than most sleeping visions were.

"Of course," the gargoyle said, licking a stone paw with a stone tongue and waiting while she brushed herself clean. "You are in *his* domain now."

She shrugged.

"You aren't afraid, are you?"

"No."

Pause. "You *aren't*?"

"No one could have a servant like you and be all that terrifying."

The gargoyle hissed, but this time she was ready; she stepped to one side and let its paw float harmlessly past.

"I guess you wait here." Jewel started toward the bridge that seemed surrounded by a glistening fog.

"I can go where I please," the creature said, pacing her. "Not like *mortals*."

She frowned. "Are there mortals here?"

"Not anymore," the creature said. "They used to come *all* the time. They whined and sniveled. They kept us awake with their crying and screaming." He shrugged. "We killed the ones we could catch. She killed the rest, if they were lucky."

Jewel stopped walking.

"Who is 'She'?"

The look of surprise on the creature's stone face was almost comical. The look of momentary fear as its great head swung from side to side in a frantic attempt to make certain she hadn't been overheard was less amusing. "Don't *say that*," he hissed.

"Don't say what?"

"Not even as a *joke*."

"What was funny?"

"Nothing. Come. We're late."

"But I asked you a—"

The cat stepped on her foot. It *hurt*.

"Little human," he said, his voice quiet and gravelly, "the Winter King is sometimes merciful and sometimes forgiving; he has been known to forget. But the Winter Queen forgives nothing, forgets nothing, and knows no mercy. If her servants were to hear you now, you would never leave here."

"I'm not here," Jewel replied.

"And you are. There are ways to trap the sleeping. There are ways to trap the dreamers who don't know enough to stay inside of their own dreams." The rise and fall of the feline syllables was almost soothing. The words certainly weren't.

"Why exactly am I here?" Jewel said.

The creature turned to her, and then said, in a voice that was as deep as any she had yet heard it use, "Watch. Listen." and the gargoyle *roared*.

The grass bowed before the voice of the beast; the flowers bent and gave off petals. This she noticed in a glance, no more, as she raised her hands automatically to defend her ears.

But she stopped; the roar died, and the unnatural wind that had followed it died with it, allowing the flattened grass to slowly unbend.

Across the stretch of field, the castle proved her wrong: It *was* made of glass, not brick.

And cracks and fissures had opened along the walls, from the ground to the tip of the highest spire. The flag, as pale in color as glass, toppled groundward. Great, curved sheets, beautiful in the light that she suddenly realized—as one did in dreams—was sunset, began to fall.

There was a music to the crash of glass, a display of light as sharp edges deflected pink sky that was not unlike fireworks. But save for that, it was eerily silent.

"Was it empty?" she asked, minutes later, when the glass itself was only expensive—and dangerous—rubble.

"No. Come." He began to walk, and she followed, placing her feet where he had placed his before she realized that glass probably wasn't going to do that much harm to stone pads.

He led her through the debris until he reached something that still stood: Four pillars of gold. In their center, on a throne that was, as the palace had been, of exquisite glass, sat what was left of a man.

He had died, she thought, a hundred years past. His face—for she was certain it was a man's face, and she accepted this certainty for what it was—was shriveled skin over a very fine skull, a wide jaw, sunken eyes. Armor encased it, and the armor, like the castle, was a thing of glass—or perhaps ice. The sword that hung loose and touched floor wasn't made of glass or ice, at least not as far she she could tell; it remained sheathed. As she approached the corpse, she felt the *cold*.

Winter King.

"Master," the cat said, in a voice unlike any she would have thought to attribute to a cat. "I brought her."

And the corpse opened its eyes.

She stifled a scream. It was a near thing, and part of what helped her was the regard of the giant cat. She had a feeling—if something as sharp as a weaponsmith's dagger could be called a feeling— that fear, or more precisely, terror was something that must not be shown in front of that cat.

"I can smell it, you know," the cat said conversationally.

"Shut up," she replied, batting it with the flat of her palm. It lifted a paw to return the blow, but the not-corpse on the chair sat up, hands falling to the smooth, clear rests beneath his palms.

Had she thought that glass was the symbol of wealth and power? It was here in abundance: Beneath his feet. At his back, over his head, beneath his lap. But it lay in shards as far as her eye could see; in sheets that would make windows Terafin could only dream of, if they dreamed that large. She recalled the glassworker as a practical man, but also a highly paid one. Wondered why such mundane details returned to trouble her, or perhaps comfort her, here. She was certain, surrounded by the demise of more than he could dream possible, the glassworker would have been weeping.

The man on the throne still looked dead, although his eyes— from the single glance she gave them—were very much the eyes of the living. His lips, flesh dried almost to nonexistence, moved slightly over teeth that still managed to retain their hold in his jawbone. A smile? Hard to tell.

Jewel knew etiquette. She had learned it, with great pain, at Avandar's hands. Had learned some very little of it at Ellerson's, years and years ago. It was Ellerson's etiquette she chose to use now, by instinct: the bow of a complete nonentity in the presence of royalty.

She would have felt better about it if the cat had been elsewhere. Although it pained her to admit it—even to herself as there was no power on earth that could force her to admit it where the cat could hear it—she hated the loss of dignity being near-splayed out on knees and hands, with forehead almost pressed into the ground, usually caused. And to lose that dignity in front of a cat who was going to sit on his haunches and offer the respect of mere silence—well, it was galling. She hated cats.

"Rise," the Winter King said.

His voice should have been paper thin; it was not. It was strong and full, the voice of an older man at the peak of his powers. Not a youth, never that; he had a voice that measure for measure matched Avandar's.

Great. I'm thinking about Avandar's voice. Cormaris, she thought, invoking the God of Wisdom, *I could use a little help.*

On the other hand, she was pleased enough to follow what was definitely a command.

"How come you to be here?" he asked. "This is the Winter land, and you are unhunted, your name unrevealed; the dogs do not howl and the cats—my cats, not hers—do not shadow your flight across the broken ground."

He rose. She had been afraid he would do that.

His shadow fell directly across her face, and in its darkness, the age that she had mistaken for death vanished. She met eyes of a startling shade; they were blue, shot though with a silver that seemed to shine like glass. He was tall; the shadows filled out his armor, and the sword that girded him no longer seemed a relic for grave robbers to drool over.

She preferred the shadows here, to the light.

"You see much," he said, although she hadn't spoken out loud.

She wanted to say something flippant; that was how she dealt with authority that made her nervous. But the words felt wrong, and she couldn't force herself to utter them. She swallowed and nodded instead.

"I have not seen another mortal in centuries. In millennia." He stepped toward her, and as long as she stayed within the confines of his cast shadow, he seemed more and more human. It occurred to her that this was dangerous.

"My appointed time has come, and it has passed; does she not remember her quest and her oath?"

"The Winter Queen," Jewel said, answering the question she was about to ask.

"Indeed," he replied softly. "I had thought, when I first woke, that she had finally come to keep her oath. But when I searched my realms, they were empty of all save a dream of you. And I know my dreams, little one. They are all I have now. You, I have never seen in the flesh."

She shook her head. "I'm sure I'd remember . . ."

"Do you live in the waking world?"

She nodded.

"And you are under the mountains, in the vastness of the Stone Deepings."

"I'm—I'm not sure where I am. I didn't see an entrance, and I haven't found an exit."

"There was one," he said. "But millennia ago, it was taken by magical force; sealed. I thought the mage foolish indeed who would attempt to deprive the Queen of her retreat. But I have since discovered that the fool was not he." His eyes became all reflected light, and she knew it was steel, not glass, that lay beneath the glow. "From the mortal world I was riven; from all worlds."

"Could mortals . . . reach you here before the—the mage?"

"None," he said, "save those I or my Queen invited. They were foolish, of course; but I do not judge them harshly. They have paid with their lives, and the eternity they were foolish enough to wish for. And I? I have paid. But I have not paid the promised price.

"I am the Winter King," he said. "But there has been no Summer King to succeed me, and I fear, no Summer Queen."

Jewel was silent. The weight of his earlier words had finally settled. "What . . . promised price has the Winter Queen not paid you?"

His smile was grim indeed. "I was a hunter, little girl."

"She's not *very* little," the cat said conversationally. He sidled over to the Winter King, and a gloved hand reached down and began to stroke stone head. "She is *older* for a human, not a half-child. She might be *stringy*."

"You'll never know," Jewel snapped back. "Because you'll never get the chance to eat me."

The cat hissed and raised a paw. Jewel raised a fist—which, given the circumstances, was stupid, as she knew if she hit the cat all that would happen was the sacrifice of a few layers of skin, all of them hers.

"Peace," the Winter King said. "Girl, can you travel in your waking world?"

"I'd better be able to travel."

"And which god claims you?"

"Pardon?"

"Which god protects you?" The lines of his brow creased; his eyes narrowed. He spoke more slowly, as if the words were meant for an imbecile. "Who do you serve?"

"I—I don't think things work the same way they did the last time you lived on the outside."

"Oh?"

"The gods don't *claim* anyone. If we choose, we follow their suggestions, and in the end, if we've learned enough in this life, Mandaros lets us pass through His Halls rather than sending us back to learn more."

"If you choose?" the Winter King said. "And are you from the Cities of Man, then, that you can be so bold?" His head rose and fell as he examined her carefully. "You are dressed like a slave," he said at last, "and not a finely trained slave at that. You do not smell of magic or magery, but I sense a depth of power in you that might be trained. In the Cities of Man, you might find freedom if you are canny."

"I—I'm sorry," she said, because she suddenly was. "But I don't know what the Cities of Man are. I come from a city on the coast that two Kings rule. They're god-born, so there are no wars for succession."

"And where do their parents reside?"

"They live in the heavens, or wherever it is gods live."

The silence was long and cold. And into it, not disturbing it in the least, were intimations of a different mortality. Jewel thought of Henden, and *Allasakar,* and what Meralonne had said about the time before the fall of Vexusa. *The gods walked.*

The Winter King returned to his throne and sat there, stiffly.

"I came," he said, "from the Cities of Man. From Tor Haval. I was a man of power and rank, and the Winter Queen paid court to me. She offered me my desire and her power, and made clear that the reign was to be for the Winter and the Winter alone."

"And at the end of the Winter?"

"It was not a mortal Winter, not that small a time, but at the end—at the end, she would take from me my life, in the Hunt, the full Hunt, if she could. And if she could not, she would release me to the world without, all knowledge and all memory intact. I asked her how many of her consorts had survived the reign and the Hunt, and she smiled, and her smile—" His expression was lost to memory, and in the shadows, he was handsome. He was young.

"Her smile was so very cold. It was answer enough. 'I will not come for you in Summer,' she said, 'I do not choose the strongest for the Summer Court. Mortals are the Winter Kings.' I came. I wanted her, and I wanted the challenge of the fight that she offered at the end. These," he said, lifting a hand, and pointing at the gray gargoyle that now stood at such perfect attention it might well have *been* a statue, "were my masterpiece, the making unencumbered by the least of her influence. They are undefeated, although they have never been tested against her."

He was silent. His silence was intense, awkward, disturbing.

At last, Jewel said softly, "I don't know who the Winter Queen is."

The cat hissed.

The man, frozen, said nothing for a long time. When he did speak, he said, "The gods are not dead."

"No."

"Then she is not dead. But she is Winter, and the Hunt is the most terrifying thing you could ever see. The most beautiful. She brings the Winter with her; the shadows and the promise of eternal ice. She rides with her host, She hunts with her beasts; She is undeniable, inevitable. If she hunted at all, you would know it, you would know of it. Your world—it must be so pale and so lacking in wonder.

"I should have known, when she did not come, that there had been changes we had never dreamed of."

She started to answer. Stopped. Thought about a palace of glass and a cat with stone wings, about pillars of stone with branches that grew into great, solid arches at their heights, about leaves of silver, gold, and diamond. About the wild, wild magic that seemed to glimmer beneath the transparent surface of everything she could see in the room, both standing wall and the ruined shards beyond.

"Lacking in wonder, yes," she said, thinking of what it must have been like to live in the age of gods. Thinking, and *knowing*. "But not in life. Not in justice."

"And you are then one of those who would trade beauty for safety." He did not keep the chill contempt from his words. The answer was obvious enough.

"You chose beauty. Live with it," Jewel said, and turned to walk away.

His laughter stopped her. It was, indeed, beautiful. "Well played, well played, little mortal. That would have cost your life in another time, on another day."

"You want something from me."

"Yes."

"I'm a merchant. I know when to walk and when to talk. You want to talk? I'd suggest a little change in attitude."

"You have dreamed of my Lady," he said. "I can feel it in the words you can't even think of saying."

"You know what I've been dreaming?"

"You are dreaming now, and you are in my lands, and I know what is thought in my lands if I bend my mind to it. I do not know the whole of the dream, but the dream itself has the taint of truth to it. I will not believe the Winter Queen dead.

"And if she is not dead, you will take three things to her, and a fourth will come, and you will remind her of her oath. Tell her that the way has been opened just enough that if her hunters are competent and not the fools they once were, they will be able to find it."

"I think I'll reword that, if you don't mind."

He laughed. "As you please. The night of the Hunt is coming. It is coming. The host will ride." He laughed, yes, and the sound would define laughter for years, it echoed so deeply inside. As if her ears had trapped it, hoarding it for memory. "I will gift you, child, if you will carry this message."

"With what? If I guess right, you'll be dead."

The cat hissed. Loudly.

The man did not blink. "With the Summer Queen," he said. "For the Summer Queen and the Winter are two very different creatures, different sides of the same coin." He rose. "There is a man who is calling your name. He calls it loudly, and he stoops to magic." His expression changed. "It is a familiar magic. I would ask you to kill him, but I fear that you will never find my Lady if he is dead.

"Go." The shadows left his face in a rush. The life left it; he was skeleton once more, strewn like a corpse in a glass throne that sat in the center of four golden pillars. Trapped here, and aware of it.

She nodded.

The cat said, "Only do this, and we will be grateful."

Jewel waited until they had left the presence of the Winter King before turning to the cat and saying, "And that would be helpful how?"

He didn't have time to answer; he disappeared in a flash of blinding, painful light. She cried out; the pain stopped.

Avandar Gallais sat beside her, in her bed, one hand on either shoulder. She could see the traces of magic, wound tight around those hands like multihued, delicate nets.

"Let go," she whispered, as his eyes widened.

He did as she bid—rare, but beside the point.

She fell backward. Felt something dig into her skull. Rising swiftly, she walked to the oval mirror that was one of her few prides. The glass, silvered so perfectly, had been a gift from the Terafin. Reflected there, she could see quite clearly in the tangled mess of hair it would take *hours* to comb out, if it could be tamed at all without judicious clipping, three leaves. One was silver. One was gold. And one, of course, was diamond.

"Wait!"

He was halfway across a room that seemed suddenly too small before her word bit him. He turned, his expression dark. He was, of all things, angry. "I have a matter to attend to, Jewel."

"No, you don't."

Shock robbed him of words for a moment, and she took that moment, leaving dignity behind, to do the run around him and end up in front of the room's only exit.

"Do you know what those leaves mean?" he asked her, his voice almost as cold as her memory of the Winter King's.

"Better than you think. Probably better than you'd like."

"Jewel, let us have this conversation after I've seen to the defense of my citadel."

"No."

His smile was chill. She wondered if the mountains themselves held some taint of Winter; she could not remember Avandar's expression ever being so frosty at home, although he had never been a warm man. "You *will not* tell me what to do in my own domain."

"I will," she replied evenly, *"Domicis."*

The slightly crimson tinge to his skin paled. She watched, unblinking; she had his attention now and she wasn't going to let go. Tenacity wasn't her middle name, but back when they named children for stupid character traits, it would have been a good bet.

"You don't understand," he said softly. "Those leaves—"

"They came from the forest of the Winter King."

He closed his eyes. "Yes."

"He's still there, Avandar."

"He will *always* be there."

"He won't. She'll hunt him. I get the impression that something *you* did," she added, without bothering to take the accusation out of her voice, "prevented the Winter Queen from actually finding him."

"And from hunting him, and sacrificing him. He should have been grateful."

"Avandar."

"You do not understand, Jewel. The Winter King isn't just a man, isn't even a man imbued with the powers she grants. He's an aspect. The man who speaks—and I assume that was the nature of the dream that held you—is a servant to the aspect, not its master; he sacrificed the essence of his mortality when he agreed to become the consort to the Winter Queen. He could no more walk these roads than the gods could, not now."

"He's trapped there."

"Yes. Whether or not he is given reign of these lands. These . . . were not his. But they are on the true road, and had they been what they were before I . . . stumbled across them . . . they would have led to him. And to her."

"We have to free him," she said.

"Everything is simple for you. Do you not understand? She will choose another to take his place. He will be what he was; the geas laid by the title itself is more powerful than the force of a merely human life. Free this human, as you desire to do, and she will merely find another to take his place, and another after his death, and another. There will be a stream of sacrifice.

"Let this man remain upon his empty throne, and there will be no further deaths."

She hated choices like this one. Hated them. But she didn't move out of his way.

"Jewel," he said, using the most persuasive tone he had—which, given his general imperious arrogance, wasn't all that impressive. "He can't hurt *me*. There is nothing at all that he can do to injure me. But you are vulnerable. Do you think she chose the kind, the just, the honorable, as her Winter Consort? She chose the hunters. She chose the powerful. She chose the merciless. You offer this . . . man . . . a kindness that he would despise.

"And I will not have him take advantage of you. I will not have his magic go where—"

"Where yours can't?" She lifted her wrist, exposing the scarlet S.

"Jewel—"

"We need to do this," she said softly.

He caught her face in his hands, cupping it and pulling it up before she could move. She saw his eyes flare; orange light, and green, and a hint of white, swirling just at the edges: magic. She held her ground, but it was difficult; his grip was strong enough—she was certain it was unintentionally so by the look of concentration on his face—that she clung to the ground by the balls of her feet.

"Very well," he said at last, lowering her. "You are not enspelled. This is merely your usual foolishness."

"No," she said, and she was certain, suddenly, that it wasn't.

Years had given him the key to her tone of voice. His eyes narrowed.

"He offered me a gift."

"You refused it, of course."

"He offered to give me this gift *after* we'd given him what he desired."

"And his desire?"

"Just the Hunt," she said softly. "Just the Hunt and, I think, the death. Not more."

"If he expects death at her hands—"

"He'll get it," she snapped. "He'll get it. She might use others that way, but she won't disgrace the title of consort. Not *this* consort. Not this King." It was there again, the steel in the words, the edge of them cutting away all that wasn't truth. And the truth was her gift, her curse. Seer-born.

"I did not know that you knew so much of the Winter Queen."

"I don't. I don't want to. But—but he mentioned the Summer Queen."

Avandar looked away.

"Avandar."

He did not meet her gaze. She studied the shuttered neutrality of his expression; no way in there. So she did what she usually did. She kept talking.

"The Summer Queen must be the opposite of the Winter Queen, and maybe—just maybe—she'll help *us.*"

"You understand so very little; you're like a child with a large sword. You have the weapon; you know the edge is sharp; but you are incapable of wielding it, of even understanding what wielding it *means*. *Yes,* Jewel. There will be a Summer Queen. But She is no mortal Queen, and even as the gods could not, She can hold a soul without mercy."

"She won't be the Dark God's friend."

"The *Winter* Queen is not the Dark God's friend. Nor will she ever be. They contest the same land, They struggle for the same Dominion."

"And won't we be better served if it's the Summer Queen that fights that war?"

"The seasons of the Firstborn," he said coldly, "are not the seasons of creatures who march toward death with the passage of time."

"You haven't answered my question."

"I have." He walked to the desk that adorned her wall less usefully than the mirror did. Placed his hands, palms flat, against its surface. "Those leaves," he said softly, "are part of his domain. And all that *he* was, was granted by her. Her power demands its price. You have taken something from her lands. I seek to protect you from that theft."

"It was hardly theft."

"You do not understand the Firstborn," he said coldly. "But I am your domicis, I will do as you command."

"The Summer Queen?"

"*Yes,*" he said, spitting the word out as if he could no longer abide its taste. "Yes, it would aid us and our cause."

"Then let's take the leaves. I have a feeling that we'll find our way out now. You said—you said we couldn't leave because it was *me* you worried about. I don't think, if there's some bar on some gate or some door, it will stay closed against me. He wants her attention."

"Yes, and you propose to draw it how?"

"By going to the Tor Leonne," she replied.

He closed his eyes.

And she, standing in front of the door, slumped against it, mouth suddenly dry. "I didn't—I didn't mean to say that." But her dream was there. The strange, compelling woman riding at the head of a host.

He opened his eyes, met hers. "Jewel," he said, and for a moment the ice melted slightly. "I *am* sorry."

"The war." She spoke as if she hadn't heard him; as if the vision was as clear and detailed as a solid tapestry before her eyes. "Is about to start in earnest."

"Yes," he replied, lifting his hands from the desk's surface. "And the most bitter thing about those words is that you don't even know what they mean."

12th of Scaral, 427 AA
Tor Leonne

The masks were very good.

Alesso inspected them carefully as they were offered to him, their makers kneeling into the hardwood of his audience chamber, heads bent so firmly into ground they might leave indentations. These men were not the finest of craftsmen, and it was obvious their gifts were seldom used at the request of the high clansmen; he could smell the sweat and dirt of the day's labor. No scented oils, no musky perfumes, no clothing pressed and preserved for a meeting of this nature, and *only* this nature.

Still, they were dressed well for poorer men; their presentation was a product of their class and not their respect for his station. To make certain that any of the watching clansmen appreciated this fact, he let the maskmakers kneel against the wood while he turned the product of their labor over in his hands, examining it. It was a very plain, very elegant mask, its surface not quite as smooth as he would have liked, but its features otherwise in every way the same as the first of the four masks the *Kialli* had offered— and ordered—for his people.

He seldom conducted any business of import in these chambers. Or rather, he had seldom done so. But today, in the full white and gold of his station, his hair drawn back and pulled in a tight warrior's knot, the line of his brow broken by crown, he did just that. Six months had passed since the crown of the Tor had been placed upon his brow, but he was still under constant inspection. That would stop only when he won his war—the war that Markaso kai di'Leonne had lost all face, and arguably his life, losing.

It was close enough to the night of the Festival Moon that the high clansmen, Tor and Tyrs all, had, with few exceptions, arrived at the Tor Leonne. They were given leave to hunt—by hawk or falcon, of course—within the grounds; they were given leave to practice their weapons skill, to ride, and to partake of the hospitality of the Tor itself.

They were also given leave to litter the sides of the audience chamber in which minor matters of governance were decided, and Alesso had been four days without opening those chambers. Sendari had—as he often did—brought this oversight to his attention, and they had argued full into Lady's shadow. In this case,

Sendari had been able to persuade the General that his position
was correct: Hospitality required a convening of the court. Hospitality and the need to show all in attendance that his court was as
fine, as important, as significant, as the court of his predecessor.

Alesso desired a change in that particular overture of hospitality, but too much had already changed; he would not slight or
offend men whose alliance he might need over the simple dignity
of craftsmen such as those who now knelt perfectly at his feet.

He handed the mask back to Sendari; Sendari handed it to the
Widan Mikalis di'Arretta, a man Alesso did not quite trust. There
was something about him, a nervousness or a fear, that spoke of
risk. He could ill afford risk at this time.

But he could afford ignorance even less.

"Sendari?"

Sendari di'Sendari turned away a moment from his magically
silent speech. "Tyr'agar?" he responded, offering so perfect a
bow no one watching—Tors and Tyrs all—could fail to note it,
or its significance.

"The masks?"

"They are, in Mikalis' opinion, flawed."

"That was our intention, was it not?"

"Indeed. He wishes to speak a moment with the craftsmen
when you have finished to ascertain that they used the correct
materials in constructing the masks."

"Done. Gentlemen, I will accept your generous gift with
appreciation." Alesso turned from his adviser to the rough silk of
merchant craftsmen's bent backs, the gleam of their dark hair.
Only the oldest of the men had been colored by the white of
wisdom, but it was he who lifted his head and shoulders first
when the Tyr'agar granted them permission to speak.

"You honor us, Tyr'agar," he said. He rose gracefully, gra-
ciously, the motion belying his age and his apparent rank. His
beard brushed the ground as he sat straight-backed, knees bent
beneath him in the second half of the subordinate posture. His
apprentices had little grace, they rose clumsily, their movements
full of youth and strength. It did not matter; they had shown that
they could bend. "Stay a moment," he said, tendering the dismissal that would allow them to rise from the ground. "My
adviser wishes to speak with you."

"Tyr'agar."

But he was no longer concerned with masks, with the makers

of masks, with the obeisance, correct but of poor quality, that those craftsmen displayed.

The Tyr'agnate Eduardo kai di'Garrardi had entered the room, with four of his Tyran.

By Tyrian law he was allowed four Tyran, but by custom a clansman entered the presence of his Tyr with half that complement. It was a public gesture of trust in the liege of one's choosing, and although there was never any trust between two men of power, the appearance was—as all appearances were—important. Eduardo di'Garrardi was not a man concerned with the import of appearance. He was allowed his swords in the Tyr's presence in *this* room, and he wore both openly. This was not a slight. What was: his sheaths were war sheaths, simple and unadorned.

"Alesso," Sendari said as he began to rise.

He stopped. For a moment—just a moment—he understood Cortano's anger, Cortano's vast impatience, with men whose passions were invoked by mere women.

"My apologies, Ser Sendari," he said, too softly for any but his friend to hear. "Tend to the maskmakers; I understand their task is the task of import. I will see to the Tyr'agnate."

Sendari's bow was perfect, instant, and stiff as steel. "That," he said quietly, "is what I fear."

Alesso made no reply.

"Tyr'agar," the kai Garrardi said, surprising him slightly. Flanked by his Tyran, he approached the room's only chair, the curved half circle with a high back graced by the gold of the sun's rays. It had the advantage of serving as throne. It had the disadvantage of forcing its occupant to sit.

Alesso was immediately on his guard. He was, as a matter of course, armed. Hard to be ready for combat from the curved seat of a chair, a throne. But not—never, for a man like Alesso— impossible.

The Tyr'agnate of Oerta did not bow, although he inclined his head.

Alesso acknowledged the lack of respect with a very slight smile. It was a smile that Sendari would have recognized had he not been involved with the matter of masks; men had died on its edge. Sendari might have tried to blunt it.

Alesso did not particularly regret his absence. "Kai Garrardi," he replied.

* * *

When Sendari heard the two words side by side, he stopped speaking. The sentence he had been in the middle of dangled a moment, like a display of ill-temper, before the man listening realized it would not be finished.

He lifted a brow in curiosity, in confusion. As a craftsman from a humble clan, he was not conversant with the nuances of the court.

"Ser Sendari?"

In reply, the Widan lifted a hand; ruby caught sunlight the Lake had released, glimmering there. The merchant began to speak again, but his lips stopped before the words left them. A good sign.

Sendari turned. From his vantage, he could see the profiles of the man who ruled the Dominion and the man who ruled Oerta. Their faces could have been chiseled by the same stonemason.

There was, about the two men, a power that could not be ignored; it drew the attention, and held it. Alesso di'Alesso had taken the Lake of the Tor Leonne. Crown and Sword were symbols—but the Lake was the Tyr's heart. He held it.

Eduardo di'Garrardi held Oerta. That in itself made him notable; he was one of the four Tyr'agnati. What made him remarkable was the fact that he had taken the Lord's title at the last Festival of the Sun, killing several of his opponents so that he might win his way to the side of the Lord's Consort. That he wanted her was not in question. Eduardo di'Garrardi's passions were ill-concealed, and once revealed, they were followed. Had he not sold an entire village, and more, for the purchase of a single stallion? Sword's Blood.

But it was acknowledged that Sword's Blood had no peer. It had been acknowledged that the Serra Diora di'Marano likewise had no peer. Had his rival been any man other than Alesso, there would have been no question of the outcome.

It comes, Sendari thought bleakly. He had watched and waited, thinking Eduardo kai di'Garrardi far more patient than his reputation implied. Thinking Alesso di'Marente more of a fool.

And thinking that, no matter what, his daughter, his treacherous, beautiful daughter, would be one man's downfall and the other's prize. He did not want her to go to Eduardo for her own sake, although Eduardo was not so foolish a man to claim such a prize and destroy it. But he did not want Alesso to win her either, for although Sendari bore none of Diora's cursed gift, he could hear the death in her voice.

For Alesso.

For Cortano.

For himself.

Alesso and Eduardo were both the Lord's men.

They had been allies, but in six months that alliance had become something dangerously close to a sword dance. No one doubted that they would see the end of it—the only question was in what circumstances. Armies had been gathered for less.

For a woman.

For his daughter.

He had not thought of her mother for months. *Alora.* She had given him no sons, and for that lack alone he might have replaced her without fear had he been a different man. Could he criticize either Eduardo or Alesso? He had almost given up his destiny—he *had* given up his power—for her sake, merely because she had asked it.

And in return she had given him a daughter, and that daughter had grown thorns, like all roses do: She had become the Flower of the Dominion. The Lily. The wife of the ill-fated heir. He had adored her at birth; he had adored her when she became wife, then widow. He had adored her until the moment she spoke with Teresa's cursed gift, to wound them all, in the hearing of every clansman of import in the Dominion who had not yet decided against them.

Ah, she had shown herself to be his daughter, then; to be Teresa's niece. Alora's ferocity had never turned to treachery. He had thought to kill her, but the rage had guttered. The pain had not. Now he thought to see her die.

He had done so much to prevent that.

A lesson, he thought bleakly. What was love in the end but foolishness and loss? He had learned this lesson once, but obviously, demonstrably, he had taken so little out of it that he would be forced to learn it again

Diora.

"Ser Sendari?" the maskmaker said, touching his sleeve.

He pulled away immediately, drawing himself up to his full height—which was considerable, but not obvious until he so chose.

"The Tyr'agar asked you a question."

And how much easier it would be to finally, *finally,* have an end

to it. To have nothing left to lose but the game itself. The pause
between question and answer would mean much to the watching
court. What was infinitely worse was the fact that he had not heard
the question. He bowed to Alesso, catching his eye before he fell
into the proper posture.

"The request," the Tyr' agnate said, breaking the silence with
his usual intemperate tone, "is not unreasonable. I am a Tyr; she
is the daughter you have promised me as a bride. But you have
been ... elusive, Ser Sendari; too often my messages find no
one to receive them. My apologies," he added, with brittle insin-
cerity, "for bringing this matter to the Tyr'agar."

"My apologies, Tyr'agnate," Ser Sendari replied immediately,
and far more gracefully than Eduardo's sullen temper warranted,
"for being unavailable. I am, as you have no doubt heard, fond of
my daughter. But I have undertaken the responsibility of counselor to the Tyr'agar at a time of great changes; his fate has taken
precedence over hers."

"Indeed."

Sendari had seen ice form. The experience was rare enough
that he remembered it clearly; he had, after all, sought it out. But
he might have saved himself the time and his father's expense;
he watched it again on the living countenance of the ruler of
Oerta.

"Then let me trouble you no longer with such a petty request.
Tend to your matters of state. I will guard my own interests."

Clumsily said. Sendari started to bow, but Eduardo had turned
away from him, both figuratively and literally.

"Tyr'agar," the Tyr'agnate said, drawing attention as fire did a
moth's, "I wish two things."

The Tyr'agar was absolutely silent.

"First: I will see my intended. She is her father's daughter, but
she is—it is rumored—under the guard of your Tyran. A House
such as Marano can ill afford guards of such caliber, and as she
is the Flower of the Dominion, I find myself taking no offense at
this liberty." Eduardo waited. He waited in vain. After a moment
he continued. "Second: I will have this business finished before
the end of the Festival of the Moon. The Serra Diora di'Marano
will be en'Garrardi when the sun sets on the first Lord's day."

Sendari bowed his head.

The first Lord's day was to be the day that Alesso di'Alesso
finally declared his intent: War upon the Northern Empire. Such
a war had not, of course, been declared, but the Tyr's intent was

an open secret. It would have to be: the armies of Raverra were mobilizing on the Northern border of the Terrean; they faced Mancorvo.

The armies of Oerta had been promised for that day.

Eduardo, you are a fool. But an intelligent fool; a cunning one. The threat had been made, the matter decided. Alesso could not move North without the Oertan armies. With Eduardo as enemy, rather than ally, he could not afford to divest the heartlands of their protection. He could gamble on the Tyr'agnate of Sorgassa, but if he left Jarrani's men behind, he would not have the power to defeat both Lamberto and Callesta. Not even with the aid of the *Kialli*.

Well-played, Tyr'agnate.

The Tyr'agar rose, divesting himself of the trappings—the trap—of the chair.

"And if she is not?"

The silk of Sendari's robe was, of a sudden, as heavy as stone and earth. But his posture was perfect, his face more of a mask than the confused, common craftsman standing before him could conceive. *Alesso, no.*

Two hands touched sword hilts. Eight hands followed. Tyr and Tyran faced each other across the length of a hall littered with spectators, none of whom were foolish enough to stand between these two men.

"Your pardon, Tyr'agar," Ser Sendari heard himself saying. Having spoken, his choice was made, but his voice did not please him; he modulated it. "But the Tyr'agnate's request is my concern." Eduardo did not turn to him; to his chagrin, although not to his great surprise, neither did Alesso. "I will arrange, as I can, to fulfill my obligations. Tyr'agnate," he said, bowing as low as he might without actually falling to his knees, "I had hoped to spare myself this. You must understand that I come poorly prepared for the ceremony a man of your station requires. I had hoped to acquit my family in a fashion suited to your rank, and I find myself unable to support that at this time."

Alesso said nothing.

"The fashion of her arrival is not of import, Ser Sendari." Eduardo's words were cool.

"One does not insult the station of Tyr without reason," Ser Sendari countered. He was aware of what this would cost him. "But my fortunes will be made with the war. I had intended to honor your request, and my agreement, appropriately after our victory." Oh, yes, he was aware of what it would cost him: the tongues of the court were already wagging at his open humiliation. He had exposed his throat as a dog did, declaring himself the weaker.

But better that, better that than the war that was *almost* declared. He held his breath, his face white with effort.

And Eduardo kai di'Garrardi turned, slowly. Reluctantly. "Very well," he said softly. "Had I realized your . . . situation, I would have been less intemperate. Your daughter could arrive by Voyani caravan and be exulted within my home, Ser Sendari. She would make humble any dwelling—as she did this one.

"I would see her, if that is acceptable to you."

"Of course," Sendari replied.

"We may discuss, privately, the matter of appropriate arrangements."

"Of course."

The Tyr'agnate raised a hand. It was the hand that had rested upon the hilt of his sword. His Tyran did likewise so quickly the two motions—master and guards'—seemed continuous. "Tyr'agar," he said, and his bow was almost perfect.

To Sendari's great regret, Alesso di'Alesso did not speak a word.

Alesso was angry. Sendari expected no less.

When the two men met at the Lake's side, they offered each other the stiffness of perfectly correct greetings, although there were no Tyran, no high clansmen, to witness them. Formality, as any weapon, could be used to either defend or wound.

Sendari cast his spells to protect their conversation from being heard by all but the most powerful of listeners and wondered, as he did so, if there would even be a conversation. There was a quality to Alesso's silence that he had only rarely witnessed; it was not, it could not be broken by any but Alesso himself.

But he had sacrificed his dignity for the sake of Alesso's war. He spoke.

"The maskmaker confirmed what Mikalis di'Arretta suspected. Ground or broken bone must have been blended with the *Kialli* clays used to construct the masks' faces. He has changed the composition of the clay, but has retained the weight and shape of the whole. He, and his sons, believe they can create replacements for the masks so generously donated by the Shining Court, but he is not confident that he can replace them all without aid.

He has asked permission to seek out those with similar craft and skill."

Alesso shrugged.

"Even so, he feels there is some chance that you will need to use some of the masks that came from the Court if you wish to preserve the numbers. He therefore asks which of the four styles of mask you would like him to concentrate on first. I took the liberty of telling him to start with the most expensive and work his way down."

"Which pleased him, no doubt."

"No doubt."

Containing his growing irritation, Sendari said softly, "There are already rumors in the streets of the Tor about the Lady's Consort. It works against us, Alesso. I believe that while we disperse the masks—as we were *ordered* to do—we may *also* disperse the rumors."

Alesso stood with his hands behind his back. His profile had not shifted once; it faced into the wind that blew across the Lake.

The Widan ceased to speak; he listened. Heard the wind's voice. War was waiting.

"Alesso, I had no choice," he said. "You of all men should appreciate this. War is your game."

"We already discussed this," Alesso said softly, speaking at last, his gaze upon the waters of the Lake. "We agreed. Your daughter's role in this war was decided the moment she lifted the Sun Sword from the lake's waters and showed it, newly gleaming, to the clansmen."

"Garrardi made clear he abided by no such decision."

"So it would seem."

"Alesso—"

"This will cost us, old friend."

"Will it cost us more," Sendari replied, his eyes narrowing at the way the words "old friend" took on an edge and a sharpness that made of them an attack, "than losing Garrardi's army? At best," he added. "At worst, the army would be pillaging the Tor Leonne. We would have to travel *with* Diora to protect her. Is that what you want? To fight rearguard action against—"

"I understand war."

"Yes. And you understand politics. You understand power. What you chose to do today is therefore deliberate, rather than the unfortunate result of youthful ignorance."

"You go too far, *old friend*."

"Tell me, then, Tyr'agar, what you would have had me do."

Silence.

Alesso di'Alesso, Tyr'agar of the Dominion of Annagar, did not condescend to answer.

CHAPTER SIXTEEN

12th of Scaral, 427 AA
Evereve

They stood at a door that Jewel had never seen before. It was twice as tall as Avandar, with a face smooth as glass and broken only by hinges to one side. She couldn't tell what the door was made of: wood, stone, steel. It looked like a thing of shadow, and it glowed very, very faintly. There were no handles, no rings, no knobs, no visible means of entry or exit; there were no windows at which watchful sentries might peer out to ascertain the identity of visitors.

Which made sense; she didn't expect he got much in the way of visitor traffic in these parts.

"Not now," he said, frowning at the door's smooth face. "But you would have been surprised had you been here when the citadel was first wrested from the mountain fastness."

"What exactly are you doing?"

"I'm finding," he said, with a slight gritting of teeth just in case his annoyance wasn't obvious, "my reflection."

"And that's going to help us?"

"Only if you consider walking through the door alive helpful."

She took the hint. Shut up, although it wasn't easy. The time passed; she loss track of how much as her eyes were drawn—for no reason she could think of—to the door. Watching Meralonne cast his spells was a special entertainment; he was alive with a glow of shifting colors and his magic, netlike, sparkled with power's confinement. She liked to guess the nature of the spell before the spell itself was cast. With Avandar, it was never so simple; she was usually involved with something like survival when he was casting his spell. And at the moment, he appeared to be doing nothing but grimacing, which was only entertaining for the first five minutes. "Avandar?"

"Yes?"

"Why does the door have no color?"

"No color?" He turned, the edge of his jaw more pronounced, the curve of his fingers that flick of muscles away from being a fist.

"I'm pretty sure that's what I said." It had no color the way shadow had none, except shadow was usually a soft shade of black, or a shade of whatever color it happened to be hiding from light. She frowned. Stepped forward slightly. "It's—it's like glass," she said. "No, it's like water. Flat water. Still water. I can see—"

"Enough, Jewel. Stand aside."

But she couldn't. Out of the nothing that was framed by the shape of a door, she saw darkness, and out of that darkness, surfacing slowly, eyes closed, lips half-parted, arms bent at the elbow and palms face out, was—herself.

Herself leached of color, but not form.

She opened her eyes.

Caught by herself, frozen by the hardening reality of skin that had seen a bit too much sun, of hair that was becoming a flyaway wild brown, of eyes that were becoming large-pupiled and dark-irised, Jewel ATerafin had the presence of mind to utter a single word.

"Avandar—"

The woman who wasn't her image, and who was, reached out, arms snapping with sudden energy, face twisting into an expression of glee and malice that Jewel prayed had never crossed her own face.

Her fingers, so like Jewel's own that Jewel could no longer tell them apart, were point-to-point with the fingers that Jewel hadn't realized she'd raised.

The other Jewel opened her mouth, lips moving slowly, skin stretching and releasing around syllables. *Mine.* Jewel's eyelids were extraordinarily heavy. She struggled with their weight; seer-born or no, she would have known it was a bad idea to sleep here.

The other image, the other her, let her fingertips drop; hands that were completely foreign in their familiarity reached up, up, caressed her cheeks. She opened her mouth. Jewel knew what she would say.

Funny thing, though. She spoke with Avandar's voice.

"Jewel!"

Coruscating blue light traveled down the length of Jewel's arms.

Both of them. They screamed, and as they did, their voices, inseparable to start, slid into a harmony of pain and complexity, and from there into a discordant wail, a single voice.

"I trust," Avandar Gallais said, in the silence that followed, his voice inexplicably close to her ear, one arm behind her back, the other beneath the crook of her knees, "you will listen in future."

"No, you don't," she said.

Her wrist was burning. She lifted her arm, and saw it for fact: the cuff of her shirt had been split and blackened, and the angry red mark on her arm was glowing with heat.

He said nothing. But when he turned back to the door, he did not set her down, and she drifted into uneasy sleep waiting— with a certain smug defiance—for his arms to give beneath her weight.

When she woke, she discovered that Avandar Gallais did not give. She opened her eyes and saw two things: the underside of his chin, exposed, as his gaze went out and slightly up, and, above him, a crown of stars, pale and luminescent against the perfect darkness.

She couldn't have said why, but she turned her face into his chest and cried quietly, forcing her body into that peculiar stiffness that was supposed to pass for calm. Gods, she was *tired,* to cry like this, to even be able to cry like this. She was going to be a woman of power; she had promised The Terafin—Amarais, standing like a slender dagger, her eyes incapable of doing what Jewel's were doing right now—no less. She was no idiot; she knew the truth, knew it better than she knew how to do anything but breathe. Show *no* weakness.

Amarais had never done her the disservice of putting that dictum into words. Avandar had. All of the time. When she lost her temper. When she was afraid. When she laughed out loud. When, in short, she expressed *anything* to *anyone.* She learned to keep her self *to* herself whenever she was forced to suffer the services of her domicis. But now, just now . . . She was tired. She wanted her home, nest of political vipers notwithstanding.

He said nothing at all. He did not even acknowledge the fact that she was awake.

She had never thought him capable of kindness.

"Where are we?" she asked, when they had stopped for the day and Avandar had chosen some crevice in between huge formations of slightly worn stone as a reasonable place to eat and sleep. She had taken to the ground as if walking were third nature and not the second that it usually was to uninjured adults; he prudently failed to offer comment or criticism.

He was silent for some minutes as he worked, calling magic for the fire that seemed both necessary and profane beneath the vastness of the night sky. He worked with care; she saw the lines of his power come up through his skin as if that skin were a porous layer of something insignificant beneath which only power resided. She had seen him use magic before, and he had never looked like this.

Her silence must have been unusual—and if she were painfully honest, it was—because he stopped what he was doing and looked up at her. Up. She was standing above him, but she had rarely felt so much smaller in comparison.

His eyes were the color of night sky made liquid, and like the power that now called on flame from the elemental wilderness, the night beneath the sheen of iris and pupil seemed eternal. Endless.

"What do you see?" he asked her quietly. Almost every word he had spoken since she had woken was quiet. It made her nervous.

Almost any act of kindness did; she was well enough versed in the arts political that she knew kindness for the facade it was. *Not true,* she told herself, the dialogue between youth and adulthood a continuous bickering match. *There's Teller and Finch.*

But they don't have any power.

They don't have any political power. It's not the same thing.

Wind blew, carrying the aroma of roses, thick and heavy in the fullness of bloom. But everywhere she looked there was rock. She'd never much liked roses; the thorns had cut her several times as an unwary child, and when she looked at them now, those thorns were all she saw; the blossoms, fragrant and softer than skin, were an incidental, like hat or clothing; something easily shed.

"ATerafin?"

"I smell roses," she said without thinking.

His frown was instant, a deepening of the lines around mouth, a narrowing of eyes.

"Where are we?"

He rose. "We are in the Stone Deepings. Under the mountains."

"We can't be under the mountains," she replied, turning her face to the night sky, the glorious, perfectly clear Northern sky. "There," she lifted a hand. "Can't you see it? Fabril's Forge."

"I see rock," he said quietly, although his eyes didn't leave her face. "I see darkness and shadow. The light I carry here," he held out a magestone that was an unusual lavender, "and here," he touched his eyes, "is the light we are navigating the path by."

"But the path," she looked to the North—she was certain it must be North, she knew the constellations so well, "is clear." The crevice they walked in was made of rock as high as the eye could see from one side to another, but it was wide and flat, and she saw no hint of the heavy snows that plagued the mountains and made passage through the Menorans so treacherous at the wrong time of year.

"Jewel," he said, and she heard the power he put into her name as clearly as she had seen it beneath the thin layer of his skin, "you are seer-born. If I could, I would blindfold you and have you walk in utter darkness, but here in the Deepings, I do not think anything as simple as a blindfold would spare you vision. Let me lead. No matter what you see, no matter what you *hear*— and you will hear much, I think—do as I tell you."

His voice was a stranger's voice. It was deeper than Avandar's, fuller, richer; the words were chosen with care, and not in anger.

"You've been here before."

"Yes, of course. I came here to find the place that would become my citadel." He knelt again, cloth bending at knee and elbow as he spoke to the fire in a voice that crackled like kindling being consumed. She had never heard the magical words spoken so . . . clearly.

She repeated them.

His eyes widened. His power flared as the fire leaped in jagged blades of flame: orange, yellow, white, and blue. He spoke, words a crackle now, power no longer interior illumination but harsh, red light. His words girdled the flame, constricting it. Forcing it into the shape and the utility of insignificance: campfire.

Her mouth hung open, as if the fire had come from her throat and not the ground upon which Avandar had been so delicately working. Fire had singed his flesh. She knew it without asking, the scent was so sudden, so strong.

He spoke in a language she didn't understand.

"No one else survived it," she said softly.

He tended his burn in silence, taking his dagger and applying it cleanly to the edge of the robe he wore. "In the bag," he said, "there is a salve. Please."

She did as he bid automatically, searching through the jars until she found one that contained a thick unguent consistent with treating burns. But her attention was trapped by fire, by the shadows fire cast. People's shadows.

"They died on this path."

He took the jar from her pale hand. "Yes," he told her quietly, as he coated the ugly patch of skin, "they died on this path."

"Do you believe in ghosts?"

"No."

"Good. I don't either."

His smile was grim. "There are far worse than ghosts to be found on this path, and I fear we will find them all. But if it is in my power to protect you, I will protect you." He was silent for a time. When he spoke, it was grudging, and the very nature of the reluctance made her smile. "And he protects you, in a fashion."

She didn't ask who he meant; she knew.

The Winter King.

13th of Scaral, 427 AA
Tor Leonne

Serra Fiona en'Marano seldom visited the outer reaches of the harem. The harem's heart was her demesne, and if she did not quite rule it, she was nonetheless accorded a reasonable measure of power and respect by the women who jointly did. Her plaintive warblings to Sendari aside, this had been a life in which she'd found a certain satisfaction. It was better than being unmarried, as Serra Teresa was; better than having no home of one's own. But as she listened to the words of a pale Alana en'Marano, she knew that that comfort was coming to a close.

"Alaya," she said softly.

The seraf, like shadow but far more pleasing, was at her side at once. She held brush and comb in her perfectly still hands as she knelt at the feet of her Serra.

"Yes, the jade comb. And the green sari, the one edged in white and gold. But *quickly,* child," she added, although Alaya was fast outgrowing that endearment. She rose, and Alana helped her unwind the informal silks of her private chambers. The deep blue, unedged and unembroidered, surrounded her feet in folds of soft warmth; serafs would take it, clean it, and fold it neatly for her later use. "Alana, have you told the others?"

"They know," Alana replied, evasive as she often was in matters concerning the other wives. It had offended Fiona once; now it was merely fact. She had survived them; they had survived her. Time built different bonds than affection, but it bound nonetheless.

"Good. I will speak with Diora."

"Thank you, Fiona."

She missed the lilies.

Her father's wives, when they could, brought her the thick, white blossoms from the Lake's edge—but they were not so perfect out of their element; they were a beauty with no context.

Still, she had not yet asked Alana or Illia to stop their infrequent gift-giving; she could hear, in their voices, that they found relief in the ability to provide her what they considered to be some small comfort. They were allowed so little, otherwise. She had been forbidden their company, except on those rare occasions when they were granted permission—by her father directly—to bring her one of the two daily meals she was allowed.

She thought she might have lived without food, although she knew it to be a pensive fancy.

Still, lilies, wives, fathers—these were things she had been deprived of before. And perhaps her father, in his great anger—and it *was* as great an anger as he had ever felt toward her—understood this. Perhaps he understood, finally, the cost of his treachery. There was only one loss—and it a minor one, but it was all that was left—that he could inflict upon her.

He had destroyed her samisen and her harp.

Standing there, in the middle of this room, he had had them brought; had taken them in his shaking hands. He had spoken little; a word or two that was not, and would never be, strong enough to bridge the enormity of the silence between them. And then he had called the Widan's fire.

If she closed her eyes, she could hear the snapping of strings, the sudden harsh *crack* of wood. The fires were not extended; that was not her father's gift. No, they were sharp and sudden, and they left once their work had been done.

Throughout it, she showed Ser Sendari *di'Sendari* all she was willing to show: the absolute serenity of her expression.

Father, she thought, then and now, *I know how to wait.*

Her hands, folded in her lap just so, had not even shaken. She had endured much worse than this.

When she heard the screens slide open, she slipped into that deferential posture that gave nothing away. Her knees touched the plain mats, and in the lap that formed, she placed her hands, one over the other. She straightened her shoulders, and let her chin dip forward so that she might see the floor more clearly than the screens.

But she lifted her head again when she heard the Serra Fiona's voice.

"Diora."

"Serra Fiona?"

"I've come," she said, as Alaya closed the screens at her back, "to give you news." She smiled brightly, but there was a hesitancy to the whole of her expression that spoke far more than her presence did. Diora waited.

"Your father has arranged for a visitor. For you," she added hastily.

"Serra Fiona, I—"

"It is the Tyr'agnate Eduardo kai di'Garrardi. He—he has demanded the right to see you, and your father has granted it."

"I have seen the kai Garrardi before this. We have spoken."

"Yes. But not as his intended."

No, not that. As a captive; as a prisoner; as an enemy that still had the power to fascinate. Diora's smile was perfect.

Fiona's became so. "Forgive me, Diora." Her voice gave away what her expression no longer would. Fear. Concern. Envy. Pity. It was a human voice.

Had she ever listened to voice and ignored the nuances of its power, the musicality of its cadence, the roughness, the depth of its feeling? Yes. Of course, yes. She was certain that she would never do so again. That had been the most humbling truth about captivity. She wanted Fiona to continue to speak, and she almost despised herself for it.

"I should let them tell you, Diora. But I know it won't make any difference; you won't give anything away.

"Eduardo di'Garrardi has demanded the rights that your father granted him at the Festival of the Sun. Your father has acceded, although if I am any judge of character, it is at the expense of the General's anger.

"You are to be married to the Tyr'agnate of Oerta before the sun falls on the Lord's first day."

* * *

There was about the Serra Diora di'Marano a quality of perfection that nothing marred; he would have recognized her in any setting, and in any style of dress. As the Lord's Consort, certainly. And as the lowest of the Lady's serafs as well.

The former, he had seen with his own eyes, and the latter he saw now: The Serra Diora di'Marano, shorn of all conceit, knelt before him as gracefully, as gravely, as the most perfectly trained of serafs. Her sari was so simple, in fact, the serafs of the highborn would have escaped its use. She had no combs, and wore only the simplest of rings—something the eye could pass over and forget instantly.

But her hair was long and perfect in its drape across bent back, and her face was the same face—measured, neutral, perfect in shape, in size—that he had, once seen, desired.

It was a desire which had been rebuked.

Worse, her father had chosen to accept the suit of the Tyr'agar's heir. He remembered her wedding night. There was almost nothing he would not do to rid himself of that memory.

"Serra Diora," he said, bowing formally.

She did not look up; her posture, delicate and perfect, made a shield of submission. He knew her well enough to understand that no wilting shyness marred the strength of her spirit; beneath all trappings she was as wild, as willful, as Sword's Blood. But she was more cunning.

"Ser Sendari," he said quietly, "I understand your desire to hide your daughter, but your attempt to transform her into a common seraf is less than laudable. She is not to be the wife of a common clansman; she is to be my wife, and I expect her to be attired in a manner appropriate to that station."

"She is not yet your wife." The Widan's voice was mild; his expression was as neutral as his daughter's. There was no doubt in the Tyr'agnate's mind that the daughter favored the father in intellect. He did not recall ever seeing Sendari's first wife—he knew, as they all did, that she was dead—which meant that she could not favor the wife in looks. There were some pairings that were fortuitous.

"She is not yet my wife, no. But as she will be—and soon, soon enough—I . . . request . . . that you respect my wishes. If money is the sole reason you have chosen to hide your daughter in every possible way, let me alleviate it for you." He removed a large bag from the folds of his robe and had the privilege of seeing Ser

Sendari's shuttered face stiffen into something hard enough that it might be steel.

It amused him to drop the money squarely in front of the Serra Diora's bent form.

"Serra Diora," he said softly, the two words a command. She heard it; she lifted her head.

He knelt before her, reaching out with his ungloved hand. "I have been patient," he said softly. "I have been as patient as any man can be." His hand hovered an inch away from her cheek.

She pulled back.

He caught her chin in that hand; caught her hair, the back of her head, with the other. She had too much dignity to struggle. "Do you understand?" he said softly, too softly for any hearing but hers. "I have waited since the evening that you were given to the kai in waiting. Ser Illara kai di'Leonne. I have waited patiently since he made the mistake of telling me a single glimpse of you is all I would ever have.

"And I remember that glimpse," he added; her face was very close to his now, her lips ever so slightly parted, her eyes involuntarily wide. "There is not a night that has passed since then when I have not thought of you.

"I would not treat you so harshly; I would not offer to others what they have no power to take for themselves." His hand tightened in her hair; she could not look away. The most escape the grip afforded her was the simple expedient of closing her eyes. She did not disappoint him; if there was fear in her—and there was; he could smell it—she did not allow it to rule her actions.

"You have already refused me once, little Serra. But there will be no General to intervene on your behalf—and no interfering kai el'Sol. You will be my wife in a few long days.

"Do you understand what this means? You will be my wife. You will make my harem. You will bear my children. And you will *never* play games of refusal with me again."

Before she could answer—and he suspected that she would not, for she was so finely mannered, so perfectly graceful—he brought his lips to hers, holding back just that extra second so that he might feel her draw a sharp, short breath.

She did.

He cut it off with his mouth, pulling her to him with handfuls of hair so soft it might have been the folds of silk unwinding. Her hands came up; she rested them against his chest.

He might have laughed had he not been otherwise occupied;

she pushed. She pushed him back, her palms flat, her arms as weak as any woman's.

He had waited so long he was not yet—not quite—willing to be put off; he kissed her more fiercely, bruising her lips, wanting to bruise them so that he might see them at their fullest when at last he chose to withdraw.

If he chose. He closed his eyes. This was as close as he had ever come to the Serra Diora di'Marano. He wanted, suddenly, to be a little closer; to touch a little more; his hand slid down from her chin to stroke the length of her throat, the nape of her neck, the perfection of her pale, pale skin.

Not enough. Never enough.

Her tongue fluttered against his like a trapped butterfly against the walls that confined it; he was gentle, but he was unyielding. She would come to understand and desire what he offered her. She had never desired the kai Leonne.

His hands brushed silk, folds of silk. Of a sudden, he wanted to remove it. Her eyes widened; this close to her face, he could not miss it.

The hands that had been open palmed became fists—but she did not strike him; did not otherwise fight.

Nor did she need to.

The fire did.

The fire was his strength. Of the Widan's many spells, it was the first to have come to him. He could remember few moments as clearly as this: The lighting of the first candle.

That candle, round and low, had been his hurdle. A thing of yellow wax, it had been set upon the small Widan's table by the hands of his reluctant wife.

"Sit," he'd told her. And then, unmanning himself because this was the most private of his chambers, he had added, "Please."

Her smile was like the flame, almost as precious, possibly more beautiful. Even then, even marred as it was by her rare display of unease. She had never loved the Widan's craft, but because he had asked it of her, because she had loved *him,* she sat by the side of the low table, her hands cupping the candle.

She had done this for four weeks.

And on the second day of the fifth week, her hands around cool wax, her eyes alert although she'd sat almost motionless for the better part of two hours in the summer heat, the fire finally heard his voice and answered.

All images, all memories, of any strength were as complicated as these. The fire was his strength.

But so, too, had Alora been before her death. His strength and his weakness.

The only person in his life that he had loved as much— although the nature of the love was different—had also betrayed him. *Diora.*

His daughter.

He did not think. Had he thought, he might have stayed his hand. But the fire sped down the length of his arms, contained within him until its spark left his fingers. Every Widan described the art differently; every Widan communed in his own way with the source of his power. And every Widan learned, immediately, that power without control was death.

Yet he did not control himself, not here.

The power came automatically, summoned by a fierce protectiveness he would have said—had any dared to ask openly—had died on the last day of the Festival of the Sun. Worse, rage was there, beneath the surface of the fire, and it was a rage that Eduardo's disgraceful behavior could not quite explain.

"How dare you?"

The Tyr'agnate cried out in pain. It was not quite a scream; there was too much anger in the mix, too much outrage. His hands left Diora's face, Diora's body, in the blink of an eye, and Sendari's daughter—his unperturbable, steely child—leaped clear of Eduardo, trailing seraf's silk, her face turned away from them both.

The sword rang out.

The fire crackled.

Death hung in the air between them: One man's death. Or two.

It would have been a better death than Sendari had faced in years, a cleaner one. He could have stepped into the flow of the wind, have become just another screaming voice in the wind's maelstrom. He could have discovered, for himself—because no matter how great the desire for that knowledge, it seemed no Widan was capable of answering the question and returning with the information—whether or not the winds ruled the dead, or the Northern gods did, or the Lady. And he might see the wife that he had loved and hated in his time, the only woman whose light had been as bright as the fire's.

Eduardo di'Garrardi swung; Sendari dodged the blade, drew his own. Steel against steel was meant as a distraction, and it succeeded; the kai Garrardi was not trained to fight Widan. He called fire. Fire came as he parried the Tyr'agnate's blow and staggered back. The ferocity of the attack was astounding.

They had come here without Tyran or cerdan.

They had come to the chamber that had been her prison.

And now, the ground at their feet hazed by red light, the air overpowered by the scent of singed hair and singed flesh, they were fighting as men fought: with swords. She thought the roof might burn away, seared into nothing by the Lord's vision, the Lord's gaze. His work, this. His work, as all misery in her life had been.

She gathered the silks more closely about her; Eduardo had pulled at the sari only briefly, but his hands were strong enough to loose their binding.

She had thought—she had thought her father would not intervene. Her hands shook as she crouched against the wall, her face turned groundward in a semblance of the humility so necessary in a Serra's posture. Better that, though, better that than that either man should see her face before she had time to compose it. She was numb with the mixture of fear and humiliation that only men could cause, and it was slow to leave her.

But when the sword skittered across the fine, fine floor and stopped six inches from her bent knees, something stronger took its place. It was her father's sword.

She looked up then. Looked up to see the Tyr'agnate's armor, bare of surcoat, bare of detail by the grace of fire. His hair, his skin dusted black by ash, his face in profile, he stood over her father's prone form, and her father—her Widan father, her powerful father—lay weaponless beneath him.

Before thought could assert itself, before recent history could remind her of everything she had never thought she could forget—even for an instant—her mouth was open, her lips full and then narrowed around a single word.

A single powerful word.

"NO!"

He stopped at once, his sword in mid-arc above his head, his arms extended beneath its weight. Vision, when he fought for his life, took on a clarity that could only be the Lord's gift: All things moved more precisely, and slightly more slowly, as he watched them. He could choose what to react to; could override the instinct that had saved his life more times than he cared to count.

Her word struck him like a forceful blow; a Northern archer's arrow aimed slightly off true while he stood, both hands on the hilt of a sword, the killing blow already begun. He almost staggered with the effort it took to heed her.

But he saw clearly.

The Widan Sendari di'Sendari was at his feet, a second from death, his Widan's fire split, like a wall made of kindling, by the use of the sword that had been the clan Garradi's since the founding. *Ventera* hovered a moment as he weighed his options.

As he weighed them and found Sendari's death wanting.

If he killed the Widan, he would be declaring himself for the North. Politically, Alesso was astute—but the entire Dominion knew of his almost legendary friendship with the Widan, and a smaller circle of men knew of his desire for the Widan's daughter. Sendari's death would be all the excuse he required.

And the war?

To go to war, the Tyr'agar would turn his forces first South, to Oerta, and then North. There was no doubt in Eduardo's mind that Jarrani would support Alesso in this. The Sword's Edge would support Alesso. For aid—should he choose to ask it—he would be reduced to seeking alliance with either Mareo di'Lamberto or Ramiro di'Callesta. As it was Callestan lands that he sought for his part in the war, it was a poor exchange.

On the other hand, Ramiro di'Callesta had *never* dared to strike him with anything more careless than a duplicitous word.

He wanted to kill the Widan.

He wanted the Widan's daughter.

He knew that, having already shown how seriously she took the duty to husband—what man could now doubt that, after hearing the depth of conviction in her speech on the last day of the Festival of the Sun?—she would be no less the dutiful daughter.

And if he was her father's killer, husband or no, he would be forced to kill her.

All these things occurred to him in a rush of thought and clarity as he stood above the prone form of Sendari di'Sendari. All of them.

Such clarity, at such a moment, could only be the Lord's vision, the Lord's gift. Almost before the sound of the Serra Diora's voice had faded into nothing, the Tyr'agnate, Eduardo kai di'Garrardi, lowered his sword.

But he offered no apology for his transgression; he was clearly the victor, after all. For his own reasons, he granted the older man his life. But it was clear to Eduardo, indeed, it must be clear to them all, that that life was also his to take.

"I can be patient," he said, sheathing *Ventera,* "when I so choose. On the morning after the night of the Festival Moon, Widan." He turned to the Flower of the Dominion. "He has his life because of my high regard for you, Serra Diora."

She bowed her head, hiding her face from view. The desire to pull that face up by the chin and force her to meet his eyes was strong, but so were other desires. Better, at the moment, to wait.

He was not completely certain that he would survive the Widan's fire so easily a second time.

He knew what she had done.

He did not know why.

Speaking at all took effort. But he might have read whole treatises flawlessly, argued with Alesso for weeks, brought the Sword of Knowledge to order less painfully than he spoke a single word. *Na'dio.* Almost, he said it. But he could not expose himself to her in that fashion.

He chose, instead, her given name. Her adult name. It was, after all, as an adult that she had become inscrutable. Perfection had destroyed the delicate, trusting child as surely as it did all Serras of highborn clans. It had turned her from daughter to wife almost before he could turn to witness the transformation.

And he had helped.

He had asked the Serra Teresa into his harem. And when Alora had died, he had given Diora into her care.

Teresa would never have raised voice to save his life. He felt certain of that. But he had been more certain that his daughter would not have.

He wanted to ask her why.

But he was a coward; he acknowledged the truth without particular fear or shame.

"Diora." He did not make any effort to disguise himself, to flatten his voice, to keep the truth from it. He wondered what she would hear.

He was no longer certain himself.

The woman whose power was words had none.

Her face was once again the perfect mask, and if her hair was

in disarray, her sari carelessly arranged, her chin darkening with
a bruise that would require the judicious use of powders to conceal, she rose above it all. She was the Serra Diora di'Marano.

Na'dio.

Oh, her dead spoke.

They spoke with such terrible voices. When she could imagine
them as angry, they hurt her the least; in anger, they were harder
to face, harder to yearn for. She had embarked upon the Lord's
path, under the Lady's guise, so that she might hear their anger,
face it, and not be shamed.

And so, of course, the Lord let the wind whisper in other ways.

*Na'dio, we each have gifts for you, but if you accept them,
they demand as much back in return.*

Her hands became fists; the nails of her exquisite fingers cutting crescents in the flat of her palms. She *would not* think of this
here. Not here, not where any could witness it.

It hurt her. She had not desired death—which of the wives
had?—but she knew, now, that death would have been far, far
easier than the life she had chosen. She would not have had to face
life alone, her arms bereft of the child she had done nothing—*no*—
nothing—

Death would have been hers, and peace with it, if not for the
man who lay, bleeding from two wounds, neither fatal, on the
ground in the room's center.

You condemned me to this, she thought, summoning her anger
as if it were a creature from the Hells and she a Widan. But like
a creature from the Hells, it twisted, defying her command,
becoming not a shield behind which to view her father, but rather
a blade upon which she might cut herself. Deeply.

She had *saved* his life.

And he had helped destroy hers.

She was numb. She had spoken with *the* voice. She had stopped
the fall of the Tyr'agnate's sword, using a power that she had not
once used in her own defense against him. She had raised voice to
save her *father* even though she had sat in the dark of the only
true night she had ever known, listening to the screams of the
dying, her hands in her lap, her head bent forward, her body perfectly still.

"Diora?"

The body in the room's center moved.

And her father spoke. He spoke with fear, with hesitation, with the curiosity that had always been the strongest element of his speech, and with something that she would not name.

She had nothing to offer in return but silence.

427 AA
Stone Deepings

Jewel had always disliked it—a matter of principle rather than practicality—when Avandar was right. But he was right about the stars. They didn't move at all; they didn't change. Hours spent walking in the great stone crevice under their cool guiding light had not dimmed or deepened the night blue sky; it had not brought dawn or moon. The stars, like the stone, were fixed in place.

She liked them better, but she found them disturbing. "Why can I see them?"

"The stars?"

"The stars."

"I don't know."

"Liar."

"If you are going to ask me a question, do me the grace of believing the answer I give you."

"Avandar, I can *hear* the lie in your voice. Learn to lie better or don't bother."

"It is not a lie," he replied, through teeth that were gritted in a comforting and familiar fashion. "I have some suspicions—and before you ask, no, I won't share them—but I do not know for certain."

"But the stars aren't real."

"No."

"And you can't see them."

"No."

"And you *know* that my gift has always made me pretty much impervious to illusion."

"Jewel, I am not ignorant."

"I wasn't lecturing you; I was thinking out loud."

"Think more quietly."

She subsided. Thought quietly. If what she was seeing wasn't illusion, and it wasn't real, what *was* it?

Why are they weeping, Oma? Her grandmother's face was still, the lines of it, cut—as her grandmother said—by sun and wind, scars from a South that Jewel had never visited. A South she was walking toward, if *Kalliaris* was in the mood to smile.

Her grandmother and her father—not her mother, not her Southern-born mother—stood on the edge of a large circle of people, all dressed simply, all carrying either clothing or food or offers, word offers, of shelter. Waiting for the Voyani merchants to unload their forbidden cargo: people.

They started to tumble out beneath the heavy flaps of canvas, rolling and stumbling as the bolts of fabric, the cords of Southern wood, the bottles of spice or exotic perfume, were removed and their hiding places destroyed: Men, women, children.

We have to offer them shelter, her Oma had said, *and you are old enough to understand this now. They come from a land that is harsher than Mandaros when he's angry. You remember what you see here. You've the blood, child. It's no sin against pride to take what you need to survive. But it's a sin not to offer it in return when you have it.*

Jewel, silent, had reached up to grab her grandmother's hand. That leathery hand, bent with age into curves that were both comforting and clawlike, had gripped hers a little too tightly as she watched the men and women continue to stumble from the wagon. They were thin, worn; some of them wore women's clothing although they weren't women. They were all younger than her grandmother.

They are weeping, her grandmother had said, *because they are free.*

No, they aren't, Jewel said.

You shouldn't argue with your Oma, her grandmother had said, breath sudden and sharp. *Come home.*

But you said I was old enough—

Come home now. She began to drag Jewel away.

This was the first time that Jewel remembered *knowing* something so clearly. She was pulled upstream, against the current of bodies, of people—like her Oma—who had come to help these people lucky enough to escape from their evil Southern masters. Gods, things were simple then; the good and the evil so clean. She said, because she was young, because she didn't understand her grandmother, except as the source of all wisdom, sharp words, and comfort: *No, Oma, they're crying because the babies died.*

And her grandmother had stopped in the streets, clutching Jewel's hand, grip so hard that Jewel was almost in tears. She'd turned back, letting Jewel go.

Jewel understood it now, but the child that she had been and the woman that she was existed for a moment in the same place, the fear of one, and the terrible pity—the unwanted pity that would have so angered the old woman—of the other in perfect harmony.

Kalliaris smiled on me, Oma. What you taught me—I never forgot it. I never will.

And the old woman answered, "I know."

CHAPTER SEVENTEEN

"Avandar," Jewel said, trying to keep her voice conversational. The problem with that was volume, which was for all intents and purposes nonexistent. She knew it and tried again, louder.

"Avandar?"

"Yes?"

"That was you, right?"

"No."

"But you heard it?"

"Oh, yes," was his quiet reply. She turned to face him, but halfway to familiarity was stopped by a woman she had last seen propped up by cushions in a flat, wide bed.

"Oma," she said, the woman dissolving into the girl, the girl on the verge of tears.

"Jewel," the old woman replied.

Jewel knew better. She *knew* better. But she walked toward her anyway, her steps picking up speed as they came, each faster than the last; she lifted her arms to shoulder height, wide, as if she could catch—as if she could catch—

But her Oma held out a hand, and her lips took on that thin, compressed line that was a clear signal of annoyance. Avandar's shout meant nothing compared to that disapproval. Jewel stopped again.

"Not here, Na'jay," she said quietly. "Never here. I will take you to where you cannot go, but must, if you are to do what you were born to." A faint hint of pride in the sheen of those eyes. Those familiar and entirely unnatural eyes. "Walk with me, or walk beside me, but *do not touch anyone* you see on this path. Do you understand me?"

"Yes, Oma," Jewel replied meekly. When the old woman started to walk, Jewel took up her place at her side as if it were natural. She paused to look behind her; Avandar walked in his customary position. "This is—"

"The Warlord," her Oma said. "I know."

"Uh—that's not what *I* call him."

"It is not what he is *called* that matters," her grandmother replied, not even turning to acknowledge the man they spoke of, "but what he *is*. He is the Warlord, Jewel. And you will thank *Kalliaris* in your time for bringing him to you—although I am not sure he will."

"Oh." She absorbed the sound of a voice that resonated with the familiar, and she understood, then, why she saw starlight where Avandar saw rock.

"Yes," her grandmother said. "Memory has always burned its way into you. You hold on to everything so *tightly*. Everything. Every loss, Jewel. Every death. You will see others where we walk, but I am the first."

She froze. "I don't think I want to see others."

"This road was your decision; you are under the geas of one of the undying. You have no choice, so you may as well not whine about it."

Her memories of her grandmother were always of kindness and wisdom, but this sharp sting of words was just as real. Jewel winced. "Yes, Oma."

"You have a remarkable way with words," her domicis said dryly. "I may take lessons. I have seldom had such an effect."

"You are a man," her Oma said with a shrug, "and the only men a woman should trust are her brothers or her father."

Jewel laughed, thinking of Teller, Carver, Angel; of Torvan, Arrendas; of Morretz—and even, in a fashion, of Avandar himself.

"Yes, I notice you didn't pay attention to *that*," the old woman said. "But you've managed to survive most of your gullibility."

"Oma—"

"Never mind, never mind, not in front of outsiders, I know." The old woman shook her head. "You should be grateful I was first," she said softly. "I'll be the easiest thing you face." She turned, her eyes glowing faintly, her skin luminescent but still somehow her skin. "You," she said softly, and Jewel realized she was speaking to Avandar, "be careful."

Avandar frowned. "I have crossed this path before," he said quietly. "And I have nothing to fear from it. My dead do not return to haunt me."

She laughed. It wasn't a particularly kind laugh, although

Jewel knew, the minute she heard it, that she had heard it before. Memory, buried so far beneath the surface of her daily life that it might as well have been forgotten, spoke in a language that had no words, but it spoke truth. This woman was her grandmother.

"Your dead don't have to return."

14th of Scaral, 427 AA
Shining Palace

"Lord," Garrak ad'Ishavriel said, kneeling. The damage done him by Anya a'Cooper had been quick to heal, physically. Had she had time, had she had leisure, had she had focus and desire, he would have born scars for eternity. And the *Kialli* did not easily scar; it was not in the nature of their forms. Anya a'Cooper had learned things in her tenure in the North that not even Lord Ishavriel had meant to teach her.

It worried him, at times. Pleased him as well. She was easily the most dangerous thing he owned. Certainly the most costly.

And she was still missing.

She was not dead; *that,* he would have sensed. But she was not at his side, and the gate that her power had been crucial in the opening of now waited in the limbo of lesser magi. The Lord of the Hells was ill pleased. His was the only power superior to Anya's, but that power had been bent to other tasks, tasks that Ishavriel privately suspected were far less monotonous, but of lesser import. Allaskar did not have that option now, if his armies were to be built. He anchored the riven gate, sustaining the foothold that Anya had built in rock and ice. *Kialli* spirits still came through the portal, shuddering to a stop in the substantial reality of flesh and form. He had watched them arrive for days on end, fascinated by the way they formed bodies outside of the containment rogue magi controlled. Fascinated, as well, by the changing shape of the gate, the rip between worlds that Anya and he had taken such pains to widen, day by day. The world fought them. Proof, if it was needed, that the old earth was alive.

The armies were still gathering; they had lost a day due to the disruption of the misplaced throne, no more. But still, the Lord was not pleased.

No *Kialli* Lord, be he once a duke of the Hells, could survive the Lord's displeasure for long. Therefore Ishavriel's considerable powers were now bent to one purpose: finding his charge and returning her to the pentagram that anchored the Lord's gate.

Or rather, to almost one purpose.

He condescended to notice Garrak. "You arrive early. Report."

"Lord," Garrak said again, kneeling, the ridges across his spine extended in a way that must have been uncomfortable. "I have two things of interest to you."

"First: The Voyani woman you asked of. She is . . . missing."

"Missing?"

"She was, you said, in the keeping of Cortano di'Alexes. If he still has her, she is farther beneath the earth than my powers are capable of reaching."

"Dead?"

"That is a possibility. But it is doubtful. I have heard rumors; the slaves speak, if their masters do not. But the slaves speak of an attack—upon the chambers of the Sword of Knowledge himself— by either assassins or demons. In these tales, the Voyani woman is never among the victims. I do not believe that the slaves knew she was present."

"The Sword's Edge has not seen fit to bring this information to council."

Garrak said nothing; he had nothing to add.

"Very well. I want that woman, Garrak."

"We are searching, Lord. We are hampered by daylight."

"Understood. But remain hampered. You are not to show yourselves until the night of the Festival Moon."

"Yes, Lord."

"The second piece of information?"

"Only this," Garrak ad'Ishavriel replied. He rose slightly, and Ishavriel saw that he carried a small cloth sack. There was a deep splash of drying blood across the length of the rough cloth.

"Your orders," Ishavriel said softly. "There was to be *no* harvesting until the night of the Festival Moon, and even then it was to follow my *explicit* instructions."

"I have broken no dictate, Lord. I have obeyed you."

"And the blood?"

"A simple death. With mortal blade."

"And the others?"

"No one else has made Telkar's mistake, Lord. I have seen to it myself."

"Very well. Telkar has been . . . an embarrassment. I have suffered two in the last three days, and if I suffer a third, I will destroy you all at my leisure."

"Lord."

He took the bag that Garrak ad'Ishavriel held in a perfectly
steady outstretched hand. Opened it. Drew from it a Festival mask.

"I recognize the design," he said with a slight smile. "And this
is of note?"

"Yes, Lord. This mask was created by the humans."

"The humans?"

"I believe that they are replacing the masks that were your
gifts."

"I see." He turned the mask over in his hand examining it
carefully. "Humans are consistently clever, are they not? Very
well. You have done well, Garrak." He rose.

Only when Garrak ad'Ishavriel left his chambers did Lord
Ishavriel, *Kialli,* part of the Lord's Fist, smile.

427 AA
Stone Deeping

The wind was a sea wind; hot and heavy with water. The sky was
a night sky, cool and very Northern. Jewel struggled with the di-
chotomy between two very real sensations.

"There isn't any point in questioning it," her Oma said tartly.
"It's as real as I am."

"And I'm having enough trouble with that."

"You shouldn't, you know."

"Easy for you to say."

"True. Everything is, now."

They fell silent; Avandar did not seem eager for the company of
an old woman whose tongue was razor sharp, and whose claim on
Jewel's affections was so much stronger than his own; he kept to
himself. Which was a pity; Jewel found the walk disquieting. Her
grandmother seemed to expect something from her; it was implicit
in the quality of her silence.

She didn't want to talk about expectations; they led to responsibilities, and no doubt her grandmother's sense of responsibility
would not mesh well with Jewel's. So she said, searching for
social words, that most despised of things, "Where did I see these
stars?"

"These ones? On my lap," the old woman replied, her voice
softening into the voice that Jewel best remembered—that, truthfully, had been all she remembered clearly until now. "They
aren't the stars over Averalaan."

"No. Not quite."

She was silent, looking at her grandmother in the light of moon and stars. The shawl she wore was suited to a cool night; it was soft and worn with age, thinning but not yet patched and repaired. It covered her shoulders, ran down the length of her back; ended a few inches above the bend in her knee. Jewel knew it well. It had been given to her after her grandmother's death.

Had been sold by her, as well, when things had gotten grimmest in the streets of the city. Food was more important than warmth. At least when it wasn't cold.

"You do what you have to, to survive."

"I know, Oma. You taught me that."

"And you be damn proud of surviving."

"I know." *I know.* "But there's more to life than survival. And sometimes—sometimes the definition of survival leaves a bit to be desired." She glanced sideways at the old woman's sharp profile. "Wasn't it you who said life on the knees was a seraf's art, not a woman's?"

Her Oma shrugged, half irritable. "You see? You remember everything." She shook her head. "It would go better for you if you didn't."

"Why is that? There's no point to life if there's no memory, Oma. Memory's what connects the bits and pieces. It's what gives strength to history."

"And history should be strong, is that it? Our bloodiest battles are fought in *history*. Our worst atrocities—things *you* can't even dream of, and you with your head in the sand—are buried, forgotten, and best that way. Some young fool will always steal from history, as if history was its own justification. Ask *him,* if you don't believe me."

"I would appreciate being left out of this conversation. If, that is, a diatribe can be considered reciprocal enough to *be* a conversation."

"I'm not arguing for or against *all* history, Oma. Just the personal."

"But personal history is what binds us, Jewel."

"It can also free us."

"Can it? I'm glad to hear it," the old woman replied. "You can tell *her* that." Voice sharp with sarcasm—and an Oma's sarcasm at that, sharp to wounding—she lifted what would have been a frail arm had it been attached to a different person's shoulder and pointed.

In the darkness, in the middle of the widening path between

the mountain walls, stood a dark-haired young woman with a glint of light at the top of a closed fist.

"Hey, Jay," she said.

He had never seen Jewel freeze so abruptly. He had seen enough, in the decade and a half in which they'd negotiated their fragile peace, to understand the texture of all of her fears. Strong fears made her grind slowly to a stop, as if realization took that long to take root, to grip her.

Nah, she's just too stupid to know when to be afraid. Carver's voice, a glimmering edge in words that were otherwise wholly affectionate. It surprised him when the words of any of her den— each member so insignificant he would not have noticed them had he chosen any other course in life—came back to him.

Words seldom deserted her, and when they did, she substituted action in their place, usually anger or rage-driven flinging of pots and pans in the kitchen that served as her inner sanctum, her throne room, her place of judgment.

But here, on this empty road, silence took everything: movement. Word. Breath. The woman by her side, peppery in speech and a hair's breadth from the ill-temper that was so common at a certain age, fell silent as well. He had thought it prudent to keep his distance; he now felt it prudent to do otherwise. It was the simplest decision he had made since leaving Averalaan. Even packing for their trip to the South had been fraught with temper and the fragments of memory that would not leave him.

He walked to her side. Saw, as he did, that the old woman's eyes were keen and bright, like a ferret's when it scented food close by. Jewel's eyes were wide, her mouth half open, her face, muscles stiff, skirting the thin edge between terror and the hope that is so wild it cuts and rends with its multiple uncertainties.

Unfortunately for Jewel, and perhaps for Avandar himself, he could not see what caused it. She was still for so long it surprised him when she took a step forward.

He put a hand out; caught her shoulder.

The old woman she called *Oma* held her differently, and perhaps more effectively. "Na'jay," she said.

But Jewel, held by them both, was only peripherally aware of their interference. She said a single word.

"Duster."

He tightened the grip on her shoulder.

"You know the name," the old woman said conversationally.

"I know it."

"Did you know the young girl?"

"It was before my time," he replied. He whispered a word, and another word, both sharp and short in the cavernous darkness of the Deepings. The light that he saw by, unnatural in every possible way, nestled like moss across the surface of worn rock, touching the stone that came up from the floor and hung down from the heights like either half of a great maw open to let them pass because they were too insignificant to devour.

Jewel had spoken of stars; there were none. She spoke of a path at their feet, and there was one, tortuous and narrow. She had not misstepped once, although he had watched for it with care; he had seen the result of misstep once before, and he was very anxious not to see that mistake repeated. The old woman at her side had taken no missteps either—if one assumed that passing through solid rock was a matter of confident footing. He had watched, waiting for the moment his magical guidance might prove useful. As she so often did, she wounded what vanity he had: she denied him purpose.

He was no longer what he had been when these paths had devoured the merely mortal. Jewel was.

He could not see with her vision. He doubted that there was another man alive who could, and although he understood the legacy left the Voyani, he suspected that the Matriarchs could not rival her raw power.

It had long since ceased to anger him that she refused to tend to the talent that was her neglected birthright. It had never greatly worried him until now.

He turned to the old woman, and he spoke, and magic reared like mythic serpent in response to his spell; a cascade of orange light spilled harmless from her head to her toes, to be swallowed by the shadows that pooled at her feet. "Don't," she said coolly. "I am not here for you, and I do not serve your purpose."

"But I see you," he said, as Jewel continued to stare at the path ahead, oblivious to the two who were slightly behind her. "You are not a manifestation of her gift and this path."

"No."

"Let her go."

"I am not what you think I am," the old woman replied, as cross as a harried market-goer.

"And I—"

"You are the Warlord. I know you. I know of your history; I

see your dead walking behind you, and within you, with every step you take. Nothing is hidden from me here. Nothing."

"This is not your road."

"No," she replied, that voice gentling, bleeding itself of power until something placid and undefined remained at the base of her words. "It is Jewel's road, start to finish, and I have some hope that she will survive it." A wrinkled, sun-worn face turned to his, and the eyes that stared unblinking at him were like no living eyes he had seen—and he had gazed upon the gods in his time. "The gods are walking," she said, "as you prophesied. The paths cannot contain the Firstborn."

"They are contained."

"You understood her vision far better than she, and if you spent time lying to yourself about its significance, you're far more of a fool than you look. Which isn't saying much." He frowned.

"Duster."

"Na'jay."

"Jewel."

The first person she'd met in the Deepings had been her Oma. That had felt so right she hadn't really questioned it.

But the second person . . . funny, that it would be Duster. She lost Fisher and Lefty to the maze beneath the old city before Duster had met her end at the hands of the demon. She had lost her parents between her grandmother's death and theirs.

But truth? Even though she had cried for days after her father's untimely and unexpected death, something about Duster's death had been sharper, uglier, more painful.

Awful confession, that. She was glad she'd never had to make it out loud. The slender knife that glinted in the moonlight was Duster's trademark threat. Not that she wasn't big with words; she used 'em, sometimes to good effect, sometimes to bad. She had the worst temper because it ran so deep and it was so hard to turn *off*.

And she almost never pulled that knife when she wasn't angry. Truth. "Duster," she said, her voice as dry as the name. She wanted to say more, but the real words couldn't get past the true ones: *I sent you to die.*

"Yeah," the shade said. "You sent *me*. To die. And I did." She took a step closer. "You want to see?"

Jewel saw her clearly enough; the shadows robbed her of

nothing. There were times when you saw something—and Jewel knew this was one—and it became the only thing in the world. She'd heard love talked about, in syrupy, stupid words, just as if it were like this: She couldn't breathe, couldn't move, could barely think.

If this was love, she'd give it a miss. A wide miss. In fact, she'd turn her back and walk away as quickly as dignity allowed. When she remembered how to breathe. If she ever could again.

There was no blood on Duster's face. No slash across her skin, no scars that hadn't already been there. She wore what she'd worn the last time Jewel had seen her alive—something she hadn't thought about much until she'd known for certain she'd never see her in it again: Undyed wool, carded by the hands of a sour old woman who'd managed to find the mangiest sheep in existence to shear. It was rough in texture, and too large. Jewel bought everything too large back then, because she hardly ever had money to buy clothing and everyone grew out of everything so damn fast.

"Bloody miracle," Duster said, "considering how much we had to eat. Hear you guys did real well for yourselves after you got rid of me."

She came closer.

Jewel stood her ground. She'd almost run out to meet her; at least that's what she thought she'd done. Stupid. Stupid move. She could see that now. Dagger and Duster. Duster and Death. Avandar's unwelcome hand was on her shoulder, a reminder of the life that Duster had had no chance to be part of.

"You here to kill me?" she asked quietly, shrugging that unwanted hand clear.

"Na'jay," her Oma said, voice as sour as vinegar.

"Maybe." Duster's shrug was more pointed than Jewel's, less useful.

"Maybe?"

"Maybe."

Silence. Heavy with the unsaid. Jewel struggled for that elusive breath. This *is* what love was like. Damn foolish. Be honest. Be honest, for once. You didn't love her in spite of the fact that she was a killer, you loved her *because* she was one.

Because she could do the things you were afraid to without thinking twice. Because she could do the things that *had to be done* without flinching, or throwing up, or looking over her shoulder and waiting for the hand of Mandaros to descend from the heavens in judgment.

Because her mother, some backstreet whore who had gone home with the wrong man and had never come out again, hadn't invested her with the same guiding principles that *Oma* and Jewel's mother had; because Duster, wild and dark, eyes and hair like shadow, voice like fire, was a freedom that seemed like power.

She looked it, now: Thin and unbowed, her lip dimpled by some old knife fight that had happened before they'd met. Her eyes, gods, her eyes, larger than full crowns, expressive enough that you watched them no matter what they told you. And they told Jewel a lot, almost as much as the dagger did.

"Yeah," she said, was saying, as Jewel stared. "I think I want to kill you."

"Too bad."

Duster raised a dark brow. "You and me in a fight, and you think you'd win?"

"Not much. But I couldn't have won then, either. See the big idiot to my left? He's smaller than Arann, but still. Mean sonofabitch."

Duster spat. "Too pretty."

"Well, yeah. But he's mean anyway."

"And he's hanging with you? Not that bright. Or didn't you tell him what happens to most of your followers?"

She flinched. Shouldn't have. Knew it. She'd had to walk the edge with Duster more than once, and Duster knew how to find all the weak spots. "Not most of 'em."

"No." She shrugged. Threw heavy hair over her shoulder. "Just the killers."

"You want to get this over with?"

"Nah. I'll keep you guessing. You have to walk past me sooner or later." Duster laughed. "Besides. You can't call the hired help. They can't *see* me."

Jewel grimaced. The starlight was as clear as the knife's edge, the walls of the cliffs to either side sheer and daunting in their barren beauty. "Avandar," she said quietly, not taking her eyes from Duster, which wasn't hard. "Please tell me I'm not talking to myself."

"Not only will I not tell you that," he replied, "but I will also insult your intelligence by pointing out that it is extremely easy, in the Stone Deepings, to commit suicide. In fact," he added softly, with an edge to his voice that she'd always disliked, "it's the only way to die here."

"Great." She shrugged. Started to walk. "I hate you, you know that?" The knife's edge shadowed her face.

Duster laughed. "Yeah. I know." She fell into an easy walk beside her. "Hate me enough, and I won't be able to kill you. Hate me too much, and you won't be able to kill me."

"You were never this smart," Jewel snapped back.

"Of course not. I was never *you*." And she pulled the knife back and shoved it forward so suddenly Jewel only had time to bleed.

14th of Scaral, 427 AA
Desert of Sorrows

The night was not very black. It seldom was in these lands; no cloud seemed to settle across the sky for long, and the stars were piercing in their clarity. Nor were the nights long. The Northern Wastes had that as their advantage, although the Lord Ishavriel preferred the Southern desert to the Winter one. For one, there was life in the South that the Wastes did not boast, and where there was life, there was hunting.

But at night, the life was hidden.

Lord Ishavriel turned from his contemplation of the night sky. The constellations, unlike the world itself, had not changed much in the long absence of the *Kialli;* he therefore took some obscure comfort in naming them all. Humanity named the stars, attaching the brightest of their lights to the oldest of their stories. Even when the stories faded, the names remained, shorn of the depth of meaning.

But not shorn of all power.

The longest night was coming.

He had witnessed it, time and again, in the isolation of the Northern Wastes. He had marked its passing in the Lord's basin, while the Lord devoured what he had forbidden them: mortal souls. Lord Ishavriel had seen the brightest and the darkest of souls offered as sustenance to Allasakar. He had also destroyed a handful of his followers when the sight had driven them to the edge of madness. None of them were among the *Kialli*.

The *Kialli* had memory to sustain them. Memory of those places. Memory of these ones. Memory of the coming night.

But although they had marked the night, they had not *used* it. The seasons had been slow to return to them. The Northern Wastes, in particular, seemed a continuous piece of winter and winter's unchanging cold. But sooner or later—sooner, in Ishavriel's case—the sense of the old seasons returned.

The Winter road would be at its strongest when the night was longest.

In the South, they called it the Lady's Night. Arianne, in all of her glorious finery, might have approved. He wondered, briefly, where she was. If she still survived. They had warred, her people and his.

But never on Scarran.

No, on Scarran, they had often turned their time and attention to this: the desert. Because once, once before mortal memory, where the desert now stood there had been *life*. A gathering of mortals so vast it was almost impossible to believe it had dwindled into the pathetic Southern Terreans and the inscrutable Voyani caravans.

It was almost enough to cast all memory into doubt. Almost.

And that was a direction in which he did not wish to travel. He had much work to do, and little time to do it in. There was power here, buried in the same way a human heart is: beneath the flesh of the world and the cage of the desert. The other *Kialli* had not been wakened sufficiently; they did not seek from the desert what he did.

But in *this* desert, and only this one, all memory played him false. His Lord had decreed, and in anger, the desert had responded. The Cities of Man had been devoured. Lost to the world, lost to the men who had graced both wall and home, they had become part of the desert's heart.

And no one, perhaps not even the Lord Himself, knew where that heart now lay.

But those with the magic waking—waking quickly with the passage of days—were developing ambitions of their own. He knew that now he could find the resting place of at least one of those cities.

He began to cast.

To his great surprise, the desert resisted.

14th of Scaral, 427 AA
Tor Leonne

She woke from her troubled sleep with a start and rolled out of the bed, coming up against wooden planks on her heels, with both daggers gleaming in the moon's light.

"Steady," a familiar voice said.

The shadows resolved themselves into the shape of Elena. Elena with two daggers and no lamp.

She took a deep breath, and the daggers found their sheaths again. It would be minutes before her heart's beat returned to the steadiness she was familiar with. "What are you doing here?"

"You obviously didn't hear yourself shout," her cousin said, snorting at either end of the sentence. "I'd imagine we'll see—Ah."

In the moonlight, Kallandras the stranger had pulled back the flaps of her wagon. He stood like the definition of shadow, his face hidden, his hands free of the daggers that Elena had armed herself with.

Weaponless or no, she knew he was the more dangerous of the two.

"Matriarch," he said, and he offered her a Northern bow. "You are well?"

"Well, yes, and half-naked. Do you mind?" She stumbled into the edge of the pull-down table the wagon boasted, cursing. Her mother had never left it down.

"Here," Elena said, handing her the shirt that had become a pile beneath that table. "And here." She paused. "It's freezing, Margret. Are you wind-taken?"

"No. I'm tired of wearing last week's shirt."

Kallandras had not moved.

"Bard," Margret said, as she struggled into the shirt, teeth beginning to chatter as the truth of the night's chill bit a little more deeply. "If you were one of mine, I'd've broken your jaw by now. Can you learn to take a hint?"

"I can," he said. "Do you know what you said, Margret?"

"Said? I was sleeping!"

And then, at his back, she heard a voice that made his sound welcome. "You were sleeping, yes, but in sleep we're at our most defenseless, and the visions we can ignore while waking strike then."

She cursed as she struggled into her shirt and wound the sash over it, but she cursed *quietly*. Elena had already bent, albeit briefly, in two. "Yollana."

"Tell him," Yollana said.

"There's a slight problem with that," Margret replied, catching her unruly hair and knotting it.

"Which is?"

"I don't remember myself."

"You spoke in the old tongue," Elena prompted her softly. "And you sounded—"

"Terrified," Kallandras supplied, when Elena's groping for an appropriate word extended that hair's breadth too long.

"He's right," her cousin said. "Terrified. I didn't recognize your voice at all."

"You thought I was murdering someone in the privacy of my wagon?"

"Wouldn't be the first time you'd come close."

"Ha ha ha." She closed her eyes. Opened them almost immediately. Narrowed them. You could do a lot with eyes. "Matriarch," she said, to the oldest woman in the crowded wagon. "There is no circle here."

"No."

"And if someone listens to what we say?"

"We will be heard."

Margret nodded. She was silent for a long time, but it was obvious that she was thinking; her eyes had closed again. When she opened them, Elena, Kallandras, and Yollana were still waiting, clustered around her, and she had a sense, suddenly, that she had been in this room before, and would be again, with these three. There was a fourth shadow that was indistinct but present. She wondered whose it was.

"I was fighting for my life. I was bound," she added. "but the binding itself did not make me feel entrapped. It was as if—as if the binding were clothing or armor; I couldn't move while I was in it, but the fact that I couldn't move made me feel safe." She shrugged. "Not something I'd try when I was awake. I take no responsibility for any stupid thing I do in my dreams."

"Start," Yollana said unexpectedly.

"Pardon?"

"Start taking that responsibility." The old woman's voice was pinched and grave. Much as her own mother's had been when she was being peculiarly serious.

She *knew* that tone of voice. It was Matriarch business.

Frustration made her bite her lip, and then chew on it. Yollana knew it was Matriarch business, but Margret *hadn't.* Hells, Yollana wasn't even Arkosan.

"And finish," Yollana insisted. "The dream."

Margret counted to three. Calmed down.

"Did I mention that I couldn't see? No? I couldn't see. I

couldn't speak." She slid on her boots in the darkness. Took a deep breath. "Lady, I'm glad this isn't a story circle."

"Don't be. If it were, you wouldn't be in it for much longer."

"Thanks, Cousin.

"Let me start at the beginning." She closed her eyes. Let the edges of sleep return to her, as if it were a vast ocean and she a child, forbidden the water, playing with toes at that water's edge. "I—I can't see. I am lying someplace dark and warm, but the warmth is unnatural; the cold is waiting. But I'm comfortable with the cold, the same way I'd be comfortable with the idea of hunger just after I'd been very well fed. It's—" she hesitated a moment. "It's night."

"Yes," Yollana said softly. "It's night. During the day you would feel the heat at a distance, not the chill."

Margret nodded slowly. "You've had this dream."

"Yes. But I've never woken from it the way you did. You screamed, Margret."

"Because something was trying to let the cold in," she replied. Her eyes snapped open as she stared at the older woman's face. It was said, among the Voyani, that dreams were significant, and as Margret had been daughter to the Matriarch, she had never had cause to doubt it. She wished she could. "Do all Matriarchs have these dreams?"

"Yes," Yollana replied, "And no. This is your first?"

"No—not the first. I've dreamed of this before, but never so strongly."

"Mother's daughter," Yollana said softly. "We do not speak of the dreams among ourselves. It is enough to know that they speak to us in different ways, but they speak the same language."

The wagon was dark. The night, cold.

"I dream of it," the Havallan Matriarch continued softly, "as being wrapped in a great cocoon, one of my own making. It is the labor, not of years, but of centuries, of millennia, and I am content. I have been born. I am waiting, in the warmth of the darkness, for rebirth."

"And it is *not* the time."

"No, Margret. It is not." The old woman bowed her head.

"*That's* what I screamed."

"Yes."

"In the old tongue." She could feel the words, thick and heavy in her mouth.

"Yes."

"Because something was trying to destroy that cocoon. To force me into the world before my time. To kill me."

"Yes."

"What was it? What was I dreaming of, Yollana?

"Arkosa."

She started to speak. Stopped. Her face was as pale as the moon, but shadowed in the poor light. At last she said, "Is that what this is about? Is that why my mother—"

In her voice, he heard the sudden strength of certainty. And fear.

"Yes," Yollana replied starkly. Her voice hid much, much more than Margret's. Oddly enough, her face did not.

The younger woman folded at the knees; the thin, flat bed that was, among the Voyani, a luxury caught her weight with a creak.

"Yollana—"

The older woman lifted a hand; the gesture demanded silence. Margret was a young woman, the youngest—for now—of the four Matriarchs. She obeyed.

But only for a moment. Then she began a mad scramble in the darkness, opening the drawers of a large chest that hunkered against the wall, its line softened by night. Cloth went flying like heavy, formless shadow; some of it fell at Kallandras' feet.

Almost absently he bent to retrieve it, but his gaze in the scant light did not leave Margret's face. He was surprised at the very fine feel of silk against his palms; the Voyani did not often acquire such material for personal use.

But she found what she sought; she stilled suddenly, the flight of clothes ended. "Yollana?"

"Turn, Margret."

She did, again as ordered. In her hands she held the round, fat stub of a candle; wax drippings had changed what must have been cylindrical in shape before fire's touch.

The Havallan Matriarch spoke a sharp word, a soft one, a sharp word, a soft one. Then she lifted her hands, cupping weathered palms in a single motion.

Fire came, caught there in the smallest of sparks. She opened her hands and it leaped, as if for safety, to the candle's wick.

"This will protect us a moment or two, but not more."

"And not," the older woman added quietly, "if anyone with true power is intent upon listening. It is not heart's fire."

"No." Margret set the candle down. "Yollana, not long after

the Festival of the Sun I met a clanswoman. She spoke to me of my mother's fate."

"That would be the Serra Teresa?"

"That would be," Margret said, her expression wry, "the Serra Teresa. But while we spoke, another came to interrupt us. He was—he was *far* too handsome. I never trust that in a man."

"I never knew you *noticed* it in a man," Elena muttered. Margret did not choose to hear her. Or perhaps she couldn't; Kallandras' hearing was second to none.

"He said, 'We have the keys to Arkosa, and we are willing to grant them to its rightful owners.' "

"You did not believe him."

"How could I? You *know* the fate of the Cities." Her voice was stark, stripped of almost everything that made her voice her own. Kallandras turned in the darkness. Elena's profile had suddenly become as stiff, as cold, as the daggers she still carried. Elena, the heir to Arkosa now that Margret was Matriarch, and without daughter. "But she told me. I should have known."

"She?"

"The blue-robed witch."

"Ah. What truth did she offer?"

"She told me that the Lord of Night . . . was here." Margret lifted a hand; encompassed the outer world with a sweeping, a shaking, gesture. "Who else?" she asked, almost whispering. "Who else has the keys?"

"Margret, carefully."

"No. I would see Arkosa destroyed before I would let Him open the door." She turned to face them, her face orange in the candle-light; orange and black but somehow as bright as new silver in sunlight. Faces lit from within, Kallandras thought, were filled with light, and beautiful for it; the light cut. "I didn't know it. I didn't know it until tonight."

Yollana was silent for a time. They might have been kin, these two, the older woman and the younger. Between them, the candle suddenly sputtered. A reminder.

"That," the Havallan Matriarch said, breaking the silence that bound them, "is the choice of the Matriarch; you've made it, without vows, without oaths, without bearing witness to the ancient truths. Arkosan blood is strong in you. Aie, Margret, what you've said. What you've dreamed." She lifted a hand to her forehead. Kallandras had known her long enough to know it was not a coincidence that she covered her eyes. "We cannot afford to wait for the heart to find us; we must find it, and quickly."

"Easier said than done. If it were that easy—"

"It *is* that easy, compared with what you will face. I don't know why our ancient enemies chose Arkosa. I don't even know, for fact, that it is the only family chosen. But I *know* that it will be tried first. And if it fails, we fail."

"No."

"Yes, Margret. You will have to trust an older and wiser voice in this. And if you will not trust my voice, trust this: I am the strongest of the seers the Havalla line has had since Michaela the Blind. I *know* it to be true. We are coming, now, to our final test. Fail, and the *Voyanne* means—and meant—*nothing*."

"And if we pass?"

The old woman did not reply.

"Yollana, Matriarch, if you have seen—"

"Matriarch," Kallandras said, lifting a hand and turning his head slightly to the side.

"What?" Her impatience was almost lovely; it brought an odd fire to her eyes, a vibrancy to her voice, that the high clansmen never showed.

"I believe you have visitors."

"Do I want them?"

"I don't believe," he replied, "that you have much choice." Then the door burst open and a large, bearish man with a burning torch filled its small frame.

The fear left Margret's face as the light from the torch graced it. Her shoulders became a stiff line, her lips an even stiffer one. She paused only to snuff the stout candle that stood on the flat, narrow table.

"Stavos," she said.

"Matriarch."

"He did it." Flat, flat voice. The fear was gone; the uncertainty, the dread. Replacing every hint of emotion in her voice: anger. And the pain that caused it.

The old man bowed his head until it was almost level with the impressive line of his shoulders. After a moment it became clear that that gesture was to be his answer.

"Where is he?"

"We have him."

"Here?"

"Outside the wagon."

"Take me to him."

The old man lifted his head just enough to nod. He turned and walked into the night; she followed, covering the distance between his back and the crowded wagon in two lean strides. She stopped just long enough to say a single word.

"Elena."

Her cousin sheathed the daggers in her hands—but they were there now in the fire of her eyes. She became the Matriarch's shadow as they left the wagon together.

Yollana watched her go. "I pity her," she said to the Northern bard. "For this night's work."

"For a dream, Yollana? You have had darker."

"I have had darker dreams than even her dream of the desert," the Havallan Matriarch replied, staring at the door that the passage of two women had left ajar, "but there is no dream as harsh as what she faces now."

"And that?"

Yollana turned back to him. "If we do not have family, if we cannot trust family, we are nothing. You cannot understand this."

He smiled. And he smiled without allowing the bitterness that took him by surprise to show.

His face was bloody. Nose bent at an odd angle—and bleeding—left eye beginning to swell in a way that would end with black and purple before it faded. His hair was sticky; she saw that as she approached him. He would have bent his head—he struggled to do so, to avoid her glare—but the man at his back held him up by the hair.

Two men held his arms.

"Matriarch," Stavos said.

She did not listen. Instead, she approached Nicu. Her cousin. Her favorite cousin.

Her hand moved before she could stop it; she struck him hard enough that he would have flown back a full body's length had he not been held by either arm.

"How *dare* you?"

Silence.

No one spoke. No one spoke to stop her, and she knew that no one would. Not even Carmello, Nicu's best friend. But her aunt, Donatella, appeared in night's shadow, carrying a torch she held slightly higher than anyone else's.

Light ran in trails down the older woman's face, flowing from her eyes over the sun-worn lines of her cheeks. She looked ancient, at that moment, and so weathered by wind and sun that she shouldn't have had any water left to cry with. Had she spoken at all, had she given voice to the mute plea her presence made, Margret's anger would have known no bounds; it was sharp with new pain, and new pain was a wild and restless creature.

But she didn't speak. She understood that what Margret did, this night, was not only her right but her duty. A weak Matriarch meant a weak clan.

And Margret now knew that at no time in Voyani history—save at the very foot of the *Voyanne* itself—could a weak Matriarch be less afforded.

"I forbade you the sword, Nicu. I let you keep your own counsel—against my better judgment—about its origin, but I *ordered* you to stay away from it."

He lifted his face, and beneath the damage done to it, she could see the willful, and wild, and the petulantly handsome youth that had urged her on in most of her childhood escapades. She wanted to turn away.

"And you've become so good at following orders, you expect the rest of us to fall in line?" he said under his breath.

This time, Stavos struck him before she could.

It was probably a good thing. Her hands were frozen at her sides. He was right, of course; Margret, Nicu, and Elena had spent a lifetime thinking of ways to thwart her mother and survive. When he lifted his head again—or more accurately, when it was lifted for him—new blood ran down the length of his face. He wore undyed cloth, a shirt his mother had made; its laces, undone, were sticky with blood and made a string painting across the canvas of his clothing.

"None of the games we played caused deaths." She knew better than to speak. She didn't have to justify herself to Nicu; in fact, it was entirely the wrong thing to do. She knew it would be costly. But she had never just walked away from an argument with Nicu before, no matter how stupid. No matter who had started it.

"And mine have? It's just a sword, Cousin."

"You will *be silent* until the Matriarch gives you permission to speak. She is not to be questioned here—*you* are."

Oh, Stavos, she thought, as she saw the stone that had, just this afternoon, been his warm and expressive face.

"Is it?" She spoke as if Stavos had not, her eyes narrowing. Her arms were across her chest before she realized she'd crossed them. "Where did you get the sword, Nicu?"

He was silent.

"Nicu, you know how this will play out. In the end, if I want the answers, I'll get them. Save me the time."

He said nothing.

"Nicu, am *I* your enemy?"

At that, his eyes met hers; they were dark, and although at least one would be purpled with bruise for weeks by the look of it, they were still his eyes. It cut her.

"Nicu, answer me. Am I your enemy?"

His gaze dropped. But she saw that the question burned him. She wasn't surprised when he answered it.

"No."

"Then why all of this?"

He glanced to either side.

"Nicu, I gave these men direct orders. I gave you the same." She unlocked her folded arms and forced them to her sides, hooking her thumbs into the perfectly tied folds of her sash. Elena's gift. "Tell me. I let it go, tonight. I shouldn't have. I see that now. Tell me about the sword."

"It was—it was a gift."

"From whom?"

He hung his head again. When he didn't lift it after the passage of a half inch of candle, she nodded at Stavos; grabbing a handful of hair, he lifted Nicu's head for him.

"Nicu, *from whom?*"

She saw the shame in his face, although it was hard to separate it from the anger. His gaze slid off her, past her, to her left.

To, she knew, Elena.

Pity stabbed her more strongly than anger.

"From someone who knows our history and cares about us more than—" He fell silent. Chose silence. It was the first smart thing he'd done all evening. "He offered me the sword. He said it would make me—make *us*—strong."

"And you took it."

"Yes."

"And what did you give him in return?"

"Nothing."

She felt it, then. He was telling the truth, yes, but it was the type of truth you told when you were lying. He knew what she

wanted him to answer; he chose how to best use the words to
thwart her. He wasn't stupid enough to lie to a Matriarch. At least
he had that.

"So you accepted a sword from a stranger."

"Yes."

"A sword that didn't see you into adulthood, a sword that hadn't
been offered your blood, and your family's name."

He flinched. "Yes."

"You used a boy's sword."

That stung; she could see new red in his cheeks, and he pulled
at the men who held his arms, breaking his slump.

"I used a boy's sword? Maybe, Margret, I *finally* used a *man's*
sword. Maybe that's what this is all about. I used a *man's* sword.
I fought like a man."

"Like a clansman," she countered, cold as desert night. "Is that
what you want? The life of a clansman? Sorry, I can't offer you
that. I can offer you the death, though.

"Who was the stranger, Nicu?"

"I don't know."

"Who?"

"Damn it, Margret, if you're going to have me killed, kill me,
but I'm telling you the truth. *I don't know.*"

She cursed; she had wished for the Arkosan heart, but never so
strongly as now. She hadn't her mother's gift or her mother's
talent; she hadn't Yollana's famed sight. All she had was herself,
her instinct, her experience. Wasn't what she wanted for a situation like this.

It would have to do. She was certain he spoke the truth. "What
did he offer you, Nicu?"

"Nothing."

And that, that was not.

"Did you trust him?"

"I didn't think about it."

Truth.

"The sword is off-limits. I won't have my men—any of my
men—use a sword that confuses which of the two, sword or
man, is the wielder, and which the weapon.

"But I told you that. You didn't listen.

Now, the only drawn breath in the clearing was her own, and
she wouldn't have bothered if she hadn't needed the air to speak
with. The night was cold, the stars clearer than they had been in

years, or so it felt. Her hands were numb and shaking, they'd been balled into fists for so long.

Stavos was watching her. Stavos, uncle, adviser, trusted ally. She saw his face, saw how hard the lines of it were, saw how dark the eyes. She was no expert. She didn't understand people all that well—Hells, she'd grown up with Nicu and spent more than half her life in his company, and she couldn't understand him at all.

But she *knew* what Stavos expected of her. She *knew,* then, what the only thing she could do was. It was a test.

And it was an *easy* test. No trick questions. No stupid games. This was as black and white as it came. She had given Nicu an order, a direct order. A serious one. He had disobeyed it.

He had disobeyed it, risking them all. He had chosen the Lord's ways over the Lady's at a time when the children—their future, their only true future—had not yet made their way out of the Tor Leonne.

What other choice could there be?

"Take him," she said, more to the two men who held Nicu than to Stavos himself. "Leave him in the wagon circle. Wait until after the Lord's height tomorrow." She looked at Nicu, and then away, her gaze like a glancing blow. Hard, that. Harder, though, to look at Donatella. Donatella, whose gaze, tear-marred and wide-eyed though it was, was measure for measure the same as Stavos'.

She could not turn to look at Elena; all she heard was Elena's drawn breath. Long, slow, steady—a sign that she was controlling either her tongue or her temper. Rare enough it might have been worth seeing—on any other night.

A test. Yes. A test of the new Matriarch.

What do you do when your kin won't follow your orders?

Yollana's answer hung in the air between Margret and the cousin she had grown up fighting with. But she was Evallen's daughter; not even at four years old would she have been stupid enough to ask for another Matriarch's help with her family.

She knew what must be done. Knew what her mother would have done, although she wondered bitterly if her mother's orders would ever have been treated so casually.

So stupidly.

She drew a breath as deep, as slow, as Elena's had sounded. And she faced her cousin's bruised face. It wasn't the first time it had looked like this. She couldn't actually remember the first time he'd gotten into a fight; the first time bruises and swelling had taken the edge off his wild, pretty face.

But she remembered fighting him for a place on Uncle Stavos' knee. Remembered fighting him for a doll that had been his mother's birth gift to her. Remembered how fearless he'd been—how stupid—when he'd saved her life from clansmen raiding what they thought was a small Arkosan caravan. They'd taken heads that day.

Nicu had been fourteen.

He'd also been incensed that he wasn't allowed to keep the head he'd taken.

"Margret—" Nicu began.

"Shut up. Just shut up." To her uncle she said, "Bring the whips tomorrow. I'll flog him myself." She turned away.

Because this had been a test, yes, and she knew she had just failed it.

But she couldn't kill Nicu.

CHAPTER EIGHTEEN

427 AA
Stone Deepings

"Na'jay," a voice said. Her grandmother's voice. She opened her eyes, or tried to; everything was dark. "Na'jay," the voice said again. The first of the familiar things returned to her: the smell of her grandmother's hair when it hung, long and pale, the soap not quite gone with the jugs of water she'd helped to heat and pour. The second followed quickly: the feel of the rounded swell of legs widened with age beneath her cheek. Her Oma's lap. She opened her eyes.

"I can't see."

"I know, dear," that comforting voice said. "I thought it best. It will pass."

"Duster?"

"She's gone."

"She's not."

"Yes, she is. You have far too much power and far too little knowledge to be traveling this path. Lucky you aren't travelling it alone."

"Avandar—"

"I wasn't talking about *him*. He was right to be afraid to bring you here. Do you know where you are, Jewel?"

"The Stone Deepings."

"Yes. But do you know what the Deepings are?"

Darkness. Beneath her hands, the chill of hard rock, broken into jagged rubble. Beneath that, smoothed by time or water, the path.

"Would she?"

"Would she what, Jewel?"

"Would she kill me?"

"It's not for me to answer. I never knew her." The old woman heaved the sort of sigh that could be heard across a crowded dining hall. "You didn't kill her, you know."

"I sent her—"

"You sent her because she was the only person you thought could succeed. *She* failed *you*." Jewel's face scraped stone as it was unceremoniously dumped off the old woman's lap. "Get up. Start *seeing*. You've got a long way to walk in this darkness, and you'd better get good at it. I can only take you so far."

Jewel stood in the slow awkward way a person does who's afraid of what she might stumble into while denied sight. "Where's Avandar?"

"Him? Oh, he's frantic. He's shaking you by your shoulders until your teeth chatter, and you're about to wake up."

"I'm sleeping."

"You're dreaming the dreams of Stone Deepings," the old woman said, and her voice was suddenly cool. "You are the key; find the lock before the path kills you."

She was glad she didn't have a mirror. It was one of the vanities that she'd refused herself over time, that leaning toward femininity that seemed either above or beneath her, depending on the time of day, the phase of moon.

"Next time," she said, through teeth that felt as if they'd been chipped, her jaw was so sore, "wait."

"Jewel, I've walked this path. Waiting is tantamount to—"

"Is that my hair? Is that my hair I smell?"

"I . . . attempted to get your attention by slightly more drastic measures than I generally use."

"You *burned* my hair?" She got up. Her knees hurt; dampness had settled beneath skin and muscle into the heart of bone. "Oma?"

"She is . . . gone."

Gone. Just like that. Jewel felt an old twinge: failure. Consequence. Fear. She put it aside. "How long have I been lying here?"

"Long enough." He pronounced each syllable with painful exactness.

"Can't be that long. I'm not hungry."

He offered no reply. Certainly not the reply Carver or Angel would have: exaggerated shock. She was always hungry.

The stars were now an aurora of light, shifting in place in a curtain of pale silver. *They aren't real,* she told herself, but she stopped as if spellbound by their beauty. She probably was.

"Jewel." She shied away from his outstretched hand; he dropped it at once. Old habits, his and hers. "Do you now understand the nature of this path?"

"No. You're telling me you do?"

He didn't answer. Answer enough. Her eyes narrowed until they seemed closed; until the only thing she could see was Avandar.

"Tell me."

His gaze was remote and cool. "I am your domicis, Jewel Markess ATerafin. I owe you nothing more personal than that."

"It isn't what you owe her, Viandaran, but what you will *give* her, that fascinates the objective observer." Jewel had often heard voices described as velvet before; she had never actually credited the description as anything but lazy poetry. She apologized now to those of bardic bent; the words had a richness and a depth, a soft smoothness of cadence and tone, that made a listener want them to be physical.

Orange light flared like the most beautiful of magework, framing Avandar as if he were a gem and it the setting that would bring out his true worth. Burning and incandescent, he stood in its ethereal heart, fire's gift. Fire.

"Hello, Calliastra." His voice was like ice.

For no reason she could think of, Jewel was afraid. Of the stranger with a voice like one of those exotic drugs that were forbidden for good reason. Of Avandar. Of what she could see in the fires that he wore like the raiment of kings.

That's because you're not a fool; no one of my blood could be a fool. Oma's voice.

Jewel hated to be afraid.

"And the objective observer is?"

"Jewel, stay *exactly* where you are."

She started to think of something clever to say and lost the words as the objective observer in question stepped into full view. Avandar had been cloaked in fire, the element of the magical protections he chose to summon. But the woman who spoke in a voice that weaker women would have spent fortunes to keep listening to was cloaked in something entirely different. Shadow and darkness, the absence of light.

She had seen something very like it in Kiriel. Very and nothing.

Jewel swallowed. Or half-swallowed; the walls of her throat had dried out entirely and clung together, which had the side effect of making her breath thin and short.

Avandar, damn him, turned slightly and raised a brow; she thought he was amused. If she'd been certain, she'd've hit him. Just as well.

"The objective observer," the woman said softly, "is Calliastra. And you, child?"

"No, I'm sorry," Jewel managed to say, "but child is ten years ago." Her voice sounded thin and shaky to her ears; she cringed when she thought of what it must sound in comparison to the stranger's.

"You are in the Deepings. Time does not have the same meaning here." She had dimples in the pale white of perfect skin. "My dear, you are ... worried. And in such capable hands; how unusual." Gods, Jewel could *see* the rot beneath the surface of her perfect face, her perfect teeth, her perfect skin; she could see the cruelty and the ice, the heavy weight of earth over the dead. But *seeing* it, seeing made no difference. She could not look away.

The woman laughed, and the sound was—was so heartbreaking in its beauty Jewel raised her hands to her ears without thinking.

Not without thought, Na'jay.

Yes, Oma.

The laughter tightened, becoming stronger and deeper in a way that denied beauty while encompassing it.

"The objective observer," the woman said, "is Calliastra. Come, Jewel Markess. I don't believe we've met, and I miss human company."

He caught her wrist, his hand plain and rough in comparison to Calliastra's, nails short and blunt, fingers just too ordinary. She pulled away. Or tried to.

"I'm afraid," he said, tightening his grip, "that I must advise you against what would be so brief an acquaintance."

She pulled. Pulled hard.

Na'jay, her Oma said, and she heard the voice, understood the warning in it, and still couldn't stop herself. For the first time in her life she not only understood the progression of compulsion, addiction, death, she felt herself pulled into the rush and current of its passing stream.

She didn't like the understanding; in fact, she was barely aware of it: she had to move forward, and Avandar Gallais stood in her way.

Jewel, no.

Avandar's brows rose fractionally. The subtle transformation of his face was instant: She had surprised him. But she'd surprised herself, too. She recognized the knife in her hands. The last time she'd seen it, it was in the process of being buried in her chest by the ghost of a girl she'd once—

Loved.

Long blade. Thin and wavy. Duster had liked to think of its form as a Southern conceit, and although Jewel knew that Southerners carried more practical daggers, she'd never seen fit to correct her friend. They'd built a life on the things they shared: Southern blood, a life in the tougher streets of Veralaan's grand city.

But they were separated by other experiences. A father. Family. The ability to control both temper and desire.

Duster's dagger.

"Jewel," the woman said, and she turned, and she saw in the eyes what she'd seen in Kiriel: Duster, some part of Duster come back to her, death notwithstanding. Those eyes, those perfect, black eyes, narrowed slightly. "Impossible," she said softly, drawing back a moment, losing the velvet that clothed the steel without once losing the appeal.

"No," Jewel said faintly, "I know who you are."

She laughed, the laughter thawing the chill of her expression. "And who is that, exactly?"

"Allasakar's kin."

The silence was slow and smooth; the surprise on the woman's face replaced by a gradual pleasure. Jewel felt her cheeks warm with the approval, and hated it. "Viandaran," she said, "I should have known you wouldn't bring a mortal of little note or worth when you traveled *this* path." She sauntered—there was no other word for the casual, hypnotic way she walked toward them—as if she owned the path, and the Deepings, as if she had waited for this opportunity and no other.

Nonsense. You've a head, girl. Use it.

Yes, Oma. For the first time in living memory, Jewel wondered if her life would, in fact, have been any better had her grandmother survived.

Put the dagger away.

Jewel stared at the knife, and beyond it, at the man she had almost threatened with its use. He was expressionless; bad sign. It meant he was preparing for a fight.

"I'm sorry," he said, as she hesitated just that little bit too long.

She wanted to tell him the hesitation was because she had no idea *how* to put the damn knife away, but she was Jewel; she didn't lie easily, and that was only enough of the truth to be plausible to anyone who hadn't laid eyes on the woman who called herself Calliastra.

And because the truth was complicated, and because she barely understood it herself, she didn't get her words out before he spoke his. She forgot about trying.

Fire answered his call in a way that breathing answered hers; naturally, inevitably. Red ringed by blue, it circled her arm, singeing skin so quickly the mark left was white.

Jewel screamed.

The fire had come not from Avandar, but from her: from the mark she bore. She understood what his mark meant then, and she would—in a fury that was inarticulate because words were too simple to express them—make it clear later.

Now?

The dagger fell from her hands as if her hands belonged to him. Her fingers opened, her palm dipped; light struck stone and glittered as the metal rang its odd, skittering chime. She took a step back; another; and a final one; her back came to rest against the chest of the man who was pulling the strings.

If she could have killed him then, she would have.

She'll kill you, her Oma said, voice completely devoid of sympathy. *And you, you fool, you'd walk straight into her arms.*

She said nothing. Calliastra continued to walk toward her, hand outstretched in an offering of something that wasn't quite friendship and wasn't quite sex. Jewel knew both well enough. She tried to look away. She couldn't. She didn't even know what Calliastra was wearing, because she couldn't look away from her face, but the impression of a long, simple dress that circled a long, perfect body and fell straight to the ground stayed with her in the shadows.

Avandar's arms closed around her, crossing at the wrists just above the hollow of her neck. She had always known he was larger, but she felt dwarfed by him, shunted back into an age she had never particularly liked—not quite woman, definitely not child. She opened her mouth to bite him, and her teeth snapped shut.

There was worse. Far worse.

He said, *I'm sorry, Jewel. Believe that I* am *sorry.*

But she didn't hear it with her ears; she heard it in the same way that she heard her dead grandmother's voice.

As if it were a part of her, as if it resided where both guilty and treasured memories did. She had *never* shared anything that personal with Avandar before. She would not have chosen to now.

Calliastra approached them, Jewel now as silent and still as stone, and just as warm. She reached out with a hand that was not a child's hand, and not a young girl's for all that it was smooth and unblemished. It was a woman's hand, in much the same way that The Terafin's hands, placed palm down on the tables in her vast library, were. Power in them.

"Calliastra."

"Viandaran, do you think to threaten me?" She didn't even sound angry.

"No, Lady."

"Good. I have a fondness for you that would not prevent me from behaving in a manner appropriate to your station."

He said nothing; she drew closer. "Jewel," she said thoughtfully, "what a perfect name. I imagine that children ridiculed you when they first heard it."

"Not more than once," Jewel murmured.

She laughed. "You are wasted on this one. What did you call him? Avandar? Come."

"She cannot," Avandar said.

"Truly?"

Magic was thick as fog in the valleys her grandmother had once called home. Thicker, and colder as well. Magic had a color in Jewel's particular vision; watching it take shape and form—as halo, as glowing orb, as flickering ethereal flame—told her much about the nature of the spell, and the nature of the caster.

There was literally too much information in what she saw now; she froze, trapped by vision, by color, by a sense of textures that moved so astoundingly fast she only barely held on to their essence at all, piling one impression upon another until all she understood was the power that lay behind the structure of the magic itself.

Avandar's arms tightened. His knuckles came up as he pulled her closer; his hands, hard now and fistlike, rested so tightly against the base of her throat she felt hostage to his desire. Whatever that desire was.

"She is already claimed," he said.

Jewel opened her mouth: silence followed the movement of lips and air. She could not speak. And she *knew* he had forbidden it. Her body resonated with a command so deep it didn't need words.

The subtle sensuality of this woman's expression shifted on an edge; the danger came out to play. "Then release her."

"No."

"You are being tiresome, Viandaran, and I have spent long enough in the godforsaken Deepings, that any company, no matter how pathetic or weak, should have novelty value enough that I am not bored by it." She stepped forward. He made no move to avoid the hands that she laid against Jewel's exposed cheek.

Jewel *screamed.*

The contact was done in an instant; surprised, the woman pulled back.

"Apologies, child," she said, tilting her chin down to examine the lines of Jewel's face. "The pain . . . was illusory, and it was not of my making."

Jewel struggled to breathe. The air came in quantities that didn't quite reach the bottom of her lungs; she fought with it, and with the tears that marred her vision, that rippled the perfect face of pain.

"She is not for you," Avandar said.

"Why? She is not the first you have brought upon this path."

He said nothing.

Jewel thought she couldn't feel worse, but she did; some ground had fallen out from beneath her feet when Avandar Gallais had used his magic to take complete control of her body. What very little sense of stability had been left was completely destroyed by the words she *knew* would follow.

"It's been such a long time since you've tired of a wife or a child—I thought you had given up on them altogether."

He said nothing at all.

"You do know what I do, don't you, child?"

Jewel said nothing, not in mimicry of Avandar but because she had no choice. She would have sworn in the name of seven different gods had she just had her voice.

"I am the daughter of, as you guessed, Allaskar." Her smile was gentle and soft. "You are talent-born; that much is clear. But it surprises me that you see the darkness and think of the god; he has had very little presence in the world of man, and the memory of men is notoriously short."

"She means," Avandar said quietly, "that she is forgotten."

"Yes, I am. But I will not remain so. The paths are crumbling, their edges fraying to reality. I hear the horns and the Hunt, and they are being called this Winter, with a power that I have not heard since the fall of Moorelas.

She lifted her perfect, her beautiful, face, and glanced to the North—to what, in the darkened night of the Deepings, should have been North—and said, "I am my father's daughter, and my mother's. Her hand is not so easily seen, is it?"

"Gods died," Avandar said conversationally.

For the first time, Calliastra was angered. "Viandaran," she said, speaking to Jewel although the words were clearly meant for the man who held her, "has the distinction of being the only mortal lover I have ever taken who has lived to speak of the experience."

"And I did not."

"His survival was a . . . surprise to me," she said quietly. "And I am so unused to surprises. Imagine it, the daughter of Allasakar and the daughter of Laursana."

Jewel knew the name; she'd heard it often enough in the halls of the Terafin Manse, in the breathy whispers of young women, young girls, in the mournful prayers of awkward young men. At that age, Jewel had prayed to *Kalliaris,* and trusted to herself. But she'd had that practical bent about her: food was more important than love. Clothing was more important than love. She'd had both, and while lack of love had made her *want* to die, lack of food had almost killed her.

She understood why people prayed to Laursana, but she'd learned the hard way that loss wasn't really worth the momentary happiness. It wasn't being alone she was afraid of. It was what would happen to leave her that way. Better not to take that risk. Always.

All this passed as she stared at the woman's enormous eyes, at her perfect skin, at the expression—one of complete attention—that she turned upon Jewel. Somehow it managed to sink in.

"You're the daughter of *two* gods."

"Yes."

It was vaguely disgusting, like finding out that your parents did more than just sleep in their bed. She almost couldn't conceive of the union between two gods. Then again, she couldn't really conceive of the union between a god and a normal person, and she was living under the reign of two of them.

"Viandaran was the only one of my many lovers to survive the night."

Avandar still said nothing. Jewel had often found his silence frustrating; it was a wall that, short of losing her temper and doing something childish and intemperate—like, say, throwing a pot or a large tureen—she couldn't breach, and in his foulest mood, he retreated there, beyond reach.

He was not in a foul mood now, but she had no way of reaching him.

Not true.

All right, she amended, her grandmother's sharp words forcing a different truth from her, she had no way of reaching him that she was willing to attempt. Not here. Not in this place. Not when she couldn't even move—and best not to think about that. Truly.

Don't judge her, a different voice said. Avandar's. *She is the victim of her nature: her mother seeks and grants love and her father seeks and grants death, of a type. She can no more change what she is than either of her parents can: they are eternal. We are mortal.* She stiffened.

Get out, she told him, or hoped she did, the words as distinct as she could think them. *Get the Hells out.*

Silence.

"He brought them to me," Calliastra said softly. "When he stopped loving them, he let me love them a while."

There was malice and madness in the words, and beneath both a terrible hunger, not only emptiness—vast and perfect and completely natural—but a fear of emptiness, a desire to fill it. Imagine it, the goddess had said—for what else did you call the child of two gods?

Avandar's unwelcome answer hit her like a crossbow bolt: *The Firstborn.* yes. That was what they'd been called. Imagine being born to darkness and born to love. Imagine that love always ended, and always in death, before any of its promise had been fulfilled. Better a god of lust as a parent than one of love. Better, she thought suddenly, *any* other god.

Jewel was speechless with something that was akin to pity but larger. And pity? Gods, why pity? This woman was a monster, she could see that, nature or no. *We are all so much slower to judge,* she thought, *when beauty is involved.*

15th of Scaral, 427 AA
Tor Leonne

Sendari stared at the bent head of his wife as sunlight dappled her hair, lending it silk's sheen. That hair trailed down her shoulders, pooling like liquid against the surface of outdoor mats. She had chosen, this morn, to wear white, white and gold with a touch of a lovely turquoise that removed the colors from the Lord's Dominion. He should have been suspicious, then. The Lord knew that he had suffered all his adult life from the intervention of women he could not trust.

Wearing a sari that had been his gift when he had been granted a clan's name, she had seemed particularly lovely. She still did; the supplicant posture was absolutely correct.

But Sendari was a man who could appreciate loveliness without being moved by it at all.

The rocks in the garden, the small stunted trees, the flowers whose tints were delicate, rather than gaudily brilliant, moved him more at this moment than the Serra Fiona.

He had never been so close to killing a wife. He might stand on the other edge of that act but for two things: First, he had learned, over time, not to act in anger. Second, and more relevant, he had promised himself—in a youth that was so distant from him there were times when he could not believe it was his own—that he would never make killing an act of passion. The seeking of knowledge, yes. Love, yes. Not death.

"How *dare* you?"

She spoke to the mats when she finally spoke.

"I am sorry, my husband. I am truly sorry. I did not realize that the Serra Teresa was not welcome in your harem."

"How dare you invite her—from Mancorvo no less—without my *explicit* permission?"

"I have no excuse, my husband. I am sorry. I judged poorly."

"And she is to arrive when?"

"This evening, if the roads permit; tomorrow, otherwise. She sent word."

"Not to me."

He watched as her pretty, feminine fingers curled slightly

around the handle of her closed fan. She had taken to ground so
quickly she had not divested herself of her adornments.

"I am sorry, my husband. Forgive me. Forgive me. But the
Festival draws near, and it is my duty—because the Tyr'agar
has no wife and he has chosen to grace your house with the
responsibility—"

"I-am-aware-of-my-responsibilities."

"Yes, my husband. Forgive me. I—I—there is so much to do
for the Festival of the Moon; so much has changed in the Tor.
The Tyr'agar has cut down the trees and widened the paths; he
has changed the pavilions and the platforms by the Lake. What
was designed for perfect beauty and privacy has become . . .
more open.

"I am not worthy," she continued. "I have tried to prepare the
Tor, but my skills—" She swallowed. He heard it, rather than
saw it.

Eyes narrowing, he said, "Fiona, you may rise."

Nothing in his voice offered comfort; he knew it when he saw
her lovely face. He wanted to see her speak.

Tears had darkened the corners of her eyes where kohl gathered in the creases sun had worn there, year after year finding
some minute purchase that spoke of time's passage.

"Continue," he said softly. "And Fiona? Do not attempt to lie
to me."

"No, my husband."

"Good. The Serra Teresa."

"When I arranged the Festival of the Sun, she arranged the final
details, but it was in the details that the Festival was made. It was
Serra Teresa's coordination, Serra Teresa's expertise, and Serra
Teresa's knowledge that graced these grounds so memorably.

"I wished to have the Festival of the Moon to myself. I wished
the world to know that it was Serra Fiona *en'Sendari,* the chosen
wife of the Tyr'agar's first counselor, who arranged for the displays and the ceremonies of Moon night.

"But so much has changed in the Tor I—I do not feel I am up
to the task. And if there is a failure, it will be attributed to your
house. This is your *first* year. I did not—I could not—take that
risk. I tried to tell you," she added, "but you have been so busy
with the Sword's Edge and the Tyr'agar you have frequently forbidden interruption by any of your wives." She bowed her head,
although she did not flatten herself to the ground again. "I am
sorry, my husband.

"The Serra Teresa has never granted me my due, but I must grant her hers: There is no one in the Dominion who could do as well by the Tyr'agar as the Serra Teresa di'Marano.

"I should have mentioned it. I should have said something at once. But we have had so little time together—"

"Enough."

Watching the tears—and they were few and delicate—trail the length of her face did not, in fact, lessen the desire to kill her. But it changed the nature of the desire into one he had lived with, on and off, since the birth of their son, and the nature of *that* desire was more weariness than passion.

He had thought that marrying a stupid woman would save him from the fate of his first marriage. And to all eyes, Serra Fiona was the finer choice: Younger, more beautiful, exquisitely graceful in all things and—more important—able to bear him a son.

Alora had always regretted that. When she regretted nothing else, that one lack shamed her. Had he desired a son? No. He had loved Alora's child as he had never, and would never, love another child. Mother and daughter.

Everything came back to them.

Ah, the Festival of the Moon was coming. He could feel the Lady's fingers in the shallows of morning; her grip was tight and cold; as merciless as he felt himself to be. No; more so.

"I am not pleased, Serra Fiona," he said coolly. "But in this case, I cannot argue with your motivation. I will . . . greet the Serra Teresa when she arrives, and I will give her permission to remain within my harem.

"But in matters of such import you are, in the future, to consult *me*. To make certain that you remember this fact, you may remain here, and in that position, until the Serra Teresa does arrive."

She looked, of all things, grateful. Relieved.

Perhaps, he thought, as he turned from her, she was not as stupid as he believed.

15th of Scaral, 427 AA
Voyani encampment

They came by day, gathering in a silence that was almost funereal. Grim-faced, clad in their hair-bracelets and the dusty shades that were Voyani mourning, they gathered at the heart of the encampment. No wildness, here; no drinking, no discussion, no little burst of conversation that meant an entertaining argument was about to start. The Voyani tied back their hair, removed all rings but oath rings, hid or removed their necklaces, their bangles, their silks. Thus did they protect themselves from the envy of the newly dead: they made their lives as unattractive as possible.

For three days and three nights they would dress in their poorest clothing, and hide their adornments; they would walk hand in hand only with the youngest of children, and mute all displays of open affection; they would speak openly of their sorrows and their losses.

Because the dead, of course, could see everything that could be more easily concealed from the living, and seeing how they had to live, the wind-taken would leave their lives with less regret, and the wind of their passage would be the breeze and not the sand-laden storm.

There were two exceptions to this unspoken rule, this governing convention: The Matriarch and her cousin.

Margret had chosen to face the wind's envy. She was not, after all, going to kill her cousin, and there was nothing beyond that to mourn.

Oh, to be angered by his betrayal, yes. To be saddened for his mother, yes. But to mourn?

She wore red, a brilliant color that drew all eyes, trapped in the shape of a long-sleeved shirt. She wore a gold-embroidered sash—the sash that had been part of her mother's unofficial uniform. She wore her birth-ring, her adult-ring, the necklaces that had been a gift for every year of life she had managed to survive, each of them flattened gold that varied in length and weight. Some years were better than others.

Nicu wore his birth-ring, his adult-ring, and his normal clothing—although the blood that had dried there would be hard to remove.

He was anchored to the ground by a large collar, but beneath that, beneath that she saw glints of gold. He cast a short shadow; the sun was almost at its height. This was an act of the Lord; such floggings—extremely rare among the Voyani—were always performed as close to the sun's height as possible.

"Matriarch," Uncle Stavos said, stepping forward. "He's secured."

I can see that. But she bit back the sarcasm that was second nature to her—or first nature if you asked Nicu or Elena—and settled for the formality the somber situation demanded. "Thank you."

He bowed. Then he rose and barked a quiet order to another man. Andreas stepped forward and handed her the whip. Her hands shook as she took it.

"Steady," Elena whispered.

She shouldn't have looked, but she did, glancing to the side to meet her cousin's eyes. They were shiny-bright, the dark bird's baubles.

"Elena—"

Elena shook her head. Turned away. It was only then that Margret realized that she was doing everything she could to avoid looking at Nicu's bent back. His bent, unbroken, unscarred back.

She pulled her arm up. Back. The whip came with it.

She sat on her mother's knee; Elena sat beside her. But her mother only had two legs. Nicu sat on the ground at her feet, throwing his long hair out of his eyes. He'd refused to let Aunt Donatella cut it; he wanted, he said, to be like Margret and 'Lena.

The Matriarch had the *best* stories. Everyone said so. And on days like this, with no clansmen, no clan war, no merchants to fleece and no townspeople to scare with hints of a dark future, she was actually willing to sit down and tell one.

Margret got to pick the story. She picked, of course, the one she liked best. *The three brothers.* Because she was young, and not yet the Matriarch's daughter in anything but name, she was indulged by parent and unrelated adult alike. All Voyani children were.

And the particular indulgence she always craved when she was told this story was that the three brothers be called Nicu, Margret, and Elena.

Her mother would begin:

There was a contest in the heart of Raverra, for the Tyr had decided that his daughter would marry not the usual court-born high clansman, but rather a clansmen beloved by the Lord, and he therefore set a challenge that would kill almost all of the challengers, weeding out the strong from the week.

At that time, the Arkosan caravan was passing through the Tor Leonne, for during any Challenge, there are fortunes to be told and money made, and the three brothers—who, the Matriarch said gravely, and this was Margret's favorite part—went *everywhere*

together, were in the Tor Leonne when this contest was
announced, and they saw not only the Tyr but a rare, rare glimpse
of the daughter he wished to marry off.

That single glimpse was enough.

"Look at her! Have you ever seen a woman so beautiful or so
perfect?"

"She is a clanswoman," the oldest brother said. "And she is not
for us. She could not walk the *Voyanne*. There are women within
Arkosa who are as beautiful, and as accomplished in their own
fashion. Look elsewhere, Brother."

Nicu was the name of the handsome brother who approached
the Tyr to win the hand of his beautiful daughter. He was in love,
and sick with it, and if he did not win the hand of the beautiful
Serra, he would perish. His two brothers, Elena and Margret, had
forced him to eat what they could, but they knew the Lady's grip
on their brother's heart was hard, and cold, and permanent.

The whip fell.

Elena was the name of the smart brother, Margret the mysterious wise one. Years later, Margret would understand why her
mother smiled that odd, lovely smile whenever she told them the
names of the three brothers, but at that time it had all made sense.

Margret and Elena loved their brother more truly than most of
the Voyani love their kin, and they saw, clearly, that the Tyr was
not pleased with Nicu's suit.

"He will try to kill our brother," Elena said to Margret.

"Yes. But Nicu loves his beautiful, cold daughter, and if he
does not have her, he will die. Therefore, we must do what we
can to help him win his goal."

Elena told him what he must do: Who he must watch, and who
he must never turn his back upon.

"You must be careful," he said, "of the daughter. She has your
heart, but you do not have hers. You are Voyani, and not the
clansman she has come to expect, and you will never have the
finery she desires."

"But she is so delicate and so perfect!" Nicu replied, seeing
nothing. "And in time I will win her heart, not just her hand. Tell
me what I must do."

"Do not partake of any food the Tyr offers you," Elena replied.
"And although you wish to please her, do not partake of any that
the daughter offers you either."

* * *

She drew her arm back again, her face dry as stone and just as expressive.

Margret, the oldest, was silent.

But he loved his brother and wished to see him happy. "Here," he said quietly. "Take this sword."

"But it is your sword, Brother."

"Yes. And it is special; it has both a gift and a curse. Wield it, and you will never be defeated in battle."

"But you never use this blade!" her brother Nicu said, lifting it, marveling at its perfect edge, its perfect crescent curve. He had never looked at the sword so closely before, for his brother so seldom fought.

"There are some battles," Margret said—and she had never understood this part as a child—"that are best not won." He was, her mother told them, very, very wise.

It made sense to none of the three who listened, but it was Margret's favorite story anyway.

The whip fell.

Nicu grunted, and his back, his unbroken skin, was red with welt and blood that had come to the surface in the wake of leather's passing.

It came to pass, her mother would say, the moon in her words and the sun in the warmth of her lap, that Nicu took the sword, and entered the Challenge, and won every battle set for him by the Tyr, no matter how difficult.

The Tyr was a proud and powerful man, and he saw that the young Voyani was going to win the Challenge unless the rules of the Challenge were changed. And although he had desired a man beloved of the Lord, he was still of the clans, and he wished his daughter to be given to no Voyani.

Nor in truth did the daughter wish it, for the three brothers were Voyani, and she would be forced to live their life of hardship on the endless road.

And she said to her father, "You have asked for a man beloved of the Lord, Father, and indeed you have found three. Let us now ask for the second proof: a test of the rider."

And so it came to pass.

* * *

She lifted her arm again. Again. Again. She counted each stroke as it fell and she *forced* herself to watch.

"They will try to trick you, Brother," the middle brother, Elena, said. "And we are not so fine at riding as we are at walking; we value the strength of our own feet, and we stand on them well."

But Nicu would not eat or sleep, and at last Margret came to him. "They will not allow you to bring your own horse," he said softly. "But bring your horse this." And he held out a very strange leaf. "Give it to him and he will obey your every command almost before you have made it, for he will understand your word as if you spoke his language."

"Do not," Elena added, "use a saddle. They will bring you a horse that is ready to mount; tell them it is the way of our people to ride bareback, and remove the saddle over any protest they might make."

He cried out. It was not quite a scream. She had thought, she had prayed, that he would remain silent. Confronted with the failure of prayer, Margret of the Arkosan Voyani hesitated a moment.

But only a moment.

It came to pass that Nicu, with the leaf in hand and the advice of his brothers, rode the horse the Tyr had chosen. The horse was wild and willful, but when it accepted his offering of leaf and was free from saddle and bridle, it carried him like the wind carries sand.

"You see, Daughter," the Tyr said, for he was an indulgent father, "the young man has won both the test of the Sword and the test of the Rider. I have given my word to the whole of the Tor Leonne, and I will not be forsworn. In three days, you will become his wife."

Because she was a very fine Serra, she said, "Yes, Father." And planned.

Elena did not lift a hand; did not raise her voice, did not speak. But Margret felt her cousin's presence one step to the left, and she wondered if Elena the wild felt, at this moment, as sick, as angry, as horrified as Margret the Matriarch.

There were two bitter Voyani things, her mother had said, that every child endured. There were three things that every Matriarch endured.

* * *

The night of the race, victory was celebrated across the length and breadth of the Tor, but nowhere near as loudly as it was in the Arkosan camp.

And it was to the Arkosan camp that the Serra, accompanied by only two of her father's Tyran, came. She wore fine veils and a very fine sari indeed, but her expression marred her beauty.

Nicu heard of her presence at once and came to her, leaving his brothers to the Lady's shadows. But the Lady's shadows are the strongest weapon of the Voyani, and the brothers found places to hide in it, that they might listen to the Serra's fine, fine words, for Margret and Elena were wise men and did not trust the clansmen.

First death.

The family was everything, and when someone betrayed the family, they died for it. Every child knew that, and accepted it as a hard truth.

But what every child did not know is that betrayal comes not from the hated and the scorned—if they exist among kin at all—but rather from the loved and the trusted.

Margret had seen her first death.

She wanted to raise her hands a moment to stop Nicu's trailing scream from reaching her ears. She was almost done. She wasn't certain she would be able to finish. Important, not to lose count.

"Seven," a voice said, words carried by wind to a place that was deeper than hearing. "Six more, Margret. Be strong." Kallandras' voice. A stranger's voice.

She should have felt anger at his interruption. She couldn't. He was the only person in the camp who could offer her any help at all, because his help was invisible and unnoticed by the men and women who would follow her into death, if she demanded it. Not even Elena could interfere, and Elena was the woman that she depended on for almost everything.

The Serra's hair was as dark as the Lady's Night, and it fell about her face like a gleaming ebon mantle; her skin was white as the softest of silks. Her eyes were dark and filled with mystery; she was delicate and she was perfect.

Nicu of the Arkosans, the youngest of the three brothers, stood frozen with desire and fear. She crossed the distance that separated them, and then, lifting her face an inch from his, exposed her lips by pulling the veil back. He bent, his own lips drawn down to hers by the gravity of youth, and she lifted her delicate fingers to his mouth.

"You have faced both of the contests of my father's making, and you have won his permission to marry."

He nodded; her presence had deprived him of not only clever words, but any words.

"But although no daughter's permission is ever needed in a marriage, I will promise you this: I am not chattel, to come and go at the whim of just any man. I have seen you, Nicu of the Arkosa, and I think it is possible that in time you might love me."

"I love you now," he said.

Her eyes widened delicately, deliberately, and she smiled. "Would that that were true."

"It *is* true," he replied, stung.

"You love others far more than you love me."

"There are no others, Serra."

"I would have you prove that to me."

"Prove it?" Nicu said, catching her delicate wrist in his strong hand.

"Yes."

First death.

Every child who survived the clansmen's raids and the family wars that occurred once a generation or two between the Voyani bloodlines learned to wield a sword in the defense of their families and their futures. They trained, usually with Uncle Stavos or men like him, large bears with easy tempers and a penchant for a humorous comment at the expense of a poor student.

And every child who had witnessed death was shocked the first time—the *first* time—they dealt it. Some were savage and wild, some angry, some deliberately cruel. The measure of the man could be taken in the manner of the first death.

Margret's first death had been all business, and after the witnesses had scattered word of it all over the caravan, she had finally been accepted in truth, as she was in fact, as the Matriarch in waiting.

But, Lady, afterward, after the victory celebration, after the eating, the drinking, the song and the dance, she had retired to the woods around the camp and she had been so sick she thought she would never recover.

She could still see the blood of that clansman on her hands, and on his face, where the sword had left the mark that killed him.

"You love your brothers more than anything in the world, and they treat you as a child. They tell you what to do and you do it without thought.

"If they were to tell you to leave me or to disgrace me, you would do it, and I will not live with that shadow, Lady forgive me."

Ah, the younger brother was wild with love of her. Crazy with it. "I love *no one* as much as I love you. I will send them away."

"They will return," she said coolly. She nodded to one of the Tyran, and he handed her a stoppered flask, a very, very fine one. "This is Lady's sleep," she said, as she took the flask into her own delicate hands. "Only grant your brothers her sleep, and I will be your wife and will serve you faithfully no matter where we travel, and on which road. Do not grant them this sleep, and *I* will seek it before I will marry you."

He was ashen, gray as bark that has served the flame fully. But he couldn't bear the thought of her death, so he reached out and took the flask she offered.

And Margret and Elena watched.

First death.
Every child saw both deaths.

Margret of the Arkosan Voyani would face the third. Her mother would hardly speak of it, but she understood why: it was *this.* This killing of kin. The Matriarch was the mother of them all, and she was harsh as Lord's Sun, cold as Lady's Night. Into her hands fell *justice,* and it fell in the shape of a sword, a whip, a noose.

This last of the three deaths was the only one that she had never faced. And it was the only one that she felt, as the whip came up, as the stranger, speaking in a private voice that only her ears and his would ever hear, counted the strokes, that she *could not* face.

The killing of kin.

And the three brothers, who loved each other as kin must love or else be forsworn, sat down at a low table together with wine that Nicu had brought them. Elena did not touch the wine set before him, but Margret—who was wise, after all—did, lifting the goblet swiftly and easily to his lips.

"To your victory, Nicu," he said softly, "no matter what the cost."

Nicu lifted the cup as well.

Lifted it in shaking hands, and then, before Margret could drink, threw the cup across the table. The unexpected blow knocked Margret back, and his own cup flew wide, the contents spilled across both the coarse fabric of his shirt and night's grass.

She could not face this last first death.

"Ten," Kallandras said. She lifted a hand; wiped the sweat from her forehead, her eyes. Looked at the length of the shadow she cast. At anything but the bleeding mess of her foolish cousin's back.

She *knew* she should kill him.

Knew it, hated it, denied it.

And the three brothers embraced.

Nicu went to his wife, and told her the deed had been done, and he claimed her for a single night, for she thought him so simple that it never occurred to her that he might be lying.

And in the morning, when the Arkosans left the Tor Leonne, they left this half-used wife abandoned at the palace gates, where all might see her and know that she was no longer fit as wife to any other man.

"And for that reason," Evallen would say, finishing the story, "the hatred of the Tyrs for the Arkosans has always been strong."

"Eleven."

"We are brothers," Margret would say, or Elena, or Nicu. "We are brothers, and Lady bear witness, nothing will come between us but death."

They would cross hands, right hands, one on top of the other, a jumble of childhood skin and childhood oath.

"Twelve."

Her favorite story, sitting upon her mother's knee. But her mother was dead, and the gift of title now rested upon Margret's aching shoulders.

She lifted the whip for the last stroke. Brought it stinging across his skin. Lifted it again.

Threw it, although she knew it would be seen as the weakness it was, across the length of the open circle where it fell at the feet of an older Voyani woman. Caitla. Stavos' sister.

The expression on that woman's face froze Margret in place. Elena's hand, a sudden weight on her shoulder, provided her the same steadiness. She wanted—Lady, she wanted—to drop to her knees at Nicu's side, to beg his forgiveness and his understanding, to wash the blood off his injured back and bring the salves that would both soothe pain and stave off infection.

And she could do none of these things.

None of these things for her brother.

She would never sit at her mother's knee again. Never choose that story, never hear it spoken aloud. And she would never trust him enough to drink from a goblet he offered her in the Lady's Night, with the object of his desire as the prize for her death, no matter what they had promised so intently, and so honestly, as children.

Margret of the Arkosa Voyani did not weep. The closest she would allow herself to come was to lift her heavy, heavy hand and grasp her cousin's—Elena's—as if nothing else would provide an anchor for the wind's aching howl.

CHAPTER NINETEEN

He thought to have more warning.

Teresa, although she was a mere Serra, was accounted wise by men of higher station than he, and she traveled—at their kai's insistence—in a fashion that suited that unspoken, unspeakable regard.

At Festival season, such fashion dictated a procession that would, in earlier years, have beggared Sendari di'Marano. Cerdan in great numbers—and worse, their horses—preceded and followed the serafs that bore her palanquin and the caravan that followed with her saris, her sandals, and the other strange accoutrements that were a part of a woman's mystery when they weren't examined too closely: scent and color among them.

As so often happened when a woman of import arrived, be she at the side of her husband or no, the streets of the Tor Leonne would become dense with the idle: small children, their elderly watchers, the women and men who were *just* free enough they had been born on the right side of the clan-seraf divide. They would point at the flapping clan colors the standard-bearers were responsible for, and they would speak the name of the occupant so carefully hidden from the damaging glare of the Lord's heat as if it were part of a guessing game.

It was, often enough.

And such a caravan might take an hour to pass through the streets of the Tor Leonne; it might take more, depending upon the graciousness of the occupant who held the highest rank. And by the time that occupant arrived at the gates of the plateau, her name had been carried, by wind and the poor alike, as if the multitude of blended voices were better heralds than their own.

Yes, Sendari expected to have more warning.

But the Lake was silvered by the Lady's Moon, the sky broken by the rich, pale light of Her veil, and he, broken in a different fashion, was utterly alone.

Alone, as all men were alone when they chose to visit the Lady's shrine. Leonne, for all that it was a weak clan—perhaps because of it—had had a better, a deeper, appreciation for the Lady's service than Alesso did, or would. Under Leonne's care, Her shrines, small and hidden as they were by carefully cultivated trees and bushes, by flowers and rock formations, had had an aura of privacy. Each man who made his evening trek to such a place was asking for, and was granted, the isolation of Her audience.

And of his own thoughts.

Under Alesso's care, if care was a word that could be so applied, they had become merely hidden places, little wildernesses of neglect rather than oases of privacy. Yet for all that, sweet water glimmered in offering bowls, reflecting, in their total stillness, the lines of her changing face.

Diora.

He knelt. It was comfortable to kneel; the Lord could not see the gesture of supplication, and he therefore could not judge it. But the Lady's gaze was keener, sharp enough to make a man bleed if he hoped to keep his secrets from her notice.

Sendari had learned, long ago, that the Lord's lack of mercy was simple death; the Lady's, complex and terrible, was much, much less pleasant. He therefore bowed to the greater power when that power was displayed.

And he had heard it.

In Diora's voice.

She had saved his life.

Ah, Lady, Lady, she had saved *his* life. Had spoken with a power that had done what shield and sword could not: it had stopped the blade of the Tyr'agnate of Oerta.

He should not have been at the shrine.

He should have been with Cortano. With Mikalis di'Arretta. With Alesso di'Alesso. The Festival closed upon them like an enemy army, and the masks were as yet unmade, their mysteries unresolved, their danger held at bay by a deception that, privately, Sendari thought unlikely to work.

Somewhere in the Tor, he was certain, the *Kialli* spies gathered in ones and twos, assured of safety by both their own power and the power of the Court that ruled them; if he was not at the side of the men who made masks their study, he should have

been with the Widan who made secrecy theirs. They had been
working, under Cortano's merciless—and tireless—direction,
upon a magic that might, with the Lady's dark blessing, grant them
the vision necessary to detect the demonic beneath the human
visage.

The death of Cortano's Widan in the capture of the Voyani
woman had damaged the research of that fragile magic almost
beyond repair. But it had provided the Sword's Edge with a
burning, a terrible, incentive, and Sendari thought it likely that
Cortano di'Alexes would find the power to reveal the essence of
the *Kialli* before any of them would piece together the puzzle of
the masks.

He should have been at Cortano's side.

But he was here, in this shrine, bent before a bowl of water
drawn from the Lady's Lake, his daughter's name a silent motion of lips.

And when the light of the Lady's face was disturbed as it lay
against the surface of water that men killed and died to claim as
their own, he knew that time had run out.

Because, warning or no, as inevitable as the dawn that must grow
from the heart of the Lady's Night, the Serra Teresa di'Marano
stood by his side, shattering the privacy that the Lady's shrine promised. The promises of the Lady.

He was not bitter. The time for bitterness had passed. Rather,
he was numb.

She dropped to her knees at once; abasing herself before the
water, the moon, and her brother; he turned to acknowledge her
presence only after long minutes had passed in the treachery of
her silence.

And he was shocked into his own by what he saw. Shocked
into the speechlessness that he so often used as his only defense
against the power that had destroyed not only Teresa's life, but
his daughter's as well.

Serra Teresa di'Marano, the Serra whose refinement was
valued by the high clansmen and clanswomen who would form
not only Alesso's court but all courts across the Dominion, was
dressed not in sari and fine, fine jewels, but rather in soft leathers.
Her scent was not jasmine, not wild rose, not moon water, but
rather the dust and sweat of the open road, and her hair, long and
fine and defiant of a thing as inevitable and debilitating as age,
was pulled so tightly back from her face it might have been a
warrior's knot.

But her eyes, her eyes as she sat up and turned her face toward him, were no eyes but hers; nothing diminished them—and nothing warmed them. That had not always been the case, but Sendari was now at a remove from the anger that had driven his relationship with this most difficult of sisters. As it so often did, weariness had seeped in to take its place.

The Festival of the Moon was coming, and it cast long shadows.

"Serra Teresa," he said stiffly.

"Ser Sendari," she replied. She was as cool as desert twilight.

"There is no war between us." He bowed his head. Light glimmered off lake water; the weariness was greater now than at any time he remembered in his life. Not even the test of the Sword of Knowledge, from which he had emerged bleeding and barely victorious, had been so completely exhausting, so numbing.

It had been almost six months since Diora's betrayal.

It had been over six months since she had spoken a word to him that had not been cool and quiet and completely proper.

At least, he thought bitterly, *she grants me that.* She knew he was not a fool.

But the Serra Teresa lifted her head. "No war, Brother?" she said softly. Knife's edge, those words. He did not understand it.

"My . . . wife is long dead," Sendari replied, eyes on the light. "And her daughter—*my* daughter—is beyond me. If I lost the mother to you, the daughter was, I believe, my own doing. It was not my intent." The words were his words; the voice, his voice. He recognized neither, in this moonful night, this darkness of the Lady's making.

"Would you have let her perish with Leonne?"

Silence. Then, "Did she summon you?"

Silence again. But the quality of the Serra Teresa's silences were matched only by the quality of her voice; they were immaculately timed, and they said what she intended them to say.

Yet he saw her lower her head; saw her, in the darkness that pale fire illuminated, lift arm and hand to see the road's work, and not the weaver's. "I have come, this eve, for just one purpose," she said at last, "It is night and I will be . . . honest with you."

"In a fashion."

"In a fashion."

He wondered, not for the first time, what she would have become had she been born a man.

"Diora did not summon me; she has no power with which to do so."

"She bears your gift and your taint."

"Yes."

"And from what I understand, you could speak to her now and she might hear you."

Silence. She broke it with his name. "Sendari," she said. "You've been studying."

"Yes."

"But without the aid of the bards."

"They are not . . . bountiful in the capital at the moment. They were not present for the Festival of the Sun, and it is unlikely we will see them, except perhaps as spies, for the Festival of the Moon. Next year; perhaps the year after. Perhaps never."

He saw the straight lines of her perfect profile. The road could not take that from her. In truth, it could take nothing from her if one knew how to look, and Sendari had seen this woman all his adult life. One cannot judge a blade when it is housed within its scabbard, but if it is the *right* blade, once seen its edge is never forgotten, no matter what scabbard adorns it.

"She cannot summon me across such a great distance."

"She could have asked the wives to—"

"The Serra Fiona summoned me, Sendari, as I believe you must know. There has been no great love between us. She would not lie."

He felt, suddenly, that he did not wish the honesty she had offered, and he rose, letting his lap fall away as his knees lost their bend. Silk, heavy and full, rippled with the Lady's light; the night was unseasonably chill.

"I will aid the Serra Fiona as I am able, on such short notice. I came quickly; I journeyed in haste."

Her words made no sense; he let them sink in, examining them in detail until he understood their essential wrongness. "You did not travel with Adano's permission."

"I could not afford to ask it," she replied, and her eyes were as dark as night. He saw the effort of the journey then, because she let him see it. Immediately wondered why she had chosen to expose that much. They had their strengths and their weaknesses. His eyes fell from hers; there was, about her stare, a strength that he found disturbing.

But not so disturbing as this: her hands were bare. She wore no rings at all.

The emerald had always been Alora's gift, an oath ring, a symbol of—

Love.

And Teresa did not wear it.

The desert night was falling. The Festival of the Moon, like a sweet and a terrible doom, had already opened to envelop them both.

"There is," his sister said, "war between us, Sendari."

He wanted to ask her what that war was, but he was afraid, suddenly, of her answer. "Do not," he said, his voice as heavy with menace as he could force it to be. "Do not enter this fray."

"What choice have you left me?" she countered. "What choice have you left even the least of us?"

"The least of you?" He felt an old anger rising. Interesting. He had thought it dead. "You have offered me honesty, Serra Teresa. Do me the grace of offering less insult with it. You have spent a life hiding behind the facade of powerlessness; it has never been more than facade."

"Not true," she replied. "I have never been able to escape the gift and the curse that my father and my brothers found such a useful weapon at their convenience. And I was powerless to save Alora's life, the one life I would have exposed all to save."

"You did not try."

"I *knew* it would fail. A healer cannot be forced to that healing."

"It was *within* his nature!"

"Does it matter?" Her voice was desert night, his day's height.

It did. It *did*. Because if Teresa no longer loved and honored that memory, no one did. He acknowledged it, beneath the Lady's Moon. In every way that he could be, he was forsworn. The Alora of his youth, the Alora of his early life, would look at him now and see nothing at all to stop her gaze, to hold it, to catch it.

Unless it be the man who would harm her daughter, her only child.

"Are you forsworn, Teresa?"

Her eyes narrowed. "I?"

"You—" He turned away. Anger, he could give her. But this was too complicated to be anger.

She had offered him honesty. "I do not wear the ring in fact, but it has never left me in any way that matters. She was only your wife, Brother," she added. "To me, she was everything."

"I would have given up my life for her."

"But not for her memory. Not for your word to her memory."

"If her memory were not so sullied by you, perhaps I might

have." But as his words left his lips, they had, for the first time, a bitter, bitter taste, a cloying texture, a defensive quality that robbed them, in the end, not only of strength but also of truth. He was lying. And he knew that she would hear that lie even had she not been gifted. Cursed.

"I have come," she said quietly, as he knew, as he suddenly *knew* she would, "for Diora."

He was silent.

The weight of the Lady's hands were upon his brow and around his throat; he could not speak. Had he stood? He no longer clearly remembered when.

She was his sister.

He had hated her in his time. But the ties that bound them, blood ties all, had stayed his hand. He had never willingly exposed any weakness that she might exploit, but he had never feared death at her hand.

Death might have been easier.

He knew her well. "Serra Teresa," he said, striving for formality.

"Ser Sendari," she replied, bowing her head to the ground a moment in perfect grace.

He thought to escape, but the moon's light was as sharp as the Lord's blade. Colder.

"Cortano will kill her."

"This is not the appropriate place for such a discussion. And you, a Serra, are not the appropriate person with whom to have it."

"He will kill her," Teresa continued softly.

"Teresa, you go too far."

"No. No, I have never gone far enough, and perhaps that is why we are here, we two, at this shrine, in this wilderness. We have hidden much, Sendari."

"I have never successfully hidden anything important from you." Bitterness. Truth sometimes held little else.

"But you have, Brother. You were—you *are*—the seeker of knowledge. I did not realize that the search was only a means of leaving behind what you were afraid of knowing."

"Teresa. Enough."

"No." She rose. She rose without even the patina of proper respect for their differing positions.

"We are no longer children in our mother's harem," he told her. There was warning in his words, but worse.

"No. We are children—we are all children—in the Lady's harem. And it is night, and the Festival is coming."

"Wait, then. Wait until Festival Night when the truth—when all truths—are forgiven."

"That, Sendari, is precisely why I will not wait."

He could have turned and walked away, but he, ungifted, heard the threat in her voice: the voice itself. She had never dared to use it against any of them: father, kai, or par. Never yet.

He bowed to the inevitable truth that governed the Dominion: It was better to have the semblance of choice, even if both parties knew it was entirely illusory. Because if she forced him to turn, there were only two outcomes that could follow from her action.

His death. Or hers.

He could not be certain that she would be so unwise; she had never been a reckless woman. But certain or no, it was a risk, this eve, and he was not willing to face it.

"You will not wait because you will not see the truth forgiven?"

"There are some truths that cannot be forgiven."

"Teresa—"

"Cortano will kill your daughter. Have you told yourself otherwise?"

"Perhaps you have not heard. She is to be wed to Eduardo di'Garrardi on the morning following the Lady's Night."

"I have heard."

"Then this is—"

"Do you think that will protect her?" She paused. "Do you think that you have left her any choice? The Festival Night will occur, and it will be either the first of its kind or the last for many, many years. She will be forced to act. Cortano will be forced to kill her.

"And *I* gave my word to Alora, and my word means something. I have come for Diora, Brother. How will you stop me? Will you call the Lord in the Lady's Night?"

He was silent. "You know."

"There was a time when you would have had the courage to tell me yourself. There was a time, *Brother,* when we might have planned together the safest course to follow."

"You would never have agreed to this," he said flatly.

"No. But perhaps, had we spoken, you would not have agreed either."

"And you tell me that *I* am untruthful."

All masks, gone. All trivialities, all niceties, all rules. They stood, the anger between them growing, as if they were children,

with the rawness and the passion, the immediacy and the purity
of emotion, that that state implied.

"Tell me that you are not."

"I owe you nothing."

"Truth." She paused. "And lie. You believe it as you say it,
but it is wrong."

"Teresa—"

"You have always said that you did not desire power. That
you desired love. I watched you with Alora, and I believed you.
I watched you attempt to refuse your daughter to the Tyr'agar's
son, and I believed you."

He was silent. The storm was gathering sand.

"But you do not love your daughter, Sendari, except at your
own convenience, and you have *never* loved her."

"How *dare* you?"

"You sold her to Leonne; we understood it. You wept, and we
felt the pain of your loss. But that's all it was: *your* loss. You
wring your hands, you twist your beard, you suffer. You. And
Diora?

"She has lost far, far more at your hands than at any man's. It
would have been more honest to kill her when you slaughtered
the clan you forced her to join."

"I saved her life."

"You saved her life because you could not bear to accept the
truth: Your love has always been a matter of convenience. You
think your suffering hallows it. It doesn't. You mourned Alora
because you let her decide your life, your life's course, rather
than choosing it for yourself. And when she was dead, you
turned to Alesso, and gave your life, and responsibility for your
life's decisions, to *him*. Your daughter, mourned or no, became
an object of barter.

"As all daughters are, when their fathers seek power."

He turned then. His hand rose of its own accord, the ice of
desert night burned away in a flash of fury. "Do you know what
I have sacrificed for her? To save her?"

She was made of stone. He struck her; she teetered back, but
lifted no hand in her own defense. And she would not be silent.
She spoke through the pain he had caused, and he knew he had
caused pain; the marks of his hand across her dust-adorned face
were already blossoming.

"And you no doubt wept for yourself because she did not love
you for the gift of her life. You wept for yourself without ever

once recognizing the depth of her love for her wives, for her husband's child. The depth *of* love.

"The time for weeping is done. The Festival of the Moon approaches and in it all things will be laid bare. You have invited the Lord in to visit, and he will not leave so easily. I thought—I had hoped—for better. But it is done. You have betrayed us all."

"Teresa, I warn you—"

"What warning have you for me but death? And what death could be worse than the death the Lord of Night brings?"

"The death," a soft voice said, "his servants bring."

They both turned, then.

And in the pale moonlight, a lone man bowed. "Widan Sendari," he said. "I suggest you retire."

His face, in shadows, was of them; long, slender, dark. He was taller than Sendari; taller than Alesso. He wore clothing appropriate to the station of high clansmen, but he wore no colors, no crest, and Sendari expected none. But he did not recognize the man.

It was clear, from the sudden stillness of his sister's face, that she did. "Sendari," she said, the nuance of the spoken word so complicated he almost didn't understand anything it encompassed.

"This is a private affair," he said to the stranger.

"No. It *was* a private affair. But the rules of the Courts are clear. She is an enemy, and she has knowledge that she should not have."

The shadows lengthened, lengthened, lengthened.

And Sendari, slow to understand anything through the haze of the pain Teresa had inflicted, understood at last that those shadows were a darkness that even the Lord's gaze could not pierce; they were not of, and not for, the Lady.

"You have not been granted permission to hunt in the Tor," he said softly.

"No. But we have been granted permission to protect what is ours: secrecy. Silence."

"This is not your affair."

"It *is* my affair. Go, Widan. Or stay and witness. It makes little difference to me."

"I would not advise it," the Widan replied. The pain fell away as the Lord's gift filled him: the clarity of battle. The imperative of life or death, and only life, only death.

The whole of the creature's attention turned to him. "Do you seek to give me orders? I am ad'Ishavriel. I follow the commands of no mortal."

"You will follow mine, in this."

"Or you will use your pathetic magery against me?" The creature smiled.

Sendari had seen just such a smile, many times, on the face of his closest friend. It had always ended in victory for Alesso. He stopped then. Considered his options. Clearly, the Shining Court understood some part of his measure, but how much? How much of his magic had he displayed in the presence of the kinlords? He would not risk the fevers in a gaudy, and useless, display.

And would he risk them for Teresa?

For Adano, yes.

And for Diora, although her words—her cutting, her terrible words—would haunt him in the doing.

But for her?

She was his sister. They were kin, clan, blood. He lifted a hand.

And she lifted her head, the tilt of her chin so slight only he and Adano, their kai, might have recognized it for what it was. His face was a mask now; the presence of a stranger bled it of emotion until all emotion was once again as it should be: hidden. Unreadable.

"I will not use my pathetic magery against you," he said quietly. "If you have made a study of me, you understand that I am not, in the end, driven by pride."

"No. But I have discovered much by listening to your conversation; you are governed by worse: the weakness of affection."

It was meant to sting. It stung.

"Perhaps," Sendari said, conceding the obvious truth with a mild shrug, a mild nod. It was easy, after all; clean. This creature wished to see him squirm, and he offered, in return, bland acknowledgment. A parry.

Teresa, his terrible, his much hated, sister, wanted so much more from him than mere pain.

"You have no taint of attachment to this one. Leave her with me, and I will rid you of a difficulty."

The Widan shrugged. "My apologies," he said, although whether it was to the demon or to the sister, he could not say.

Teresa nodded. She straightened the line of her shoulder,

shedding anger and emotion just as Sendari had done, but fully. Finally.

He stepped back; stepped outside of the circle of the Lady's shrine. The moonlight was extraordinary in its brightness, given that the Lady still wore some part of her veil.

The darkness approached his sister. Lifted a clawed hand to her exposed face. The motion was as graceful as a caress, as seductive; Sendari shivered, seeing it.

Serra Teresa did not. She raised her head so that she might see, fully, the face of the demon who meant to be her death.

And she spoke three simple words.

"Do not move."

Hearing them, Sendari forgot to breathe. Or perhaps breath was forbidden him. He had heard the gift in her voice before, but never like this. Wind was in her words. Death. The desert heat. The sandstorm.

Had he ever thought he understood the depth of her power? He knew, now, that he had seen the sheathed sword, and only the sheathed sword. She drew the weapon, revealing herself. Exposing herself.

She stepped forward; he saw a flash of pale light that disappeared in the darkness, and then he heard the surprised grunt of Lord Ishavriel's creature, cut off in its entirety as it lost first throat and then head to the clean precision of his sister's long knife.

She had turned her back upon Sendari, obscuring much of the rigid demon's form, but because she had never been tall, he saw the creature disintegrate from headless neck to shoulder, crumpling slowly inward as if her blow had hollowed the whole. It shouldn't have been surprising—he'd seen it before in the Court—but it was. Perhaps because he had never stood so close to it; perhaps because he had never seen the kin fight outside of the great stone halls of the Shining Palace, or perhaps because his sister, hand shaking slightly, resheathed her long knife without hesitation.

The wind was her servant.

The ashes were carried away, and the night settled into the quiet of the Lady's contemplation. He had seen so much of the Lord of Night's power. It had seemed like the sun, like the wind, but stronger, more certain, an inevitable end to the life they had led. For what other purpose had the god himself come to earth?

"Your compatriots do not trust you," she said softly. "But

then again, no man of power trusts another who possesses it, no matter what assurances are offered." She did not turn.

He did not speak.

"This," she said softly, "is an ending, Sendari."

He bowed; his clothing made the noise, rustling at both fall and rise, that his words could not.

Her shoulders became a single line, and he saw that, from a distance, she might have been . . . a man.

Teresa.

He had never seen this, but he had always seen it in her. Numb, he watched her leave, wondering what she said to Adano, if she had said anything at all. Wondering when, and how, he would see her again. Worse, if he would survive it. He was surprised at how much the question hurt.

They had never been friends, but they had not—quite—been enemies, and he had thought that strange hostility would endure for the length of their lives.

He lifted a hand.

Surprised himself. "Teresa."

She stopped; although she had moved, as she always did, with grace and certainty, she had not walked with speed. She did not turn. "Widan Sendari."

Night voice.

"Do you realize what you've done?"

"I have killed an enemy," she said quietly, "of the Lady." And then, before he could speak again, she added, "Yes, Brother. I know there is no return."

"You do not have to do this. No matter what has passed between us, I have never betrayed my clan. I would never betray you. Return to Adano. Return to your life."

Her head fell slightly; her shoulders dropped. She drew a breath that seemed endless.

And then, beneath the sharp light of the Lady's growing crescent, the Serra Teresa di'Marano turned to face him. "You have betrayed us all," she said quietly. "If it is not your hand that draws the dagger across our throats, it matters little; we are dead, or worse, if the Lord walks."

"The Lord?"

"Sendari, I have treated you as many things, but never a fool. Tender me the same grace. Adano does not know, and I have not told him; I think it would break him, in a fashion, and the Lambertan Tyr will *need* Tors of strength and integrity.

"War is coming. I knew it at the Festival of the Sun, and you knew it then as well. But I could not be certain, not then, what price *you* were willing to pay to not only start the war, but win it. I . . . had some warning. I have thought of little else since I received it. But I had hoped. . . .

"I would have said many, many things of you, but I did not see you as a servant of the Lord of Night." Her face was particularly beautiful in the dull glow of lamp and the pale silver of moon. "But that is my weakness; I saw the truth, and I planned for it, but not well. I hoped that the plan itself would be unnecessary. I waited, Sendari. I spent time that we did not have if we are to stand against the Lord of Night.

"You've chosen your master, and I do not think, having made that choice, you will be able to turn from the descent you've begun; your path is steep, and it pulls you down at ever greater speed."

He watched her face for a minute, two, three. "Why," he asked at last, "are you telling me this?"

"Because, having chosen your master, you will still be yourself. You would not lift hand to save my life, but you will not take it, and you will not lift hand to see it taken."

"You are so certain of this?"

"Am I wrong, Brother?"

"Teresa—"

"I tell you this," she said, voice low, "because Alora loved you. And I tell you this because, in my fashion, I loved you as well; of my brothers, you were the one I most favored. You and I—we were ill-loved by the only man in our lives who had power. You were a scholar, a Widan-Designate, not a man. I, I was merely a woman."

"Yes."

"She saw it."

He did not speak the name of his dead wife, but the breeze that stirred as Teresa's words ebbed into silence carried it. *Alora.*

He could almost understand, seeing Teresa stripped of the finery and the mannerisms that had defined her in the eyes of the Dominion, what Alora had loved in her. And that was difficult.

Almost as difficult as what she said next.

"I told you I came for Diora, and do not mistake me; I gave her mother my word that I would watch over her, and death will break that word before I will. But I could have continued that task in the safety of anonymity.

"I came to say good-bye, Sendari."

"We should have let you have a life," he replied.

"Yes. So much harder, then, to walk away." She bowed. A man's gesture.

He could not quite offer her the courtesy that she offered him; he did not bow.

And as she walked away, beneath the changing face of the Lady's strongest moon, he said no farewells. As if, he thought bitterly, hoarding the words would change the truth.

The moon was bright enough to cast long shadows, but none of them were new; he stood in the darkness he had chosen, feeling a peculiar numbness as he listened to the rhythmic movement of water against the dark stalks of rushes.

Diora.

Teresa.

And then, unnaturally, *Sendari.*

427 AA
Stone Deepings

He would not let Calliastra near her.

He did not have the power to send the child of gods away, but he had the power to prevent her from touching Jewel.

Mostly, that was a good thing.

But the road, still bowered by distant stars, was long, and the walk tiring in a way that it hadn't been when she'd had her Oma by her side.

"Jewel," Avandar said softly, when she stumbled and he righted her, "let me carry you."

"You've been walking as long as I have," she snapped, "And you're older. I can take care of myself."

"Or you could let me help you," Calliastra said. There was no menace at all in her voice; there wouldn't be, Jewel thought, until a moment before death, if at all. Death had never had much promise, but when she looked too long at Calliastra's face, she understood the allure of suicide.

Hated that.

Calliastra took the refusal in stride, although there was a delicate shift in her expression at each refusal that Jewel came to understand meant hurt. Pain.

"Jewel," Avandar said softly.

"You could offer me a blindfold."

He laughed. It was jarring to hear that laughter; the path was quiet and suffocating with the presence of Calliastra, and that presence had strangled all mirth. Well, all of hers anyway, not that she'd recently had that much to spare.

"And that was funny how?"

"You are seer-born," the goddess replied. "Blindfold or no, you would still understand what my presence entails; you would be drawn to it. If you could not see me, my voice would become that much more distinctive, that much more compelling; if you somehow managed to deafen yourself, the ground would slope toward me, the air would carry my scent. You, seer-born, must learn to accept what you *do* see; to run from it in any way—"

"Is impossible," Avandar replied.

In perfect synchronicity.

"Is it true?" she asked, although she knew the answer.

"Is what true?" Each word as light as mountain air, but not as crisp, not as sharp.

"Did you feed her your wives and your children?"

He shrugged. Offered her silence by way of response.

The stones beneath her feet grew sharper and taller; she concentrated on walking in the shadows at his side as the silence widened the gap between them.

When she had given up on getting an answer—or rather, an answer that involved words, since the texture of his silence was often answer enough—he surprised her.

"Yes."

It wasn't the type of surprise she liked. And what was worse was this: She wasn't certain if she was surprised because she had hoped to believe that Calliastra was lying, or because she had never expected him to willingly surrender that much knowledge about his past and his personal life.

He's got nothing else to lose, she thought, silent in the face of the implications his words made. *I've seen the place he called home. I might have been party to enough of a change that he loses it entirely. What is there to hide?*

Another voice spoke, so much like her own she would have thought she was continuing her dialogue if her thoughts hadn't been headed in a different direction.

Everything.

She thought it would be impossible to sleep. She fought it for as long as she could. But in the end, stone or no stone, night or no night, goddess or no goddess, she was drawn to a place that Avandar and Calliastra could not—directly—touch. She slept.

"You keep interesting company," a voice said, stretching the word "interesting" so that it sounded feline and unpleasant.

She opened her eyes. Shrugged. "Goddess. Whatever Avandar is. I don't have much say in the company I'm keeping."

A stone paw came down gently on top of her foot. She felt the growing weight of stone. "I wasn't talking about *them*," the gargoyle said. "I was talking about *me*."

I hate cats.

"The Winter King and the Firstborn are enemies," he continued conversationally.

"I listen better when I'm not in pain," she replied, staring pointedly at his very large, very stone paw.

"Everybody else's pain is always more important," the creature replied, rolling its eyes, its face a study in exaggerated disgust. "I was sent to tell you that Calliastra will not help you."

"How surprising."

The big cat hissed.

"She is the enemy of the Lady of the Hunt."

"Oh. And she is?"

A louder hiss. "The Lady," he said. "The Winter Queen. You are not at *all* the right sort of human. You have bad manners, and you are scrawny and stupid. But I'm not allowed to eat you or even play with you a little bit until the door is open. So pay attention."

She snorted.

Laughed.

"If you want me to help you, offering to make me a cat's toy isn't exactly incentive."

"But we're bored," the creature complained, lolling its massive head in a circle as if easing itself of some hidden tension. "And the Winter King is impatient. We can't have *any* fun until the Hunt begins."

She started to speak, and found herself flying through the air. The ground at her back was hard, and the flight winded her.

The cat took off, muscles carved in stone fluid beneath stone's surface. She couldn't imagine the enchantment that had created this creature; couldn't imagine the strength it took to move that much weight into that flight.

But she found that she could imagine the effect that much weight would have when it landed; she cried out and rolled as quickly as possible into the lee of a large stalagmite.

That rock snapped like a thin icicle as the cat clipped it and continued to circle. "We don't like being bored," it said, its voice as irritating as ever, its presence a danger now, not an annoyance.

"She will help the enemy," he continued. "Do not speak to her, do not speak of her, and do not give her any part of yourself. You are too valuable."

Right, Jewel thought, *until I open that stupid door.*

"Very good," her Oma said.

The cat snarled. Her Oma frowned. "Get away, you impudent creature. What she had in mind when she granted permission for your existence, I don't know."

The cat's hiss was different. It didn't land, and Jewel realized that the hesitation had something to do with the presence of her Oma.

"You *do* know," the cat miauled back.

Her Oma shook her head. "No, I don't. Oh, I know what the effect'll be, but I don't know what she was thinking. I can guarantee she won't be happy with the results." Her Oma's smile took on that spicy, Southern edge. "Of course, neither will you, little cat. She'll play with you the way young boys play with flies."

The cat's hiss was a full-throated sound that was *so* unnatural Jewel thought it would end in a hacking, awful cough—which was deserved. It didn't.

The cat left, and quickly.

"You just have to know what to say," her Oma explained, rubbing her hands on her apron the way she did after she'd finished any job worth doing. That apron, old and graying, worn and patched, was like a map to the woman's life; a bit of food here, sweat and dust there, dirt, creases from her lap, from the bend in her knees when she worked on her hands. It also wasn't what she had been wearing when she'd first appeared in the mountain pass.

Great. Ghosts need clothing? But she remembered both things clearly, and wondered how much of what she saw was fabricated, was fabric, of that memory.

"Let it go," her Oma said.

"I can't. History makes me what I am."

"Yes. But you know the price of making that history an excuse for what you *can* be."

"It's not just my own history I'm concerned with," Jewel said softly.

"Of course not. I didn't raise an idiot. But if you can't cleave to the Warlord's shadow, other shadows will devour you. There is no light on *this* road, and you've chosen to walk it."

"Not much of a choice," another voice—a voice she had never heard before—contributed. She looked up to see a woman sitting in the v made of twin rock formations. There were flowers in her hair; leaves that trailed like willow swatches down the side of her face. "Not much of a choice at all if she wasn't told the nature of the road before the walking."

"Busybodies everywhere," her Oma said, turning just as Jewel had done. "You're not wanted here."

"No?" She stepped onto the path, and where she walked, stone gave way to earth and earth to flowering plant. "You must be Jewel," she said.

"You know me?"

"I didn't. But Calliastra has been calling you, loud and long, and we all have ears to hear with. There hasn't been this much activity on these paths since the gods walked." She smiled, and her smile was beautiful in a way that Calliastra's wasn't. There was nothing to compel in it; nothing to attract; nothing to make a person uncomfortable with the unsaid, unacknowledged sensuality of a first meeting. "I'm Corallonne."

"And Corallonne is?"

"I'm Calliastra's . . . cousin," the woman said with a smile. "And not all roads lead to where you are going."

"Her road *does*," Jewel's Oma said emphatically.

"Well, then, I guess that's that," the woman replied lightly. "I never argue with an old woman. I hope to see you again, Jewel, or your kin; the road shouldn't be traveled, but since it will be, let it be traveled well. Take from my garden, or rather, from the garden that will grow where I have ventured, and be comforted."

"I'm not in need of comfort."

"But you are, child." Her smile was reminiscent of Finch's. "Let me tell you something you would know if you were willing to think about it: The Warlord gave his wife and his children—some of them—to Calliastra."

"I already know that, but thanks for the thought."

"It was a death they earned when they attempted to bring about *his* death, and it was a kinder death than he would have suffered.

"But," she bent down, reached out with her hands, and came up carrying round fruits that looked a lot like apples, "all things grow, if they know life and if they are mortal. All things change."

"He's not, strictly speaking, mortal," Jewel's Oma said.

"He is," Corallonne replied. "Mortal through and through, with no ability to acknowledge it anymore, not in a way that counts. You know it, and I know it."

"Mortality, by definition, involves death," her Oma snapped, sharp as vinegar.

Corallonne frowned slightly. "He is not the man he was."

"He has been many men."

"Indeed."

"And he's failed at being all of them."

Corallonne's frown deepened. "And *we* can judge? What is failure? What is success? There is birth and death, and the Halls of Mandaros, where we—you and I—will never go." She turned to Jewel, who was bound by their words as if her life depended on them, although indeed both women were calm and peaceful. "Judge him if you will, but judge with hope."

"Hope?"

"Where there is damnation," Corallonne said quietly, "there is also redemption."

"Na'dio."

She sat, composed, in a darkness alleviated by nothing but the memory of the moon.

Sleep had proved elusive, but this was common. Uncommon, and more painful, was the reason. She had saved her father's life. Of all deaths, his had been the one she had least desired. But she had desired it. The dead, her dead, spoke with the voice of a wind that scours rock to smooth facelessness.

The screens that slid by day to admit food and the rare, rare visitor would remain closed this night, as they had all nights since the death of the kai el'Sol. But there were some things such doors could not keep out.

"Ona Teresa," she replied, matching words of power with words of power, smoothing the guilt and the anger out of the voice that spoke them. **"I had not heard that you had arrived."**

"Nor, I fear, will you."

Silence. **"You are not staying in the Tor?"**

"No."

"But I—"

"I will be here for the Festival of the Moon, child," Serra

Teresa replied. "But I will not help to plan it; I will not wear the silken sari or bear the silken fan; I will not wear gold or jade or . . . emerald. I will have no retainers save one, be protected by no Tyran."

"I . . . I do not understand."

"It is time, Na'dio, that we leave the Tor Leonne."

Ona Teresa.

She had trusted her aunt as she had trusted no one but her wives. She considered the words, hearing the command inherent in them. Hearing the fear, the wildness beneath their surface.

Her aunt, she thought dispassionately, was worried. Afraid.

"When?"

"When?"

"When do you desire my departure from the Tor?"

"This eve."

"The night of the Festival Moon is one week away, Ona Teresa."

"The night of the Festival Moon will be, I fear, far too late. I am coming for you, Na'dio."

There was only one thing she desired more than she desired the feel of the moon's breath across her upturned face. She had planned, after all. There had been so little else to do.

"Ona Teresa."

"Yes."

"Not tonight."

The silence was long. Full. At last it was broken, and Diora felt her breath return to her in a rush although, until that moment, she hadn't realized she was holding it. "Na'dio, the games played here are—"

"Men's games. Yes, I know. And you have cautioned me against their play."

"Indeed. I will caution you again, but your victory at the Festival of the Sun speaks for itself. If you are not ready to leave, I will accept that. But I must warn you: I am not nearly so certain of my ability as you are of yours. The night of the Festival Moon will be a . . . difficult night."

"It will be the night," Diora said coolly, "before my wedding."

"Yes. And preparations for that wedding will necessitate the presence of far too many people. Will you not reconsider?"

"I . . . cannot. I cannot leave the Tor without taking an old friend with me, and she—she will not be ready to leave until that night."

"Na'dio—"

"Will you tell me the price of failure?" Diora said, soft as the moon's light and just as cool.

The pause was as long as the question had been. "No."

"I cannot leave here alone, and my friend is not yet ready to travel. I can make no plans until the Festival itself—and perhaps not even then. It is a moon night, but the traditions and the freedoms of those nights have not been offered to me this year."

"I will wait," the Serra said.

"Thank you, Ona Teresa. I—" She fell into silence. Silence had always been her only protection.

"Yes?"

"I—I should tell you something you may not be aware of." Her aunt waited with the patience of a Marano. "Kallandras of Senniel, Kallandras of the North."

"The North, as the South, prepares for war—and that war, I think, will be *the* war. If you have not heard, Ser Anton di'Guivera now serves the last of the Leonnes. He will travel South in the boy's company."

"I have heard . . . little. But I remember the first time I saw Kallandras: It was during the Festival of the Moon, in the year that the Tyr'agar declared war against the Empire." She did not add, because she did not need to, that that declaration, and the loss that had followed in battle, had probably cost the Tyr his life and his line.

"Yes. He is here?"

"I do not know where he is, but he is in the Tor Leonne, or very near it. His voice is strong."

"Thank you, Na'dio. I will bespeak you later. You have planned, and I have planned, and as all plans must, they will require revision."

The silence was long, had been far too long.

"Ona Teresa?"

"Yes, Na'dio?"

"I . . . must sleep."

"Sleep, then." Pause. "I am here, and I will not leave you behind."

The silence was terrible.

"Ona Teresa?"

"**Yes, Na'dio.**" Not a question.

She could not ask. She could not see the moon, had been forbidden the harem's heart and the comfort of the women who had been her mothers in the absence of the one who had died birthing her, had been given to sunlight only when those responsible for the deaths—the deaths that drove her like the sand-laden storm— decreed it. And she could not ask for what she desired, not quite. Was she not the Serra Diora di'Marano? Was she not her aunt's perfect daughter?

So she chose to ask a different question, and in its fashion, it was just as terrible.

"**Did you know?**"

The silence, as always, was marked. The Serra Teresa di'Marano understood her meaning at once. "**You have never asked me that question.**"

"**No.**"

"**Were you afraid of the answer?**"

"**Can't you hear it?**" Diora asked. "**Can't you hear it in my voice?**"

"**I hear much, Na'dio. Much. But you are distant; perhaps that protects us both. Let me answer. Listen well. Understand that we two cannot lie to each other; our gifts are too strong and our training too poor.**

"**No. I did not know. I believe your uncle, Ser Adano kai di'Marano, did.**" Her voice was smooth, cool, distant; perfect in every way. "**But I am also certain that he did not understand the whole of the game; it will hurt him much when he finally does.**"

"**And will he?**"

"**He, of the three of us, comes closest to being a fool. But not, sadly for him, that close. Yes. He will.**"

Diora's fingers ached. She had always played the harp or the samisen when they spoke in such a fashion, and the absence of music—as comfort and retreat—had created a hunger that was almost as great as the one that had driven her to ask the question of her aunt.

She did not acknowledge it.

She had been taught well, and taught most by the woman to who she spoke.

"**Na'dio,**" that woman said, voice soft as the river silks, and strong as the desert wind. "**You must sleep.**"

"**Yes.**"

Silence. And then, perhaps because captivity and silence changed all rules, perhaps because her knowledge of voice and word was so much greater than Diora's own, she offered her almost-daughter what the younger woman could never have asked for: she sang.

The sun has gone down, has gone down, my love, Na'dio, Na'dio child.

And in the cradle of that voice and those words, time unwound in the dim and cramped room. The Serra Diora di'Marano offered her aunt no greater acknowledgment than this: she slept.

CHAPTER TWENTY

When she woke from her sleep, there was fruit in her hands. Round and unblemished, like the ideal of an apple and not the fact. She had not been hungry until she felt the firm curve of fruit against her palms. After which she was, of course, starving. She expected no less. It was what would have happened in a dream, and often did, things turning on an event or a sensation, branching in a way that felt totally natural while you were trapped in it, but made no sense when seen at a safe remove.

That was what had been bothering her, dimly, since she had first seen her Oma. She had not, in fact, felt as if she had truly been awake since she had left the streets of Averalaan.

She felt, more than saw, the grin of a big, gray cat. *Not as stuuuupid as you look. But that would be imposssible.*

She hated cats.

So: she could doubt reality while hunger gnawed away at all other sensation. She could doubt that she'd seen Duster; that she'd seen her Oma, that she'd seen someone who claimed to be the daughter of darkness and love—*liar*—but there was one thing she could not, did not, doubt: That Avandar had killed wives. Children. Friends.

He is master here.

Aristos' stone voice, grating and rough, which was fitting given his fate.

He's not my master.

What is he, then?

He had saved her life more times than she cared to count; enough that she had long since stopped questioning The Terafin's wisdom in choosing Avandar as her domicis.

The hunger that had curled her over with its strength was gone as she thought of the woman to whom she owed everything in her present life. The woman that she would never see alive again.

You promised her, her Oma said sharply. *And you know how I feel about promises.*

Does any Voyani feel any differently?

She snorted. *You've got the blood but not the upbringing. I feel promises are important.* They *feel promises are important as long as blood ties bind them. Don't forget it. You've got power, but you've not the blood—you belong to a family that* left *the* Voyanne *for the safe streets of the Northern city.*

Safe. Safety was the child's dream.

And sometimes, the adult's. She looked up from the food in her hands and saw the only companion she had on the road if you didn't count a disembodied voice or two.

His back was her wall. His shoulders, broad, were unbent; his neck was straight, spine more like spear than like bone; he stood, unarmed, the way an armored member of The Terafin's Chosen would have stood had they been guarding The Terafin herself.

She wanted to ask him how old his children had been. Remembered what Corallonne had said, and didn't doubt it: he had given them a kinder death than they would have offered him. But even so. Had Duster tried to kill her, what would she have done? Everything in her went against the killing of kin. Well, her own at any rate.

Beneath her, spread out and wrinkled in a way that would have made silk merchants cry, his outer robe. She hated this road. She could not clearly remember falling asleep. Could not, in fact, remember whether or not she had fallen asleep in the cradle of his arms.

"Avandar?"

"Jewel," he said in a low voice, turning toward her. "You've been—" He stopped, tensing as his gaze fell to her hands and what they carried.

"I haven't eaten yet," she said, the wryness of her smile instinctive. It surprised her when he relaxed visibly. "You do realize I'm starving, don't you?"

"Of course."

"And it would be a bad idea to eat?"

"That food, and here, yes. Although I am by no means certain that the intent was harmful."

"Which means you know where the food came from."

"There is only one place it could have come from, on this road," he said softly. "But there are worse people to meet than Corallonne." He looked back—or forward—and Jewel saw Calliastra's shadow.

"I suppose if I ask you if we're there yet—"

"I would tell you that you'll know when we arrive."

"I was afraid of that."

His smile was a glimmer of his old smile; thin and easily broken, but present.

"Will you?"

"Will I what?"

"Will you know when we arrive?"

The smile deepened. She'd hated it, back home: it was the smile reserved by adults for children who had done something precocious, and she was *well* past the age where precocious described any part of her behavior. But because it was familiar here, and because she—weakling that she was—desperately craved the familiar and the *real,* she accepted it almost happily.

"They have not come for me. Calliastra came for you. I see that Corallonne was wakened as well. Truly, Jewel, I thought that I would define the path we took. I would not have risked you otherwise. But there is something in you that sees far too clearly, and *here* those who see clearly are clearly seen.

"Your question is a wise one. No. I do not think I will know we have arrived before you do."

The words slowly made sense, and when they did, she didn't like them. "You do realize," she said, slipping into irritable incredulity, "that this is the worst case of the blind leading the blind I've ever seen?"

He laughed. His laughter filled the canyon the pass had become while she slept, and the rocks shivered with the passing touch of his voice.

15th of Scaral, 427 AA
Tor Leonne

"Kallandras."

He would not have said he had been waiting for her, but when he heard her speak he felt no surprise, none of the minor shock that accompanied unexpected recognition. His gentle inquiries—guarded and admittedly few—had led him to believe that the Serra would not make the trek to the Tor Leonne for the Festival of the Moon, no doubt a punishment of sorts devised by the younger of her two brothers.

But the Festival of the Moon was *her* festival.

"Serra Teresa." The Serra's voice carried her presence across the miles that separated them, and it was only many years of experience with the voice—and the dialogue of bards—that prevented him from falling into a flawless Southern bow.

"Forgive me," she said, her words so completely controlled they changed the meaning of the word power, **"for this late interruption. I had not expected to see you at this Festival, and I myself—**

"I am newly arrived in the Tor Leonne. I have taken little time in my journey and perhaps I have been imprudent; I sought out no information until after I had completed the first of my errands. It seems that the city is not to be graced with the presence of the Voyani."

"Your information is correct; it is not safe for the Voyani to venture into the Tor Leonne, greater or lesser, at the moment."

Her silence was the silence of thought, not leave-taking. **"I find myself in an awkward situation,"** she said at last. **"And I ask your pardon if the awkwardness and the urgency conspire to rob me of grace."**

"Serra Teresa," he replied, completely truthful although such flattery seldom was, **"I cannot think of the situation that would rob you of grace."**

"Southern grace, then," she replied, and he heard the momentary smile in her perfect voice.

"I would forgive you much."

"I had intended—I had hoped to find Yollana of the Havalla Voyani within the Tor."

"Ah. Was she expecting you?"

"She had received warning that I might travel upon short notice; word does not travel quickly or perfectly between the clansmen and the Voyani."

"I can carry word to Yollana for you, if you wish it."

"I do," the Serra Teresa replied. **"But I find myself, none-theless, in an awkward position."**

"May I be of assistance?"

He read the hesitation in the pause, but the answer itself was firm. **"Yes."** And bold. Surprising.

"Only tell me how."

"I . . . if you are able, I would be honored if you would meet me in the city."

"The honor would be mine. Where in the city?"

"Perhaps by the Eastern Fount of Contemplation?"

He heard the levity in her voice; for his own part, he laughed, and let the wind take the sound to where she stood—wherever that might be. **"Most certainly. But I warn you now, I desire a kinder reception than I received on the previous occasion I agreed to meet you there."**

There was much about that night and this that was similar. The night was cool but clear, the wind evident in the way it brushed strands of hair into and out of his eyes. He could see by the light, but the shadows were longer than he would have liked, and he did not desire the attention a lantern would lend him.

The Fount itself made more noise than he did; water trickled up and down in a thin stream encircled by a stone basin. Once, there had been gold highlights across the stone's face, but time and desperation had worn such adornments away: the rock remained, and the water it contained.

He paused by it a moment; there was a single person by the Fount, and he, seated cross-legged in the center of the circle of contemplation. The circle itself was scuffed and dusty; that would change in scant days as the men and women responsible for the city's face worked their way from the center out in preparation for the Festival.

For a festival, he thought, that would be quiet and strained enough that the wild honesty it encouraged might never come to pass.

"Serra Teresa," he said quietly.

The person in the circle shook off silence and stillness. "I would not have thought I was so easily recognized; I have taken pains to be otherwise."

"There is very little about you that is easily hidden," he replied, bowing in the correct Southern fashion for a man meeting a Serra whose family outranks him when that family—father or husband—is present.

"Say, rather, that there is very little you miss."

"At your insistence, Serra." He rose. "Remember, I have seen you dressed in such a fashion before; the years are not enough to distance me from that experience." He offered her a hand; it was a Northern gesture. He was mildly surprised when she accepted it. "I have taken the liberty of finding you accommodation."

"Let me take the liberty of accepting it." Her voice was grave, as still as the waters of the Lake on a windless night. He saw the moon in her eyes, or across their surface. She paused, and he saw her lips move, but heard only the movement of wind.

"Ramdan?" he asked.

"Yes, and two of my brother's cerdan."

"That . . . would be impolitic."

"I have considered this. I accept the risk."

His turn to pause; his turn to turn voice to wind. **"Margret."**

She could not reply, but he knew how to leave pause for reply between his words. **"We will have not only the Serra Teresa as visitor, but also her oldest servant and two of her cerdan. Prepare yourself, if this displeases you, and tell Yollana."**

He turned back to the Serra. "I believe it is time that we leave this place."

"I put myself in your hands, Kallandras of Senniel."

"Follow, then." He turned moonward, then back, seeing much in her face and the Lady's that was similar. "You will not be returning."

A brow rose, dark against white; no skin was as pale as hers unless it belonged to a Serra of clans that could afford to keep her, unspoiled by sun and obvious labor, within the confines of a harem. "I am so very obvious."

"Ah." He smiled. "I take no credit where credit is not due; it was Yollana's guess."

Yollana met them as they approached the camp's outer edge. Her arms were folded in such a way that she could prop herself up on a cane by the weight of her elbow, and her face, at this distance, was as sour as wine left to air. She stood not ten feet from Margret, and Margret, flanked by Elena and Tamara, waited impatiently, arms folded across her chest, a younger version of Yollana, whose similarity at that moment was marred only by the lack of a cane. She had no other obvious guards, no brothers who had stepped out of shadows to add their strength to hers.

But Kallandras knew there were at least two men with crossbows in the shadows the wagons made of moonlight. He assumed they would be trained on the cerdan who followed at the Serra Teresa's back.

"You took your time," Yollana said, as they approached. Kallandras noted, with some wryness, that she reserved the sharp edge of her words for him; to Teresa, she offered a surprisingly genuine nod of head, as much acknowledgment as a Voyani matriarch ever gave an outsider.

"Accept my apologies, Matriarch," the Serra replied. "It took . . . longer than we had hoped to leave the Tor without pursuit."

The older woman shrugged. "It's not my caravan," she said. "You can grovel to the Arkosan Matriarch to your—or more likely her—heart's content, but do it on your own time." Her gesture belied the careless sting of her words; she stepped forward and reached out to the Serra Teresa.

Without hesitation, the Serra Teresa offered her both hands. Those hands, ringed and ringless, locked as the women stood facing each other.

Yollana was not diplomatic. They were, in Kallandras' opinion, the most powerful people in the small clearing. He wondered, privately, if that was why Margret had chosen to denude herself of guards: Yollana, Havallan, was nonetheless *the* Matriarch in the camp, and the younger woman wisely wished to spare herself exposure to the too obvious comparison.

"Aie, Na'tere, look at you. You're indecently young."

"It is the moon's mask, no more. The Lord's gaze has treated you no less harshly."

Yollana's laugh was a crow's laugh; jarring compared to the softness of Teresa's. "And you lie so poorly; I expect better from a clansman." She lifted her head, but not her hands, and looked beyond Teresa's shoulder. "Ramdan. You're still in her service, then."

He bowed.

"You've not thought the better of my offer?"

Teresa smiled. "Matriarch, you embarrass him."

"Ha. I've tried. It's not possible. Now you, maybe you could."

"I," the Serra replied, with perfect gravity, "have never tried. I will leave you to your contest of dignity." It was, Kallandras noted, the Serra and not the Matriarch who pulled her hands free first. She looked up, past Yollana to the woman who waited, arms pressed more tightly against her chest.

"Matriarch."

"Serra."

The Serra Teresa offered a very correct Southern obeisance, but the perfection of its lines was ruined by the clothing she wore; men's clothing, all, and made for the road.

He did not require his training or his gift to read Margret's mood; it was written—poorly and plainly—across the breadth of her face. He had passed desert nights, without the benefit of Voyani hospitality or shelter, more warmly.

He had expected no less; Margret's feelings toward the clansmen were legendary among the four families. He had not often met her mother, but Evallen of the Arkosans had considered it a point of concern; she herself, as any Matriarch, had no great love of the clans, but she understood their uses, and when necessary was able to "hold her nose," as she put it, and deal.

And as she spoke, her glance had passed over her daughter, lingering there just long enough for a man of Kallandras' training to note her unease.

"Serra," that daughter said. "I did not expect to find you here."

"I did not expect to be here," the Serra replied smoothly—and without rising.

"Have you been to the plateau?"

"Briefly, Matriarch."

"And did you—did you speak with your niece?"

He heard the fear and the loathing, the desperation and the terrible hope, that weighted each word.

"We could not speak freely," the Serra Teresa replied. "She is kept in isolation, and she is watched."

The hope left Margret's face; its absence hardened the lines around her eyes, her mouth. "Then why have you come at all?"

In the moonlight, Yollana's face was blanched of emotion, but Kallandras knew her well enough; the older woman was angry at the exchange.

"I was forced to either come in haste, or come late," the Serra replied. "There was no opportunity for me to attend the Festival of the Moon otherwise."

"I don't care if you attend the Festival," Margret's voice was low. "But you—you of all people—have access to—"

"Margret." Yollana's bark was, for Yollana, mild.

"Matriarch?" A warning there.

Yollana heeded it as she heeded all else. "Don't you understand what you see?"

"Exactly what do you expect me *to* see?"

"The clanswoman has traveled without her retinue, and in unseemly haste."

"Yes?"

Yollana smacked her forehead with the heft of her palm. Had she been dealing with one of her own, Kallandras knew it wouldn't have been her head she smacked. "She has traveled without permission."

"She—impossible! She's a *clanswoman*. They barely breathe without permission, and when they draw such a breath, they do it so no one notices."

She was, Kallandras thought suddenly, absolutely correct.

"Someone will notice," Serra Teresa said quietly, unmoved by Margret's distaste. "There is much between us, Evallen."

The younger Matriarch opened her mouth and closed it quickly. Wise. "What do you want, then?"

"Shelter, for the moment; a chance to help you in your current struggle."

"Oh?"

"We desire the same thing."

Margret's laugh was bitter and a little overlong. "And that?"

"The liberation of my niece. She has what you require, and she has capabilities and depths that you will find useful on the road you must travel."

"I'm not taking *her* with me. I only need what she carries."

The Serra Teresa bowed.

Margret turned and began to walk away. Turned back. "You can stay until we get it." Kallandras had seldom heard words more grudging.

"She is . . . perceptive," he said as Serra Teresa rose.

"Oh?" The word was cool. Private.

He understood a warning when he heard it. He had offered her the private voice; he offered her silence in its stead.

Because Margret's unvoiced suspicion was—and this surprised him—correct. That the Serra Teresa could have met with her niece had she not chosen so drastic a course of action was not in question.

What he had not questioned until this meeting was the inverse: That she could have avoided the drastic course of action and in so doing, met with her niece. She had forsaken both brothers and the life she had led in order to avoid that early, simpler meeting.

He wondered idly if the Serra Diora di'Marano truly understood the depth of her aunt's commitment. For by avoiding Diora in such a fashion she had forced from Margret at least two things: an alliance, and the offer of hospitality. By taking advantage of that hospitality, and Teresa's aid in Diora's rescue, Margret opened herself up to the debt of Matriarchs. She would owe

Diora and Teresa safe passage, at the very least, to the Terrean of Mancorvo or Averda for their part in the return of the Voyani heart.

Teresa, safely ensconced in her brother's harem, needed no such hospitality. But the Serra Diora would need it—and more. There was literally no other way that she could cross the Dominion in safety. No clansman would dare offer her shelter.

Whether or not Margret would honor that debt, on the other hand, remained to be seen.

How much do you know, Yollana?

The sun was high. Beneath the wide brim of leather hat, the Serra Teresa hid her face from both the Lord's gaze and man's. But the Matriarch of the Havallan Voyani passed the masks Kallandras had brought for her, one at a time, into the shadows before the Serra's face.

The Serra did not speak, but Yollana nodded anyway; it was a conversation of sorts, but it offered no satisfaction to eavesdroppers such as he.

He would not have thought that Teresa would expose her abilities to anyone who could not divine them for themselves: the bard-born, those afflicted in a similar fashion. He was surprised; he had underestimated her, and the Serra Teresa was a difficult woman to underestimate.

"Serra Teresa. Matriarch." He spoke more to give them warning of his presence than to offer any politeness. They stopped in their inspection to acknowledge his interruption with a nod. "Are we closer to any understanding?"

Mikalis di'Arretta offered a frustrated nod in return. "Closer. But not close enough." He rose, agitated. "The Sword's Edge, and the Tyr'agar," he said speaking through his teeth in just such a way that Sendari knew immediately how little sleep he had been allowed in each of the past few days, "were ill-advised to set themselves against the Voyani."

Sendari looked up from the comfort of cushions and mats; this work, they did in the privacy of the halls reserved for the Sword of Knowledge. And Cortano's halls, muted and sparsely decorated, were nonetheless quite fine. Mikalis seemed out of place in the room; his face unshaven, his clothing unwashed, his hands flecked with dirt and clay, moist with sweat. He had no proper quarters upon the plateau. Sendari did, and his appearance—cool and exact—reflected that. "Perhaps. Perhaps they had a choice between the Court and the Voyani. You know the Lord's law: choose allies among the weak, and you will join them."

"I know the Lord's law," Mikalis muttered, "But let me add the Lady's advice: Choose carefully that which you designate as weak."

"That is not the Lady's—"

"It is the essence of her words."

The masks lay before him like a public accusation.

"Mikalis, you have my apologies. I have spoken to Cortano."

"About?"

"You have slept some three hours in the last two days, or so rumor has it."

"Rumor is not usually that accurate." The man grunted and sank back into the cushions, his restless pacing halted by the smoothness of Sendari's words. He gripped his neck in the palm of his hand and strained against taut muscle awhile.

"The dead drive the Sword's Edge now."

"The dead make bad drivers."

"Oh?" The sarcasm in the single word was mingled with something more raw and less complicated. It was something Sendari knew too well; he backed away, as was prudent.

Mikalis di'Arretta relented; he had that type of grace. "I want what any good clansman wants: revenge. I am not a great warrior; had I been, my early life would have been simpler. The only hope I have of thwarting our enemies is this, this work. I do it." As he spoke, he stared at his hands, turning them palm in and palm out as if they held some secret he could only define by such close inspection.

"Some of the older magics were based on odd principles, and it is generally thought that they were more religious in nature— and vastly less effective—than the magics we practice today."

"You believe this magic and that magic are connected?"

"Either that or the masks mean nothing; they're a clever trap to draw our attention from a different form of attack."

"I've considered that," Yollana said, wiping the sweat from her forehead almost absently. "But a shadow has fallen across all of these faces. Can you not feel it?"

The Serra Teresa met her eyes, tilting her chin and exposing her face a moment to the Lord's gaze.

Yollana laughed. "I forget myself. You are nothing at all like the Voyani, Serra, but the *Voyanne* has nonetheless scarred your soul; I recognize the look. And because I do, I treat you as one of my own."

"And I welcome such hospitality," the Serra replied, "when it does not involve the friendly blows I've seen you deliver to those closest to you."

"Who could hit such a face?"

But the Serra Teresa had fallen silent.

The silence stretched; her gaze had been caught by the gaudiness of the finest of the four masks. Feathers dyed in delicate blues and brilliant reds crowded eyes that were wide, gold-circled, round. The nose, beaklike, had a ferocity about its joining with the mouth; it spoke of cruelty, the essence of all power when it is unbridled by such a trifle as affection. She lifted it slowly, turning it front to back in a slow circle.

"What would happen," she asked the Havallan Matriarch, "if I were to wear this?"

"I wouldn't advise it."

"No?"

"No. I'd be hesitant to let most of the men and women in this camp even touch it."

"Could you make this mask safe?"

"Not safer than the replicas you've had made."

"And the replicas?"

"They are as lifeless as the clay they are made of."

"But these—could we have someone wear them?"

"Sendari, I have told you what I know. I have examined these masks in great detail. I have drawn upon all the knowledge I've gathered in my life on the edge; I am only barely able to touch the enchantment. It's almost as if—as if—"

"You cannot remove these enchantments."

"No."

"Could you make this mask safe enough?"

Yollana's expression shifted. It was subtle work; the lines of her face—and her face was lined—grew heavier, deeper, as if she had momentarily freed all suppressed age. She had eagle eyes and she had vulture eyes; all Voyani women did. But it was not as hunter that she turned on Teresa now, although she had the intensity of the hunter that feeds a whole tribe.

"I forbid it, Teresa."

And the Serra Teresa, stranger, student—and if Kallandras was any judge of the quality of the interchange between the two, an excellent one—said quietly, "In this camp, that right is not yours."

"As if what?"

Mikalis was silent for a long time. At last, and with a hesitancy that Sendari understood the minute he began to haltingly speak, he said, "I do not know how you . . . express . . . your power. My first teacher—an older man who did not survive the fires—"

"You were taught by a Designate?"

"My clan was not as powerful as yours, Sendari."

"My apologies. I—please. Continue."

Mikalis drew breath. Reached, for the first time since Sendari had been in attendance, for the sweet water that had been drawn from the Lake at Alesso's command. That water refreshed, and while it did not obviate the need for sleep, it removed the effects of its lack for some small time.

"His name was Coramir."

"I do not remember him."

"You wouldn't. He was a Widan-Designate only after he was careless enough to get caught." An old anger burned briefly, lighting Mikalis' features from within. Sendari had never seen him so animated.

"But I digress. Coramir explained two things to me. First, he said that power was so personal even sex was uniform and bland by comparison." Mikalis' grimace was informed by affection, but it was a grimace. "Second, he said that our way of 'seeing' power sometimes narrowed what we saw."

"This is not so different from my own first teacher."

"He told me about his vision."

"*That* is very different."

"I will not protect him now; his voice is the wind's voice and he has no use for his secrets. His own use of magic was sedate, simple, subtle: His search for power was like his search for a book in the library of a very rich man. He might wander down the aisles, casually picking up title after title, perusing the contents and setting them aside."

"I am surprised that he managed to cast at all."

"He did. But . . . slowly.

"He said there were times when a book he picked up was

written in a foreign language; it was still a book, it was obviously meant to be read—but it was not meant to be read by him."

"You think that is how he would have seen these masks?"

"Yes. And he would never have gone beyond them. He was convinced that the language barrier was a protection, a guard set by the Lady so that magic of malign nature might see no moonlight."

"I find it hard to believe that someone this superstitious was almost Widan."

"We all have our superstitions."

"My apologies, Ser Mikalis. I meant no disrespect. I was thinking out loud."

"I had great difficulty learning from Coramir in those early years. His vision was so enticing, I would look for 'books' when it came time to draw power and focus."

Sendari nodded. It was a common student's mistake, and it was a mistake that most students would never rise above. This was one of the main reasons most masters kept their paradigms to themselves.

"But my focus was much, much less civilized, much simpler. And I will tell you now because I cannot see what it reveals of me and my magics."

"I am . . . honored."

"No. We are desperate." But his smile, brief though it was, provoked the same from Sendari.

"I am a juggler, of sorts. I see power as small, round balls."

Sendari's brows rose.

Mikalis reddened. "There are reasons why our internalizations are so seldom exposed. When I reach for power, it has a curve. The size of the curve tells me much. Over the years, I have learned that if the 'ball' fits the 'palm' of my hand, I will summon a magic I can easily control. I can draw less—find something the size of a pebble; I can draw more, and find something whose curve matches the size of that basin." He was quiet a long time. "That basin, or perhaps something larger than that, will kill me if I am not careful."

"But there is more, and this is something I was able to . . . expand upon during my travels with the Voyani. I can sometimes touch the curve of another's power. Sometimes, when the mage is a man of Cortano's capabilities, I touch a wall, no more. He guards everything.

"Sometimes, when a mage has what I believe is *your* paradigm, then beneath the surface of the globe, I feel fire, flame, heat; it is uncomfortable enough that it makes any other discovery more difficult. But I still *feel* the roundness in my own hand, or in both. You are a powerful Widan, Sendari; more powerful in measure than you are in respect, at least among the Widan."

"You would do well to keep this to yourself."

"I would. I have. But not now. Not with the Lady's waters between my lips and the certain knowledge that when these masks are worn we will—"

"Yes?"

Mikalis hid himself behind the Lady's water. "Let me go back to the example of Cortano. His power is such that he guards *everything.* When I touch any spell of his working, I touch a wall; flat in every possible way. I am incapable of gaining information that he does not wish me to have: I do not know the intensity of his power, the cost of its use. Only a fool would try to gain more than that from Cortano."

"We are all fools, in our time."

"Aye, we are all fools at least once," Mikalis said wryly. The wryness twisted his lips for an instant, no more. "But I can tell you this. When I touch the power that exists as *potential,* the power that exists before his casting, I feel it."

"Lady's Moon," Sendari said softly. He was silent with the enormity of what he'd been told. Surprised that Mikalis had been open enough to speak of it at all.

"Yes. It is . . . hard work. Intricate and difficult. And it almost never applies to something that has been created. It is also," he added, his lips dimpling in pained smile, "the only reason I survived the test of the bridge. I am not, by nature, a man of power."

He met Sendari's eyes again. *Ah, Mikalis,* he thought. *And you think I am such a man.* It stung.

"I assumed that these masks were created by a master of just such magic," Mikalis said, unaware of the effect his words had.

"Interesting. I can feel nothing at all. No heat. No light."

"I know. I thought, until yesterday, that I could feel nothing. I thought that they were expertly protected. I was wrong. These masks are *not* magical as we understand them; they are not magical as the Voyani would understand them. They are a spell whose last component has not yet been cast: the potential, but not the finality."

"You mean—"

"Yes. They are not, in and of themselves, magical—but there is magic about them, half-finished, trapped, and waiting. When I touch this magic, this working, I feel something, in both palms, that is almost flat." He waited a moment.

Sendari sank slowly to the floor. "You mean—"

"You are faster than I was. Yes. I thought they were protected, as Cortano is, from detection. I was wrong. It is not a flat wall I feel; the curve is there if I traverse the power for long enough."

Margret was not happy.

"The choice is not yours to make," the Serra Teresa said quietly. All eyes suddenly turned to the younger of the two Matriarchs. Teresa's reminder was unwelcome, but it was there: Margret was the undisputed—ha!—ruler of the Arkosan Voyani, and both Teresa and Yollana were her guests.

Oh, the woman could be a bitch. Smart, vicious, cold as desert night.

As Lady's Night.

"How can she even start to make these safe if she doesn't understand their power?" Her voice. She was hedging. Anyone watching would know it, but Matriarchs were expected to be cautious.

"I didn't say I didn't understand it," the Havallan Matriarch replied. "I said I didn't—and don't—understand the purpose the power is put to."

Ah. "Not the same thing."

"Not at all."

"Yollana, we're in this together. You've no right to withhold information."

"No?" The older Matriarch pushed herself to her feet, teetering imperiously as she gained solid footing with the aid of a cane.

"This is not the Lord's power."

"No. That we would all recognize—Widan, Radann, and Voyani alike. They know us well enough to know that, Matriarch."

"Then what is the power that drives this mask?"

Yollana bowed her head a moment. When she lifted it, her face was somehow sterner. "I believe it is a magic that was lost before the *Voyanne* opened to swallow us all; it was old, even then, and wild."

There was a minute pause between question and answer, one

they all heard. But only Margret could fill in the words that Yollana could not speak aloud: Before the fall of the Cities.

"Yollana—"

"I can touch it, yes. I can manipulate it to some small extent, for reasons it is forbidden to speak of. But the power at work here is vast and almost endless." She spun in a slow circle before adding, "If I am not mistaken in its source."

"What is it supposed to do?"

"I . . . cannot be certain."

"Yollana!"

Yollana turned a critical eye upon the Serra Teresa; an appraising eye. "They cannot, themselves, be certain that the masks will have all of their intended effect."

"What is that effect?"

"I believe," Yollana said quietly, "It is a summoning." She was silent a moment.

"Matriarch." Yollana turned at the interruption; Margret turned as well, but not as if the title fit her. She recognized the voice. The fire of the heart circle she had build let no word out that she did not wish heard, but it let word in when that word was carried by her blood relatives.

Adam stood respectfully at the fire's edge, his eyes orange with flame's reflection.

She spoke the words that would break the circle just long enough to allow him entry. She saw his eyes narrow a moment; read the thought that stabbed him in passing: *Mother used to do this.*

Aie, yes, this had been hers, and the fact that she didn't rule the circle was sure proof, if it were needed, that she was gone. *Everything* Margret would do from now until her own death would be certain proof that she was gone.

"Adam?"

This close, and without the heat to distort him, she saw that his chest was heaving.

"Is it Nicu?"

"Nicu?" he frowned. "No. Nicu's with Donatella and Tamara."

She relaxed slightly. "Then what?"

"The clansmen."

"Adam, *please*. Faster."

"Stavos set us to watch, Alanos and I. We've been in the streets of the Tor. He's still there. I had to come to tell the Matri—to tell you."

"Tell me what?"

"There are lineups in the city streets. Long lines, patrolled, sort of, by the Tyr's cerdan. We don't look that different from most of the people in the Tor, so we joined one."

"Risky, you idiot."

"Stavos said—"

"I'm your sister. You listen to me, not Stavos. Go on."

"Alanos thought maybe it had something to do with food."

"Alanos thinks everything has something to do with food."

"Anyway, we joined the line. It took a while to really start moving. There was some man at the head of the line, and when he finally reached him, he took our hands for a minute, and then he, well, he gave us each something."

"Adam!"

He jumped at the tone of voice; she could squeeze a lot of expression into his name. Years of practice. She could also squeeze a lot into other forms of expression, and he was less fond of those: Matriarch's privilege, and one that their mother had practiced more often on Margret than on her brother. He pulled something from the folds of his shirt. It was pale, flat clay, whitened by heat, shaped like the undetailed upper half of a face. A mask.

"It is not a god's magic; we would know it. Both of us have studied the antiquities, but where you have chosen to remain in the South, I have traveled. Bluntly, I have touched the working of the Northern 'gods,' and I recognize the feel of their power.

"If this were the work of the Lord of Night himself, it would chill us; his work could not pass beneath our hands so disguised. It is not in his nature; it is not in ours."

"Mikalis, what you've said—"

"I know."

"We must speak with Cortano."

"Indeed," a third voice said quietly.

Both men turned at once. They were seated, but before they could leave mats and sparse cushions, the Sword's Edge lifted a hand, silently negating the need for the gesture his rank demanded. "What have you discovered?"

Mikalis replied, speaking smoothly. Smoothly, Sendari thought, and with vastly less comfort. Sendari understood why; it was risky to say that one knew anything—anything at all—about Cortano's power.

"Ah." Cortano's expression was unreadable. In another man, that would have been a bad sign; Cortano was often unreadable. "It happens, gentlemen, that your discovery is relevant to . . . current events."

"You have news," Sendari said. Not a question.

"Perceptive."

"Is any of it welcome?"

"Be the judge, Sendari. We now have no choice. Not only must we understand the magic the masks are part of, but we must also be able to counter their power."

"Counter it?" Mikalis interrupted, hands curling into tightening fists. "But—"

"Two headless bodies were found in the Tor Leonne yesterday. They had been disposed of carelessly, and perhaps too casually. The heads, we did not find; nor could we find markings or rings of any sort that would give us a clear indication of who those men were."

"Not serafs, then."

"No. We assumed that someone would eventually lodge an inquiry or complaint."

"And there have been none?"

"No. It had only been a day, judging by the condition of the bodies themselves. But the Tyr'agar is a man of . . . instinct. He had the bodies brought to the Sword of Knowledge, and he demanded answers."

"From headless corpses?"

"Indeed."

"You found them."

Cortano's brow rose a half inch. Sendari cursed himself inwardly. He was usually far, far more politic than this. Far better able to hide the extent of his knowledge of the abilities of the other Widan.

Diora. Here, where he could least afford it, weakness.

"We found answers, yes."

Sendari did not speak, smoothing the lines of his face into neutrality, into the safeness of silence instead.

"The Radann have been sent out. The Hand of God."

It took Sendari a moment, a long one, before the words made any sense at all.

Mikalis di'Arretta, however, did not understand the exchange, and he was not so well-trained or well-schooled that he knew better than to reveal his ignorance by asking. "Why?"

"Assume that we were able to put face, and therefore identity, to the bodies in question. There had been no inquiries—and there would likely be none for some time—because the two men who belonged to those bodies were demonstrably not dead."

"My apologies, Sword's Edge, but I do not understand."

The Sword's Edge gestured; magic's fine arc lit hands that were rarely exposed to the Lord's glare with a glow that was both white and violet. A cloud rose in the near-airless room, sparking and struggling as if seeking a life of its own.

They waited; as folds of billowing light coalesced at the cloud's heart, they were given the beginning of an answer to Mikalis' question. Two men stood, arms folded, expressions both wary and anticipatory. They were not tall men, but not short either; they had dark hair and the beards of the clans, but their manner of dress put them near the bottom of the clan heirarchy.

Sendari recognized them at once. The maskmakers.

"They were not dead?"

"No, indeed. They have been working, at *our* request, on the masks that were to replace those given us by the Shining Court."

"And the Radann?"

"We have not received word, but I expect it shortly."

"You suspect—"

"Yes."

CHAPTER TWENTY-ONE

427 AA
Stone Deepings

She woke with a start to the sound of horns.

She was tired of waking that way; stumbling from the darkness of sleep and the certainty of nightmare into a waking world that was distinctly not better.

Avandar was at her side before she had left all of nightmare behind. His face, in the constant gloom of star-broken night, was pale. "Calliastra," he said quietly, "is gone."

That should have been good news. Jewel's lips had started up in the reflex of a smile before they froze there, stupidly.

The horns, dirgelike and loud, gave meaning to the phrase *shattered silence*. Avandar did not glance up; did not so much as look in the direction that she thought the sound came from. She did. And then she turned, as the first notes were answered, in the distance, by a second set, by a third. At her back, the wind howled, and above it, carried by it, she heard the frenetic growling of stone: Gargoyle.

She knew, then.

"Jewel?"

"What would scare Calliastra off?" Jewel asked softly, in the momentary lull between the rise and fall of the horns' voices.

"Very little," was his quiet reply. "She has . . . angered many in her time, but is proof against almost any retribution."

"And that *almost* would be?"

"She would not tempt the wrath of her father."

"Okay . . . let's try for the less obvious. As in, someone *I* wouldn't know." She matched his silence for a moment, and then said, "Avandar, what do the horns mean?"

He closed his eyes. "I would never have brought you here," he said quietly, "had I known what you would meet on this road."

"Tell me."

"Tell *you?*" He laughed, the laughter in time with the strongest of the horn calls. "Jewel, of the many I have lost to this road, a handful have met one of the Firstborn. You have met two: Calliastra and Corallonne. I can protect you from Calliastra, and to my knowledge, excepting only situations in which her gardens are threatened, Corallonne sheds no blood that is not her own.

"But even I have not met what I fear you are about to on this road."

"Avandar—"

"They call her Arianne, the Winter Queen."

"That's what I was afraid of."

His turn to look nonplussed.

"I met the Winter King, remember?" She lifted her head. "Why all the horns?"

"The horns characteristically mean two things. She is on the trail in a Hunt or she is gathering her host. She does not hunt—she cannot now that the ways are closed—except at the height of Scarran, the Old Winter, when her power is at its peak."

"When is Scarran?"

"By Weston reckoning? The fourth Motherday of the month of Scaral."

"The twenty-second of Scaral. Why?"

"In the lore of the heavens," he replied, in the tone that indicated she already had the information she was asking for if she wasn't too lazy to think about it, "it would be the shortest day of the year, or conversely—"

"The longest night. I get it. Can I assume it's not—"

"You can assume nothing within the depths of the Deepings, but the Stone Deepings are the least treacherous that way. I do not believe, however, that it is Scarran."

"Which means she's gathering her host."

"Which means, indeed, she is gathering her host."

Jewel looked down to the road that lay beneath her feet, broken by rock and bracketed on either side by the faces of sheer cliff dusted with snow and ice. "Tell me," she said softly, "that there's another way through here."

"There is another way through here," he responded obediently.

"Good."

"But if you can hear her horns, she will not be taking it."

"What?"

"She is summoning the host," he replied, staring into the darkness, "to *this* road, or you would not hear her at all." He turned, having absorbed that darkness into the core of his eyes, until the darkness seemed to be all that they were. "Why you?" he asked her.

She stepped back.

Stand your ground, her Oma's voice said, snapping like a whip's lash.

Oh, right, Jewel replied, sarcasm asserting itself. *What's the worst he can do?*

He stepped into the space she defined as her own, and, taking about half a second for deliberate thought, she slapped him. Hard.

It was almost worth the look on his face.

Reality reasserted itself; he was ashen, and the smile he offered her was the grimmest of the limited set he used. "I would never have thought," he said softly, "that you possessed so much power. A pity. In times gone by, that power would have saved your life, and more; you might have stood shoulder to shoulder with the men who ruled the only human citadels to stand against the power of the gods and survive their hubris unchanged.

"You will, of course, never realize that potential in these diminished times."

I'm going to slap him again, Jewel thought, compressing her lips into a thin line. *Arrogant sonofabitch.*

She heard her Oma's grim laugh. *He won't let it by, this time. He's not your servant, whatever else he's promised. Don't cross that line, Na'jay; he is far older, and far more accomplished in those particular games, when he cares to play them.*

Games? she thought. But she held her hand.

16th of Scaral, 427 AA
Tor Leonne

The dwelling was humble. In appearance, it was poorly kept; the mud clay that formed and protected the outer wall had cracked and crumbled from years of poor care. Odd, that; one would expect men who worked with their hands, who worked, in fact, with clays and muds, to keep their domicile in a fit state. But it was not, in the end, the cracks in the worn walls that caught his attention; it was what they surrounded. A door.

Doors such as this—heavy, solid wood—were rare; they were

found in the studies of most of the Sword of Knowledge; they graced the shrine of the Sun Sword; they graced the private entrances of the palace and the temple of the Radann. But they seldom graced the dwellings of poor clansmen, who lived packed cheek by jowl in crowded, small places. No, the heavy, colorful hangings woven—usually with a claim to clan's colors—by low-born women were the norm.

The Radann kai el'Sol, unattended by the usual servitors who performed—as free men—the essential duties of a seraf in the Lord's name, stepped forward. Lifted his hand to knock.

Light flashed over the entire surface of his hand, like a thin sheen of water across the skin of a man newly risen from the Lake. Heat. He did not cry out.

None of the men who watched did.

"Kai el'Sol," Marakas par el'Sol said softly. It was a question.

"Yes," Peder replied, dropping his hand to the hilt of his sword. *Saval* was hot to the touch. He looked down; frowned, looked back up at the door—"

And dived out of the thin, flat-dirt road.

The door followed, thrown off its hinges with enough force it appeared, for long seconds, to take flight. In the distance, he heard a crash, a scream, another scream. None of that mattered.

Because although the door was gone, its frame was not empty.

"Did you think," the creature who filled it said, "I wouldn't notice your stench?"

"There are four faces," the Serra Teresa said, repeating an obvious fact. "Kallandras, where did these masks come from?"

"They were distributed in the Tor Leonne," he said quietly, "by men who purported to serve the Tyr'agar."

"Purported?"

"I heard the voice," he replied softly. "I think the Tyr'agar's allies—if they are allies at all—work without his permission. It was a single day, perhaps two, and few enough of the masks were given to their intended bearers before the distribution was stopped completely."

"Ah." Teresa held up the finest, and the simplest, of the four, searching for moonlight through the holes meant to surround the eyes. "Four faces. Four principles. Yollana, could they be somehow elemental?"

"You are . . . learned for a clansman."

"Indeed. And I had a fine, if somewhat brusque, teacher."

The Matriarch shrugged. "I've thought about it. It seems to me that they'd more likely represent the four faces of mortality."

"The four?"

"Birth. Life. Death."

"I apologize; I am slow. The fourth?"

"The soul itself, fully freed. Wind. The most dangerous breeze blows on the Festival Night. You've heard it."

"I have seen deaths on Festival Night before."

"And you've not seen the wildness that follows them? The stir of the wind, the restless movement of fire, the shuddering of earth?"

The Serra's fine brow rose delicately. "I have felt none of these things."

"Then the death you saw took place in some other city," the older woman replied. She rose, stumbled, and accepted Kallandras' help as if it were a natural occurrence.

"This city has significance?"

Yollana's eyes flickered like fire as they met Margret's.

"We are in the heart's circle," Margret said softly.

"And we are accompanied by two strangers; two who are not, and will not be, of the blood."

Margret shrugged.

"You're too casual." Yollana's frown was a momentary heat in the lines of her face. "You'll make mistakes."

"I am not the one who invited them."

"You drew the circle, Matriarch."

"And I should decide. I know. You've made this clear." She lifted her head. Met the Serra's gaze. Turned slightly and met the gaze of the man who stood watch beside her. Kallandras of Senniel. Kallandras of the North. Kallandras of the Lady. Against her will, she thought him handsome, but in a cold, cold way.

"Trust them." Her voice. Her words. "And trust me," she added, humor creeping into the words just enough to rob them of gravity. "I haven't heard this either."

"I know," the Havallan Matriarch replied gravely.

There was blood on the creature's hands; blood across the breadth of his chest. But both hands and chest looked human in appearance.

It was the face that made a mockery of humanity. Eyes were in the right place, but they were as black as the ebony that adorned the sheaths of fine swords or the kohl that emphasized the eyes of fine Serras.

"You are such pathetic fools," the creature said, his voice the storm's voice. "Did you think to stand against the will of the Shining Court? You will learn better, in time." It was not the display of teeth—and there were many—that was disturbing; it was the expression itself. The smile that spread across his face grew beyond the simple boundaries of his almost human appearance. "You are too late. The masks are gone."

Peder kai el'Sol smiled; it was an expression the Lord would have recognized. And approved of. "We did not come here for masks."

"Oh?"

He lifted *Saval.* "We came here for you." At his back, Marakas, Samadar, and Samiel fanned out.

"I'm sorry to disappoint you, but I am summoned to the Court, and I—unlike your master—know better than to disobey."

Shadows engulfed him in an instant, defying day and day's light. Defying natural darkness.

He was gone.

"There is, well, there was, a belief that the four elements and the four faces of mortality were somehow linked. It is an old belief, and sadly I have seen it transcribed exactly twice, both times in a language that was dead before the *Voyanne* was born."

"And when did you learn how to read at all, never mind a dead tongue?"

"You sound like your mother," Yollana replied. "But she eventually stopped whining and started studying as well. It's an art that even the clansmen practice on occasion. Do you want the story or not?"

"I want the story more than I want the nagging."

"Then don't interrupt me. Birth was tied to the element of water. Life to the element of earth. Death to the element of fire. And the spirit, of course, to the element of air."

The Serra was silent. She still handled the mask with care. "That would make sense, Yollana. And yet . . ." She turned the ivory face over, seeking its interior. It told her nothing, of course. Very much like the people of the Dominion themselves. "You have not told me why you feel that a death in *this* city on the night of the Festival Moon would usher in the wildness."

"Perhaps," Kallandras of Senniel said, "it is better not to speak

of it at all." He might have added more, but something about the
quality of her silence enjoined him to be silent himself.

She was listening.

Mikalis was pale. Pale as moonlight, as if the Lady's grace had
descended, and he had consumed, and been consumed, by her.
"Sword's Edge," he said, after a few minutes of silence, awkward
and crowded with the unsaid, had passed.

"Yes?"

"I have not—I think it—You—"

Cortano was a patient man, in a fashion. He sought power, but
in all else was as much unlike Alesso di'Marente as a powerful
man could be. He was also less merciful.

"I do not mean to criticize your choices," Mikalis managed to
say at last.

"No. You have always been wise. Wise enough, in fact, to surprise us all by surviving the test of the Sword." It was a threat.
All three men in the uncomfortable and well-protected room
understood that.

"The woman you held captive—the woman you tortured—we
need her."

"I doubt that there will be much of her left if the *Kialli* have
chosen to question her; they take poorly to failure, and they are
not as patient as I. Nor as careful."

"She is not without power."

"She was without power here."

"You are not *Kialli.*"

"Enough," Cortano said. An edge of irritation lined the single
word, sharpening it.

Mikalis continued anyway. "We need the Voyani."

"And their rustic, half-fraudulent magics will accomplish what
the Sword of Knowledge cannot?"

Tread carefully, Mikalis. Sendari was silent, weighing the cost
of speech.

Or he should have been gone. That much was clear from the
mild consternation that rippled his ebony brow. But the shadows
parted like harem silk, exposing him.

Saval was in the hands of the kai el'Sol. Peder could hear—as
if at the edge of a conversation—something that sounded like
words; they were cold as steel in shadow.

"Oh, very clever," the creature said. The shadows that had surrounded his body did not disperse; they grew dense with shape, heavy with gathering power. In just such a way, the clouds gathered water and lightning before the storm. "We were told that you would not be a threat. Luckily, no one in the Court trusts the word of the man who holds your leash."

"No one in the Court," Marakas par el'Sol said unexpectedly, "trusts anyone else in the Court."

"I will grant you that, mortal. Accept it; I will grant you nothing else, no matter how hard you plead."

The words were so slow, so languid and sensuous, that Peder kai el'Sol barely had time to parry the claws that came within a fine silk's thickness of the middle of his chest.

His armor would bear the scar in his stead.

The Serra Teresa looked past Margret, past Yollana; Ramdan knelt at her side and unstoppered an entirely unremarkable waterskin, offering it to her. She drank from it slowly, gathering her words as the sky paled above them, never taking her eyes from Kallandras.

Kallandras of Senniel College.

"No," he said at last, waiting patiently for the question until it became clear she would not ask it. "Whatever it is you hear, or think you hear, Serra Teresa, it is not a voice that speaks to me."

"Perhaps," she replied gravely, "that is because you do not carry the mask."

"I have carried them."

She held out one ivory hand; he could hardly tell where the line of her skin ended and the line of the mask began. The gesture, perfectly graceful, was a command; she was a woman of the Dominion, and as one, she had learned the fine art of giving a command that involved no words.

He, as a visitor and a bard in a strange land, had mastered the art of accepting such commands with as much grace as they were given. Thus was the surface of etiquette unperturbed.

He took the mask from her hand. Held it in his own, turning it, front to back, back to front. There was something odd about the feel of the clay beneath his fingers, but he had grown accustomed to that strangeness in these masks. He waited a moment.

Then he knelt, still circled by fire and allies, against the flattened grass.

"Kallandras?"

His eyelids fell, as curtains might, shutting out the world and

its visual detail. That left the subtle senses: scent, the muskiness
of sweat, the sweet burning of the Matriarch's fire, the faint but
unmistakeable aroma of Lady's oil and wine; touch, the cold,
hard curve of clay in his palm and beneath his fingers as they
traversed half a face. He had touched corpses before. He knew
death when he felt it.

But touch, scent, sight—these were the senses that his training had honed into weapons. Hearing, he had been born with.
Lady's gift.

He listened.

"I am sorry, Serra Teresa, but I hear . . . nothing. Nothing at
all out of the ordinary."

"I . . . see."

Then, deliberately, coldly, he lifted the mask to his brow.

The Serra Teresa inhaled sharply; Yollana shouted his name as
if it were a curse, a plea, or a command. These things he heard,
but peripherally.

Stronger, much stronger than these was the pain that lanced up
his left hand in an arc of blue light, storm's light, sparking and
hissing as it burned a thin trail along the surface of his pale flesh.

But he heard it: the wind's voice. *Mine,* it said.

It did not speak to him.

The creature was canny. Unlike the demon named *Telkar*—
first kill—he knew their worth as enemies; he used the door and
the short stone hall behind it to narrow the fight. One man might
stand against him with ease; two, if they were careful and understood each other's combat style well enough to take advantage of
the slender space.

The Radann were not sword-dancers; they were warriors; they
kept their skills to themselves.

Peder kai el'Sol stepped forward. *Saval* burned, and he burned
with it. The claws of the creature struck out; he parried the hand.
The strike of demon flesh against steel was oddly musical. His
arm shook with the strength of the clash.

Hands shook with something more.

He had desired power. That was truth. He accepted it. Accepted
that that desire had bent and shaped him until it had become the
definition by which all men were judged.

All men.

Saval's light was fire. He held it.

The creature struck again; both hands moving in a blur of ebony, claws extending so far they looked like slender, long daggers. Hard to parry them all; the shadow devoured surcoat, scratched armor. The armor was strong; it had saved his life a handful of times before this, when strength had been contested. When power—Lord's power—had been proved.

At his back, he could feel them: Samadar, Samiel, Marakas. Men chosen by a different leader. They stayed their ground and bore witness; he knew that no matter what the outcome of this fight, they would not flee. *This* was the purpose of the Radann.

Had he never seen it?

Saval's intensity should have scored his vision; it was brighter, stronger light than the Lord's own. But it left no trail across his eyes; it illuminated.

Fredero kai el'Sol had put his hand into the heart of the Lord's fire.

He, of all men, had known the Lord's law.

Power. Yes. Power . . .

He had chosen to divest himself of power because it was the only way to wake them—but their waking had been slow.

Radann Peder *kai* el'Sol fought like a man possessed. It was the only way to repay his debt to the man he would think of, for the rest of his life, as *the* kai el'Sol. He had incurred that debt willingly, but without the knowledge of just how much his part in the death would sting, would cut.

Had he let it, the wind would have torn the mask from his hands and shattered it against distant rock. The scent and taste of Cenera Pass, the only way through the rough, deadly chill of the Menoran mountain chain, overpowered the stillness of the heartland's languid night.

But he had not summoned the wind; he had not offered it his edged and reluctant alliance. Here, he was master. The summer returned.

"You take a risk, Bard." Yollana's clipped words were like blows; he heard the anger deepen with every syllable. She brought a smile to his lips, a rare one: it was genuine.

"There is something to what you say," he agreed, turning his attention to the Serra Teresa, who had not moved a muscle or spoken a word since he had lifted the mask to his face. She relaxed as he spoke.

The mask in his hand was cool as desert night. He turned it over. Looked up.

"Adam," he said.

The boy nodded.

"You said they had resumed distribution of these masks?"

He nodded again. His hair fell over his eyes and he lifted a hand to push it back, a gesture very much like Margret's. It made Kallandras wonder, perhaps for the first time, how old Margret actually was; the sun had weathered her skin, the road had toughened it. No Matriarch ever looked young.

"Yollana, Margret, Serra Teresa." He rose. Bowed.

"What is it?" the oldest of the women said, sharp as a dagger's edge. "Do you know what they do? Do you know what their purpose is?"

"No. But I know," he added softly, "what night they will be worn on."

"The Lady's Night."

"Yes. And it is a night that has no significance in the Empire for anyone but the student of antiquities. The twenty-second day of Scaral, the shortest day of the year, was once called *Scarran*. The Dark Conjunction."

"We know of it," Yollana replied, her words so tight he wasn't certain if the "we" had anything to do with present company. Judging by Margret's frown, he thought not.

"Yollana, I am not Widan; I am not Voyani Matriarch; I am not Northern mage. But I am not a fool; these masks number in the hundreds. They have been distributed to the people of the Tor Leonne, and try as he might, the General will not be able to retrieve them all before the night of the Festival Moon. Whatever they do, whatever they *will* do, they will do it at a time when the ancient magics are strongest, and the protections between our lands and older ones weakest." He set the mask against the silks, keeping it, as the Voyani did, from touching the earth beneath them.

"I have walked the Winter road," he said. "I know what power it holds. And if you feel that a death on the Festival Night brings its own wilderness with it, we must assume that one of the conjunctions between our world and the old one is someplace within the Tor itself."

She surprised him, then. She lifted her hands in a circular motion, completing a gesture that was said to protect the soul from the howling winds.

"Margret," she said, turning to the younger Matriarch, "we must speak."

Margret waited. So did everyone else, with the exception of Kallandras, who rose.

A minute passed before Yollana snorted. "What was I thinking? Margret, you've yet to train your people, and I don't have time for idle chatter. That," she said curtly, "was a hint. Let me make it clearer: Everyone else, leave *now*."

Fingers shaped like finely honed blades had drawn blood. But so, too, had a blade shaped like the curved crescent of the slender moon.

The creature summoned fire.

And fire, liked a trapped soul, writhed and twisted in his grip. "Be honored," the demon said, as he ripped the fire in half and forced it to take two shapes, sword and shield. "You will be the first of your kind that has survived for long enough to merit my sword and my standard." the demon lifted a shield made of living flame that nonetheless seemed to bear runnels the eye could recognize as a pattern.

Peder kai el'Sol nodded grimly. "It is good," he replied quietly, "to know who one's killing."

The demon snarled. "You are not so very powerful; if it weren't for your swords, you'd be *nothing*."

Truth was always the most effective weapon.

Peder stepped back into the street.

He judged correctly; the creature, bearing sword and shield, followed him into the wider corridor the buildings made of the street. Samadar stepped to Peder's left, Samiel to his right.

Marakas, healer-born, waited in grim silence at their backs. They had seen fire before. But they had never borne so many of its scars as they would this day.

Peder lifted his voice in the battle cry of the Radann. The streets were graced by blinding light, scoured by fire.

"We walked these roads," Yollana said, the intensity of her voice belying the banality of the words themselves. "We walked." She had been staring into what was left of Margret's fire, speaking the same words over and over, as if they were breath and she was drawing them.

"Yollana."

The Havallan Matriarch looked up at the sound of her name. Studied Margret's face as if Margret were suddenly a stranger.

"We walked these roads," she said at last, but before Margret could interrupt her again, continued. "When they were desert sand and desert sun, and the creatures that call themselves *Kialli* sought our destruction. We traveled from the ruins of our homes, bearing children the road—or the kin—took from us, and at last, when our numbers were far fewer than they are now, we came to this place.

"It was not just Havalla." The fire illuminated her face; Margret realized that the sun was falling only by the orange glow across Yollana's cheeks. "Arkosa came. Corrona. Lyserra. Drawn here, to a place that we would never willingly have approached when we sat in our seats of power." She shuddered. "This is an old tale, Margret, and you are unblooded."

Margret snorted. "I had my first courses when you could still bear children."

"Aye. But that is not the meaning of blooded to the Matriarchs, and you will come to understand, to your sorrow, what it *does* mean." The fire absorbed her vision, she had none left for Margret. "We came to a place the demons would not travel to easily. We came seeking either death or salvation. It was . . . it was long ago. An old story." But her hands opened and closed convulsively as she spoke. Margret had seen dying men; they had shuddered in just such a fashion.

"Yollana—"

"I know. People dwelled here." She turned her head. "The Lady dwelled here."

"The Lady?"

"The Lady," Yollana repeated faintly. "And because we fought Her enemy, because we brought them to Her cohort and She was . . . amused . . . by the battle that resulted, She took only a little from us for our trespass, and She granted us . . . Her miracle."

"She saved our families?"

"Oh, yes," Yollana continued distantly. The fire, it appeared, had become more and more compelling.

"Why are you telling me this?" But Margret felt it; the chill of knowledge. She suddenly thought she understood why Yollana was so fascinated by the fire: It offered warmth. "It was here."

For the first time since she'd begun speaking, Yollana lifted her gaze. "Yes."

"In Raverra." *She granted us Her miracle.* "No. Upon the plateau."

"Yes. The Tor Leonne was built around the Lady's jewel. The Lake itself. It was a gift, of sorts. She created the Lake from the blood of Her people. And ours. We had a mutual enemy. You know the law: the enemy of our enemy." Darkness, shadows, age. All pulled at the lines of Yollana's face, shrouding it in mysteries that Margret had not yet begun to approach. "We respected the Lake. The Tor itself was built long after the war was both won and lost, and the roads were closed."

"Yollana—"

"But closed or no, when a death is offered Her here, She feels it."

"But, Yollana, the clansmen say—"

"What? That the Lake was made for Leonne? Leonne was a pup with gift and vision, no more. He was shown the Lake's secret because he was the leader who could unite the clans against the *Allasakari*. The servants of the *enemy*. Of the Lady. Of the Voyani." She snorted. "He was a clansman. He made it his own, of course. Lake *and* myth."

Margret let the words take root, turning them over as if they were physical objects. "I don't understand."

"Of course you don't understand," Yollana replied irritably. "Which part?"

"If summoning the Lady saved us the first time, why would the *Kialli* risk summoning Her again?"

"*Assuming* the Lady saved us the first time." Which meant, of course, that she didn't know. Yollana rose. "Get Kallandras." The words hung between them a moment before she had the grace to add, "Matriarch."

The Lord had no use for trophies; they were as useful to Him as clothing. But men often took trophies when their victories were costly or grim. A reminder, not of supremacy, but of survival.

The Radann understood why the taking of trophies counted so little with the Lord: the battles in which survival was noteworthy were the very battles that made trophy taking impossible. The *Kialli* left no bodies.

At least, Peder thought grimly as he stepped through the ruined doorway of what had once been a maskmaker's home, no bodies of their own. The Radann began their inspection of the creature's living quarters.

He was silent. He bore witness.

But he thought, as he forced distance to come between what he saw and his reaction, that although war was indiscriminate and left seraf and warrior alike at its back, there was a special horror about the death of children.

Especially so long and so messy a death.

Marakas par el'Sol was white. He had long been called the weakest of the Hand of God; it was easy, witnessing the strength of his reaction, to understand why. He was physically sick. Visibly. His body shook with the force of his emotion.

He did not speak. His silence was joined as they walked from room to room. The bodies they found were not always whole; Peder privately thought the creature had eaten parts of its dead, although it was widely believed demons had no need to eat.

It was Samadar who broke their silence; Samadar, oldest and arguably wisest of the four.

"The masks?" he asked quietly.

If there had ever been masks in this slaughterhouse, they were gone.

"It is a time of change."

The Serra Teresa sat beneath the nearly full moon, her voice as soft, as perfect in cadence, as it had been in the harem of her oldest brother, and her father before him. She sat upon grass beneath the open sky, the soft drape of a loose shirt all the finery she would be allowed upon the road she'd chosen.

But at least here, she could loose the bindings across her breasts.

Ramdan, as always, was there before she had begun her task. She lifted her arms, and he helped her raise the shirt, taking care to keep the folds of silk from her hair. It was habit, not necessity, that guided that action.

"This will be a different life," she said softly. It was as much a plea as she could make.

He put his hands upon her shoulders and massaged muscles that were stiff with the tension of both riding and disquiet. His answer.

The sun paled the sky; the moon's light dimmed; the shadows—all but those cast by Teresa and the only man she had ever, and could ever, completely trust—withdrew. She wanted to know what he was thinking; she had often wanted to know what he was thinking.

But that conversation was not for a Serra and a seraf, and she knew that even if she could offer him his freedom, he would not take it. He was a seraf at heart: the Lady's chosen seraf, the man whose service was perfect.

He surprised her, as he sometimes did. "The Lady," he said quietly, "has been kind to me. She has given me a master who makes a seraf's life an honor, not a burden."

Morning, the edge of it so wide Sendari and Mikalis di'Arretta could ignore its slow arrival, for its arrival meant the lessening of their time by one precious day.

The sun was an unwelcome sight, but it was glorious nonetheless. Had they been successful, had they been closer to understanding the scope, or the nature, of the spell the masks were a part of, neither man would have noticed; they were Widan after all.

But if they did not have success, they would take a moment to have beauty, to find some small solace in the fact that the sun rose at all.

CHAPTER TWENTY-TWO

The sun was low, but it was present; the Lord, in pursuit of the Lady, had given in to gaudy display. Only at dawn and at dusk, when the Lady bore witness, did He clothe Himself in colors: radiant pinks, deep oranges, pale purples. The Lady was unimpressed, or so the story went, but this one evening, dusk seemed to last forever, lingering like the grains of sand that cling to an hourglass.

The day had been long, and only partially fruitful.

His cerdan, spread thinly through the city streets, were searching for the masks that had been the gift of the Shining Court. Twice now, the Court had undermined his efforts to keep the masks where they might be safe.

There would be no third time. Safe or no, he had made the decision to have them destroyed. The masks were, in Cortano's estimation—and in this, the Tyr'agar trusted the Sword's Edge—Ishavriel's purview; they served the kinlord's ends, and not his Lord's.

Or so Alesso di'Alesso now hoped.

Choose caution when dealing with the masks. You do not wish to offend the Lord of the Shining Court.

He will be offended, in time.

He will be offended, Cortano had replied, unruffled by the heat of Alesso's tone, *in a time of our choosing, when our allies have substantially changed. Be wary of forcing His hand; it may be that the masks serve that goal, and no more. Ishavriel is cunning.*

Does it matter? A man is cautious as circumstances dictate, and I have been cautious. I will not be fearful.

He would destroy the masks. If they could be found.

He sat by the Lake's edge, upon the Pavilion of the Dawn,

the cushions beneath him a scattered fan of colors that matched the grace of dawn's light; about him, nattering like cast-off harem wives, the peripheral members of the court he had risked all to rule.

They, like the cushions beneath him, were brilliant in their display. Cool, calm, arrogant, they had the demeanor of men who knew they lacked power, but desired it nonetheless. Such men as these did not define the Tyr, but they bolstered him, for by their sycophantic behavior, they showed others where true power lay.

The waters of the Tor Leonne were legend. They were also a weapon. At the Radann kai el'Sol's suggestion, he had begun to serve the water to *all* of his guests, great and small. Only one guest had refused to drink. Not even the ashes of his clothing remained, and the Shining Court had one less spy in the Annagarian court. Satisfying, that; so little else was.

Other information had filtered in, where the masks had proved elusive. The most telling, of course, was this: No other city had been so gifted with the work of *Kialli* craftsmen. The masks had come to the Tor alone.

There were two possible reasons to account for this lack. The first, and least likely, was that the distribution of such masks required the cooperation of the Tyr or Tor who ruled the city, and the *Kialli* could be certain of no such cooperation.

The second, and more likely, was that the Tor Leonne itself was significant.

A seraf appeared, noticeable as the flickering of a shadow that the light couldn't quite cast, and refilled his goblet. He allowed this, but lifted a hand when the seraf offered—by gesture alone—the wide, colorful fans that were used to add movement to the stillness of humid air. The serafs disappeared, reappearing at the side of the dignitaries who had chosen to grace the pavilion. Had any of them been tolerable, Alesso would not have sought the special isolation that comes only within a crowd.

"There are no women here." The words drifted to him. Had another man spoken them, he would have been certain they were meant to be heard. This, this was just laziness, stupidity, or the very fine wine that was imbibed freely by men whose means might otherwise have forced them to abstinence.

No women. No grave and graceful presence, none of the cool, soft beauty that were the marks of a great man's harem. *I have had no time,* he thought, rehearsing the argument. It was a poor rehearsal, but men in power did not require perfection in such minor matters. Less minor was the fact that he had been offered concubines by any of the great clans, and had demurred.

He waited, he told them, for a wife who could see to the details of such a portion of his life; war was the only mistress he chose to dally with at the moment.

Had it amused the offerers? Jarrani kai di'Lorenza, certainly. His kai, Hectore, certainly not. Perhaps they knew the wife he waited on. And he did not wish to think of that here; war was the more comfortable of the two.

He therefore turned back to war, to the waters of the Lake itself. Because the *Kialli* defined arrogance, and they had no use for human titles, human geography. They would therefore not consider the Tor Leonne significant because it was the seat of power in the Dominion; that title counted for far too little.

No; there was only one thing of significance in the Tor, but that one thing made the Tor unique.

They chose my city, he thought, his gaze absorbed by the beauty of light broken by water, its harshness softened only by the round, white flowers of the lilies that seemed to have, and know, no season.

Of course.

He rose; at once, a dozen men rose as well; they cast unpleasant shadows against exposed wood grain and silk. "Gentlemen," he said softly. "The Lord's face has changed; I am called. Please continue without me; I will find you by the Lake at the platform of the Lord." He did not bow; it was not required, and the gesture no longer came naturally to him. So soon, he had excised it from his life.

He sought the man whose friendship—inexplicable and unquestioned—had seen him from captaincy to Tyr. He found him. There was really only one place that could contain him at the moment.

But the Sword of Knowledge had drawn blood in the past few days; Sendari's face looked as if it had never been graced by sun's light. His back was bent; his knees and feet were pressed into the carefully cultivated moss that adorned the rock gardens. He cast a long shadow; in it, another man toiled at his side, mixing something in a small urn. Mikalis di'Arretta. The Sword's Edge was nowhere in sight.

A warrior could not be approached by a man—any man—without being aware of his presence; even if he chose not to acknowledge the visitor, little signs of his sudden attention were evident to one who knew how to look. A slight stiffening of back, a straightening in the line of shoulder, a minute change in the tilt of chin.

These two were not, and had never been, warriors. Not until his shadow passed over the face of the closest man did one frown and look up.

Sendari di'Marano squinted at the sun's edge, lifting a hand to his eyes. It was not a particularly graceful movement; certainly not a powerful one. Alesso found it disturbing; he had seldom seen Sendari look so much at the mercy of age as he did at this moment.

"You need the Lady's water," he said carelessly, speaking as one spoke not only to friend but to blood.

"And you," Sendari replied, his eyes narrowing enough to hint at irritation, "need answers. Shall we sacrifice your needs for our own?"

Alesso laughed. "Well put, old friend."

If possible, Sendari's eyes narrowed further. He put a hand on Mikalis di'Arretta's shoulder; the mage started and looked up. Alesso seldom observed the Widan at work; it still surprised him that anyone could be so firmly entrenched in their study that they could not be moved without physical contact.

It was amusing to see the Widan's eyes grow larger as he all but dropped the slender pestle in his hands. He found the proper posture quickly enough, his mortification adding to the length and depth of his bow.

Sendari offered the gesture without the mortification—observing form for the Widan's sake, and not the Tyr'agar's. In privacy, between these two men, gestures of formality were used as rebukes. In public, not even children failed to observe protocol in the presence of their fathers, if their fathers were men of power and influence; it demeaned the father.

"I believe," Alesso said quietly, when both men had risen, "our concentration has been too narrow."

"Oh?"

"We still do not understand the purpose of the masks." The question was in the words; Sendari heard it and shook his head. "But let us understand their target instead."

Both men frowned, and the frown was similar; it lent a furrow to brow and a sudden, particular absence to expression. They glanced at each other. Glanced at the mask. Glanced at the urn. There was a delicate ceremony in the silence of their questions.

Surprisingly enough, it was Mikalis who broke it.

"Need there be a target?"

Alesso frowned.

"We are dealing with the *Kialli,* and if the Voyani lore is correct—if our own lore is correct—the amusement of death and confusion is a goal in and of itself."

"If they sought merely death and confusion, they would have an easier time of it in the small villages of lesser Tors. They have chosen the Tor Leonne."

"Indeed," Sendari said, speaking for the first time. "I would therefore add humiliation and assertion of the superiority of their power to Mikalis' goal."

His tone of voice implied all previous discussions. "Sendari," Alesso said quietly, "seek the Lady's grace this eve."

"Our research—"

"Will keep."

Silence. Then, "Have you come to aid us?"

"No. Nor to interfere. I come to confer. If we assume that the *Kialli* are intelligent—"

"Alesso—"

"There are two things within the Tor Leonne that make it special." He waited a moment.

Mikalis frowned.

Sendari said, stiffly, "The Lady's Lake."

"Yes." Alesso smiled; it was brief, but the sun's light did not extinguish it. "And the Sun Sword."

"Their action can have no bearing on the Sword itself." Mikalis spoke with the flat tone of absolute certainty.

"They could destroy it."

"They could not destroy it without aid. It was made to stand against them. The Widan, working in concert, would have trouble destroying that blade." His tone implied that they would fail for their trouble.

"Very well, Widan. I accept the knowledge you offer." He waited. The Widan exchanged another glance.

"The Lake," Sendari said at last.

Mikalis lifted the mask on the mat at his feet and brought it up, clutching the chin in a half-fist of frustration. But he did not argue with the two words; once spoken, they had the weight of the self-evident.

"The Lake is an artifact of the Lady," Mikalis added gravely, "and one of the few proofs of Her existence. They dare not even touch the water; how are they then to harm it?"

"Bend your thought to that task," the General replied. "Because if we cannot stop the use of the masks—and it appears we will be denied that ability—we may well stop their effective use. If the water *can* be harmed, let us guard it."

"Elena."

She stiffened. She didn't need to stand or turn to know who spoke. She did neither. She had had trouble even meeting his eyes since he'd tried to steal what Margret had forbidden him.

No, be honest, Elena. Since she'd flogged him. If she closed her eyes for longer than a blink, she could see the stretch of his back broken by leather thong and rising blood; could see where he would scar.

Could see, if she pulled back, the shaking hand that drove the whip. It was the only hint of weakness Margret had shown, and it was one that Elena was fairly certain no one else had been close enough to catch.

Lady, the cost of it.

"Elena, we need to talk."

"We need," she said, grunting as she heaved the sack up and over deceptively strong shoulders, "to feed our own."

"That's not your job. You're the heir, now."

"That never stopped Margret from working her fingers to the bone."

"Margret's not Evallen."

"Not yet, she's not," Elena snapped back, "but she's working on it."

She took a step. Two.

Then the bag of ground corn meal wasn't the only thing on her shoulder.

"Nicu," she said, through clenched teeth, "remove your hand, or I'll do it for you."

His fingers tightened, a reminder that he was the stronger of the two. She wondered who needed the reminder more: herself or Nicu. The flogging had taken something from him. She wasn't certain how desperate he was to get it back.

But she was certain she wasn't going to be the way he did it.

"Elena," he said, changing tactics. His hand fell away, and his

voice developed that ... dimple, that fold in the middle of her name that fell just short of whine or plea.

She tightened her grip on the heavy sack and turned to face him. "What?"

"We need to talk."

"So talk."

"Not—not here."

"Nicu, you're starving our children. What do we need to talk about that can't wait until after dinner?"

"Everything."

She turned away. Started to walk. Remembered two things, one easy and one difficult. Easy: the fact that the sword was still in the camp. Difficult: that he was her cousin, that she had grown up with him, that once upon a time they had been closer than siblings. All those bonds, built then, still had the power to cut when struggled against.

She stopped struggling, wondering whether or not he'd've even tried to steal the sword back if she'd given him the time he'd been begging for.

She stopped wondering as quickly as she could because she didn't like the answer she was getting too close to. Nicu had always been strongest of the three. And he'd always been weakest.

"All right," she said at last. "Let me just go talk to Donatella, and I'll be back."

"Why do you want to talk to my mother?"

"*Nicu.*"

"Why?"

"Because," she said, forcing her jaw to relax although she couldn't keep the irritation from the words, "the children have to be fed."

It was women's work, the feeding of the children. The Matriarch—Evallen—said it was a natural extension of the fact that women had breasts. Men could be trusted for many things, but they were short on attention span and shorter on patience. The children *had* to be fed, or there was no Arkosa; it was one of the highest responsibilities any woman in a caravan could be given.

Elena privately thought the Matriarch crazy; the men in her life had been far more patient—with the single notable exception of Nicu—than most of the women, and far less likely to raise their hand and lash out in annoyance. But they had also been far more indulgent and therefore more likely to be late with food or angry about the waste of it. The latter was necessary, because no matter how hungry the family was, children were peculiar creatures with odd likes and dislikes and a propensity to choose play over sustenance. They had to learn to take what they were offered *when* it was offered; they had to know, as they grew older—and they did that so quickly—that any food they ate was less food for the men and women who protected them from bandits, clansmen, and Voyani raiders. To waste it was a slap in the face, and worse.

During the hungry season, men died to protect food. Because, of course, in protecting their food—and water—they were saving the lives of the children.

You didn't throw away food. Not even as a two-year-old throwing a tantrum.

"Elena?"

"Donatella." Elena dropped the sack neatly in front of the older woman's bent knees. "I hate to do this, but—"

"But I need to talk to her, Momma."

Nicu. Voice where she least liked it: behind her back, but close enough to her ear she could feel it tickle her spine.

"Nicu," she said, forgetting for a moment that she stood in front of his mother, "*go away.* I'll meet you desert-side in five minutes if I can."

"But—"

"If you don't, I'm going to feed the children. You decide."

He made a big display of drawing breath, but she could only hear it; she didn't bother to turn around. She also heard the heavy tread of his feet as he dragged and stomped them across the flat brush.

Donatella's face had taken to shadow since the flogging. She had spoken no word against the Matriarch—and she never would—but she had spoken no word *to* her either, and Elena knew it hurt Margret. She also knew Margret would swallow her sword before admitting it, and you talked about Margret's pain at your peril. Her business.

The older woman rose. Her back was more bent than Elena remembered it, but her hands were just as strong. Age wouldn't deprive her of strength, although it would probably try. She reached out for Elena's hands; caught them.

Like Margret's, these days, they were shaking.

"I'll feed the children," she said quietly. "You speak to my son."

The tone of her voice drove a dagger a hair's breadth to the side of Elena's heart. *Lady, Nicu. All this pain for a sword. Didn't you even think?*

To his mother, she said, "I will, Donatella. I will. He's not a bad boy. He's just wild with anger. Who wouldn't be? The clansmen—"

"Enough, Elena. I know my boy."

She'd thought the shaking hands were bad. "I'll talk with him," she said, backing away from the words.

Ai, Nicu, there's not enough pain in the world, you have to cause more of it? It was a graceless thought, and she tried to rid herself of it before she met him. Because he was so much like the children that she'd been about to feed: willful, easily wounded with sharp words, in need of direction. You could manipulate him into doing what he needed to do—but it was work and it took patience, and the older he got, the less patience she had with him.

And where had that led?

Broken back. Scored flesh.

He'd hurt them all.

But not half as much, not a tenth as much, Lady, not a *hundredth,* as he'd hurt them if he tried something like that again and Margret was forced to kill him.

The streets of the Tor Leonne had opened before him and closed at his back as if they were liquid and he a diver. He spoke the right words to the right guards and they nodded him through gates. Of course he spoke with a voice that was, as he was, more than it seemed, and he spoke words that they would lose to the undertow of memory almost before they'd finished listening.

He passed from gates through the various pavilions that were—finally—being richly and deftly built in the city that was closest to the Lady's heart on Festival Night.

Silks, some deep with color that seemed like it must have been set in cloth by a blend of tradition and magic, others pale with light and sun, were being hoisted up on poles to make something that would be called tenting when composed of a lesser material. Men worked, straining against both weight and time; very few of these bore seraf marks.

He lingered only a second or two at each, listening to the tenor of men's voices. Fear, but it was masked, and remote enough to be due to the orders of a more powerful man. Anger, but again muted enough to be part of the life of a man living in the Dominion.

There was no joy. No hint of the wildness that was promised on the night of the Festival Moon. He wondered, then, if any of them believed it would come to pass.

He was certain, but he understood—as they did not—that wildness could not be denied. It was as old as the Lord's gaze, as old as the Lady's full face, inevitable as dawn or dusk. Nowhere did men speak of masks.

Instead they spoke of demons.

They spoke of the Radann, the swords of the Radann, the work of the Lord. As if their words themselves were a harmony—several harmonies—to an old, well-known song, history blended with politics, past and present coming to a single, sharp edge. Someone would be cut by it; someone would bleed.

But it was enough, at the moment, to know that person would not be Kallandras of Senniel.

Not, that is, if he performed the task set for him by Yollana of the Havalla Voyani.

She had not told him what to look for. She told him little, hoarding the texture of her aged and perfect voice as if aware of how much of a gift it was. It was, of course. Nothing slipped past Yollana. Nonetheless, Kallandras knew what he sought: Corronans. Lyserrans. Men who bore the marks of the Matriarch's van. They were not easily detected among those whose feet never walked the open road.

His had. He understood the Voyani better than most men. After all, they were a people defined by lack of home, their penance for past sin.

"Not all roads," she said softly, "make Voyani."

He felt the spark of the storm touch the tips of his fingers and hover there. "No," he replied, without turning, her voice more distinctive than any vision of her face would have been, "Some roads are far harsher."

"I can't believe how much you change as you get older. You live behind your experience. You probably don't even realize how different you are. But I just saw you twenty years younger, and I wouldn't even guess you'd become who you are now. You were so angry. At me. You could be so cruel . . ."

"That any kindness seems out of character?" She was, he thought, not much past thirty. It surprised him slightly; he had not heard this much youth in her voice for long months. He turned to face her.

Her hood was down about her shoulders like a cowl, her chin framed by the depth of a blue the silks upon the pavilions he had just passed couldn't hope to match.

"You change," he said softly, "as much. More, perhaps. One is never the best judge of one's own evolution."

She snorted. At this age, shored up by the certainty of youth and the confidence of experience, she was the most open. Younger, and her anger was as great as his had been, perhaps greater for the fact that it was so aimless. Older and she had begun to delve into the mysteries, to shoulder the burden of power that would either redeem the choice that she had made at the beginning of her adult life, or prove it to be a waste and a conceit.

Here, now, she was almost beautiful.

With Evayne, now was all one had, and perhaps there was a lesson in that. "I . . . did not expect to see you."

"Oh. I thought—I thought Yollana would tell you."

"Tell me?"

"I met her for the third time tonight. She's not as intimidating when she can't walk." Her grin held warmth, self-knowledge, no fear. When she was older, she was wiser. "I thought I'd been sent to you. No, I was certain. But she was there instead."

"Unusual."

"She's—she's gifted."

"Yes."

"She said you'd left something for me?"

It was Kallandras' turn to raise a brow. "Evayne," he said gently, "the heart of the crisis is not yet upon us. I did not think to see you yet, if at all." Had she been younger, he would have chosen his words with far more care.

"Oh."

"What, exactly, was I meant to have left for you?"

"A mask."

"I . . . see. What else was I meant to have said?"

"That these were magicked in a way that you didn't understand and the Voyani didn't understand either."

"Slanted, but truthful. Go on."

"It had the right feel to it. Her words, I mean. I took the mask."

It had the right feel to it. He wanted to ask her what she meant.

But asking would remind her that she spoke of things she should not—or could not—speak of. He kept his silence.

Her eyes had that pale tint that often added a touch of coolness to an otherwise warm face. As they narrowed, he thought them very like a shade of purple steel. Her grip tightened. Very carefully she turned the mask over.

"I was still holding it," she said, her voice dropping enough that he was forced to step closer to catch the words that followed. He looked at the interior of the mask. "When I stepped off the road."

Silence.

"Evayne?"

"I walked into a slaughterhouse. It was dark and stuffy and airless; there were bodies, parts of bodies, blood. I—I dropped the mask."

"Did it survive the drop?"

"I don't know," she replied, neutral now. "Because when I picked it up again, it was covered with blood. From the inside. It was wet with it." She pulled a hand from the folds of her voluminous robe. In it was a very fine, very complicated mask; the contours of face—eyes, nose, the ridge of broad cheekbones so particular he was certain it was meant to be the likeness of a living man.

"Was there fighting?"

"There was fighting," she said faintly. "But in the distance. The moon was full. It was . . . outside, for all that it felt like the inside of the royal slaughterhouse."

"Where were you?"

"I'm not completely certain," she replied. "But I think it was here."

"Where we stand?"

"Or somewhere like it. In the Tor Leonne."

"When was it?"

"You know."

He did. He bowed his head a moment. Then he reached for the mask. She handed it to him. "This is not the mask I left you."

"No."

"Evayne—"

"I couldn't find it; I was searching for it, but the dying—" she closed her eyes. "I took one false step and the path carried me away."

"To me."

"No."

"To further information?"

"Yes." She drew a breath. "To Meralonne APhaniel of the Order of Knowledge." The sun's light at this time of day was unforgiving, but it cast the darkest shadows, and those shadows were so much a part of her expression he withdrew, physically, to give her the privacy of that darkness.

"The mask . . . is not the one I dropped."

He waited; she had turned her eyes from his, and he now watched the profile of her face, seeing where youth strengthened it, and age weakened it; seeing, as well, the converse: the uncertainty and the power. The sweep of her lashes hid the clarity of violet; she could have been—for just that moment—a Serra, pale-skinned, dark-haired, troubled by things she could not speak of.

"But Meralonne said it had been." She turned the mask over again. "I'm sorry," she said softly.

"Sorry?"

Hands shook as she turned the mask from exterior to interior. "The blood." Her voice was quiet. "He said—it wasn't there before the mask was donned."

"Will you—can you—travel with me?"

Her smile was sharp and bitter; youth and age. "I can try. Why?"

"I am sent to rouse the Voyani."

"Sent?"

His brows rose slightly at what he heard in her voice.

She had the grace to blush, but only slightly.

"It seems it is my fate to follow the orders of women with vision, no matter how unpleasant those orders are."

"And these?"

"Are unpleasant."

"Kallandras—"

"You, Evayne a'Nolan, have never met the Corronan Matriarch."

17th of Scaral, 427 AA
Essalieyan, Averalaan Aramarelas

A world away.

Time had been both kind and unkind in the passage that separated them: this world and the world that he knew best.

Meralonne no longer found it unsettling to see Evayne, and

this surprised him. He was, after all, made to carry a grudge. It had been his signal pride as a younger man, although perhaps he had called it by some other phrase. *Honor* came to mind.

She had been his finest student. Subtle, brittle, jumpy, she had nonetheless had the vision to pierce the veils that magic throws up in its own defense. She had will, and anger to fuel it; she had just the right respect for power.

Seeing her, mask in hand, hand shaking in the shadows of his tower, Meralonne could almost forget that. Perhaps that was why he felt so little of the anger her presence always stirred.

Smoke from burning leaves curled around his beardless chin, a hazy frame.

Someone came. The knock at the door irritated him, but it often went away if he ignored it. He ignored it. It went away.

The tobacco burned down to ash as he fanned its embers with drawn breath, exhaling in ovals that thinned and spread very, very slowly in the still air. The season was a thing of rain and humidity. He endured it in the same way he endured all such trivial details: he failed to notice it.

Except at a time like this, when triviality prevented one from thinking about larger issues. There was a tactile comfort in emptying the pipe; in tapping the bowl, gently but firmly, and emptying it of ash. It was almost ritual, and there was otherwise so little ritual in his life that he clung to it.

He would be forced to give it up soon.

Evayne.

The mask was gone. She had handed it to him, slick with new blood, and some of that blood remained on his fingers. It had not yet dried to stickiness—a fault of the humidity—but just this once, he did not wonder who had shed it. The mask itself had answered the question.

It was not a spell he had ever cast; no member of the Order of Knowledge possessed the skill and the vision to do so.

"You said Kallandras gave you this mask?" he asked.

"No—not this one. I said—"

"My pardon. You said he had given you a featureless half-mask."

"Yes." Her eyes were narrow; sharp. The shock of blood was fading quickly, and because he had now seen her at so many ages, he knew it would be replaced by simple determination. "This mask—that mask—you're saying they're the same."

"No."

Momentary clenching of jaw. "You're saying that *this* mask used to look like the one I was given."

"Yes."

"Meralonne—"

"It is an old art. An imperfect one, let me add." He turned. "It is from a time of schism and unrest, and even in the annals of the antiquities, one might find a single mention, or two, and both oblique."

She was quiet for longer than the situation demanded. He wondered, as he often did, what she was thinking.

This time, as she rarely did, she let him know. "Which annals? Which books?"

"Evayne," he replied, only barely able to keep the edge in his voice from changing the tone of his words, "you were the best of my students, but not even you were privy to all of the knowledge I have secured."

Her eyes narrowed, expression sharpening until it was as cool as his words.

Pale violet and pale gray clashed in the stillness. At last, she said, "Perhaps one day you will forgive me for my lack of choice."

"Perhaps." And then, because he wished to make certain his meaning was clear—with the younger Evayne it had never been certain, "We all have secrets."

She frowned. "I have never attempted to hide mine behind so obvious a ruse. I am what I am. You are—"

"Short of time." He rose. There were questions she had never asked him. He wondered if she knew their answers.

But knew, conversely, that she didn't. Not at this age.

And not when she could bring him this mask. "Where did Kallandras obtain the mask?"

"From the Dominion." She paused, and then glanced away. "The masks were not manufactured by the Sword of Knowledge or the Voyani; he suspects they are *Kialli* in origin."

"Now?"

"I don't—I—when is this?"

"This is the seventeenth day of Scaral, in the year 427 after the advent."

Her minute hesitation angered him. Anger served to further chill his expression. The coolness, however, was slow to be reflected in hers. The shift in her age, a shift that Kallandras seemed to accept without pause, was difficult for Meralonne. People changed with age, certainly; it was an accepted and acknowledged truth. But as one tended to age *with* them, the changes were buried by time, made less obvious to the intimate observer. History and memory dictated how clearly the changes were observed.

Evayne was bound by no history and no memory. She was, quite literally, a different person every time she entered his rooms, and he had—after ten years of inconvenience—chosen to give up the protections against her entry by focusing his spells, not upon her person, but rather upon the robes that person wore.

At times he regretted it.

He rose, reaching for his pipe. Aware, as he did so, that he would not have responded with this anger or this annoyance had she been at the zenith of her power—if indeed he had ever seen her at the height of her power. Aware, as well, that she had been brought here for a reason.

Abruptly, as it sometimes did, the anger left him. He was not above the vanity of thinking himself beyond petulance. Nor was he deluded enough not to recognize petulance, even be it his own.

The mask. He reached across the desk, lifting it gingerly between two fingers. The face was light and delicate, a disturbing contrast to its expression.

"What does it do?"

"Now? Nothing. It has served its purpose."

"What *did* it do?"

He gazed across the table he used to separate himself from most of the visitors he received. "You are familiar with the concept of naming."

"Yes. It's how a mage takes control of the demon-kin."

"Indeed. The power of names over the *Kialli* is absolute. The ability to find a name they are forced by their nature to recognize is where the practitioner's power is proved. But I digress. The power of naming is not limited to *Kialli,* or rather, it was not.

"There was a time when such a power was used to define mortals as well."

"My name has no power over me."

He raised a silver brow. Smoke tangled with air as it left his mouth in a thin stream. "Spoken as a young woman."

She was old enough, however, that being called young no longer irritated her. He let it go. "Naming is sometimes a wordless affair. This mask, when put in place, becomes the face by which a man—or woman, or child—will be known; it reveals their truest self."

She frowned. "I don't understand."

"No." He rose, his pipe cupped in his palm. "Nor do I. The time when such a mask would be relevant—Evayne, *this* mask, where did it come from?"

"If you mean when, I'm not completely certain; I didn't have the time to find out."

"Was the moon full?"

"Yes."

He rose. "The masks were sometimes used on Scarran."

"On—" Her voice lost all strength. "The Dark Conjunction."

"Yes."

"But—"

"Yes?"

"That doesn't make any sense. The demons don't need masks to bring out the mortal soul—they can see it."

"I know," he said softly. He found his way to the window and began to draw the curtains; when they were halfway open, he couldn't remember whether or not he wanted to let the light in or deny it. "But that wasn't always the case."

"Meralonne?"

"You cannot speak to yourself," he told her quietly. "But if you have some other way of conveying a message to your older self, tell her this: her power is needed in the Tor Leonne on Scarran."

"When is that?"

"The night," he replied, his voice momentarily the irritated voice of a teacher who knows his pupil is capable of better than she's offered, "of the Festival Moon."

"Will you—will you go South?"

"I am drawn to the South, it seems, for many reasons." He turned away from her fully, his eyes on the familiar streets below the full glass panes. "But no, I will not go South. Not for Scarran. Not now."

"Meralonne—"

"I think it is best that you leave."

"But I—"

"Now."

427 AA
Stone Deepings

She was not sure when it happened—although that wasn't much of a surprise as she wasn't sure when *anything* happened in this

place—but something in the air changed. The sound of the horns—
and the word sound had rarely been guiltier of such poverty of
description—grew louder and richer until the mountain valley
resounded everywhere with the question and answer, the supplication and demand, of their music.

It reminded her of something; she struggled a moment for the
memory and then let it go. In the distance, beneath the breath of
the horns, rise and fall of notes collapsing into something more
complex than harmony but never so discordant as cacophony,
came the sound of hooves against rock and road.

"Stand your ground," Avandar said softly. He put a hand on
her shoulder, and she didn't bother to shake it off. It wasn't that
the contact provided her with any comfort; it didn't. What it did
provide—what she *knew* it would provide—was protection. She
stood under Avandar's shadow, and she knew, because he had
been recognized by Calliastra and by Corallonne, he would be
recognized by the riders who, from the sounds of hooves, approached from the road ahead.

"They ride to join Her," she said softly, without pause for anything as useful as thought.

His grip tightened, but he said nothing.

She wished that she didn't suddenly feel so plain and dowdy,
and didn't bother to wonder why: the host had come over a ridge
that, until they crested it, she hadn't noticed in the road ahead. They
didn't ride horses. Nothing as simple and practical as that. They
rode stags, or what would have been stags had deer been the size of
Northern moose, and astride what was clearly the largest of these
beasts, a man in armor rode.

She could not see his face clearly, but she saw the fall of his
hair in a single, silvery braid, saw the breadth of his shoulders,
the straight line of his back, the ease with which he rode.

"You know," she muttered to Avandar, "if *we* rode anywhere
with hair that long—not that any of us could actually *grow* hair
that long—we'd have caught it in the saddle or the damn spurs.
Or something."

His fingers were momentarily painful, but he did not tell her to
shut up; he knew her well enough to understand the bravado that
was her den's particular exorcism of nervousness.

They came toward her, and with each passing step they took—
and they traveled quickly—she felt their regard grow more pointed,
more certain. The lead rider, who bore horn and not sword, lowered

the horn; one less voice in the vastness of the Deepings, and hardly likely to be missed.

She heard a cackle in the silence; her Oma's voice, and at its least pleasant. *It'll be missed, all right,* she said, *but I imagine he's not stupid enough to think otherwise. You're as safe as you can be, on this road, right where you are. Even if he wanted you, he wouldn't dare to take you—not without her permission.*

And she is *most definitely on the road.*

And I'll be safe from her?

Her Oma didn't offer an answer, which was answer enough.

"This is my dream," she said quietly.

"Pardon?" Avandar asked.

"My dream," she repeated the words. "The dream I—I left The Terafin for."

"No," he said quietly, "it is not."

"Look—"

"Jewel. They hear almost every word you speak."

"And I should care?"

She felt, rather than saw, his momentary smile in the easing of his grip. She also subsided.

The mounted man—no, not that, but something very like— lifted a hand and the small host ceased as if it had been moving in time to his movement, as if it were dependent on him. Perhaps it was.

He lifted the visor of the helm she would have said was decorative it was so fine and thin. The smile on his face dimmed in that instant, but it lingered in memory: the expression of a predator, who, catlike, plays with its food. She did not like the look of his fine, fine features any better on closer inspection.

It irritated her that the breaking of the smile had had nothing to do with her; she had seen the gray gaze flicker up over Avandar's face and freeze a second before falling.

The silence that engulfed them was no longer underscored by the voice of the horns. She suspected it was magical in nature.

Very good, Na'jay. Very good.

"You are strangers on this road," the stranger said. "And ignorant of our ways, no doubt."

"Indeed," Avandar replied, before Jewel could.

"Therefore I will ask you to give way on the road; we ride to meet our Lord, and She is neither patient nor forgiving of the intrusion of strangers into lands She has claimed."

"Indeed," Avandar said again, his voice even softer.

The man's mount took a step back, and then another, before he brought it to bear. She wondered what Avandar's expression looked like at that moment, because the creature was definitely frightened.

Which was good, because Jewel *knew,* as she watched him, that there was no way for her to leave this road in safety. She said, as quietly as she could, "Avandar."

His fingers brushed the curve of her collarbone in warning. She did not shake his hand off—hated that she couldn't.

"Avandar?"

"Jewel."

"We can't."

"We can't?"

"We can't leave this road. If they're to pass, they can go left or right; they can dig a damn tunnel through the rock or build a stinking bridge. But *we* can't surrender the road."

His silence lasted only a moment longer than it usually did, but that was enough. Acknowledgment. "You are," he said, and she was certain that *his* voice didn't carry, "such a rarity, Jewel. Had I found you at the height of my power, and not this nadir, had I found you at the peak of this world's glory—

"You are correct. Which will require a change of tactics. Come, stand by my side. You will see the circle I draw upon the ground; no matter what is said or done, *do not* cross it. Do you understand?"

"Perfectly."

"You've never been particularly good at following the orders of others," he continued, as if she hadn't spoken, "not even when your life depended on it. Pretend, for a moment, that it is not *your* life that depends on it, but *theirs.* And obey."

She took a step back and to the side, swallowing more than just words. "What are you going to do?"

"With your permission."

"As if you need my permission?"

He said softly, "I do."

"But I—"

He stared down the road at the waiting riders. She had never seen that expression on his face before, although Avandar's face didn't exactly define the word expressive. He seemed on the verge of words, but when he finally spoke them, she had to strain to hear them, they were so low.

"Arann, Carver, Teller—especially Teller—or any of the rest

of your den with the possible exception of Kiriel—could act
without your permission on *this* road. I believe The Terafin could.
I . . . cannot."

"I don't understand."

"Perhaps not consciously. And I would lie to you and tell you
that our time grows short, but you have always been a difficult
person to lie to."

"Except by omission."

His brows lifted in surprise, fell in amusement. "Except," he
said, nodding quietly, "by omission. Your permission?"

"Yes."

He turned. Lifted his arms as if to strike the air, and at that, in
a way that would kill. It wasn't his way to warn her, but the gesture itself was warning. She flinched, but did not jump, when
blue-and-orange light burst up from the ground in a coruscating,
visually abrasive wall.

She started when the light grew bright enough—in literally an
eye blink, bad timing on her part—to momentarily blind as it
traveled up, and up again, toward the stars that Avandar said
were not there.

But she *did* cry out when that power bent back toward the
earth like a whip's lash, crackling and branching out as if it were
a living tree, but one formed in the heavens of lightning, and not
for the benefit of the ground below.

The man on the stag's back was engulfed by it; she heard
screaming, a terrible, terrible wailing that grew louder as the seconds passed and her vision returned to her. But she didn't realize
that she'd jammed her hands up against her ears until Avandar
touched one of them.

"Make it STOP!" she shouted at him.

His face was as warm as stone. She understood from this that
he expected her to be strong, where strong was defined as either
not caring that someone, anyone, could be in *that* much pain, or
in Jewel's case—because he wasn't stupid enough to expect a
miracle—at least not showing it.

But it was just *so* bad.

Na'jay, her Oma said, voice as gentle as Avandar's expression. *Don't.*

Don't tell me what to do, Jewel snapped back. *He needs my
permission, and I* don't *give it. Not for this.*

She turned to him. Caught his very fine robe; clenched the arm
beneath, and shouted words to that effect in his ear, or as close to

his ear as she could get when he made no move to meet her halfway. Gods, she hated tall people.

He's wrong about you, you know, her Oma said, subsiding into irritability. *You would never have survived in his time; you would have been devoured whole by his enemies.*

Fine. We're not living in his *time, thank Kalliaris. We're living in* mine. *And I'll damn well define part of it.*

She felt the words leave her lips; she couldn't *hear* them.

Avandar caught her by the arm—one arm, the way one would catch a careless thief and *not* a member of the House Council—and shook her slightly. It had the effect of forcing at least one of her hands from her ears. And when she did: silence.

Sudden silence. In it, all eyes—his, and the mounted riders ahead—were turned to her. The road was blackened and scarred by the magic Avandar had wielded; there was a pit about a foot deep that ran the road's breadth, and seemed edged—slightly— in an angry red glow.

In that pit's center stood the leader of the strange host: His armor was blackened, and his skin somewhat darker for its exposure to Avandar's power, but he was otherwise untouched. He was staring at Jewel.

From the ground.

The mount on which he'd ridden was nowhere to be seen.

I'll be damned, her Oma said quietly.

Isn't that already decided one way or the other?

The old woman's laughter was a warmth and a comfort. She tried to hold on to it. But it was a pale echo in the silence.

Only two faces were exposed: Their leader's and her domicis'; both were inscrutable.

She hated that. Hated the silence, and did what she usually did when silence made her uncomfortable: she broke it. "Well," she said, squaring her shoulders as Avandar released her arm. "Uh, we'd like to get past, if you don't mind."

The silence got worse.

This time, she decided to be prudent; she bit her tongue and squirmed, but quietly, quietly. *Gods, what was I thinking?*

You weren't thinking, her Oma replied, but without the sting such words should have had. *That's the point of the path you've taken, Na'Jay.*

Well, I'm going to start now, if no one minds.

Voice dry as autumn leaves, her Oma said, *I don't believe that the Warlord would mind, and I certainly would be pleased to have raised no fool.*

The stranger said, "Viandaran. Warlord. Tell her what she has done."

"Lord Celleriant," he replied, inclining his head as he cast off the polite fiction of being unknown, "I am disinclined to take your orders."

Silence. The man stepped from the pit in the road's heart.

"Avandar?"

"A Terafin?"

Wonderful. "What happened to his mount?"

"A very good question," he replied. "And I believe that Lord Celleriant is about to demand an answer to it."

"Which means," Jewel said, in a voice that was becoming quieter and flatter as she spoke, "That you don't have any idea either."

"None whatsoever." The two words were polite and conversational, neither of which Avandar generally was. She flinched; she couldn't help it. "And before you ask," he continued, again in that pleasant tone of voice, "no, I did not attack his *mount;* my spell was aimed directly at Celleriant. But you will come to understand—if you are unlucky—"

Which means it's certain, Jewel thought.

"—that the mount and its rider are bound in a particularly unpleasant fashion, especially for the mount."

"It was the mount that was screaming."

"It was, indeed, the mount."

"But—but I heard *it.* It *wasn't* a deer's voice—if deer even *have* voices."

"No."

"But it—"

"Yes. I'm surprised that you didn't see it."

"See what? What do you see?"

"I? I see what you see. But I do not have your gift. This close to High Winter, my dear, you could hear the truth. But on Scarran, you will see what these mounts actually are, if you are ever foolish enough to be in the path of the Hunt during the Dark Conjunction."

"Or perhaps," another voice said, "she will become more intimately acquainted with the truth than that, and sooner."

The voice was a woman's voice.

If blood were water, Jewel's would have frozen. She turned,

slowly, to that part of the road that she had left behind, and there, at her back—and at Avandar's—was the most beautiful person she had ever seen in her life.

And, inexplicably, the most terrifying.

CHAPTER TWENTY-THREE

Avandar bowed at once; a signal.

Jewel started to, but her knees locked in place—and not just from terror, although terror would have been a good excuse. It would have been helpful if she'd understood why she couldn't bow; she'd done her share of bowing and scraping in her time, and had learned not to take the protocol personally. But she was fighting against an instinct as strong as any she'd ever felt, and she'd never learned to beat her instincts. She struggled for breath, found its rhythm, forced her lungs to adhere to it.

The Winter Queen.

The lack of obeisance did not escape her notice.

"You are bold," she said softly, "and boldness is not always unpleasant."

"Just now," Jewel replied.

"Indeed." Her hair was not as long as the hair of the rider Avandar had named Celleriant, but it was like silver, and not like ice or snow. Her eyes were gray, and her skin pale, and she was taller than Avandar; taller, in fact, than any woman Jewel had ever met. Her gaze narrowed and slid off Jewel's face. "Warlord," she said softly. "We are destined to meet on strange roads."

He rose then, at her acknowledgment. Jewel would have found it galling in any other circumstance; it seemed merely natural now, which was warning enough. "As you say, Lady."

Her smile was genuine, but it was not warm. Nothing about her was warm. "You would have been a King without compare, Viandaran."

"You honor me, Arianne," he replied, bowing again. "But I flatter myself: I believe that I was a Warlord beyond compare."

"You were. It is a surprise to find you here, and so diminished."

His facial expression did not change at all, but Jewel knew that her words had found their careless mark. She did not wish to fence with the Winter Queen, so she offered no defense of the man whose service she had reluctantly accepted so many years ago.

But Avandar needed no defense.

"Come here, child," the Winter Queen said, and Jewel started to walk. Started, and stopped. Avandar's hand was on her shoulder, and her foot was an inch away from the magical line that was still glowing incandescently against the rock at her feet. She had failed to note it. A very bad sign.

"Viandaran, I will offer you warning: do not interfere."

"I have pledged," he said, "my service. Understand that that pledge would have had meaning in your court not through your power or your guarantee, but through my own sense of honor. It has that meaning here, Arianne." He bowed again. "And I have made no pledge to you or yours to break."

"No. But there is wisdom, Warlord. The political extends to all realms, wherever power gathers."

He bowed again. Jewel didn't think she had seen him bow this much before in her life—even if you counted every half nod that acknowledged an authority greater than his own.

"I say to you again, do not interfere."

"I understand, and thank you for extending your grace. It is with great regret that I must refuse you."

"So be it. It is noted." She turned back to Jewel. "You have taken something that is mine, little mortal, and I will have it back, or I will have an equal measure of obedience and servitude from you in its stead."

Jewel felt her breath lurch, and she steadied it again. "I'm sorry," she said, and she truly was, "but I don't know what you're talking about."

"No?"

Avandar closed his eyes.

"No."

"Perhaps, Warlord, you might care to explain to your charge the nature of her crime."

He turned to Jewel then, as he had not done when Celleriant had offered a more roughly worded and less dangerous order. He spoke quietly, but he looked just to the left of her eyes, and she could not read *anything* in the cast of his expression. Avandar was not a histrionic man, but he was not a subtle one; by word, lack of word, or stiffness of bearing he made certain she knew exactly what the right—and the wrong—thing to do in any given situation was.

And she realized, as she waited upon him for a signal that it slowly dawned wasn't coming, that she'd come to depend on that. That she had, in fact, grown dependent on a man she had never much liked, and truthfully didn't like much now.

It pulled her up. "What laws, exactly, have I broken?"

Neutrality answered. "Celleriant is a rider in the Queen's service."

"Not anymore, he's not."

"Yes, and that is the problem. The creature that he was riding *was* the Queen's creature; gifted and bound to Celleriant by her magic. In . . . expelling the creature . . . from this realm, you have stolen property that she has claimed as her own."

A claim isn't the same as ownership, she thought; she wasn't stupid enough—not quite—to expose the words by speaking them. She chose instead to speak a less difficult truth. "I didn't choose to expel it. It was expelled. There is a difference."

"There *is* a difference," the woman he had called Arianne said quietly. "But in your case, while you speak what you believe to be the truth, you lie. I do not understand how, because the art is long lost, but in walking this path, you have made it your own."

And what you own, you have power over, her Oma said, in a voice that Jewel almost didn't recognize. *It is a lesson that Arianne understands better than any of the Firstborn. You would do well to heed it.*

Jewel glanced quickly at Avandar, lifting one brow.

"There is no other way," he said, answering the question she hadn't bothered to put into words, "to have torn the creature from the grip of the Winter Queen. Her power is tantamount except where she does not reign; in lands unclaimed or unowned, the . . . binding that grants her power over her subjects is—"

"Unbreakable," the Queen said quietly. "You have therefore taken from me something of mine. I will have it back, or I will have something in return that I value as much."

"If the bond were unbreakable, it couldn't have been broken." Jewel straightened her shoulders. She would have rolled up her sleeves if she'd been in her kitchen; would have rolled them up if she'd been heading into a tricky political encounter.

Of course, Avandar would then berate her for ruining the sleeves of the garment he'd chosen, but there were certain habits that were ingrained. "All right, Queen of Winter," she said softly, and with as much respect as she could put into what was, essentially, a counterthreat. "Maybe if these lands *were* unclaimed, I might have committed some sort of crime. But if I understand what you're saying correctly, these lands *are* claimed. By me."

Avandar's face might have been made of stone; he did not flinch, he did not smile, he did not nod. But he did not take his hand off her shoulder, and the line he had drawn in the ground was glowing as brightly as a living flame.

"Viandaran."

"Lady," he said quietly. But this time, he did not bow.

"Tell your mortal that she plays a dangerous game."

"Does it matter," Jewel countered, "as long as I win it?"

A gleam of a cold smile touched the most beautiful face in creation. "No," the Queen said softly, "it does not. But this is the only place in which you might have the smallest of chances to win, and you cannot remain here, in this pass, for eternity. My memory is long."

"Actually," Jewel said softly, lifting a hand and gently prying Avandar's fingers free, "this is the one place that I *can* stay for an eternity. I don't really need to eat. I don't need to rest. Sleep is a permanent state. Anyplace else, and you could wait me out."

She motioned her mount closer.

"I wouldn't if I were you," Jewel said quietly.

"You could not conceive of what it means to be me," the Winter Queen replied. She motioned the mount forward, and it obeyed her. The two closest riders made to follow, and she raised a hand without looking back; they froze in place.

"Do you know who we are?"

"No."

The word was so blunt and so forceful Jewel thought the two who had stayed at their lord's command might charge forward. But Arianne lifted a hand again and continued to edge her mount forward, until it stood at last on the edge of Avandar's circle.

"Do you know who I am?"

"No."

"Viandaran, please."

"She is one of those called Firstborn," Avandar said quietly. "The Firstborn are children of the gods."

"Fair enough. Some of the people I respect most are children of gods."

Arianne's smile was chill. "They are children of neutered, tame creatures, they are not children of *gods.*"

"Before you speak again," he said, lifting a hand, "let me say that the neutered, tame creatures she refers to are not the human parents; those are completely beneath her notice and her contempt. She refers to the gods that are worshiped across the Empire of Essalieyan."

"And am I so forgotten that my words must be explained?" the Winter Queen said. "Then it is time to be *remembered.*" Her foot, covered in leather that seemed very thin and very supple, dug swiftly into the sides of her mount—but Jewel *knew* that the gesture was entirely for show; the creature did not need to be visibly forced to do anything. It existed at her whim, at the convenience of her thought.

Brace yourself.

She did not need to be told.

She had taken Avandar's hand from her shoulder; he did her the surprising grace of leaving it at his side.

The light on the ground did not change, but at the last, at the last, Arianne drove her mount *across* it.

The creature screamed. Jewel recognized the scream, although it was distorted slightly because a different voice uttered it.

Inches away from her face, kept from collision by the grace and protection of Avandar's spell, she could *see* the creature's face. Stags, she had thought them, and she wished—incoherently—that she could still think of them that way. But no: The face that was burning in the light of Avandar's flame was a human face, distorted by shimmering spell and blood and fire's scoring, but recognizable for what it had once been.

She stepped back. She bit her lip and swallowed blood to stop the sound that was curled in her throat from escaping.

Avandar, damn him forever, turned to her as she stared unblinking at the face of a horror she could never have imagined, and said, "Your command?" in a voice as cool as ocean water. Light glinted across the surface of his eyes like light across the flat of a blade.

She understood the lesson he meant to teach her. She vowed that she would never willingly submit herself to such teachings again.

She did not raise her hands to her ears and she did not order him to drop the barrier that protected them. That was the point of this particular form of attack: Jewel's weakness. Well, she was weak. Didn't tell her anything she didn't already know about herself. She was weak in a way that Avandar and Arianne were not—and she refused to be ashamed of it. But weak or no, she wasn't stupid. Avandar's magic stood between her and the once human creature whose face was wilting—and while she might, for pity's sake, have saved it the agony of Avandar's magic, on its back, the true threat waited: The Winter Queen. Jewel could not quite bring herself to abandon all defense in the face of that threat.

But the screaming was *terrible*.

Jewel had been beaten in her youth; all the care and caution in the world couldn't prevent the streets from taking their toll. That had been better than this: the pain had been visceral, immediate, her own. She had thought, then, that she would not survive. She was afraid, now, that the memory of this moment would outlive her; that she would carry it to Mandaros' Hall and be scarred enough that it would echo down the length of the lives she had left her until she made her final choice.

She could not afford to show it, although she knew Arianne knew. A test. A game.

Gods, she *hated* these games. Hated Avandar, for playing them so well. Hated herself for learning them.

She had bowed her head. Wasn't sure when, but she could see the bright line of the ground, Avandar's magic neatly cutting the flow of the creature's blood. She would not order him to withdraw the magics that protected them both.

But she didn't have to stand by and let Arianne define all the rules of the game. If Jewel understood what she had done—or rather, *how*—with the other creature, she would have done it again, although her gut instinct told her that this time, with the Queen herself as rider, it would be impossible.

All right, it was impossible.

The fires were burning; she felt them touch her in the darkness; they *hurt*. And they liberated.

She wasn't helpless.

Jewel Markess ATerafin lifted her head. Stared a moment into the face of the screaming creature, and then, looked up and beyond, into the face of the Winter Queen.

She said, words as direct as arrow's flight, "You want to get through. Well, all right. I demand a price for passage, and if you continue this game, it will be beyond your ability to pay."

She didn't shout. Had she spoken in a whisper, she was certain the words would be heard. But she waited another heartbeat—and hers were coming thick and fast—and then said, "You lose a day."

Another beat.

"A second day."

Another.

"A third day."

The screaming stopped.

As simply as it started, it was gone. The creature's face, burned to bone and scoured by flame into a charred blackness that should have been beyond pain but wasn't, jerked up, out of the barrier. It stumbled as it took a step, and the silence that followed the stumble was profound.

But what followed made Avandar stop breathing in mid-gasp.

The Winter Queen dismounted.

17th of Scaral, 427 AA
Tor Leonne

Kallandras wasn't certain that she wouldn't disappear; with Evayne, one couldn't be. Nor was he certain—for he had to turn his back on her several times during their journey through the Tor Leonne—if she didn't disappear, that she wouldn't age or diminish by the time he turned to face her again. It had long since ceased to matter to him what Evayne looked like or who, in fact, she was. Over the years he had developed enough of a familiarity with the woman at any age to be at ease with the suddenness of her changes.

It had started idly enough, and it had become a puzzle, a challenge, filling in the steps between terrified adolescent to serene, powerful woman. He had heard all of her voices; seen all of her faces. He knew the exact moment—in the chronology of her life—she had become a killer; knew that she would never lose the ability, as some did who visited that precipice and then withdrew. He knew how to anger the Evaynes it was possible to anger; knew how to comfort the Evaynes it was possible to comfort.

But he did not know if she would be at his side when he finally found the woman he was searching for.

He felt a hand on his shoulder. Smiled. The older Evayne carried her warnings—if she offered them at all—by words. It was amusing. In her youth, she saw him as the shadowy, dangerous assassin whose eyes missed nothing, no matter how well hidden. In her prime, she saw him as a peer, and as such, presumed that anything she noted with ease would be likewise noted. Only at this age, between the two and confident of her own power, did she seek to warn him when no warning was necessary. "I see them," he said quietly. The hand withdrew.

Two men lounged idly in the midday heat, like many of the Southern clansmen. The hour was right for it, but the wind wrong; it was, as the Tor Leonne went, a cool day. Sweat, here, was a fact of life when the sun reigned.

They wore sturdy clothing that had probably seen better days, but could certainly see worse; uncolored cottons and brown vests, wide sashes, long pants. Swords adorned hip and rested off to one side, a foot above the ground. They weren't likely to be drawn.

But the daggers already had been; they were clumsily but deliberately concealed. He approached them, but kept a comfortable distance.

"Gentlemen," he said, speaking flawless Torra.

They glanced at each other; the older man, bearded and slighter of build, frowned. It was the younger of the two—heavier set, about three inches taller than Kallandras or most of the men one could see in the streets of the Tor Leonne—who chose to answer.

"Not usually."

Evayne came from around his back. He saw the mask in her hand as if it were a natural extension. The younger man frowned, and once again turned his gaze to the older for a quick, silent consultation.

But the older man's eyes, caught by Evayne, were held there. Interesting.

"Kallandras," Evayne said softly. It was a question. A request. He nodded.

"Gentlemen," he said again, and this time the older man nodded slowly. "I am a stranger to the Tor, and I am . . . lost. I have been told that you guard one of the fairest merchant trains in the city. Perhaps you might offer me the kindness of your hospitality."

"The Tor," the younger man said, before the older could reply, "isn't known for hospitality."

"No, indeed. Nor is the open road, but I have found hospitality there in my time."

"And such hospitality as you have found," the older man said, speaking for the first time, "is offered in less dangerous times."

Kallandras nodded, but he did not offer an answer; he was, for a moment, moved to silence by the unusual richness of the stranger's voice. It was a deep voice, and it had layers to it—of anger and joy, of wariness and abandon, of sadness and determination—that were muted in other voices, when present at all. There was intimacy in it, or hints of intimacy; there was friendship, or the promise of friendship, and there was, distinctly, death. It was, he thought, a brother's voice.

But a brother did not serve the dictates of the living.

He bowed.

The older man raised a brow.

"Indeed, in less dangerous times. And by a family other than Corrona."

"You are . . . observant."

"No doubt. We," he said quietly, nodding to Evayne without taking his gaze from the stranger, "have come to deliver a message from two who have offered us their hospitality."

"And that?"

"It can be delivered only to Elsarre."

"That is not the way things are usually done in this caravan."

"It is the way things are done," he said, interjecting the faintest note of apology into words that, on the surface, held none, "in the entourage of my mother."

"Your mother?"

"Yollana," he said quietly.

"A common enough name." It was not to Kallandras that the man's intent gaze traveled, but to Evayne. "You have been on the road a long time," he said at last, his eyes never leaving her face. "And if you desire it, I will speak on your behalf."

"The message can only be delivered—"

"So that the woman for whom such message is meant might be predisposed to listen."

"Dani—" the younger man said, surprise and anger highlighting the two syllables.

But the man called Dani raised a hand, no more.

The gesture had the full force of an order. An order given by a man with the authority to give it.

"We desire it," Kallandras said, speaking for Evayne. "And we will be in your debt."

The man raised a brow. Nodded. "Follow, then. But follow quickly."

He moved.

Kallandras was not surprised by his speed. He wasn't surprised by his silence, either; the Voyani belonged to the shadows the Lord cast; they were used to running or hiding. What surprised him was the grace of his words; he spoke like no Voyani—especially no male—that Kallandras had ever met. That he traveled the *Voyanne* was not in question. Not in this caravan, not with this train. That he was born to it? Highly doubtful.

But the Voyani as a rule did not take in strangers, and on the rare occasions they did, they still distinguished between charity and blood. Family was family, and everything else was a matter of convenience.

Dani led them through the maze of narrow streets that the poorer clansmen who served the Tyr called home. He stopped occasionally to speak to his companion, his expression shifting with the careless wildness of a man who's drunk almost too much. The younger Voyani responded by shying back with a mild look of concern mingled with disgust; it was clear to the casual observer who was responsible for whom.

And it was a common enough sight in the streets. Kallandras frowned and drew the young woman at his side closer; she in turn pulled the folds of her hood farther down about her face. They walked as a loose party, one of several similar parties, the Lord's gaze upon them, the preparations for the Festival of the Moon crowding streets that were seldom so busy.

He smiled as they came to a narrow doorway, replete with long hangings and a garland that hung from the height of the stone frame. No one but Elsarre would live like this in the Tor Leonne. Or rather, no Matriarch.

They entered the dwelling, and then Dani turned and bade them wait; he did so with an economy of words—precisely none—that was astonishing among the Voyani. In spite of himself, Kallandras was curious. It had been a long time since he had been simply curious.

When Dani returned, he said, "She will see you now."

He led them down the long hall into a wide, round room; a room that was lit by lamp and hidden by hanging and shutter from the sun's light. The hanging, he pulled aside, holding it back as if he were a seraf. The gesture made him invisible and Evayne passed him by without a backward glance. Not so Kallandras; he stopped a moment to nod. Dani raised a brow and gestured, by nod of head, to the room.

There, seated upon a bench that rested against the unadorned stone wall, sat a woman. She was not alone; not quite. To her left—at the bench's edge—stood an older man, his hair white, his skin dark and cracked by sun and wind. To her right, seated, was an older woman, shawls pulled up about her head as if she were a clanswoman. Her hair was still dark in places; curls crept out beneath the edges of cloth framing her face, with its severe, suspicious expression.

But the seated woman did not trouble herself with such severity. She was younger than Kallandras, although she was old enough that she no longer deserved to be called young. Her face, unlike the faces of most Voyani women of her age, was almost unblemished by exposure to the sun; it was plain that she did not choose to face the Lord often. She wore red and yellow silks, much to Kallandras' surprise; they were fashioned in imitation of the saris that high clanswomen wore, but they were not as restrictive.

She wore a sword as well, although he judged it decorative rather than practical; she could not fight with competence in what she had chosen to wear. Nor in how she had chosen to present herself: her hair, long and thick, fell in a straight line from head to bench, rippling against the wood as it caught the light.

All of these things were seen, judged, and consigned to memory in an instant. Elsarre, of the four Matriarchs, had always been called the wild one. He better understood the naming now.

"You," the seated ruler said to Evayne.

Kallandras, standing beside her, heard the shift in her voice. She was momentarily confused, but she knew better than to expose herself to this woman.

"My apologies," she said softly, "for interrupting you in this fashion."

"It is hardly an interruption compared to your last visit." She lifted an arm, waved it to take in the whole of the small room. Kallandras kept the smile off his face; her look was luxuriant and elegant; her voice and her manner were distinctly Voyani. "You gave us portents and signs and warnings, and we traveled here in the secrecy you counseled wise. We have been *waiting*," she added.

"You know that I do not come at my own choosing, or in my own time. I travel at the Lady's whim."

"Oh, indeed," Elsarre replied, her words so heavy with sarcasm they could have damaged the floor had they been solid.

Evayne stiffened. "If you did not believe my words," she said, her voice the sudden breeze that takes heat—or warmth—from a room, "you had no cause to travel."

"It was not your words, but my own instinct, that brought us here."

Careful, Evayne, Kallandras thought. But he knew what his apparent position was in this room, and he stood as her shadow; attached, but silent, unremarkable.

"Then confine your anger to where it is due."

Elsarre lapsed into a silence that indeed confined her anger. Kallandras was momentarily impressed.

"I come with information," Evayne said, breaking that chilly silence.

"No doubt it is urgent."

"I do not seek to second guess the wisdom of a Matriarch," the seer replied, smoothing the ice and irritation from her voice. "It is information; your sense of its urgency will decide, in the end, how urgent it is." She turned to Kallandras.

He bowed. The younger Evayne would never have been so politic because she would never have been so capable of judging the mood and character of a woman she had only just met.

He was certain that this was the first meeting for Evayne; her voice betrayed surprise, confusion and, overriding both, determination. Dislike. He wondered which Evayne had spoken with Elsarre, and what she had said.

But he did not wonder long. Elsarre's eyes were upon him, and she—the youngest, until the death of Evallen, of four Matriarchs— did not have the easy patience, or temper, that Yollana did. He knew better than to keep her waiting.

"Your information?"

"I have been sent," he said quietly, "with no words."

"Stranger, I warn you—"

He reached into the hidden pocket of the robe he wore. At his back, Dani moved, shifting position and changing his status of unarmed observer to armed one so quietly Evayne didn't turn at the noise.

When Kallandras opened his hand, Elsarre froze.

"This cannot be," she whispered. Her eyes narrowed, her gaze slid past him, flickering a moment like candlelight.

He *moved,* turning, his palm snapping into a fist, his free hand dislodging weapon from sheath. When it came up, it came up beneath the chin of the man called Dani.

To his surprise he found a slender blade a hand's width from the center of his chest.

He looked up; Dani's eyes met his. There was a flicker there, of recognition, perhaps of respect. A nod.

"Elsarre," Evayne said, her voice as cold as Northern winter. "This is not a game. It would pain me to deprive you of an obviously trusted ally, but I'll do it in a heartbeat if he doesn't lower his weapon."

The Matriarch rose, ignoring the seer's warning. Obviously, Kallandras thought, a better judge of character than he had given credit for. "Where did you get that?"

He held out his hand. The ring gleamed in his palm, band broken from beginning to end by russet etching in a bleached, pale white that Kallandras thought, from the look alone, must be bone. Except, of course, no simple bone could survive as long as this ring must have: it was etched with symbols the like of which he had last seen when the Kings had opened a cenotaph and their armies had descended into darkness, and the darkness beyond it.

"From the hand of Yollana of the Havalla Voyani."

She spit. Not at him, not quite, but the derision, the disbelief, could not be contained by a simple snort. She dressed like a Serra, but that was all that they and she had in common.

"She says the place is—"

"I will know the place," Elsarre snapped back. "If you do not lie, I will know it."

"Matriarch—"

"Dani, watch him. If he speaks another word, kill him." She turned to the woman at her side. "Ona Elisa?"

A volume in those two words.

The old woman met his eyes. "Your weapon," she said to Kallandras, no softness in her voice although she spoke quietly.

"Yes."

"It is the Lady's weapon."

"Yes."

"Swear by Her."

"What would you have me swear, Ona? All vows to the Lady have their price."

"Swear that the Matriarch gave you the ring."

"So sworn," he said softly. His eyes flickered off Dani's dagger hand as he made his decision. He lowered his own blade; let it bite palm. Hoped that the demon within it drew no sustenance from the gesture. "By the Lady."

She nodded grimly. "Trust him."

"But he—"

"You know it yourself, Elsarre. Trust your instincts."

"But a stranger's hand has *never* borne that ring. How could she take such a risk? I tell you, Elisa—"

"Tell yourself," Elisa replied, her voice firm, "that time is of the essence."

But she was not to be shamed—or corrected—in front of a stranger. She turned on him; he expected no less.

"You are a messenger, no more—and an ill chosen one. Speak of what you have seen, speak a *single word* of the thing that you carry, and I will have you hunted down and killed for sheer pleasure. Is that understood?"

"Well understood," he replied. He put a hand on Evayne's shoulder as he spoke.

It did no good. "You will have no pleasure from it, but perhaps the Corronans will be led, thereafter, by someone with temperance and wisdom."

"Evayne—"

"Are you threatening me?"

"No more than you threaten him," she replied, voice so cold it burned.

"Evayne," he said, speaking with the bard's gift to the seer's ears alone, **"this is pointless. I am not offended by the threat. I am not threatened by it. If it annoys you, let it annoy you on your own time. This is not the only journey we must make this day."**

He thought to chasten her, and perhaps it worked. Perhaps not. But she fell silent.

Elsarre's complexion was ruddy, her lips thinning with the effort to leave words unsaid. He recognized the expression. Before Evayne could speak again and break the fragile silence, he bowed.

"I accept the burden of silence that you have placed upon me," he said gravely. "And I understand the burden of trust that the Havallan Matriarch felt necessary, by circumstance, to bestow. I will honor both to the best of my ability; all else leads away from the *Voyanne*, into shadows that the Lady has never claimed."

"You do not follow the *Voyanne*."

"No," he said speaking so low she would have to strain to catch the words that left his lips, "But I, too, have walked away from my home for the sake, and the fate, of man."

She was silent. But the color left her cheeks; the flames receded. She said quietly, "Dani." Her acknowledgment of his words. And her command.

Dani sheathed his long dagger.

"We will meet again, you and I," he said quietly.

"Of that, I have no doubt. I do not know what the ring's message is, but it is clearly a summons."

"Dani," Elsarre said sharply, "show them out."

She could not have said *shut up* any more clearly. Dani grimaced.

But he showed them out.

"I hope," Evayne said darkly, speaking just loud enough to be heard by the men who served Elsarre, "that she grows up."

"I would not say your own response was worthy of you," he replied. "But she has long been the most difficult of the four. She feels her age. This may diminish with the death of Evallen."

"Great. She'll have someone else to push around."

"You haven't met Margret."

"Oh, yes, I have." She grimaced. "Of course, she was eight years old at the time. Or nine. I'm not good at judging the age of children."

"You will see more of her." The sun was bright, but the day was not overly hot; it was the Lady's season. He brought his hands to his eyes.

"Good. As long as I see less of Elsarre."

"Evayne."

"She was threatening you!"

"And I was not threatened. I fail to understand your particular sense of ownership in this case."

She had the grace to flush, and he thought that would be the end of it.

"I don't feel any ownership."

"No?"

"Kinship, maybe."

A cloud passed over the sun; he felt it, although he could not see it. For just a moment he wanted to turn on her, to grab her, shake her, even strike her. *Kinship.*

She saw it. She saw it in him, although he had become well versed in hiding from her over the years.

Her face paled. "I'm sorry, Kallandras. It's just that—"

"We have work."

"I forget sometimes," she continued doggedly, "that I forced you to take this road."

He laughed. The sound was more bitter to his ears than he would have liked, and far too honest. When he spoke again, he spoke with the intimate voice, the unassailable privacy. "No, Evayne; that is the fiction I told you—and myself—in my youth to attempt to deny the magnitude of my betrayal.

"But you could not force me to leave my brothers. Nothing could have forced that upon me but my own choice."

She was silent for a long time; the streets, roughly packed dirt giving way to the stone of the wider roads, passed beneath their feet as she kept her voice from him. She had learned, over the years, that her voice was the window through which he examined all her fear and motivation. At last she said, "I was offered a similar choice." He heard it; she so rarely spoke of the beginning at this age that he was surprised by the depth of the anger in the words. "So I know how little choice there really was."

"Evayne—"

"We all have to live with ourselves. We all have to *live*. If someone says to you, 'Do what I say or I'll slit the throat of this infant,' and they happen to have a knife at the throat of an infant, you have a so-called *choice*. But I'm not sure you can be judged by the quality of the choice you make in those circumstances."

He wanted to be gentle with her. That surprised him, as it so often did. He remembered the night, three months ago almost to the day, that she had come to him, bloodstained, and so very, very young. She knew that he was her enemy, or that he had been, but her fear and her anger were greater than that knowledge.

Kinship.

He had offered her comfort then. She had been too weary and too terrified to refuse it; familiarity, in that case, had meant more than the actual history that created it.

He closed his eyes. In the darkness, he heard a name he did not recognize, each syllable rich. Resonant. Silent. Someone had been sworn to a death, in the Lady's name.

This was no memory; it was event. What he had sworn decades past at labyrinth's end, when he had passed the last of the tests

and had finally proved himself worthy, had given him the world
of the *Kovaschaii,* and not even his betrayal could sunder the ties
the Lady built that day. Only his death would, and perhaps—
perhaps not even that. For She would not come to return to him
the name She had taken when he had offered Her his obedience.
Or so the Lady had promised.

And without that name, he had no way of finding the Halls of
Mandaros. Would he scream? Would he weep? Would he hover
on the edges of the *Kovaschaii* forever, a grim warning to all
who pledged their service?

Would he, in the end, succeed so that there might *be* brothers
to whom one could give such a warning?

"If someone held a knife to an infant's throat," he said, pausing
a moment, the name of a dead man passing from event into
memory, "and they offered me a choice, I would continue without
pause. Unless," he added softly, "prevention of that infant's death
was our goal at that time and place."

"Kallan—"

"Remember what I was," he said, words cool in the day's heat.
"Remember what I *am.*"

"I've seen what you are."

"Yes and no. A knife was held to the throat of the only thing
that would either move me or force me to hold my hand." He
turned, in a daylight shorn of cloud, and met her eyes. The wariness had returned to her face, her posture; she knew she had
offended him in some fashion.

They walked a while in the silence of the Lord's light; the
streets widened and narrowed. Twice, he pulled her into courtyard or fount as the wind carried the heavy footfalls of armored
men. He expected her to vanish at any time; to be gone between
one step and the next.

But an hour passed as he searched for the Voyani who would
lead him—or point him—to the Lyserran Matriarch, and she still
walked at his side, in his shadow.

"You're the only one," she said, her voice muted, a harshness
beneath the softness of the tone.

"The only one?"

"I've seen you at so many ages, I know you don't die."

"Evayne—"

"You're the only one I'm certain I don't destroy—and you're
the only one who was smart enough to hate me. Maybe they're

connected." She swallowed. "Maybe it's why I feel as if I—as if we're—" Looked away. "We're working toward the same end, Kallandras. And you know as much as I do, maybe more."

He had thought it odd that she had stayed, to saunter along this path on his search for Voyani.

He understood, as she could not, why. It was time.

Twenty-five years.

He wondered if his life as Kallandras, bard of Senniel College, might have been enough to satisfy him if the bonds that defined the *Kovaschaii* had died with his obedience. Certainly the anger and the loss would have sustained him for years. Two. Five. Ten. But a quarter of century?

The name of a man who was dead and who did not know it echoed in the still, hot day.

"And in the end," he said softly, "it was not your hand that held the knife. You showed me the truth. I blamed the messenger. I am not . . . proud of that. But it was . . ." Worse than death. "Kinship?" He caught her hand; pulled her to a fountain's side, where he knelt and began to polish brass and marble.

"It wasn't a good choice of word," she said, joining him, her robes shifting in shape and shade until they looked very much like the robes of a seraf owned by high clansmen.

The cerdan who passed not ten yards to the North spared them a glance, if that. Serafs of note at the time of the Festival Moon were as worthy of attention as the stones of the streets themselves; they were so much a part of the scenery they were hard to distinguish from the background.

"No, Evayne," he said softly, almost to himself.

Her robe, alive a moment with magic and movement, reformed in its own image, shaking as if the deception was unpleasant. "I know. I'm sorry—I wasn't thinking. I know that we don't—"

"Not yet, but soon."

He turned.

Saw her, frozen in place, her eyes widening slowly as hope— he could see it so clearly now—stripped her of defense. In her youth, her anger almost as harsh and all-encompassing as his own had been, she had been so hard to hurt. He had tried. Perhaps that was why he had seen so little of her as youth, so much as older woman.

"Kallandras," she began, looking up.

She took a step toward him.

She was gone.

* * *

Elena's shadow was longer than it had been; so was her face. She caught a glimpse of it as she passed by the mirror that Voyani Matriarchs possessed, but seldom used. She suspected the mirror was part of a stage act, a way of convincing the gullible—and even among her own, she was willing to admit that fools were legion—that the Matriarch had special powers without resorting to the powers in question. She did not want to speak to Nicu.

Why?

Because she was afraid she knew what he was going to say, and she didn't know what she'd do if she heard it.

It's not my fault, she thought fiercely. She'd been having the argument, in all its variations, since she'd agreed to speak with Nicu. Rehearsal. She knew Nicu well enough to play his part.

So did Margret. But Margret did not mention Nicu and Nicu was not mentioned around Margret. It was almost as if he *had* died. Maybe it would have been better.

And would it? What would you have done if she'd called for his head? No answer, there. Or an uneasy answer she didn't want to look at, which was pretty much the same thing.

She and Margret shared blood, but they weren't cut from the same bolt. Elena knew, on some fundamental level, that she could deal with the hard things when they came up. She could wield a sword. Could birth a difficult baby. Could take a life, either in anger or as an act of mercy. Could sell herself, if that was the price of survival.

She had done it all.

If she was faced with Nicu's death, she would find the strength to deal with that as well, but there were darknesses one didn't go into gladly, or at all, unless one were forced.

And Margret?

Elena's hands did a slow, tight curl until they were shaking. She remembered, on the edge of anger, the days when she and Margret used to fight for Nicu's attention. She remembered the days—she, just off her mother's knee—that she thought they would all grow up and get married, take vows, be inseparable. She remembered the earnest vows they had made then.

" 'Lena?"

She was angry.

She didn't want to be angry, but she'd swallowed the rage; it was inside her. She didn't want to pay the price of keeping it there.

Her hands would not unclench; they tightened at the sound of her name in his voice.

They stayed that way until she saw his face.

" 'Lena?" His voice broke between the two syllables. His face, his too-beautiful face, was yellow and purple where he'd been ungently handled, but no lasting damage had been done.

"Nicu—"

"I know you're angry," he said. "I—"

"Nicu—"

"I wasn't thinking. I *know* she's the Matriarch, but—"

"But what?"

"But she's Margret. She's always told me what to do. I've never had to listen." His eyes were wide as cat's eyes, broken only by the spill of dull hair.

She was still angry, but he'd managed to break the back of the worst of her temper by exposing his throat. If she could've been certain he'd done it on purpose, she'd've hit him, hard. But this Nicu, this Nicu she knew well. The contrition and the fear—of her disapproval, of Margret's—was as real as the temper and the hubris and the arrogance. That was Nicu's problem. He did everything with his whole heart—and nothing with his head.

"Nicu—"

"I know. I know. I—"

"What did you want to talk about?"

" 'Lena, don't be mad at me. I—you don't understand."

"No. I don't."

"We're always on the bottom. The clans rule *everything*. This was our chance."

His eyes shifted slightly and his glance strayed groundward. "Nicu," Elena said sharply.

"Never mind."

"Nicu, if you're really sorry, you'll tell us exactly where you got that sword."

"I did tell you."

"You just took a sword from a man you've never laid eyes on? You accepted an unblooded blade from someone who isn't even kin?" She couldn't keep the scorn and the disbelief out of her face—or she assumed she couldn't; she didn't try very hard.

He flushed. "Do you *know* how many clansmen I killed?" He said, voice low, chin slowly rising. "They would have been ours."

"We weren't in danger—or we wouldn't have been if you hadn't started killing them in their own home!"

"I was *tired* of hiding and mewling like a weakling!"

She felt her jaw lock. She raised her hand. Lowered it. "Nicu," she said quietly. "We don't have anything to say to each other." She turned on her heel.

He caught her by the arm and then leaped back when she spun on him. As if he expected the fist to be wrapped round a dagger's shaft. "Don't ever do that again." She turned away. Thinking. Not wanting to think. Hoping to escape before he said the words she didn't want to hear.

"But I did it for you—don't you understand?"

Lady, please, not this, Lady, not this. She kept walking.

"Elena!"

She turned. She almost hated him, but something buried deeper than affection made his pain unbearable.

"I did it because I love you."

"Nicu—"

"I did it because you deserve better than this!"

She started to speak. Stopped herself. Something twisted at her stomach with claws as sharp as any knife that had ever broken flesh. For just a moment, less, the scenery, shifted, breaking and regrouping as if it were a vessel and it had been shattered and rebuilt by hands that had a deeper understanding of clay.

She saw Nicu's face, eyes sightless but open, robbed of expression, of the ability to express itself. Circling him, dark shadows, burning him—although he was well past sensation—the unadorned face of the Lord.

And weeping, weeping into the desert, voices that she could not bear to listen to, because one of them was her own.

He'll do it, she thought, numb because to feel at all was suddenly too dangerous. She closed her eyes to hold back tears, and when she opened them again, he was standing before her, ruddy faced, bruised, defiant. Young and—Lady help him—so very, very stupid. Had they let him be so stupid? How?

But the stupidity was precious because it was Nicu's, and because it meant he was still alive.

She opened her arms. Just as she had when they had been younger. She saw him, suspicion withering almost before it had a chance to take root—stupid, stupid, Nicu—greed overcoming sense as he swept in to take what he desired most.

What all children in pain desired most: comfort.

He smelled of sweat. He was the wrong shape—too tall now,

and too broad—and she the wrong height. But she was 'Lena, he was Nicu.

Don't you do it, don't do it, Nicu, she thought, the words like a prayer she didn't dare give voice to because the wind was capricious and might take the words to ears not meant to hear them. *Don't make her kill you.*

CHAPTER TWENTY-FOUR

17th of Scaral, 427 AA
Tor Leonne

Finding the Lyserran Matriarch proved challenging. Had it not been so close to the Festival of the Moon, Kallandras would have assumed that she had wisely chosen to forsake the city by which the Dominion would be defined for generations to come. But it *was* the Festival, and the Matriarchs, who avoided the cities of the clansmen at any other time of the year, made the trek to the Tor Leonne.

It was the Lord's City, for the man who held the City was the ruler of the Dominion. But it was the Lady's City, for it held the Lake that had been Her gift and their salvation. It drew them all: the people who claimed power by His law, and the people who claimed power by Her mystery.

He found her, not in the poorest sections of the clansmen's city, but in one of the wealthiest; found her, not as an obvious ruler within her own caravan, but as a guest, of sorts, within another's, and at that, a clansman's. A merchant clansman.

"Aiya," a man said, his voice a voice that, while soft in seeming, had been trained to carry the distance. Kallandras did not immediately look up, but he stopped a moment to admire the pale silks that had been painted for the moon's season. The work was very fine. Edged in gold—as most silks were that made it this far into the heart of the Dominion, it was adorned by no central work. Instead, the delicate impression of lilies had been created by minimal strokes of white and pink and a green the shade of muted jade.

"You seem to be a discerning man," the merchant said.

"I am," he replied, and this time he let his gaze move across the panoply of bolts and up.

The man he faced was large. Dark-haired, dark-eyed, dark-skinned; in all things, Annagarian. He spoke Torra as if he were a clansman, a sure indication that he was used to trading with moneyed men. He wore desert clothing, the heavy robes of the sandtraders, but his hands were ringed in fine gold. Heavy gold; his fingers were not small.

"The bolt you were looking at," the merchant said with a practiced smile, "was made as a special gift for a young Serra. But she passed away not two weeks ago and as the family is one of my best customers, I did not choose to press the issue of payment or delivery. If you desire it—"

"It is very fine," Kallandras said, with a smile that was far more natural—and far more practiced—than the merchant's. "But it is too pale and too youthful a pattern for my taste. I have no young daughters."

"No, indeed. Nor have I. Sons," he added. "But they are strong and useful. You have no wife?"

"I had one." His tone made clear that the subject was not open to discussion. "I seek a silk," he said, in case the merchant was not skilled at reading such a tone, "for a woman who will reach her prime during the Festival season. Something darker or cooler than these, less fancy, more elegant."

"Elegance such as that will be seen as poverty."

"I am not a man who lives by the opinion of other men. Those who know will know; those who do not will not. Neither concern me."

"Ah." The merchant nodded sagely. "As long as you understand that the price for such silk will not be much less than the price I must charge for these."

"I understand it might be more. But I am weary of searching. I have seen the very finest that three merchants have to offer already, and I am determined to seek the fourth. I will, I hope, end my quest here." He frowned. "These silks, these are all you possess?"

The man spit to the side in derision. He clapped his hands and two young men appeared from the flaps of the tenting at his back. They had much of his look about them, but they were as grim-faced as guards.

"My sons," he said. "You, Jonni, you sell these while I'm gone. This customer is looking for something special."

The son so addressed nodded.

"Mika, go to your mother and tell her, be ready."

The second son nodded.

The merchant turned to Kallandras. "Follow me."

"Your sons," Kallandras said, "will make fine warriors."

The merchant looked pained. "They require some experience at the more gentle art of selling, yes. But they can be brought to smile."

"I'm not certain I'd like to see that."

The man shrugged. "All right, you're right. But at least they're marriageable, and they'll bring me daughters who might teach them some of the social graces." He grimaced. "If, that is, I can afford them."

He led them through a market that was thin with people. It was, indeed, the market at which the clansmen stooped to barter, and as men did not demean themselves by open discussion of something as vulgar as money, it was perfectly natural for the merchant to lead Kallandras to some private dwelling where arrangements might be made.

Equally natural was the presence of the Serras with their cerdan, Toran, or even Tyran. Wives were allowed by custom to trade with merchants—so long as they had the appropriate clan presence to preserve the aura of propriety. Even so, merchant wives often dealt with the Serras of the high clans. Or daughters.

The merchant, however, who claimed no daughters obviously intended to deal with Kallandras himself.

There was no merchant authority in the Tor Leonne; no laws that governed the merchants in the way the Imperial laws governed the various merchant guilds. But there was an old dwelling, the finest of the buildings in the city that existed beneath the plateau. Here, the ruling Tyr of the Terrean had once made his home, and he had made it out of the bones of the earth: stone and clay and wood.

No Tyr claimed it now; the stone and wood had protected the Tyr from all enemies save time and a weak heir. The man who had succeeded the weak son had in his turn been betrayed—by blood.

Songs had been written and sung about the fate of the men who had chosen to value their dwellings over their prowess and in the end—through some path that was not clear to Kallandras or most of the bards who carried this Southern tale—the building had come into the hands of merchants who managed, barely, to work in concert. They were, after all, men who valued money over the warrior ethic; a breed necessary but in the end as valued as women.

Seeing the merchant Court—unofficially called the whorehouse by many of the Southern clansmen, all of whom notably did not have the right to cross its threshold—he could well believe it was money that was the worshiped god within the building's confines.

The high clansmen had, about their lives, a starkness, a simplicity that was at once elegant and profound. The difference between the Tor Leonne, situated upon the plateau, and the merchant Court was the difference between an unbroken oath ring and the gaudy, jeweled creations so valued by the newly rich; the one was a statement of quiet power and endurance, the other a statement of riches. And power, of course; even in the Dominion, money and power were not easily separable.

The stairs, as wide across as three lesser buildings, forced those who would enter to acknowledge the lofty heights of the men who were privileged to call the Court their home. At the height of the stairs, stone leveled out, giving way to a mass of flower beds on either side. These flowers, watered and tended as the men in the streets below were not, were the merchant symbol: they thrived, no matter what the season, or the condition, of the world that lived at the foot of the stairs.

"Ah," the man said. "Here we are."

Kallandras stopped, his hand hovering an inch above the wide, gold-laced rails that punctuated the stairs in three places.

The merchant smiled, clearly pleased with himself. "I am," he said, "Tallos of the clan Jedera."

Tallos. A shadow passed over the sun.

"Have I said something to offend?" the merchant asked, looking somewhat annoyed by the lack of expected reaction.

"No, Ser Tallos. I—had a compatriot in my youth who perished in the war. He bore that name."

"Tallos is an overused name," the merchant replied, somewhat mollified.

"I think it, rather, well used. You are of the clan Jedera."

"Yes."

Tallos. Tallos di'Jedera. The name was vaguely familiar. The clan itself was not one of the warrior clans; it lacked the antiquity of Leone, Callesta, Lamberto, or even Marente, and the sons of Jedera blood would therefore never rule.

But it had *money,* and the prestige that money could buy.

Among the merchants, that prestige was a seat in the hall of the merchant Court, and a right to use the halls and courts, the baths and parlors, at the height of those grand stairs.

"Come," the merchant said. "When the business at hand is a matter of significance, or the client a client I feel will be of import in the future of the clan, I prefer to retreat to the Court. There are very, very few who would question the authority of the merchants within their own halls."

"Indeed," Kallandras said softly. "And the clan Larantos perished because they likewise understood that custom had the force of law, and they sought to force that issue with the ruling Tyr."

"An interesting phrase. The force of law."

Kallandras paused an instant, gold warmed by sun beneath his palm. Misstep.

Without pausing, the merchant who called himself Tallos took the steps, leaving Kallandras with a simple choice. He could follow, or he could leave. He followed.

"You will find," the merchant said, his voice thick with accent as he slid from Torra to Weston, "that the word law in Torra is very rarely used."

"It is often used," Kallandras countered, still speaking the Torra that had been his birth tongue. "But it goes by the guise of power."

"And in the North," the merchant said, abandoning the obviously foreign tongue, "the guise of power is indeed baffling. But it is there, if one knows how to look."

Kallandras smiled. "Money, Ser Tallos, is more valued in the North than in the South."

"Less valued," Tallos replied. "But more openly."

"You have traveled."

"The clan Jedera deals heavily in the goods that come through the Terrean of Averda. We had hoped to . . . take more active control of those interests." He shrugged. "The clan Callesta is more interested in things monetary than we would like. But who knows? The winds of war are coming, and may sweep them entirely from the plains and valleys."

"Many of their allies will be caught in that gale."

"Indeed, it is so." The merchant shrugged. "But men of money make poor allies, or so it is said."

"It is, indeed, said."

The flower beds passed beneath three large arches, the facades of which were gilded and painted in deep blues. Bright light and dark intertwined in swirling patterns that, only when viewed at a distance coalesced into a meaning that was not merely a visual delight: *Those who are willing to pay the price, enter.*

Seeing where his guest's gaze dwelled, the merchant said softly, "I think you have already paid."

Kallandras raised a brow. Games were a part of his art, but he was suddenly weary of them. The day was wearing thin; he would not be at Yollana's side again until dusk, and then only if he moved quickly.

"I have," he replied in Weston.

The merchant's raised brow mirrored his own.

"Take me to her. We have very, very little time."

There were four Halls of Gold: the Lord's Hall of Gold, the Lady's Hall of Gold, the Golden Hall of Dawn and the Golden Hall of Dusk. They formed a quartered circle in the center of the circular grounds beyond the impressive, arched walls: the symbol, in the South, of an oath made between equals.

There was something appropriate in that; the men who had made both building and oath had perished, but what they had wrought remained. Legacy. He was not certain where the merchant led him, but his path crossed the Lord's Hall, where those merchants of power who wished to make a statement by presence alone might choose to spend a portion of their day.

The Hall had been built by a warrior; it was built for warriors. Commerce, like one of the forgotten arts, had devolved onto the shoulders of lesser men, made Tors for the most part in an effort to insure that such devolution did not engender dangerous disloyalty.

Titles seldom produced that effect among men of ambition; Kallandras wondered idly why the gambit was so often tried.

Or perhaps the sense of the attempt was too Northern in origin; perhaps the titles were an attempt to dignify the import of duties that might otherwise remain hazardously untended. Men of worth, after all, hungered for many things, but tending money, much like tilling fields, was not one of them. Perhaps the only incentive that *could* motivate a free man was the title itself. He could not be certain.

What he could be certain of was this: The Hall was vast, and half of its visible surfaces were covered in gold. The arches, fanciful and fancy, through which the flower beds had passed were forsaken here for the absolute lines of a rectangle that stood the

height of the ceiling on either end of the hall. Smaller doors
punctuated the massive stretch of walls to either side, but they
had been designed to blend in with the grim and exotic face of
the walls themselves: In cold, golden relief, the battles of Tyrs
were played out for the Lord's pleasure.

"Do you recognize that?"

He looked back at the hooded expression of his companion.
"The battle? No. I confess that my studies were less military in
nature."

"Ah. Well."

"You are familiar with it?"

"I? I am merely a merchant," Tallos di'Jedera said.

His answer was carefully neutral.

Too careful.

"Are those doors ever closed?"

The merchant frowned. "Doors? You mean the arch?"

"It is not an arch—or rather, it serves that function but it has
hinges built into the stone."

"An interesting question."

"And one to which you don't have the answer."

"I would have to say no," Tallos continued, as if Kallandras
had not spoken aloud. "In my tenure, they have never been
closed. It is an odd question."

"Odd?"

"I have brought many guests through the triad and into the
Halls of Gold—although I have left many more in desire of such
entry at the stairs—and most of them fall silent when they enter
the Hall." He shrugged, turning toward the rectangular doorway
that had been the target of such idle curiosity. He began to walk
again. "Those who do not fall silent fall into their own catego-
ries. There are men whose need to impress is so great they trivi-
alize the wonder they see. There are those who simply cannot be
silent—and among merchants, that number is legion. And there
are those who cannot contain the sudden awe they feel; it strikes,
and they respond before they can stop themselves.

"But I babble. Come. We must pass through the center, and
from there, the Lady's Hall. We have little time."

The center was, itself, a hall of a type. Four large arches, each
in a different style, entered it, and for that reason it had a chaotic,
an uneven look to it—one that no detail in the Lord's Hall would
have hinted at. Of the four entrances, the Lord's was the boldest,

the simplest, the tallest, its line unbroken from floor to height by so much as a bend.

Opposite the Lord's arch was the Lady's. It was tall, of course, but not so tall as the Lord's; wide, but not so wide. It was, however, splendid. One could see where the architect had started with the simple shape of a door, but no mandate had confined him to its line. From the floor to two thirds of the full arch's height, it rose unimpeded. But from there, it traveled up in a trefoil whose peak was adorned with opal and diamond. Gold lined the wall in profusion—to be expected of something subtitled Hall of Gold—but overlapping the gold, a colder metal, like new silver. Or platinum.

Engraved in the width of the stone wall that supported the arch were words in old Torra. He could not pronounce them, not cleanly, but he knew what their symbols meant. Birth. Joy. Sorrow. Love. Hatred. Loss. Death. Dominion.

The Lady's domain. He paused before he passed beneath the arch. Bowed once, although the day without was bright and the sun high. Windows, glassed and leaded and supported by the work of architects the like of which the Dominion had not seen in decades, let that daylight in, where it spilled across expanses of gold and stone as if daring mere men to rise to the challenge of poets in an attempt to describe it.

Tallos passed beneath the arch and paused there, waiting.

Kallandras nodded slightly. Followed.

And then, before his foot touched the tiles beyond the arch, he leaped forward in a sudden surge of movement that ended with the merchant.

Tallos di'Jedera swung 'round; Kallandras held him firmly by shoulder and throat, using him as a shield.

It happened in an eye blink; the merchant grunted as a crossbow bolt hit him in the fleshy upper arm. He spun again, but the merchant shouted an order in sharp, harsh Torra, his voice a bark.

Kallandras did not speak.

"Very well," the merchant said softly. "My apologies, but I had to be certain."

"And now?"

"I am certain. *Mika.*"

The second son appeared from behind one of the glorious columns of light the windows above made of stone. His crossbow was unfired. "Father—"

"It is enough."

"But he—"

"Will you shame me further by arguing in front of a stranger?" He made no attempt to shrug himself free of the hand that held him.

Which was just as well.

"Jonni!"

A second man appeared. The merchant relaxed.

"There are three," Kallandras said.

"Mika—"

"He's lying. There were only Jonni and I." Truth, in that voice. And not a little fear, although the surface of the words was unbroken by it, and a man with little talent might have missed it altogether. He was certain, then, that Mika actually was Tallos' son.

Ser Tallos was silent a moment. Then he said quietly, "The third is not mine."

"No," the third voice said, stepping out of the shadows that light also made. Her face was the color of ivory, her hair was pale, and her eyes were like the winter sky. Her crossbow was armed; she held it firmly, with the casual familiarity of one who has used it often.

"I believe," she said softly, "that you have something of value to me."

He met her eyes for a moment.

"I believe," he replied, "that we have grounds for discussion. May we repair to a less public venue?"

"It would be hard to find a less public venue than the Lady's Hall." She lifted a hand, swept it in a wide semicircle. "The Lady's Hall—and the Lord's—are not as venerated as they once were within the Court."

"I . . . see. Nevertheless, I must ask."

"I thought you might." She put up the crossbow. "Come, then. We were expecting you."

She led them to the North wall. Paused before it. Bowed deeply, the movement so exact it had the feel of ritual. Kallandras was afraid that Mika might try something unwise, but his father's terse command seemed to keep him in check.

The stranger put her hand to the wall. Said three words. The words themselves were perfectly clear and completely meaningless to Kallandras' ear. Magic.

He nodded to himself as the door, unseen and indistinguishable until that moment from the flat panorama of gold and blue that was sunset over the Menorans, slid open.

"Enter," the woman said quietly, "and accept the hospitality of the Lady."

"Thank you," he replied, releasing the merchant.

Tallos di'Jedera, bleeding from the bolt that he had not yet retrieved from his arm, straightened himself to his full height.

"I believe," Kallandras added, as he turned his back upon them all and walked into the small enclosure, "that you are the woman I've been searching for."

There were no benches here; no chairs; none of the furniture that one associated with a Northern room.

But there were also no mats, no pillows, no low tables and no fans. There were no torches, and no windows, no openings from above through which light might fall.

Yet the room was not dark, and it did not feel empty.

"You take your risk," he said softly to the woman.

"This Festival," she replied gravely, "I felt as if there were little choice. Tallos," she added, speaking to the merchant for the first time, a real note of anger in the calm of her voice.

"I had to be certain," he told her, shrugging. "You know what they've offered for you."

"They?"

"The Tyr'agar has expressed a desire to meet with the Voyani. Or we assume that's what incarceration in the Tor proper means." Tallos shrugged. "Unfortunately, given other disturbing rumors, Maria has elected to remain . . . remote."

"I see. A wise decision. So, too, have the other Matriarchs, although not one of the three is as well hidden as the Serra."

She raised a brow at the title.

He bowed in return. "Apologies, Matriarch, but were it not for the hand of the sun upon your skin, I would not guess by voice or gesture that you were a Matriarch. There is a roughness that seems to elude you, or a polish that eludes them, but having met the three, I would say the former is the more likely truth."

"I accept your apologies," she said, with the faintest hint of a smile, "but I do not believe they come from any accidental slip. You knew who I was."

"It is a failing of my profession."

"It is a failing of one of your professions."

He froze then.

"My thanks, however; I realize that Tallos could just as easily be dead as wounded at your hands. He required some proof that you were as I said you were."

"And that, Matriarch?"

"Does it matter? You have come to us, and you have passed any test we have set for you. You have a message."

"You do not know what that message is."

"Although it grieves me, no." Truth.

Yet she had known he would come to the market, to Tallos di'Jedera. So she had some of the Matriarch's gift, and the ability to use it.

He slid his hand deftly into his robe; extracted Yollana's message in the curve of his fingers, and withdrew it. "Just this," he said softly.

The poor light in the room flickered erratically as his fingers exposed palm, and the contents of hand.

She was as unlike Elsarre—as unlike a Matriarch—as any woman could be. He saw her skin pale beneath the surface; saw the sudden stillness of chest, heard the extra layer of silence that it provided. She offered him no more. Until she lifted her own hand to take the ring he held out.

The arm trembled. She could not stop it.

"I see," she said softly. "There were rumors that Yollana was taken. Exaggerated?"

"No."

The ring looked so fragile in her hands. She turned it over, and over again. "I have never had such a summons," she said at last, and although her words were as cool as any Serra's might be, beneath the surface her fear lay completely exposed.

"Bard," she said softly.

He raised a brow.

"I see you. I saw Yollana. I saw Elsarre. I saw the face of a young woman, and not the woman I would have . . . expected of this summons. Evallen of the Arkosa?"

"She perished in the Tor Leonne during the Festival of the Sun."

The Matriarch of Lyserra closed her eyes. "So. It was her."

"You attended the Festival of the Sun?"

"Yes," she said softly.

"Unusual."

"No, not so very unusual as all that."

"Maria—" Tallos began.

She lifted a delicate hand to his lips. Stalled the words that spilled from them with a smile. "Tallos is the kai Jedera."

Tallos looked slightly offended that she felt it necessary to make that clarification. Hard to tell how genuine the expression was.

"And I am his Serra."

The silence that followed the words—his, her husband's, the man he had called son—was the sudden hush of men who expected revelation to bring immediate danger. She, however, continued to speak, allowing them only that briefest of pauses. "You must forgive us our lack of hospitality."

"You—you are the Serra en'Jedera?"

"Even so."

"But you are—"

She smiled. "Yes. And sometime, sometime I will tell you the story. Suffice it to say that it was not my mother, but my mother's sister, who was Matriarch before me. My mother died during a clan raid, and I was . . . raised by hands other than Voyani for much of my young life. We have compromised much, Ser Jedera and I, in order to maintain what we have built."

The logistics of their life seemed far too complicated to succeed. In spite of himself, he was curious—but not so curious that he could not wait.

"You will see the fruit of that compromise. It is not a well known fact, but among the Matriarchs, it *is* known. I am not, and I will not be, respected or trusted. Even my own fear my absences.

"But my daughter bears no such taint; she is Voyani, start to finish."

He looked at the ring that she held in her hand. "I fear," he said softly, "that her taint, or her lack, will not be in question. The Festival of the Moon is almost upon us."

Something in his tone caught her by surprise—and that, judging by the chilling of her expression, an unpleasant surprise.

"What did Yollana tell you?"

"She need tell me very little," he replied softly, his gaze sliding off her face to a point beyond her shoulder—and beyond the walls that kept them all hidden. "I have long known that the Festival of the Moon and the High Winter night are the same, and I have been forced to walk the Winter road."

"You have walked the Lady's dark road?" She brought her

hands up in a complicated gesture that ended with a single word
of denial—a word in an ancient tongue.

"We do, in the end, what we must. That is the way of it. There
has never been any other."

"You are not what I expected."

"What did you expect?"

"A brother," she said, using the Voyani word for kin, "dark
and fair."

"And I?"

"You are fair and fair; like light upon cold water." Her hand
curled into a fist, and then opened. "Take back what you have
offered. My answer will be known." She turned to the man she
called husband, although the Matriarchs *never* had husbands, and
said, "You must leave."

"I will not leave without you."

"You will."

"Maria—"

"Tallos." Her hand caught his; his eyes narrowed.

"He has frightened you."

"Do not," she said, warning him. "He is messenger, no more."

"Men kill messengers who bear bad tidings."

"Then they are fools. Some tidings can only be carried by men
who understand enough of their weight to persevere. You must
take our sons and leave the Tor Leonne."

"But I—"

"Now."

"And our daughters?"

"They will take care of themselves."

"Mother!" the man called Mika said, for just that moment
sounding like an aggrieved young son. He drew close, as close as
Ser Tallos.

"They are not bound by the rules of the clans, my son," she
said, lifting a hand to touch his face. "And your sister leads her
people. She can no more find safety—even if it's the only intelligent thing to do—than the Tyr'agar; not without loss of face
and power."

"But we—"

"Have no such power to lose. I . . . did not see the danger. But
the message Yollana sent can only mean one thing."

"And that?"

"Tallos." There was warning, gentle but unmistakable, in
the word.

"Maria—" He caught her face in his hands; she let him. They stood that way in a silence punctuated by the sullen worry of their son. At last, gruffly, he said, "I should never have freed you."

"I'll be careful. I always am."

"Because you are lying to me out of worry, I forgive you," he replied, brushing his fingers very gently across her brow. "We have seen so much together." He kissed her, quickly. "And I want to see more. Aya, Maria, I have never seen you so—"

"Take my sons and leave. Promise me this."

"But I—"

"Promise me, Tallos."

"Or you'll stay?" He chuckled. She did not.

"I have to do this. I cannot guarantee that I will return, and I will not attempt to lie to you again. But if I am to go, to do what must be done—"

"Maria, *what must be done?*"

Her fingers brushed, and closed, his lips. "I wish to know at least some part of my life and my heart is safe."

He was silent. At last he said, "You, dark brother." He had not turned; had not taken his eyes off the face of his unyielding wife.

But he had called Kallandras by his oldest title. No, not title; a title was a thing that could be walked away from, ignored, repudiated. He had called him by his oldest self, and that self, forsworn, nonetheless answered.

"Yes."

"I know what I must pay you to have a life taken, Lady-willing. But what must I pay in order to have a life preserved?"

Kallandras chuckled. It was not a humorous sound. Dry as the summer heat, he said, "We are not preservers of life. If you wish a life spared, bespeak the Lady. Your Serra has told you—I am certain she has told you—that there is no safety."

"If you cannot preserve a life, and can only take it, what must I pay you to take the lives of those who would harm her?"

He started to say, *More than you have,* but the words fell short of his lips. This man probably had enough. "I am not," he said, "a protector."

He was surprised at how hollow the words sounded to his own ears. *Does it come to this?*

"Kallandras," she said, speaking a name he had not given her. He didn't ask where she had learned it; he could guess. The tone of her voice, the texture of the name she spoke, made her meaning plain. *Lie to him.*

Expedience, he understood. Lies, he understood as well. He had accepted the title the merchant used as his own, although he had no right—and had had no right for a majority of his life now—to claim it. And yet.

He bowed. "Inasmuch as I can, I will protect what you value. I do not guarantee success; I cannot make that protection my mission. Compensation is therefore not at issue."

"Maria—"

"Go," she said quietly. "Go to your daughters."

The Widan Cortano di'Alexes was immersed in the ancient studies by which he had made himself a power to be reckoned with. At his side, two of the lesser Widan toiled, poor substitutes for the men whose loyalty and expertise he had lost to demon hands. He was not a man of many words when the subject was anything other than the heart of his studies; he had said his economical farewells by the sides of dead men whose bodies had then become evidence, things to study and dissect in search for proof and truth.

But he had said other things as well; oaths of a sort, and they had been graven in air—as so few things were—by the force of his anger. That anger drove him now, and very, very few of the Widan were reckless enough to step in its path.

But every congregation has its fools.

What surprised him, as he broke the flow of his concentration with a brief look that should have killed, and in fact might have, had the protective magics surrounding the bearer not been so strong, was the identity of that fool.

Sendari di'Sendari.

Surprise pulled him back from the edge. He returned to the powder he was grinding in a large pestle.

"We have a problem," Sendari said.

"You have a penchant for understatement. How rare, in these times."

Sendari did not answer the irony with any irony of his own. In fact, he did not answer at all.

Cortano continued his work. "Mikalis," he said. "Willem. Leave. Now. Return in no more than an hour, and no less than a quarter of that."

They bowed at once, hands steeped in blood and dust, and obeyed.

"As you have deprived me of necessary labor, you might consider joining me while you speak."

"There have been reports."

Cortano glanced up. "All reports come through me."

"Reports to do with *Kialli* activity or reports that have filtered back from our spies within the Shining Court, yes."

"And these?"

"They have come to us from the common cerdan in the city below."

Cortano frowned. "Sendari—"

"There is trouble. Fire—and worse—in the streets."

"And worse?"

"I believe the man spoke of the earth cracking, and the ground taking form and shape and swallowing a man whole. His screams, apparently, could still be felt in the vibration of the earth that enveloped him for some time."

"Rogue."

"Indeed."

"Sendari, I warn you—"

"But worse. The Blasphemy is spreading, and I am not certain we have the resources necessary to contain it."

"What blasphemy—speak plainly, Lord scorch you!" He was exhausted. They were all exhausted. That was the only excuse he could give for so plainly misunderstanding what would otherwise have been obvious in Sendari's words.

"It has long been said, and long been believed, that the power of the Sword is the province and the privilege of men, although there is ample proof to the North that the truth is otherwise. We have our own reasons for maintaining these beliefs. They have served us well.

"But the evidence—dramatic and sudden as it is—works against us here. The power of fire and earth, of wind and water, is being wielded by a woman."

"By a—Lady's blood."

"Yes. Anya is in the Tor Leonne."

CHAPTER TWENTY-FIVE

She had told him to leave her alone. More than once. She told him and told him and told him. But he followed her, speaking Southern gibberish, and when she got annoyed and told him to go away, he shouted at her. In the Court, that would have meant his death right there, and no one would have spoken two words for him, except maybe ones that meant he was stupid.

But Anya wasn't stupid; she knew that the rules of the Court—the Shining, secret Court—were different from the rules of the rest of the world, at least until Allasakar revealed Himself. She had to be careful. She had to be *nice*.

But when he *touched* her, when his words, which smelled a pale, ugly green, accompanied the taste of black, she couldn't remember what nice meant. It was only for a minute or two. It was such a *short* time. But the ground here was so *soft* and the people were all so frail it reminded her of—

Of things she hated to be reminded of.

Just a glimpse of her mother's face, her father's stern expression weakened by affection, and both of them useless, helpless—she couldn't think of them *here*. They might find her. And what would they do if they found her? What would they say?

She remembered to be nice now, but it was too late; the earth was broken and the ground was all black and the rock of the fountain—there had been a fountain, she'd been sitting on the edge of a fountain—had melted beneath her feet, but not before the heat on the inside cracked it and sent splinters flying everywhere.

Blood.

Dead people.

Screaming people.

She didn't like the screaming. It reminded her of other things she didn't want to remember, so she had to make the screaming stop—and when it stopped, when it finally stopped, everything was just *too* quiet.

Anya a'Cooper stood in the center of a large crater. The sides of the homes that had cramped the old streets had been either splintered or melted depending on how close they'd been to her fire. She could see whole living areas, barren of life; could see blood being absorbed by dirt that never got quite enough moisture.

She knew Lord Ishavriel was going to be angry with her, and she was—just for a moment—afraid.

Which made her angry.

She hadn't *come* here to kill all these people. But that man shouldn't have touched her. He shouldn't have touched anyone. He shouldn't have shouted.

She didn't like the open sun and the heat and the cloudless sky. But she'd come here looking for something and she didn't want to go home before she found it.

She didn't remember what it was.

As she walked away from the mess, a little child reached up and grabbed the edge of her robe with his three-fingered hand. She started to yank herself free, but stopped as she looked more closely at the face. It was a little girl's face, her dark, long hair sheared by fire's touch, her skin bruised and reddened, her eyes terribly wide. She opened her mouth, but no words came out.

Anya understood children. She had always liked them. She had planned to have them herself, lots of them, before—No. No, she wouldn't think of that, not here. Not yet.

"It's all right," she said, as she bent at the knees and picked up the little girl. The child drew sharp breath. "You're *hurt,*" Anya a'Cooper said softly. "Don't worry. I'll help you. I'll take you to where it's safe." She propped the child up on her shoulder; heard the girl's muffled exclamation of pain, and winced in sympathy. "He won't hurt you, you know," she said. "He won't hurt anyone anymore. He's quite dead."

427 AA
Stone Deepings

Na'jay.

  Not now, Oma.

  Now.

  Not now.

She stood beside Avandar, or rather, in front of him. She allowed herself to be grateful that he had chosen to be her shadow; it seldom happened, and she hoped it wouldn't become habit, but if she labored under any other illusions, her ability to survive this encounter without him wasn't one of them.

His magical line burned the vision but not the ground, and the host of the Winter Queen stayed on either side of it: Celleriant, on foot, and the Queen to the side of a wounded creature that seemed to be healing as Jewel watched.

Na'jay, her Oma said again. *You can keep her here until the sun sets on High Winter. But you don't have the power to hold her for longer. The Warlord might—but I wouldn't bet on it. If you use your head, you'll let her pass. You've proved your point.*

Fine.

The silence that followed was a little warm for Jewel's liking. The child that lay buried beneath years of responsibility didn't remember her Oma being such an interfering nag. *I'm not sure what more you want,* the old woman continued, after the silence had done its work. *She did heal the creature.*

That's not what I asked for, and she knows it.

Would you have her approach the Winter Hunt without a mount?

I'd have her forget the Hunt altogether if it were in my power. It's not. Na'jay, let it go now.

But she was looking up at the night's scattered face, little glittering lights strewn, as if thrown by some careless deity, across the dark heavens.

"Mortal," the Winter Queen said, her voice as much part of the heavens as the stars. "The Winter is coming."

Jewel nodded.

If it were in my power.

She looked at the ground beneath her feet, wondering why she had chosen to see a mountain's pass beneath the open night sky. Avandar's gift, perhaps; he had spoken of building safety beneath the mountain's vastness. She had seen what she expected to see. Wondered what Avandar truly saw.

She closed her eyes for an instant.

He had built safety out of what was hidden beneath the mountain. And she? She had built as much safety as she could, in a different way. She had never thought to leave it. Jewel ATerafin began to roll up her sleeves. This was her road, this was the path she had chosen. She wanted to make it her own, and she knew that she could.

Difficult, though, to know exactly what that meant.

She had thought she would build Terafin, as she had in Avandar's fortress. She had thought she might see the perfect, ancient masonry of its walls, the cultivated, necessary privacy of its grounds, bisected by Avandar's magic, but otherwise familiar, her own.

Instead, beneath the thick soles of her boots, the stone was changing shape, and texture—but it was still hard. The cliff walls to either side began to shift, losing substance and form until they appeared very like the clouds that Meralonne APhaniel birthed illusion from.

Na'jay. Her Oma's voice. Harsh and sharp.

Her Oma.

We always see what we want to see. She looked at the ground. There, beneath her feet, cobbled stone that had seen better decades, but was still serviceable, still practical. The walls that formed out of mist were the exterior walls of tall, narrow buildings, grouped together in a haphazard way that spoke of both age and lack of street space. A sign, paint faded—but not so much that it had to be redone—hung over them all.

Her eyes fell from sign to sign: Arianne's frown was the most sensuous expression of disapproval she had ever seen. It did not mar her face at all; perhaps the opposite. It added warmth. Of a type.

She felt a hand upon her shoulder; Avandar's. But he did not seek to restrain her; his fingers applied a distinct, but faint pressure, no more. She turned to look back at him, met his gaze, saw the warning in it. She opened her mouth. Shut it. Wondered if he'd appreciate the rarity of her silence.

As she wondered, she realized that he hadn't used her name once since Celleriant and his riders had answered the summons of the horns. *Names have power.*

There is a danger in what you do, her Oma said, in a very distinctive voice. *You have avoided giving the Winter Queen your name—more due to wisdom on his part than yours, but for now the reasons don't matter—but you give her more when you do this: You give her a glimpse of yourself.*

Of my history, Jewel said.

That is all you are, the old woman replied gravely.

Yes. But that's not what you are.

Silence, the quality of it very different from any silence she had yet offered. *What do you mean?*

I mean, Jewel said, *that you're no part of my history, but you*

*know it well enough. I should have known. Avandar couldn't see
Duster and Duster almost killed me—but he could see you. You
aren't my ghost.*

The streets grew harder and sharper; memory supplied the
smell of the sea and the cracks in the stone and the feel of sweat
in the heat of a summer sky.

The passes were gone; the Winter was gone—momentarily—
with it. Surrounded by Summer in Averalaan, Jewel looked up at
the Winter Queen.

"You need my permission to pass, and you know what my
price is: Free him."

"And go unmounted into the Hunt?"

"And go unmounted."

"Or you will do what? Wait until Winter is upon you?"

"Wait until it is upon us both," she said grimly. "Or should I
say, upon us all?"

Her gaze did not waver from the face of the Winter Queen; it
was the Winter Queen who broke first, her brows rising like perfect, pale crescents, into the line of her hair. *"You."*

Jewel turned to one side to see the woman she had mistaken
for the dead. "It almost worked," she said.

"It worked well enough. But you benefit in this case from
being both gifted and untrained."

"Oh?"

"You see with your heart, which is not uncommon. But your
heart won't let you see what you want to see; it forces you to see
what is there. An unusual combination." Her face, her much-
loved, wind-cracked face, began to lose all wrinkles, all signs of
age, all peppery lines around eyes and mouth that spoke of
ferocity of expression, both in anger and joy.

"Hello, Arianne," the woman who had been Jewel's grandmother said.

"Very clever," the Winter Queen replied. "I should have seen
your hand in this."

So easily dismissing Jewel's. Jewel knew she would see all of
these women again. She *knew* it. The woman whose name she
did not know, but who had known *her* well enough to take the
face of the dead grandmother who had been as close to Jewel as
her parents. Calliastra, Corallonne and Arianne.

And if she was going to be part of their future, and they were
going to be part of hers, the groundwork was going to be set in a

way she could live with. Yes, she was mortal. Yes, it was a flaw that they didn't possess.

But she wasn't about to be disregarded out of hand because she only lived a handful of years. One minute and the right weapon could destroy eternity.

"Did you know who she was?" she asked Avandar softly, her gaze flickering between the Winter Queen and the silent woman who stood at her side; the two had become absorbed with each other's presence, to the exclusion of all else.

Avandar said nothing. "Avandar?" Jewel turned, ready to take her temper out on the only safe target in sight. But when she saw that he was staring at her, she subsided.

"No," he said quietly.

"Did you guess?"

"No."

Silence. Then, "Who *is* she?"

"Firstborn," he replied.

"I mean, what is her name?"

"Name? She has none that I know of. There were whole sects devoted to either her worship or her study when man's power was at its height."

"Oh." Pause. "And what did they call her?"

"Fate. Destiny." He shrugged. "The Oracle."

The Oracle. The two words held a sudden power that stood out in a landscape that was rich with it the way a bolt of lightning might claim attention coming from the heights of storm-laden sky. What had Evayne said? *You must walk the Oracle's Path.*

As if she could hear the words, spoken as they were in another woman's voice—and in memory, that fortress of privacy—the stranger who had worn her Oma's face turned. Her eyes were like Kiriel's eyes; shrouded in darkness and shadow. The effect was curiously unlike the effect Kiriel often had.

"You have not begun to walk my path," she said, her voice completely devoid of the familiar cadences.

"But I will." Not a question.

Full lips curved in a smile, but the Oracle's eyes were unblinking, and unchanged. "Oh, yes."

"How did you know?" Avandar asked.

Jewel shrugged. "It was the only thing that made any sense. You didn't see Duster. There had to be some reason for that." *Duster.* "It's too bad. Duster, you'd've liked."

"She was a member of your den?"

"Yeah. She defined it," Jewel added softly, "by being everything they weren't. Except loyal. I suppose all rulers, no matter how decent they are, need their killers."

"You are not—"

She lifted a hand. Waved it, batting away the words as if they were mosquitoes. "Don't. Doesn't matter. What matters is that you can't really see my ghosts. I should thank *Kalliaris* for that."

"Oh?"

"Means I can't see yours, and I have the strong feeling that I'm grateful for that."

"Na'jay," the woman Avandar called the Oracle said quietly. "You have served my purpose, Arianne's, and your own on this road. It is time to leave it."

"No."

For the first time, Arianne's expression broke into a semblance of warmth and amusement. "You see? I have told you, and told you frequently, that humans make poor tools unless you shape them."

"Or inform them," the Oracle said, completely unruffled by Jewel's blunt refusal. "What do you wish, child?"

"I want to know what's happening. Who are you, and why are you here?"

"I am as the Warlord has told you. Of the Firstborn. But what he has not told you, perhaps because he does not know it himself, is that I am *the* Firstborn. I existed before any life that was not the wilderness we called gods, and I will exist beyond it as well."

"Which means, of course," the Winter Queen said quietly, "that she has seen some element of all of our fates. Those of us who have power have never willingly lived, ignorant, in the shadow of her knowledge. Come, tell the child how she has served *my* interests. It might be amusing to both of us, since I believe that neither of us can see it."

"Indeed, neither of you can. I expect no better from you, little sister," she said. "You choose your ignorance carefully and willfully. And you, Na'jay, you are a child; you are learning. And you will understand this, in time."

"In time for what?"

The Oracle smiled. She didn't answer.

"Very well," Arianne said. "You are a pawn, and you will therefore suffer a pawn's fate, and not a willful enemy's—if you but leave the road now."

"I'll leave the road," Jewel responded, "When you—"

"Enough." The Oracle's voice was cool.

Jewel knew a warning when she heard it; she'd heard them enough. But the gravity in the Oracle's voice was astonishing because her expression was so mild. This woman was not, like Arianne, exquisitely lovely, but there was about her face a depth and a certainty of knowledge that implied true safety and not just safety's illusion; that implied the ideal of a mother's comfort rather than its reality.

Jewel didn't want to say no to her. Inexplicably and suddenly, she wanted to nod obediently and follow.

She even turned away from Arianne before she stopped herself. It had been a long, long time since she had obediently followed anyone just because they had told her to. The person she had followed, and the person who *could* follow that unquestioningly were both dead.

And besides, Jewel had something to settle.

"I'm sorry," she said, turning back to the Winter Queen, "but we haven't finished yet."

Arianne did not look surprised or perturbed. She nodded, as if expecting no less—or perhaps no more—from one merely human. At her back, the host, horns silent, swords sheathed, mounts restive, waited upon her word, moving in time with a slightly mistimed breath. "What do you hope to gain?" she asked calmly.

Jewel said nothing.

"Riches? I have none that would not destroy you and your kin. Power? The only power I have left to grant one of mortal kind is not a power you could be trapped into accepting if you are marked by the eldest." Her smile was thin. "And I believe you are one of the few who would refuse the gift of immortality; perhaps there is some wisdom in you after all.

"If there is, find it now. I am not what I once was, thanks to the interference and the trouble caused by your kind. But I will not be diminished in my world. I have nothing to offer you but death, and if you have gleaned truth, that I cannot offer you death on this road, understand this: the eldest has commanded you to *her* road, and on the way to that one, you must cross many of *mine*. There is no place you will not be hunted in my lands if you pursue this.

"You forsake the wisdom of the eldest in order to make an enemy," the Winter Queen said. "Be aware of what you are doing. On this road, there is no illusion."

"This road is only illusion," Jewel countered.

"As you will. I say to you again, do not press this."

"You didn't drive that beast into my circle for nothing. Congratulations. You won. You got what you wanted: I'm upset. Happy?"

"ATerafin," the Oracle said quietly.

"What, you're still here?"

"Yes." She looked to the woman she had called sister. "The Winter is coming, and you have much to do before it arrives."

"Take your human from my path."

"The human is not going from your path without that—that creature," Jewel said quietly.

The moments stretched, and stretched again. And then Arianne smiled. The expression transformed her face. Jewel was instantly on her guard—which was hard, given she'd thought she couldn't be more wary.

"Very well," she said. She moved away from the beast, every ripple of cloth, every movement of hair, every clink of armor noteworthy, fascinating.

"My Lady," the man closest to her said, dismounting at once. He made his way to her side, taking care never to pass her, and knelt. The joints of his armor against the stone were resounding, bell-like. Magical. She could not see the face behind the helm, but the voice was compelling; almost as beautiful in its way as the Queen's, but infinitely less cold.

"No," she said to the kneeling man. "For I have already lost Celleriant, and I will not lose another."

"Avandar," Jewel said, although she knew Arianne could hear every word, "what does she mean by that?"

Avandar did not reply. As if he were one of Arianne's followers, his gaze was fixed upon the Queen's every movement. Jewel knew this because she forced herself to tear her own away to look at him.

"I do not believe you wish the answer to that," he said quietly. "But you will receive it. I do not understand what has happened here. But something has changed. Be wary of accepting what she offers you."

"But I—"

"Be wary."

"Celleriant," the Queen said, her voice passing between Jewel and Avandar as if it were the wind in the highest of the passes through the Menoran chain. Celleriant knelt at once into rock that Jewel would have sworn hadn't had the time to cool. His hair hung long, obscuring his face, but before he bowed it, Jewel thought she saw him pale.

"Avandar—"

The Queen handed the reins of her mount to the man at her side. "Take him," she said, "to his new master."

"My Lady," he replied, hanging on to the reins of his mount in one hand while retrieving hers with the other.

"You have served me well," she said to the stag. "In all ways. I have received pleasure from the Hunt, both of you and with you; serve your new mistress as well and perhaps *she* will grant you what I never would." She reached up; touched the tip of his magnificent tines, and pressed hard; when she drew back, her hand was red with blood.

Jewel was shocked.

For some reason, she'd expected her blood to be a different color, if it ran at all.

Or perhaps she just never expected to see it run. Arianne had, about her, that complete invulnerability that allows for no injury, acknowledges no pain.

The Queen's rider brought the beast. The beast followed, docile, without a backward glance at the woman who had been—who was, in some sense—his absolute master. The rider brought him to the edge of Avandar's circle and stopped there. His face looked vaguely familiar; Jewel was almost certain she had seen it, or its kind, before—probably in a dream. Which she thankfully didn't remember.

"I am Celleriant's brother," he said. "Called Mordanant in my youth by mortals. We are of the Firstborn, and of the First family, and you have harmed us considerably.

"When the day comes and the road is open, the Queen may forgive you." He dropped the reins of the Queen's former mount with contempt. "I will not. Winter court, or Summer, there is blood to be shed between us."

"That sounds like ritual," Jewel said to Avandar as the rider wheeled his mount with a vicious tug to the bit and rode back to the side of the Winter Queen.

"It is," Avandar replied. "A ritual of the Arianni. You've made an enemy today. I will, however, be impressed if you make only one."

She stared to reply, but the beast was walking toward them, and her words were swallowed whole by the expression on its face. The humanity that had showed through the wall of Avandar's magic was gone—and coward or no, Jewel thanked every god in the pantheon for its absence.

"Avandar," she said, "what exactly is it doing?"

"It is coming," he replied, "to its new master."

"Me."

"Yes."

"But I don't—"

"Jewel."

What she'd been about to say was lost to the shock of hearing her name. She turned, saw that his lips were closed. Realized that he was speaking to her in a way that didn't involve sound at all—and that she didn't particularly like. She started to say something, stopped. Turned.

The beast loomed above her, beyond the magical barrier Avandar had laid. This close, and bereft of agony, it was absolutely silent, great eyes unblinking and either depthless or endless brown-black. Intelligence, in those eyes, and something else. Madness, maybe. She really didn't want to think about it.

"What do we do now?" she said softly, not to Avandar, but to the stag.

In reply, he lowered his head. Tines as tall as men—or so they seemed to Jewel in the not-quite-real environs of the path the Firstborn walked—were lowered, not in challenge, but not in greeting.

Mute, she tensed as the uppermost tips of the tines, sharp and pale as the sun-bleached bone that sometimes made its way up through seaweed to sand, breached the barrier. Fire flared where it touched what Avandar had built, but the blood on the horn's tip glowed as brightly as flame, and this time there was no screaming.

"You are meant," Avandar said softly, "to mark him."

"Pardon?"

"You are meant to mark him. The tine," he added. "Lift your hand."

She did as Avandar bid, feeling it: a sudden pull, a warmth beneath the skin of her palms. For a moment, just a moment, the stag stood as a knight might, as a member of the Chosen, as one who stands to swear service with his life as his oath and his death as its end.

She had no sword to swear by, no ritual to bind the moment with, to hallow it or to grant it meaning. But she had understanding. She brought the fleshy part of her right palm to the tine the stag lowered—the only part of its antlers that had breached Avandar's protections—and biting her lip, she pierced her skin.

As the Queen had done.

Fire shot up her arm; Avandar's magic, seeking and finding something foreign within her. She refused to show the pain the spell caused; on some level she had expected no less, and besides, she could not take her eyes from the face of the stag.

Beneath fur, beneath the width of open, clear eyes, beneath the weight of tines that must surely count, on this road, as a far greater burden than any crown, she could *see* the face of the man that had once offered just this oath to the Queen of all Winter. It was not a young man's face, but not an old one's; it was the face of a man at the peak of his power.

She wondered what crime he had committed, if any, in the eyes of the Winter Queen. Wondered what he had done to catch her attention, or if power—and he had possessed it once, she was certain of it—had been enough.

"You don't understand what you've accepted," the Oracle said quietly.

But Avandar placed a hand on Jewel's shoulder and said simply, "Of all people who have walked this road, I believe that this one, better than any, understands the weight of the burden. She has agreed to bear it."

"Are they all like this?" Jewel asked quietly, unable to look away.

"I cannot see what you see," he replied quietly, "but if I could venture a guess, I would say no. The mount the Queen rides is in all ways special."

The rider who had delivered the stag into Jewel's keeping said, "The bargain has been kept, mortal. You will stand back now, or you will be driven from the path by the force of the Old Laws." He lifted his helm a moment, and his expression made clear which of the two choices he favored.

He lowered the helm; she had seen what he intended her to see; a glimpse of his perfect, of his beautiful face, forever beyond her. He rode to join his Queen, and his Queen nodded. Although she alone was on foot, she was not diminished by the height that separated her from the riders who waited upon her word.

Their silence was heavy; they waited.

"Celleriant," Arianne said, looking *through* Jewel as if she had become—had never been anything but—inconsequential. "You have failed me."

"Lady."

"Let your failure serve a purpose; let it be a warning to those who might fail me through their carelessness."

He was absolutely silent. Jewel looked back at him once, but he did not move, and she was certain that he wouldn't. She gave the whole of her attention to Arianne. Not hard to do. The Queen, alone of her host, was unmounted; Mordanant stopped before her and made to dismount a second time, and a second time she denied him, by gesture, this sacrifice.

"Understand what you are seeing," Avandar said softly. "Mordanant offers to go into exile for the sake of his brother. Exile or worse." When Jewel did not speak, he continued. "There are rules that bind the Hunt, Jewel. It is forbidden for the Arianni to go unmounted."

"Forbidden by who?"

"Arianne, of course. They are hers, and she is theirs. Celleriant lost his mount to you. You are mortal; he is not. He has proved himself unworthy of her host."

"And if she wanted to save him?"

"I believe you already understand some part of her nature; she has made the law, and the law rules her. To unmake the law is to unmake the Arianni, and that, she will do by dying, if at all."

"She's going to kill him?"

"No," he said quietly. "I fear she will do far worse than that."

Jewel had never been young enough to wonder what was worse than death. She was silent.

And in the perfect silence, the words of the Winter Queen rang out with the weight of geas. "Celleriant of the green Deepings, you have failed me. Let me give your service to a mistress whose demands may be up to your lesser ability. In my stead, you will serve the human who bested you."

"My Lady—" Mordanant's voice. Celleriant did not speak.

"Denied," she replied, without looking back. "The Winter is almost upon us, and I will not be hampered by the weakness of affection. Your family has long suffered the stain."

"Lady."

"And if I don't want his service?"

"It matters little what you desire. It is what *I* desire that defines the Arianni. Lord Celleriant has failed me, but he *is* of the host, and perhaps he will serve you well."

I doubt it, Jewel thought, daring a backward glance at the man who was not quite a man, and who had not moved an inch from the supplicant posture he had taken while awaiting the outcome of her decision.

"You are fighting our ancient enemies," the Winter Queen said quietly, "and it may be that I have been . . . merciful. Lord Celleriant will be recognized should he choose to use the power that is his birthright."

"Lady," Mordanant said.

The lightning fell.

Celleriant lifted his head as its absolute brilliance lit the night sky beyond the summer day Jewel had created as harbor for herself, Avandar, and the Oracle. Mordanant was pale with the unsaid—but she had left him his mount. And his life. He did not interrupt her again, and Jewel knew he would not. But in spite of herself she felt a twinge of respect, of kinship, with the only one of the Arianni to speak for his fallen comrade. She wondered if the brother—hard to imagine that these men were brothers, as brothers seemed a thing of flesh and blood, of messy family fights and reunions—would have done as much if their positions were reversed. Had a bad feeling she would find out.

Lightning left silence.

Into the silence, Arianne spoke as if she were a god and this were some strange dreaming over which her power was growing. "Celleriant, if you will be of mine, you will follow my orders."

"Lady."

"Serve this girl as if she were, indeed, your mistress in all things. Suffer this humiliation with honor and in a manner that only the Arianni can, and when she is dead, if you have acquitted yourself with dignity, I may yet choose to find you a mount and a place in my Hunt."

The man who had called himself Mordanant bowed his head. It was a very subtle movement, and easily missed; Jewel would have missed it but for the edge of his helm, which caught the light of Jewel's sun, Jewel's waning sky.

What if I won't take him? she thought, but she found herself mute.

Avandar spoke unexpectedly. "You set a high price for his return, Arianne."

"Oh?" The word was the cool Northern wind, rolling in from the mountain's height. Night was falling, even in the streets of Averalaan. "A mortal's span of years is very short in these diminished times."

"Four Princes were set just such a task, and for greater cause, and they failed in far less than the span of years you would have him serve."

"Viandaran," Arianne said, in the silence that followed his words, "you are indeed still the Warlord; you seek the weakness you perceive, and you strike where you can. I dislike the reminder of past failures, as you must. I will not, however, return the favor by asking about your consort—any of them. The curse that guides you still shadows your brow if one knows how to look.

"I have never lied; it is not my nature; a lie is beneath me; it is a tool of those whose truths are not powerful enough. I promise what I promise and I honor my oath; it is the willfulness of mortality that seeks to make of my oaths something that they are not."

He bowed. He bowed low. "Indeed, Lady, mortality is willful. But I, too, understand the power of oath. I serve my Lady, and I accept, in her name, all that you have offered in return for passage."

"Too many," Jewel said.

"But I believe," he continued, as if she hadn't spoken or as if he hadn't heard her, "that even with gifts such as your personal mount and a lord of Celleriant's worth, you undervalue the worth of your host. You may, of course, pass; in that, my Lady is like you: she does not lie."

A complaint of his. A frequent one. Funny to hear it praised, and in such company.

"But you have gathered a Hunt such as the world has not seen since the divide," he said quietly. "And where roads have been held by my kind, no such host has ever been granted passage, save once." He rose from his bow. "This is not that time."

"Warlord, I forget your roots, you have been almost one of us for so long. But you are in part what you were. Can you not feel His shadow? It stretches from one end of the road to the other, growing and gathering strength. We swore, and we were divided, the immortal from the mortal, gathered and pressed into places small and wild . . . and limiting.

"But for the sake of my father, we swore, and we abide by the oaths that were given." Her smile was sudden, beautiful; Jewel literally could not breathe in the face of it.

Jewel knew what the oaths were.

She *knew* it.

"Yes, seer-born, little disciple of the eldest. We swore that we would cleave to the old and hidden ways just as the gods themselves did."

The words settled slowly, starting at the top and finding depths in Jewel that she hadn't suspected existed. She did not say the name aloud, but it came to her as a perfectly aimed arrow might have. *Allasakar*.

"The tide is turning, and not in your favor. Our ancient enemies are rising; they gain power over the earth and the wind, the fires and the waters, while we treat like beggars or children upon a road that will soon have little meaning."

"Understood," Jewel said softly. "But understand as well that it makes no difference to me who does the killing—you or the *Kialli*. Because the dead will still be dead." She paused a moment to look at the stag that the Queen had so casually thrown against Avandar's barrier. "And the living don't look like they're much better off."

"Perhaps not," Arianne replied, as the night at last descended, "but think on this: is it better to give me the one life to take or enjoy as I see fit than it is to give *all* life to our enemy?"

Jewel looked at the stag. "I don't know," she said at last. "Maybe we should ask him."

"You may. But he will never answer." She inclined her head. "You are surprising; perhaps your sight is clearer than you know, or perhaps you are foolish because we have been absent from the world for so long. It matters little. The winds are coming, mortal. But this is the first Hunt of this scale that we have seen and I am loath to miss even a moment of it. I will take the smaller party.

"And I will remember your face. Keep your name hidden, and hidden well, or perhaps you will carry a greater burden than you carry now."

Jewel understood. She'd won.

But winning had never felt so dangerous, so empty. She made to step aside, but paused a moment as Avandar began to draw his magic in a tighter, more personal net. With a gesture—for drama's sake, because it really didn't make any other difference she could see—she dissolved the image of home: the streets of Averalaan faded into mountain's pass, cold and lifeless beneath the perfect glitter of evening stars.

"Why?" Avandar asked her softly, as the Arianni began to gather at their Queen's back, to be chosen or discarded.

"Why what?"

"Many things. But for now, a simple question. The land; you let it go. Why?"

"Because whether or not it's illusion, I couldn't bear to watch her ride with her host through the streets of *my* city." The wind, indeed, was rising. She lifted her head and let it shove unruly curls out of her eyes. "Come," she said softly. The stag obeyed her so silently if she closed her eyes she would not have heard his movements.

"And the other?" Avandar said, uncharacteristically gentle.

She started to say something sarcastic; she was good at it, after all. Years of practice.

But when the rider looked up and met her eyes, his expression inexplicably dulled the edge of the words she might have spoken. Still, she was surprised when she said, just as softly, "Come."

He rose, silent as the stag, and together, Avandar, Jewel, and the two gifts that would be her lasting legacy from the Winter Queen, stood by the road's side and watched the Hunt ride into the darkness of the unknown.

Only after they had passed did Jewel realize that the Oracle was nowhere to be seen.

CHAPTER TWENTY-SIX

19th of Scaral, 427 AA
Tor Leonne

He did not choose to allow the serafs to enter his personal quarters. Food and water, when they were desired at all, were brought in basins designed and blessed by the strongest of Widan's craft and left beyond the simple, sliding doors that it had become death for all but a few to pass.

Alesso di'Alesso, the Tyr'agar of the Dominion, was not, however, shut in: the walls opened to grant him a view of the world without; one made splendid by the hands of gardeners and carpenters, of master weavers and painters, in preparation for the Festival of the Moon. Here, the sheen of fabric catching the Lord's dying light, he could see white and gold and deep, deep blue; Her colors. The Lady was coming.

And with Her, in the cover of Her night, his allies. His enemies. It had been a long time since he could easily separate them.

"Alesso."

But, as always, such sweeping statements demanded their exceptions. He turned at once, almost pleased at the interruption. Sendari di'Sendari waited in the span of the open doors. He had aged ten years in the course of the last ten days, his beard streaked with the white blanket that served as both warning and shroud. "Come," he said, nodding. "But the door—"

"It is secure."

"Good." He gestured.

Sendari, as any other visitor, went immediately to the low table, a stark, flat block in the center of the room, its surface interrupted by only two things: A perfect clay vessel, its thin walls bearing three strokes that suggested the long, slender leaves that bore rushes, and a matching cup.

He poured, as carefully as the Serra Teresa herself might have done, and when he was finished, he drank.

The waters of the Lady's Lake touched his lips; Alesso watched him swallow and then turned back to the view, the breadth of the plateau upon which the Tyr's power depended.

"She has vanished," he said softly. "Thirty people dead in her wake. They are speaking about her now: She has become either the Lady or the Lady's avatar, come to show her displeasure at the changes the new Tyr is making. They are saying that—"

"That a Tyr of Leonne blood would not be in this position."

Sendari fell silent.

"Old friend," Alesso said quietly, "they are correct. Markaso kai di'Leonne would never have been in this position. His power was his by right of birth; no strength or weakness marred it."

"Alesso—"

"Not here. We must plan, and we must plan with care."

"You believe that Anya was sent?"

Alesso's laugh was brief and dark. "No more than any rabid beast can be sent or commanded. Her role as the opener of the way is of tantamount importance to the Lord of the Shining Court; I do not think He would willingly give her up so that she might kill a handful of clansmen and their serafs. The least of His demons could do so with ease."

Sendari nodded, his face carefully neutral. "That was my thought."

"Can Ishavriel be made to contain her?"

"We do not know. Cortano traveled in haste to the Shining Court, and to no one's surprise, that Lord is not in attendance. Nor is he expected before the end of the Dark Conjunction."

The latter surprised him. "Where did you come by this information?"

"The Lord Isladar."

"And you believed him."

"Cortano believed him. Lord Isladar has little to gain from the lie."

"The *Kialli* lie as a matter of course; they speak truth when they have something to gain. And they see into a future that contains our grandchildren or great-grandchildren; our own fates are, of necessity, of limited import. We cannot see what they have to gain; our own lives will not encompass it." There, the Lady's banners were being laid out against a field of green. Grass was the most difficult of things to grow and tend; it died with ease in weather too dry, but if left to grow even half an inch too long, it coarsened. The flowers that had been planted a year, or two, or three previously blossomed and died, growing in place but moving by tendril and leaf so that the whole drifted in a pattern that suggested the freedom of life within the containment of order.

There had been so little freedom in the last few months.

He had thought the sacrifice insignificant; after all, power was the only guarantee of freedom a man could have in lands the Lord ruled. But he better understood the price to be paid now. While he watched the facade of the Festival unfold, he understood that he would never again be part of it. And it pained him.

"Why did Cortano not bring this news himself?"

"He has not yet returned from the Court; the journey was costly enough that he would be at risk were he to travel immediately. He sends word that he will arrive the day before the Festival at the latest."

Alesso nodded quietly. There were spies enough within the Tor that the Sword's Edge—feared far more than a simple warrior who stood with the crown across his brow—could not afford any display of weakness, any obvious lessening of power.

But the Tyr could ill afford to be without him.

"The masks?" he asked.

"They are out there, in the lower city. Quite possibly in the hands of serafs and lesser lords upon the plateau, although we have concentrated most of our recovery efforts there." Sendari bowed.

And with his face still groundward, he added, "The Sword's Edge has been summoned by the Lord of the Shining Court."

"Oh?"

"The masks, Alesso."

Silence.

"He wishes the masks to be worn."

Alesso was quiet. Very quiet. At last he said, "We knew the risks. They will not, of course, be worn."

"Of course. But I believe that Cortano would be much pleased," Sendari said, rising, "if you were to inform the Lord of that fact in person."

In spite of himself, he smiled. "I believe that he would, indeed, be well pleased." The smiled dimmed. "He is . . . well?"

"He is unharmed for the moment. The Lord's attention was drawn away, fortuitously, by a more dangerous breach in his own plan."

"Oh?"

"Anya a'Cooper is no longer within the walls of the Shining Palace."

Alesso closed his eyes.

"Yes," Sendari said. "We will feed our own to her, and perhaps in greater numbers; she will damage us by her presence because people will wrap her in the Lady's myth at our expense. But her absence has saved us from the greater danger. For the moment."

"For the moment," Alesso said softly. "Where are our Northern enemies? Why have they not gathered? Where are their forces? Without them, we have no balance of power."

No balance.

Sendari rose. "I do not know, Alesso. I have seen nothing but masks for these past several days. The war has become a thing of dream; it lacks substance." He ran a hand across his eyes.

"And what do the masks reveal?"

"Masks conceal," he said, the words tired and graceless. They hung a moment between the two men. Then the lines that exhaustion and sun had carved into Sendari's face shifted, cutting his expression.

"Old friend?"

"Masks conceal," he repeated, but he spoke the words as if they were foreign, the syllables weighted and heavy. "They conceal." He walked to the window, to stand beside Alesso, to stare at the Tor beneath them both.

"Sendari?"

"I am . . . remembering," he said quietly.

"And you desire privacy?"

"I desire impossible things, but lately privacy is not one of them." He lifted a hand to his beard. Let it rest there.

They're all wearing masks, his daughter's voice said, coming, beloved and perfect, from the remove of more than a decade. He could feel her hand in his. Could feel her weight—not inconsiderable for all that he desired to pick her up and hold her for the eternity of the Festival Moon—in his arms. Her mother, his shadow, dead. Her aunt, as cursed as she, at a safe distance. Nothing to separate them as they walked into wonder, into the Lady's Night.

And what had he said?

Lady's hand on his shoulder, Lady's voice in his ear, the weight of the ruin he had brought upon his daughter—*the last woman alive that he had loved, had promised to love*—so heavy he could barely breathe beneath its pressure.

And because they wear masks, they can be who they are, as the Lady decrees.

"Alesso," he said, seeing his daughter, "I must go."

"Sendari?"

"From the mouth of babes," he replied quietly. There was no fire in the words; Alesso saw shadows everywhere in his friend's face. Age. Weakness.

"The masks?"

"I must speak with Mikalis. It is urgent."

"And Cortano?"

"You are correct. He must fend for himself. But I believe, before the Festival's end, it is *we* who will be tested and tried in the Lord's hottest fires."

"And if we survive?"

Sendari said nothing. His robes swept the spare surface of unadorned, uncovered wood as he turned. When he reached the doors he stopped, his hands upon the frames that had been magicked by Cortano himself to withstand all form of intrusion save that of greater power. He turned. "Sometimes the winds devour us," he said softly, "and all we can do before they tear us from the monuments we have built is to write our names where men can see them; to write our histories where men can be emboldened by them."

He did not turn.

Alesso could not see his face. "Sendari?"

The doors opened. The man who had been captain, General, Tyr, and friend could have ordered him back—but the last title was a title that robbed a man of some of the ease of command. The Widan did not choose to turn, and the Tyr'agar did not choose to press the issue.

"I don't understand," Diora said.

She was so rarely given to any acknowledgment of ignorance that Alana en'Marano, the oldest of her father's wives and the de facto mother of his entire harem, although Fiona was technically Serra, stopped in open surprise.

Diora's frown was slight, and as she met the gaze of her father's wife, it melted into the perfect, flawless countenance expected of a woman who had once been the wife of a Tyr. "Is something . . . out of place?"

"No, Na'dio. Not anymore." And nothing was. Her hair, beaded with strings of jade and held by three combs that locked together in a triad of intricate golden leaves, framed a face that had been paled by powder and lack of exposure to the Lord's light. Too little light, in Alana's opinion. But that opinion had carefully not been asked.

They all knew that Diora had worked against her father, somehow; that her incarceration was punishment for her betrayal—whatever that betrayal might be.

"Tell me, Alana. Why?"

Alana looked at the face of her favorite daughter. Cupped it in her hands because they were both hidden in the heart of the most private room in her father's harem, with the possible exception of the room in which he practiced his Widan's art. "I don't know, Na'dio. Your father said only—said only that—you needed time to prepare for the Festival of the Moon." She took a deep breath. "We have heard that the Widan Cortano di'Alexes has traveled and will not be in the Tor Leonne for the next few days."

"You 'have heard'?"

Alana said nothing.

"Ona Alana, please?"

"No. No, Na'dio, and that face, that perfect, beautiful face, will not get answers from me. There are some questions that are never asked."

"But my father—"

"He told me himself, child. Be comforted."

She felt Diora stiffen, if steel could be called stiff, and she let her hands fall away. *Child,* she thought, seeing none of the child she had once coddled in her harem daughter. *Your father loves you as much as a man is capable of loving any child.*

But how much was that, in the end? He would give her to Garrardi; no one doubted it. And the life she would have?

No one doubted that either. Alana bowed her head to hide the momentary bitterness that twisted her lips. She would have railed on—she did—in the company of any of the other wives. But it was pointless to worry her Na'dio further when they both understood the truth. She waited the space of three breaths, and then forced herself to speak of more pleasant things. "You are to have escort if you desire it."

"I do not desire it."

"And that escort," she continued, as if the Serra Diora di'Marano had shown the grace of good manners and offered no interruption, "is to be the Radann Marakas par el'Sol."

Diora's perfect eyes widened, and then she bowed her head.

"Na'dio," Alana said quietly. The winds were so strong in the stillness of the room that she wanted to sweep her harem daughter into the momentary safety of her arms. She didn't. All safety was momentary, and Diora did not need a reminder of that fact.

"We must hurry," Alana said, not bothering to gentle her voice. "The par el'Sol will be waiting, and we are under strict orders to waste none of his time."

"Whose?" Diora asked softly, although she followed the woman who had been one of her many mothers with a docility that was uncharacteristic.

Na'dio, she thought, *has your captivity changed you so?* But she said nothing at all; she caught the young woman's hand in hers and fell silent at the ice of it, the chill beneath the summer skin.

"Alana," Diora said, the delicacy, the hesitancy, of her voice a surprise to the older woman. "Where is Ona Teresa?"

Alana's shrug was a lie. The words were a lie as well, and although she had not been able to lie successfully to this strangest of daughters, she said, "Your Ona Teresa is with her kai in the Terrean of Mancorvo, and a good thing, too. There is much that is strange about this Festival, and the Festival of the Moon was always of great import to the Serra."

The younger Serra had often accepted such lies. The older one met the wavering gaze of the harem's oldest wife, held it a moment, and then let it go. "Come," she said, voice now as cool as her flesh had been, "we have scant hours before the dressmakers arrive with the gown I am to be wed in; the kai Garrardi has made it most clear what the price of their failure to create the perfect setting for me will be."

Has he made most clear, Alana thought, *what the price will be if you fail to be the gem that lives up to that setting?*

The sunlight everywhere was astonishing; there was a newness to it that defied all shadow. She felt as if she had not seen it in months, perhaps years; that the shadows and darkness at a remove from sun's light had sunk roots and taken nourishment from her. It was not the truth; this feeling—as feelings often were not. She had but recently met with the Serra Fiona, had spoken beneath the open sky at the grace of Fiona's ability to plead prettily with her father. But she had felt—that day—the confines of her father's bitter anger.

No—Lady, no, she had felt the confines of her own. The desire for death, his, hers, *everyone's,* as a way of ending the horrible sound of her name screamed in accusation by the distorted voice of the woman she had most loved.

That memory cast its shadow now, working at wounds that had never closed, and by the grace of the Lord, never would. Diora bowed her head, seeking anger, and seeing—seeing the rippling dance of the light on the Lady's water. Seeing, because she so desired to see them, the floating blossoms, out of season, of the lilies on the Lady's Lake, their perfect white petals unmatched anywhere across the breadth of the Dominion. She hated her weakness, for just that moment; the desire for *beauty* so strong she could feel it rise above all other desires, even the desire for death, for justice—as if death and justice could be separated in the Dominion.

A Northern wind blew the artfully arranged strands of loose hair across her flawless skin. She bowed to the Lady's Lake. "Alana," she said softly.

"Serra Diora," Alana replied, bowing as low as the difference in their ranks publicly demanded. "Your escort is here." She fussed a moment—a departure from the strict etiquette their public excursion demanded—arranging and rearranging the wide-brimmed hat across which hand-painted silks were stretched as a protection against the covetous eye of the Lord—and also, always, as a statement about the worth of the Serra beneath them.

Then her hands fell. She stepped back, falling at once to earth in a position that was not different from that a seraf would have adopted.

A reminder of a painful truth: Alana was a seraf, no matter what freedom she had found for herself behind the broad back of Sendari di'Marano. Sendari di'Sendari.

"Thank you," Diora said, seeing not the rich silks with which Sendari's wives were now always burdened, but rather, the bent back beneath it. "Will you accompany us?"

"No, Serra. I have matters to attend to with regard to the Festival; the Serra Fiona has, in the absence of a wife for the Tyr, been put in charge—mere days ago—of the appearance of the Tor Leonne, and she cannot do without me."

Her father was cruel in his fashion. A younger Diora would have smiled and derived some satisfaction at the discomfiture of a rival. There was no smile now. She saw the rising of the sun and the slow march of time toward darkness, toward the day when the sun would both rise and fail to rise.

"Na'dio?" Alana whispered softly. "Please. He is coming."

And he was. She could see him, resplendent not in the ceremonial robes that she expected but in armor, and at that, armor that had been blackened and scarred in ways that cleaning could not repair. He wore two swords, but he had done her the grace of raising his helm.

She saw his eyes, and wondered who he was, although Alana had called him Marakas par el'Sol. For a moment, just a moment, she knew fear.

I am not the person I was, Diora thought bitterly. How could she be? She had *saved* her father's life. And now, as if she were a favored pet, some small, wild creature who had soiled an item of value without understanding or intent and had only just been forgiven, he granted her this—while his own master was away on some errand. Freedom. Freedom and the only escort in the Tor that could be absolutely trusted not to be in the pay of the Sword's Edge.

The cost. The cost of it.

She knelt, carefully folding her knees into dry grass; automatically preserving the illusion of folds of silk as she arranged the fall of her sari in her lap. Her hair, so carefully, intricately bound, cast shadow upon grass at the feet of the Radann Marakas par el'Sol, where it escaped the rich shadow of silk, the brim of a hat fastened by pin and comb to her hair.

He offered her a hand.

It was unmailed.

She lifted hers, and then let it fall, remembering the last time she had been touched by this man. He must have remembered it as well, for he said, in a voice that was barely a whisper, "There is no lack of trust between us on my part, Serra Diora di'Marano. What is yours, is yours; my word that I will not use the Lady's gift against . . . the Lady's servant."

She said nothing.

He held out his hand again, and he waited. The time stretched, the silence became uncomfortable, and it was her duty or her responsibility to alleviate the tension; she was, after all, the woman. But she remembered: He had, under the guise of offered help, attempted to reach what she hid beneath the surface of skin through the powers with which he had been gifted, or perhaps cursed: healing. To ascertain what her motivations were. To reach her thoughts.

There were some walls that she would not allow to be breached.

She *knew* that Alana was close to fainting, and that thought amused and steadied her, leeching the edges of her anger into something calmer and smoother.

"Serra," he said softly. "Meet my gaze. I will not be offended or judge you unworthy for boldness."

She stared up at his face, lifting her head slowly, her hands unnaturally still in her lap. She saw a face that she had seen in shadow and the unnatural light of the Sun Sword on an evening that she had also seen demon and death. It was the same face, but it was not; there was an edge to it and a fire to it that she was suddenly aware could burn.

There were worse things than fire.

"I will never again attempt to take what you will not offer. The war is larger than that." He bowed his head to her. Lifted it again.

This time, when she saw his face, she saw a different man: the only man who had been close to tears—although those tears remained unshed—when the man she must always think of as *the* kai el'Sol—Fredero, born par di'Lamberto—gave himself to the Lord's cause by drawing the Sun Sword where all might see the power of the Lord's edict: that only those born of Leonne blood had the right to wield it.

That man, fire reflected, rather than internalized, she understood. And that man had been chosen by Fredero kai el'Sol, as par, against the advice of the rest of the Radann; she knew this because her husband's mother had made certain that information trickled down into her harem.

The harem that had been such short glory, such perfect happiness.

She took his hand.

It was strong and dry as it closed around her slender fingers. "My gratitude, Radann par el'Sol," she said, lowering her eyes. But as she rose, she felt a sharp pain between her breasts; a hardness and a heaviness that almost dragged her down. Because her aunt had trained her, she did not stumble; did not in any way expose awkwardness of movement. This man might be her ally, but what was an ally in the Lord's eyes? A man of power who desired power and in the end, might find use to make of yours.

"Where do you wish to travel?" the Radann par el'Sol said.

Serra Diora di'Marano did not answer immediately; the freedom of such a choice had not been a possibility and she had not planned for it. Silence, when such lack of foresight became a difficulty, was the wisest course, and Diora had always been pronounced and judged wise for her age.

She was surprised when she spoke.

"To the Swordhaven," she said softly.

"To the—" He bowed, then, his silence more awkward and less practiced than hers. "You will be watched."

She nodded. "And I will be watched, as well, when I venture to the Lake, and when I venture beyond Lake and plateau into the merchants' palace to find the mask and the dress that I will wear for the moon's full face."

"I am," he said softly, "the cerdan to the Serra's command for this day; the kai el'Sol himself has ordered no less. Come. Let us pay our respects at the Swordhaven; the day is short."

She opened the doors herself.

Marakas moved to aid her, but there was something solid about the feel of old wood against the flat of her palms that she desired, and in as polite a way as one could possibly be rude, she waved him away and put her own slender shoulders into the work of opening the door.

There were eyes upon her back; the Lord's, and perhaps the Lady's. She pushed and the doors slid inward, creaking slightly on hinges that had once been perfectly silent.

Dust rose at the eddies of the sudden breeze; it settled again, but the accusation of neglect had been made. Wind's voice. Here.

As if he could hear her disapproval, the par el'Sol said, "We have been busy, Serra Diora. There are demons in the streets of the city, and we have lost men to them."

Demons. Servants of the Lord of Night. She closed her eyes a moment. Nodded. She did not need to straighten out the lines of her shoulders, the lift of her head; they were perfect.

Nothing about the haven had changed; the braziers still stood astride the steps that led to the case itself; the doors, heavy, were still open to those who had either the rank or the temerity to view the sword. They were few; the reigning Tyr'agar had little use for the sword and the viewing of it by clansmen who visited the plateau had become a political gesture. Few indeed were the men who wished to risk the wrath of their new ruler; a new ruler had no choice but to be brutal and swift in reprisal. And complete.

But the Radann could make no statement more political than the kai el'Sol had made by dying with this sword in his hands;

they were expected to at least pay polite respect to the Sword and its haven.

"There is no fire," Diora said quietly.

"No."

The braziers were dark, and almost empty. The torches were guttered.

But from the windows above, light streamed down on the Sword, accentuating its lines in the shadows windowless walls made.

"Please," she said softly, "wait here."

He bowed. Bowed. To her.

She walked to the steps that led to the sword, and she knelt there, knowing the dust would leave its mark on her knees, but willing to be so marked.

She could not easily remove her hat, or rather, she could remove it, but could not replace it; the pins and combs were intertwined in such a way as to seem a natural part of her hair except where gold and jewels were meant to make a statement of their own about her father, or her husband, or her owner. She hesitated a moment, and another, and then, with shaking hands, she began to remove what Alana had, with such care, placed there.

She was surprised to hear the footsteps at her back. Surprised when she turned to see Marakas par el'Sol, standing as Alana might have stood, as Ramdan had always stood for Ona Teresa.

"Here," he said, "let me help you."

"But you are—"

His expression was strange; she could not be certain that she saw it clearly, the light on everything but the Sword was so poor. "Serra," he said quietly, "I was a clansman, one step above seraf." He bid her, by movement of hand, turn her back to him, and something in his face made her comply.

Sorrow, memory; things that demanded privacy.

Yet although she had turned her back, she could not give him the gift of her deafness; she heard what he did not say in the cadence and the texture of the voice he offered his words with. She might have asked him to be silent, but she did not.

"My wife," he said, as his hands gently touched not the hat's rim, but the binding combs, "had such lovely hair. She was not so fine a Serra, and would have been a poor seraf for your Ona Teresa or your father, but she had a rough grace, and a wildness I fostered.

"We could not afford serafs. We could barely afford not to become serafs."

The wife was dead. She heard it in the words; dead but not dead, as her mother had been for most of her father's life: dead but not dead. She hadn't understood it before she had lost her own wives, lost Deidre's beautiful baby, *her* first baby, the child Diora had dared to call son.

You could learn to hate the living, if you had to. You could learn to force them away, or force yourself away, from the things they stirred. Not so the dead. The dead would never again irritate by ugliness or pettiness or simple change and age; they were like the steel of the Sun Sword, tempered in fire.

For just a moment, his hands on hat and hair, she wondered if there would ever be a time, again, when the living drove her, not the dead.

And she hated herself for wondering it.

Because she had saved her father's life.

"I used to do this, for her, because we had no serafs," he said; she had missed some of his words, but none of the feeling behind them. "I used to tell her that I was her seraf." He laughed.

"And she would tell me that I was a clumsy oaf; her hair, unlike yours, was so very fine and so easily broken or tangled." His hands were gone. He had lied, of course; she had never called him clumsy, or an oaf. He had done for Diora what Alana had done, but swiftly and almost unnoticed, his hands healer's hands, light and certain.

She wanted to ask him about his wife, because she suddenly wanted to know who had been graced by his devotion; who he had thought worthy. But the Sword beckoned, and there would be time for questions—if time existed at all after the passage of this terrible Festival—later.

She lifted a fold of the winding cloth of her sari, and dutifully began to drape it over her hair, her face. She bowed, once to the East, to the Lord's beginning, and once to the West, to the Lady's; both were proper; she was proper.

Marakas par el'Sol stepped back from the stairs, granting her privacy, and after a pause to take a breath, to still the questions his action left her, she began to mount the stairs.

It had always taken effort to mount those stairs, but this was different. No smoke burned in the braziers as an offering of some theoretical respect or obedience; no Radann waited in the silence of their attendance upon the Sword. She had nothing to offer but the intensity of her inspection.

She stood before the Sword on its golden platform, the light from the Lord above creating an echo in this, His weapon, and His scepter of judgment.

Stood, and then began to unwind the sari that hid her face, that protected her hair, that kept her from the full force of the Lord's judgment. She heard a sharply drawn breath and she froze, but the Radann Marakas par el'Sol said nothing, and into the strange quality of his silence, she made her first gesture of denial, although she did not know it for that until later.

She stood.

She said, "I have a warrior's heart; I have dealt my enemies a blow; I will die fighting your greatest enemy. Judge me, if you will, Lord. Find me wanting. The wind claims us all in the end, and no wind can come that can hurt me, no death that can scar me, as I have already been scarred." She took a deep breath and uttered words that she had heard not from her father, but from grandfather, long, long dead: his stories to the sons of the kai, had been there when she chose to catch their edge. They had never been for her; he had never had the desire to make a man of the women in his family—because that would have been its own shame.

But she had been stirred by the stories of daring and sacrifice and tragedy, and in the end—in the end, whose life was more bitterly marked by the Lord's gauntlet? She was the Serra Diora di'Marano, and in her heart, words meant to guide young boys into the ferocity of battle were the only words she could find to say. "I will face any death you offer, gladly, if it be over the corpse of my enemy." She reached out with the flat of her palm.

And she felt pain, like a spreading blossom, start at a point between her breasts where, hidden from sight, another burden lay: the pendant given her by a woman whose death had been an act of mercy—by the hand of the Serra Diora di'Marano.

"Radann par el'Sol," she said, pitching her voice, reckless now, so that only he might hear it.

He came at once, as if his name were a summons or a command. "Serra Diora."

"The Sun Sword—has it been tampered with?"

"The Sword itself could not be tampered with." He spoke with certainty. She was comforted by it; there was no doubt at all in his voice. "The scabbard?"

"It, too, was a gift from the Lord." But there was less certainty in those words.

"And the stand upon which both rest?"

"I . . . do not know." He closed his eyes. "Serra Diora," he said quietly, without opening them, "we are now involved in a war; my Lord and the Lady against a Lord whom the Radann will never willingly serve again. What you see here you must never see, do you understand?"

She nodded, the perfect Serra, and then realized that he could not see the gesture. "Yes, I understand."

Fire grew in his hands, left and right, as if an artist of exquisite skill had chosen to paint a representation of the Lord's strength where His earthly power resided: in the hands of the Radann. But it did not stop; it grew, brightly, darkly, until his hands were of the fire and not of flesh.

His face was *white*.

He reached out to touch the scabbard in which the Sun Sword lay, and the fire guttered at once, doused as if shadow and darkness were liquid.

He curled his hands into fists and drew them close; she had no doubt whatever that had she not been present he would have screamed. But he—even he—could not be so unmanned. He held the pain until he could speak through it. She was certain a candle would have burned down by half before the first word came.

"You are . . . perceptive, Serra Diora. And we . . . are lax. Come; before we continue our errands, I must deliver a personal message to the kai el'Sol."

Her expression of concern—and it had been there because she chose to reveal it—was gone; she was the Serra who had once been wife to a Tyr; cool and distant and perfect. She bowed low.

The Serra Diora di'Marano had vowed that she would never think of Peder par el'Sol as kai, for by his treachery—redeemed, in the end, by the grace of the kai el'Sol and the par el'Sol's commitment to God, if not to honor or loyalty—Fredero kai el'Sol had gone to a death he might well have avoided.

But when he was brought from the confines of the temple the Radann occupied at the behest of Marakas par el'Sol, she did not recognize him as the same man. There was a leanness to his face, and the presence of three wounds, two of which, in her opinion, would leave scars. Both of these, that gaunt look, those wounds, transformed him: he had become the Lord's man. Gone, the political games by which all men—perhaps even Fredero, although she could not conceive of how—achieved power at this pinnacle of power in the Dominion. He wore his sword by his side, and the scabbard, red with blood, was unadorned by so much as a leaf of gold, facet of gem.

So, too, his robes; gone silks and the perfect seams of master tailors; he wore armor, and the armor itself was without exaggerated shoulders, paint, or color. He was not dressed for display or parade; he could have been any cerdan, and Toran, if not for the fact that his surcoat bore the sun ascendant. Only two men had the right to wear it, and Diora doubted that she would see the Tyr'agar again before the day of her wedding.

He was not Marakas par el'Sol. He would not, she thought, ever bow to a woman who was not in the ceremonial position of being the Lord's Consort. But if he would not acknowledge her in a way that debased him, he acknowledged her by two things: first, when she began to lower herself to the ground in the full supplicant posture, he stopped her by a single, sharp gesture, and second, he nodded and met her gaze fully.

She should have looked away. She began to; the lessons of years turned her muscles gracefully, exposing the side of her face to his inspection in as pretty, as perfect, a way possible. But something in her tightened; some imperfection, some part of her that had been broken by the truth:

That perfection, that obedience, never guarantees safety. That *good* and the reward of being *good* were for the discipline of children. She had done everything as it was to have been done; had been everything she had been taught to be; more.

It had given her everything, she thought, only so that she might learn what loss was.

The Serra Diora di'Marano met the gaze of the Radann kai el'Sol, and held it. His brows rose a fraction, a fleeting gesture of distaste at what she guessed must be her boldness.

"Serra Diora di'Marano," he said, "the Radann have been told by the Tyr'agnate Eduardo kai di'Garrardi that you are to wed the morning after the night of the Festival Moon.

"Accept our apologies for our rough state; we have seen the beginnings of war, and it is not from the direction we would have expected." He paused then, to look to the North. To the North, where the traditional enemies of the South lay in silence, their movements unascertained because the spies and the scouts of the Tyr were in the streets among his own people.

The words that he spoke next were not for her; they had that faraway quality that spoke of unguarded thought. More than anything else he had said or done, the lack of caution surprised her. Frightened her. He said softly, into the wind. "Where are they?" It was almost like . . . a prayer.

And the wind twisted the heavy flap of his surcoat, pulling it in the direction where their historical enemy lay in silence.

CHAPTER TWENTY-SEVEN

427 AA
The Stone Deepings

"You must let yourself relax," a familiar voice said in a darkness sharp with nightmare. The words, calm and wise, could be heard with ease over the dying sound of a scream. She shook her head. Opened her eyes.

She'd been dreaming, of course. All she did on this road was dream; what made it hard was that she could not remember—ever—falling asleep. Her journey had been one of waking from nightmare into crisis; waking from nightmare into crisis. The act of sleep itself had deserted her.

She found her breath with difficulty because she was waiting for familiar sounds that would—of course—never come; Finch's light step, Carver's cursing, Angel's sharp words, and Teller's quiet *Are you all right?* But from them, only silence. She had no room, no bed, no wing; there was no House Terafin, no manse, no shelter. The road was open and she felt as if she would never leave it.

Wise, wise child.

Oh, shut up, she snarled.

But at least one thing hadn't changed: Avandar stood at her feet—which was probably as close as he could come to the foot of her nonexistent bed—carrying a lamp, or rather, the magical outline of a lamp whose heart was white fire. His own.

And when she shook sleep off, she found that the other shadows had not left her: The stag, horns heavy, stood to one side of the sweep of the rock strewn path, and Lord Celleriant stood against a rocky outcropping, his sword unsheathed, his back toward her. A sentry, she thought, but against what? The worst of the dangers had ridden, abandoning him to her care.

"Jewel?"

She nodded. No kitchen to go to, but she stood anyway.

"Where are we going?" Avandar asked her quietly.

"I don't know." She started to walk.

"Jewel, may I—"

"No." She stopped and began to roll up her figurative sleeves; the ones she was wearing wouldn't easily roll into the loose folds of cloth she best liked. It was time to *wake up*. "Is any of that money real? Any of that gold?" She reached down and gave the front of her tunic a sharp tug. Felt real enough. "Am I going to walk off this path and end up stark naked? Because this isn't the weather for it, and even if it were, it's probably not the right country."

"Jewel."

"Yes?"

"Your dream."

"I don't remember my dream. I haven't remembered a dream since—" Silence. The stars were so bright she couldn't believe they were an artifact of memory.

Believe it, a familiar voice said, almost too softly to *be* familiar. *But believe that it is not* your *memory that makes them so, but mine. The world was young, once. I was young.*

You remember that?

I remember everything, was the quiet reply. *And you remember more than you know. You were dreaming, child, and your dreams are a part of my gift and my curse to the creations of the one who would not be trapped by a name.*

Starlight. Bright. And beneath it, the movement of men, of hundreds of men, thousands.

"I do remember." Jewel said. She tried to keep the accusation out of her face when she looked up at him, his chin lit by the lamp he held, his face cast in shadows. "How did you know?"

"Because you called out two names," he replied quietly.

"And those?"

"Valedan."

"That's one."

"Kiriel."

She shuddered. "It was Kiriel who broke the dream."

"I . . . guessed. I have rarely heard you so terrified, and I have borne witness for so many of your nightmares I have lost count."

"Kitchen," she said, without thinking. And then, scanning the landscape—such as it was—added "Ledge." She pointed with her head. "You, pretty boy, sheathe that and follow. And you, four legs, if you've got a brain in there, you might as well join us."

"Jewel—"

"What? She told me they were *mine,* and in the end, there's really only one way to *be* mine. No, don't make that face. If you disagree, tell me I'm wrong. Go on. Tell me."

"I believe that you do not understand the danger of what you suggest," he said, but after a long pause. "But you accepted Kiriel where I would have killed her—if that is even possible now—and you have not yet been proved wrong."

"Meaning you think I will be."

"To your lasting regret, yes."

"Let's just say this is a matter of instinct and leave it at that."

"Let us, then." His lips were tight. It was a familiar expression, and she was very happy to see it. She walked to the ledge and stood to one side, propping her chin up by the use of elbows and palms. "Okay," she said, looking the almost-human newcomer squarely in the eyes, "these are the rules. It's late. I've had a nightmare. It's what I call a true dream."

The pale, silver brows of the most beautiful man Jewel had ever seen rose a fraction. *I'm going to have to do something about those looks,* she thought. *He cannot stay that pretty and be part of my group.* But she decided that particular set of changes could wait.

"You have the Sight," he said at last, as if speaking to her was a distasteful but necessary evil.

"More or less," she replied. "You're used to pomp, circumstance, ritual, and sadism. Guess what? Life's a lot different where we live, and it's going to *stay* that way, if I have to send everything that isn't human to the Hells permanently."

"Jewel."

She ignored Avandar.

The pretty man was only marginally less pretty when haughty; he was haughty now. "You really don't understand what's happened, do you?"

"Yes, I do. Dark god that we all don't name because we're afraid He'll hear us has managed to get a teeny-tiny foothold into our world. We don't want Him here, and we're going to send Him back to the Hells. Simple."

"Something is being simple," he said coldly.

She slapped him.

Just like that, hand snaking out and back in a movement that surprised them all. His sword was out of its scabbard so fast Jewel wouldn't have bet money that he'd ever sheathed it.

Avandar was faster still; lightning met sword as if it were corporeal. But the sword stopped.

The man who had been Lord Celleriant closed his eyes. Jewel could see the mark her hand had left on his perfect skin. She wondered, then, what sun would do. What age would do—if he would age at all when they left this place. "Do you think," he said, moderating his tone with such obvious difficulty Jewel wasn't sure whether she should be grateful for the attempt when the failure was so great. "That you can stand against a god?"

"If I remember my history," she began.

"You don't," Avandar said. "You remember your legends. History and legend diverge in details both great and small."

"If I remember my *legend,*" she said, throwing Avandar the look he deserved for the interruption he'd given, "Moorelas—"

"Called Morel of Aston," Avandar said, speaking directly to Lord Celleriant now, "in your time."

"I know well of whom she speaks, Warlord."

"Good. I can do without the interruptions. Avandar, take a hint.

"Moorelas rode against Allasakar."

"And?"

"Well," she said, frowning, "he won, obviously, because there are no dark gods—no gods at all—wandering around making our lives miserable. Not that we're not good at doing that ourselves."

"Is that the tale that is told now?" he said, not to her, but to Avandar.

"Lays are sung about the Shining Lord and the Shining City," was Avandar's quiet reply. "But this is known: That Moorelas rode into the shadow, and in time, the shadow lifted."

Celleriant frowned.

"It is also known," Avandar continued softly, his words weapon now, and cold. "That he was to have ridden with the four princes of the Firstborn. Four, sworn to fealty.

"But he dared the shadow that they would not dare."

"Not so." Celleriant was stung. "There are only three sleepers."

Avandar frowned. "Death takes us all."

"Or almost all. Maybe this will be your battle, Warlord," the tall immortal said. His lips turned up in a smile that Jewel had seen before. Once before. On the lips of a demon. "Or perhaps not; it is said that your curse and your skill are one and the same. Perhaps you must hide with the rest of the cattle in order to achieve your—"

Blue light flared in Avandar's hands, but it wasn't his hands that concerned Jewel; it was the light that seemed to pour, like gouts of multicolored flame, from his eyes.

"Avandar! No!"

Celleriant's sword caught the lightning, but his armor absorbed the spell, and of the two, Jewel thought the spell the more dangerous. Celleriant grunted with pain; the magic drove him back into the rock. But it didn't kill him, and that surprised her. His armor, however, was shredded in a way that she wouldn't have thought possible for something metallic.

"Avandar!"

Celleriant brought his sword 'round in an arc. It was a great sword; it had reach and weight, and he had the height and the strength to wield it as if it were a long sword.

There was a clang of steel against steel. Somehow—she had no idea how, and a strong sense that she didn't *want* to know— Avandar was armed.

She had never seen him fight before. She had seen him kill and had reason to be grateful for those deaths. She had seen him use his magic, briefly, in the Common against the demons. She had seen him pull the leash that he held, invisible but absolute, when she had been surrounded by statues that didn't seem to have her best interests at whatever was left of their hearts.

There had been no question of his power.

But this: this was power shorn of facade; it was contest shorn of any experience but the immediacy of the battle itself. And she had seen it before. Once, long ago, hiding behind the banisters of the largest stairway she had—up to that point in her life—ever seen, her den at her back, breaths held, waiting on her command. Waiting.

The clang of steel.

Someone was going to die. If she didn't do something, someone was going to die.

And she knew who it would be.

It shouldn't have mattered to her, but, curse everything, it *did*. She froze a moment on the road, the wilderness and her own helplessness bearing down on her. And then she turned.

Turned to where a set of round, unblinking eyes observed everything: The fight, the swirl of steel, the aurora of magic that haloed both men as if they were angels. Or demons. She had hoped that what lay behind that soft fur, beneath that crown of tines, was animal. So much for hope.

But the creature dipped its massive head, and she understood at that moment exactly what to do. Jewel, who *hated* riding and avoided horses whenever possible because of the embarrassment the inevitable comparison between her skill and the skill of those born to leisure always caused, grabbed the neck of the great stag, catching the antler nearest her for support as he shrugged her onto his back. She had seen—just once—Duster and Carver try to kill each other. It was ugly. It was one of the ugliest memories she had, and she didn't take it out often for just that reason. But the ugly things, like things of great beauty, had power; they stayed with you no matter how much you tried to dodge 'em. She'd stopped them then.

She sat.

Took a deep breath.

The stag said, *hold on.* She nearly fell off.

And then it lurched forward, and somehow, lurching or no, she realized that it would not let her fall. Its tines, like the swords' light, glowed.

She remembered Duster, Duster her killer, Duster the member of the den that she was always most attracted to *because* she was a killer, circling Carver, dagger extended, taunting him. Remembered Carver, wary, but cheeks flushed, his anger overwhelming his sense. You couldn't make Duster stupid with anger. When she was ready to kill, you couldn't do it. The quiet was ugly with her determination and her pleasure.

And how had she broken them up?

Arann's help.

The stag's muscles tensed beneath her. Ready to leap, she thought. Ready for flight.

Except that flight implied *away,* and she wasn't going away. Arann's help, yes. But it had been Jewel, in the end. Jewel in the center of all things, where tempers had frayed and blood was being spilled in scratches that threatened to become something irreparable.

She *heard* the strike of swords against tine; heard the creature she was on *growl*—and would wonder, later, how a stag could growl—and then she was off the beast's back, hands tangled briefly for both leverage and swing on the lowest of the beast's antlers before she found her feet there, in center ground, in the middle of a fight that should never have happened.

Wouldn't have happened if she hadn't slipped, if she hadn't been intimidated, if she hadn't been tired and afraid.

The swords rose and fell, but they fell slowly as both men realized what they would strike—if they struck.

She wanted to smack them both. That's what she'd done to Duster and Carver after the sheer terror and anger and shaking had finally left her. And not a Northern slap, nothing weak and simple about it; a good, Southern slap. Like her Oma would have given 'em, had she been alive then.

But these two—these two were beyond that. Mostly. For now.

"Avandar." He stared past her and past his name to the face of the equally intent Lord of the Arianni. "*Avandar.* I'm talking to you."

"I . . . am listening."

"Do better. Pay attention."

The moment stretched out. She curled her hands into fists, forgetting his dignity for a minute. Forgetting her own, not that it mattered as much. But perhaps, sensing what was about to follow, Avandar remembered *his* dignity. He turned to her.

"ATerafin." Obviously angry.

But in the anger department, he had nothing on her. "Okay," she said, hissing on the sibilants, "*he's* an idiot. He has no idea what it means to be one of mine, he's probably lost the only thing he really cared about having—not that it makes any sense, but that's beside the point—he's got an excuse for being an idiot. What's yours?"

"I see, Viandaran," the Arianni Lord began, in a tone of voice very like Duster's would have been.

He didn't finish. Jewel nodded at the stag and the stag very swiftly—*very* swiftly—butted him. His sword came up, but he staggered back; the point was made. Jewel glanced sideways at the stag; had the sword not come up, the argument would have ended, and not in a way that she liked.

But could she judge? No. She never wanted to know what the stag had gone through. Never.

And he had a voice to tell her with. It was very, very dark, for a moment, the light seemed to bleed shadows.

This was not the den she would have put together on her own. But with her own so damn far from her, it was the only one she had.

"Lord Celleriant, you're going to have to come up with a different name."

"Oh?"

"Yours is too—too—well, to be honest, it's the type of name

a child would choose because it sounded either magical or important."

His brows rose; his cheeks darkened. "It's not like Avandar's going by his real name either," she reminded.

"He," Avandar said with quiet dignity, "is going by the name as it would have meaning in your current tongue."

"Not my tongue."

"One of them."

"Whatever. What should we call you? What do you want to call yourself?"

"Celleriant," he replied.

"Why don't we just shorten it to something *I* can remember."

A white brow rose.

She looked him straight in the face. "Let's get one thing straight. I don't give a damn if you think I'm stupid. I don't give a damn if you think I'm anything at all *except* the woman whose orders you *follow*. Clear?"

His brows rose a fraction and he looked over the top of her head—which was easy—at Avandar. *"This,"* he said, his voice no longer dripping contempt because a very real curiosity had edged its way between the words, "is what you have chosen to serve?"

"She surprises me constantly," Avandar replied. "She is not what I thought to serve. I . . . had other plans for her. I thought to guide her to a position of power."

"I don't like your definition of power," Jewel snapped; it was an old argument. "It doesn't mean I don't want power."

But Avandar wasn't speaking to her. He put up his sword. So did the Arianni Lord. "Good. If the two of you children have stopped slinging rocks and can sit at the table like grownups, we've got things to discuss."

Celleriant's brows disappeared into the line of his hair—hair that was momentarily less than perfect because he'd bled on it somewhat. Or Avandar had. They both looked as if they'd been fighting for their lives. And they both looked, damn them, as if they somehow enjoyed the unguarded ferocity.

"Come on," she said, her voice as dark as the night, "the ledge. Now. Any more shit, and I'll—"

"You'll what?" Avandar said pointedly.

"I'll discharge you both from my service and leave you here. Him," she added, nodding in the direction of the stag, "I'll take."

Avandar said nothing. He was used to her. Lord Celleriant was used to something else from humans, and from the looks of his face, it was a lot closer to groveling and pleading than Jewel was capable of. He started to speak. She cut him off.

"You want an easy death, or you wouldn't have started that fight. We both know damn well that you're no match for Avandar." It was meant to insult; it insulted. Jewel was not above temper herself. "Well, guess what? I gave you an order, *follow* it. You don't get an easy death when you're with me."

His bow was heavy with irony. And armor.

"And while we're on the topic, this is the first rule: No fighting among den members. You're one of mine. You *don't* fight with anyone else who's mine. Clear? Good."

"Two: You're used to the kill. Fine. I won't judge you for your past. Okay," she added, glancing to and from the stag, "I'll try real hard not to. Past is past; you're here. So: I don't care what you want to kill, I say *stop,* you stop. Is that clear?"

"Do you wish me to exercise my own judgment?"

"What did I just say?" She sat down in front of the rocky outcropping. "Okay. Speaking of dens: You're part of my den now."

"Den?"

"Yeah. Group of people who do what I say. Sort of like your host, but less—just less whatever it was *she* was."

He said nothing, but for just a moment, the expression on his face made her pity him in spite of her best intentions. "You won't meet the rest of 'em—if they're lucky—for a while. They call me what you can call me. What everyone but Avandar calls me."

"And that is?"

"Jay."

He was silent.

"Wait, don't tell me. You're another one of those people that think a name is defined by how many syllables it has."

He didn't dignify her comment with an answer, but looked to Avandar. Then he said, "I will call you what you suffer your other powerful servants to call you; nothing less."

"All right. Call me Jewel."

"Jewel is . . . a more interesting choice of name."

"It wasn't my choice."

"Indeed." The Arianni took his place in front of her. But he sheathed his sword; she wondered how he managed to get it into the scabbard across his back without nicking the side of his neck—but she always wondered that with the big swords. They never seemed practical. She also wondered how he'd drawn the blade in the first place.

Avandar's sword was nowhere to be seen, and she didn't ask. She cleared her throat. "You," she said, frowning slightly, "will have to be Teller."

Avandar took his place at her side and slightly behind; the stag took his place behind them all—which was just as well because there wasn't any room for him at the small ledge.

"And what of me?

She rolled her eyes. "You clean the blood off your face and your arm, and then you—"

"No, Lady—Jewel. What do you wish to call me?"

She was silent for a long time, looking at him. Thinking that the names that had come to her for her den had come because half of her den didn't know their real names, or couldn't wait to leave them behind. In the end, she'd named them—half in fun— and the names stuck. As if they had power. Teller. Finch. Carver. Lefty—dead, with Fisher and Lander, dead with Duster. Arann had survived with his own name intact because only Arann was so much himself she couldn't change him.

"Killer," she said quietly.

If something as graceful and perfect as Lord Celleriant could roll eyes, he would have. His expression was damn close. "Killer."

"It sounds close enough to the first half of your actual name, and it's descriptive. I could go for stubborn, arrogant fool, but that would probably bother you, and it's too many syllables."

"Jewel." Avandar's voice sounded as normal as it had since they'd left Terafin.

"And another thing," Jewel said to him. "You never mentioned my name while *she* was around."

"No. It's not . . . safe. Not during the Hunt."

"But you'll mention it to him?"

"She gave him to you. He is yours. He is incapable of betraying you. And, if the truth were known, I believe him incapable of understanding you well enough to use your name in the fashion of his kin."

"If they were incapable of betrayal, Moorelas might not have fallen. Or so legend says."

"Jewel," Avandar said, almost sharply, "you speak of things you do not understand. Celleriant is Lord; they were Princes; she could not bind them in so simple a fashion. She could command, yes, but she could not compel. Celleriant *will not* betray you, although he may well do everything within the bounds of his ability to resist.

"Oh. Good." She turned back to the Arianni Lord. "Well, Killer, this is what we do. I have a dream. I tell you what it is. You listen. That's it. Teller takes notes, and I'd let you do it—but I suspect you can't write. Weston," she added quickly as the clouds moved in on his expression. "You can't write Weston."

"Very well," he replied, tone mirroring expression.

Gods, could things get any more difficult?

"Dream."

Avandar set a "lamp" on the table; a thing of fire that had the rough shape of the lamp Finch or Teller so often carried. She stared at it, wondering if the fight had driven the dream back into whereever it is that dreams—thankfully—went when she woke. But Avandar spoke quietly.

"Valedan," he said.

And she saw, in his fire, the heart of the dream: the young man's face, his high cheekbones exposed. He wore a helm, its visor above his face; lines of sweat trickled out from beneath his dark hair. That hair was drawn back; it vanished into the edges of light. His eyes were narrowed; he was intent upon something, but it was something that she could not clearly see.

There was a scratch across his forehead; it had healed, but the russet stain of blood was caught in his eyebrows, just visible against his skin. Sloppy cleaning—or quick. Hard to say.

"Jewel?"

"Valedan is staring at something. I hear a voice. He's annoyed, but it passes. I see him. He turns." She swallowed. "Gods, Avandar, they're in a valley, I think it's a valley—not sudden and sharp, but I can see where the trees and the hills rise on either side—"

"Averdan valleys?"

"How the Hells should I know—Shut up, I'm losing it." She didn't want to hold on to it. But it was strong. "There are dead all over the place. I see a standard; its pole—it's been snapped in half, but someone managed to keep it up. It's flapping in the wind, but—but I can see it." She stopped speaking. "The standard-bearer's dead."

Her discussion with the Terafin spirit came back to her, and she froze because all around her she could see the dead. She could smell them, and she had never been on a battlefield that she knew of; she could hear their bitter cries.

Their cries were almost enough to drive her back. Almost. But she'd gotten tenacious over the years. The dying hadn't woken her.

"Two crowns," she said, her voice breaking and reforming between the syllables. "Flanked by swords, and beneath them the Sword and the Rod. The edge of the flag is singed."

"The Sun ascendant?"

"I—I don't see it." She swallowed. "I'm looking. I'm—oh, gods, no . . ."

He didn't speak. No one did. Had they, she wouldn't have heard them.

"The screams are . . ." She shook herself. She didn't want to find the words to describe them. Swallowed the ones that were halfway there. "The dying are dying. I can't hear 'em anymore because the living are screaming. Screaming. I—I've never heard that before. Not from—" She stopped again, mesmerized, the dream in control now. "Someone's warned Valedan to pull back. A mage, I think—he's gone too quickly. Valedan says . . . says no. The—" She stopped again. "There's a monster on the field."

"Jewel, tell me exactly what it looks like. *Exactly.*"

"I don't know. It's—the sun is in my eyes; I can only see its shadow and its shape. It's just—it's so damn big—I think its jaws are as wide as a man—wider. I—someone's riding it. Someone's on its back. I can see—I can see the reins."

"Reins?"

"The beast it—it's reined, somehow . . ."

"How?"

"There's a rider."

Silence.

"There's a rider. I can—I can see him. No, wait, I can see . . ."

No!

"Jewel?"

No. . . .

"Na'jay?"

She looked up. They all did. Standing in the road wearing her god-born, immortal beauty but speaking in the cracked, wind-broken voice of the old woman Jewel had loved and trusted, stood the Oracle.

"The time has come to find your own road," she told the younger woman quietly. "You see the truth," she said. "You will always

see the truth. But understanding the nature of truth is a difficult
business, and one learned only after walking the true path. You
will find your world. From there, you must search for me in *mine*.
Come to me, Jewel. She will tell you when."

   Kiriel.

   "Wake now, Na'jay. And come. The Festival Moon is beginning to shine in the streets of the Tor Leonne, and you will be
missed if you are not there to greet the Festival's start."

   "How long until the Festival's height?"

   "Clever child. Let me answer the question you have not asked.
Scarran is the third and the last of the Lady's Nights."

   She began to walk, and without a qualm, Jewel followed.

   She would remember that later.

19th of Scaral, 427 AA
Tor Leonne

Moonlight.

   So close to full, only the trained eye would know the difference. Sendari di'Marano's—for in truth, although he had been
responsible for the deaths of many in order to merit a different
title, this was still the name with which he felt most comfortable,
and to which he returned, by slip of tongue or careless pen, again
and again—was trained, and in both ways; he understood the
moon and he did not look away from its slow arc across the sky.

   Mikalis di'Arretta was his sole companion, but this was not a
vigil. He stared at the masks that had been laid out against enchanted parchment. They had been oiled with something Mikalis
had concocted—a salve of sorts that contained not a small amount
of his blood. The wounds had been deep but controlled.

   Sendari was no fool; the pallor of his friend's skin was not due
to loss of blood alone. He had offered his own blood to the mixture, and Mikalis had rejected it flatly.

   The Widan did not ask why. This was not an art that the members of the Sword of Knowledge practiced. It was not, judging by
the ease with which Mikalis worked—none at all—an art that
Mikalis practiced. But it was one that he had stumbled across, or
had been gifted with, in his travels.

   What, he thought, *did you offer the Voyani that they shared
their art with you?* He wondered it frequently. He dared, in the
strain of the weeks of fruitless searching, to wonder it aloud.

   Mikalis had looked up, eyes red with sleep's lack, jaw clenched in a perpetual frown that made his face a landscape immune to joy. "I wondered that myself, and often," he said, in the voice of a man who has arrived at a truth he doesn't like. "But I think. Sendari, it was simply this: The Voyani see deeply and see far.

"It was not anything I had done that was considered worthy of their teachings."

"No?"

"No. It was what I *would* do, if the time were right and the portents . . . as they are." He was pale. He was old. Sendari thought that he would not regain the youth he had lost in the last week. "There is no love lost between the Voyani and the clans, and they understand that history better, I fear, than we."

"Mikalis?"

"They see far," he had said then.

And now, gaunt, he simply said, "Widan, your gift is fire. I ask you . . . I ask you to do me the grace of using it when the time is right."

"When will that time be?"

"You'll know," Mikalis said, and he smiled. It was not a pleasant expression. "But you must satisfy my curiosity. What made you suspect that the masks served a purpose opposite to their function?"

It was a question that Sendari did not want to answer. But he was Widan. "It is the Festival," he said softly, turning away to protect himself against involuntary facial expression. "And we wear masks during the Festival of the Moon so that we might do as we desire. So that we might reveal our true selves without fear."

Sendari turned his attention to the masks. Four—one for each of the designs—lay in a quartered circle that had been drawn in more of Mikalis' blood. A battle, Sendari thought, would have cost his friend less.

The significance of the circle was not well understood, but its history lay at the founding of the empire; the crossed circle was the highest symbol of the oath between two powerful men. Mikalis, after anointing the masks, handled them almost carelessly; he forbade Sendari to so much as touch them, even with the magic that was his art.

"There is never a time," Mikalis said softly, "when we can reveal our true selves without fear. But, yes, there are those who prey on our hopes and our illusions. Now," he said. "Watch."

Fire took the edge of the parchment, but slowly, the flames

held back by some power invisible to Sendari's trained eye. *Mikalis,* he thought, *They taught you much.* For he was looking, and he could see no sign—but the obvious, that of moving fire— of magic. He said nothing.

The flames crawled in, delicately curling and blackening paper until they hit the line the Widan had drawn in blood and unguent. Then they leaped into motion, dancing higher and higher until they seemed a warm, sensuous wall, a red veil that tantalized without concealing.

"Watch now," Mikalis said, pale as the moon.

Sendari's hand found his beard and began to stroke it absently; all thought was focused on what Mikalis was achieving by dint of a knowledge that Sendari did not possess. The contours of the masks, lit by this coruscating, eerie light, were consumed, or so it seemed, by the heat of the flame.

Another man would have asked a question; would have said something. But Sendari was trained. When the contours of the masks began to change in the dance of fire, he said nothing at all, but his face grew as pale as the face of the Widan who had offered his blood for this rite.

The simplest mask changed first, taking on the features of a child, pert nose, expression pensive. Where the eyeholes had been, Sendari could *see* the ghost of a child's eyes, pain in them, tears on the verge of being shed. He hoped for the boy's sake those tears would never fall; he had learned the hard way that they invoked a punishment far worse than whatever it was that had caused the tears themselves.

But all boys who survived to be men learned that lesson. All boys.

He started to speak—a mistake—and stopped. The second mask had begun to take shape. A youth's face. Defiant, even angry, but with an anger that knows fear. He had seen that expression before, but never so clearly from the outside; it was almost uncomfortable to look at. He cast a sideways glance at Mikalis di'Arretta. The Widan stared straight ahead, his expression so rigid it gave away everything and nothing at the same time.

There was something about that youth's face that was familiar; some breadth of cheekbone, some shape of forehead; it had no hair, of course but the eyeholes were again full, the eyes narrow and dark.

He knew the face.

Closed his eyes on the knowledge, but the spell had been cast;

it went on, whether he chose to witness or no. And he was Widan, in the end. He opened his eyes.

The third face was a man's face. Scarred in two places, eyes wide, expression shocked, hurt; vulnerable. He had to look away; he had to look away because he could not bear to see a friend unmanned so completely.

But it was a younger face; he told himself that. A younger face, a face that had been left behind by the man he knew as Mikalis. He turned then. To watch the last face. And he understood, as it took on the contours of Mikalis' face—the lines, the wind-worn crevices in skin around eyes and mouth—that there was much, much more than mere appearance about it. It had been a slender, magnificent, monstrous face, a thing with feather and gilt, and a nose hooked like bird's beak, but grander, more ferocious.

That was gone now; it melted into a thing of flesh. Into a thing that was familiar and worse: There was something about it that promised to reveal everything to Sendari's curiosity. Every indiscretion. Every fear. Every weakness.

It was as if—as if the real Mikalis was being stripped of essence, as if the mask was somehow absorbing him, becoming him, becoming what he would be without the polite and necessary fiction of social grace.

Sendari turned to look at his friend; his friend was transfixed, utterly transfixed. The hands that had drawn blood and spilled it, had mixed it with herb and unguent and potion, had circumscribed the circle in which the four masks might be contained, their magics examined, now lay almost flaccid in his lap, trembling at the loss of self.

Loss of self.

Or the revelation of it.

The truth in that thought was profound: in the Dominion of Annagar self was like secret: the revelation destroyed its essence. He had watched deaths with less horror than he watched this unraveling.

Mikalis had asked him to be ready with fire; to use it when the time was right. If the time existed it was *now,* but he could not lift hand to destroy that mask, that face, that *man.* He could more easily destroy the man beside him who seemed to be leeched of color and life.

Paralyzed, as he had so often been paralyzed by death or tragedy, his gaze jumped between the two, trapped on either extreme by Mikalis di'Arretta.

His father had said he would never make a warrior. His grandfather had said worse, favoring Teresa or Adano easily over the awkward Sendari. And he recognized the truth of it in the paralysis. Anger, and something very like what was on the face of three of the masks he now stared at, filled him; it was as if he now *wore* those faces, they had become so much his own.

But he was not a child.

He was not a youth to be bullied by either bigger boys—or worse, the large, unwieldy horse and the men who had nothing but contempt for a boy with a fear of horses.

He was not a young man, and the loss of his wife was in the past; her death had opened the door to the only thing he now possessed with any certainty. Power.

Power.

Sendari di'Marano had learned to be a political man; had indeed become so politic and so polished as a Widan that his early awkwardness became simple memory. He had embraced power and the study of power, calling it knowledge. He had followed the trail that was set by curiosity; had turned that curiosity into the heart of the fire that he contained now, waiting for the moment. Waiting for the time that Mikalis had promised he *would know*.

Waiting.

And unbidden, while waiting, while seeing these truths about himself and about his friend, while fire burned everywhere, a name returned to him: *Na'dio*.

His daughter had saved his life.

And—if his ill-loved, clear-eyed sister was correct, and Winds take her, Sun scorch her, she so often was—he had destroyed hers.

Fire.

Flame.

Moonlight.

"Oh, very clever," an unrecognized voice said. "My Lord was right about you. You are not as stupid as it appears you must be. But I'm afraid what you've discovered dies here. With the two of you."

Sendari turned, fire gathered in his palms and in the center of his chest, burning there like elemental anger. Like elemental pain. "Oh?"

"Do you think to threaten me? *You?* You who are less than servant to the Sword's Edge? Do you know who I am?"

"You are probably," Sendari replied in a mild voice, "*Kialli.* I doubt Lord Ishavriel would send anything less for a mission of this import."

"Clever indeed. Not powerful, of course, but clever. I enjoy the deaths of clever people because they understand exactly what is happening to them. Unfortunately," he added, his features elongating in a way that suggest a jaw that was serpentine and no longer human in nature, "we have so little time. Your friend is dealing with magic that is a bit before its time. Or a bit before our preferred time.

"The Sword of Knowledge is famed for its curiosity," he continued. "A great pity for you, Widan. You would have seen magic that has not been seen for millennia. Perhaps in another life." His laughter was slick and unpleasant. "No, let me be truthful. Most certainly in another life, but perhaps you will not be in a position to appreciate the results." He stepped forward, hands elongating into lovely, slender blades, jaws lengthening yet again. Nothing human remained.

He turned to the motionless, sightless Widan who knelt on the floor in front of burning parchment, helpless.

Sendari di'Marano said something. Or thought he said something; his lips moved; his throat constricted and sound filled the room.

The fire that he had contained in bits and pieces for so many years, the anger at mockery, the pain at loss and betrayal, the desperate desire to fill the void with something, with the only thing he had ever been competent at, destroyed reserve entirely.

His weaponsmaster would have humiliated him publicly, and with ease, at such a loss of control. That had been his first lesson: Never lose control.

It was gone.

It had been his second lesson as an aspiring Widan, as a seeker of knowledge.

That, too, was gone.

What was here: a demon, an enemy, a target—something to look at that was not *himself.*

When the fires came, they were almost beyond him.

And unfolding slowly in that flame, the *Kialli.* It was an almost perfect moment. He had never heard a demon scream quite that way before. He listened, the fires burning, the ground now scorched and blackened at the creature's withering feet, until the cry was only a memory.

A man stepped around the flame.

Not Mikalis, although Mikalis had shakily gained his feet; not Cortano, although Cortano was the only other man to have easy access to this room of Widan study and contemplation.

No: It was Alesso di'Alesso, the Tyr'agar. His sword's flat reflected the lamp that now seemed a poverty of light's expression. "Sendari," he said, over the crackle and hiss of flame and burning demon. He said it again, and again, as if he expected the word to have meaning.

I am not Kialli, Sendari thought, *to be controlled by the use of a name.*

But he looked at Mikalis and he understood that a whole life's truth, more complicated and much more difficult to retrieve, could be taken from him and exposed as the masks would expose all. He wondered if, looking at the face of a man who wore such a creation, he would be able to name him.

Wondered, and knew the answer at the same time.

Yes.

"Sendari," Alesso said. He lowered the blade.

Sendari understood. At last, he understood. The flames guttered instantly. The chill began to set in.

Do not let the fire control you, his former master had said, *For the fevers will devour you in its wake. You have power, Sendari di'Marano; but you have something more precious to me as a teacher: common sense. Wisdom. Use them. Do not let the power use you.*

Shaking.

He fell to a knee before the only man in front of whom he felt no need to be ashamed of such weakness. "Why . . . are you here?"

Alesso di'Alesso sheathed his sword. Smiled, the corners of his lips quirking in a way that they had not done since he had taken the crown and the Tor. "To have a fight," he said, "but it appears I was late."

"You are not . . . allowed . . . entry here. Cortano—"

"Is not here."

"How . . . did you know?" Alesso's arms were beneath his arms.

"Enough, Sendari. I will answer your questions when you are able to ask them."

"But I—"

"Enough. I think, if I am any judge, that you have the answers that we need."

"No," he said. "Alesso—a favor. I was too weak to do what had to be done."

"What favor?"

"Destroy the circle."

"The circle?"

"The burning circle. The masks. Do not look at them—just—destroy the circle."

Alesso's eyes narrowed.

"A favor," Sendari said again.

It was as much of a plea as he had ever made to anyone who was not his wife or the man who could have saved her. Alesso closed his eyes. Nodded. Turned, letting Sendari's knees crumple.

From the vantage of the floor, Sendari di'Marano saw his only friend lift *Terra Fuerre,* the sword which Alesso had promised would leave its mark in the history of the Dominion, and destroy fire and masks without hesitation.

He wondered if Alesso could not see what he had seen, for Mikalis was there, alive, in the faces the masks had become. Alesso missed little; Sendari wondered how he could raise and lower his sword with such destructive ease, but he did not ask; the favor had been granted; the cost was Alesso's to bear.

As was the weight of the Widan who was his friend.

CHAPTER TWENTY-EIGHT

20th of Scaral, 427 AA
Tor Leonne

The streets were busy.

They were always busy during the Festival season, Sun or Moon, but there was, in the hurried movements of the crowds that streamed through the grip of frustrated merchants, a tension and a furtive silence that was unusual given that the Lady neared Her time. The dawn came; the Lord prepared to give way for the three days that ended with the full Festival Moon. Lady's gift, that final night, although the spill of wildness often began, hesitantly, on the night prior to it. She was, after all, nearest Her ascendancy; She forgave much.

But the Lady was angry this year; there were dead to prove it. And the Tyr was no Leonne; the streets whispered the truth, the cobbled stones carried the words. No man could be heard to speak them—no clansman—and no one listened to the whispers of the women or the mutterings of the serafs, but the words traveled, wind-borne, like the locusts that occasionally destroyed whole harvests beneath the Lord's careless gaze.

Even so, the serafs cleaned the founts; they polished brass and silver; they cleaned and repaired the banners and flags, the hangings and tapestries, the tenting and the awnings that were a part of the Lady's Festival. Wine came in barrels and on wagons; merchants—the less timorous, or those with the tacit alliance of one of the older clans—dragged their horses or camels—depending on the direction they traveled into the heartlands from. Some were turned back by the Voyani warnings, but many simply didn't have the luxury; die by the Lady's hand or the Lord's—starvation was starvation—and the Festival season could make or break a small merchant family's fortunes.

But the large merchant families worried no less.

Behind the gated entrances to homes that would impress even the Tyrs, surrounded by the best cerdan money could buy, swathed in their silks and surrounded by things which drew the attention of men of quality and power, it could be argued that they had more to lose.

By some.

But the worries, in the end, were the same: family first, then fortune. "Maria, I *don't like it.*"

The Serra Maria en'Jedera bowed gracefully to her husband. In fact, to his great annoyance, and the amusement of her younger son—the carefully hidden amusement—she fell into the full supplicant posture. It looked very strange, coming as it did from a woman dressed as a barely free merchant's mother.

Mika, her oldest child, was thundering around the circumference of the most private of her chambers, lifting the mats with his heavy thumping stride. "You should listen to Da," he said, the words heavy with an anger that was a thin covering over fear. "Not mock him!"

"Na'mi," she said gently, lifting herself from her position without her husband's permission, such as it was. These were, after all, her rooms, and in them—in them she was allowed, as all Serras were who did not have the misfortune to have married monsters, some control of her life. And such a small space to have control in. For a moment she pitied the clanswomen. But only for a moment.

Mika blushed. The rebuke in her use of a child's name was enough, for at least the span of one long breath, to stop his heavy tread. And in truth, the elegance and grace of a Serra was no deception; she disliked the loud and the ugly wherever she saw it.

It caused her difficulty among her kin. She lifted a pale hand to the chain at her throat; the heart of the Lyserran Voyani beat there more strongly than her own; it was as if, this night, it absorbed breath, and blood, and spirit: everything she was. Everything she had to offer.

Or perhaps it was as if it demanded no less.

But unlike the other three Voyani Matriarchs, Maria's path had led her down a life that was split between the two Dominions: the one ruled by men like the clansman she had married—paler, lesser versions, of course—and the one covered in the crisscrossing web of the never-ending *Voyanne.*

"Maria?"

She looked up at her husband, and tightened her palm around a gem that Ser Tallos kai di'Jedera had *never* been able to see, although Mika and Jonni could see it quite well, and Aviana, her eldest girl, could sense it when it was within the building. Lorra was sensitive to it as well, but she said nothing; Aviana was Matriarch's daughter and heir, and Lorra adored her; she did nothing to draw attention away.

Or perhaps, Maria thought, she was like her mother and knew it: she was not quite of the *Voyanne,* and the clansmen resented what they saw as the obvious domestication of their own. Had Maria not been found by the Lysseran heart—a story in its own right—she would never have been accepted by the Voyani.

As it was, they were uneasy around her, as if she might break with a loud word, a badly drawn breath. And she had learned to put an edge into her words; to reveal more of herself; to be open with her grief and her anger—but to hide, to always hide, all scent or trace of fear. In that, at least, the clans and the Voyani were alike.

The heart steadied her. It brought back the memories of the childhood that lay buried beneath the memories of her induction into the graces of the Dominion's high society. "Tallos," she said, in a voice that was rougher than he liked, and gentler than she should have been, "what choice do I have?"

"You know what I want, Maria."

"And you know, my love, that you *cannot* accompany me. The summons was clear."

"*What* summons? I heard no word, I saw no magic; I saw a *bone* ring. That was all. What would make you risk this night, these streets? The Tyr is *looking* for the Voyani Matriarchs."

"And he has found one, and she escaped him. She escaped the Widan, and the Tyran, and the cerdan; she cannot be found. Who will mistake me for Voyani? My own do not," she added, keeping the trace of bitterness out of her voice. "My hair is like the mountain peaks, and my skin, almost the same, and I am too thin and I speak too little and when I speak, it is too softly." She smiled a moment, and the smile was cutting, "Yet I am not merciful enough." She bowed to her husband.

"Your boys—"

"No. The only person with a right to attend is Aviana, and I will not risk her."

"Maria, *please.*"

She stood. Straightened out the dress that she wore, a serviceable sari of a heavier fabric than she was used to. "I have my guard," she said.

"Oh?" Her husband's demeanor changed. She had angered him. "Who?"

She bowed her head. "Enter," she said, not even pitching her voice to carry. Her huband was nonplussed.

But the stranger entered the room anyway. He bowed, very low, to Ser Tallos kai di'Jedera, as if this meeting occurred not in the heart of Ser Tallos' harem, but rather in the main chambers in which dignitaries of lesser note were gathered.

"My apologies," he said smoothly, as he rose. "For presuming, but I offer you my word, Ser Tallos, that I will guard your Serra with my life."

Ser Tallos di'Jedera had gone from concerned to grim with a twitch of a few muscles. He stared, unblinking, into the face of Kallandras, the Northern bard. His Serra waited, lips moving up in a pained, fond smile that was absolutely genuine. "Tallos," she scolded gently. "Was this not what you requested? Has he not proved the ability that you doubted?"

"Maria—"

"If I do not go, we will all die, and I will not risk my husband and my sons." She had no wives; it was not the Voyani way, and in that, blood had proved stronger than upbringing. "Not to that certainty."

"And he is to be given you what you what you deny your own family?"

Kallandras raised a brow, turning to face her, the expression his question.

She chose to answer it. "Protection," she said quietly. "It is not only their duty, but their right."

"Serra," he said, bowing. "It is early yet, but I am not certain how long it will take us to arrive at our destination; if there is difficulty at all—"

"Understood. Wait a moment beyond the hanging; I will join you." He bowed, accepting the command so gracefully she felt he must have followed the orders of women all his life.

When he was gone, she simply said, "Na'mi, come and hug your mother. Na'jon, you, too."

The older boy held back a moment, as if incapable of believing that she intended to go on without him. But the younger son, her boy, came quietly and put his arms around her slender shoulders. "You'll come back?" he asked.

"Yes," she replied softly, "although I wish your father would take my advice and leave the Tor."

"Mother," Jonni said, reasonably, "he has his duty and you have yours; he cannot leave the Tor without losing all hope of position within the new order."

"And what good is position without life?" she countered, but with neither fire nor edge. She accepted with grace the risk that she asked her husband to accept. In that, they were different.

He accepted gracelessly.

When her oldest son had finished his fierce, brief, wordless hug, her husband proved that he and Mika were cut from the same cloth.

"Where would I find another wife like you? You drive me to madness, you make a fool of me, you unman me in a way I'm certain no clansman would be unmanned; you let your blood relatives turn *my* daughters into useless harridans—and it doesn't matter. If you are this Voyani Matriarch, then you are what you are. But let it cost your life, and Jedera will war against the Voyani until there are none of either. Do you understand?" His grip on her arms tightened. He shook her to punctuate each of the last three words.

In return, she lifted her hands, framed his weathered face between them, and kissed his brow. It was her promise, or as much of a promise as she would make and be bound to. And he closed his eyes after a moment and leaned into the kiss, defeated by it.

"Tell the bard," he said, as she turned to go, "that I'll kill him or have him killed if you are harmed." Cold voice now. No doubt at all that he meant those words.

As she left the room, Kallandras joined her. They walked some distance in the silence of that good-bye; she was certain he had heard all that was said; equally certain that the truth and the vulnerability that had been expressed had been absorbed into his silence, to remain there, undiscovered by even the strongest of winds. She was that comfortable instantly; a poor sign.

But the fact that Yollana favored him with her trust was a reasonable one, and it excused some of her ease.

"How shall we proceed?" she asked.

"Cautiously," he replied, and then he said, "expect trouble, Matriarch."

And she said, "I know."

Over her heart, pressed into flesh as if it had grown spines, the Voyani heart burned.

* * *

But trouble did not dog her steps, or his; in the open air the worst of the difficulties they encountered had more to do with frayed temper and poor wine than any machinations of their chosen enemy. She paused to look at their reflection in the still water of the Western Fount, and she smiled at what she saw there. He was patient; she was grateful.

"It is . . . hurried for a Festival."

"Yes."

"But even so, I think the spirit of the city cannot be suppressed, fear or no. Feel it: Timidly, or no, the people of the Tor are beginning to blossom."

"You have a touch of the bard in you," he said with a smile.

"The early bard," she replied, her words lifting in question, "whose love of words is perhaps as gratifying to an audience as a small child's love of attention?"

His smile caught her by surprise, for he seldom smiled. "There are bards who love the florid, Serra Maria, and bards who love the spare; and they speak, each, to their audience."

"And you, Kallandras of the North, who have somehow earned the trust of the most suspicious of the Voyani Matriarchs, which do you love? To whom do you seek to speak when you speak as a bard does and not as—" She stopped.

"I have . . . sung . . . before at the Festival of the Sun," he said softly. "At the behest of the wife of the Tyr. And it may be, Serra Maria, if you were not of rank to have heard me sing then, that you will be when this situation is resolved."

She nodded gracefully. Two children ran past her, knocking each other roughly into the folds of her skirts. She caught one by the ear and shook him sharply, her lovely smile still fixed upon her face. "Put it back, child, and my companion will allow you to keep your ear."

The child squawked something rude, took a closer look at her companion and became completely still. Her companion had *his* friend by the throat, and his friend's face was changing color.

She shook her head softly. "You know the penalty for robbing a clansman," she said softly.

"You're no clansmen," the sullen boy said, "and he ain't neither." He shrugged. His friend's hands were clawing at Kallandras' hand with no visible effect. "It's Lady's Festival, Serra," he said, changing his tone and striving for the near-groveling politeness that would save their lives.

"Indeed," she said. "My things."

He returned the small pouch in which money was usually kept; returned as well, the powdered silks that were meant to dry the skin and face if the sweat became a visible problem.

She let him go.

He sized up Kallandras; she watched him a moment, surprised that he didn't immediately flee. Then, keeping her eyes on the boy, she said softly, "It *is* the Lady's Festival, and boys will be . . . boys."

"As you say, Serra," the bard replied, dropping the young would-be thief. "Although thieves generally learn the error of their judgment in a more permanent fashion."

The two boys ran; she noted that the older boy—the boy she'd caught—stopped to grab the younger boy's hand and pull him to the safety of crowd and distance.

She wondered if they were her own, or Yollana's, Elsarre's, or Margret's. Or if they were the sons of very poor clansmen, or worse, orphans who narrowly escaped becoming serafs in a greater man's home. "Lady be merciful," she whispered, drawing the Moon's quarter circle across her heart. "As we desire, so shall we be."

"You, Serra, are a surprise to me."

"And if I believe that," she said softly, watching the human wave the boys' flight made through the crowd until even that evidence of their existence was gone, "I would not be the wife of one of the richest of the merchant clansmen." Her smile was, as her expression, sad.

"I would feel no pity for them," she said, "but it is clear that they understand family. That boy was terrified but he was afraid *for* his own, not for himself."

"He was afraid for himself," Kallandras replied. "There are sacrifices we cannot make and face ourselves again in the quiet of any evening the Lady keeps."

"Indeed," she said. "But you think deeply, and I think they do not; they respond from the heart."

"And their own needs, yes. But how is that different from what we do? Come. We have at least an hour's travel to the gates, and beyond."

The sound of singing was not particularly pleasant. But it was loud, and it would get louder still before the Festival's abrupt end. Maria felt comforted by it. The shadow of Yollana's summons had made all shadows seem menacing and dark, and the very ordinary activity of the rough men of the Tor eased her.

Kallandras kept them at bay, providing her a casement through which to view the world. She could smell the food and the fire in the air; could see glimpses of the jugglers and acrobats as they prepared for the following day, marking the way to their various platforms. She could see—and she stopped for just a glimpse before Kallandras ushered her on—two men, trapped in the dance of the blade, oblivious, or so it seemed, to all others.

"This city," she said softly, lifting a hand to her pale throat, "is important to me."

He nodded.

"It is not important to any of the others; perhaps the opposite. I think there will be some argument about its fate."

"I believe you are correct. But perhaps the argument will not be as clear as you think it. The clansmen so despised by the Voyani have made the Tor Leonne their seat of power—but if you destroy the Tor Leonne, or allow it to be destroyed—"

"So much more than the clansmen will be lost," she replied. But it was of the clansmen, not these desperate, traveling merchants and performers, that she thought.

She had seen the streets of the city strewn from one end to another with their broken bodies; fires had gutted whole buildings. The Voyani gift was strong in Maria; much stronger than any but her husband knew.

She stopped a moment in the broad, wide streets the lesser sellers used. Froze there.

"Serra?" The bard's voice, like a breeze, brisk and cool.

She answered him when she would not have answered any other, not even Tallos. "I saw a child's ball, there. It was a first year toy, one that grandmothers make for their grandchildren to celebrate their survival. It was not a fine ball; made of scraps of clothing but seamed with enough care that it was dirty and worn and still in one piece. A bit flattened."

"Serra—"

"And it was on the ground, beside the child—" she turned to look at those stones, as if memorizing the crowds that now milled across them would somehow erase the deeper vision. "Not everything I see comes true," she said, and this time she turned to him, to meet those clear eyes, to look at skin that, beneath some thin paint, was paler than her own, "And I will do whatever I can to make that vision a false one."

"Even if the child is not your own?"

"I am a Serra," she said softly. "I see death everywhere. Among the serafs I was taken with, only a handful have survived, and not one has reached a station equal to my own." She gazed up at the face of the indifferent sun. "And I hate the Lord for it. I am the Lady's in all possible ways. If not for the grace of Tallos, I might be that child's mother—"

She closed her eyes, smiled weakly. "I could never bear to listen to my own cry. It is *such* a weakness."

"Serra," the Northern bard said, unexpectedly, "do not speak of it as weakness. I have seen your sons, and I have—although I will not tell you when—seen your daughters. Your children are what I believe the Dominion's children might one day be: of both the Lord and the Lady, the Sun and Moon. But perhaps in a different land, where the power that you have is not granted by husband, and by husband taken away."

Her smile was bitter. "Power wears odd faces."

"Yes, and this Festival it will offer odd faces: the masks."

"Yes." She shivered. Seeing a woman, face *made* of the clay that she had donned, blood everywhere, and beside her, confused and terrified, holding that first year ball as if it were all that she had in the world, a pretty child in a Festival dress.

And it was, Maria knew, all she had in the world. Brief world. Her arms ached. She could hear Aviana say, "Mother you are *too* damn soft." Yes. She was.

And she hated the visions. Hated the gift. Hated the responsibility of being Voyani and Serra both, when all she desired was a home with the indulgent husband who had, quite probably, saved her life in every meaningful way.

But she wouldn't let her daughters run from their responsibilities.

"If I could see," she said softly, "how these masks killed their wearers—"

"Not now, Serra Maria. Not now, but soon."

It took four hours. Four hours, through crowds that thinned suddenly as the East gate came into view. The gate was an old one, and the city had spilled beyond it, but it was manned now, and the merchant wagons had been stopped before they could pass the rebuilt guard post. The barrier between the new Tyr's cerdan and the old Tyr's Festival was wide and tall, for all that it was intangible.

The only moment of difficulty that they encountered was at

the gate itself. A cerdan wearing the rayless sun stopped them; three others joined him before he had finished asking the first of his droning questions. They were armed, but they did not draw their weapons, and Maria, a merchant wife of some standing, prepared to wait them out. Ser Tallos was a man who navigated the bureaucracy with the skill of an eagle hunting desert mice; she did not feel threatened into foolish action by the mere presence of armed clansmen.

But her companion did not feel a pressing desire to play such waiting games, and perhaps wisely. Had she been any other Matriarch—Elsarre, for example—she would have actively resented the fact that he seemed to know more of Yollana's plan and mind than she, a Sister in kind.

Or perhaps it was because she lived in a world of men, and in it, men dealt with men and the women circled like beautiful birds of prey, or even vultures, watching and learning but never interfering without confidence of privacy.

For whatever reason, he spoke, this Northern bard, his perfect, fluent Torra such a joy to her ears she would have listened to him speak while the Tor burned. She wondered, not for the first time, who he truly was, and how he had become the Lady's servant. She wondered what his gift was when the cerdan, four men who were trained to be wary, accepted the explanation that, to her ears, was weak and fanciful.

But she was thankful for it; as a Matriarch prepared for difficulty she was a match for the four, but no Voyani sought Lord's light where shadows would do.

Kallandras brought the Lyserran Matriarch to the encampment slightly earlier than the agreed upon hour. She greeted the Havallan Matriarch as if it were an acknowledged fact—and not an unacknowledged truth—that Yollana was their leader. He wondered if she made the gesture so open as a reminder to Margret of the differences between them, but decided against it; Serra Maria was a practical woman; she had pride, but she was graceful, and she understood the practicality of necessity in a way that one not raised by clansmen could not.

The greeting she offered Margret was different; laced with sorrow and quiet respect. He understood, then, why the Voyani— even her own, perhaps especially her own—were so suspicious of her. All the scouring and scraping the winds had done she hid beneath a placid surface—and the Voyani were not a placid people.

Yollana said, "Well, Margret, will you build the heart's circle, or will I?"

"I think," the Serra Maria—and he thought of her this way, although she was indeed Mother of Lyserra—said quietly, "that this discussion is of a nature, Yollana, that such a fire should be built by eight hands, and not two. You have summoned us; we have come."

"Not all of us," the older woman said sharply. "Kallandras." Pepper, her words, and salt. He smiled. She called him the way most would call an errant child or a stupid but well-loved dog, and he came. "Where is she?"

"She?"

"Don't play stupid with me. You found Elsarre?"

"Yes, Matriarch, I found her."

"You gave her the token."

"Yes."

"Then where, in the Lord's fire, is she?"

"She's probably," Serra Maria said, with the faintest hint of a smile—and not a friendly one, "making an entrance." Her gaze rose to the sun's height; fell to the sun's shadow. "She will not be here for at least another half hour, if I am any judge of her." Her smile diminished slightly. "Matriarch, if I may be so bold, I believe it pointless to be angry; it is what she desires. If you offer her no reaction at all to being kept waiting in this fashion, she will have failed in her goal."

"And if this is more complicated than we think, she'll have *cost us* ours."

"She is young."

"She is an idiot."

"Yollana, I realize that she does not always keep your favor, but I must ask you—for this particular meeting—that you keep your distaste to yourself. She is rash, and she is impetuous, but she is *also* Matriarch, and if your summons is not an over-hasty reaction, she is necessary. Please."

"And I should bend?" Yollana snapped. "I should bend when that clansman's get—"

"Yollana, *please.*"

Margret, notably, chose to say nothing. She was both youngest of the four and childless, and more aware of each as the shadows grew longer. She knew that Yollana expected Elsarre late; knew that she had given orders that Elsarre arrive early, and knew as well that she knew they would be disobeyed. It seemed pointless and circular, especially given that Elsarre, attractive and wild, had never been easily contained.

"Easy to say," Elena said quietly, when Margret mentioned it in passing, "but be as calm when Elsarre lords it over you as the youngest and the weakest of the four now that Evallen is gone."

"She wouldn't dare."

Elena laughed grimly. "We all have our weaknesses. Are we to gather wood?"

"No. We're to wait. Yollana and Maria have decided that the circle must be built by fire, and the fires blessed by four, if we are to speak freely, or at all."

Elena nodded. She was quieter than usual, which normally made Margret suspicious. "What's wrong?"

"Wrong?"

" 'Lena . . ."

Elena turned to her cousin. "I don't know how to say this, Margaret, but all I see is fire, everywhere I turn. Heart's fire, Lord's fire, dark fire. I—I don't want to do this. I don't want to be here. I've never attended a meeting of the Matriarchs before."

"You used to say—"

"Scorch what I used to say! Can't you feel it? It's in the air, we're going to lose our own to this, and we *don't even know what we're doing*."

Margret slapped her.

Hard.

She didn't think; she just lifted her hand and heard the sound as if it came from a great distance. It went on and on.

"I guess," Elena said, when the thunder of the gesture had finally passed, "You really are the Matriarch." Her smile was lopsided, but it was genuine.

"No," Margret said, shrugging. "But *I'm* the one who worries and panics, and you're the one who shrugs and laughs. Don't panic on me, 'Lena, or we won't survive it."

"Margret—"

"I mean it. You're heir, until I have children—and if we're gathering like this, there's a good chance I won't survive to—"

"Don't *say* that," her cousin snapped back, voice like a slap, hand raised. But Margret's temper was legendary; a true Matriarch's temper; Elena's temperament was legendary, but it wasn't the same thing. She let her hand fall. "Margret—"

"I'm lucky," her cousin said, looking as if she felt anything but. "I've got an adult heir. A partner. Don't fall apart on me, 'Lena."

"But I've been seeing—"

"I know. I know what the visions are like. I started them after I started first blood."

"I remember that. That was when Stavos was trying to get you to spend time with his nephew—"

"The great hulking idiot who was in love with his muscles and his little bits of dried body part trophies. Yes, I remember. He said we would make strong sons. I said we'd make no sons because I'd castrate him first." She laughed. Elena laughed.

They struggled to hold onto the laughter for just that extra minute, but both of their glances strayed to the camp. The Lord had left his heights. The night was coming.

"I'm sorry, Elena," Margret said. "I should have warned you—but I didn't think—I thought I had the visions because I was her daughter not because I was her heir."

"I was younger, but I was prepared. I should have known you'd start having those flashes. You're like me. We *are* blood." She knotted her fingers. What she didn't say, what neither of them could, was that a third of the knot was missing.

But she said, "What did you see?"

Elena met her gaze without blinking and said, "Nothing important—but it was unsettling anyway. Come on. I think I see the Serra and her entourage arriving."

"She's already here."

"I was talking about Elsarre." Elena grimaced. "Maria, she doesn't put on airs, she just makes the rest of us feel old and wind-burned and ugly by nature. Elsarre *is* like the rest of us but does her best to try to rise above us and look as young and perfect as a Serra." She shrugged and shook her head. She had never cared for Elsarre.

Margret looked, and across growth flattened by wheels and heavy steps she saw Elsarre and her companion. She whistled. "I wouldn't travel with *him*," she said as she looked the slender, dark-haired man up and down.

"No? He's really pretty," Elena replied. "*Really* pretty. I wouldn't push him out of my wagon. Why wouldn't you travel with him?"

"I make it a rule never to be involved with anyone prettier than I am," Margret said with a laugh.

"Well, that would explain why you've stuck me with the position of Matriarch's daughter."

The slap that Margret offered was a much better-natured one; they started up the hill together. "Come on, Cousin," Elena said, as she picked up her pace.

"What are you hurrying for? Elsarre isn't going to."

"I know. But I don't want to miss a minute of Yollana's reaction when Elsarre finally does get to the circle."

Elena was to be disappointed. She had so hoped for a fight, something that might put Elsarre in her place—which place, it was lucky no one asked Elena. And it had started out with such promise: Elsarre had sauntered in—no other word for the casual gait—taking the time to be *seen* by the Arkosans in the fine, fine silks she wore. Her hair was still dark, and long; so much about Elsarre was rooted in vanity, and it would have been nice—for Elena, who couldn't stand her—if that vanity had been misplaced.

It wasn't, of course; that was the way the winds blew. Elsarre was striking, lovely, the lines of her face elegant enough.

Not only did she come in finery that would have been costly for a Serra, but she also brought a companion. Where the Matriarchal heirs were of age, they were expected to be included in the meeting of the Matriarchs that occurred during the Festival of the Moon. Elsarre's companion was *not* her heir, which was, strictly speaking, a breach of protocol. A breach that had also been committed—and it was clear that she knew this well in advance—by Yollana's use of Kallandras. This man, this newcomer, *was,* on the other hand, striking; pleasant enough to look at that Elena wondered why he didn't have better sense than to spend his life guarding Elsarre.

For it was clear that he was there as her shadow; that he put himself, subtly, between her and anyone who approached her save the Matriarchs themselves.

Perhaps his presence threw Yollana off—although Elena doubted that anything threw the old woman off—but the explosion expected by both Elena and Margret did not come. Yollana spared Elsarre a glance—half a glance—and then said, "We make the fire."

Elsarre was thrown off. "Pardon?"

"What we discuss today we discuss at the heart of a fire built by the Voyani as a whole. Gather," the old woman said, her words clipped, her tone so matter-of-fact and flat it almost defied argument, "and return."

"We are gathered," Elsarre said, stumbling over the words as if speech itself were an obstacle.

"The wood," Yollana replied, speaking slowly and as if to a fool.

The finest and most expensive powder in the Tor Leonne couldn't hide the ugly flush that stained the younger woman's cheeks. She started to speak, cut herself off two syllables into Yollana's name. She cast a cool glance at Margret, ignored Elena entirely, and stared for much longer at the Lysseran Matriarch. Then she started, as they had all done, to roll up her sleeves.

She was not dressed for the gathering of wood or the making of fire; she assumed—as Elena and Margaret had done—that the heart's circle was the Arkosan responsibility because it was the Arkosan camp.

"Elsarre," Margret said, before Elena could stop her, "I would hate to see you ruin those beautiful silks; the forest where the wood has fallen is dense. Might I offer you—"

"No." The second youngest of the Matriarchs removed herself from the circle, nodding her companion in the direction of the woods. "I dress like a Serra, but I know my duty and I can do it without changing clothing."

She passed a scornful glance—if anything that short and dismissive could be called a glance—at the Lyserran Matriarch; the woman returned the most gracious nod Elena had ever seen.

It made the younger woman feel ugly and dirty and heavy and ungainly. She turned her head slightly and met Margret's eyes; then she burst out laughing, it was so obvious they were thinking the same thing.

"And what exactly does the Arkosan daughter find so funny about our current situation," the oldest and least gracious of the Matriarchs snapped.

Elena tried to swallow her tongue. "Nothing, Matriarch."

"Perhaps the Arkosans don't realize the gravity of the situation," she continued, showing them all that a woman with hobbled legs and the weight of years of responsibility for her family was a force to be reckoned with. Unfortunately, it was a fact that had never been in question. Elena could almost feel the cringe that Margret kept hidden.

"Don't just stand there like useless sons, go out and gather the wood!"

"Yes, ma'am," Elena said.

Margret cringed.

Yollana's frown grew extra creases and her eyes narrowed to slits. "You'd do best, Matriarch," she said to Margret, "to watch *this* one carefully."

Before Elena could say anything else, Margret grabbed her by the arm. "Wood," she said, in as severe a tone as she ever used with Elena, "now."

"And I, Matriarch," Maria said, "would offer you any aid you require if I did not fear the same tongue lashing the Arkosan daughter received."

"You'd get worse if you offered me that," Yollana said.

Maria smiled. "I will tend to the fire, as Elsarre and Margret do. I will leave you to your companion, and will thank you for his aid."

Yollana nodded. "We've got an hour," she said. "Maybe two. Donatella's cooking."

"Who is feeding the children?"

Yollana's smile was unkind. "One of the Arkosan men."

"The men? He is braver than many Lyserrans would be."

"Yes. The children call him Uncle Stavos." Yollana bowed her head a moment. "We sent the Northerner out on the roads, in search of safe passage from Raverra, but the Tyr has been gathering his army. We keep the children here, and we hate it."

Maria's smile dimmed, but her forehead didn't wrinkle, her expression didn't sour. She and Yollana seemed to be opposites in every possible way. "Yes," she said softly, "the future is in their hands, and we risk it. Your daughters?"

"Safe. Yours?"

"Safe as well, if that has meaning in this place and time."

"Good. Wood, Maria. I tire of your endless grace; it wears me down and makes me feel as old as I actually am."

She watched them go; Kallandras watched her face, the lines of it losing the mockery of true anger. In its place, skin cracked and weathered by as long a stretch upon the *Voyanne* as any Matriarch had been known to have, something pensive, something like fear. "Matriarch?"

She nodded. "I miss my daughters." It was unexpected. "And

the children here, it's too easy to get attached to children, even when they aren't your own."

"In the North, the Mother—the Lady's harvest face—calls all children Her own. Perhaps you approach the wisdom of our gods, Matriarch."

She snorted. "No, just the age. And is it 'our' gods now?" She snorted again. "Come. You'll have to carry me if I'm to make good time. Bring the Serra with you."

"The Serra?"

"Teresa."

He paused a moment.

"And show some of those flashy Northern manners, Bard. Speak in a way that I can hear." She paused, grunting with the effort of pulling herself to her feet. "She does."

"She must trust you, Matriarch."

"That or be desperate. Or both, more fool she."

The Serra Teresa emerged from the wagon that had been appropriated for the Havallan Matriarch's use. Dressed as a Voyani, she was very like the Serra Maria en'Jedera: unable to shed the grace and the elegance of her upbringing when she donned the clothing. "Yollana," she said quietly.

"We go for the wood," Yollana said. "And the herbs; the flowers we want will not blossom here until sunfall, so we'll skirt night's edge and wait."

"You told the others to be here in an hour."

Yollana stared pointedly in the direction that Elsarre had wandered in, and smiled—a brief, sharp quirk of the corners of her mouth. "They can wait on us."

"Teresa?"

"Yes, Yollana."

"There, under those leaves."

The Serra who had commanded the best trained serafs in the Dominion bent, graceful and delicate in the motion, and turned over the heavy, low leaves of a plant she didn't recognize in the deepening blue of evening. They felt odd beneath her fingers; a texture of something at once supple and swollen.

"Be careful not to break them. What's beneath them?"

"Flowers, Matriarch; but small and white."

"Good. Take the leaves—break them at the stem; take care that they are otherwise unbruised—and the blossoms." She paused to curse. She cursed frequently. Her fingers were splintered from the exercise of cutting wood, and the Serra Teresa di'Marano, accustomed in all things to a grace and gravity of manner when exposed to the open air, found herself smiling.

She had not offered to help Yollana wield the heavy knife that would take the wood's heart; it was forbidden. Yollana had obliquely taught her much in the few times they had met, and one of the things she had learned was that the cutting of the wood was in some ways the act of the heart that sparked the magic that not even her hearing could pierce. Nor, in the end, had she offered to support the old woman while she cut, balancing her weight on feet that might never right themselves after the injury done them; Kallandras was adept at avoiding the sudden danger a stumble caused when the knife slipped.

She did not understand why Yollana would not use an ax; the handle was longer and the blade far shorter, and in the end it was lighter than the tool she chose. But she had her way, and—like the most ancient of wives in a good harem—those ways were indulged and unquestioned by a younger Serra.

A younger Serra so very much out of her element.

"Yollana," she said quietly.

The old woman took the leaves from her hands and wrapped them—with great care—between two folds of cloth. "This is the last of 'em, Teresa."

"Ah."

"Not that you're looking at the flowers," the old woman said, wiping her hands on her knees.

"No. I see light, I think, from the plateau."

"You see light," she agreed. "It's the first night, and the Tyr probably has to show off some; he's new and he's not secure in his position. Lady willing, he won't ever be."

"Lady willing," she said, but her heart did not give the words weight; the man that was now Tyr was her much hated—and much loved, and that was the truth and the pity of it—brother's oldest, and truest, friend. He had killed a wife; he was not a man that she herself would have tangled with in any way, and he had *hurt* her almost daughter so much she clung to life by the hatred of the hurt, and not for any love of existence.

And yet, he was Alesso di'Marente, and a flash of the spirit that moved him, the loyalty that bound him to those whom he chose as friends, moved her. She wanted him to fail. But the fate that she wished upon his allies she did not wish upon him. Aie, weakness.

She had seen the Festival of the Moon from only two places in her life: the Lambertan city of Amar, or the Raverran city that defined the Dominion. The Tor Leonne.

Wind blew at strands of her hair, her unkempt, unoiled hair; she felt the last of the dying sun across her skin.

The Serra Teresa di'Marano, refined and learned in all things courtly, had long been confined by rules of the life she had been born to. Denied wives and children of her own by the curse and the gift she'd also been born to, she had wondered for forty years why the Lady had seen fit to curse her in such a fashion.

Darkness answered her now.

And at the heart of the darkness, light on the plateau. She felt the wind again, and she turned to look at the Northern bard. He did not blink; his eyes in the darkness seemed like captured water from the Lady's Lake; his gaze fell full upon her. As if he understood some small part of what she felt.

No, more; as if all of what she felt—the sense of loss and the sense of terror at a freedom she had both dreamed of and never desired—were an echo of the winds that drove him. How could they not be?

She had seen him call the winds.

She had seen the winds obey.

And yet they were here, crouching in shadow, fearing both daylight and night sky. She shivered, acknowledging the truth of her fear: That if a man who could control the wind's voice with the strength of his was afraid, what could *she* do in the battle to come?

Lady, she thought, wondering if perhaps she had been rash; wondering if her strengths, those ties so carefully developed and cultivated through the years of empty court life, might have been better used there, upon the plateau. But no. No.

Night thoughts.

Lady's thoughts.

She bowed her head.

Together, she, Kallandras, and the unusually quiet Matriarch of the Havalla Voyani made their way back to the heart of the Arkosan camp.

Four women.

Four Matriarchs, the chosen of their line. And not by birth

alone, although birth defined it. There were Matriarchs in the history of the Voyani families who had died abruptly and without children; those who had—although it was very, very rare, died in birthing those children. There were Matriarchs who, like Evallen, had died, but with her daughters by her side.

The hearts, either immediately or slowly, but in either case with certainty, found their way to the women who were meant to wear them: To Yollana of the Havalla Voyani, early to her title and her mystery, and late to reign against the desire—some said because of the desire—of wind, sand, and clansmen. To Elsarre of the Corrona Voyani, later than to Yollana and she less adept at charting the political course, less able to cast off the desire for the approval and the love of her people. To Maria of the Lysseran Voyani, unexpected and unlooked for, a burden and a gift with so many complications she accepted it the way women must accept all: gracefully and with pleasing humility.

The only person who did not bear the heart of her family beneath the folds of her clothing was Margret of the Arkosa Voyani. She was acutely aware of the lack at the moment, which was surprising as she hadn't thought her sense of inadequacy could get any worse. Hadn't. Now she was certain, as they each began to lay the logs at the base of what would be their fire, that the night would bring new lows.

Yollana laid down her heart wood first; by age, Maria followed, taking care to nestle the logs in the dirt in such a way that between them they formed two parts of what would be a cross; oath markings. Elsarre was next; she took the wood from Dani and bore it carefully to ground. Then she rose and took her place at its end, facing inward. Margret was last. She wondered if any of the other women were as nervous as she felt. And doubted it. But she took her place; they stood, Elsarre to the West and Margret to the South, Maria to the East and to the North, where the shadows and all their ancient enemies lay, Yollana.

Elena and Teresa were allowed to be of aid; they brought the containers that had been so carefully prepared by silent Matriarchs, handling the earthenware as it passed from hand to hand as if it were made of the finest of crystal, the most delicate of northern glass. To Elsarre, the largest of the vessels, heavy and fragrant with a wine that would have made poor merchants in the Tor at this season weep for joy if they happened to obtain it; to Maria, glittering with the light from the low moon, the next largest vessel, its contents so clear that were it not for reflection and weight it might have been empty. To Yollana, a small flat jar, with a heavy, coarse lid that the old woman did not bother to lift.

And to Margret of the Arkosan Voyani, a shallow, empty dish. Because she was Arkosan, and this was her camp, and therefore her home. She was to be the anchor.

"Come," Kallandras said quietly, when the vessels had been delivered to the women who would use their precious contents. "Stand outside of the circle."

Margret, having never seen this ceremony performed, wished very much that her mother were the one to perform it; she wanted to say all the obvious things and get the muted and whispered answers to the questions inherent in them. For one, there was no circle. For two, how did he know there was supposed to be one when she didn't, not really? What did his eyes see? What did he hear? Why was he trusted by the Havallan Matriarch in a way that not even the other Matriarchs were? As a girl, as a daughter, she would have been forgiven much and her questions—some at least—given the half-answers that would be understood as truths later in life.

But she was trapped by the necessity of her role, and her role had been narrowly and clearly defined. She waited upon the actions of the other Matriarchs.

Elsarre of Corrona poured the wine, following the line of wood she had laid out to the center of the cross, where she carefully emptied the contents of the jug. Maria of Lyserra poured the water, but more carefully; she walked a line without spilling a drop, and at the end, in the center, when she made the last libation, she murmured a prayer that the wind took from Margret's ears. Only the quality of her voice remained; musical, low. Desperate. A prayer, then.

Yollana's turn next.

She lifted her head; nodded imperiously to the two Matriarchs who now stood beside their empty vessels in the flattened grass. Maria—it was so hard not to think of her as Serra, and Margret loathed the women of the clans—acquiesced at once; Elsarre waited that extra minute to make clear that she was doing this of her own accord and not at Yollana's command. Aided now by the Matriarchs, and the Matriarchs alone—Yollana of Havalla anointed what had once been living wood with the fine paste she had made from the forest's harvest.

They helped her back to her place at the end of the stretch of wood she had cut.

And that left Margret. She knelt by the empty, flat bowl and rolled up her left sleeve. She *hated* this part. It was ritual. It was ceremony. It was a tradition that was so old the stories about when it started were almost the same as the stories that mothers used to get their children to behave properly.

She took the dagger from her side, lifted it; held it in front of her face where it could catch and reflect moonlight, as if waiting the Lady's inspection. She was slow and deliberate because her hands were shaking and she was embarrassed by it. But she did not like to cut herself; certainly not deeply enough to fill the shallow dish and paint the line from here to the heart of the fire.

She knew it was childish, because her mother had cut herself many times, bled herself for the sake of her people, and it had always looked easy. But she wished that this meeting had been anywhere else—Elsarre's caravan. Maria's. Yollana's even.

She bit her lip.

And she hissed as she drew the knife across the vein. But she did it. Hoped she hadn't cut anything useful, like muscle. She held her arm over the bowl, let it fill—and it filled too quickly, she thought—and then grabbed the cloth between her knees and bound the wound as tightly as she could. Donatella had, bless or curse her, spread ointment on the cloth; it burned where it touched the open wound. *Fire,* her mother would say, *is good. It burns away the disease.*

She wanted to cry, not for pain—the pain was liberating and she held onto it because it was so much in the present—but because she was truly, completely, and utterly alone: her mother was no longer Matriarch, and she would never come back to be so. The winds had taken her, as they had taken everything else.

And Margret stood in the gale without the heart of Arkosa, arm throbbing, as she crawled along the line of cut wood, anointing it with her blood, which was after all, the product of the years of Arkosan history. She thought about her mother, and then because that was painful, Elena. But Elena brought Nicu, and Nicu was a memory she didn't want to face.

Blood now. Death later.

Damn. She'd cut too deeply. She could feel that dizzying spin that loss of blood caused. *That* would be the final embarrassment, and at a time when she wouldn't just be failing her own, she'd be failing them all. But it would be her life. It would be her luck.

Lady, she thought. *Lady, we're doing Your work as well as we*

can. She swallowed. Got back on her knees. Tried to keep the
line her blood made as straight as possible. It was hard; the fire
had not been lit—it could not be lit—until she had finished this,
this final step.

But she *knew* she had to finish. That she could not stop or
pause or leave the last of the ceremony undone. She had dreamed
it, and the Lady, unkind, sent true dreams to haunt and harry her.

She saw Elena move; saw the bard—the Northerner—reach
out and grab her by the upper arm. Was very surprised that he
kept his arm; Elena went for her dagger almost instinctively.
They were all on edge.

They were all afraid.

She'd cut too deeply. She was an *idiot.* But she crawled. She
crawled, and it came to her, as no doubt the Serra Maria's prayer
had come: that she would crawl and suffer if she could save the
children, their future. That she would die, willingly, if by doing
so she became a part of the foundation that would drive back the
Lord of Night.

The dreams were terrible.

"When can we help her?" she heard Elena shout.

No one answered.

"Margret!"

"I'm—fine, 'Lena. You're . . . embarrassing me."

"Well, it's good you should let someone *else* do it for a
change," Elena snapped back. Only her voice carried. Fear. They
were afraid. She was tired of fear. Did the enemy know fear?

He could smell it; could taste it; could almost touch it, thick
and tangible as it was. But he did not dare; not there, not when the
powers they were summoning, half understood but still primal,
were so close to fruition. He could not walk cloaked into that fire,
although he was not so diminished, not as a Lord of *Kialli,* that
the fire would destroy him, spell or no.

It would destroy his seeming.

It would destroy the careful humanity, so close to his natural
features, and so far from it, that he had endured for decades.

He longed to stand for a moment at the heart of that fire: It
would reveal all that he was; put him in danger of entrapment for
the seconds the four frail women survived.

And that was a fool's game; he had not lived to become a Lord
in the Hells by such self-indulgence. He shook himself; the world

drew him. Life, its variety, its lack of predictability, had been all but forgotten, and the lure of its delicate enjoyments became harder to resist.

In that, he was willing to admit—where no one could hear it—that Isladar had been correct in his concerns. Had it been the choice of that Lord, the *Kialli* would not now exist upon the plains of the frozen North, nor dwell within the grandeur of the Shining Palace.

Lord Isladar, not coward, not fool—and yet, not a power. The enigma; the *Kialli* who somehow stood beside the Lord's throne without being devoured.

No *Kialli* in existence accepted subjugation. They sought power, all of them; some with more subtlety than others. But Isladar's game? None comprehended it. He was a dangerous Lord to have as an enemy, and in the end, a difficult one to make, for he was devoid of the pride and the desire for dominion that informed, that *defined* the *Kialli* Lords—therefore the act which would make an enemy of him was not always clear or logical.

Yet Ishavriel was certain that Isladar was behind the appearance of Anya, so inconveniently, in this city at this time. This, after all, was Ishavriel's moment. The masks had been of his crafting; the summoning of the four women who could prove their destruction—to a city in which theirs was assured—was also the fruition of a plan some human years in the making. The masks that the human General—and he was impressed, in spite of the short span of years and the general ignorance that Alesso di'Marente displayed—had eventually decided to destroy had been spread about the city as artfully or artlessly as the occasion demanded.

He was annoyed, of course; there was no magic that they could have possessed that would tell them what the purpose of the masks was, and even if they understood it, they would not understand: these were a people broken by the loss of the truth of their history.

He should have had the moment to savor; the victory his own to enjoy.

Instead, he had been summoned by his Lord to deal with the difficulty the most powerful and least predictable of his vassals might cause.

Yet he stood, watching as the fires were built, the fear of the four women he considered the most dangerous of threats as alluring as the cries of the damned, but sweeter in their promise.

It had been so very long since he had heard the cries, attenuated and harmonic, of those who had chosen their fate and delivered themselves, in the end, to the eternity only the *Kialli* could provide.

But there were other ways to enjoy fear, other ways to plan for it. Lord Ishavriel turned his face to the evening wind, scenting and anticipating. He had taken a risk, to come to this camp at all. Because it was a wild night; a night when the forces that not even gods could tame—and it had been tried, and tried again— were loosed upon those sensitive to them.

These mortals, they could sense its tide and time, but were not a part of its current; they watched from its banks, and only if they were foolish enough—and powerful enough—to enter the current—were they carried and changed by it. They dabbled now, as if they could chart their course through that wildness with safety.

And he watched, called by their fear.

Soon, of course, their fear would be nothing. The subtlety of it, the anticipation of events that they would never fully understand, would be overwhelmed by the viscera of immediate pain, immediate death.

But he was fascinated, as many of his kind were often fascinated, by those who knew death as a part of their natural life; who could be tainted by wildness but never made part of it, and who could—in a fashion—tame wildness for a time. He watched, at a safe remove. Watched, impressed in spite of himself, that these diminished, helpless children could invoke the heart of a power they did not understand, but were descended from.

The girl who crawled on the ground had power. She would never realize it; it existed as potential, revealed only at moments like these, when the wildness brought their mysteries to their fullness. She was almost finished. A few moments from now, these grounds would not be safe.

But he was interested in a young man who resided within them, and he would not leave without speaking to him.

In the darkness—and what darkness could there be in these lands of moon and stars?—he found the human. The injuries done him—surprising injuries—were obvious although they could not be seen; the air was heavy with the scent of dried blood.

He sat by the side of a wagon; at a time when his kin slept, he was sleepless. The weight of his anger, like the scent of his blood, was tangible to the *Kialli* Lord; more so than the heavy wooden wheel at his back or the damp ground beneath the blankets he sat on.

"Nicu," Ishavriel said.

The man looked up, and the *Kialli* Lord could clearly see the boy in his face. The suspicion was instant; the anger that had been turned inward, leaped out.

"You!"

He could have crushed the boy's throat before another word escaped, but he allowed himself to be touched; to be pushed; to be shoved back.

It took all of the self-control he possessed, so close to Scarran, to be treated so by a mere mortal. His fingers sharpened; his teeth elongated; he could feel his skin losing its mortal softness. He fought; he fought it back. The feeding would come, and soon. He could wait.

"Nicu," he said again, putting power into his voice.

The man who was more boy than not stopped.

"Did I not honor my word? Did I not give you a weapon with which you could slay enemies? How have my actions betrayed you?" His voice contained intent and power, and this pretty young man with the darkened eyes and the gaunt cheeks had prickly edges of desire that cut him no matter which way he turned.

It was really almost too easy.

"Your children are important. I will make you a hero, but you must listen, you must listen with care."

The suspicion was there. The boy was wild with desire and the certainty that he had no worth, but he was not quite stupid. And the children were the one thing—or so Ishavriel had managed to glean from his limited study—that mattered to the Voyani. They were called the heart of the tribe.

He intended to give the boy a moment of heroism.

Staged, planned, crafted.

He had decided that the youngest of the Matriarchs would survive the slaughter because he needed *one* Matriarch. And he had decided that the young man who had survived the loss of her trust by the grace of her affection—for he watched them all, making his plans—would win both back. Would have to before he was of use again.

"What do you want?"

"Want? I want to help you, Nicu. I want you to have what is rightfully yours."

Nicu winced. "Your back isn't scarred," he said at last. That surprised Ishavriel.

"Yes," he said softly, "it is. You cannot see the scars, they are so old, but I made my choices, and I paid for them; we all must." He turned to leave, and then turned back; the man's eyes, unblinking, were upon him.

"I came only to warn you," he said. "The Lord of Night is coming. You've heard the whispers, surely. You know that's why the Matriarchs have gathered."

Nicu's lips thinned.

An overstep on Ishavriel's part. He was outsider, and in the heart of their camp. He immediately changed his posture—an act of will, again, a test of the resolve that was his plan—and let his shoulders slump slightly; bowed his head and upper back.

"Forgive me this intrusion," he said softly. "I did not realize the effect the sword would have upon your Matriarch. I thought, perhaps rashly, only of your people. And I am outsider; I do not know their ways."

Silence. Long and hard.

"But I will give you no weapon; not this time. You have a sword, I have been told, that bears your adult blood. I offer you only a shield that will protect you from the magic of your enemies—or from the enemies of your Lady. You may take it or you may set it aside as you desire. You may run to the Matriarch and tell her of what has transpired.

"I leave the decision up to you."

He stepped back as Nicu continued to stare at him, his expressions changing so rapidly no single emotion had dominion. No fear. Ishavriel did not smile; instead, he bowed low, and let the cape he wore slip open. Beneath his arms, held wrapped in a heavy, rough cloth, was indeed the shield of which he spoke. It pained him to touch it this way; uncovered, it burned, and the fire that it started could not be stopped by anything but magic wards. Obtaining the shield from the room of antiquities had injured one of his most powerful lieutenants; it was, however, meant both as a test of his lieutenant's power, and a way of diminishing some of that power while Ishavriel was not within the Palace to guard his political interests personally.

He wondered if the mortal would appreciate the enormity—and

the danger—of the gift. The construction; the design; the magics, all ancient, and all inimical to one of his kind. To one, in fact, who was not mortal. A gift manufactured in the forges of the Cities of Man, taken as trophy—and as object of study—by the *Kialli* before the rift.

The perfect gift.

Be a hero, he thought, dropping his difficult burden and stepping as far away from it as he could. "I must leave. My time is short. Decide for yourself what to do, Nicu of the Arkosans. But I will say now that you will *know* when the moment is right to use what you have been given."

Nicu's eyes fell to the cloth-covered curve in the grass. Hunger there, but caution and pain as well.

Lord Ishavriel winced; his attention was taken from the boy, from the grass, from the interplay of hunger and desire, of depthless shame and uncertainty, by something powerful. He felt it. The youngest Matriarch was almost at the center of the cross.

She had been wounded before.

She had been wounded before, and more deeply than that, and she hadn't had the cloth on hand to bind herself with. Elena had *seen* it. She knew it for truth; hadn't she been part of the same fights? Hadn't she suffered similar wounds? Hadn't they held each other up while help came, held each other's hands, spoken while they could as they waited? Yes. There was no way that Margret could be so weak so suddenly unless there was something wrong with the blade. The blade was poisoned. It *had* to be. The wind was wild where she stood, and the Lady's hand, sharp-nailed on her shoulder. But so, too, was the foreign bard's.

"Do not," he said, his words so heavy with the weight of command it did not occur to her to disobey them—not immediately.

But he was outsider, and she was family. She shrugged herself free.

And was caught again before she could take another step. Margret was struggling. She could see it; she wasn't even certain that she was going to make it with that bowl to the center of the cross.

"Let me go," she said, without looking at the stranger.

He didn't answer. And anyway, there was only one answer she wanted: His hand off her shoulder. The Voyani were not a patient people. She counted one, two, and then in silence, she drew her dagger.

It was out of her hand and across the grass before she could move, silvered by the turn of flat in the moonlight, but the hand on her shoulder—as far as she could tell—hadn't shifted once.

"Let me go," she said, letting the snarl transform her voice.

"You cannot go to her." He shook her slightly to punctuate the words. It was the most animation she had ever seen from him, except strictly speaking, she couldn't. See him, that was. She turned, and this he allowed, lifting his hand. "You do not understand. The wood was cut, yes, and the wine and water and unguent of forest and earth placed upon pine to summon the fire. But the fire that you are summoning here is an old fire; the protection you demand demands its price. Your cousin is *not* bleeding to death."

But Elena watched her slow crawl. She knew what Margret looked like when she was in pain, and she *was* in pain.

"But you—"

"She is paying the price that the fire demands. She will survive it."

Something in his voice. Elena's eyes narrowed. "Or?"

He raised a brow. "You have . . . exceptional hearing."

She turned around again. He placed a hand on her shoulder. "Do not force me to stop you, Matriarch's heir." Something in his voice was as black as the Lady's longest night. As merciless as the Lord's glare, but hidden by cloud, by pretty features, by a soft voice.

"Don't force me to choose between your threat and my cousin," she shot back, although she was chilled. She'd seen death before, and she recognized it here.

"Let me force you instead, Matriarch's heir, to choose between your cousin and the Lord of Night; your cousin and the children.

"Help her, break her concentration, take her away from the giving, and there will be no fire."

Elena could be swayed by pretty faces; a weakness of hers she readily admitted to anyone who would listen. But this man's beauty was shorn by the ice of his words into starkness that she could not trust. His words, however, were true. She felt them settle and take root, and she turned away from him again to watch.

At least the argument had served one useful purpose. It had spared her the watching.

Margret was almost there.

*   *   *

She had never had to crawl this far. Not physically. Not emotionally. Her mother, as mothers will—or as she assumed they all did—had put her through her tests; endurance, patience—she failed that one frequently, but her mother was indulgent enough because, well, it was in their blood—and subterfuge. She had crawled because crawling was a way of hiding. She had crawled because it was a way of moving when too injured. She had crawled when her mother had dropped the bones, branches, smooth stones, and rings that she used to make herself look either mysterious or gaudy, depending on how much the clansmen could be taken in by appearances, her face to the ground because each of the fallen items was precious, some bit of history, some important artifact of Voyani life.

And she had crawled as a baby, a time of her life so long past memory that only the motion itself remained true: the struggle to get from one place to the other without falling face first or having one's knees slide out. Why? She couldn't remember. Maybe to get to her father's side, her long dead, much-loved father; maybe to get to her mother's—because surely her mother might pick her up, might offer her comfort? Might drive away the terrible, terrible fear that pressed her into the ground as if it were a foot getting heavier and heavier against her back?

Inch by inch she spread her blood against that wood. She had never been much for smell, but there was salt in the air, and wood was so tangy in scent, so fresh, it overpowered her a moment. But only a moment. Fire was for burning, and she had to get to the center.

She was Margret of the Arkosans.

If she couldn't walk—and she couldn't—she'd crawl. And when her body became too heavy for that; when the lights had dimmed until she could follow the wood by touch and smell alone, she dragged herself along, lifting the dish with care, moving, always moving, toward the center, dabbling her fingers in blood that had cooled but had not yet become sticky and tracing its pattern—her pattern—into the grain.

Lady, she said, as she crawled, or she thought she said it, she couldn't tell for sure whether her vocal chords had the energy to express the sound, *Lady, we are Your servants; the darkness is coming. We have cleaved to the road; we have followed the Voyanne into the darkness and out of it. If it leads us into darkness again, we will follow; we will fight it, we will never again be its subjects, slaves, or allies.*

So swear the Arkosans, so swears Margret of the Arkosans as their Matriarch.

I ask for no mercy. I offer no mercy. But as we enter the darkness, save our children. Show me a sign that they will see light if they follow the road. Show me a sign that the road is our home that the road leads to home that there's life if we follow your road.

The wood ended. Suddenly. Just like that. The trail she had laid was gone; the center open before her. All she had to do was offer the last of her blood, and the fires could be summoned.

Give me, she tried to open her eyes, and to her great surprise, succeeded. She lifted the dish, holding it as far out as a shaking arm would reach. Emptied it. Refused to let it fall to earth where it might somehow be damaged. *Give me a sign.*

Light flared as she squinted into its radiance. The Matriarchs had not yet summoned the fire, but Margret had summoned something very like it: A nimbus of white light that burned vision as it spread upward and out like a beacon in a darkness that she had been afraid would be without end.

A sign.

From the light a hand reached out, and a voice that sounded very, very human said, "I'm not sure where we are, and I'm not sure who you are, but you look like you could use some help."

She started to say, *It's not allowed,* but the hand seemed a sign from the Lady.

She took it; felt its very firm grip, and felt strength come down through this unknown woman's palm into her own. Shakily, she rose, blinking back light as light died into night sky and the stillness of held breath.

"I'm sorry," the woman said quietly, "I've been traveling a very strange road, and I didn't know where it would finally end." She had hair, dark and tangled, like a Voyani's, but her skin was paler. She was short; too short for a miracle, but there was something about her eyes as she looked around the clearing, taking in the four women and the carefully laid out logs that led—to her.

"If you don't mind, I think I'll get out of your way for a bit."

Margret was on her feet. "I—I don't think I mind," she said shakily. She looked to the other Matriarchs.

But the young woman, the stranger, eyes narrowed, looked beyond them all. And her eyes stopped, her expression shifting between surprise, pleasure, and oddly—relief.

"Kallandras!" she shouted.

The Northern bard that Yollana trusted did something strange: He smiled. "ATerafin," he replied, nodding quietly as his strangely soft voice carried the distance. And then, "Jewel. Well met."

"Which means," was her dry response, "that you knew we were coming. Gods, I hate that woman."

"That woman?" Margret had to ask.

"Evayne," was Jewel's curt reply. "And if Kallandras is here, I have no doubt whatever that you've already met her."

CHAPTER TWENTY-NINE

"She has indeed," Evayne replied. "I am acquainted with all of the Matriarchs in this generation, and in the last."

They looked up, almost as one person. Four Matriarchs, and those who had been chosen to witness or aid in the building of their historical fire.

Her cloak was dark; it stretched in either direction like enemy shadow; her hood was low. Margret had not seen her many times in her life, but at no time had she looked like this. She was frightening. The youngest of the Matriarchs almost embarrassed herself by taking a step back. Almost. But anger held her in place.

Because *this* woman had robbed her of both mother and heart, and she never came without demanding—and receiving—her price. And what did they receive in return? Cryptic comments. Assurances that there *were no other choices.*

It was too much.

And it was Margret's camp.

"What," she said, almost losing the word as this Evayne turned, hooded, to meet her gaze. But anger was her shield and her prize; she held on to it; held it up. "Have you come for now? Have you finally come to give *us* the help that you've demanded from us for as long as I can remember?

"Or have you just come to make sure another one of us dies?"

"Margret," Elena hissed, but Margret was past caring. It was as if anointing the heart wood with her blood had cleansed her of something. Not fear, not exactly. But something.

Blue robes twisted in the stillness of the night as if the wind was wild and dangerous. It seemed that that would be the only answer the midnight woman offered. But when she spoke, Margret *did* take that step. "There is death, there is death coming."

Kallandras, the bard from the North who seemed to serve all interests that involved Evayne, stiffened. "Evayne," he said.

"The road," she said softly. "It is wide, this year; darker and longer than it has ever been."

"You traveled—"

"Do not ask. I have come with my message and my warning. I have come bearing gifts."

"And the price?" Margret said, although her voice was shaky; not the voice she would have liked to use. "The price for those so-called gifts?"

"It has already been paid," the woman responsible for her mother's death said. Margret wondered by whom. And she heard a strangled voice ask the question, and it was her own. She *hated* this woman, for just this moment, at just this time.

"Shall I tell you their names?" Evayne said coldly. "Shall I tell you the names of their families? There were four, Margret. Do you want to know what their deaths were like?"

She stepped back. Stepped back. Stepped back.

But Yollana stepped forward until they were shoulder to shoulder, and although it was a breach of etiquette, Margret was almost grateful to have that bent back to hide behind.

"No, Evayne a'Neamis. We have no desire to know how they died. Or their names. Or their families' names. There will be deaths in plenty to weep over. She is young. She has not been tested. Do not test her here, where we have power."

"Yollana, you do not seek to threaten *me?* I have traveled a long road, and there is a power here that will take that threat gladly."

"Then take it," the old woman said, the steel in her voice. "But there are four, Winter Lady, and we are stronger together than apart."

"I don't understand," Elena said. "She's our—"

But Kallandras' hand on her shoulder was so sharp she lost voice. He said, "Evayne." And then, when she did not turn her attention from Yollana, said again, but in a different voice, **"Evayne a'Nolan."** Her head turned. Her robes, wild twist of night, turned with her. "You have swallowed Winter, remember it. **You** have swallowed **Winter.**"

Her breath changed. It became labored; the breath of someone struggling *to* breathe. She looked up, and they could see, for just a minute, that her eyes were of blackness; they were not human. But her expression was—aged, and tortured—she reached out with a shaking hand, and they saw it: fear. That was worse than menace. Worse than darkness.

She said a single word, and it was a prayer.

"Kallandras!"

He spoke, his word a song, the tone and texture of it so beautiful that Margret could forget the sense of raw power she felt when the words left his lips. She wanted to weep with sorrow, sudden and sharp, because she could not understand a single word.

The words were all for *her.*

The darkness did not leave her. But the wildness left her clothing, the struggle to breathe became breathing, simple and spare.

"I have not much time," she said, in a voice that was menacing but somehow almost normal. "Take these. Do not light your fire until the night itself. Gather your children, all of you—if they reside near the Tor—gather them here, and light fire only when the sun has fallen completely from sight. Send out those that you trust, and those with the power; you must search out the four Founts that sit on the points of the city circle, even as Matri-archs, you stand upon the points of this fire. Those Founts must be whole; the waters cleansed with these," she took from her robe a crystal decanter with a silver stopper, and a small clay jar. "There will be circles of gold or brass; they must be from start to finish unbroken. These things must be done before the night of the Festival Moon, for it is upon that night that your enemies will be at the height of their power; they must not catch you—as they expect to—unprepared.

"Then, only then, and quickly—must you summon the fire; it will be a fire such as you have never created in Arkosa, Havalla, Lyserra, or Corrona. You will summon the living flame, the wild fire. When it burns, when it burns and it understands what it can and cannot devour, you must take what I give you and go to the ancient places of power."

Margret frowned.

Yollana said, as if she could see the frown, although she did not take her eyes from Evayne a'Nolan, "The Founts."

"Yes. And when the time is right, you must don these." And from her robes, she pulled four masks.

For the very first time, Jewel spoke. "We'll know when the time is right *how?*"

"The Hunt," Evayne said coldly. "The Hunt will pass through the city, and those trapped by it will die."

This stranger, this Jewel, frowned. It was as if the darkness did not disturb her at all. "I'm afraid," she said coldly—as coldly as Evayne had spoken, "that's not acceptable."

"Then stop it, seer," Evayne said with contempt. But she stopped. Frowned. "You are different," she said, and before Jewel could reply she reached into her robe and pulled out something that should have been familiar to the watchers.

But although it was rounded and fit between the curve of her two palms, it was also dark as night; the shadows were trapped in it; the light devoured. The Northerner drew a sharp breath and took her first step back.

But the seer did not notice.

She looked into those shadows, those moving clouds; for the first time in her life, Margret had no desire to be this mysterious powerful stranger who by presence alone commanded her mother's respect, fear, and obedience. There was nothing, save perhaps fear of the death of the children, that could force her to look into those depths. Because she knew enough to understand that ball was the soul crystal, the physical manifestation of self that seers in legend—and Matriarchs as well—nearly died to extract from themselves. It belonged to Evayne a'Nolan and it mirrored the woman.

That woman said to Jewel ATerafin, "You have walked the path."

"Yes."

"And you have met the Oracle."

"Yes."

"She has not asked you, yet, to pay her price." She looked up, her eyes like the ball, a darkness and a danger. "But she will. Oh, she will."

The Northerner did not reply. Evayne smiled, and the expression was like nothing Margret had seen before on the face of a mortal; but in depictions in the few books the Matriarchs possessed about their ancient histories, the cruelty of that smile was found on the face of the *Kialli*. Demons.

"Fine. I'll deal with that when I get to it," Jewel said after a space that was just a little too long. "You don't mind if I borrow your bard, do you?"

"And what do you intend to do in those streets, ATerafin? You are not even trained. Will you hold back the tide of the Arianni by yourself? Will you stand in their way when they ride?" She laughed. "Will you face the Winter Queen?"

And Jewel ATerafin looked back at Evayne, and she said, in a quiet, steady voice, "Look for yourself. Have you not seen?"

Evayne surprised Margret. She was certain, in fact, that all of the Matriarchs were equally surprised; the seer did as she was bid. She searched.

The silence was long; when the seer looked up, it was not at Jewel but at the man who stood, just far enough away from the Northerner that Margret was certain there was no intimacy between them, but close enough that it was clear he was her protector.

"I see," she said quietly, and some of the night bled from her voice. An expression like regret but colder and harder touched her features. "Yes. Take my bard. Take your domicis. You want to save them all, ATerafin?" She laughed, and the laugh was chilling.

"Try. Try with my blessings." There was no question whatever to Margret that the words were a curse, meant to cause pain; they implied certain failure, and the amusement of the powerful at the pathetic struggles of those doomed to fail.

Margret was afraid of this Evayne. She had been afraid of Evayne before, but she had never realized, until this moment, that *this* night defined her fear; all of it was new to her, but all of it, someplace where thought and memory couldn't easily reach, was *old*. A touch of the Matriarch's gift. A touch of the gift that had transformed the woman before them. She started to speak. The woman named Jewel spoke first.

"Evayne," she said. Her voice held no power and no song, but it caught the attention anyway, "I *will* try, and with your blessings. That's all we can do. Me. You."

"You compare yourself to *me?*" the older woman cried. Light flared and danced, an orange rain.

Jewel stood, untouched, in its wake, her face pale, her eyes unblinking. She was not particularly beautiful, but Margret could not look away from her briefly illuminated face, even when it was claimed by night and moon again. The Northerner who had appeared to offer Margret a hand from the center of the fire's cross, met Evayne's gaze, waiting.

It was the seer who broke away first. "Kallandras is right. I have swallowed the Winter to travel before the host, and I must fight it now, and I must fight alone." She took a step forward and was gone.

"Bitch," Elena said shakily, to no one in particular.

But Jewel looked up at the word. "Don't," she said softly. "Don't judge her."

"You *saw* her. How can we trust a woman who comes carrying the darkness?"

Jewel turned to look at Elena. "What would you carry," she

said softly, the words like a well-sharpened blade, "to save the children?"

Elena said, "The children will die before we join with our enemies again. And if you can ask that question, you don't understand the *Voyanne*."

Margret said, "Shut up, Elena. Of course she doesn't understand the *Voyanne*. She's never walked it."

But as she looked at this Jewel ATerafin in the moonlight, she wondered whether or not her parents or grandparents had.

"Come on," Jewel said quietly to Kallandras. "You're on loan. Avandar?"

"I am . . . ready." They turned; this silent stranger's eyes were fixed to the spot at which Evayne had disappeared.

There was something comforting about weeds tall enough to smack you in the side of the face, and burrs that were solid enough to force you to sacrifice a handful of hair to get rid of them. She was less thrilled about the mosquitoes, but even the mosquitoes—once squished—had a charming sense of the real about them. This place—far, far from the political turmoil of Terafin—was nonetheless hers.

She was profoundly grateful for the absence of a mountain pass that had never truly existed.

"Avandar," she said, after they had walked for a while in the silence of her newfound sense of wonder, "was any of it real?"

"It was all real."

"The Mountains weren't. You didn't see them."

"I saw something else," he replied, nudging the weeds that still fascinated Jewel to one side with what she thought was a spurious use of magic. "but I saw it at your side."

"And the . . . the Winter Queen?"

"You don't have an imagination that is that deep or that dark."

She slapped a mosquito at *just* the wrong minute. Frowned. "And the others?"

"The Oracle and Corallonne are certainly also real, in their fashion."

She rolled her eyes. "You're being obtuse on purpose, right?"

"Indeed." She thought he smiled. Hard to tell, the expression was so brief. "If you mean Celleriant and the stag, then I cannot answer the question. Our return was by a road they could not follow."

"What?"

"They are not of this world. If they could follow us, Arianne and the rest of the Firstborn could also arrive in a similar fashion. The ways between worlds are protected, and they open only at the appointed hour."

"Oh. Damn these bugs—there's hardly any water, where are they all coming from?"

"A good question, although I feel I should point out that they aren't biting anyone but you."

"Thanks."

"Pretend they're a dream, if you will, Jewel ATerafin; they are, in a fashion." But to dream she needed sleep, and to sleep she needed to finish a few things first. She rolled up her sleeves, and there, on her arm, was the Warlord's mark: red broken by gold and silver.

20th of Scaral, 427 AA
Tor Leonne

His existence depended on hers.

Word had reached him, quickly, and at some cost; the messenger had traveled just ahead of the Lord's wrath. Anya had not returned to the Shining City. He had informed her of the import of her participation at the "big party" as she called it; he had told her, had promised, that she would have a lovely dress—much prettier than Lady Sariyel's finest—and color for her lips and her cheeks, if she so desired. He had made clear to her that she would be the center of attention; that she would be the most important person in the Lord's retinue, and that, for her service, He would be *grateful*. That seemed to have meant something to her, then.

She had been so excited. So very excited.

It had not occurred to him that she would miss that party. But she was not in the Shining City; she was here. And the Lord's anger, when she failed to answer His summons, was impressive. Impressive enough that the kinlord was . . . concerned.

The frown that touched Lord Ishavriel's lips lingered as fireworks took to air, a signature of the largesse of the Sword of Knowledge. He had been told that it was customary for such a display to occur only during the night of the Lady's Moon itself, but an insecure Tyr could perhaps afford the expense of a more generous display.

It was a poverty of beauty compared to the stark and natural dance of the borealis across the Northern Wastes. A poverty, a thing he could reach by the simple expedient of magic, and by the simple expedient of magic, dispel. No; this act had pretensions of grandeur, and any attempt to capture beauty that fell so short was contemptible.

As were the people

Certainly such display had its effect; the streets were crowded, and if there had been tension in the Tor, it was suspended while the lights played across the face of the sky. He had sent out three of his most trusted vassals to insure that, in the morning, the night would be remembered for something darker and infinitely less pretty.

It had been his hope, his desire—a sign of weakness, but hidden, concealed—that he join his lieutenants in their subtle hunt. He had been so long from the chase; so long from the skill by which the *Kialli* had been blessed and cursed: the causing of pain. It was sustenance, for those who had chosen to follow in the Lord's steps; the only sustenance allowed them.

He would hunger for a little longer. Because of Anya. It did not please him. Not when the streets were alive with the souls, glimmering dark and bright, of those who had not yet chosen; whose domain was neither the Hells nor the thing that even gods did not understand. Oh, they dressed; they wore silks or cottons or rough, heavy fabrics he could not identify. They wore gold and jewels and long feathers that had been died or painted by delicate brush; they wore paint on their eyes, their lips; they colored their hair. But these things, noted, were the ephemera, just as they themselves; the flesh was a means of causing pain, but it was also merely casement; the frame for what was of value.

And tonight, that window was shut; denied him.

Very well. He had grown used to denial. No *Kialli* could rise in power who could not exercise control. But likewise, the indulgences, where they were appropriate, were sweet.

He paused a moment. People moved past him; some fast, some slow, their scents strong and cloying. He could kill with a touch. He did not.

Somewhere, Anya was in the Tor, and he did not trust her not to get in the way of his plans. She was literally the only completely mad person who had ever held rank or power within the heirarchy of the Shining Court; the rules that governed the *Kialli* or their ancient enemies were not rules that she even understood. The humans did, in their diminished fashion, but *Miara* guided and protected Anya, and *Miara* was a god not even the gods understood; drooling, mad, sly, frightening because she lacked the basic predictability of understandable desire. Power meant nothing to those completely blessed by *Miara*.

Yet it meant something, some small thing, to Anya.

She was terrified of their Lord—but only when she was forced to be in His presence; her mind was not even capable of a child's intelligence and fear.

And Ishavriel had not yet found her.

He suspected that she had chosen to hide from him; she had learned, only two years ago, that she could break all the tracings that bound them. He built better ones; she built better ways of breaking them. Twice, she had almost died in the dissolution of that magic, and had he desired it, she would not now be the problem that she was.

But she had her uses; her power was without equal, and it could be directed in a way that a sane person's power could not. He had hoped that almost dying would teach her not to force the bonds he had built.

It had not, although she had, in fact, learned. Learned the cracks in the walls of his powers; the weaknesses in the more hidden streams that flowed like silk chains between them. She understood that distance was, indeed, a factor; understood that there were places she could go in which his magic could not survive.

He had had to be subtle. He could not be the direct cause of torment or pain, although if his protections did cause pain, this was acceptable. And when her life was truly in danger, he had always intervened, becoming in fact her savior. She desired that from him—but she was canny and wise in a way that made no sense. She did not trust him.

She was far too powerful.

Far too unpredictable.

He wondered, this night, after years of playing the game; of having Anya slip his gentle leash, of leashing her again, of losing her, whether this particular and unpleasant game had been encouraged.

There was only one other Lord who could influence Anya at all. Isladar. And if she were part of Isladar's game, he was of concern. But not of much concern; Lord Isladar had failed. He had attempted to gain power by the expedient of the bastard child who had escaped the city after causing so many deaths.

So many very surprising deaths. Lord Ishavriel was still impressed. Kiriel was, in her fashion, as deadly as Anya; she had, as advantage to her enemies, a less cluttered insanity. Predictability. Weakness. The two were friends, in the way that mortals formed friendships.

He had taken much of value from it; Anya could not be silent and she was a source of information when it came to Kiriel's abilities, and Kiriel's activities.

Until, of course, Kiriel had so abruptly departed the city.

He paused. The crowd no longer flowed, roughly or smoothly to either side of him; it stopped, in a series of jagged but concentric circles, men lifting children to shoulder height so that they might see what was not immediately obvious to a man of Ishavriel's height. He did not have difficulty clearing a spot for himself, although he chose the nuances of expression over overt magic; the wildness was close, and he was on the verge of its great hunger. Caution.

Caution.

Within the smallest circle, he found what had captivated the attention of so many, although he had heard the strike and slide of blades long before his eyes witnessed what lay behind their song.

Two men were dressed in white and black in such a way that they looked not twinned, but in opposition. One wore white shirt and black collar, the other wore black shirt and white; where one sash was ivory silk knotted carefully at the back; the other, again, a deep blue-black. They wore the same boots; they had about them the same fluidity of motion, the same easy grace. And it was easy to judge that: they did not stop moving or spinning; they lunged and leaped and managed to be where their blades weren't for just the split second necessary to avoid shed blood. The two blades in this odd dance were, in weight and length, of a kind. He thought they must be forged by the same maker; certainly sharpened by the same stone.

With a small gesture, accompanied by a word spoken in a language of power that he had learned so long ago it was almost easier to remember when he had first drawn—and last required—breath for sustenance, he caused one of the men, spinning on the point of a toe, to stumble.

He smiled as he heard the intake of the crowd's breath; smiled as he anticipated the blood; the end of the dance.

Frowned when it did not follow.

Misstep, and misstep, but somehow the blade that should have

pierced him was not there to cut skin, and the stumbling motion
was mimed by his partner, built into the dance, made one with it,
a part of the odd beauty of their animal rhythm.

He could have pressed the point, but the pressure lacked the
subtlety he'd desired, and one of the most powerful of the *Kialli*
Lords turned, the dance forgotten, the failure remembered. He
was not here, could not be here, for his own enjoyment. The task
had been set by his Lord.

Anya was no longer bound to him. He could not be certain
where she was unless she desired to be found, and clearly she
did not. She could lead him on a chase—if she was aware that
he looked for her at all—for a very long time. And if that chase
somehow occurred during the night of the Dark Conjunction
itself . . .

He looked forward to an eternity in the Hells with her, although
her soul was not bound yet for a place in which the Lord had
dominion.

The moment the Lord's gate was open, and the forces of the
Kialli could finally return to the world unhindered, he would kill
her at his leisure. Although he doubted there would be satisfaction in it; the deaths of the mad were . . . unsavory. *Miara* protected her own against the predations of his kind.

A woman offered him food; something round and artificially
bright. He took it, wondering what it was. Wondering and remembering. The air was heavy with scent: sweat and wine, joy and
fear, silk, cotton, leather; plant, leaf and vine creeping—at the
behest of clever gardeners—in just such a way as to frame what
did not grow, and did not change: brass. Stone.

For a moment, surrounded by these, jostled on all sides by
those too careless to actually meet his gaze, he felt like the brass
or the stone; unchanged, unchanging, the life moving around him
like a halo or an aurora of its own. He felt a fascination, a
hunger, that had no possible existence in the Hells; the dead were
dead, and as unchanging in their fashion as those who had
chosen to accept the responsibility of long justice.

For a moment, that hard fruit in his hand, that young woman's
hesitant face before him, he could remember a time before this
time; a time when that sense of justice had meant something
other than pleasure and indulgence and joy at the pain of the
damned—

He killed her quickly. Efficiently. Her basket fell, scattering fruit
along the cobbled road.

One nameless red item rolled along the ground, caught in the crevice worn by feet and wheels between the stones, until it came to rest at the base of the Western Fount.

Water caught light's reflection; it would be some time before her body was discovered. His magics had made certain of that. But he found himself by that Fount, bent over, his hand around the redness of a food that he had been promised he need never eat again.

And he cursed Isladar as he had not cursed an enemy in millennia.

Festival Night.

There were festivals in the Empire. The Challenge season, with its merchants, its would-be heroes, its barbaric Southerners and its aloof Northerners, was perhaps the closest to this mix of bodies—but the atmosphere in the Tor was very different from Challenge time: It reminded Jewel of the last six days of Henden, called the six dark days, a commemoration, in ritual, of the devastation of the Empire in the wars of the Blood Barons before the return of Veralaan with her sons: Cormalyn and Reymalyn, called the Twin Kings. Jewel suspected they'd never particularly looked alike, and weren't born at the same time. History left these details to the imagination.

Many things were left to the imagination.

She walked behind a silent woman, a woman who, in gait and movement, might have been a slender man, hair pulled taut and slicked back in a warrior's knot; sword half visible beneath the swell of cape, pants wide for ease of movement, boots flat, ugly, practical. She walked slightly ahead of them, cocky, an arrogance to the freedom of her movement that spoke of rank and power. She had it; the clothing that she wore was simple but costly. Jewel's favorite kind of clothing. She had no doubt that the sword was the same, although she only caught a glimpse of it. Wondered if the woman—introduced by Kallandras as Serra Teresa di'Marano—knew how to use it. It was hard to imagine, watching the ease with which she navigated the crowds—mostly by staring down her slender nose until the people unfortunate enough to be standing in her way moved—that there was anything she couldn't do well.

And that type of person always made Jewel feel either sick or inferior. Or both. It would have been easier if the Serra was friendly; she was not. She was cool and distant and her manners, whether woman or man, were elegant and refined. She made Jewel feel clumsy and awkward without saying a single word.

Jewel navigated—a pretty overstatement which meant that she was dragged along—the streets behind Kallandras. She had been given two choices: bind her breasts—a painful but swift process— or travel as a poorer clanswoman. Jewel had chosen to travel as a clanswoman and spare herself the pain, but she decided, the fifth time that Kallandras gently corrected her position so that she was walking slightly *behind* him, that she should have gone for the binding and passed, in the faded evening light, as a young man.

Then again, she'd suffer by comparison to the Serra Teresa, and she wasn't much interested in that.

She had originally planned on traveling as one of the Voyani women; she was good at that, and her Torra, imperfect when it came to dealing with the high nobility of the Dominion, was much like the Torra the Havallan Matriarch spoke. But she hadn't counted on that being unsafe in the city; the Voyani *always* journeyed to the Tor Leonne for the two Festivals. Or they did in the tales her Oma used to tell her when she perched on the lap bent legs made.

The streets here were both exotic and familiar. The buildings, flat and white from ground to oddly tiled ceiling, looked nothing like the brick or wood that she was used to; there were no grand trees, no merchant Common, no large temples to the various deities who did not make their home on the Isle. But there were votive offerings, she thought, and small fount-stones, which bore fruits and flowers in deliberate, delicate array; she assumed these must be places where the Lady was worshiped. Night places.

And there were serafs, marked and unmarked, who bent back under the watchful eye of overseers to do the real work this Festival demanded. Polishing brass and cleaning tile, their clothing simple but of a quality that reflected the status of their owner, they seemed much like any laborer to Jewel; some harried, some quiet, some happy.

It made her wonder about the nature of freedom. ·

Until she saw the young boy being beaten. She could not see the boy's face, but she could hear his whimpering pleas, and she wasn't about to walk away from it. It had been a long time since she'd had to.

She was wrong, of course. But the memories it brought back were the least pleasant of all her memories. The helplessness. What was the point of having power if you had to stand back and watch people being beaten or killed? What was the point? Kallandras caught her arm as she started toward the man with the cudgel. She knew by the type of grip he used he would not let go.

And that he was *right,* damn him. She was a clanswoman of low birth, and that man had every right to do as he wished. Festival or no. She hoped, come the Night of the Festival Moon, the seraf had the right to slit his master's throat, if they had Festival at all.

The Serra Teresa returned, stopping a moment before she came to stand beside them. It was the first hesitation that Jewel had seen, and she didn't like what she thought it meant. But the Serra offered no criticism; in fact, all she said—when she chose to speak at all— was, "These are the Lord's lands. On every day, every night, but the one we approach, the laws that govern our lives are His."

She spoke flawless Weston, and in the mix of that flawless voice, Jewel thought she heard, faint and distant—and cool as desert night was supposed to be—pity. For her. And gods knew, Jewel wasn't the one who needed it.

"But that boy—"

"Not here," Avandar said, and she knew no one else would hear his words. What she wanted to say in reply, on the other hand, would probably be heard by the entire Tor. She bit her lip until it bled. She'd done it once or twice at very irritating political meetings—a comparison she felt instantly guilty making. "Make him stop," she said, as quietly as she could, "Or I will."

"At your command," Kallandras replied, and his voice was so smooth, so incredibly soft, that she wasn't certain if it held sarcasm or not.

He left her side. She stopped; Avandar came to stand just in front of her, hiding her from the easy view of unscrupulous men— or at least, she thought that must be the so-called reasoning behind this stupid half step behind movement that was so unnatural she had to work to maintain it.

Kallandras walked quickly to where the boy alternated between sobbing and screaming beneath the shadow and the arm of the man who clearly owned him. In the evening light, she saw no mark across his face—no brand except the bruising, the split lip, the bleeding. Brand enough.

She started forward again, convulsively, and Avandar caught her arm as Kallandras had done. Exactly the same grip. She wondered if killers so confident in their ability that they didn't need to strut like peacocks were all alike; steel and silence.

"Watch," Avandar said, shaking her. "Understand subtlety. You *are* capable of it on occasion."

"But I—"

"Jewel," he continued, "you will never learn to lead if you cannot trust those you give orders to follow them. You have given an order. Learn to rule."

"That's leadership?" she hissed, pressing him, pressing herself. "Telling everyone else what to do while you do nothing?"

The look he gave was contempt mingled with something that she couldn't quite name. "No," he said at last. "It is partly choosing the men and women who will follow the orders you have given, but will perform them in a way you could not.

"Watch," he said quietly.

What else could she do?

But she wondered, as she watched Kallandras depart, if Avandar's words and his almost unquestioning acceptance of her command were part of the same lesson. Wondered if, in fact, he knew what she had accepted as her last order from The Terafin. He probably did.

What have you seen? she thought, not of the bard but of the woman who was arguably his master. *What have you seen for me and mine, and when will I know it?*

He stopped, Northern bard, hair darkened by Margret's swift work, skin colored, but still somehow a thing out of place in the Tor. It was his movement, she decided; graceful and lithe, he was completely silent. His feet against the uneven ground gave no hint of his approach; he hoarded all information that might grant an enemy any leeway.

Jewel realized that he meant to be out of place at that moment; she had been in a gathering as Kallandras' companion before where even she had had trouble telling him from the crowd when she was *with* him.

She wondered whether or not he would kill the man; she hoped, fiercely, that he would—although some part of her knew that it would be profoundly disturbing to watch; there was something about Kallandras that was so cold-blooded she was afraid to bear witness to his killing. The fear was misplaced.

Death in such a fashion would not have served their purpose, and she *knew* that he chose a purpose and served it with both ferocity of intellect, and the coldness of intellect.

He touched the arm of the man who was beating the youth.

That man, Jewel saw, was not large; he was not particularly muscular. The boy was his equal in strength, in size.

But better to take the beating than the consequences. Better to risk the chance of death than to risk certain death. She said nothing. Avandar's grip did not change. They knew each other that well. For the first time, she was glad she had left her den behind.

"Jewel," Avandar said, voice by her ear, and she realized that she'd turned away.

She turned back; the bard was speaking slowly and softly to the man. She could not hear what he said; could not in fact hear his tone. But the man's heavy hands fell slowly, and the cudgel— or whatever it was—fell with it.

"I understand," Avandar continued quietly, as the man nodded, again slowly, at the bard's words.

"No," she replied with conviction. "You don't."

He was silent.

"You've never particularly cared if you had to watch a stranger suffer and die. I imagine, with a title like Warlord, you might have even enjoyed it."

"I did," he said, the two words without inflection.

But she heard the truth in them, and she hated it.

Kallandras came back to her. The man barked an order to the slave, and then turned away and left him there. She wanted to intervene somehow; it was a Festival Night.

"Yes," Kallandras agreed, "it is a Festival Night. But it is not *the* night, ATerafin, and the cerdan of the Tyr are between every house in the city, watching and waiting for the extraordinary. Let it go. Let it be. We must see the Founts, and if the circles there are broken, we must repair them. That is our goal, this eve; it is our only goal."

"No. It's *their* goal. Mine is different."

"Do you think," Avandar said, his impatience so familiar she thought she would never dislike it again, "you will see enough in the city streets in *one night* to end the coming threat?"

"Maybe," she replied. "We don't even understand the nature of the coming threat."

"You walked the road," he said, "and it has changed you, Jewel. No one walks that road, claims a part of it, and emerges unchanged. Think."

She was. She was thinking, as she froze a moment, of the last words Evayne had said. *I have swallowed the Winter to travel before the host.*

"They're coming," she said quietly.

"I believe that is so."

"To what end?"

"Who can say?"

"You can. You know more than I do about that Lady and her cursed host."

"Not here, ATerafin, and perhaps not ever. I do not know why she rides, but if you are here, brought by the Oracle; if the seer who travels through time came here, brought by her own curse and her own vow, I cannot believe that you met the Winter Queen on the road by chance. Come."

"But—"

"But?"

"We've—we've lost Elena." Jewel looked from side to side; the crowds were thin in places, and between them, fire and light shone across the surface of gold and brass, dimpling the stillness of water, the offering to the Lady on this night. They would offer her wine tomorrow.

And on the Festival Night? Jewel could see the dead all around her if she closed her eyes for even a second; the vision was *that* strong. Unfortunately, not closing her eyes caused them to tear painfully.

"Elena is not lost," Kallandras said softly. "She is here. But she waits. The Voyani do not risk their lives in open conflict, and you are not of their number. Nor I, nor Avandar. She will join us as she sees that our stop here has brought no unwanted attention."

"They always do this?" she whispered.

Kallandras turned to face her, eyes clear and dark as water in the night founts. "They are Voyani," he said, as if that explained everything.

"Some allies," Jewel snorted.

Avandar and Kallandras exchanged a single glance; it was as if they spoke in a language that she had heard often enough before she could recognize it, but had never—and would never—master.

Elena joined them, walking with the polite and hampered gait of a lowborn—but free—clanswoman as if it were natural for her. Jewel had seen Elena casually slap a youth who'd gotten just a bit too familiar—and had seen that youth, face reddening in an area the size of her palm and fingers. She couldn't believe the easy way she took to the role of a meek clanswoman, cramming her hair and her expressive movements into this drab bundle of heavy, almost colorless sari.

Avandar gave her the look that clearly meant: *If someone like Elena can accomplish this task so easily, you should be able to do better,* and she tried very hard to meet that expectation. She did try.

But she cursed under her breath—or as under her breath as she ever did—while she walked through the city streets. Avandar, behind them as always, cast a long shadow.

Margret had been in fine fury—and Jewel understood it so well she'd have caved in an instant to her demands—when she was ordered to remain in the confinement of the circle. But Yollana, the Matriarch of the Havallans, made it clear that her responsibilities lay with the children, and with the fire they had been told to hold, and hold at ready, for the three days.

She was worried, was the old woman; Jewel knew it, looking at her face. The lines lay heavily across it, pulling her eyes down so that they looked closed. Margret, mutinous, had opened her mouth to argue, and it was Jewel who found herself saying, "They need you here because you're the heart of the fire.

"The fire should have come tonight. It's waiting. It'll try to come tomorrow. You'll have to hold it back."

And the four Matriarchs had stared a long while at her in the silence that followed her words. It occurred to her, walking in the streets of the Tor Leonne, hundreds of miles from home, that those four women had taken an awful lot on faith.

She tried to imagine how she would have reacted to her own appearance in the center of that wooden crucible, Avandar dressed in gaudy, expensively jeweled clothing at her back, and she as herself, whatever that might mean to the four ruling members of the Voyani families. Nothing she had ever heard about the Voyani from her merchants led her to believe that they were particularly trusting.

Especially not the women.

But they accepted her as omen; and they *were* superstitious.

"You've walked a hard road," Yollana said at last. "But you see truly. I name you, as I name Kallandras, roadbound; you are not of the *Voyanne,* but you have in truth walked it, and if I see well, you will walk it until it ends."

The striking, dark-haired woman gasped.

The pale woman, equally striking, but in a much more understated fashion, became utterly still; Jewel realized that she had stopped breathing.

"Margret," Yollana said, her expression taking on a sharpness that Jewel wouldn't have liked at all had it been directed at her, "when you walked your path to the fire's heart, did you ask for a sign? Did you pray, did you pray to the Lady?" She slapped the leather loop she wore for emphasis; herb pouches lifted and fell, punctuation.

"And you didn't?" Margret snapped back, whip-crisp, hands finding her hips.

"Oh, I'm sure we all did," the old woman said. "But you're the fire's heart because this is Arkosa. *Your* prayer was answered. Now live with the answer, you ungrateful wretch, even if you don't like it."

"And how is this the answer, that I'm supposed to stay here?"

"You heard her. You heard what she said. You have to contain the fire. *You.*" The woman, fingers now tucked into that wide, long loop, turned some of her sour attention toward Jewel Markess ATerafin. "What happens if she goes?"

"Goes?"

"Goes with you."

"Goes with me?"

"Are you an idiot, you don't understand Torra? Goes with you *there.*" She jabbed her finger in the direction of fire in the night sky; the Tor Leonne, lit at the center beneath their view by Festival lights. "You look at me, girl. Look at my eyes."

"I would if you'd stop squinting," Jewel said.

Silence.

Long silence. It was broken by laughter, which in turn was broken by a longer silence.

"If you were one of mine," Yollana began, but she let the rest of the threat go. It wasn't clear to Jewel that she was actually angry. "What happens if she goes?" she said again, lowering her voice.

And this time, Jewel let herself relax into the question because she could *feel* the answer there, something unpleasant and heavy, like the residue herbal brews often left on the tongue. She was very glad, as she met the lined and wrinkled face of the Havallan Matriarch, that she wasn't Havallan.

"If Margret doesn't stay, the Fire will come."

"And?"

"It will devour you all. It has no target. It has no . . . enemy. Not yet."

"And we—the rest of the Matriarchs—won't be able to stop it?"

"No. You are four and you have called the fires from the quarters; you have implied your oath. But she *has paid the heart and the blood price."*

"The children?"

Jewel looked away. She looked away and did not look back, and she closed her lips on the answer and her eyes on the vision.

"You're not going," Elena said quietly to a very stiff Margret. "But I'll go. I know what you're thinking. That Evallen died there. That this is Arkosan business. Okay. It is. But I'll hold up your end."

Margret, face as red as the fire she was supposed to contain, seemed to have missed whatever the other two had heard in Yollana's earlier words. She stormed about the small clearing cursing in a broken Torra that Jewel only half understood. Half was good enough. When she'd stopped, she said to her cousin—in Torra, but quick and sharp, "You better come back in one piece. You're all I have, and I need you here."

And Elena shrugged. "Lady's Moon," she said, her voice softer than her cousin's and infinitely less angry, "how could I not come back?"

" 'Lena—"

"Learn to live with it. The children are here," she added, her voice taking gravity as if it were a weapon. "What else do you need to know?"

Margret had nodded.

And here they were, in the middle of a crowded city, streets alive with both wonder and something like fear, but unnamed, unacknowledged. Acknowledgment, after all, had its costs.

The Serra Teresa was their guide. Jewel thought that Kallandras had more than a passing acquaintance with the streets of the Tor Leonne, but he seemed content to let the Serra lead; he followed, Jewel behind him, and behind her Avandar and Elena.

Teresa stopped twice at the fount-stones that were tucked into rounded curves in the walls; kneeling until her chin rested just above the water, her nose near the blossoms that had been so carefully cut and placed. Jewel was used to private prayers, but there was very little privacy in the Tor. It was not as big a city as Averalaan, but she felt the crowd much more keenly.

"Come," Teresa said softly, rising. "Tonight, I think it best that we find the Northern and the Western Founts." She lifted her head and then stood; lowered her gaze until it fell across the still water in the fount-stone.

Jewel nodded.

She had thought there would be more drama. There was about the night a sense of storm, something dense and invisible that hovered in the air. But there was also a solidity, a reality, to the stones beneath her feet—flat and perfect in a way that the stones of Averalaan's old city seldom were—that refused to give menace easy purpose. There was continuity in her life. She did not lurch from waking moment to waking moment and wonder where the sleep had gone, and when it had taken her.

The wind, when it came, was fresh; it held a scent that the mountain pass had lacked. Unfortunately, not all of that scent was pleasant—with this much wine, and this many people, it couldn't be—but the night was cooler than it ever got in Averalaan, and it was drier as well.

She turned when Avandar placed a heavy cloak around her shoulders. Started to thank him and frowned. "This isn't what you were wearing," she said softly.

"No." He had changed his attire from the gaudy and the impossible to something that suited a subdued clansman—a gift of sorts from Margret, and by extension the Arkosans—but there was something about Avandar that just didn't subdue easily.

"Avandar . . ."

"You will have to learn," he said in perfect, flawless Torra, "to accept kindness with more grace."

"I don't expect kindness from you," she replied. But she was cold and she was practical. She'd get angry about his flagrant use of magic later—if they even had rules about flagrant use of magic here, which, come to think, she highly doubted.

She watched as Serra Teresa examined first the Fount itself and then the markings across the ground around it.

"I don't understand," Jewel said, speaking out loud. Speaking in Weston.

"No." Avandar replied in Torra.

She took the hint, switching between the two languages with ill ease. Her mother's language, and her Oma's language, were tools that she used, but they were no longer as natural a part of her life as Weston had become. The language of thought, for Jewel, and she thought aloud. "No what?"

"No, you don't. I do not think any of us do. But the Serra Teresa, although she is not of the Voyani, has been sheltered by them, and taught in some fashion by Yollana. That one," he added softly, "has more power than a Voyani Matriarch has had in some generations. And vision. Be wary around her."

"Not hard," Jewel said.

"But it is. You are already comfortable. She could slap you, and you'd rub your cheek as if you were one of her children and she a short-tempered mother who had that right."

"Avandar, you take the fun out of everything, you know that?"

He raised a dark brow; did not dignify the comment. It was not the type of thing she would usually say to him. She fell silent and watched as Teresa and Kallandras traced the circles. They seemed almost like kin; tall and lithe and slender and silent; they worked at opposite ends of the Fount until Teresa nodded. "The West," she said softly, "is secure." She took the things that Evayne had given them and very carefully apportioned a small amount of the liquid from the crystal flask. This she poured into the water. Then she unstoppered the clay jar, and she frowned.

Jewel froze.

Avandar's hand caught her shoulder.

"Jewel?"

"Where did she get those masks?" Jewel said softly.

"Pardon?"

"Evayne. The four masks, Avandar, where did she get them?"

He was silent. But as she watched the gray powder fall into the waters of the Fount as Teresa murmured, she knew that it was ash, and that it had once been human, and alive.

CHAPTER THIRTY

He watched them from the darkness. This had been his game from the start, and although he could not have foreseen—for that had been little part of his talent—the direction the game would take, he found it interesting. Fascinating. Too much so; the Lord of the Shining City expected all of His subjects, with the single exception of the Lord Ishavriel and his chosen servitors, to attend Him at the midnight hour of the Dark Conjunction.

Lord Isladar had survived millennia by understanding what the word exception meant, and when he might reasonably expect to use it; this was not that time.

But the moon across the face of the mortal world was cold and white, and the night chillier than the nights in the Northern Empire's capital, where the greatest threat to his Lord lay; the elements were wild with a whisper and a song that had not been properly heard, or joined—

He bowed his head.

One day and one night away; the world was poised on the brink of a conjunction that would be invoked for the first time in centuries. Longer. And Lord Isladar, without mission or order, was left to spend his personal power both in leaving and in joining the City again.

Lord Ishavriel was in the city, searching for Anya a'Cooper; his scattered minions spreading the masks of such importance to his plan. He was clever, the Lord Ishavriel, and understood human ambition, human greed; he understood the mask of power that the men who ruled the Dominion wore, and he assumed that he therefore understood the men themselves.

A flaw. A flaw in his reasoning.

But Lord Isladar of the Shining Court did not feel responsible for pointing out such a flaw; it would be perceived as—would be, in fact—an insult. Isladar's smile was soft and perfect in the light of the Tor.

The *Kialli* disliked a particular type of subterfuge. To hide, in human guise, among the humans, was particularly odious to most of them; a trial that only the command of a more powerful Lord would be sufficient incentive to endure. But Isladar found it interesting. Here, as seraf, he was invisible in a way that magic could not detect; in a way that clansmen and women of power would be above noticing. He noticed everything, touched very little, polished brass and swept stone.

He had found it expedient not to kill a seraf and replace him; he merely became another possession in a powerful and stupid man's keep by the expedience of magical suggestion. In all things, Isladar did what was not obvious to the *Kialli* and many of the kinlords found him either beneath contempt or worthy of constant scrutiny. It was almost . . . human . . . to distrust the obvious outsider, or to dismiss him, so thoroughly.

It amused Lord Isladar. In truth, he felt the same hunger the *Kialli* did; the desire for the pain that lingered, the final reward for those who had made the choice of the *Kialli* so long ago it was not even a whisper of memory to the weak of will. He, too, desired an end to the self-imposed centuries of restraint. But it was not the only desire that ruled him. Isladar was among the oldest of the *Kialli* and he remembered.

He remembered the voice of the old earth. The crackling shout of the fire; the voice, heavy and cumbersome, slow and cool, of the ocean that was so close to the shores of Averalaan the desire to lose days standing at the foot of its near silent ebb and flow had been almost paralyzing. The air had come to him first, because *the* Lord had chosen a home in the Northern Wastes, and the winds howled fiercely, untrammeled by tree or lake or rushing water. But the other voices, slow to waken, quickened now; as if they could sense, in the *Kialli,* what the *Kialli* sensed in their Lord: freedom, a way back to power.

A costly promise. In the Hells, the kinlords had felt it a certainty: what other gods now walked these lands to thwart the power of their Lord?

But His manifestation here, on the plane forbidden Him, had been weakened, the vessel damaged, by the interference of just such a god. One god. The Oathbinder. The Oathtaker.

The kinlords had cause to resent him; desire, and more, to see him trapped in animal state, sentience denied him except for a few days of the mortal year. Yet, although they had planned everything perfectly, much had not come to pass.

Isladar did not believe in coincidence. He was *Kialli;* he did not believe that the plan itself had been wrong. So much of it had been, through subtle machination, his own. And yet; they were here. Kiriel, gone; the number of the Kinlords decimated by her hand, and in a way that had been difficult to recover from. It had occasioned a change of plan; although he had argued against it.

And so he watched, his desires thwarted, the child whom he had caused to be born—the biggest risk he had ever taken—in the hands of the Northern humans His Lord feared most. She was not in the Tor Leonne; he would sense it immediately; she could not hide from him.

But Jewel ATerafin, the woman he had tried and failed to kill because her influence had threatened what had been built, stood not at Kiriel's side, as he had feared, but rather at the side of an old, old ally, and an old enemy: the Warlord. A man who understood the *Kialli* as if he'd been born to them, bred by them. Bred for them.

Perhaps he was part of the puzzle. And perhaps not. But certainly, the puzzle was changing face again. He watched; the two mortals walked the perimeter of the old circle, they cleansed the water; they spoke in a language that he could not hear, although he could see their lips move; their eyes flicker a moment to each other and back as they acknowledged what had been said. Interesting.

The girl was seer-born. But she was young, and she was untrained. . . .

Untrained. He looked at her, eyes narrowing. There was about her some difference, a darkening of aura that *Kialli* eyes might be sensitive to if they knew what to look for. He regretted the fact that she still lived, not because it was a personal failure, but because she was an element at play that he no longer understood.

But he understood all else.

Isladar took his risk, to come this distance and watch this play unfold; his hand was not invisible in it and it had been many, many years since he had deliberately undermined the efforts of his kin.

In fact, he had only taken an obvious risk in one way in all of his years of service at the side of the Lord of the Hells. Only one: the rearing of Kiriel, lost for the moment in the streets of some far-off city, but coming, in the end—coming to him, via the war that would start on the morning after the Festival.

He smiled as the circle was made. He had never been witness to this particular rite, although he had once—from a distance—seen it in play. He was curious.

Lord Ishavriel's plan, in this instance, was counter in some fashion to his own. He desired balance to the war, and for balance to be achieved, the mortals had to have some say in their destiny.

For the time being.

He bowed to them: ATerafin, Warlord, and the two strangers who worked at their side. One of them looked up, the movement as natural as all movements had been.

For a moment, no more, they locked gazes; Isladar looked away, as any good seraf should. Impressed, in spite of himself. That was the beauty, had always been the beauty, of things that knew birth, growth, death, and decay: nothing was static, and occasionally the change in the cycle between birth and death was beautiful, deadly, fascinating.

He bowed again. And he left quietly.

The Northern Fount.

Of the Founts, it was the finest, although this changed in season and with Festivals. The North and the South were aligned with the Lady; the East and the West with the Lord, or so it was said; tonight, moon almost full and the sky so clear she was glad no window separated them although she loved glass, Jewel believed it was the finest.

There were flowers in the Fount itself, white, delicate lilies of a type that Jewel had only seen once—and then, in the cultivated wilds of the footpaths in *Avantari*. In the center of those lilies, a statue rose from the waters; its features were muted; a suggestion of detail rather than its embodiment. That face, rather than looking unfinished, seemed to be the face of every woman, eyes suggested by a dimple in stone; lips by a swell, cheeks and chin neither remarkably high nor remarkably shaped. You might, Jewel thought, see yourself in that face should you choose to come here for comfort. If you could find the room to pray.

It was busy.

That was a problem only until Kallandras nodded quietly to the Serra Teresa and unstrapped the instrument Jewel would have said he wasn't carrying. He moved as if completely unencumbered, and it hadn't occurred to her to inspect him. But Salla was there, his weapon and his enticement, and he moved out of the gates which at other times of year protected the Fount, singing. In Torra. At her Oma's knee, she had heard stories about the bard-born who led whole villages to the slaughter, and when she was old enough to finally meet real bards and recognize them for what they were, she had doubted them; she knew enough about the powers of the voice to know what it cost to force a single man to do anything against his will. But watching Kallandras sing, she wondered.

And she wondered if, were it necessary, he would lead the people who listened, entwined in his words and music like flies in a different web, to their deaths. Trusting in beauty, she decided— for his voice was hypnotically beautiful—was so often fatal.

But the people of the Tor did trust in it, and they left, and even before the last man was gone, his hands loosely holding a wineskin, his cheeks flushed with the effort of actually moving, Teresa had already begun to inspect the perimeter of the circle. She knelt. Rose.

"There is a problem," she said.

Jewel came forward at once.

"See? The circle is cracked."

"It's old," Jewel said. "But I'd've missed it."

Teresa looked up. "Yes," she said at last. There was about the word a vague air of disapproval. "We must heal it." She rose, pushing herself up with the flat of her palms. "Or cause it to be healed."

"Cause it to be healed?"

The woman waited patiently. Very patiently. Jewel frowned. And then she smacked herself in the forehead. "That old witch knows everything, doesn't she?"

Teresa raised a dark brow. "Everything? No. But enough. She knows that he serves you, and that his skill will serve us if you request it."

And she turned to look at Avandar, who had not moved, but who had clearly listened intently to all that had passed between them. "Can you fix the circle?"

"With ease," he replied, no trace of pride or hubris in the two words.

"Then, please—fix it. I'm tired. I want to go back to camp. I want to go to sleep someplace where I can remember the before and the after."

"You won't forget," he said quietly. "You have . . . accomplished something, Jewel ATerafin. But as in many such journeys, the world you left and the world you returned to are the same; it is you who are altered."

"Humor me."

His smile was so faint she wasn't certain she'd seen it. But his bow was exaggerated and obnoxious.

She found it oddly reassuring. He knelt by the circle. "Do you understand what this does?" he asked Jewel quietly when she finally understood that he meant for her to bear closer witness.

"No."

"It encloses the Fount."

She rolled her eyes.

"The Founts were meant to stand at four very specific points," he said softly. "This city was planned as a . . . shadow . . . of older cities."

"A what?"

"These were designed as a way of keeping enemies out."

She gave him a look that could best be described as skeptical. If one were being polite.

"Trust me," he said.

"I do," she replied. And then she knew she was in trouble. Because she meant it.

He knelt beside the Serra, and she quietly watched as he laid hands on the circle. He spoke a word. Two words. Three. Then he smiled.

From beneath the flat of his palms, Jewel could see light. She was used to seeing magic as light; she had learned, with practice, to discern the general nature of the spell being cast by the color of that light. But it had been a long time since she had seen that particular light, and she didn't like it.

Gold.

The Summer color.

It spread from his hands in a circle, following, she realized, the circle embedded in the stone. "Avandar?"

He did not speak. He did not, in fact, seem to know that she was there at all; the light that left his hands seem to be fleeing him, and with it, his awareness of the world. She had seen him cast spells before, but he had never been quite like this: deliberate, almost contemplative. His spells were cast either with a

precise energy and motion—which was usually necessary since
when he used his magic it was often in her defense—or a nonchalance that was a grating part of his natural arrogance. But
this . . . this was different.

She looked over her shoulder; Kallandras was still singing, his
voice sweeter than the spill of golden light around the Northern
Fount.

Avandar rose. He was pale.

"Come," he said quietly. "We are done here."

She frowned, and then saw that the Serra Teresa had indeed
finished stoppering the crystal decanter and the small clay vessel
that contained ash and death. She said, "I'm not sure Kallandras
has finished."

"He hasn't," the Serra said quietly. "But he will, and he will
join us. We should return, ATerafin. Tomorrow we must complete
this task, and it is already late. See? The sky is slowly paling."

It was true.

Jewel nodded, and together, they left the city. Only later
would she remember that the Serra had waited, as Avandar did,
upon her nod. As if she were the one in charge.

21st of Scaral, 427 AA
Tor Leonne

"Very well," Alesso said, lifting one hand.

Sendari di'Sendari and Mikalis di'Arretta did not appear to hear
him the first time. He had, having witnessed the peculiar and
boring discussions of the Widan over the minutiae of their studies,
expected this level of attention, and had taken it upon himself to
preserve both his dignity and the lives of either the two men or
any seraf who might witness their lack of paid respect. He had
summoned them to his personal chambers, had seen that those
chambers, fitted for dignitaries, were well supplied with both food
and cushions, had ordered warm water and the towels that were
used to sponge and refresh oneself before either food or discourse
in an informal setting, and had sent the serafs away.

Sendari and Mikalis had been late.

A bad sign.

They were studiously avoiding each other's gazes, which he
considered a worse one. They swept the room, each man taking a
side, as they searched for magic, or the traces by which magic
might be recognized; they found nothing, although a small out-

burst about methodology occurred there. Alesso did not know whether to be amused or surprised; he had literally never seen Sendari so . . . imperfect in his manner or his presentation. Mikalis came from a poorer family; Alesso expected neither elegance nor grace from him; obedience and respect was enough.

But while obedience was offered perfectly, respect was sadly lacking, at least for each other. The men were arguing about the exact meaning of their discovery, and using words that Alesso imagined would only make sense to other Widan, if that. As Tyr, and as General before that, he had done much to learn about the Widan's art—but this esoterica, this type of discussion, had always lost his interest, to Sendari's abiding regret.

"Gentlemen," Alesso said, lifting his hand for a third and final time. He settled upon amusement at the lack of attention paid his first two attempts, but it was a thin veneer; it would not survive a third.

They turned.

"From what little I consider to be intelligible in what is clearly too heated to be a discussion," he said softly, and Sendari had the grace to flinch and then straighten up, adopting his usual posture, his familiar neutrality, "You are saying that the nature of these masks is to reveal, yes?"

"Yes," they said, as one person. Mikalis threw a glance at the side of Sendari's face, but having been reprimanded in this fashion, Sendari chose to exercise his control, which was—or could be— considerable.

"But you have not yet decided why this ability—unmanning as it appears to be—will actually be *useful.*"

Silence. Sendari spoke; Mikalis hiccuped half a word into the flow of Sendari's sentence and then, as if only just realizing where they both stood, fell silent. Which was good. The Festival Night— the night they now feared was the significant night—was one day away. And these two men, and their kind, were all that stood between the unknown plans of the *Kialli* and the Tor Leonne.

"No, Tyr'agar, we have not. You have posited, and we have considered, that the Lake itself must be significant; but we have also taken into consideration that this is, regardless, the seat of power in the Dominion, and as we understand the society of the *Kialli,* were it a barren rock, it would still be of interest to them for that reason alone."

"Trust my instinct, old friend." It was not a request.

"Regardless," Mikalis said, not quite taking the hint, "we cannot understand the use of masks or the way they will harm the Lake." He bowed. "We posit that the demons themselves, in old texts, are known by, and to an extent, controlled by the nature of their name and their naming. Perhaps they so little understand the nature of mortals, they have crafted a weapon against which a demon would have little recourse. Perhaps this is a way of making a *name* known."

Alesso stood. He found the cushions confining, and the necessity of privacy meant that there was no easy egress to the outer world. Everything about this discussion, this dilemma, was interior. He paced, pausing only to lift a fine glass that contained the water of the Lake which had made the Tor the chosen seat of power in the Dominion.

"Having seen the effect of the mask itself," Sendari said quietly, "I would concur."

"And you were . . . discussing?"

"How that would be useful. I believe that with judicious use of the masks we might, ourselves, gain power if a demon were forced to wear one under the correct circumstance."

"An idea, Sendari. A good one. Do not destroy them all."

"No."

"Tyr'agar," Mikalis broke in, and Alesso understood at once the nature of the argument, "I believe it unwise. There are forces which we do not understand; with imperfect understanding, we cannot control them. They will control us. Our enemies will find egress into our private spheres of magic should we attempt to avail ourselves of theirs."

"Oh? Sendari?"

Sendari's shrug was dismissive. "There is a danger," he said, although the acknowledgment was at best theoretical; it was certainly not conveyed in the tone of voice that he chose.

"And that danger?"

"Is, in my opinion, purely theoretical."

"You have done *no* studying of the arts you think to use," Mikalis broke in. "I have done very little—but enough to be granted some recognition. I am not a half-wit Designate, Sendari—I am fully Widan, and I know of what I speak." He turned before Sendari could reply—and it seemed, to Alesso's admittedly familiar eye, that he was about to, and addressed the Tyr'agar directly. "Magic," he said, "is like armor, but there is a personal element to it. When two Widan struggle in a contest of magic and power, they reveal much about themselves to each other *unless* one of the two is much more powerful, in which case he has the magical resources available to conceal some part of his own talent or ability. The Sword's Edge is such a Widan. I, and, I believe, the Widan Sendari are not.

"And the Sword's Edge is not here."

"You would take this risk, if he were available?"

"No," Mikalis replied.

"And that is the point. He has said himself—"

"I said that between *two Widan*—"

"*Gentlemen.*" They quieted. "I will think on what you have said. It is of interest. But it is not of as much interest as the use of the weapon itself. Is it sword? Is it bow? Is it garrotte? What is its function?"

To that, they had no answer.

"Mikalis, understand: We do not throw away any weapon we are offered. Your objections have been heard, and they will be considered. They will not, however, be repeated. Do you understand?"

He bowed immediately.

"Good. Find out what they will do. Speak with the kai el'Sol."

"But—"

"Do it. The Lake and the Sword have been their purview for centuries; perhaps it is time that they showed us the deeper understanding expected of their position." He paused. "No, Sendari, not you. You are to retire to your chambers."

Sendari let the mask fall. Only then did Alesso realize exactly how *much* control his friend had been exerting. He was impressed; he did not embarrass his friend by openly admiring the restraint shown previously; there was no way to do it without pointing out its loss.

"The . . . demon took much out of me," he said quietly.

"Understood. Let Mikalis talk to—"

"He does not maintain the proper perspective."

"He will have to do. Sendari, do not mistake me. That was not a request. It was a command."

"Tyr'agar."

20th of Scaral, 427 AA
The Shining Palace, The Northern Wastes

The Sword's Edge had left word that his return to the Tor Leonne was imminent before he received word that it was also forbidden.

The first words were a use of power that was not, given the distance between the Tor and the Shining Palace, trivial. The second, however, were far more costly; they were not his, and he was not a man to suborn his will to another's with grace or ease.

But Lady Sariyel had brought the word, white and trembling, to his doors, and she loitered in them, waiting for his reaction. More significant, she had been used indirectly as a messenger from the Lord of the Shining Court.

"Are you," he said at last, "to carry word back? The nature of your statement did not seem to imply a request on the part of the Lord."

"No," she replied. "I—I'm not to carry word back. But do you—" She gazed to the side; the gaze was furtive. They were not protected here. To cast the magics necessary to truly ward a conversation from prying ears was almost to draw attention to it, the *Kialli* were so sensitive to magic. She swallowed. The Northerners were always vastly more expressive when upset than the Southerners.

Expressive enough that he understood that she was about to take him into her confidence. They were not friends; he found her almost offensively forward, graceless for a woman, displeasingly bold for a *person*. But he was willing to acknowledge—here, outside of the Dominion, where neutrality was the law—that her actual power was substantial and worthy of respect.

Had she been Annagarian, he would have had her killed, or perhaps have killed her himself. She was not.

She stood before him, hands bunching in the skirts that were so oddly functional in the North, the furs settled round her shoulders and face, framing the delicate paleness of her skin. The garish color of her lips, the bruised look of her eyes. This was, he supposed, attractive to someone. Certainly it had been many years ago to the unfortunate Lord Sariyel.

He found that with Lady Sariyel, in a certain situation, one could use silence as a weapon; he used it now. Subtlety was not a shield that she could use in defense. The waiting stretched; he watched her expression shift, and shift again; fear fought with fear. The silence worked its way inward until she felt forced to expel or break it. She was so terribly obvious.

Yet he could not offend her completely; not now. For she had carried an order that forbid travel to any of the human mages now within the confines of the Shining Palace. He did not think that, should the Lord desire their deaths, they had any hope of avoiding them.

"Widan," she said softly, "you came to the Court with word that Anya a'Cooper had traveled South."

"Indeed." It was not the expected subject of discussion; he segued smoothly, forcing even the faintest trace of frown from the lines of his brow. "Lord Ishavriel, I have been assured, is in the act of containing her."

Lady Sariyel was silent a moment. "Containing her?" she asked at last, "or returning her?"

"Lady," he replied, with the exaggerated politeness that would have been recognized for sarcasm in the South, "You have no doubt a much better acquaintance with Anya a'Cooper than any of us."

She stiffened. "She does not, as you must know, reside with the humans; she is Ishavriel's curiosity and pet; she resides with him."

"And she is his responsibility." He measured the silence, trying to discern which outcome would please her least; which would encourage fear, and therefore a further exchange of information. It was difficult. She had never particularly liked him, and he had never desired a change in that state of affairs. He did not desire it now. He watched; she waited; he made his decision.

"But she eludes him and we suspect she will continue to do so; our only concern," he added smoothly, "is that she not interrupt our plans for the Festival Night."

Apparently the decision he had chosen to make was a wise one. She sagged visibly; her breath literally stopped. She could not, and some part of him found this vastly amusing, speak. He almost wished that Alesso di'Marente were by his side for the sheer pleasure of her momentary silence. But she recovered. That was the interesting thing about the Lady Sariyel. She always survived. He did not therefore dismiss her now.

"If she is not found," Lady Sariyel said, "then you will *personally* have far more to lose then the convenience of a successful plan in the Tor Leonne."

"Oh?"

"Why do you think we have been forbidden travel?"

"I have," he replied, with complete honesty, "no idea."

Again, the furtive glance to the door. Then, after a moment, she reached a decision; she stepped into the room and pulled the door closed at her back.

It was his nature to be suspicious; it was as natural as breathing. But the very subtle magic he used was repulsed by her easily, and her expression shifted a moment, her hand hovering behind the fall of brocade near the door's handle. The situation was obviously dire; she let her hand fall. "I am here under orders, yes, but what I tell you now is no part of that errand." She leaned forward, as if secrecy and intimacy were entwined. He did not step back, but it was an effort.

"We did not desire to distract you," she said quietly, "but there were reasons for choosing the Northern Wastes as the citadel from which our Lord might plan His victory over the Empire and the Dominion."

"You did not desire to . . . distract us." The man who had lived with the sun and sand at the edge of civilization all his life had learned how to imbue his voice with Northern ice. "How . . . considerate."

She flushed, and then drew herself up. "And you," she said coldly, "you have bothered us with every detail of plans which do not concern *us*."

"And this plan does not concern us?"

She shrugged. "No. If you truly serve the Lord and depend upon His ascendancy, it does not. It is another step, no more." She turned. Turned back. He was reminded of trapped or restless children who expect—but are not certain they will receive—a beating.

"And this step?"

"You know that He has been building the gate between our worlds."

"Yes."

"You know that many of His own generals and lieutenants have come through, but that the passage is not instantaneous."

"Indeed."

"You know," she continued, and he found it both fascinating and mildly insulting, "that He had a way of anchoring the gate to this world so that they exist in some fashion in the same space and time?"

He stopped finding her babble mildly insulting. "No." His mind raced. "We—Lord Sariyel and I—had discussed this possibility briefly a long while ago; but it was theoretical."

She nodded quietly. "I saw his notes. It was theoretically possible under very special conditions. First, whatever power the god contributed to the casting of the spell had to be met by a matching power that was anchored in this world. Second—"

"That power had to exist in the same vessel as the matching

power, an echo of the magical melding He wished to accomplish. And third—and the most problematic of the triad—that the ground upon which such a spell was cast must already have the properties He wished to cement: they must exist in a realm outside of this one, but be part of it."

She looked at him expectantly. "Scarran," she said, and when his silence grew impenetrable she added, "The Dark Conjunction."

"If it were simply a matter of Scarran," he replied, "the Lord would have cast His spell years ago."

"He did not have a mage of requisite power until a handful of years ago."

Understanding, then. "Anya."

"Anya. Understand that her absence has already cost Lord Ishavriel two of his most powerful lieutenants."

But it still did not make sense. "No," he said at last. "Even with Anya, the advent of Scarran does not guarantee him any purchase between the worlds. You are speaking, I assume, of the old roads? They barely exist, and they exist only when the First-born choose to use them."

"No," she replied quietly. "That was our misunderstanding, our misreading of the signs."

"Our?"

"My Lord Sariyel's," she said, meeting his eyes in a way that men would not have dared to in the Dominion, given the differences between their ranks. "And my own. Or did you think that I merely amused him sexually while he worked?"

"There is nothing mere about you, Lady Sariyel. You have chosen to play your role; I have chosen mine. But we mask power in our own efficient ways." He started. Stopped. Took another risk. "I have underestimated you in a fashion that you are no doubt aware of. I had assumed—Lord Sariyel let it be assumed—that the work, indeed, was his."

She lifted her shoulder and let it fall in a delicate shrug. Or as delicate as a shrug could be in the rustle of heavy and coarse brocade. He was not certain if that inelegant gesture was a Northern acceptance of a tacitly worded apology; he was certain that she did not understand the personal significance or cost to himself to make it.

But she continued, staring now at a point beyond his shoulder. "The old roads exist; we are certain of it. There has been evidence gathered—firsthand—by some of the previous servitors of the Lord in their summoned state, that those roads and the barriers that divide the two worlds are remarkably thin on Scarran—but although we chose the Northern Wastes, and the basin, because it was once a seat of power along the hidden way, we have personally found no sign.

"And then, we felt it; seven years ago; a resurgence of the power along the way. And because Lord Isladar was present, he was able to tell us something that we ourselves could not discern: The horns were being winded."

"Horns?"

"When the Hunt rides," she said softy, "the Queen of the Hunt takes to the road. They are her roads, and when she walks them, they . . . respond to her presence. But she hunts infrequently. We do not understand the old roads clearly; the *Kialli* are unwilling to discuss what happened before the gods left our world; but it is conceded that the Queen of the Hunt—whoever she is—is one of the godlings left behind."

"Godlings?"

"The gods were very corporeal at one time. The Northern gods," she added. For just a moment, her lips curved up in a full, and a very lewd smile. But it faltered as it met the stone of his gaze. "You are so very, very cold," she said plaintively. But her eyes were as cold as his demeanor. "The gods, however, were not. They coupled," she continued. "And they had children. Let me assume that you understand the mechanics." She walked away from the door and began to pace the perimeter of his rectangular carpet. Carpets here were thick and heavy—but they were necessary. Nothing about the Shining Palace exuded warmth.

"Those children are—we believe—called the Firstborn. They were many initially, but they warred; there were few in the end, and the few that remained were either powerful, reclusive, or both. The Queen of the Hunt was most certainly the former. We believe she is the oldest of the Firstborn, but again, the *Kialli* will not discuss what they know with the merely mortal. This is conjecture.

"Conjecture is dangerous in its fashion." She shrugged. "But when the Queen of the Hunt is mentioned, the *Kialli* tense. I believe that she and they were not friendly; that they warred in some fashion. Sor na Shannen, a kinlord in her own right and one of the few of her phylum to rise so high, encountered the Hunt on the Scarran—or the Winter—road. They fought; she escaped.

"But that year, that year there was also the tangible sense of a meeting of worlds."

"But Sor na Shannen was in the Empire."

"Indeed. That is when we realized the geographic distance means nothing; the road is like a single body, a living thing. The Queen Hunts or she does not.

"However, having said that, it took us time to understand that the solidity of the path is provided not only by the Queen but also by the victim she chooses. When the *Kialli* and Queen met in combat, we believe the old road was eclipsed again." She paused.

He was not a slow man; he absorbed her words, examined them, toyed with pretending to be slow to understand. But pretense was all he had to offer, and he wished some confirmation; he also wished to see the notes she had taken and the path she walked to reach the conclusions that she had.

"It was Lord Ishavriel," she said, after he nodded, "who pointed out that the points that drew the old road and the old world together were both elements of the Hunt: the immortal and the mortal. He posited that if the host hunted, and in greater number, we might see such a grounding of the road as we had never seen, and take advantage of it.

"It was also Lord Ishavriel and the *Kialli* craftsmen who created the masks that were sent to the Tor Leonne." Her glance slid from his face. She swallowed.

"The masks?"

"The Tor is a special place. The Lake is—according to the oldest and most powerful of the *Kialli* lords—an artifact left by the Queen of the Hunt for her loyal subjects in their battle against her chosen enemies."

Cortano grimaced. "That is not our telling of the tale."

"No." Again, her expression hardened. "But even you do not believe the Southern telling of the tale."

He brought hand to beard. "Perhaps. The Lake is significant?"

"Yes. Because it exists in our world no matter what the time or season, and not in hers—yet it retains some elements of her gift and power." She swallowed. "I believe that it indicates that when the Queen of the Hunt roamed freely, she returned there, to the heartlands of the South; that some residual element of her power resides there still—and that, with the right tools, she can—like the *Kialli*—be summoned."

He understood, then. "The masks."

"Yes."

And he wanted to kill her. He almost did.

"If the masks summon the Hunt, they will Hunt in the Tor?"

"The Tor, if we guess correctly, will *become* a part of the road that she travels; neither here nor there, but both. It will be the strongest anchoring of that path in this world since *our* tenure here began in earnest.

"And on such a platform, the Lord might build His throne; might sit without being forced to devour the scraps that his demons bring him from the towns or the kingdoms where they might be little missed."

"Very well. And our tenure here?"

She frowned. "Do not play games with me, Widan. You understand the significance of what I have said."

He did. He nodded, fingers stroking beard. "Anya a'Cooper is acknowledged as a power without parallel. She has no mind, of course. But she has power. She was to be the vessel?"

"She was."

"Would she have survived it?"

"Does it matter? If you mean would it have killed her? I think it unlikely. Would it have damaged her mind further? How would we be able to tell?"

He understood all. All.

"If she is not found, *we* are to take her place."

"Yes. And there are few of us; most of the talent-born are scattered across the North and West. You are here, and I; there is one other."

Three. Three fully trained mages. "And you are concerned? Lady Sariyel, just *how* powerful is Anya a'Cooper?"

She looked up at him through wide, darkening eyes.

"What will happen to us if we are forced to take her place in the ceremony?"

She didn't answer that question directly. But she said, "Cortano, she must be found."

"I will . . . do my best to make certain that she is. Anya . . . leaves a trail. It is not hard to follow."

"We have very, very little time. The Lord plans, and this is the only time that we will have this opportunity."

"The ceremony can wait a year, surely?"

"No. We believe that if the Queen of the Hunt Hunts in the Tor, when she leaves, the power of the artifact will leave with her."

"The artifact?"

"The Lake. The waters of the Tor will no longer be blessed by her and left by her; they will once again become part of her world when the Hunt is withdrawn."

"What?"

"Lord Ishavriel believes that the power of the Lake will be reclaimed by the Queen of the Hunt when she withdraws at the end of the Dark Conjunction; it will become ordinary; we will therefore have no way to summon her again, because there will be no focal point for her power; no beacon."

"I . . . see." He did not smile. He knew that he had lost color, and he knew that she would assume it was for the same reason that she had. "I . . . thank you for this information. I . . . will converse with Alesso at once about the urgent nature of our business.

"Where is Ishavriel?"

"He is supposed to find her." She frowned. "He did not seem concerned."

"He would not," Cortano replied absently. "He is *Kialli;* concern is an act of weakness. Lady Sariyel, I must ask you to leave. It is not our way to enjoin our superiors to act with haste in the company of women. I apologize if this is foreign or even repulsive, but I assume you want me to be at my most effective."

"Understood," she said, curtsying. She looked almost pretty for a moment as she withdrew.

Almost.

Cortano stood, alone, in the center of his chambers. Aware now that he had a choice to make. He did not particularly like these rooms; he would have found some ease with such decision had he been given a different venue in which to make it.

They understood so much about the desire for power, these *Kialli* and the Lord they served. They had a fundamental understanding of pride. But the complexities that marred the absolute desire for power . . . the way that pride hindered or aided that search . . . they were fine points. Wasted.

He had desired to live forever. So, too, had Alesso di'Marente; but the General who had risen to unheard of heights thought of immortality writ in generations: his name, a clan that bore it, a history that remembered it.

Not enough, for a man like Cortano; he had desired to *see* the passing of those generations; to discover for himself what history remembered and what it forgot; what it chose to elevate, and what it chose to misplace—and whether in fact any truth remained buried. He was willing to lose much to gain that.

The *Kialli* understood that.

But they did not understand that there were limits to what he was willing to lose. He had seen the *Allasakari* come, their minds no longer their own, their bodies inhabited by Lord's Shadow that would eventually devour everything of substance.

He had no doubt that that would be his fate.

Unless Anya were returned to the Shining City.

And then what? He thought of it: the moral authority of the new Tyr'agar completely destroyed by the loss of the Lake, by the inability to wield the Sword; an easy target, a man who could take the blame and be cast aside. Alesso was too difficult; too independent. The *Kialli* would have little problem finding a more complacent replacement.

Cortano was certain as Sword's Edge he could personally survive the transfer of power intact. But in the end, would it matter? The Southerners were to be useful as a distraction for the North; the *Kialli* would have that, regardless.

It galled him; he was—as Alesso was—a proud man. Cortano had seen Sendari swallow almost greater personal insult and continue; he had always wondered what it would take to force him into the same position. To make of him the same man. His pending death?

Perhaps.

But . . . he knew now with certainty that Annagar had always been intended as fodder. The Northerners had been informed of the use to which Annagar would be fully put. The Southerners had not. Which outcome was to his best advantage? To theirs?

As Sword's Edge, the Widan Cortano di'Alexes was accustomed to quick and silent decision.

He readied himself for the conversation to follow.

21st of Scaral, 427 AA
Tor Leonne

Morning on the Lake.

He knelt before it, knees against the smooth wood of the pier. The dawn's beauty had suffused the light with a color and a delicacy that a man could only appreciate serenely in isolation. That had been the intent behind this, the Pavilion of the Dawn. It was nestled behind a stand of trees, and behind the cover of the master landscaper's artful rushes; it could see all, but could only be seen, and in passing, at a distance. Distance, for a ruler, was everything.

He knelt in isolation, silk of the very fine surcoat that made a statement of his position artlessly arrayed before him. The counselors that he most desired would be some time in arriving; he desired no other and had sent the graceful pedants of his own court scurrying away like rodents underfoot. And in time, if he had time, he would regret it; it was rash.

But time was a luxury. And it was, Alesso thought, almost gone. He did not cede victory to his enemies, but he did concede that they had maneuvered artfully, playing him against his desire; feeding him the information that he expected, and dealing well with his discovery of the information that had been concealed.

The Radann had found and destroyed four more of the demons in their search, and they had become a powerful symbol of the Lord in the city streets. How powerful, he could not say; he did not expect to be able to leash them in the aftermath of the slaughter, unless they perished in it.

The combined forces of cerdan, Widan, and Radann had found, and destroyed, some hundred masks. They had, against the better judgment of Mikalis di'Arretta, kept a handful. But the handful they kept were not the the only masks that remained. They knew that for fact. What they did not—could not—know was where the rest of the masks lay.

Whose hands had lifted them; whose hands had carried them home either as poor prize or rich gift; whose faces would bear them, and in bearing them die so that the Tor Leonne—and the man who ruled it—might lose the one thing that had always set it apart from any other city in the Dominion.

The Lady's favor.

The Lake.

The *Kialli* would destroy the Lake, the Tor, and his people. He wondered, idly, if he had been meant to survive at all. His hand found the hilt of *Terra Fuerre* and rested there a long moment; he bowed his head, exposed as he was to the Lord's gaze.

He heard footsteps. They were heavy, slightly uneven. He rose at once from his contemplation of sunlight across the rippling water. The Widan Sendari di'Sendari came into view. Taking the wineskin from his own sash, Alesso knelt over the pier's edge, filling it with water. He was no courtesan, to move with elegance of pleasing grace, but he moved quickly. The skin passed between them and after a perfunctory politeness, Sendari di'Sendari drank.

"Garrardi," he said without preamble, when the water had cleared his throat, "is demanding an audience with you."

Alesso shrugged. "He will have what he wants; he can wait to receive it. I have summoned you here to ask you a question."

"And I have come," Sendari replied, an odd expression on his face, "to offer you an answer."

"You intrigue me. If I did not know you better, I would say that you find some levity in this situation which escapes me entirely. Share the joke, old friend."

"It is no joke," Sendari said quietly. "But it is absurdly simple."

"What?"

"Here." He reached in his robes and took out a leather satchel whose smooth, brown face had been broken in several places by runic symbols.

"You brought . . . a mask?"

"Indeed. I wish your permission, Tyr'agar, to utilize the waters of the Tor."

Alesso's face darkened. "It is for that reason that I have summoned you. I had word from Cortano early this morning."

"He bespoke you? I was not informed."

"No. It was done in haste, and with cause. Protect us."

"It has . . . already been done." He lifted his arm; it was encircled by a bracelet. "Not by my skill, however; I thought it best to . . . recover."

Alesso nodded. Another time, and he might have asked how such a bracelet had been created, or more precisely by whom. But their shadows were shortening as they spoke; he could almost feel it; the slow swing of the pendulum; the fall of the grains of sand. "Tell me of your discovery."

"Mikalis discovered it. We were . . . late at work."

"I ordered you—"

"You *requested,* Tyr'agar. And I thought it best, given the urgency of our situation, to use my own discretion. You ordered me not to speak with the Radann."

"Sendari."

"Alesso."

Alesso laughed. Truly laughed. For a moment, here, on this pier, surrounded by water and sun and enemies, he felt young again. His pulse quickened; his senses sharpened; he could see the variegated light, sharp and distinct, across the water; he could smell the rushes and the lilies on the breeze; could feel, for just a perfect moment, the heft of a weapon he had not drawn in battle for months. Sendari's frown deepened his laughter.

"My apologies, old friend. Please. Your discovery."

"It is merely this. Your permission?"

"You have it; you have always had it. Let us not stand on formality when we are so close the end of all plans."

"Very well, Tyr'agar," Sendari replied. With care not to touch the mask itself, he walked to the end of the pier. And upended the bag.

Alesso watched, surprised, as the mask fell, spinning once in the air as if it were clutching for purchase. "Sendari—"

The water burst into flames as the mask touched its surface. It did not have a chance to sink; the golden, glowing fire, brilliant and brief, devoured it, made ash of it. Absolute denial.

Alesso was silent for a moment. When at length he was ready to speak, his voice was no longer captive to the wild edge of amusement. "So," he said softly, "our allies gain two things: The foothold they desire in the world, and the destruction of a weapon that is very effective against their magic."

"Against the *Kialli*," Sendari replied. "You have never attempted to throw one into the Lake; I suspect it would last as long." He bowed. "I apologize. We were intent on discovering the masks' purpose; it only occurred to us afterward to seek a method by which they might easily be destroyed."

Alesso smiled. "Let me change the subject, old friend. If I asked it of you, and if there were none to stand in your way, would you take the title of Sword's Edge?"

Sendari was silent for a long moment. "Tell me," he said quietly.

"It appears," Alesso replied, looking at the place where the mask had almost fallen into the water and the water had denied it, "that the masks are tied in to the destruction of the Lake. And worse."

"Alesso—"

"Anya a'Cooper is no longer in the Shining City."

"We knew this."

"Yes. We have some idea of where she might be; there are two reports. But that is beside the point. The Festival of the Moon is significant in its fashion to the Lord of the Shining Court, and He had His own plans for it. Cortano feels that there is a chance that if Anya a'Cooper does not return to the Shining City before the rising of the Festival Moon, it will mean his death."

He paused a moment for Sendari's comment, but the Widan knew him well; he waited for the rest of the story.

"It is however also Cortano's considered opinion that it will

mean our doom if she returns to the City in time for the Lord to
do anything other than utilize her directly."

"I . . . see." Sendari was tired. After a moment he said, "The
Lord's attention is turned toward Anya."

"Indeed."

"And if Anya returns to the Shining City early, he will turn his
attention to the masks and the Tor. And the destruction of what is,
essentially, the true crown and the true throne of the Dominion."

"Indeed."

"You will tell me how?"

"I do not understand how. I know only that the destruction of
the Lake is byproduct; that the masks themselves are a beacon
that will summon someone Cortano calls the Queen of the Hunt.
She *must* be summoned; the masks provide the sacrificial fodder
for the hunting party she will lead. Her presence here somehow
affects the . . . land . . . that the Lord has chosen as His gateway.

"He needs Anya in the Northern Wastes in order to take
advantage of the Hunt here. Her loss is of great concern to Him,
because without her, He cannot complete whatever spell He
hopes to cast."

"And this affects the Sword's Edge how?"

"He will attempt it anyway. Using the mages he has."

"Attempt *what,* Alesso?"

"The spell," his friend replied, with just a trace of frustration.
"She was to be vessel and containment to the Lord's power. He
will use what He has in her place if He cannot find her."

Sendari said quietly, "We need Cortano. He *is* the Widan; we
cannot be guaranteed that the man who becomes Sword's Edge
in his stead will favor us or our alliance." He met his oldest
friend's hard stare, and said simply, and with an honesty beneath
most clansmen of note, "I have not the power, Alesso, or I would
take the title for your sake and at your command. But among the
Widan, as among any who rule, power is key."

"You are certain?"

"As certain as I can be. We do not know or reveal the full
extent of our talents—but it would kill me to cast the spell that
carried Cortano to the Shining Palace."

"And the other Widan?"

"I believe there are one or two who may rival, in raw talent,
the current Sword's Edge. They are politically neutral; they have
avoided testing their skill against his. Mikalis was correct; it
would reveal their strengths, but it would also reveal their weak-

nesses. Neither at this moment desires that; Cortano is strong. Should he perish, there will be a contest of a type; the winner will take the Edge; the loser, the grave.

"But I am not that winner."

"Understood, old friend. Understood. Be prepared, now, to play a dangerous game."

"What game could be more dangerous than this?"

Footsteps. Sendari turned; Alesso drew his sword.

And Lord Isladar of the *Kialli*, kinlord without demesne, walked around the grove of small trees and into the shadows they cast. He smiled. "All games, Tyr'agar, are dangerous. But in this day, and in this age, with so much at risk, life is a game."

CHAPTER THIRTY-ONE

It was good to wake up in the same place where she'd gone to sleep. It was less good to wake up to the sound of an argument, but there was something about it that reminded her of her childhood; older woman's voice raised in annoyance, younger woman's in defiance. She had forgotten how much her mother and her Oma argued when she was a child. She hadn't, however, forgotten the particularly sharp sound of a slap.

The wagon was dark. The flaps were closed. She sat up a bit too quickly and smacked her forehead against something hard. Her cursing brought light; someone lifted the flap. "It's about time you woke up," a half-familiar voice said. "We'd've woken you, but the guy at the side of the wagon started threatening to torch circles in the grass." It was Elena, Margret's cousin. Her face was lit from the side by day; she looked haggard even in the shadows cast by tarp. "Food," she said quietly, "and then work."

Jewel rubbed her forehead. There was a ledge above the flat bench she couldn't quite bring herself to dignify with the name bed. There were books on it. And bottles. Great place to put bottles. "I'm coming."

Elena took her to where there was a small horde of screaming short people running around. Two of them attempted to enmesh her in their game of catch-me; she failed to project the correct aura of deathly gloom because they didn't let up until Elena shooed them away. They did not, however, go near Avandar.

"Teach me that," she said out of the corner of her mouth as they took a seat at a table made of platform planks.

"Teach you how to kill children?"

There was something about the tone of his voice that made it clear that he was only half joking. Bitterness. Anger. Pride.

"Never mind."

"At your command."

That set the tone for the day. She saw him as he was—but she also saw him as he had been. Beneath the mountain. On the path. She couldn't forget it.

"Uh, Jewel?" Another voice. "Is that you?" She looked up into the face of a dark-haired, bright-eyed young man. Handsome, in a Voyani fashion, his skin dark but not yet cracked by sun or wind.

She nodded, and then realizing that everyone else was talking with their little cheeks and mouths full, said, "That's me."

"Good." His shoulders sagged with obvious relief. "The Havallan Matriarch is looking for you."

"So tell her I'm here," Jewel said. But she was being mean, and she knew it. "No—never mind. I'm joking. I wouldn't send you to a fate like that; you're a perfect stranger. You've done nothing to offend me. Yet."

He laughed. "And I'm not going to, either—not if that's what you do to people who *do* offend you! I'm Adam," he added. "Margret's brother."

"You're the Matriarch's brother? Funny," Jewel said, rising quickly and setting aside the breakfast that was about to be grabbed by an energetic child whose age she couldn't quite guess. "You don't look like you're covered in bruises."

He laughed. "I'm faster than she is."

It did not escape her attention that she was being fed with the children. And the significance of that, if not the actual experience itself, was flattering. She briefly considered wresting that flatbread away from the ill-mannered child. Decided against it. Indeterminate age or no, he looked decidedly too skinny.

Yollana was not amused that they took their time coming, where the phrase "took their time" in Jewel's opinion roughly translated into the Weston "weren't here instantaneously." Her frown lines were distinct and pronounced; it was clear that they were either the same lines that she used for smiling, or that she didn't smile a whole lot. Either way, Yollana of the Havalla Voyani was a singularly impressive presence, all of it simmering.

"We were—"

"Don't bother making excuses," she said, lifting a hand sideways as if the edge of her palm were a weapon. "You've wasted enough of my time. You," she added, her frown becoming more pronounced, "you watch over *her,* clear?"

"I have," Avandar replied, his voice as dry as desert air, "made that oath."

"Good. Keep it. You'll travel with the Serra and the Northerner into the city tonight, but you two are staying there. They come back."

"What?" It wasn't Avandar who spoke.

"I don't know why," Yollana snapped. "It sounds stupid to me. But you two don't come back with the rest of 'em. And I'm hoping it's not because you can't."

"But we—"

"So I want you to take these. Pay attention, girl. I'm tired and I need my strength."

"Uh, Yollana?"

"What?" Whip-snap sharp, that word; the old woman's hands froze at the flap of a generous pouch.

"You were captured, right?"

"Yes."

"And you weren't expecting to be captured."

"No."

"And so you couldn't have prepared to be here, right?"

"Yes."

"So how is it you have anything to give me?"

"That's very clever. If you were Havallan, girl, you'd be rubbing your cheek right now."

"Which means you aren't going to answer me, right?"

"Clever, as I said. We need these back. Just to make you comfortable, the penalty for stealing them is the death of your clan."

"That would be easy; I don't have one."

"We'll improvise. We're good at that."

"I bet. All right. They come back."

"But if they're lost the *right* way, you'll probably scrape by with groveling and sniveling."

"Good to know. What are they?"

She took two objects out of her pouch. One was a small silver horn; it was straight from mouthpiece to bell, and it was so delicate Jewel wondered how it had survived being carried in Yollana's pouch; it certainly didn't seem padded or cushioned. It was about as long as the stretch from her index finger to the inner edge of her wrist. "I suppose if I ask you how to use this, you won't answer?"

"I could give you a guess, girl, but I have a feeling that you'll know how to use it if it needs to be used."

"Great. So do I." Jewel very carefully slid the horn into the pouch she carried. After all, that was the way Yollana had carried the damn thing, so it couldn't be that fragile. It couldn't be.

"Second, take this."

The inspection of the horn had pulled her attention away from Yollana—who looked about as pleased as one would expect—and when she looked up, she saw that Yollana had a thick, very plain silver bowl, about the size of two cupped palms, in her hand.

"And this is?"

"A bell."

"A bell."

"Yes."

"It looks like a bowl."

"Gods help you if you eat out of it, girl," the old woman said darkly. "Anyone that stupid would get the fate they deserve. And we have enough stupid people here," she added, spitting to the side. "We don't need another one."

"Yes, Matriarch."

Yollana frowned. "That's it, then."

"That's it?"

"That's it. It's getting late. Go and get ready. Both of you. I'll see you again."

"When?"

"That would be telling. You've got the gift, don't be so damn lazy." That was her exit line. But she didn't get up and walk away; she glowered at Jewel until she took the hint and dragged Avandar off.

"It is not a surprise to me," Avandar said quietly, "that the clansmen find the Voyani Matriarchs so difficult."

Jewel laughed. "Oh, I don't know. From where I look, her position is the one to reach for—she can say whatever she thinks and people have to take it exactly as given. None of this political garbage."

He raised a single brow. "If you believe that the Havallan Matriarch is not political, then you still have some of that charming naivete about you."

"On the other hand," Jewel continued, "Maybe I just like the position because if *I* were in it and you said that, I could just slap you instead of answering."

"And you haven't?"

She was silent. After a minute of high-stepping over weeds

that would not be tromped flat no matter how hard she tried, she said, "Come on. She's given us warning. Let's pack."

"And this meets with your approval?" The Radann kai el'Sol glanced up from the table upon which only an unscarred, flat medallion sat. It was round; in diameter slightly larger than the widest part of his palm; it was perhaps an inch and a half thick. But it was heavy, solid wood, and the Tyr'agar waited, his hand on the hilt of his undrawn sword.

"It meets with my approval," the Tyr'agar replied quietly. "It was my suggestion."

"I . . . see."

"You do not trust me."

The Radann kai el'Sol said quietly, "I cannot understand what could be gained by this, but it is, in principle, a ceremony that I approve of. You have been very security conscious; it is by your will that the gates and the grounds of the Tor have been turned from pleasant landscape and architecture to fortification.

Alesso laughed. "This is not fortified, not truly. But I wish to open the Lake for the day and perhaps the early evening. My reasons are my own, but you have been a staunch ally, and I therefore choose to explain them. There have been troubling rumors in the streets of the lower Tor. We are not proof against their travel; wind takes them everywhere.

"It is said that I consort with the Lord of Night."

Peder kai el'Sol said nothing.

"Therefore, I wish my respect for the celebration of the Lady to be well known. I wish the populace to come to the plateau and see that there *is* no truth to the rumors of a Lord of Night as Consort. I wish my eminence as Tyr to be remembered. Therefore I wish to open my Lake to the Festival goers, so that they will be blessed by the gift of the Lady."

"And that gift will be remembered as yours."

"Indeed."

"And you wish us to participate in the ceremony?"

Alesso frowned. He was not used to being questioned by the kai el'Sol. But his alliance had shifted dangerously; where he had planned for weak Radann, he now needed strong ones. For a moment the wind on the Lake was strong; it caught his hair, and the fallen petals of the flowering trees whirled about his face in a gentle dance. He might have thought it a sign, were he a religious man. Or a superstitious one. The petals were the color of Northern snow; the color of sun on water.

"I wish you to preside over the blessing ceremony."

He was gratified when Peder's expression cracked before he could shutter it. Surprise. "And what, exactly, do you see as our role in such a blessing? It is not the norm and we are not the Lady's servants."

"It is not the norm," Alesso agreed, prepared now to be genial. He drew his sword slowly and kept the edge toward ground. "And it will not become the norm. But your actions in the day—and the evening—will be in the service of the Lord, no matter how gracious the gesture appears to be."

"Oh?"

"I wish the *masks* blessed."

Peder kai el'Sol raised a brow. And then he laughed. "General," he said, deliberately accentuating the title that Alesso had held before the slaughter, "in my considered opinion, if the Lord had to descend from the heights to bless sword and bloodline again, it would be yours he would bless. Markaso kai di'Leonne was not, and would never have become, your equal." His smile thinned. "And for the Radann?"

"The Radann will be strengthened by this, as you know," Alesso said quietly. "And I will give you my word, taken by blade in the the Lord's plain view, that I will do nothing further to weaken them."

"And your allies?"

"We will deal with the allies," he said softly. "I have the Dominion. You have the Radann. In the end, is that not what this alliance was brought about to secure?"

"And the war in the North?"

Alesso lifted his sword over the circular medallion. "That is a necessity. I have made my offer; you will accept it or reject it, but you will do so now."

Peder kai el'Sol unsheathed his sword; it caught the light sharply and perfectly. He raised it; lifted it; held it a moment suspended above the wood that would seal his vow. And then he brought it down.

Ishavriel was furious.

The conversation drifted past, heavy with excitement, the fluid syllables of Torra exchanging information almost fast enough that the individual words were lost to the sense of the whole.

But the excitement was tinged with awe; it was almost as if a miracle had occurred. And it had. The Tyr'agar upon the plateau—a plateau unattained by most of the citizens of this city in the course of their meager lifetimes—had, in a moment of insane generosity, invited those people who celebrated the Lady's Festival to visit the Lake by which She had made Her favor to *this* city known.

He did not want foreigners unless they, too, were willing to celebrate the mysteries and the wildness of the Lady's longest night; he therefore asked only one thing of the would-be revelers who sought to visit the Lady's Lake, and to perhaps even partake of the waters therein: That they prove their intent by bringing the masks which would hide them in the Lady's darkness.

Hide them and allow them, therefore, to be their truest selves.

Lord Ishavriel had underestimated the former General. Twice. It angered him, but he felt a certain admiration for an enemy who could, with such an apparent lack of information and skill, and so very little maneuvering room, still manage to outmaneuver him. The kinlord would make certain, however, that that admiration did not extend to a third such event.

He understood what Alesso di'Marente hoped to achieve. It was, indeed, a clever ploy on his part, and Ishavriel had not yet decided how best to deal with it. Which was unfortunate, because as difficult as it was, it was the least of his concerns.

The greater still showed no sign of resolution.

Twice, he had almost crossed Anya's path. He was certain of it; her use of magic had a telltale signature that hung a moment in the air if one knew how to look. There were no obvious deaths; no obvious scarring of landmark or melting of stone—a thing that she often did out of sheer boredom. But there was something, something like taste, but more tenuous, that hovered on the edge of his awareness.

It was almost as if someone, someone capable of hiding obvious influence, of sublimating all sign of his power, was aiding her in her deception, in her forbidden flight. On a different day, this would not have mattered; on a different day it might have amused him to pit his skill against an unknown other's. He would, of course, have to kill the other for his unwarranted interference, but that necessary death would have made the hunt more interesting.

Today, however, the Lord's anger was vast.

Anya had not returned to the Shining Palace. She lingered here, somewhere, causing difficulty in the Tor.

Ishavriel had impressed upon her—inasmuch as the very broken fragments of her intelligence could take an impression—the importance of the Scaral night. He had also stressed her own importance, her central role, the fact that the Lord Himself was depending upon her considerable power. Flattery often produced what threats could not.

She had seemed so very enthusiastic.

He cursed. She was possessed of an intelligence that was so splintered it seemed nonexistent. Until, on a day like today, one cut oneself. There was no illusion whatever: If he failed to return her, *he* would pay.

And now he stood in the streets of the Tor; the sun, brilliant, the dawn long past. Anya eluded him.

It was time to send out the hunters, but he hated to do it; if they were miraculously lucky, and they found what he could not find, they were also very likely to perish. Anya's hatred of the kin—an aftereffect of his own plan, which had proved both convenient and inconvenient—was legendary, and with cause. Very few of his servitors could survive a chance meeting with Anya a'Cooper. He frowned.

Closed his eyes.

Sent out the words that would set them in motion. It meant that he might lose their participation in the festivities of *this* evening, but in this case they would not resist his command; they all felt it: the anger of the Lord of the Shining Court. So small a distance as the one that separated them did not afford them protection or ignorance.

The only bright note in an otherwise dismal morning was the lovely sound of screaming in the distance. One of the bodies, he thought, had at last been found.

The Captain of the cerdan was slightly gray. In no other way did he show the strain of his discovery, although Alesso questioned him at length about the details. He answered only what he was asked to answer; volunteered no opinion until he was asked for one; replied truthfully and with an economy of words that managed to convey respect rather than brusqueness or the stiffness of manner that comes from the ill at ease.

Alesso took note of the man's name; he was neither too young nor too old. The General was a judge of character, and he felt that this man might, in time, prove a worthy addition, to his

Tyran. He thanked him for his service to the city, offered him a commendation, and released him.

He missed Sendari's constant presence. The counselors that he afforded himself otherwise could not offer any meaningful guidance, being as they were unapprised of the full situation. But the Widan was still somewhat weak, and Alesso wanted—if possible— a full recovery by the night of the Festival Moon. He did not understand fully what would occur. No one did. Not even Lord Isladar would commit himself to a full prediction.

But in the meantime, this—three very grisly and very precise deaths—was the latest move on Lord Ishavriel's board. He wondered what that Lord would offer in counter to his opening of the Lake; he had his reserve planned. He expected the demons to attempt to stop anyone from entering the Tor itself. It was what he would do were the positions in the game reversed.

But the demons were, themselves, occupied.

He had to consider his options carefully; weigh the cost and the value of the pieces he was willing to surrender.

The Sword's Edge was among the most valuable of his pieces. Sentiment aside, he was of more value than the men he had not yet made generals, and of more value than the individual Tyrs. He was not, however, worth more than the Lake or the Tor; to lose either was to lose the game.

The sun's shadows were shortening as the day progressed. The gates had been cleaned and the flowers there tended. It was almost time to open them; to open them and to see who had the temerity to approach the Lake whose waters were said to grant longevity and peace.

But he smiled as he signaled an end to his brief reign in the private audience chamber.

He had made his career, and guaranteed his position, by turning a rout into a retreat—a costly retreat for the enemy. But that was when he had been forced to concede. In the Tor, he reigned, and he knew he was not yet defeated.

She had never seen so many people upon the plateau. The carefully cultivated wilderness that offered a sense of isolation and privacy to those with power and means bowed before the pressure of the hundreds, perhaps thousands, that made their trek from the city below.

Their voices were like the rumbling of distant storms, and

even when awe muted them, there were too many for silence to have strength. The Serra Diora stood in the protected shade of a copse of lovely, bent trees, and watched as the crowd traveled between the gently sloped hillocks.

Alana en'Marano stood beside her, and behind them—not nearly as far away as they might otherwise have stood—two of her father's cerdan. There was also a seraf who held a large umbrella that protected them both from the sun's full glare.

Alana was almost speechless. "I heard rumors," she said.

"But you didn't credit them." Diora's voice was soft. Almost faint.

"No."

"No matter, Alana; I do not think any of us truly did. But . . ."

"Yes."

"He will empty the Tor."

Alana was silent. After a moment, she said, "Perhaps there is less truth to the other disturbing rumors we have heard, if he truly offers the Lady's blessing so openly."

"Perhaps." The Serra Diora looked up from her inspection of that crowd and the possibilities inherent in its very presence. "Alana," she whispered, pitching her voice into the higher range of youth. Alana's face immediately snapped into the lines that meant indulgent suspicion.

"What?" Because she was the eldest of Sendari's wives, and because the Serra Teresa was not present to exert her influence, she was allowed to have less than perfect manners when no one but the cerdan themselves were present to be offended.

Diora willed her lips into a smile. It wasn't difficult; a smile, after all, was a woman's way of controlling the atmosphere of her environment; of making it light and pleasant and cheery when none of those things were otherwise evident. "Could we not," she said softly, "go now to the Pavilion of the Moon? The Tyrs will not require it but—"

"But it will give you a vantage from which to view the Lake?"

She blushed. "Forgive me, Alana, but I am very curious. I have never seen this many people by the Lake before—not even for my wedding." She paled then.

Alana's expression was sharp enough an unwary person could cut themselves to bone on it. "Na'dio," she said sternly, "I am pleased to see that you are capable of playing these games. A little more of them and perhaps you would not be where you have been these many months." She frowned. "However, they are not meant to be used against women unless you feel the woman in question is as much a fool as the men."

She bowed meekly, hiding her expression.

"But because it has been so long since you have ventured out in polite company, I will take no insult from your attempt to manipulate me. And because I am indulgent and old—and far more important, because *I* am curious—I will even consider it."

"What game are they playing?" The question was softly asked, the edges hidden. The Lyserran Matriarch seldom spoke when the Matriarchs gathered, possibly because it involved a contest of volume and raised voices, or perhaps because speech depended upon the ability to slide words into the cracks between shouting. Obvious scorn and derision didn't hurt either.

Unfortunately for the Matriarch, these skills had never been encouraged; she was very much the elegant Serra and very little the fishwife. Jewel was reminded of this, however, only when she did speak. Even at her sharpest, she was deceptively quiet.

"Not sure," Jewel said, as the Serra was staring directly at her. "But we were there. My Torra's not up to court intrigues, but I can get the small words. Kallandras and I went as far as the gates, but we didn't have the masks on hand; they turned us back. We've got every reason to believe if we'd been carrying masks, they'd've let us in with the rest of the crowd. And before you ask, everyone seemed to be leaving. Most of them were quiet on the way out—good quiet not bad quiet. Almost contemplative. Whoever this guy is, this is the first politically smart thing I've seen him do."

That got a look from Yollana that gave new meaning to the phrase "if looks could kill." She heard Kallandras whisper, *Have a care, ATerafin; Yollana was guest in the Tor, and only for the preservation of her children would she put aside the desire for the destruction of the current ruler of the Dominion.*

She had no way of questioning him in as unheard a fashion, but the emphasis on the word guest made the situation quite clear.

"There was one odd thing," she continued, letting her gaze hit the dirt within which a special fire was encircled. "They were talking about the blessing that the Lady gave or withheld. It seems that in some cases, when the Festival masks were offered to the water—"

"They were *what?*"

"They were consumed by fire. It was as if, or so the partici-
pants said, the Lake itself rejected the work." She drew breath.
"And in every case, the mask was one that had been given out for
free by men who claimed to be working at the behest of the
Tyr'agar himself. He is said to be in quiet fury, but to be grateful
to the Lady for the protection She affords Her loyal followers.

"And I have no doubt that he'll empty the Tor of at least half of
the existing masks by tomorrow morning; apparently this added
festivity is to continue until the Festival Moon shows itself.
But . . . and correct me if I'm wrong, please . . . doesn't this work
in *our* favor?"

"Indeed," the Serra Maria said, and Jewel bit her tongue even
though she hadn't used the title itself, because it was almost impossible to think of this woman in any other way, and it was the
wrong way to think in this camp. "That *was* behind my question."

"And if you'd speak half plainly, that might have been clear,"
Elsarre snapped. Probably, in Jewel's opinion, because she was
irked at the fact that the Serra Maria seemed to already have the
information that Jewel had only just presented.

The Serra declined to notice the remark; it was easy enough to
do—it had no information content that needed to be acknowledged. Well, all right, Jewel amended silently, it probably wasn't
all that easy to do; she'd about had enough of Elsarre's snappish-
ness and in Maria's position would have already returned it in
kind or hit her by now. It was the *graceful* thing to do, however.
Too bad grace was so underappreciated.

Margret snapped at Elsarre in Maria's stead. Elsarre snapped
back. They continued in this friendly fashion while Maria and
Yollana said nothing. It was to Yollana that Jewel turned.

The oldest of the Matriarchs fumbled a moment with the
pouch at her side, her hands carefully unclasping and unbuckling
worn metal. A quiet descended around her; she was unhurried,
her every movement deliberate. She seemed, for that instant, to
be *the* wisewoman, with a bag that contained magic, treasure,
mystery.

Or a pipe. Jewel rolled her eyes. But as the old woman worked
dried leaves into the bowl, she was reminded of the only other
person who consistently smoked a pipe when the discussion
turned to matters arcane—and disastrous. Meralonne APhaniel.
The biggest difference was that she didn't just snap her fingers
and summon a fire; there was a fire before her—one that had the

advantage of being made by someone else's labor—and a few
slender sticks, and she made use of both. Yollana was practical.

Practical, cantankerous, so Oma-like in her demeanor that one
could almost forget that she was also Matriarch, and of them, the
one with the most blood on her hands.

As if the stray thought were words, and those words loudly
spoken, Yollana looked across the fire to Jewel. For just a moment,
Jewel could see the menace that lines and chosen demeanor hid; the
ferocity behind the face; the woman who would do *anything* at all
to save her children.

Anything but walk hand in hand with the Lord of Darkness.
Anything but leave the *Voyanne*. It chilled her. Because the
thoughts—as they so often did—came from nowhere, and once
there, they took root. They were true. She *knew* it.

"I think," Yollana said quietly, "that the Lord of Darkness has
a short memory indeed if He expects any alliance He makes with
the men of power in these lands to prevail."

Serra Maria started, and then, to Jewel's surprise, she laughed
out loud. Her voice, rich and deep in laughter, sounded like a
stranger's voice—a hidden glimpse of a woman who only rarely
revealed herself.

"It's good to see you laugh," Yollana said, her tone implying
the opposite.

"I think," the Serra said, sobering almost instantly, "that if we
are very lucky and very successful, the Dominion will not regret
his rulership half as much as he will. He did not choose wisely
when he chose to make an enemy of you."

"He'll have other things to worry about." But watching the
pipe smoke wreath the old woman's face, Jewel wasn't as certain. "And besides, I bear him no personal ill-will."

"No?"

"No."

"Then?"

"The Sword's Edge."

Elsarre's low whistle spoke for them all. "Pick a different
enemy, Yollana. That one—"

"Enemies are made by their actions." The Havallan Matriarch
shrugged. "They are never truly *chosen*. Our enemies, by their
actions, appear to be divided. Let us move quickly, Sisters. Let us
take advantage of their division as we have always done."

Margret, who had been silent until now, rose. "The Serra Teresa and Kallandras are waiting," she said quietly. "Let us see them off, and then feed the children."

The Serra Diora di'Marano understood the powers of the Lake. She understood the properties of the water that both prolonged life and offered health to those who were powerful enough to claim it.

But the understanding that she claimed was silent, personal, private; she did not speak of it as she stood beside the oldest of her father's wives; the oldest of her many mothers or sisters. Alana en'Marano was, herself, stunned into a wary silence as they crested the hill that formed a natural crown to the Lake. The sun faceted the waters; the winds rippled them.

The Serra Diora di'Marano had been married in front of these waters; handed from father to husband in a ceremony that extended as far back as the history of the Dominion under the rule of the clan Leonne. She had made the most important move in the game that would—for better and worse—define what remained of her life standing in them, dressed in the white and the gold that had been Fredero kai el'Sol's gift to her. The dress, of course, was gone; if she closed her eyes and tried to summon it, feel or look, she could no longer clearly separate it from the equally fine gown in which she had been married.

But his last gift she could not forget—and she was torn between trying and vowing not to. That, too, had been offered her in these waters. With no blood to succor him, and no divine blessing to strengthen his hand, he had *drawn* the Sun Sword from its scabbard.

And the Sword, instrument of the Lord's indifferent wrath—and He must be indifferent, for no god could judge the former kai el'Sol's service so poorly otherwise—had devoured him; the winds had carried his ashes away.

Yet for all that, she had not given the Lake what it was given now: respect, awe, fear, hope—and tears. She found the tears both distasteful and fascinating; she had spent so little time among the common clansmen. The serafs with whom she had been surrounded would have been as disgraced by such a display of overt emotion as she herself

Although it was a miracle, it had become a commonplace part of her life; even in captivity, she had been brought the waters of this Lake from time to time, depending on the importance of the visitor.

But she watched, now, as a small child approached the ebbing flow of water between sand and rock. Each face the Lake presented was different, as was each view. The Tyr'agar had chosen the area in which Festivals were both opened and closed to accommodate those thousands upon thousands who now made the trek from the city below to the palace above, clutching masks of varying degrees of complexity in their different hands.

This small child, hands clutching something that was supple and shapeless, knelt and began pulling small rocks out of their bed in the sand. It was hard, at this distance, to tell whether that child was boy or girl; not hard to discern that he or she had been born to a level of poverty that often meant indenture in later years.

She saw so few children now her eyes were drawn to the child; held there by the determined grimace on his or her little face. It was beautiful in an entirely different way from the Lake, and it allowed for no circumstance in which such vandalism was unacceptable. The Lake was not a special lake; it was a body of water in front of which sand and stone were set for his or her purpose.

She wondered where he had seen so much water to be so immune to the awe of it, and then realized that he was not immune; he was giving the Lake the only tribute a small child can; he was attempting to play at its edge. She waited as the inevitable occurred; the child edged forward a step; two steps. The foot found water, and then withdrew, came closer, found water, and withdrew more slowly.

She heard the sudden roar of the crowd; the word *fire* carried up the hill on a dozen voices, and carried back down again on one: Alana's hands were cupped over her mouth to stop anything else from escaping. Diora looked away from the concentric circles spreading out from the child as he dropped rock into water with a grave satisfaction and watched the effects.

A man now stood cowering on the simple, wide platform that had been set up for the commoners to stand on. The people to either side of him had pressed as far into the crowd as they could; he sat alone, his hands upon his face. She heard his cries of shock and denial. Heard the terror in them; the certainty of death, the desperate, and undignified attempt to escape it.

But the death did not come.

Instead, his cries were followed by the raised voice of a man who could only be Radann. She did not recognize the cadence of his voice immediately, but it came to her: Peder kai el'Sol. The force of his oratory carried across the murmurs and the little shocked cries of his audience. She spared them all a glance, but her eyes were drawn to the boy. To the child.

He was in the water now, to his knees. The Lake lapped against his thighs and torso before she realized that he could not know how to swim. She turned to the cerdan. "Karras," she said quietly, "please."

"Serra?" His eyes were on the spectacle and not upon its fringes.

She started to order him down to retrieve the foolish child, but the words did not make it past her lips. The boy was in the water. The boy was not allowed to stand in the water. He did not carry the blood of kings in his veins. He was not the Consort. Not a priest.

"Serra?"

"It is . . . nothing."

She scanned the crowd; she could not tell who, on its fringes, the boy might belong to. In truth, he might have come up to the plateau heedless of his parents, or unaware of them; the tide of moving bodies was a strong pull.

"Na'dio?" Alana came forward; touched Diora's shoulder and arm. "Na'dio, what is it, what is wrong?" But her gaze was turned to fire; turned to the fate of the man whose mask had somehow been refused irrevocably by the Lady's decree.

"There is—" she fell silent.

"There is what? What do you hear? I'm old, my ears are poor. What has happened with that mask?"

"I think it best," the Serra replied demurely, "that we listen to the words of the Radann; he is a man of the Lord and surely fire is also the Lord's dominion. He is no doubt explaining the meaning of this miracle and this sign."

Alana's eyes narrowed, but her harem child's face was serene and beautiful; mild in the shade provided by their seraf. "Na'dio," she began.

"Alana," the Serra Diora said, her eyes upon the Lake, "it is best that we watch, I think, and speak little." So easy to say. So easy.

She watched the little boy, now up to his arms, no attention upon him. All eyes were turned to the Radann who had now mounted a pedestal; who spoke of the coming of the Lord of Night, and the appointing of a new Tyr who might be strong enough to *fight* him. Clever, she thought it, but idly.

The boy would drown.

If she did not interfere.

No mother could go in after him. Where a child might—barely—be excused such an act of sacrilege, an adult, no matter what her reason, would not. These were the waters of the Lady.

Lady, she thought, *give me a sign.*

The child stumbled.

She froze; it was the sign she had asked for, but it was not the sign she desired. She had been a fool to pray to the Lady while the Lord reigned. Her mouth opened slightly, so slightly that Alana did not notice it. Neither did the cerdan, whose attention, like Alana en'Marano's was upon the spectacle that they had come to witness.

The child fell, and when he attempted to right himself, the water's ledge deepened. She knew what would happen next. She had asked for a sign, and she was given it, and she turned away.

And then, jaw clenched, she turned *back*.

The child did not know how to swim.

But the Serra Diora di'Marano had been taught by her husband, her little loved, very important husband. He had been truly delighted to be able to teach her something she did not know; to see her graceless and flailing as she attempted to find solidity and purchase in a medium that offered none.

And she had learned, laughing with feigned delight, silent with genuine fear, to navigate the treachery of water as if it were solid. What had she learned? That it would support her weight if she worked with it, obeyed its rules; that she would sink like a stone if she did not.

But stone could be retrieved whole and unharmed from the depths of the clear, clear water; not so small boys.

She *spoke.* Her throat was too thick for words, but the words had to be forced out.

Because the child could not swim, and she could, and she could force him, through strength of will and curse of gift alone, to do what must be done.

"Do not breathe," she said first. **"Hold your breath and stop flailing."** The boy had no choice; he held his breath; his body relaxed. **"Now,"** she said, and the words stuck a moment as he floated limply in the water, **"turn over."**

He turned. He was facing the wrong direction, but she righted him, using a voice that was implacable. He had no choice but to obey her; she had no choice but to use that obedience. It no longer bothered her to watch him cough and struggle; it only mattered that he do it on land, near sand and stone, where someone—where anyone—might notice him. The waters were like the Lady; they were necessary, but in cases like this they seldom offered a second chance. No sharp edges, this; no fire, no arrow's head, no warrior-dealt death—but death, just the same.

"Na'dio?" her father's oldest wife said, but her voice, cracked by age and wind, was distant. Diora did not speak; she did not allow her voice or her attention to waver. She brought the child by slow degrees to the edge of the Lake, and then, beyond it.

She forced him to approach the crowd held spellbound by the Radann's harsh words, and she finally heard the words that would release her from her own.

But she could not quite hear what they were. A mother's words. A mother's terror and fear and guilt and anger.

She wondered what the boy would tell his mother.

And what the mother would say in return, if she said anything at all.

Her legs were weak. Not from effort, although the effort was there. Not from exertion. But she wondered if it would happen this way every time she was foolishly moved to risk herself by saving the life of a stranger: the horrible guilt, the self-loathing, as she confronted the fact again, and again: she had not raised her voice to save the people who had become the center of her life.

The wind whirled around her face, a cool and welcome breeze. And she heard, from across the Lake, something else that was almost as welcome.

"Well done, Na'dio."

Ona Teresa.

Lady, she thought, *I asked for a sign, and maybe you have no sign to give me but this.* She looked up again, and the boy, carried by his mother, was almost invisible beneath the dark length of her wild hair. His arms disappeared into it, and his face was obviously buried against her throat. She held him on the shelf of her hip, oblivious to the fact that he was wet, and perhaps oblivious to the fact that he had committed a capital crime.

The fires erupted again as the Lake denied a slender white mask not only entry but existence. But although the fire held everyone mesmerized, it could not pull Diora away from the contemplation of what she had done.

The contemplation of what was left *to* do.

She wondered where the rest of the Radann were.

* * *

Samadar's time on the front during the border war with the
Northern Empire had left him with a permanent limp; the twelve
and a half years since that battle had not worsened it. He had
learned, with will and exercise, to mask it during all but the most
grueling of physical activities, and as he was Radann, he traveled
on horseback when any great distance was involved.

But he had assiduously avoided giving challenge or accepting
it in all but a handful of cases; he was no longer young. Where he
could, he substituted prudence and wisdom for the strength, the
endurance, and the speed of youth, but he lacked the ferocity and
the *swiftness* that had once made him the most noteworthy of the
Radann.

And yet, lacking that, he managed to avoid the set of unnatural
claws that came swinging for the side of his neck and got lodged
instead in the side of a building. And when he rolled out from
under them, *Mordagar* took half of the creature's chest.

A man would have been dead.

The demon was simply angry. He *roared*.

Samadar roared back, but his voice formed the syllables of a
name. *Mordagar*.

Two people lay dead at the hands of the demon; the creature
had lain in wait—as, indeed, the kai el'Sol and the Tyr'agar had
guessed one might—along the path that led to the plateau. It was
not in the best interests of the demons to allow their masks to be
destroyed by the combined efforts of the Lord and the Lady, and
it was easy enough to scare the common clansmen into immo-
bility or flight.

The kai el'Sol had remained upon the plateau as a symbol of
the strength of the Lord; the par el'Sol now scanned the streets,
waiting, watching.

The Radann in this case had an advantage that they had previously lacked. The creature had taken no pains to hide its true
nature. Instead, it had suddenly emerged in the midst of the long
procession, unfolding to a full eight feet in height as it casually
reached out with its blade-length claws and speared the two
closest people by their throats.

They gurgled and died in full view of the people who intended
to reach the plateau. Those people hesitated a moment in silence
before the screaming began.

And by that time, Samadar had reached the demon. He wore
full armor, and as much regalia as a man could competently fight

in: the Sun ascendant adorned his chest and back, the eight rays emblazoned in gold, the curve of the sword beneath the high sun embroidered in shining silver. As background, instead of the darker blue favored by the former kai el'Sol, the Radann par el'Sol now wore azure. They looked like the Hand of God.

They served as protectors, but more: they made the symbol of both their office and the office of the Tyr the symbol of protection against the predations of creatures such as this. For the only people who did not flee—toward the Lake if they were closer, away if they were on the opposite side of the demon—were the Radann.

From a safe distance, Samadar gathered an audience.

And, taking up his sword in the empty space fear made between himself and his enemy, he became the root of legend, a part of the history of the Tor that would—whether he survived or no—be carried from the mouths of these witnesses to their children, and their children's children, and on, until it served as a reminder of valor, and a game for children to play at: I'll be the Radann. You can be the demon.

If any of the witnesses survived the Festival of the Moon.

Mordagar flashed; a challenge.

The demon smiled; with a casual flick of the wrists, he disposed of the stilling bodies. He spoke in a language that Samadar did not recognize. *Mordagar* did. Blade hit claw, claw skirted the surface of arm, ripped surcoat; they met, and Samadar forgot his age; forgot his reluctance to join battle with those who were larger and faster, who were stronger, whose endurance had not been worn, like rock, by sand and wind.

He had passed the test of the fires every year he had faced them; he passed them now with a wild certainty that he would never face them again as anything other than a child's echo of the real war.

But first: survival.

He wondered, briefly, if the others fared as well as he.

"There's trouble."

Kallandras stopped. He had been in mid-step before the words left her mouth—she was certain he had—but there was no telling now; he had come to a complete stop with ease and grace, turning to face her as if that had been his intent all along.

"ATerafin?"

"I think Avandar and the Serra should go ahead to the Founts."

Avandar folded his arms across his chest. But he did not gainsay her, and she thanked *Kalliaris*—if *Kalliaris* could even hear her in a land where foreign gods were said to rule—for the small mercy.

"And you," he said calmly.

"Kallandras and I are—"

Fire erupted a hundred yards away.

"Going there."

"Jewel—"

"Both of the circles are cracked," she told him, without taking her eyes from the flowering plume that seemed to go on and on.

Avandar did her a second grace; he took her word. "Jewel."

"Yes?"

"Be careful. It might be best that you meet us directly at the Southern Fount."

She nodded absently, her face as focused and still as it ever got. "Southern Fount. Got it."

Then she turned, and she bowed, stopping her hand from making the automatic Northern salute that passed between political equals. "Serra," she said quietly.

The fire banked; the screams did not.

"ATerafin," Kallandras called, and as she turned away from the brief farewell, she saw that he had drawn both of his weapons. she nodded and he took the lead, navigating the streets as if he'd been born to them.

And for all she knew, he had.

CHAPTER THIRTY-TWO

They found a man lying facedown upon the cobbled stone. Blood pooled beneath him. Kallandras barely broke stride to look down; Jewel's knees were at half bend when he shook his head. She stopped a second longer and then nodded to herself, but as she followed Kallandras, she thought that death should have more meaning than a curt half-shake of the head.

And it would. It would have meaning for someone else: Mother or father, brother or sister, wife, child, friend. She followed Kallandras as quickly as she could—which wasn't as hard as she'd feared. The streets, normally so busy with stall and hamper and basket, so crowded with merchants and men who couldn't keep their hands to themselves unless they were staring at guards with long swords, had suddenly emptied. Two doors slammed shut before she reached them. It angered her, even though she had no intention of seeking shelter. There would have been more, she was certain, but doors in this part of the Tor were rare. There were open stone arches, or simple wooden frames that held either hanging or sliding screens.

But these, too, were pulled close and wedged tight.

What did you expect, she heard her grandmother's voice say, the distance of years made small and insignificant by the steps of an unusual journey. *People aren't ugly; fear is. But some fears are very, very ugly.*

Maybe I'd hoped that people wouldn't give in to their fears so easily?

So says the girl who can't be killed unless she ignores all her instincts.

Shut up, Oma.

Kallandras rounded a corner. She followed.

There was almost no one in the street. Even the windows above the ground were empty—when they were open at all. Jewel could almost hear the frantic whispers or hysterical cries that the buildings enclosed. Here, it was easy. There were very few doors.

But, she thought, if she were one of the people huddled in buildings this close to the creature that suddenly came into view, she would have kept on running. She didn't trust stone or wood to provide any defense against the obviously magical. And the creature was obviously magical; there was nothing human about it. Not even its form was human in proportion. Most of the demons Jewel had had the misfortune to meet had at least boasted arms and legs and torso in roughly normal proportions. This was like a giant cat, one with scales instead of fur and eyes that were as red as poppies.

She started to speak when the second such creature came into her view; stopped moving when the third followed. And in their center, sword literally awash in blue flame, was a bleeding, armored man. He was whole; he was standing. That said something. She was certain without intervention both of those states would be rectified by the creatures who hunted him now.

"ATerafin," Kallandras said.

She met his gaze.

"Do we require him?"

"What?"

"Do we need him?"

"Kallandras, how can you even ask a question like that? He's—"

"ATerafin, we do not have the time or the luxury for this argument. My apologies. **Do we need this man?**"

"I—*yes.*"

He nodded then, and the weapons in his hands flashed. The man she did not recognize, the newcomer who had managed to hold his own against three demons, held a sword whose light was somehow compelling. She found it both beautiful and uplifting. Not so the weapons that Kallandras held. She promised herself that she'd never ask him where he got them from.

And reminded herself that she trusted him completely.

She watched him take to the cobbled field as if he were an army. He walked directly; he did not seek shadows or subterfuge. The creatures were intent on their kill, the way cats might be with mice if mice had fangs, and they assumed that any would-be help had fled.

Their second mistake. Their first had been to come here at all. She watched, fascinated, as Kallandras calmly walked up to the closest creature and severed its spine. It happened so quickly she almost couldn't understand what she'd seen; his funny long knives rose two feet in clenched fists and fell two and a half; he twisted them neatly and brought them out in those same fists— but his wrists were now crossed.

The creature *screamed* and began to writhe and twist as it turned to face its unseen attacker. Kallandras circled slowly until his back was exactly toward Jewel ATerafin; there he stopped, weapons held out to either side as carelessly as if they were gloves. The demon roared and bore down upon the slender bard; he held his ground.

Jewel watched Kallandras' back, wondering what he saw as the creature charged. She should have been afraid for him, but the bard appeared so relaxed that meeting bloodthirsty demons in the Dominion's capital seemed almost an everyday event, like shopping in the Common.

When he finally moved, he shifted position very slightly; the dagger arms came up. She couldn't actually see what followed, but an educated guess—from the way a roar stopped in mid bellow—made it fairly clear that they were now down a demon.

Kallandras stepped back. He watched the man with the sword very carefully, and after a moment, he turned to Jewel. "ATerafin," he said quietly. "I think our work here is done for now. The Radann par el'Sol is capable of—ah, you see?"

The blue blade slide through bone and cartilage.

Jewel followed the roll of the resultant bodiless head along the uneven ground. "Good point."

She turned away.

And then turned back.

"Bard!"

The last of the demons lay aground. Jewel watched it in fascination. And watched. And watched.

"Kallandras?" She was certain that the creature was as dead as demons ever got.

"I see it," he said softly. He looked up at the man who had called him by profession if not name, and nodded slightly. Acknowledging an equal, an ally, or a worthy enemy—in the Dominion these things were almost identical. And then he went one step further. "Marakas."

Jewel slapped her forehead. "Is there *anyone* you don't know?" She said out of the corner of her mouth.

"Many people," the bard replied. "And in truth, I would not

say that I know this one at all well. Perhaps once, but people change with time and responsibility. But it is too late; we cannot flee one of the Radann par el'Sol; if they choose, they can make our lives very difficult."

"I think," Jewel said, looking at the bodies that had not yet dissolved into the nothing that she associated with dead demons, "They have other things to worry about."

Kallandras smiled. There was no mirth in the expression. But he stood his ground, and Jewel noticed that his weapons had disappeared back into their sheaths. He was an unarmed, simple clansmen with hair a trifle darker than she was used to.

The man Kallandras had called Marakas par el'Sol stopped ten feet short of them both and bowed. The bow was deeper than Kallandras' nod. "I owe you my life."

"There is no guarantee that you would not have prevailed without my intervention."

"And you believe that?"

Kallandras chose not to answer.

The silence was terrible. Jewel broke it. "So," she said, "how many of these creatures have you faced lately, and do all of their bodies stay behind?"

The phrase "looked down his nose" had never been so appropriate. Kallandras said, in Weston, and in a voice that clearly did not carry to anyone but herself, "You are a clanswoman in the Dominion. Think before you speak."

Jewel bit her tongue and briefly regretted saving the man's life. But only briefly. Marakas said, "I have news. The Voyani woman—"

"We know."

The man looked away. "I did not know," he said softly.

"She knew. Her death?"

"It was . . . clean. In the end, it was clean."

"And how did she die?"

"Bard—"

"You gave your word that you would do what was necessary to protect her."

"I gave my word that I would do what was within my power. But when the time came—" The man with the sword looked away.

So did Jewel. The bodies of the demons were finally, slowly, dissolving.

Neither the bard nor the man dressed in what was left of a blue surcoat seemed to notice. Men.

She wanted to ask Kallandras what in the Hells was going on—but she bit her tongue and swallowed the words. It wasn't particularly enjoyable, and as an experience it was one she'd decided against repeating, but Yollana had pronounced her unfit to be a boy, which was particularly mortifying given that the graceful and elegant Serra Teresa strode the streets like a man. Some things made no sense.

"When the time came," the Radann said quietly, "she knew what had to be done."

Kallandras said, "Man of the Lord, *she* did not give her oath. *You* did."

Marakas par el'Sol fell to one knee in the empty street. Jewel heard the windows flap open at her back. "Kallandras," she whispered. "These streets aren't going to be empty for long."

"No." His pale eyes stayed on the face of the wounded man. "You did not know who she was, Radann, but you understood that you fought the same enemy. In her position, you would have died the same death. But you have broken faith."

"Faith is often broken," the man replied, "in dark times. She knew."

"Yes. She knew. But she depended upon you to remember your oath, for in a fashion you will be called upon to fulfill it."

"Fulfill it? Nothing of her remains, Bard. There is nothing to escort to safety."

"You are wrong."

"I *saw* her body. Had I been able to call her back from the edge, I *would have done it.*"

Kallandras smiled; it was a cool expression. "And then, Radann par el'Sol, you *would* have died. There are things that it is not safe for such a woman to share, and attached to you after the healing, or no, she would know it. She was the Mother of her family."

He looked up as if struck.

"Yes," Kallandras said quietly.

The Radann stood, and it seemed to Jewel that he stood taller. "Very well. The time?"

"I believe, if I am not mistaken, you will know. I believe, if I am not mistaken, that you already have a greater understanding of the situation than we do. You know what must be done, or you do not—I am forbidden to speak of it. But if you know, discharge your oath; the Lady is watching, and the Lord remembers what was promised."

The man bowed. "It will be as I have vowed." He looked, only then, at the empty streets. "For I fear it is our fate to perish here, in defense of the Lord in the Tor Leonne itself, and if we are gone—the Voyani and the servants of the Lady are our best hope. The Radann will never willingly or knowingly serve the Lord of Night again."

"Indeed," Kallandras said softly. "But what is done in ignorance is still done, and someone still pays the price for it."

He turned. "Come, Jewel."

"What was all that about?"

Kallandras said nothing.

"Kallandras?"

"If I am not mistaken, you will come to understand the exchange quite well."

"Great. Is *everyone* playing the cryptic game?"

He caught her arm, moving so swiftly she actually let out a squeal of shock. "It is time that we return to meet Avandar," he said quietly, "and it is therefore time that you remember your place. The streets will not remain empty, and our presence here has almost certainly been noted. We have very little time, Jewel ATerafin. When we are almost upon the Southern Fount, I will create a diversion. Take advantage of it, and flee."

"What?"

He did not repeat himself; he knew that he had been heard.

Lord Ishavriel felt the deaths of the three.

They had been his for centuries, perhaps longer; they had chosen to bind themselves, by blood and oath, to his will rather than face destruction. He had taken them as a matter of course after the death of his liege, and the taking had nearly killed him, for they masked their power and their intelligence well. He had succeeded in the binding, however, and over time he had learned to value their existence. They were mindless in their obedience— but they *were* obedient. They did not have the strength of will or mind to plot against him or to politic in the fashion of the greater lieutenants.

And in areas where obedience was of importance, he brought them.

They were gone. He was not certain of the manner of their death, although he could guess; he had seen—in the brief moments he spared them—the Radann. The blades, the old blades, had lost none of their power; they had wakened early. He had not expected that.

A day as unfortunate as this had not occurred in his entire existence in the service of the Lord's justice, in the Hells. Anya was nowhere in sight; she evaded him and she had become crafty; she no longer burned stone, no longer boiled water; no one was foolish enough—apparently—to touch her, for she had left no trail of bodies in her wake; none, certainly, as she had in the disaster that had drawn their attention to her absence.

Anya, he called.

"Yes, Anya, the child will be . . . well."

Anya looked at the little girl who, swathed in soft bandages, lay sleeping on the pallet. "You're sure?" she demanded, her eyes narrowed as she glared at the Lord Isladar. She had to work hard to remember that he was a demon. He wasn't very ugly—like Etridian or Nugratz—and he almost always spoke in Weston— real Weston, not the demon-speak that made their awful words sound normal.

"Yes, Anya, I am certain. The physician has been very careful. Please—it would be a pity for you to kill him. He has helped you save her life, and when we leave, he has promised to protect the child."

"You can't trust them." She told him this as she looked at the doctor's face. He was an old man, not as old as her father—and she didn't want to think of her father here.

So she melted a small section of the wall. Just a small section. Not enough to make it all shatter or fall down. "I promised her," she told the doctor, who was sitting with his back to the wall. "I promised that she would be safe.

"But I promised, and she doesn't look well."

The doctor swallowed.

"Why is she sleeping so much?"

He glanced at Isladar out of the corner of his eyes. *"Look at me when I talk to you,"* she told him. She made a mistake, and the wall cracked. She *hated* making mistakes.

"Isladar?"

"Yes, Anya?"

"Go and get me the other one."

There was a momentary silence. Then, he bowed; she heard the rustle of his very boring, very plain clothing. "What?"

"I'm sorry, Anya, but when you collapsed the big archway, the other one died. You can kill this one if you like, but then there will be no one to take care of the little girl."

"But where *is* everybody? There's hardly anyone out in the streets. Where have all the people gone? It was crowded yesterday."

"Yes. And the day before."

She turned to the doctor. "Tell me where everyone is."

"Serra," he began.

"I'm not *Sara*, I'm *Anya*."

Rock trickled down the wall in a lovely orange stream. She wanted something bigger, but she had to be careful not to hit the pallet the girl was sleeping on.

The physician closed his eyes. He was afraid. She knew he was afraid. It made her angry. Did he think that she was a monster? That she would just kill him?

Well, she might, if that's the way he felt about it. If that was the kind of person he was, people would be better off without him. She could kill him and—and then he wouldn't answer her question.

"You," she said.

"Y–yes."

"*Where* has everyone gone?"

He dipped his head, staring at the ground a moment. "To the Lake," he said at last. "To the Lady's Lake."

"To the what?"

"Anya," Isladar said quietly, "the man is clearly tired from his exertions. It is very difficult to save the life of an injured child, especially when the injury is caused by fire. I believe that he is telling you all that he knows; you cannot expect more."

"I can't?"

"Well, you can if you'd like, but I don't think that more will be forthcoming. I have been in the Tor Leonne several times, and perhaps *I* can answer your question. If that is acceptable to you."

She thought about it for a minute. Looked at the child whose breathing was *still* not quite right. "All right. You can answer my questions.

"But I'm hungry. Should we go home and eat?"

"As you like, Anya," Isladar said softly. "Perhaps that would be best. I believe that Lord Ishavriel is looking for you."

"Oh, that's *right.*"

"Anya," Lord Isladar said, in a tone of voice that would have bothered her had it come from anyone else, "He *is* your Lord."

"I know that. But . . . he doesn't want me here in this city, and I promised the girl I would take care of her. She isn't well, but *I* keep my promises. I said I would protect her, you know. We'll stay here. I'm sure there's food here. Tell me," she added, as she started to look for doors, "about this Lake."

She very casually made a door in the wall, protecting herself from falling rubble as she walked beneath a shaky, unnatural arch.

They met at the Southern Fount. Avandar was standing just inside the open gates which framed the Fount as Jewel approached it from the North. The Serra Teresa was sitting on the edge of the wide, simple basin into which water trickled. The statue, here as in the Northern Fount, was of a human figure, worked in stone, but where the Northern statue had been stark and simple, this was an artist's rendition of a very beautiful, older woman. Her chin was neither too wide nor too narrow, but Her cheekbones were high and Her nose was patrician; Her eyes, wide, stared out at the city that would soon celebrate her mysteries.

Or be killed by them.

"Well?" Avandar said quietly as they approached.

Jewel shrugged. "I'm not sure."

"You're not sure?"

"Well, there was a demon. Three actually."

"And?"

"There was also a man—one of the priests of the local god— who had actually managed to fend them off."

"Three?" Avandar raised a brow. "Impressive."

"Kallandras stepped in to help." Jewel glanced around, looking for the bard. "But . . ."

"But?" Avandar frowned. "Where is Kallandras?"

In the distance, as if in answer to his question, a cry was raised in rapid Torra.

Jewel cringed. "We've finished, right?"

"We had finished what we set out to accomplish, yes."

"Good."

"Good?"

"We have to get out of here."

"Wonderful. What did you do?"

"I didn't do anything. Kallandras killed a demon—but he thinks we *may* have noticed. He—" Her curls fell into her eyes as she swiveled her neck to look over her shoulder. "I think we need to find a set of masks."

"Jewel—"

"I don't know about anyone else, but I'd like to take a look at that Lake."

Avandar glanced up at a sky that was deepening in color. "It will wait," he said quietly.

"It won't wait," she replied. "Because, like it or not, I think the gates are going to be guarded against us. We can leave—but not without a big display of fireworks."

"Our work here is finished," Avandar said. He didn't add, because he didn't have to, that it no longer mattered whether they drew attention to themselves or not.

"It's not." She drew a deep breath, keeping pace with the flow of words that were taking her someplace she couldn't quite see. "But we're going to need time and money."

"Oh?"

"We can't go up the hill without a mask. I don't know about you, but the last time I checked I wasn't much of a craftsman, and I have a hunch that we don't want to cross the gates carrying something obviously magical. I could be wrong."

He frowned. "I would tell you that sarcasm doesn't suit you—"

"But you've done it so often you know better than to waste your breath."

To her great surprise, the Serra Teresa said, "There is a place we may retire to."

Avandar was less than pleased, but he was also surprised. "Serra?" he asked, speaking with a measure of respect that he seldom afforded his chosen master.

"I believe that I, too, would like to see the Lady's Lake." She looked back at the Fount; they could no longer see her expression. "I doubt I will have the opportunity to see it again, and I would like to . . . say my farewells."

Avandar offered no argument against her words, and because they suited Jewel so well, neither did she. But she heard what Avandar could not hear, and what, she suspected, no one else except Kallandras would either: The Serra Teresa was lying.

She led them to a large building that housed, from the look of it, many a poor family. The building itself was unlike the large structures in which Jewel ATerafin's den had made their home; it was open in several places to the sky and the sun, and a huge courtyard—in which children were running and screaming under the watchful eyes of a set of adults who may, or may not have been, their parents—seemed to dominate the landscape. Doors faced inward, to the courtyard, but they were Southern doors; arches with hangings. No fancy screens, not here.

The Serra Teresa did not alter her stride, and the children scattered, maintaining a watchful distance as she passed them. That distance increased dramatically when Avandar followed in her steps, and decreased almost as dramatically when Jewel, bringing up the rear, closed the feeble gate behind them.

She was not tall, and Avandar's stride was long; she had to scurry along like a small child after an angry parent. This annoyed her. So her steps were heavier than they might otherwise have been. But her obvious anger meant nothing to the children; they closed again at her back, as if they were a curtain.

They made their way to a small room, beyond which another room lay, and in that second room was a table. There was food on it.

The Serra Teresa entered the room and stared at the table. Then she lifted her face and began to loosen the severe knot that held her hair so tightly.

Jewel, hungry in spite of herself, stepped into the room and saw, beside the door, the Serra Teresa's seraf, Ramdan.

"How did you know?" Jewel asked.

"Know? That we would stay here? I did not. This . . . place . . . has been mine for some time now. My nature is such that there was always the risk of necessary and unplanned flight, and I thought it wise, many years ago, to purchase a home in the less well-traveled section of the Tor for my personal use.

"Thank you, Ramdan."

The tall man bowed very slowly. "Serra."

"Eat; Ramdan and I will leave shortly to find the masks we require for entrance into the Tor. But if we are not back by the evening, sleep; there are silks and mats in the room beyond Ramdan's back. This is a poor area, but it is not known to be dangerous."

"But—"

She readjusted her hair, and confined it again with a small smile. "No buts. We know the city; you do not. Allow us our small display of hospitality."

Jewel was hungry, and she found it very difficult to argue with the Serra Teresa. She nodded, and together, the Serra and the seraf left them in a room full of food.

"Jewel," Avandar said.

"What? It'll just go bad if we leave it."

But by moon's full height, they had not returned.

He heard the singing in the Tor, and in the procession that led to the Lake. It was a thinner procession than the Tyr'agar would have liked, but a vastly larger one than would have appeared had it not been for the intervention of the Radann. Already, the tales of their prowess had spread, enlarged and made almost ridiculous, through the city streets. It worked to Alesso's advantage.

There were six dead demons.

The Radann Samadar par el'Sol had sustained a severe injury, but it did not seem to slow him; the Radann Marakas par el'Sol had sustained only minor damage, although he had destroyed, by day's end, two of the expensive surcoats that the Radann had been gifted with. The Radann Samiel par el'Sol was bemoaning—in a stately and elegant fashion that still made him sound like a man twenty years younger than his apparent age—the unfairness of his lot, for he had seen none of the kin in his patrols along the crowded route.

"It is because," Marakas par el'Sol said, "your reputation precedes you, as ours does us. They are simply afraid to approach."

Samiel snorted. It was also uncharacteristic; the Radann, as a whole were very changed men. Even the politically shrewd and astute kai el'Sol seemed momentarily pained at the loss of opportunity his role in the Tor had necessitated. Alesso could feel it; this brotherhood that had been cemented by fire and death, by demon, by an enemy so large that politics could be cast aside.

He wondered—if they survived—how they would fall back into their old roles. Because when the battle ended, if they were left standing, that is all that would be left them. He had discovered that, with some bitterness, many years ago. But so, he thought, had these men.

Not for the first time, but for very different reasons, Alesso regretted his inability to wield the Sun Sword in the battle for which it had been forged.

"Gentlemen," he said, rising. "The moon is full. The night has come, and the clansmen are waiting. Let us take our positions again in the darkness."

They drank from the Lady's Lake; they finished the meal—sparse and perfect—that had been prepared for them. Then they rose. "It will be a long night," Alesso said quietly, his hand upon his own sword hilt. "But not as long, I think, as the night of the Festival Moon." He bowed to the Radann; it was both dismissal and thanks, for it was a very deep bow.

21st of Scaral, 427 AA
Shining Palace, Northern Wastes

Cortano di'Alexes watched from the windswept balcony that rested between the narrow spread of diving dragon's wings. The air was very cold; the night as clear a night as any the South could hope to see. Beneath the Shining Palace's height, the city, such as it was, was slowly coming to life. He could see the scuttling movement of creatures who carried long, rough poles with carefully made cressets into which a burning substance had been placed. Not wood, he thought, judging by the light—but what it was, at this distance, was not clear. He wondered if the demons needed the light to see by; there had been no evidence from past behavior to suggest it.

Ritual, then. Ceremony. These things defied sense and logic.

"What—what do they do?" Lady Sariyel's voice was quiet. Steady.

"They line the way," Cortano replied.

The Lady started to speak, and the great beasts roared. She lost all words, and all ability to speak; they seemed to drain from her along with all color. Cortano's hand tugged beard; he did not speak until the shaking of the balcony had passed.

She closed her eyes. "You do not fear them," she said softly.

"I? Any sane man would fear them, Lady Sariyel. And were I to be fed to the great beasts of the Hells, I would certainly . . . show fear." He shrugged. "Perhaps, for the first time since the Lord built this Palace, He will let the beasts rampage. But I believe He will let them go in the streets below, and not within the Court. We, you and I, are too valuable."

The trace of bitterness in the words did not escape her notice.

A knock came at the door. A third man joined them. His hair was dark with white streaks, his face as pale as Lady Sariyel's. "Sword's Edge," he said, bowing in a passable imitation of Southern grace. "Lady."

"Are we summoned?"

"Merely to dine," the man said.

"Krysanthos—I do not think I am hungry."

"Very well. But I would suggest that we eat. Remember, Lady Sariyel, where we are, and who watches. Our fate is not sealed until the Full Moon rises on the morrow." Krysanthos bowed. "I would be honored to be your escort. Sword's Edge?"

"Indeed," Cortano returned the very polite bow. They were not friends, but that was the nature of the Court; friendship could be a costly luxury when this much power was involved. But if they were not friends, they were, at the moment, compatriots by the very grim circumstance in which they found themselves.

"Have any others returned to the Court?"

"No. I believe the summons has gone out—but extricating themselves from their positions would place them in jeopardy, and I believe the Lord is unwilling to expend his power in the opening of the portals necessary to bring them here.

"There are, as you know, very few who can travel as you travel, Widan."

Cortano shrugged off the compliment. "It is unfortunate. Come. Let us eat."

They did not make it out of the room before Krysanthos said, "You have had no word?"

The Sword's Edge smiled grimly. "Yes," he said coldly, "but none that will please any of us. Let us eat. I believe on the morrow we will be . . . summoned. There is an anointing ceremony that is to take place before we can be adequate vessels in the Lord's service."

21st of Scaral, 427 AA
Tor Leonne

Ramdan watched the Serra Teresa in silence. It was a familiar perspective in many ways. He looked at the line of her nose as he watched her bend her face to her hands a moment beneath the clear sky over which the moon reigned.

"Will they forgive me, do you think?"

He did not answer, and after a long moment, she said, "Or is forgiveness, as usual, a thing one can only grant oneself?"

His bow was enough of an answer; her lips curved up in a smile. But she heard an answer, and she rose at once at the sound of the familiar voice.

"Serra," Kallandras of Senniel College said, offering her the most exquisite bow a woman of her station—her previous station—

could hope for. "I do not think they will question you, or even notice the slight deception."

She looked up. In the moonlight she could see blood on his shirt. He did not however seem willing to acknowledge injury or wound, and she was, as his bow reminded her, the Serra Teresa di'Marano. She did not ask.

They were silent as they stood together; it was easy to be silent. The crowd—thinned but not nonexistent—was emboldened by wine and Festival, and they filled the cracks between words with their unhurried noises.

After a few minutes Kallandras said, "The Tyr'agar has generously announced his intent to allow revelers upon the plateau during the actual evening of the Festival Moon."

"Yes," she said softly.

He smiled; the smile was very gentle. "Tell her, Serra."

"Tell her?"

"Tell the Serra Diora to be ready when you arrive."

She closed her eyes; he understood the nature of the deception in its entirety, and he accepted it. Nothing she had done had been done for the approval of anyone save perhaps one dead woman who slept restlessly in every memory that contained her. But she felt her throat close over the words that she might have spoken; pretty words, empty words meant to soothe or dull.

He offered her a hand, and she accepted it, dressed as she was. "I must keep watch," he said quietly. "But find what you purported to seek, and return before the ATerafin panics and sends Avandar, or worse, chooses to travel on her own. It is late enough now that they will not seek camp; they will stay in the Tor and they will travel with you at the appointed hour."

She said, "Thank you."

And because she spoke to Kallandras alone, and in a language that only he would hear and understand, she knew that he heard her; but he did not acknowledge the words in any obvious way.

CHAPTER THIRTY-THREE

22nd of Scaral, 427 AA
Arkosan Camp

Dawn. Margret woke to the sound of a distant argument; she listened with one eyelid open in the darkened wagon, heard a few telltale phrases—about food and time and marriage—and turned over on her side again. That type of argument no one smart interfered with; in the end, the shouter and the shoutee—both women—would make up and forgive each other, but at least one, if not both, would be angry at your interference for the next ten years.

Men could get that wrong on occasion. Some leeway was granted them.

"'Gret!"

No leeway, on the other hand, was granted the Matriarch.

"Go away!"

Light flooded the wagon. "I'm sorry you were too tense to sleep last night," 'Lena said, without any trace of sincerity, "but you can't make up for it this morning. The old witch is after all of us, and I'm not saying no to her. You want to tell her to piss off, you can do it in person."

"If I tell her in person," Margret said, trying—and failing—to cover herself with blankets faster than 'Lena was tossing them aside, "it would kind of defeat the point; I'd have to get up."

"Well, then, I guess you suffer."

Margret glared at her cousin; her cousin laughed. This much was ritual. But there was an edge to 'Lena's laughter that Margret had never heard before, and the circles under her cousin's eyes were very dark. "Didn't you sleep at all?"

"Yeah. Like a rock."

"Great." Margret shrugged herself into clothing while 'Lena

waited. "So we can *both* fall asleep during the most important night of our lives."

Elena laughed. "Every time I fell asleep, I started dreaming, 'Gret. Every time."

"Me too." Margret struggled with her boots and then gave up and let Elena put them on. "I dreamed that people were standing over my coffin and they didn't bloody well listen while I screamed myself hoarse."

"Screamed?"

"I wasn't dead, but it escaped their notice." She forced herself to laugh. It felt . . . fake. Lady, she was tired. "What about you?"

"I dreamed about Nicu."

"I think," Margret said, not meeting 'Lena's eyes, "I'd rather dream about being buried alive."

"You would," 'Lena replied, lifting the back of her hands to rub the sleep out of her eyes. "And we'd both rather have the dreams we had than be late to meet Yollana; come on. Donatella made us food—"

"But she's feeding the children!"

"She says, today, feeding us *is* feeding the children, because if we don't . . . because."

"All right. Food and then Yollana."

It was barely the right order to start the morning with, and apparently *no one* had slept well, at least not to judge by the extremely sour expressions on everyone's faces. Everyone's except the Lyserran Matriarch, who merely looked distant and cool.

The wind on the plain was brisk.

"Word came ahead of Kallandras," Yollana said. "The Serra accomplished her task, and if we are to defend the city itself against whatever it is that's a problem, we're to light the fire before the sun sets and then to make our way to the Founts with the masks the timeless one left us."

Margret looked at the wood. "How long is the fire supposed to last?"

Yollana's gaze was piercing, but it did not linger. "The fire," she said, "will last until dawn. That's what you asked for, didn't you?"

"I—"

"That *is* what you asked for."

"Yollana, I don't remember what I asked for. Whatever it was, it wasn't that specific."

Yollana frowned. "Enough, then. It doesn't matter; the price was paid. We won't know until the morning after the Festival Moon's fall whether or not it was high enough. Get your things; we take our position at the fire's edge and we prepare."

"What else is there to prepare?"

"Ourselves, girl," Yollana said. "Maybe you're not clear on what has to happen—but the masks that the timeless one gave us—they have to go on. Have you looked at them?"

Margret couldn't answer the question. Yollana's words had hit a weakness she hadn't known she had. "We have to wear them?"

"Did you understand nothing you heard?" Elsarre's voice, thin with the same fear that Margret felt.

"I guess not," Margret snapped back. "Maybe if there was a little less jabbering from other quarters, I might have been able to concentrate."

"'Gret," 'Lena spoke out of the corner of her mouth. Elsarre's hands lodged on her hips in a gesture that was familiar to *any* Voyani, no matter what the family. But Yollana's harsh bark brought them both to bear. They went toward the fire that had been laid out like the two strokes of an oath, and they took their places before the wood they had anointed.

And Yollana came forward, hobbling, the canes that she used to support her weight the only aid she would accept. She banished the daughters—which in this case meant shooing them off with the length of the hard wood and, as Elena pointed out, it was called a *hard* wood for a reason—and carried the bag that Evayne had given them in uncharacteristic silence.

She walked first to Elsarre, and from the leather sack, she carefully pulled the first mask. Elsarre reached out to touch it, and then cried out—with something that sounded a bit too much like terror for Margret's liking—and leaped back. Yollana, implacable as high summer sun on a cloudless day, waited, the mask in her hand.

Elsarre was very, very pale when she reached out again; she did not speak. But she took the mask. "Must we touch them?"

Yollana said, her voice unusually gentle, "We must *wear* them, Matriarch. There is no way to do the one without doing the other. The masks must be presented to the fire, or they will devour us, and we will fail in our duties.'"

Elsarre swallowed air. Nodded. She walked to the logs that she had anointed with the Lady's wine, holding the mask with the tips of her fingers, and looked at the crushed, flat brush and weeds, at the wood, at the symbolic empty vessel—at anything, in short, but the face.

Yollana came to Maria next, and to Maria she handed a mask. From this distance, it was clear to Margret that both the first and the second mask followed the pattern of the masks the servants of the Lord of Night had made: the simple face, like a child's mask, and the delicate one that might belong to a pretty youth or a pretty girl. Maria paled, but she had had Elsarre's cry as warning, and she had braced herself against what Yollana now offered.

And having braced herself, she started. Visibly.

My turn, Margret thought. Swallowed. Waited.

Sure enough, Yollana came to her next, mask outheld in weathered hand like a commandment and a doom. And this mask, this was a full face, fine-boned and yet wide enough to be either a man's face or a woman's, hair and details perfect.

Unfortunately, it was also alive.

She embarrassed herself. She screamed in a fair imitation of Elsarre of Corrona. The mask almost fell from her shaking hand. "I can't *wear* this," she said, speaking before thought could overtake her mouth and shut it.

Yollana glared at her. Margret was grateful that the old woman didn't find the words to express what she was obviously feeling. Instead she waited, patiently, while Margret gathered enough of her wits—and her grim determination—to take firm hold of the mask. Then she nodded and moved on.

Elsarre to the West, Margret to the South, Maria to the East, and to the North, where all their enemies lay, Yollana. She grimaced with distaste and took the last mask out of the bag. It was by far the finest, and at this distance, it was impossible to tell whether or not it, too, was alive.

Or perhaps it was impossible to tell without touching the mask itself. Margret stared at grass and wood and water, at anything but the eyes that watched her, bulging in pain or fear or plea—it was hard to tell without closer examination, and she didn't think she could get through the ceremony if she stopped to look at the face.

And then Yollana of the Havalla Voyani, the oldest and the wisest of the Matriarchs in this generation, knelt at the foot of the fire. She set the mask down upon her lap, and stared at it, and as she did—meeting the eyes that were present and moving, she said, in a voice that no one could avoid hearing, "Anoint the masks as you anointed the wood, Matriarchs. Lady's daughters. And then, when you have finished, anoint yourselves likewise. You will then be able to hear their voices, even where they have no mouths to speak with."

Elsarre and Margret exchanged a very panicked glance; Yollana had not looked up. She was now a rock at the pinnacle of a quartered circle. An anchor.

"You will do them this honor because, after the fires are written in wood, the lives that have been written in flesh will be offered in the stead of our children's lives. Whether they died willingly or no—and you will know, for they will tell you—they are our people, our flesh, and our blood, and the debt we owe them is a kin-debt that will know no end. It is not written in sand, nor spoken in wind; it is written here, in wood, as oaths are written between equals.

"And if you think to avoid this, do not. This *is* the price that we will pay for their sacrifice, and until we know or understand the whole of what *they* have lost, we cannot offer their lives as our own. Do you understand? You will give them their due."

Margret stared dully at the face that she propped in her lap. At the eyes that followed her every movement. She reached for her dagger, twice, and missed both times. A sign of cowardice. Or a sign from the Lady. She didn't much care which. Although she was Matriarch by bloodline, she had not yet completed the pilgrimage which would define her; nor had she retrieved the heart which would succor her.

She had never been asked the question which she knew lay at the end of the road: *What would you do to save the children?*

But looking at this face, this living mask, this life crushed into a space far too small for the living, and trapped there, she thought that she was too squeamish to give *this* answer.

She found the dagger on her third attempt; by this time she had lost sight of the others; she was alone, by a fire that had not yet been started, this face, this mask, awaiting the gift of her blood. The cut that she made this time was not too deep. But it was sharp, and she felt the sting of metal just that little bit too far beneath the skin.

She took her bleeding palm and pressed it against the forehead of the mask. She hesitated a moment; she did not want to hear the story behind the face; did not want to suffer the pain and the guilt of being—even indirectly—the cause of it. But could she do less? Could she do less when in the end, the sacrifice itself was important and no one else might know of it? No one else might carry the story, and make it a part of their history?

She swallowed; she had always disliked intense pain, especially if it happened to be her own. Then she pressed her bleeding palm into her own forehead, for the sake of symmetry.

The mask was a man's face. She knew this because she heard his voice, a thin, leathery sort of thing, the type of voice you'd expect from a man who'd taken a throat wound and had lost all ability for forceful speech, but who was still trying to bark out a command.

He said, *My name is Andaru, and I am of the Arkosa Voyani.* And inexplicably, Margret began to weep, tears of rage and fear and sorrow. If Evayne had been standing before her now, she might have tried to kill her. This man was one of Margret's own, but he was still a stranger. She listened as he spoke of his life: his birth—a story that came from his mother, for he certainly didn't remember it on his own; his youth in the wilds of the Averdan valleys, where the Arkosan caravan had chosen to stay for several years running; the raid by the clansmen that had robbed him of a father and a brother, but had made him a man in the eyes of those who survived.

He spoke of his favorite stones; rocks, flat and smooth, that he had gathered the one time they had passed close enough to the ocean that he could taste nothing but dry salt against his lips and on his skin for weeks afterward. She could not understand how he could speak of these things when the fate that they wound their way toward was this: entrapment in what remained of his face.

I am Andaru, Matriarch, he said softly, *and it is my honor to serve you; to protect the children. To preserve the* Voyanne *against our enemies. I came to you willingly, and I will go with the winds when they come. But I wish you to know my life, for when the winds come, there is no one else who will remember its final moments.*

And she wept again because his voice was gentle and she had thought that all that remained to him would be fear.

He told her about the girl that he hated on sight, she was so rough and rude and pushy. She laughed out loud when he told her about their wedding night. He told her about his children, and when he spoke of them, his voice grew somber, and she knew why: even if he had taken this extraordinary step to save their lives, they would

know loss. Not death; he had, he said, just disappeared. They
would know *loss*. They would wonder why he had left them.

He had been given no opportunity to explain, and had he, he
would not have taken it. *Because my wife, you see, she is so
brave and so terrified at the same time, and she would have
taken my place if it meant that it saved the children from my loss.*

"And loss of her?"

*It would never occur to her that she could be so important;
when they were babies, yes, but not now. They are boys, and they
make great show of not needing their mother anymore.*

"I give you my word," Margret told him, "that I will return to
the valleys in which you live; only tell me where they are, and I
will bring you—bring word of you—back to your own."

He did not speak to her of death.

She did not have the courage to ask.

But when she finally looked up, the sun had touched the
lowest edge of the horizon.

Anya did not like the masks. People wore them in the streets,
covering their faces as if they were playing a game. She didn't
like them.

"Anya," Lord Isladar said, "it is Festival in the Tor, and they
do things differently here. The masks are meant not to hide them
or to fool you—because fooling you would be very, very difficult; they are meant to fool the Southern gods. To divert the wind
and the sand; to protect the face from the gaze of the sun."

"But it's hardly sunny."

"Indeed. But the people believe that the Lord—the sun—gazes
down upon them until the last of His face has fallen beneath the
western coil."

She frowned and shifted the burden of the sleeping child. The
girl stirred, and Anya hushed her, with magic powerful enough
to draw the attention of anyone remotely acquainted with its use,
back into that state of restful slumber. "And you say *I* need a
mask?"

"No, Anya. You are special. If you choose to visit the Lake, I
am certain we will be allowed to pass without a mask. It will be
faster, and it will make you less angry, if we have a mask to
show the men at the gates, but it is not necessary."

"ANYA."

She looked up and frowned. "We'd better hurry," she said.
"Why?"

"Didn't you hear him? He's using his grumpy voice."

"Hear who, Anya?"

"My Lord Ishavriel."

"I am afraid that I find the crowd quite loud. And the music quite lovely. But I did not hear the Lord Ishavriel's voice. Perhaps it is time to answer him."

"Not *yet,* Isladar," she replied, tightening her grip on the girl. "I *promised,* don't you remember?"

"Ah, yes."

"*I* keep my promises. No demon will hurt her. No one will hurt her again. I promised. I promised her."

Her grip tightened. "He ran away," she said.

"I know, Anya."

"How do you know?"

"You've told me."

"Oh." Pause. "I have?"

"Yes, Anya."

"Oh." She smiled suddenly. "And you remembered?"

"I remember everything you tell me," he replied gravely.

"Can I test you?"

"If you'd like. But here, let us stand in line with our child and you may test my memory until I have proved to you that I always listen to what you say."

She bounced along beside him, liking him greatly, and wishing that she trusted him enough to let him carry the child; she was getting very heavy, and Anya's arms had never been quite strong enough. She thought about this for a long time, and then said, "Isladar?"

"Yes, Anya?"

"Why did Kiriel leave? I forget."

"I do not know, Anya. I had hoped she would be here so that she could answer your question herself."

"Oh." She was silent for a little bit longer, and then said, "I suppose if you *really* want, I'll let you carry the baby for a while. You used to carry Kiriel when she was a baby, I remember that now, and you never dropped her or let her be hurt."

"I am . . . honored, Anya. If you will allow it, I will carry the child." He smiled as he held out his arms. But he did not irritate her by promising to protect the girl. After all, Anya knew that men who promised that just *lied* and she hated liars more than she hated demons.

But only a little.

                              *   *   *

Alana en'Marano was sick with worry. It showed because in
the heart of her harem, with an absent husband, it was allowed
to show.

Illia en'Marano brought her the waters that Sendari's position
as adviser to the Dominion's ruler now granted them as a matter
of course, but Alana set the cup aside untouched. The dressmaker
had come and gone, and he was frazzled in a way that men often
are during the Festival season. A wedding dress on the first day
was not considered auspicious by some; by this poor, and somewhat beleaguered man it was barely considered possible.

And it was only possible because the person who would be
offended were the dress not finished and not *perfect* was the
Tyr'agnate Eduardo kai di'Garrardi, a man whose temper was as
famous as the single-mindedness with which he set about ful-
filling his desires. The dressmaker was excellent; Alana had now
been in the capital for long enough to know both his name and
his work.

But he was snappish to the point of being almost intolerable
and the cerdan now had their hands permanently affixed to the
hilts of their swords. It was difficult; they were not allowed to
actually *see* what was occurring—that would be offense beyond
imagining to their master; but they were there to make certain
that no offense was offered their master's wives.

Pierro di'Casell was offensive. Alana could see the clenching
of cerdan fists as he railed at poor Diora from behind the safety
of the screens that assured modesty when the cerdan were present. But she could see what they could not: the absolute, stark
terror in the poor man's face. This was Festival Night, the only
night given to the people at the Lady's behest that they might
express their secret joys and secret desires—but it was no longer
for him; his freedom was to spend the night by candle and lamp,
desperately beading and sewing the remnants of this gown so
that it might be ready for the ceremony on the morrow.

However terrible that fate might be, she did not think death
would be kinder; death would be kinder only if it seemed that he
would somehow fail to produce a gown that was worthy of the
bride of the kai di'Garrardi. And although his temper was sour—
understandably—the gown itself was exquisite, second only in
quality to the workmanship of the former kai el'Sol's hidden
servitor. If he completed his work, his existence was guaranteed.

But the announcement of the ceremony had been so sudden that he was not as close to completing the work as he should have been on the eve before the ceremony itself. She drew a breath as the cerdan started to turn, and offered him sweet water.

The look he gave her could best be described as rude—if one chose to be mild and polite. But she knew the kai Garrardi. And in her fashion, she was fond of Pierro, who had done such fine work for Illia en'Marano, the youngest and still the most beautiful of Sendari's wives, excepting only the Serra Fiona herself, who half an hour ago, had absented herself from this gathering in tears.

She, too, felt the pressure of the Festival, and Sendari, grim and gray from the terrible burden of the rumors that swirled around the Tor Leonne, was of little use or help in alleviating any of them. As *his* wife, the Tor had been her responsibility; but the preparations of the grounds, subtle and delicate and perfect, had been almost destroyed by the influx of so many common clansmen, and worse, their serafs.

Alana hoped that the Serra Fiona en'Marano had a mask and a destination for this Festival eve, although she doubted it. Sendari's wives were afraid this Festival was of the darkness, and Alana doubted very much that they would chance the outer world, masked or no. Too many rumors had passed from seraf to seraf, and grown—as rumors will—more significant and weighty with the passage. The darkness held servants of the Lord, and the Radann, bereft of the sunlight, might prove too weak a defense against them.

And the masks . . . the whispers that she'd gleaned in passing when the Widan—her husband of many years—spoke to himself in his most private chambers . . . how could any of them risk the wearing of such a thing?

Yet without masks, the Festival was a night like any other.

Except that on the morrow Na'dio would leave them, and for a husband far less to their liking than even the previous husband had been. But perhaps, just perhaps, it would serve her well. Perhaps she would build a harem again, and find some peace in the building, and perhaps she might choose wives who could speak to the loss and the rage that no one who had raised her could touch, it was trapped so far beneath the perfect, serene surface of Na'dio's face.

Alana wrung her hands, noticed that she was doing it, stopped, and then decided that it was *her* harem, and Festival Night at that, and she could wring her hands if she so chose. The dressmaker was pulling his hair in frustration—which was certainly less dignified.

All the while, like a statue of the very Lady, the Serra Diora di'Marano stood. Her hair was pulled back in the simplest of knots merely to get it away from the very fine silks with which the dressmaker worked; her face was devoid of all powders and creams, her lips so pale they were almost of a color with her skin. Her eyes, dark and round, were unblinking.

And she was beautiful; a beautiful adult, a stranger, a woman who did not belong in the bosom of her father's harem.

The dressmaker gathered his things and, by some miracle—mostly prayer, and at that, Alana's and Illia's—he was allowed to leave the residence with his head still upon his shoulders.

After he had left, Alana shooed the cerdan out with the least friendly words she had used all evening; they were accustomed to her, and one of them had the cheek to smile on the way out, as if he were actually a son and not a man paid by the labor of her husband. Illia, she set to tend to the last of the details: the jade combs, the strands of pearl and gold with which any daughter of means must be decorated, the rings which even now Na'dio would refuse to wear.

Only then did she turn to this statue who was her daughter, in truth, because she had borne no children for her husband, no matter how desperately she had desired them. "Na'dio," she said, to this young woman, this stranger.

And then, because it was the Lady's Night, and because she had the premonition that sometimes comes in those longest of terrible darknesses, she pulled her daughter down from the dressmaker's uncomfortable pedestal, and kissed her pale cheeks.

"Good-bye."

Diora started, then, as if the words were not the ones she expected to hear.

"I do not know which road you travel, Na'dio. I would travel it with you if I could. But I love the father that has lost your love; he has been kind to me, and to all of mine save those of his blood; Teresa and you."

"Alana—"

Moon-wise, Alana stood before Na'dio. "If you marry the Tyr, you know what to expect. But if you do not . . ." She looked at Diora's perfect hands.

"I heard what you said, or heard of it. The Lord heard it, and his servants accepted it. No matter what happens on the morrow, Lady be with you, Diora, and if the Lady is merciful, I will see you again.

"And when I do, child, you will be at peace."

She turned, then, and she left Na'dio in an empty room in the harem's heart.

Because she thought—although perhaps it was conceit—that she had somehow finally touched her almost daughter, and she wished to give her the privacy in which to shed tears, if tears were going to fall. For even as a small child, Diora had felt the shame of tears keenly.

The Radann were upon the plateau. They should have been exhausted, and if not for the sweet water from the Lady's Lake, they might well have been. But Marakas attended to their wounds— such as they were—and the Lady's bounty attended to their bodies; they were as whole, and as prepared for battle, as men can be.

Peder kai el'Sol was not among them; he was upon the platform that separated the Lake from the people that had come, masks in hand like awe-filled beggars, to partake of legend. He was not particularly pleased with the role—but it strengthened the Radann in the eyes of the people; it made them the masters and the arbiters of the Lady's bounty and mystery; it tied them together, politically, with a ceremony that otherwise had little meaning for them.

And it allowed them to claim the destruction of the accursed masks as acts of the Lord.

They should have cared. Perhaps, in the morning, they would. But this night . . . they were not Widan, but they could feel it: a wildness in the air. The sun had not yet disappeared below the Western horizon, but the Festival of the Moon had already begun.

They did not wear masks, this eve. And yet, perhaps for the first time as Radann, they felt the ultimate freedom the Lady offered: They were completely at ease with their desires; they revealed themselves as the darkness approached, and, swords in hand, they were content to wait.

Kallandras watched at a distance.

Elsarre was weeping openly; the Serra Maria was crying. Even Margret—who, he thought, had much in common with the mother she feared she could not live up to, had given in to the sentiment of the binding. Only Yollana was dry eyed. What passed between her and the face in her lap was so private, she did not voice a word.

Because a word, in his presence, revealed everything. He smiled. But the wind caught his hair and his hair, his eyes. He looked west at the colored sky. *Time,* he thought, although he dared not interrupt them. *It is time.*

But they knew.

On some level, they knew, and they were so entwined with the sacrifices made that they were incapable of wasting it. As one woman, the four suddenly snapped to attention, lifting their chins and turning, faces toward the fire that did not yet exist.

Reverently now, and with great care, they lifted Evayne's gift, so that eyes that still saw could bear witness to what would follow. They moved, again, as one woman.

He had never seen this fire lit, although there were songs sung of it, ancient and in a tongue that he could not sing with the requisite skill unless he used the legacy of his gift. He had never tried, and he thought, after this eve, he would never have to; the words came to him, and beneath them, contained but only barely by the skein of those words, music, song, a hint of harmony.

He had Salla over his shoulder; he unstrapped her as he watched, and his fingers wandered delicately over taut strings. She was, of course, in tune; he coaxed a phrase from her, something simple and direct; another, less so but with a complexity that hinted at what he now witnessed.

Kneeling, facing the fire, Margret of the Arkosan Voyani began to speak. She spoke in Torra, but in a Torra that was broken everywhere by phrases that had the feel of antiquity, the awkwardness of history being compressed into the present by someone who both understands that she is on the verge of mystery and yet cannot conceive of its depth.

The words were taken up, first by Elsarre's weepy voice and then by Maria's—and Maria's voice was as sharp as a blade, cold as steel, a surprise. But when Yollana, the fourth and the final Matriarch, finally offered her voice for his inspection, it was a revelation: Yollana of the Havallan Matriarch was beside herself with rage and sorrow and anger and hopelessness, and it infused her song with a full understanding of the words that the others struggled with. She spoke the old tongue, with its awkward cadences, and it was *beautiful;* it was, for a moment, her native tongue, her only language.

Spellbound, his fingers weaving on the loom of Salla's strings, he joined them, who should have stayed silent.

And the fire joined them as well, blazing up like a beacon and a challenge; it took the cross beams of wood at once, traveling from the West, where Elsarre clutched mask to chest, to the east, where Maria cradled; from the North, where Yollana, like Maria, gently cupped the only mask that no longer looked human, to the South, where Margret of the Arkosans waited.

And when it lapped the ends of the wood she had anointed with Arkosan blood, it *crackled.*

It spoke.

"You have paid the price, Daughter," it said, in a tongue that he understood because the bard-born understand all speech. "And I have come. What would you have of me?"

It snapped up wood, devoured it the way an effete patris devoured canapes in the Northern capital of the Empire.

And she said, "Protect my people. You are fire and light; our enemies are darkness and shadow. Let your magic be the only magic that is cast in my home; let my blood be the only blood that, by magic, is shed. Cast light great enough that my people will see by it until the fire comes up over the eastern rim."

The fire's crackle stopped; for a moment, it stood in an eerie silence, an image of fire's heart. Then it spoke. "You ask much, Daughter."

"Yes."

"And are you willing to pay the price?"

"Have I not already paid it?"

The fire roared; it was, Kallandras realized, fire's version of a laugh.

Margret did not move as the fire reached out and touched her wrist. She stiffened; she bit her tongue, and then her lip; in the unnatural light cast by the flame blood had summoned he saw blood trickle from the corner of her mouth.

And then the fire withdrew. "Yes," it said, "you pay my price."

The ring on Kallandras' hand sparked; the fire turned, seeing him truly for the first time. Kallandras bound the wind as tightly as he could, and he offered the fire his obeisance. But not his blood.

"Yollana," he said, not daring to approach the elemental, the wild, fire. "I believe it is best that we leave immediately. I had . . . forgotten . . . how possessive the wild elements can be."

She nodded.

But she waited until Margret stumbled back from the oathfire, clutching her wrist. Only then did the rest of the Matriarchs move.

"Well?" Yollana said, glaring at Kallandras as if she had not heard his words—and he suspected that she had not. "What are you standing there for? Get me my bag, and get ready to leave. We must be at the Founts by the time the moon has taken the sky." She turned to Margret. "Tend the wound."

Margret shook her head. "There is . . . there is no wound. Just . . . a lot of pain. And a scar."

"You're lucky. The fire likes you. Now. Say your farewells; tell your people to watch the camp."

"But the fire—"

"The fire will be felt by every demon in the Tor, mark my words. If they choose, they may contest. They won't win. But they may try. Tell your children to stand in the fire's light."

The light, Kallandras thought, permeated the camp in a very unnatural way.

He walked to Yollana and offered her his arm; she took it. But she was unwilling to relieve herself of the burden of her mask; none of the Matriarchs, not even Margret, set those masks aside, and he suspected that they would not, until they were either dead, or the masks had served their purpose.

Whatever that might be.

CHAPTER THIRTY-FOUR

"How will we know when to don the . . . masks?" Margret asked quietly, as they walked briskly toward the city. She carried the mask in a sash at her side, the way a woman with an infant will carry a baby. She had to resist the urge to tell Andaru what she saw, and what it meant to her; had to resist the stronger urge to bring him out and let him see what she saw. She felt that she owed him that much.

But other obligations were stronger. "Yollana?"

"You'll know."

"But *how?*"

"Matriarch, trust your instincts. If there is *any* doubt in your mind, do not let your hands act or your tongue flap. Understand? You *will* know."

Margret subsided. But she promised herself if Elsarre said a single word, she'd slap her silly.

They moved as a group of four women. Margret had chosen to leave Elena at the camp, and after a brief but very heated argument, Elena accepted the order. Yollana had no daughter and no retainer except Kallandras of the North, and she readily accepted from him the help that she would not take from the Voyani. Elsarre took Dani with her; Maria, as Margret, had chosen no escort.

They had daggers, after all, and the will to use them if it came to that—but they were Voyani, and the shadows at night were so plentiful there should be no excuse for open confrontation.

As they approached the city, they donned other masks, and Margret found them a comfort. She had always been herself until the moment she had learned of her mother's death. Then she had been forced to go into hiding. To hold back tears and fear and anger; to hold back harsh words and the pleading that she might otherwise have done with her cousins. She had become Matriarch in every external way possible, but on the inside she was only Margret, a damn poor substitute for the woman the clansmen had murdered.

Hiding her face behind something that made her one of the faceless, those responsibilities fell away. She heard the distant strum of samisen strings and the hoarse bark of a man selling expensive trinkets. She stopped a moment; they looked like gold. She lifted one, and his eyes followed her every move. Heavy enough to be gold.

She put it down. He whined at her. Both moves were perfunctory. She had no desire to tryst with a stranger; no desire to exchange some token of such an encounter. Not all of the Voyani women felt the same way, and certainly the younger girls could be a bit wild if released on an unsuspecting city during Festival—but Margret had always had her mother as leash, and her eventual role as guide.

She stopped at the wine seller, insulted something that might once have had grapes passed over it, and then scurried to rejoin the group. They walked in a circle. Kallandras took the lead, and although the crowd was dense—and no surprise, with the sun so long and the colors of the sky so inviting—they had no trouble at all moving between bodies. It was almost as if he smiled sweetly and they parted.

It didn't matter. For whatever reason, they came to the first stop in the circle. Kallandras reclaimed his arm from Yollana, and she hobbled to the Fount, taking care to cross the circle completely. She propped herself up against the ledge, so that she was near the water. "Go. I'll give you three hours. But when the moon is there, in relation to the plateau, begin." She then turned to scowl at a young couple who had chosen to perch there.

The man frowned, but the woman whispered something Margret couldn't catch, and drew him away. It was very crowded by the fountains. Margret hoped that people wouldn't interfere with magic.

Or that magic wouldn't kill them if they were someplace they weren't meant to be.

She nodded dutifully, as did the rest of the Matriarchs; satisfied, Yollana turned to face the moon; they had no question whatever that she would be facing it until it was time.

But she was wrong; Yollana looked away just before Margret turned. "Matriarch of Arkosa."

"Yes?"

"The fire marked you."

Margret frowned and touched her very tender wrist. Even though it was swathed in unguent and bandage, it ached.

"What else did you ask from the fire?"

Margret said nothing at all. But she was glad it was dark; that her face was hidden; that the others could not see the shift in an expression that, unlike Maria's, was always in motion.

Kallandras bowed to Yollana. Yollana grimaced. "We should have brought wine," she said.

"We did," Maria replied mildly.

"For *us* to drink."

Maria raised a perfect brow, but said nothing.

From the Northern Fount, they went to the East, and there, as at the circle in the Arkosan camp, Maria took her position. There were men and women here, but they were few. Those who wished to pay their respects to the Lady had taken the road up the hill, to gain their first, and probably only, glimpse of the Lady's miracle. Kallandras spoke a few soft words here and there, encouraging them to be on their way; to be hungry, to be sleepy, to be whatever it might take to get them to leave of their own accord.

Margret noticed that he had not done the same for Yollana; Yollana had been left to fend for herself. Which she did.

Elsarre noticed the same, and was put out by it, but she hadn't the energy to have a real tantrum. Just as well, because Margret hadn't the energy to stop herself from slapping her, and that would cause *real* stress between Arkosa and Corrona.

But it was just as well that Margret was left at the Southern Fount and Elsarre was taken into the darkness at the city's edge.

The sky was very dark, and the night was clear. Margret sat upon the fountain's edge and watched the people who milled around in the gated quarter. They wore masks, often simple ones, although in the streets that led to the Fount she had seen gold and glory on the faces of those who were rich enough—or foolish enough—to afford it.

They were quiet, these people; they did not understand how to revel. And she was glad of it; tonight she wished to be left alone. It was a waste of the few minutes of freedom she had, and she knew it. She took the thin mask off and set it aside on the stone lip of the Fount.

An hour passed.

People in masks drew near and then, seeing her naked face, drew away; there was a statement in the simple removal of the mask that was anything but simple.

She waited as she watched the full face of the Lady's Moon rise and extend itself toward the height of the plateau.

Peder kai el'Sol let a mask fall into the Lake. Before it touched the surface of the water, flame took it. The crowd—and it *was* a crowd—saw the light in the darkness far more clearly than they had when the Lord reigned. It should have pleased him.

But the wind came, sudden and cold, unfurling over the Lake as if it spoke with the water's voice; he felt a chill very like the one ascribed to men who looked into the waters and saw their own deaths. He wanted to hurry them then; to dispense with formality and politics; to tell all of the men and women who watched that *this* Festival, they must make certain that all masks meet the Lake or remain unworn.

But he was the kai el'Sol; he stood in the wind's path and he continued.

22nd of Scaral, 427 AA
Shining City, Northern Wastes

It was not his own blood that he minded; Cortano di'Alexes had seen his share of that. He had bled as a youth in his father's home, when his father chose to drink to excess; bled during the training that would in the end serve him poorly on all but one occasion; bled as he clung to the bridge of Winds that was the Widan's final test. At every juncture of his life, there had been blood spilled.

Even in the daily routine of his life as Widan, he had been forced to the blade's edge; he could not conceive of a time in his life where blood would be concealed beneath skin, its power untapped. He had cut himself several times for those spells and ceremonies in which blood was the only acceptable signature, and he had bled from wounds when men who were tired of his reign had attempted to end his life. They were dust; he had survived. In some ways, the act of bleeding meant that he was alive.

No; his own blood, taken from either palm, did not upset him.

But the Lord's blood did. And he was anointed very carefully with it, as an animal in a divination rite might be before its

THE SHINING COURT   695

slaughter. He could not move; nor did he waste the time or the energy attempting to do so. The Lord summoned, and he obeyed. It was as simple, as humiliating, as that.

And worse: He did not desire to disobey. There was about the darkness a rich and endless beauty, and when he gazed upon the Lord's face he understood what Isladar had hinted at, and still did: that the *Kialli* had not chosen to follow the Lord out of any compulsion other than . . . love.

The Lord gave him robes, and he accepted them; the Lord bid him close his eyes, and this, too he accepted. But his lids, thin and delicate, felt the weight and the pressure of a god's fingers; felt something warm—hot—and sticky against the membrane that protected his vision.

Heard the words that joined them, although the language was a cacophony of words in an endless stream of languages, most of which had not been heard by living man.

Lady Sariyel struggled; she fought; she used her magic unwisely and this displeased the Lord. In return for her disobedience, he bled not her palms, but her cheeks. On another day, this might have amused Cortano, for in truth he found her particular vanity revolting.

Tonight, it did not. The moon in the Northern Wastes was full and high above the Palace that had been carved out of a single piece of rock from depth to height.

"Come," the Lord said, and Cortano bowed. He bowed willingly. Krysanthos joined him. Of the three, the Northern mage accepted his fate gladly; it made Cortano wonder how much of the shadow had already devoured him. No man willingly became a vessel for the Lord's power who had not already been touched by the influence of the *Allasakari*. It was a route that a man dedicated to the search for knowledge might study but would never take, for it devoured not body but mind.

Alesso, Cortano thought, but he said nothing. They were ushered, in haste, to the tower's doors, and from there, they traveled by grace of the Lord's power to the courtyard below. There, roaring and snapping in a fury, were the Great Beasts. Cortano had been called to audience with the Lord before. He had found the conceit of a tower without stairs to be amusing, a way of weeding out the weak from the strong.

Not so the beasts at the tower's foot.

They lunged and snapped, and even when the Lord roared and

they reared back and exposed their throats, they still growled. Something, Cortano thought, would die in those jaws this eve.

And perhaps that might be the kinder, the quicker, death. The Festival Moon had not yet reached its height.

The Lord chose to ride astride one of the beasts; the second . . . the second he gave to the mages. Neither they, nor their mount, were happy with the arrangement; the beast because no one likes to be reined in by food, and the mages because it was hard to navigate the spikes of the beast's back in order to sit, let alone hold on when it began its sinuous padding movement through the city streets.

And how like city streets they were, and how unlike. Cortano had spent his youth on Festivals. He had even spent his money on the trinkets one offers to women behind delicate masks, although he had only been fool enough to do it once.

The streets then had been as crowded as they were now. He had never appreciated the diversity of the Tor, although the memories were sharp and distinct as he laid them against the demons and the imps that watched the Lord's procession.

They watched with a mixture of adulation and fear, and they did not look away; indeed the least of their kind pressed their bodies against cold, cold stone and whimpered in the language of the kin.

It was almost repulsive. He wondered how a god could actually find the obeisances and dim obedience of such creatures gratifying.

Or necessary.

He wondered if, on the morrow, he would be like one of those creatures. It was not a pleasant thought.

Alesso. Where is Anya?

22nd of Scaral, 427 AA
Tor Leonne

Anya was still missing.

The continent was not distance enough to separate the kinlord from his Lord's rage. Mountains, he thought, would fall before this night's end if Anya were not in place.

He had used every spell that he had ever designed to trace her; every call that he had ever developed to compel her; he had sent his lieutenants to in full *Kialli* form to tempt her out of hiding.

There had been no response.

Lord Ishavriel dispensed with pretense.

After tonight, it would no longer be needed.

But if Anya was not delivered to the Lord before the end of Scarran, all of his careful planning meant nothing. And Scarran was coming; he could taste the change in the air, could feel the old earth waken at the touch of his foot.

He looked into the open sky; called wind. Wind came. It scoured him of the facade of mortality, and he let that facade be taken in exchange for the elemental power.

Take this name, he whispered. *Take this name and carry my power with it.*

And the wind lifted him, sundering his momentary ties with the earth that was waking as the old world began to eclipse the mortal one.

He gestured and all mortal seeming vanished as his sword came to hand. The people in the streets of the dismal, pathetic city that was becoming less significant as the minutes passed screamed when the sword brought fire.

The wind begged him for a plaything, and he let it take a mortal or two, choosing from among the many who did *not* wear the masks of his devising. They screamed, and their cries were carried in eddies and currents of wind, along with their bodies.

It cost him; the wind did not yet have that power on its own. But in return, it gave him what he desired.

"Anya!"

She froze as if she'd been slapped.

The sound of her name ran up and down her spine as if the vertebrae were strings and a child was playing with them. She cried out in shock and pain, and she almost dropped the child—but Isladar was there to catch her. They had been taking turns carrying the sleeping girl, and it was hers.

She was *very* angry.

"Anya," Lord Isladar said, in his calm, calm voice. "I have the child. She was not hurt."

But Anya *was* hurt. And she didn't *like* it.

"Stop it!" she shouted.

Lord Isladar said softly, "Anya, you will frighten the child."

She tried to stop being so angry—it wasn't good, she *knew* that—but he shouted her name again, and it *hurt.*

So she lashed out with the thing she knew best.

Fire carved an arch of light in the deep night sky.

Ishavriel cried out as the fire struck him. It dripped from his armor in rivulets and vanished—but the effort was costly. Had anyone—*anyone*—other than Anya cast that spell, he would have hunted them down and killed them; as it was, he was almost past caring about her survival. Almost.

But the glory of the Lord depended upon it.

Lord Ishavriel had spent mortal years planning for this evening. He had subjected not only himself but the fist of the Lord to the humiliation of treating the Southerners—the descendants of the traitors—as near equals. He had enduring the insanity of the most powerful mage on the planet, pandering to her foolish whims, her idiocy. She had put a throne at the pinnacle of the gateway! It was almost inconceivable that something so powerful and so theoretically valuable could cause so much damage on a whim.

Ishavriel was immortal, but the last several decades had been very, very long. He was used to a long game. He was also used to *winning* them. Had he lost any game of power, he would not be kinlord or general.

The darkness was almost completely; the eclipse was almost done. He could hear—at a great distance—the thunder of delicate hooves.

He was about to win the game. . . .

If Anya returned to the Shining City in time.

The old ways were *strong* now. The Moon was almost at its height. It was time for so many things.

Time.

He let the wind carry him in the direction the flames had come from.

"Teresa," Jewel said quietly to the woman who was now dressed as a woman and whose face was covered by a silvered, simple mask. "Do you know what we're doing?"

"We are standing in line," the Serra answered lightly, "in order to catch a once-in-a-lifetime glimpse of the Lady's Lake."

"And those gates are the gates that take us into the Tyr's home?"

"Into the Tor Leonne upon the plateau, yes. Beyond those gates— it is said—there is a road that leads to the heart of the Empire. Small roads branch from it to either side, but the path itself is true. The lake is there, and beyond the Lake, the Tyr's palace rises. We will see it," she said quietly. "Although I am not certain we will see it soon."

"We're moving." Jewel shrugged. "We've moving slower than a baby who hasn't quite figured out crawling yet, but we're moving. Gods, I hate these masks. My face is sweating like—"

"Jewel."

"I mean, what a lovely custom." She did actually blush, which meant the masks were good for something after all.

"I am not offended, Avandar," the Serra said, and her voice made it sound like it was true. "It is Festival Night, after all, and we speak with our hearts on Festival Night."

"Jewel always speaks with her heart. It would be encouraging if she attempted to speak with more of her intellect."

"Avan—dar."

"Yes?"

"Can I have a word with you?"

"If by word you mean what you usually mean, you may have several."

"Teresa," Jewel said, as plaintively as she could, "can I ask you how you managed to find Ramdan?"

She actually did laugh at that, and her laugh was so surprisingly sweet Jewel immediately wanted to say something that would make her laugh again.

But the laugh must have startled the Serra, for she fell silent immediately and did not speak again until they had passed the gates.

"Diora."

The Serra Diora, dressed in a simple sari, knelt before a mask. It was a simple mask; it had a bird's face. As a child, she had thought it was an eagle's, but it was softer than the harsh-beaked hunter; not so wide-eyed as the owl. There were feathers in abundance across the face, some gold along the edges, and upon the beak itself. It was almost gaudy; it was certainly not the mask she would choose for herself now.

And yet, it was here, buried beneath layers of clothing, kept safe from Festival to Festival, from home to home. Aie, it had even survived the death of her wives. She should have known, then. She touched it hesitantly, her fingers brushing bent feathers.

Remembering, as if the sharp, brittle quills of such dress feathers were keys that had opened a locked door, the Festival of her fourth year, when she had been carried upon her father's shoulders through the streets of the Tor. More clearly than she remembered events of a month ago, she remembered the flash of the blades in darkness where he had paused to show her the dancers; she remembered the food he had bought for her, a light pastry with a very sweet syrup in the center, made by Northerners who had come to visit the Tor. War was very far away from her then.

She remembered that her father did not come home the next day. That all of her mothers were worried about him; that none of them would tell her what they were worried about. But she could hear it in their voices: they thought that her father was going to die.

She had tried to talk to Ona Teresa, and Ona Teresa had forbidden it; she had said it was dangerous to her father. And so she had spent a night in fear, until at last she had crept out of the harem room where the children slept. She remembered the walk between their room and his, because Alana would be angry that she was not asleep, and she didn't want Alana to be angry.

No one caught her. No one. She curled up in her father's rooms, determined to wait until he returned to them. That night had been at least as dark as this one. She had prayed and prayed and prayed to the Lady—but it was no longer Festival, and she knew that the time when the Lady would listen *best* had passed.

She had no candle for light. She walked in the dark, her hands touching familiar walls and screens with a sudden understanding that all familiar things seen in shadow were mysterious and frightening. And yet . . . she had not wondered then what she herself was like, seen in shadow.

She had found her father's room. And sleep had found her there.

But so had her father. Her clearest memory of that evening was her father's hands, red and raw and bleeding, his face, scratched, beard singed, his robes torn. It should have horrified her. She should have been frightened. But he was *alive*. He was alive; the Lady had given her all that she had asked for.

Such an easy thing to ask for. Her father's life.

"Na'dio?"

"I am . . . here, Ona Teresa. I am almost ready to leave."

"Time your flight carefully. We are not yet at the Lake."

There was a pause, and then the Serra Teresa added, **"Kallandras does not answer me."**

He heard the wind's howl; his hand sparked and flashed with its voice. A moment, no more, he ached to walk the same path that the kinlord walked; but higher, faster. He missed the wind's voice, and when it came to him, when it spoke all of his names as if those names belonged to the wind alone, he heard nothing but its song, desired nothing but its music.

But he had been tested by greater desires, and he had survived far greater losses than simple denial. He sang his regret, and the wind churlishly shredded the words into syllables and single notes.

But it did not, in its caprice, choose to betray him to the Lord who now gave it freedom to play.

Freedom to play?

Kallandras frowned.

"He will be here, if he is needed. I am . . . almost ready. I will meet you by the gate, unless I am detained."

Diora lifted the mask to her face and after a long pause, spent staring at the flat curves of the interior of that birdlike face, she settled it upon her cheeks and tied the ribbon around her hair with shaking hands. She pinned it, wrapping it in her hair so that it could be lifted but not easily dislodged.

There was a small mirror in this room, for this was the room in which she was to prepare for the wedding on the morrow. She paused a moment to look at her face in the mask a child had chosen.

And then, because she was no longer a child, she looked away. She would have set the mask aside, but it was the only one she had; the only one she could be certain was not in some way ensorcelled.

And it had stayed with her, year after year, for so long, she felt that it was meant to serve this final purpose.

She had chosen her clothing well; it was seraf's clothing—but of a fine cut and a fine cloth. The role of seraf was a part that she could play with ease, for in the end, upon the plateau, there was very little difference between the wife of Tyr and the seraf of one until she bore a child. And if that child was a girl, her status changed little.

But the freeborn mother of a *son* had power; no son who was to inherit title and clan could be tainted by the shadow of slavery.

And she would not think about sons. Not now. Not here, so close to the grave of the only son that she had ever had. All of her ghosts were restless tonight.

Festival Night.

Freedom.

She gathered a blanket—the only other possession she would take with her—and began her final journey.

The Tor was alive with people, more crowded than she had ever seen it. Here and there, the wildness of the evening had given way to more personal meetings than she desired to witness. She wondered how the grounds would look on the morrow; if the delicate dwarf trees to the east of her father's residence would be trampled under the heels of the masked strangers who now strode like giants across the landscape. Robbed of daylight and Lord's judgment, they, too, were free.

And to spend that freedom being so carelessly destructive seemed a profound waste.

But not all men were free.

As she left through the screens her father's serafs were accustomed to using when they needed to fetch sweet water, she saw the cerdan near the front of her father's home. They had elected to remain in defense of the harem, and they looked like men under siege. She wondered if any would die attempting to approach the dwelling.

She wondered how many men had died when her harem had been attacked. And how many had just gracefully given way so that the women and children they were to guard could be brutalized and slaughtered.

The rings on her fingers were large and cold; she started to shake and curled those hands into fists. Lady, Lady, *please.* The Festival Moon was so *strong,* and she had spent almost six months in isolation. *Please, not that, please.*

But it returned to her. Not the sight, not the smells, not the fire on the Lake. Not even the screaming, although that had been a living nightmare.

But the sound of her son's neck snapping.

The sound of Ruatha's raw, raw voice, twisted around the syllables of her name. It was overwhelming because she could not forget it; her gift had taken the memory and made it as much a part of her as breathing. She could turn away for a day or two;

she could think of other things—but always, unexpectedly, it returned to her.

She had not cried that night.

She did not cry this one.

She swallowed truth until she thought she would bleed from it, and she walked, elegantly, gracefully, demurely, to the only thing that offered her the hope of true freedom.

She could see the outline of trees and flowers in the silver light of the moon. And she could hear the exhortations of the kai el'Sol as the Lake caught his voice and cast its echoes across the plateau like a net. She heard samisen strings, and that stopped her for a moment because it had been so *long* since she had played and known the ease that comes only with the wordless expression of music.

And it *was* Festival Night.

But she was the Serra Diora di'Marano, and the Festival's freedom held a different promise. She slid her way between people, bumping up against a sword here and a hip there, brushing expensive silk and rough twill, running her finger through silky, thin hair when the head of a small child appeared near her hand.

But the crowd lessened as she approached the home of the Radann upon the plateau. The Radann, who served the Lord, and were not known for their fondness for revelers. They were not hostile, but they did not welcome intrusion, and even on a night when anonymity and safety were theoretically guaranteed, accidents did happen.

The crowd had guaranteed her anonymity; as she left it behind, she became more conspicuous.

Lady, she thought, her hands trembling as they once again became fists. *Lady, guide me. I am your servant.* No. That was not true, and when one begged a boon from the Lady, it was best to be honest. And yet she was not certain what honesty was anymore.

She had *saved* her father's life.

And she had begged the Lady for a chance to avenge herself against the men who had destroyed her family. Perhaps, having been given that single chance, she had failed the test, and would be given no other.

Diora!

Aiee, Lady, she thought. *Do not judge me, do not condemn me, for that alone; in all else I have proved true to my vow. Please, Lady.*

Diora!
Please.

She walked blindly and without the grace for which she was renowned; she had left behind all of the things by which she would be easily identified.

But there was one thing that she could not leave the plateau without. For she was still alive, and while she lived, she planned.

The Serra Diora di'Marano made her way to the Swordhaven. There were no Radann to guard it, and none needed; she reached for the torch in the iron ring, and taking it in a hand that she had to work to steady, she opened the door into what should have been darkness.

But the sun had descended, and now resided within the blade itself, for when she opened the door, she was almost blinded by the radiance of a Sword that had become its name.

From the heights above the city, the *Kialli* Lord could see two things clearly: Anya, who had evaded his power and his command, and Isladar, who stood beside her, human child in his arms.

"How dare you?" he bellowed, and the wind came rushing to him with the glee of a wayward imp. He sent it out, with his words.

And when it returned, it bore a message. "Have a care, Ishavriel. Anya is almost beside herself with rage, and if she chooses to fight us, she will not return alive to the Shining City.

"I have tried to convince her to leave, but it appears that she has promised the child I now hold—the child you made her drop—safety. It has a meaning to her that I do not understand, and I would be . . . gratified . . . if you would enlighten me. If, that is, you understand it yourself."

Lord Ishavriel roared with frustration.

And beneath him, quivering like animals, the mortals heard his true voice. **"It is time!"**

Margret almost slid the mask over her face. Almost.

But she hesitated and as she did, the people around the Fountain—and in the streets—seemed to start like rabbits or small animals exposed to birds of prey. They recognized magic, if they recognized nothing else, and the little fears that had built surfaced between the cracks in the silence.

As people ran or moved away, she heard a young boy ask

his Oma if the fire flowers were about to blossom across the heavens. And his Oma in reply scooped him into arms that seemed too frail to carry his boisterous weight and started to flee—

And something in Margret spoke. "Wait!" she cried.

The old woman teetered and turned, and Margret held out a hand to her. "To me," she said. *"Quickly."*

The stranger hesitated and the creature above them, tall and slender and beautiful in a chilling way, spoke again. She did not understand what he said, but she understood from the rhythm of his syllables that something was about to happen that neither she nor the other Matriarchs would like.

And yet. And yet the time was not right.

The old woman reached out. Margret caught her hand and dragged her across the incised circle, where she sat, heavily, on the edge of the Fountain. "Don't touch the water," Margret told her, almost gently. "And whatever you do, don't step back across the circle."

The boy peered out from the safety of his Oma's familiar hug. "Why not?"

"Because, you see that bad man up there?" Margret spoke with cheerful grimness.

"Yeah."

"Well, he'll kill you."

"Oh. Oma, will he really kill me?"

The old woman frowned at Margret, and Margret nodded.

"Yes, Na'simo, now shush."

He fell silent. Margret turned her face toward the moon, but her attention came back to the creature that hung suspended above the city.

In the distance, the screaming began.

The Serra Diora entered the Swordhaven as if compelled. The door swung shut at her back; she set the torch in its place in the ring on the wall and then approached the braziers. They were cool; the Radann had overlooked the heating of the fire and the burning of incense. That they had overlooked these pleasant duties to do battle in the streets of the Tor made their mistake not only forgivable but commendable, although in truth she wondered if the Lord cared at all for incense and ceremony.

The whole of the haven was silent. The Sword was white; the

light it cast a visual cry. But of what? She could not be certain. She walked quickly to the altar's stairs, and knelt there. *I have no incense to offer,* she silently told the Sword, *but I will offer you something more important in its stead: freedom, and a chance to be what you were meant to be.*

Wielded by a man with Leonne blood in his veins.

The Sword did not brighten, but it did not darken either, and because she desired a sign, she accepted its neutrality as the permission she sought.

Did they bar and lock this door? Never. For although it had been attempted, no man alive had ever survived the Sun Sword's touch when he had come with intent to steal.

Very well. It was truth; she accepted it as such. But she was *not* a man. She was the wife of a dead Tyr, a weak fool who had not, in the end, done Sword or clan—or family, Lady, family—justice. In a single evening, he had been destroyed, and his family unmade.

But for six months, the seraf granted freedom solely to be thrown as a sop to the Northern Imperials had survived. For had he been dead, Alesso di'Alesso would have taken the Sun Sword as he had taken the Lake and the Crown.

She reached the Sword, and there she knelt, pressing her forehead into her hands. This was the final test; if she perished here— as the kai el'Sol had perished—she would be truly free. At the side of Marakas par el'Sol, the stone that was weight and responsibility had burned a warning into perfect, unseen skin.

She had thought it a warning of the Enemy's presence, but she felt it now, as something else. It was still painful. Perhaps still a warning.

And it made no difference.

She touched the Sword. Lifted it from the gold-and-jade pedestal crafted for its use. There were two scabbards, and although the Sword was to travel to war, she chose the dress scabbard to house it. She could not carry both, and if she survived here, it would be necessary for the Sword to be recognized instantly.

No plain sheath would accomplish that.

Forgive me, she said to the blade, *but this is not an act of vanity; it is an act of war.*

The blade did not reply. But she, who had lifted it from the waters of the Lady's Lake after the dissolution of Fredero kai el'Sol, took silence as assent, if not approval, and she slid the blade, taking care not to touch its edge, into the curved crescent of a sheath heavy with gold and jewels. The sun was eclipsed; the room was cast back into the meager light that a flickering torch could bring. It took Diora a minute or two to become accustomed to the shadows; she took that time, holding the weight of the Sword in both hands. Then she wrapped it in the blankets that she had taken from her father's steps and turned.

There, at the base of the steps, a torch casting orange light against the wrinkles and contours of his aged face, stood the Widan Sendari di'Sendari.

Her father.

CHAPTER THIRTY-FIVE

Her hands clutched the mask; she held it as if it were a shield and not a burden. The old woman and her son huddled against the Fountain, caught between the water that Margret told them—as gently as possible—not to touch, and the edge of the circle that she told them—less gently—not to cross.

Had it been within her power to spare the child, she would have cut off all sounds of screaming, for the screams were obviously human, and the terror in them could not be disguised or explained away.

She wanted to know what was happening but she knew, now, that to leave this circle was death. Her own, and the rest of the Matriarchs; they were bound; the points of an oath. But she wasn't certain what she'd promised yet, and that made her uncomfortable. Her wrist ached with the touch of the fire.

No screams could continue forever, and the ones that they were forced to endure grew distant or worse: they broke into sobbing terror. The child's face was not invisible; she wondered, briefly, if in this evening's work he would lose his parents. The same thought must have crossed his grandmother's mind, for she clutched him tightly and the shape of her eyes slowly changed as she bowed her head, tucking her grandson's hair beneath her chin.

Margret wondered how many other grandchildren she had, but she didn't ask. What point was there?

The woman was singing.

She was singing a cradle song into the ears of her frightened charge, and his arms, tight around her neck, relaxed slightly. The song promised what she could not promise: safety. And it offered what she *could* offer: love. Comfort.

Margret had never seen these two people before, and if she survived this night's work—if they all did—she would never see them again. But they seemed a microcosm of her own family.

And she so hated to grant that much power to clansmen.

Roughly, because she was suddenly angry at herself, she said, "What is your clan?"

And the woman looked up and said, "Namarro."

It meant nothing to Margret. She looked away.

"All right," Jewel said quietly. "Here we are. That's a beautiful body of water. Well, from here anyway. And here is about as close as I want to be. Where is she, Serra?"

The Serra lifted her head a moment. Frowned. Neither she nor the Northerner had mentioned the only thing of value to the Serra. But she heard the certain knowledge in the younger woman's voice, and on this one night, she acknowledged it. *Diora.* She wondered if Kallandras had told her, and if so, how much.

She lifted her chin slightly. Called with the private voice.

Silence.

"I . . . do not know," she said at last.

She stood, the Sword that defined the Leonne clan wrapped like a babe in her arms. The moon lit the steps at her feet, but cast her shadow down the rest, like a carpet or a path. She froze there, staring.

"Serra Diora," the Widan said quietly.

"Widan Sendari," she replied, her voice the cool voice of the dutiful daughter. It was a voice she understood well, and it came naturally to her.

He stared up at her, his face as naked as the moon's face, but shorn of light and power. "Na'dio."

She stiffened. It was a rejection they both understood.

But understand it or no, the haggard man at the foot of the stairs said again, "Na'dio."

She hated him.

She hated him and she could not hate him. She desired his death and yet, when it had been offered her, she had rejected it utterly, risking exposure and death to stay the hand of the kai Garrardi when he had no desire to show mercy. She said, although all instinct screamed against it, "You have no right to call me that."

He flinched.

He *flinched.* She was wearing the mask, and he, he had chosen the subterfuge of the naked face, a sign, on Festival Night, that one did not wish to expose oneself to strangers, regardless of how anonymous that exposure might be. Yet *he* flinched. He stood, his voice stripped of accusation, of anger, of surprise, but not of emotion.

Had she not been carrying the Sword, she would have covered her ears. And it would be a futile gesture, a child's gesture.

"Will you not ask me why I am here, Father?"

"And if I ask," he said quietly. "If I find the courage to ask, will you answer, Serra Diora?"

In the worst of the isolated moments in the Tor, when she had been denied the use of the samisen or the lute, and her voice was not steady enough for naked song, she had dreamed of what she might do when she could finally confront her father.

For in the end, the others were men of power, and they played by the rules of the powerful: kill what must be killed, salvage what is of value, destroy what might be used against you.

They had not betrayed *her*. They had betrayed oaths given to and accepted by the clan Leonne, and if those oaths were honored by the Lord, they were not so honored as victory. Victory.

She intended to destroy the victory that had been bought at the expense of her family. Not her husband's family, but *hers;* the wives whose rings she would never again remove; the child—oh, Lady, her boy—

But her *father* understood the pain of that loss. And her father was the only one of them who had promised to protect and to love *her*.

She *hated* him. **"Ask,"** she said wildly, the power crackling beneath the surface of the command. She wanted him to feel that power; she wanted him to understand that no matter what happened here, he was at her mercy, and there was so little of it.

But he offered no resistance. The word might have held no power or no command at all.

Or perhaps it did not conflict with his desire. Perhaps he had come this way, to ask her whatever it was that she had commanded him *to* ask.

"I did you no kindness, did I?"

The words might have been Weston they were so foreign; she did not understand them.

He waited, and then, searching for the face that the mask hid, he said, "Would it have been better to let you die with your wives?"

She opened her mouth, but no words came out. His voice had the power; hers eluded her.

"I have come because it is Festival Night, Na'dio, and because I thought—if I have not misjudged you—that you would be here."

She stared at him, her hands rhythmically clutching and unclutching the folds of silk the Sword was wrapped in. When she answered his question, it wasn't an answer at all. It was a child's plea. "Why? *Why?*"

She could not even articulate what she desired because she did not understand it; her dead were screaming as they always screamed, and for the second time—for only the second time—she joined them.

He flinched again. Took a full step back. His eyes moved, flickering off the contours of her masked face, dodging her eyes.

But before she could force them back, they came; he stood, old now, staring up at her, and he finally raised both hands, empty hands, palm up. It was a plea.

"I wanted what men want," he said. "Na'dio, Na'dio, please." His voice was incredibly gentle. It was a voice that she had not heard for a decade.

She was weeping. She had never thought she would weep again in his presence. She could not see him for the tears. "Alora was dead. I could not have her back. I searched for a second wife, but there was no wife like Alora. Because," he added, "I was not the same man. I did not realize it then, and realizing it now does not change me; I am what I have become, and I will pay the price for it."

"And what of *me?*"

"My child—"

"They killed my wives," she said; she had started and she could not stop the words. "They *slaughtered* my wives. And my son—my boy, Deirdre's babe—they snapped his neck. Do you *know*—can you even imagine—"

"What it is like to watch the one you love slip away while no one raises a hand to save her? Yes. Yes, I know."

"*I* did not kill *your* wife. I did not destroy *your* life!"

"Yes, Na'dio," he said quietly. "You did."

The Sword tumbled out of her hands and came to rest at her feet; the tip of the blade, peering out of the silks she had been so careful with, now overhung the edge of the platform.

"She bled to death giving birth to you. We could not stop the bleeding. I sent for a healer. He failed me. He died." He did not look away; she did not; they were trapped now by the cadence of his words. "I hated you."

A peculiar numbness began to settle around her.

"And I wanted to continue in that fashion, but the Serra Teresa convinced me that you—you were all that was left of *her.*"

She bent slowly, her knees almost giving under her own weight. The sword was beautiful as it lay exposed to moonlight.

"Believe that I loved you, Na'dio," he said softly. "It did not take long before I could see her in you, and could see that you would never be what she had been." He looked away. "I did not desire this marriage. I did not trust the Tyr, and his son was not to my liking. I had hoped to protect you, but I was ordered by both kai and Tyr to give you in marriage to the kai Leonne.

"And on the day you were married, you had no desire to leave my house. It was only a year," he added softly. "I—"

"Please do not tell me that you thought I would come back to your harem unchanged."

"I will not tell you that if it is not what you wish to hear, but it *is* the truth."

She knew what he would ask next, and she did not want to hear it. It was a question she had asked herself so often the answer made no sense. She lifted the Sword. Bundled it carefully in the silks that she had brought for just that purpose. She started down the steps, and he stepped aside. But he did not spare her the words, and she had no strength to force him to silence.

"Why did you not attempt to defend yourself? Why—if you had the powers that you *do* have, did you not save your wives? I did everything within my power to save mine."

She froze; the mask was on her face, but it was less effective than her expression would have been. "Because," she said, her back to him, "I knew that there was nothing I could do that would save their lives."

"And so you saved your own."

She turned then.

"Yes," she said, voice as sharp as the Sun Sword. "I saved my own because I thought if I did, I could avenge what I could not stop."

The silence—she thought it would go on forever.

"Na'dio," her father said, surprising her again, "I have dedicated my life—what is left of my life—to the pursuit of power." He lifted a hand, extending it into the empty space that separated them. "And I no longer find it a rewarding substitute for the life I had.

"I am . . . committed. I am old and there is no way to turn back from the path that I have begun to travel. But I will tell you now that if I knew that we would be here, on this Festival Night, speaking these words, I would never have taken the test of the Sword."

"And now?"

"Now?"

"You have taken the test. You have chosen your path. And I, Father, have chosen mine." She knelt slowly and placed the Sword on the floor between them, and then lifting shaking hands to the back of her head, she carefully untied the mask she had taken such pains to secure.

In the torchlight, she met his gaze; he met hers.

"I am leaving," she said quietly, "with the Sword. There is only one way you can stop me."

"Na'dio," he said quietly. "Do not do this. Do not force my hand."

But there was no steel in his voice, no edge in his expression; he acknowledged, measure for measure, what she acknowledged; that he could not see her killed; that he could not lift his hand to kill her himself.

"Leave the Sword," he told her softly. "Take your freedom, but leave the Sword."

She placed the mask on the floor beside the Sword. Looked at its flat face, its bright plummage. "I remember when I asked you for *this* mask," she said, as if he had not spoken. She stroked feathers as if they were alive; ran her fingers over the contours of the familiar beak as if by doing so she could capture the sensation, hoard it against a future hunger which might be appeased by such simple comfort. "And you told me, so sternly, that I was a grace-less, ill-mannered child; that a proper Serra never made demands. And I knew that you were disappointed; but I also knew that you would bring me the mask."

"Your gift was that powerful even then?"

"No." She smiled bitterly. "I knew it because when I was a child, I knew that you loved me more than you loved anything else in the Lord's creation, or the Lady's Night. I knew that even though you did not like the way I asked, the fact that I asked at all would mean something to you.

"I am not that child.

"You are not that man.

"But I was that child; you were that man. I cannot take this with me, Father; I have held it long enough. But if you desire it, keep it, and remember."

She did not meet his gaze; her hands ceased their searching motion over the fine surface of a child's desire. She turned, instead, and lifted the much heavier burden. She walked to the door, the closed door, and then she turned back.

He did not look up; instead, he knelt by the mask that she had left on the floor, touching it, as she had touched it, as if he could absorb that contact.

She felt a fierce, a terrible urge, to throw down the Sword and run to him, to open her arms and believe in the comfort and the promise of his uncomplicated and unfettered love. But it passed.

"Good-bye, Father."

"Na'dio . . ."

"She is coming."

"What?"

"Diora, the Serra Diora; she is coming."

Jewel nodded absently. "Avandar?" There was something unpleasant in the air. Like the smell of burning flesh, but without smoke, fire, or victim. The wind was a little too wild; it was as if . . . as if . . .

"Yes."

"Yes?" As if she could hear the wind in the Deepings.

"Yes, you do."

"I hate it when you do that." She turned to the Serra Teresa, and asked, "Serra, do you hear . . . horns?"

The Serra frowned. "Yes."

The General Alesso di'Marente presided above the Tor Leonne in shadows. He could see the Lake; he could see the Radann. And above the city, in raiment of fire and light, he could see Lord Ishavriel. The match was almost at an end. If he lost, the game was lost. If he won, the game continued. There was little ground in between.

He waited for Sendari, and eventually, out of breath, the Widan arrived. "Old friend," Alesso said. "Are you well?"

Sendari did not reply. It was answer enough.

"This is not the game that we envisioned," the General said, lifting a goblet of sweet water in one hand, and a goblet of sweet wine in another. "But it is the only game. Come. Have we ever played to lose?"

"You have never played to lose," Sendari replied after a moment, choosing not water but wine. Alesso raised a brow in the dimly lit room. Then he put a free hand on his oldest friend's shoulder.

"And I do not play to lose now. Anya a'Cooper, against all odds, is in the Tor."

"What?"

"Do you see the person standing in the large, empty space?"

"Yes."

"He or she just threw fire halfway across the city."

"Oh."

"I cannot hear what is being said, but I would say, from the up and down motions, that Anya a'Cooper is about to have a tantrum."

Sendari raised a hand to his brow and closed his eyes. And then he opened his eyes again.

"Yes, old friend," Alesso di'Marente said. "Horns. I believe that Mikalis di'Arretta said that this was sometimes called the Hunter's Moon." Sendari was silent. "What is that, old friend?"

The Widan lifted a pale hand. In it, far too small for a grown man's face, was a small child's mask. A mask.

"How many?" The General asked softly. He waited; his oldest friend stared at the mask in hand as if it could provide answers.

"Let us pray that the Lady is merciful."

"Which Lady?" Alesso said, with an almost reckless laugh.

Moon night.

Above the city, Lord Ishavriel could see the masks that he had created. Some had survived. Enough, apparently. For in the distance of the Scarran road, High Winter was returning to mortal lands on the backs of the Winter Hunt. He could hear the song of the silver horns; could hear the hooves against the dirt. But although he remembered the Winter Queen well, he could not imagine what she might look like; it had been that long. He wished to see her arrival; indeed, that had been his role. But Anya, willful and foolish, had destroyed that triumph.

She had destroyed much. She would not destroy everything. His plan, and The Lord's favor, might still be salvaged if Anya arrived in the basin before the ceremony's start.

The boy in the Arkosan camp would have no demons to save children from, and therefore no strategic return to grace this eve; the Radann had thinned the ranks of his servitors severely enough that he could not afford to sacrifice another.

It was the night of the Dark Conjunction.

Across the thousands of miles he spoke to the Lord, and the
Lord listened.

I have found her, Lord.

From the heart of the Northern Wastes, his Lord spoke.
Ishavriel gathered the god's power and made it his own.

"Anya."

Across the city she struggled against him, but he was her
master; he not had spent the years training her singular talent
without building careful holes in her defenses against the time
when he might need to exploit them.

He used them now.

She screamed in rage and pain.

Lord Isladar said, "Anya. *Anya.* You will frighten the child."

The wild, wild anger deserted her for a moment, although the
struggle against her Lord did not. She was awe-inspiring in her
fashion, for although she was destined to lose, she nonetheless
held her ground against not only Ishavriel's considerable power,
but also *the* Lord's. "Is she awake?"

"Yes," he said. His voice was gentle and quiet. "She is awake,
but she is confused. Because you have promised that she will not
be hurt, she has been . . . happy." He gently pried the child's
arms from around his neck, taking care, nonetheless, to support
her full weight. He had done the same countless times with
Kiriel. "But when you scream like that, she is afraid that it means
that you cannot protect *her,* and then she is frightened."

"I *can* protect her," Anya growled.

"Yes. But Anya, the Lord needs you in the Shining City."

"The Lord doesn't need protecting from *anything.*"

"Ah. No, he does not need protection. He needs your help.
There is no one in the Shining City who can do what you can do.
No one who has your power. You are special. You have always
been special."

"I don't care about that," she said, tossing her hair. "I
promised—"

"Anya, we can *all* go to the Shining City together. Shall we do
that? And while you are busy with Lord Ishavriel and my Lord, I
will watch over the child for you."

"You?"

"Did I not protect Kiriel? And she was younger, and even
more helpless than your child."

"But you're a—"

"Yes. I know. And you do not have to leave. You are power-ful. If you wish to stay in the Tor, no one will be able to force you to leave. But the Lord will be proud and happy if you arrive in time to help Him."

"Oh."

Such a difficult child, Anya.

She thought about it for a moment, and then she frowned. "Can you smell that?" she said, wrinkling her nose in obvious disgust.

"Smell?"

"Yes, it's *terrible*."

"My apologies, Anya, but I am only *Kialli*. There are some sen-sations that are lost to us. I smell nothing."

"It's the bells," she said. "And the horns." She actually started to gag, doubling over and vomiting until she had emptied her stomach. Isladar watched, fascinated.

"We have to leave," she said, when she could speak at all. She wiped her mouth on the sleeve of her robes, and then said, in a *very* irritated voice, "I'm ready, why are you taking so long?"

Lord Ishavriel appeared almost instantly. He had time to smooth the lines of fury from his face, but only barely.

"You *promise* you'll take care of my child?" she said, ignoring him entirely.

"Yes, Anya, I give you my word. But I think it best that we leave now. I do not think it healthy for you to be that . . . sick . . . again."

"If you are behind this, Isladar," Ishavriel said softly, "you will pay."

"Indeed." Isladar shouldered the child who had conveniently fallen back asleep.

The shadows took them all.

Alesso nodded. "Done, old friend."

He gestured; Sendari let the spell lapse. The vision of distant kinlords became just that: distant.

"So it would seem. But in time?"

"We will know in the morning."

"Yes. And that leaves us only one other problem. Look at the Lake."

In the center of the Lake, land was rising.

Not drowned mud, this; not straggling rushes; not the sediment that swimmers might touch whose dive was clean and fast; this was an isle that the Lady Herself could claim as home. Trees, here, taller than the palace upon the plateau, and between their branches, moonlight, shadow, stars. Grass, Nightshade, rushes near the retreating edge of water.

No buildings here; none needed. All who could see it understood its meaning: This was the heart of the Tor. This was the true palace.

When Margret heard the horns, she *knew*.

She turned to the old woman and the boy, and she said, "No matter what you see now, no matter what you hear, you *must not* leave this circle. Do not speak. Do not answer any questions you might be asked. And do not interrupt me."

She drew her dagger and with a grimace that was becoming far too common, she cut herself. She submerged that bleeding hand in the water. It *burned*.

Then she turned her back upon the old woman, for the child's sake, and she carefully pulled the mask from the sash she wore. She met a dead man's eyes, and she said, "This Hunt—it's for you, isn't it?"

He said, "I am honored to serve Arkosa, Matriarch."

"You serve more than Arkosa, Andaru, and I wish—" The horns again.

"Matriarch," he said quietly, "you were my audience; everything we have to say to each other has already been said. It is my time."

"Yes." Margret planted her feet against rock and her back against rock. Then, swallowing air as if it were a foreign substance, she placed the mask upon her face.

From the land in the Lake's center, there grew a bridge that stretched to the shore; it was made not of wood or stone, as bridges are, but of moving earth; lilies were tossed aside or crushed as it progressed. The people surrounding the Lake—and they were many—began to back away. Some fled.

Alesso wished them well. He lifted a goblet to his lips and drained it. "Sendari?"

"I am weary," Sendari said. "And if strong magic is required this eve, I fear that neither of us will survive."

The Serra Teresa's eyes widened. "There," she said, raising an arm. Someone hurried toward them carrying a large, awkward bundle; it was dark enough that Jewel did not get a clear look at her face.

But it didn't matter. "Okay," she said softly, her eyes on the newly made bridge and the strange light that seemed to emanate from the ground like a processional carpet. It was, in a fashion. She *heard* the horns. She *knew* what was going to follow. "You two?"

"Yes?" Serra Teresa's voice was sharp and alert.

"Leave. Now."

"But—"

"No—I'll meet you back at the camp. Or somewhere. But *leave*." Jewel began to elbow her way through the crowd.

"Why now, ATerafin?"

"Because some of those people didn't get their masks to the Lake in time, and now—now there isn't any. *Get moving*."

The strangers left. The Serra Diora di'Marano looked at her aunt; the silence between them was profound. They had been forbidden the pleasure of each's other company since the Festival of the Sun, and they were both much changed; the Serra Teresa in her poor clansman's clothing, with only Ramdan in attendance, and the Serra Diora in the clothing of a powerful man's property. The Serra Teresa had learned with time to school her voice so that one bard-born might hear nothing noteworthy in it; Diora had learned some of that art as well.

But neither woman wished their first meeting to be full of phrases so polished they were hard and shiny, things of surface beyond which any depth was unattainable.

At last, Teresa said, "You have changed, Na'dio."

Diora offered her aunt a very tentative smile. "I have, which is one of my burdens; and I cannot be seen to, which is the other."

They did not speak in words that any one else could hear. "Who is the stranger? Is she one of your Voyani friends?"

"No. She is from the North. The far North. She is well acquainted with Kallandras, and she is so honest it is hard to believe she holds political power, although the ring that she wears is a symbol of power in the House Terafin; I have therefore chosen to overlook the quality of her manners."

"But Kallandras' are so perfect."

"Yes," Ona Teresa smiled. "And while the world ends, will we stand in the moon's shadow and speak of the manners of Northern barbarians?" and she held out her arms.

Diora closed her eyes and walked into them, shunting her burden to one side. It was an awkward embrace for many reasons, and when the older Serra pulled away, her expression was troubled.

"Na'dio?"

"It is . . . nothing. But I fear that we are not yet free."

"Ah. And I fear the opposite."

"The opposite?"

"That we are, indeed free. I have been the mistress of a domain in which all is perfectly circumscribed; in which perfection is therefore attainable. What shall I do in the wilderness of a world that knows such poor grace and such ill ease?"

She spoke lightly, but buried within each word was a grain of truth.

"Ona Teresa?"

The Serra looked at her niece's cumbersome burden. She did not speak.

"Kallandras is calling us."

"I cannot hear him, Na'dio," Teresa replied quietly.

"His voice is not . . . strong."

"Where is he?"

Diora shook her head; strands of her perfect dark hair pulled free from the knot at the back of her head. "I do not know. He says that we are *not* to travel to the Arkosan camp.

"We are to meet . . ." She frowned.

"Yes, Na'dio?"

"At the merchant Court."

The Serra looked at the retreating backs of the two Northerners. Then she nodded. "Let us go, then, and quickly. There will be time to brood over our fate and our future if we survive."

Almost before the shadows lifted, Anya a'Cooper was gone. The Lord summoned her in a voice both pleasing and beautiful, and she chose to put aside her fear and her distrust. It had been some time since the Lord had consumed mortal souls, and some portion of His memory and power had grown wild. But the wildness was less of a danger than the sentience; Anya understood it better.

She appeared in the center of a large circle, and above her, for she was in the basin, the demons crowded, glad of the distance. Anya did not care for the kin, but she was no longer terrified of them. They had become her special game; she attempted to kill them, and they attempted to survive.

It weeded out the weak and the foolish, for while she was devious, she was easily surprised and easily distracted.

The first question she asked when she arrived was directed to the Lord Isladar, and when he assured her that he had indeed kept his promise, she allowed herself to be anointed. But first, she complained bitterly about the presence of that awful Southern barbarian, and he was dutifully removed from the circle. Then, she decided that she didn't like Lady Sariyel because, you know, Lady Sariyel was often not very friendly, and she, too, was removed. And last, she decided that she did not want to share space, or in fact anything, with Krysanthos, who, she suspected, thought she was stupid.

And so she stood under the Lord's hands, her skin glowing darkly with His earthly blood, the power washing over and through her as she stood on the old road.

The kin watched.

The Lord began to anchor the ways between the worlds. And as he worked, they all heard it: the calling of the Wild Hunt. The horns sounded three times in perfect unison.

The Lord laughed with a very rare joy; for it was wild law that once the Hunt had been called, the hunters would hunt their quarry; and nothing, not god, not mage, not even the Queen of the Hunt herself could call the hunters back.

The Arianni spilled across the plateau into the mortal world, and the old paths grew *strong*.

Margret of the Arkosa Voyani lifted hand out of water in a clenched fist, and she saw it with two sets of eyes; her own and Andaru's. Her eyes saw her hand, wet, tinted pink with water-thinned blood. But his eyes saw a vein of light, white and glistening, wrapped around the darker core of her flesh. She lifted her hand as if holding it up to inspection by moonlight, and the light flew skyward like an arrow from her palm, but it left a trail that began at the cut she'd made. It stretched out as far as the— well, as far as the mask's eyes—could see. She watched, fascinated by it, and she saw that it did have an end; it met a light in the sky above that was almost a mirror image and together they formed a narrow arch.

And then from the East and the West, light also rose, and when those four trails were joined, branches of light shot out from the

center to the ground until the Tor Leonne was engulfed in a cage
made of pale-colored light. It was beautiful.

Hold your ground, Matriarch." Andaru's familiar voice
said; she felt the words more than she heard them. *"You have
just defined the boundaries of the Hunt, and the Wild Hunt
does not like to be contained.*

"And you know this how?" Margret said uneasily.

It is one of the advantages of being dead.

"And not being dead at the same time?"

*Yes. I see clearly; I see things that living eyes cannot see. And
they, Matriarch, see me. Brace yourself. They come.*

"W—what's that?" the old woman on the Fountain, forgotten
until now, said.

The earth was shaking. Margret stood up and then stopped.
"Remember what I told you: Do not leave this circle no matter
what you hear."

Jewel had seen the hunters on the hidden path. At all times,
and in all ways, they had deferred to the Winter Queen. She had
known that they would come here; her dreams had been very
precise.

She had, however, expected some stately procession, some
parade, some celebration of the Winter Queen and the fact that
she ruled them all. But the minute the eerie and disturbing
growth of earth touched the shoreline, the riders burst forward
like fire in the hands of a crazed mage. The stags which had been
still and silent on the road now stretched their long, fine legs.

Jewel was nearly trampled. Avandar pulled her out of the path
of the Hunt. The mounted stags traveled far, far faster than any
horse she had ever seen as they raced toward their destination.

"Where's Arianne?" Jewel shouted, over the thunder of hooves
that had appeared so delicate in the otherworld.

Avandar shook his head.

Jewel stood. The isle was still in the Lake, but the Winter Queen
and her cohort were nowhere to be seen. She *knew* this was bad.
Her eyes, lids suddenly heavy, closed—and she could hear the
screaming in the city below the plateau. Could *see* in the darkness
behind her lids, what the Winter Queen hunted.

Those who were not her prey lived if they left the path the host
rode; they died otherwise, but quickly. Cleanly.

But they died, *Kalliaris*, they died. And those who wore the masks—those who, by some unfair ancient rites that had *nothing* to do with humanity . . .

For just a moment she stopped breathing. And then, smacking her forehead hard enough that it hurt—which given the thickness of her skull at the present moment said something—she fumbled in her satchel and pulled out Yollana's "gift."

"Well?" she said to her domicis.

"If you wind that horn, I can almost guarantee that she will turn back."

"How?"

"Her name is etched in sixteen different languages in circles on the bell of the horn," he said quietly, "and at the moment, twelve of them are glowing."

Jewel nearly dropped the horn. She didn't. And she cursed mildly under her breath because Avandar was right. "What about the other four?"

"I don't know. Perhaps you might summon her and ask her."

Jewel shrugged.

Then she lifted the horn and winded it.

It made a truly pathetic sound.

She lifted it again, but Avandar caught her wrist. "It was heard," he said. "Wind it again and you will only annoy her."

Jewel laughed. "As if she could be any *more* annoyed with me."

But her domicis saw no humor in the words. "She will come, ATerafin, because both she and the horn are bound by the same wild law. But she is the Winter Queen, and when she ruled these lands and she was summoned by such a thing as that horn—and I would advise you to return it to Yollana as soon as this ordeal is finished, should we survive it—she was treated with the deference due her birth and her title."

"I don't know much about her birth, and I don't much care for her title."

"Learn," Avandar said coldly, "because this is not the last that you will see of her."

"But if—"

"You have walked the road, Jewel, and you have claimed—and *held*—a part of it. You will see her again." He looked up. "And soon. Be prepared, ATerafin."

Jewel looked down the road and beneath the eye of the Scarran Moon, at the head of a group of twelve mounted riders, the Winter Queen came. She wore moonlight as if it were silk, and the wind that blew through the white, icy length of her hair made her hair seem sensuous and alive. Seemed desirable, or worse, necessary. She had forgotten how beautiful Arianne was; she faced that truth squarely. Mortal memory—at least not Jewel's—was incapable of preserving the truth of her beauty, her presence.

"Ummm, Avandar?"

"Yes?"

"Isn't she supposed to slow down?"

Avandar's smile was cold. "Learn the first lesson when you deal with the Firstborn. Let me use small, succinct words."

"What a pleasant change," Jewel snapped back, through clenched teeth.

"If you have no plan for surviving what you want to summon, think twice."

"You couldn't have said that before, right?"

He laughed. "I merely wished to illustrate a point. You are in no danger." He smiled.

"They don't seem to be stopping."

Avandar lifted his hands; Jewel saw blue light follow the mound of his palms. But before it left him, something else occurred: A mounted hunter came out of the bush and took up his position in the road.

In front of Jewel ATerafin and her domicis.

"Celleriant?" Jewel said, the last syllable uncomfortably close to a squeak.

The hunter turned to look over his slender shoulder; he offered her a nod, no more. "But your mount—"

The stag turned. He dug dirt with his hooves and snorted.

"And that's animal talk for 'How dare you insult me?' right?"

"I believe," Avandar said quietly, "that Celleriant and the stag have reached an accommodation for your sake. Consider yourself honored, ATerafin." There was no humor in his voice.

"I thought—"

"You thought—"

"They didn't come with us. I thought they were—I don't know, like the rocks or the mountain pass or the falling asleep and never remembering it."

"Oh, no," he said softly. "They are quite real. But the path that the Oracle made for you and me was facilitated by our lives in *this* world, and neither Celleriant nor the Stag who has condescended—for your sake, I believe—to bear him, can claim that."

"And when the Hunt is over?"

"When the Hunt is over, they will remain."

"What am I going to do with a stag that size in Averalaan?"

"May I suggest that you wait to see if you survive to reach Averalaan before you worry about that?"

"Good suggestion. Is she going to ride him down?"

"No. Celleriant is powerful enough, even without her gifts, that she could not be guaranteed to ride him down and retain her mount or her composure. She will not lose face here; she gave him the order that protects you now."

Jewel held her breath until it did nothing but make her lungs ache. The Winter Queen and her escort came charging down the road at full speed.

"Where are the others?" she asked.

"The others?"

"The other hunters. There were a lot more than this."

He stared at her as if she had lost her mind. "Jewel, this is the night of the Wild Hunt; it has been called. Where do you think they are?"

"I don't know." She said it. She lied.

"They are hunting and killing anyone who wears one of the *Kialli* masks."

CHAPTER THIRTY-SIX

The woman who held the boy in her arms bit her lip to stop herself from screaming. She held her grandchild who had fallen, inexplicably, asleep. Better to let him sleep than to wake him for what she was certain would follow. She backed up into the Fountain's lip, and she looked wildly from side to side.

There was only one way out of the deserted yard that held the Lady's Southern Fount: the gates.

And in the gates, long and dark as shadows, eyes glinting with an unnatural brilliance, were men mounted on great, horned beasts, the like of which she had never seen.

Margret lowered her fist and looked to the hunters through the mask. She reached for the flippant words that had momentarily decided to evade her, but when she spoke, she didn't recognize anything that came out of her mouth because *none* of it was hers.

"I am Andaru of the Arkosa Voyani," the man whose face she literally wore said. "And the Hunt has not been called which can catch me. The mounts that you have are heavy and slow, and the horns that you wind are of little concern. You call yourself hunters? Then *hunt*."

Spears and the tines of great antlers tore at the gates, until, with the angry toss of antlered head, the great brass gates were uprooted. Into the hollow created by Voyani art and the willing sacrifice of Arkosan kin, the Wild Hunt came. They knew their quarry, although what they saw when they gazed upon Margret's masked face, she couldn't say. And was glad of the inability.

They circled, but their spears did not pass the circle that was etched—and glowing—in the stone. The old woman had closed her eyes. Margret wanted to offer her some comfort, because she understood that the source of her fear was the child she now held.

But she had no control over what she said.

"Come out, come out, little human," one of the tallest and most beautiful men she had ever seen said. "If you are so brave that you have just given us your name, why do you hide behind that pathetic, mortal circle? The Hunt will not wait once it has been called."

"Then leave, mighty hunters, and step on mice and rodents."

She expected fury and there was a tightening of that gorgeous face, but there was also a flicker of something in the eyes that was akin to hunger—or starvation. The man who had spoken reached down to his belt and unhooked a long, slender horn. He lifted it to his lips and just before the mouthpiece touched his skin, Margret felt a shudder take her whole body.

Lady's grace go with you, Matriarch. Protect my child.

I will, Margret said. I'm the Matriarch. All of the children are mine.

She felt something touch her forehead, light as breeze, and then it pushed off; she stumbled, lost her footing, flailed—and was caught an inch from the circle by the iron grip of a frail arm.

The mask—and Andaru's presence—were both suddenly gone. She was alone. When she looked up and met the face of the hunter, his eyes widened in surprise and then in very real anger. "Get back," he cried to the others who had crowded into the courtyard. "Mount up! He's gone!" He winded the horn, then, and the shock of the sound drove her to her knees.

But it did not bring her close to the circle's edge.

"I—"

The old woman said, "I did not recognize you, Wanderer. But you have done the Lady's work here this eve. I know that your kin and ours are not always . . . friendly . . . but I have heard it said that you do not kill our children. Or sell them."

Margret returned the grip around the old woman's arms. "And I have heard it said," she replied ruefully, "that the clansmen love their children and their families as fiercely as we love our own. And that the women seem frail but . . ." she gazed at the hand that gripped her arm.

"You did not recognize my family name," the old woman said. "And perhaps in the end, it will mean nothing. But clan Namarro is in the debt of the Arkosa Voyani, and perhaps we will save your children from hardship or grief, as you have just saved ours." She paused a moment. "This sleep . . ."

"I am no witch," Margret said quickly.

"Then perhaps it is the Lady's gift. I am . . . grateful for it. Is it safe to leave the circle?"

"Yes," Margret said quietly. "The Hunters have gone elsewhere, and I think that the hunted will lead them back on a road they should never have been able to leave."

Celleriant sat like a wall in the road; the stag upon which he sat slowly, even leisurely, lowered its massive antlers.

At the last minute, the Queen broke her stride. She looked down upon Celleriant. To Jewel's surprise he did not bow his head; he did not beg or scrape. He waited until she had slowed and then he turned to look back at Jewel ATerafin.

She swallowed and nodded, and he stepped off the road, leaving her to face Arianne.

The Winter Queen sat astride her chosen mount.

"This grows tiresome, mortal. You have not the skill or the power to make this road your own." She lifted her visor, and Jewel's mouth went dry. "It was therefore very dangerous to summon me. I have called a Hunt, and there *will* be a Hunt; that is the wild law."

Oh, good. Jewel felt awkward, ugly, small, and just verging on the edge of pathetic. Oh, and dirty.

"I have a message to deliver," she said, keeping her voice as polite and as neutral as it was possible to do.

She felt Avandar's gaze boring into her profile.

"A message? Truly? How . . . amusing. Deliver it while I am still in the mood to hear it. The night will not last forever, and the Hunt *must* be joined. I enjoy the Hunt," she added, her voice changing in texture and tone, "but even if I were to tire of it, mortal, I am of the Firstborn." Her eyes were dark and round, where they had, moments before, been the color of perfect steel. It was almost as if . . . as if . . .

"The wild law governs many things." Jewel could not take her eyes away from the white expanse of the Winter Queen's skin. Luckily she didn't have to. "You have a duty and an oath to fulfill and you are called upon to fulfill it."

The was a sudden silence; all movement ceased; it was as if the ice of Winter had hollowed out every member of the Queen's entourage, leaving stiff and frozen shells behind. Then the Winter Queen dropped hand to horn and rested it there, and Jewel understood that this was the worst of the threats she had yet made—although she didn't understand *why.*

"And you, mortal, will tell me of my oaths?"

"I am a messenger," she said quietly. "You are challenged,

Lady, to a greater Hunt than this. These people have kept their faith with you; they have followed the vows that their ancestors made."

"Indeed."

"And your presence here threatens—"

"I am aware of what my presence here may mean," she said quietly. "But the law is the law."

"Do you hear the Hunters?" Avandar asked, breaking the silence that settled around that pronouncement.

"No," the Queen said quietly. "But they have called their Hunts and they pursue them."

"Indeed. But where, Queen of Winter?"

She frowned a moment. And then she raised her face until it was full in the moonlight; closed her eyes so that white lashes brushed perfect cheeks. "They . . . are not here."

"The only Hunt that has not been sounded is yours, my Lady," Avandar said.

"And the Winter King awaits you, he says, if your hunters are capable of finding the simplest of trails."

"What did you say?"

"I said the Winter King—"

"You have seen the Winter King?" Her eyes narrowed. "Impossible."

"For your hunters, and perhaps even for you. But I . . . visited him . . . at his request."

"He owns nothing that does not come first from *me*." Arianne's fingers twitched along the length of the horn. "And he has been long hidden. How do I know that this is not a mortal game? Such tricks have oft been attempted when the alternative is . . . unpleasant."

Jewel frowned.

"ATerafin," Avandar said, his voice smooth and confident, "answer the Winter Queen."

"He didn't exactly give me a password," she said out of the corner of her mouth.

"No-o-o," a painfully familiar voice said. "He gave you something *better*."

She swore under her breath as that something flying overhead took advantage of moonlight to cast them all into shadow. *I don't believe this is happening to me. Kalliaris. I can't possibly have offended you this much in one lousy lifetime.*

Before she could speak, the shadow grew larger and darker; it happened so swiftly that, were it not for the sickening sound of snapped bones and the two bodies that lay, like cast-off dolls, against the broken red maples, she would have said that the gargoyle had never dived at all.

"Hello, stupid ground-dwellers," the winged cat said.

"*You,*" one of the Queen's Hunters shouted. "Lady—"

"Enough." She turned. "Kalliasanne—look down the road. Look, and tell me if it is possible."

One of the Hunters—and Jewel could not tell them apart, they were all tall and perfect and pale-haired, and they all had the same high cheekbones, the same steely gray eyes—turned his mount in the direction of the Lake. He moved forward slowly, pausing a moment in front of Jewel and Avandar.

Jewel nodded. He passed them by under the watchful eyes of her domicis. She wanted to watch him; Avandar apparently had no difficulty. But her eyes returned to the face and the eyes, the astonishing eyes, of Arianne. The Queen spared a glance to the fallen, no more. It was almost as if, by dying, they had served their purpose. If they were dead at all. She thought them very like demons, and expected their bodies to vanish as they fell.

But these two did not.

The rider who had approached with caution came flying back; he rode around the road to reach the side of the Queen and when he did, he dismounted and dropped to both knees. And his forehead touched earth at the foot of her stag, and he knelt thus on the ground while she looked at his bent back.

"So," the Queen said quietly. "The trail was there and you missed it."

He said nothing at all. As if aware that to offer an excuse was to also make oneself a target. "I should leave you here," she said softly. "Or let you join Celleriant in his exile. You have failed me, and in some ways your failure is the greater one.

"But the news that you bring is welcome, and I am in a mood to forgive. Someone, bring down that cursed cat."

The "cat" hissed in that dry gurgling sort of hack that Jewel associated with its laughter.

Lightning rose like a miniature storm, but it was gone between the bolts, moving faster than anything made of that much stone had any right to.

"Good-bye, little mortal," it said, elongating every syllable in the most annoying way possible. "If you are *very* good, *may*be you will see me again."

"Avandar."

"Yes."

"Help them."

He smiled. "I think it a waste of power. Listen, Jewel. You are about to hear a sound that has not been heard for a very long time."

The Winter Queen lifted her horn to her lips and pressed mouthpiece to mouth, and from the bell of the horn a cry sweeter than horn music had any right to be filled the air.

In the distance, across the Lake, an answering note sounded. The Winter King.

The Host, mounted, surged forward; they left Arianne behind. She paused on the road. "We will meet again, you and I," she said quietly. "You are marked, and I, I now walk under the same shadow." She turned to face North, and the smile on her face might have frozen water.

"But my Lake is safe, child, and for that, I am grateful. When next you see me, I will ride a different mount, and I will preside over a Court in which, should you desire it, I will grant you a place."

She turned and her mount leaped forward; her hair brushed against Jewel's upturned cheek. On impulse, Jewel reached out to touch it, and three strands remained in the palm of her hand when she opened it.

The Host followed their Queen—but it seemed to grow in number; where twelve riders had been, there were now too many to count, they flowed past so quickly.

Jewel didn't try. Instead, silent, she watched as the Queen lifted the horn again; heard its song; she could not see it touch lips, and that was just as well.

The bridge, old and wet and new, took the thundering weight of the host; the water echoed its voice; the air carried its command. They were wild, yes, but they were beautiful. Jewel's throat was full; she stared at the Winter Queen and wondered if she would ever see anything as beautiful again. Hoped not.

Prayed to.

Avandar stared at her.

Jewel stared at the long, fine hair. A poverty of beauty. A promise.

"You have been honored," he said quietly. "Although I do not understand why."

"Because," Jewel said, watching the Lake swallow the island and all trace of the Hunt, "by giving her the Winter King, I've given her back the Summer."

She turned, then, to look upon the Lord Celleriant; he watched the Lake devour his companions as the true road, the *only* road, opened in the fabric of earth, air and water to receive them. Only when it was clear, perfect water again, did the tears come.

But he wept in the silence for a long, long time.

Margret and the Matriarchs were gathered by Kallandras of the North. They were tired as children are tired, and they allowed themselves to be led. Even Yollana could spare no energy for cutting remarks. She let Kallandras bear the brunt of her weight, and when she looked, for a moment, as old as everyone thought she *must* be, she let him ease her with words that passed no farther than her ears.

Margret was curious, but she was tired, and in the end, exhaustion won out.

But she felt a deep satisfaction that had nothing to do with reality. She still lacked the heart of Arkosa; it was wrapped around the neck of another woman—a woman who had accepted the burden laid upon her by a Voyani Matriarch. But she had found something of her own in the streets of the Tor, and when she was awake and well-fed she might even understand what it was.

Her mother's ghost escorted them back to the Arkosan camp, where the fire Arkosan blood had paid for was still burning like a miniature sun. She did not speak, of course, which was very uncharacteristic, but speech was no longer necessary. Margret understood what her mother had died for.

Had her mother accomplished what she set out to accomplish? Margret was not certain she would ever know.

But she knew this: the Hunt had not destroyed the city, and the demons had not returned. She had saved the life of an old woman, and the life of a little boy. The bodies that lay in the streets were a tragedy, but they were someone *else's* tragedy for now, and that would have to do.

Diora and Teresa, shorn of title and the responsibilities to which they'd been born, wandered through the empty streets of the Tor Leonne. They stayed near shadows when shadows were present, and when they heard the heavy tread of many feet, they chose to be prudent. But the night was a new night, and the dawn would not begin the first day of a new year; it would begin the first day of a new life.

They were afraid.

They did not speak of their fear; they could not. If they began a new life, they began it as themselves, and what experience would alter—if anything indeed was altered—would be determined by time.

But there was a language they could speak, if they could not openly speak of fear.

When they reached the merchant Court, Kallandras was nowhere to be found. They called him in the way that they had been taught, but if he heard them at all, he wisely chose not to answer. It took them half an hour to decide to approach the manor, and when they did, they found, tucked neatly beside the wide flower beds, a Northern harp.

Diora's hands trembled as she lifted it. Her fingers, clumsy with months of forced inactivity, skittered off the surface of the strings as if she was afraid that strumming them would destroy them.

It was Teresa who gently took the harp from her hands; Teresa who began to play it, although in truth between them Diora was the more accomplished musician.

And it was Teresa who began to sing.

> *"The sun has gone down, has gone down my love*
> *Na'dio, Na'dio child*
> *Let me lay down my helm and my shield bright*
> *Let me forsake the world of guile*
> *For the Lady is watching, is watching my love*
> *Na'dio, Na'dio child,*
> *And she knows that the heart which is guarded and scarred*
> *Is still pierced by the darkest of fear.*
>   *When you smile, I feel joy,*
>   *When you cry, I feel pain,*
>   *When you sleep in my arms I feel strong*
>   *But the Lord does not care for the infant who sleeps*
>   *In the cradle of arms and my song.*
> *The time it will come, it will come, my love,*
> *Na'dio, Na'dio my own.*
> *When the veil will fall and separate us*
> *May you bury me when you are grown*
> *For the heart, oh the heart is a dangerous place*
> *It is breaking with joy and with fear,*

Worse though if you'd never been born to me,
Na'dio, Na'dio my dear."

Sendari di'Marano did not sleep; he watched as the dawn rose over the trampled grounds of the Tor. There were bodies, but they were few, and the only man so far who was in danger of joining them was the very hysterical man who had tended the grove of dwarf maples that had been splintered and crushed by the passing of hooved animals.

As the Serra Fiona en'Marano was very fond of the man's work, he had had him incarcerated for drunken behavior—a flaw that was acceptable in the aftermath of the Festival, but only barely.

And never in the presence of the Tyr. Enough damage had been done that it was worth the effort of retaining a man whose passion was the landscaping of the Tor Leonne. In much the same way, Sendari would have attempted to preserve the life of a physician who had seen too much in battle and had lost his temper in front of the General.

And the General was definitely here.

The Tyr'agar, Alesso di'Alesso, the shadowy figure who had been born on the eve of the last day of the Festival of the Sun had vanished in the grim morning light.

Sendari had never understood that man; he admitted, in the scant light that came before the sun was truly risen, that he did not completely understand this one. But this one had the advantage of familiarity. Alesso di'Marente—still called, for the sake of formality, Alesso di'Alesso, as if that earlier man did not exist—was in control of the situation.

A message had arrived from Cortano. It was short but sweet, notably because it had been delivered in person. Mikalis and Sendari had been furtive in their attempts to ascertain the . . . magical health . . . of the Sword's Edge. It amused him—in a very brittle sort of way—to disabuse them of the notion that he might be controlled by the Lord of the Shining Court.

He carried word from Lord Ishavriel, who glossed over the fate intended for the Tor Leonne. Sendari was furious; Alesso was not. They had, after all, failed, and the plan had been clever. He understood Lord Ishavriel's plan and purpose, but he was not particularly outraged. He could not—yet—afford to be. The usefulness of the kinlords had not diminished with their failure.

The Festival of the Moon had given Alesso back purpose and

vitality. He was as sharp as *Terra Fuerre*. Which was good; it was the only Sword that he was to wield.

The Sun Sword was gone. The Radan kai el'Sol had come with that news in the morning; he had shown neither dismay nor outrage.

After he had gone, Alesso looked across the room at his oldest friend. And then he said softly, "Sendari."

"Yes."

"Your daughter?"

"Will never marry Eduardo kai di'Garrardi, although for the sake of our alliance, I will be as horrified as you are when her disappearance is discovered."

"And who will discover it?"

"I imagine," he said softly, "that my oldest wife will be waking the Serra Diora di'Marano now, or attempting to. My cerdan will come shortly with her panicked, terrified message."

"And the Sword?"

Sendari met Alesso's gaze and held it. He said, "I am sorry, General. You were right. You should have killed her when the rest of the Leonnes were slaughtered. I think, in the end, it would have been a kindness."

"To her," Alesso asked shrewdly, "or to her father?"

"To her," her father said, "To me? I cannot say."

"Then I will be blunt. Had I killed her deliberately, it would have damaged the only friendship I rely on. We have always had our peculiar weaknesses, and we mask them, as we can, with strength. She has stolen the reminder of what I failed to do. No more. No less.

"The battle for the Tor will be decided by the Lord: we will war. And at the end of the battle, the winner *will* be the wielder of the Sun Sword."

He smiled. "There is only one Leonne left. And after his death, the Sword will be free. Come, Sendari. All choices have been made. We go to war against the North."

"It is not auspicious, if history is an example, to call for war after the Festival of the Moon."

"It is precisely because of the comparison between myself and the former Tyr that the timing is perfect. We have won a victory over our allies, and we are in control; they need us."

"Well played, Alesso."

"Indeed. And my only regret is that it was not *all* my doing."

23rd of Scaral, 427 AA
The Shining Palace, The Northern Wastes

Lord Isladar sat in the tower that had been Kiriel's home. In his
arms, slumber enforced by spell—as Kiriel's had so often been
until she grew into her power and developed the peculiar immu-
nities which made her so dangerous—was the child Anya had
plucked from the city streets.

She had woken twice, screaming in terror; he could taste it
and he was certain that every demon in the city was drooling
where it stood. But he eased her fear rather than feeding it.

He had given Anya a'Cooper his word.

And his word, given as it was to the only mage alive who had
survived such an enormous transfer of power, was worth keeping.
For now.

The Lord of Night had His throne; He had some portion of His
gate, but although He had clawed and struggled, the Dark Conjunction had failed to produce the anchor that He needed to hold
the worlds together in their drift. What He guaranteed Himself
was a place in which he might reign without the constant need to
feed in order to stay sentient.

Which was unfortunate, but not unexpected.

The child stirred, he shifted beneath her, the movement almost as natural to him as breathing was to her. Ironic, that something he had done for so short a span of years could still feel
natural.

Kiriel had taught him many things, and all of them were complicated; he had not yet done with the lessons. Nor had he finished with the lessons he wished her to learn.

He thought about putting the child down; Kiriel's bed was as
she left it, the sigils and wards still functional, although it had
been many, many years since they were invoked.

Yes, he thought about putting her down.

But he was not certain how long he would have the ambivalent
sensation of carrying her. She had been brought here by Anya,
and most of Anya's pets or toys died of neglect or her frayed and
unintelligible temper.

He wondered, if Anya hadn't already been so very damaged, if
she would have the survived the ceremony intact. It was an idle
curiosity; he would not be allowed to experiment. At the end of it,
as if completely unaware of what had transpired, she had turned

to Lord Isladar, of all people, to complain because her arms and her back hurt. The child, apparently, was *heavy*.

But his arms were not her arms, and the child that slept in them could be held forever. And forever, as Isladar knew, was a very theoretical concept.

Michelle West

The Sun Sword:

☐ **THE BROKEN CROWN** UE2740—$6.99

☐ **THE UNCROWNED KING** UE2801—$6.99

☐ **THE SHINING COURT** UE2837—$6.99

In the Dominion, those allied with the demons of the Shining Court fear the bargain they've made, for to the *kialli* betrayal was a way of life. And as the Festival of the Moon approaches, demon kin begin to prey upon those in the Tor Leonne. But even more frightening than their presence was their "gift" for the Festival, masks created not by human craftsmen but by the *kialli*. . . .

The Sacred Hunt:

☐ **HUNTER'S OATH** UE2681—$5.50

☐ **HUNTER'S DEATH** UE2706—$5.99

TANYA HUFF

VALOR'S CHOICE

"Readers who enjoy military SF will love Tanya Huff's
VALOR'S CHOICE. Howlingly funny and very
suspenseful. I enjoyed every word."
—*scifi.com*

Staff Sergeant Torin Kerr was a battle-hardened professional.
So when she and those in her platoon who'd survived the last
deadly encounter with the Others were yanked from a well-
deserved leave for what was supposed to be "easy" duty as
the honor guard for a diplomatic mission to the non-Confedera-
tion world of the Silsviss, she was ready for anything. Sure,
there'd been rumors of the Others being spotted in this sector
of space. But there were always rumors. Everything seemed
to be going perfectly. Maybe too perfectly. . . .

0-88677-896-4 $6.99